CARDEW
OF
ST. JIM'S

Cardew the Rebel
Tom Merry's Rival
Captain Cardew
Skipper and Slacker
D'Arcy's Christmas Party
The Vengeance of Cardew
Tom Merry's Foe
Just Like Cardew

Comprising GEM issues 824 to 831 inclusive

CARDEW OF ST. JIM'S

by

MARTIN CLIFFORD

HOWARD BAKER
LONDON

Martin Clifford

CARDEW OF ST. JIM'S

(The Gem, 1923, 1924)

© Copyright: The Amalgamated Press Ltd., 1923, 1924, 1972

Originally published in single issues

Howard Baker (Greyfriars Press) omnibus
hard cover edition, 1972

*Greyfriars Press books are published by
Howard Baker Press Limited,
27a Arterberry Road, Wimbledon, London, S.W.20, England
Printed in Great Britain by
C. G. Colour Printers Ltd., Gloucester
and bound by Leighton-Straker, London.*

The writing phenomenon known to the world as Martin Clifford, but who was also well known and much loved by generations of readers as Frank Richards and Owen Conquest, died at his home at Kingsgate in Kent on Christmas Eve 1961 at the age of eighty-six.

His real name was Charles Hamilton, and by the time that he died it is conservatively estimated that he had written – under one name or another – the equivalent of one thousand full-length novels.

His work appeared continuously for over thirty years in those famous Fleetway House magazines *The Gem* and *The Magnet*. Undoubtedly the most famous of all of his immortal creations was Billy Bunter, the Fat Owl of the Greyfriars Remove, whose exploits together with those of Harry Wharton and Co., appeared in the latter paper from 1908 to 1940.

Almost equally well-known was his uniquely memorable character, the Hon. Arthur Augustus D'Arcy, the Swell of St. Jim's, ably supported in *Gem* stories by Tom Merry, Jack Blake, Talbot (the Toff), Dr. Holmes and many others.

Altogether, the brilliant character studies of boys, masters, and local citizens of which he was capable ensured Charles Hamilton's permanent place in the hall of literary fame.

This great story-teller loved writing for the young and affirmed that no writer could do any better work in life. Certainly, no-one did it better than he.

Ballads of Famous Schools
No. 2
St. Jim's

ST. JAMES'S COLLEGE stands erect
  In Sussex, Queen of Counties,
And smiling Fortune has bedecked
  Its walls with wondrous bounties.
Beside it flows the River Ryll
  Which boys spend joyous days on;
The pasture round is sweet and still,
  A goodly sight to gaze on!
The dignified and stately tower
  Intact through countless ages,
Still stands supreme in silent power
  Whene'er the tempest rages.
If only that tall spire could voice
  The past, with all its glories,
How every fellow would rejoice
  To hear its stirring stories!
Kildare is skipper of the school,
  What rival can come near him?
The juniors revel in his rule,
  And all applaud and cheer him.
In every branch of sport he ranks
  A strong, unyielding giant,
Who puts his foot down on all pranks,
  And those who are defiant.
The worthy Doctor Holmes is " great,"
  A really fine headmaster;
And through his studies, long and late,
  Success comes fast and faster.
St. Jim's will ever lead the way,
  Top place we must concede her,
So long as she enjoys the sway
  Of such a learned leader!
The juniors are a noble band:
  Who has not heard of Merry?
A real good sport, whose deeds so grand
  Are keenly talked of, very!
While in the New House Figgins shines
  A most illustrious fellow,
Who causes cads and their designs
  To look extremely yellow!
Then drink, in flowing ginger-pop,
  A health to boys so splendid.
And may they never " shut up shop,"
  But ever be befriended!
High on the hills of hope they climb,
  Courageous, strong, and clever;
Their deeds, so dashing and sublime
  Shall thrill our hearts for ever!

EVERY WEDNESDAY.

The G.EM 2d

LIBRARY OF SCHOOL AND SPORTING STORIES

No. 824.
Vol. XXIV.
November 24th, 1923.

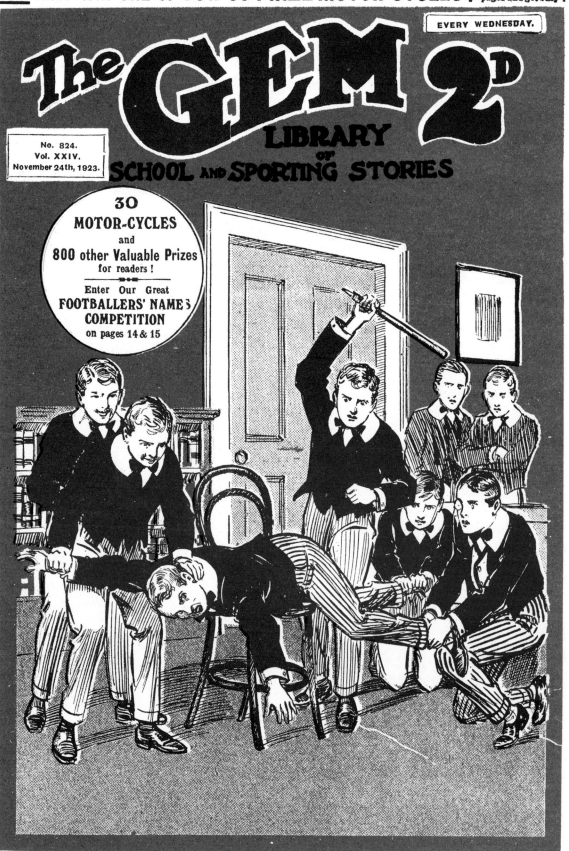

CURING THE SLACKER!

Ralph Reckness Cardew, the slacker of the Fourth Form, in the grasp of the indignant Games Committee, suffer the penalty for cutting footer practice! (See the grand long St. Jim's story in this issue.)

Your Editor Chats With His Readers.

Address all letters: The Editor, The "Gem" Library, The Fleetway House, Farring-don Street, London, E.C.4. Write me, you can be sure of an answer in return.

My dear Chums,—Only two more weeks to run! That is how matters stand with our grand Footballers' Names Competition. But though time is short, there is still a good chance to romp in a winner, so long as you make the most of the next fortnight. You can pack a lot of good work into two weeks. To those readers who have not yet taken a hand at the game, I would say get busy right away! Now is the time. The valuable prizes are worth a record effort.

"TOM MERRY'S RIVAL!"
By Martin Clifford.

This is a really great story of St. Jim's for next Wednesday. Things are moving fast at the old school. Cardew thought a lot before he definitely took up the challenge to stand for the junior captaincy of St. Jim's. That is easily understood. Time and again Cardew has shown his real admiration for Tom Merry. There have been times when it was obvious that the very last thing Cardew contemplated was to stand in as a rival to the popular young leader, of the school. But circumstances are always changing. Cardew has been egged on. The yarn next Wednesday shows an amazing change of front. On the footer field and elsewhere Cardew shows his hand. We see the self-reliant, cool-headed fellow, in his mocking, sarcastic mood. For his part, Tom Merry reveals the sturdy, rugged independence which sits so well on him. If a fresh skipper is wanted—well, let St. Jim's elect one. Cardew or another; that's Tom Merry's attitude. You will be keen, I know, on the amazing feud between the two prime favourites of St. Jim's.

OUR CHRISTMAS NUMBER!

It is top-hole. Readers drop me hints about what they want. I have done my best to get what everybody wants in the superlatively fine Christmas issue of the good old "Gem."

"MIKE MAKES A WIRELESS SET!"
By Elmer K. Arter.

Another treat for the next issue of the "Gem." We have got to know a good deal about good old whimsical Mike and his staunch chum, Billy Burton, not by any means forgetting mischievous Marmaduke. The delightful trio are found hard at it designing a magnificent radio set next week. That is to say, Mike McAndrews does most of the real, genuine, hard thinking. Mike's brain power is the wonder of the age. He is a mechanical genius of the first water, and his treatment of any deep subject which he takes in hand is invariably fresh and invigorating. Don't miss him in this wireless scream.

HOBBIES.

What are your favourite hobbies for this winter? Somebody assures me that the amateur magazine hobby is going out of fashion, but, somehow, I cannot credit this assertion. There is perpetual interest in the jolly little written-out magazine full of wit and humour, with smart personal impressions of what goes on in the world.

THANKS.

M. Lowson, 95, Gilmour Street, Thornaby-on-Tees, sends me a postcard about a certain Tuck Hamper which reached his address. The hamper in question was well and truly won. My correspondent puts it this way: "Many thanks for Tuck Hamper, which arrived this morning. It quite exceeded my expectation. Have taken your paper for a great many years, and hope to do so for many more." I am much obliged for this cheery message.

TUCK HAMPERS AGAIN!

Apropos of the above, it has been hinted to me that I ought to give a list each week of the contents of the Tuck Hampers. The menu, in short. But that would take up a lot of space, for the Tuck Hamper contains so many excellent items of provender. Seems to me we can let it go at the fact that the bi. of Tuck Hamper fare is just A1.

"THE TRIERS!"
By Jack Crichton.

A stunning instalment will be found next week. Disasters came thick and fast on plucky patient Jack Morton. His deadly enemy, George Clifton, will stick at nothing to encompass the ruin of his rival. It will come as a shock to learn of the fresh tragedy which clouds the life of the splendid youngster who has put up such a game fight. But the end is not yet.

THE "HOLIDAY ANNUAL."

There is nothing on the market to beat the "Holiday Annual" as a companion on a winter evening. We hear tell of the Magic Carpet which transported its lucky owner into strange and wonderful lands. But the "Holiday Annual" eclipses that feat. With its budget of bright yarns, and its myriad other fine features, it carries you into the jolly world of St. Jim's and Greyfriars, and shows you a heap of other cheery sights.

Your Editor.

Ralph Reckness Cardew has threatened to go over the traces—   This time he does it!

CARDEW THE REBEL

A Grand, New Extra-Long Complete School Story of St. Jim's, telling how Tom Merry, as junior football captain, is forced to take action against the slacking Ralph Reckness Cardew.

A Ripping Yarn,

By Martin Clifford.

CHAPTER 1.
Slack !

"**S**LACKER !"

"Rotten slacker !"

Ralph Reckness Cardew of the Fourth Form at St. Jim's did not answer. He did not even look up.

He seemed too comfortable to move, as well as too lazy. Being both comfortable and lazy, he did not stir.

Levison and Clive, his study-mates in Study No. 9 in the Fourth, were standing in the doorway of the study looking at him. They were looking at him very expressively, and their words were expressive, too.

"Slacker !"

"Frowster !"

Cardew smiled gently.

He was reclining on a sofa—a new and handsome and luxurious sofa, which Cardew had added to the furniture of the study out of his own ample pocket-money.

A silken cushion was under his head. In his fingers he held a cigarette, which he occasionally placed lazily in his lips. A faint blue haze of smoke hung over him.

Levison and Clive were in football rig, with coats and mufflers on. Levison had a ball under his arm.

"Are you coming down to practice?" Levison demanded.

Cardew condescended to turn his head slightly towards the doorway.

"Practise what?" he asked.

"Footba'l, ass!"

"Oh, football! No!"

"You're smoking in the study," growled Clive.

"Yes, dear man."

"Chuck that muck away and come down to the footer."

"You've often told me," drawled Cardew, "that smoking is bad for the wind and spoils a chap's form at footer."

"Of course it is—and does."

"Well, then, footer is off. I'm spoiled already."

"You silly ass!"

"Thanks !"

"Look here, Cardew——"

"I'm lookin'."

"Oh, don't be such a slack duffer, Cardew!" exclaimed Levison impatiently. "Are you coming down to Little Side or not?"

"Do I look as if I were?" asked Cardew lazily.

"Tom Merry has offered to give you a chance for the junior eleven if you shape well in practice."

"Dear old Tommy! Give him my best thanks, and tell him——"

"Tell him what?"

"That to-day we have no bananas !"

"You silly owl!"

Cardew blew out a little cloud of smoke. He seemed to find something entertaining in the clouded brows of his chums. The slacker of the Fourth was looking his very slackest at the present moment, and evidently football was far from his thoughts.

"Now look here——" recommenced Sidney Clive.

Cardew waved his hand gently.

"Go away! Run away and play! Go and lead the strenuous life you love, and leave me here to slack !"

"I've a jolly good mind to mop you off that sofa and put your silly head in the coal-locker," grunted Clive.

"Dear man !"

"I've told Tom Merry you're turning up, Cardew," urged Levison.

"Naughty !" yawned Cardew. "Shouldn't tell stories! I never do—exceptin' sometimes! I say, won't Tom Merry be waitin' for you?"

"No, ass !"

"Won't Blake be waitin'?"

"Fathead !"

"Won't Kildare of the Sixth be waitin'? I believe I've heard that he's coachin' the fags at footer to-day."

"He's not likely to wait for us, duffer."

"Dear me! I wish somebody was waitin' for you, and that you were in a hurry not to keep him waitin'," said Cardew plaintively. "This is my first smoke for weeks, and I was enjoyin' it when you put your faces in the study. Won't you take them away and bury them?"

"Look here——"

"On second thoughts, you needn't bury them. But take them away !" implored Cardew.

"Oh, come on, Levison!" exclaimed Sidney Clive. "That frowsty slacker won't stir. Let's get out."

The South African junior went on down the passage. Ernest Levison lingered for a moment.

"Won't you come, Cardew?" he said. "You know we want this study to show up well in the footer this season. You ought to play up a bit for the study."

"You two fellows play up enough for three," assured Cardew. "Now my weary eyes I close, leave, oh, leave me to repose !"

"Kildare may miss you——"

"Let him !"

"Well, you know that all Lower School have to turn up to-day, and there will be three or four prefects on the ground," said Levison.

"Leave 'em there !"

"Oh, go and eat coke !" exclaimed Levison, exasperated, and he stalked away after Clive.

Cardew grinned over his cigarette, and his head sank on the cushion again. The fact that football practice, on that particular afternoon was compulsory for all the Lower School, did not worry Cardew; in fact, it made him all the more determined not to turn up. Opposition always made the dandy of the Fourth more obstinate.

There was a footstep in the passage a little later, and a cheery-faced fag looked in. It was Levison minor of the Third Form.

"Ernie gone down?" he asked, looking round.

THE GEM LIBRARY.—No. 924.

"The excellent and strenuous Ernie has gone down," answered Cardew. "He is probably already urgin' the flyin' ball, under the approvin' eyes of Kildare, our energetic captain, and winnin' golden opinions from all sorts of people."

"Oh, don't be a goat, you know," said Frank Levison. "Why don't you come down to footer, Cardew?"

"Echo answers why."

"Lazybones!"

"Good-bye, dear boy! Shut the door after you!"

Frank quitted the study and shut the door. But it was opened within five minutes.

This time it was Tom Merry of the Shell, junior captain of St. Jim's, who looked in. Cardew sighed.

"No rest for the wicked!" he said gently. "Do you happen to want anythin', Thomas?"

Tom Merry frowned. Then he coughed as he caught a whiff of tobacco-smoke. It did not agree with Tom's healthy lungs.

"What are you frowsting here for?" he demanded.

"Gettin' inquisitive in your old age, Thomas?"

"All the Lower School have to turn up at three-thirty, Cardew."

"I know."

"Well, are you coming?"

"No."

Tom Merry eyed him.

"I'm supposed to round up the slackers as junior captain," he said.

"Leave it at that, old bean. Does anybody ever do what he's supposed to do?"

"Look here, Cardew, you'd better come."

"I agree."

"Good," said Tom. "Get a move on, then." And the captain of the Shell went on his way.

Cardew winked at the curling wreath of smoke over his head.

"I agree with the worthy Thomas that I had better go," he murmured. "That's a dead cert—I'd much better! But I haven't agreed to go. It doesn't seem to have occurred to the solid, stolid brain of Thomas that a fellow sometimes does what he better hadn't! Dear me, I hope there won't be any more callers this afternoon!"

And Cardew threw away the stump of his cigarette and lighted another, and settled down to lazy repose.

CHAPTER 2.
Called Over the Coals !

"TOM MEWWY——"

"Hallo, Gussy!"

"Isn't Cardew comin'?"

"I think so," said Tom Merry. "It doesn't matter much either way."

Arthur Augustus D'Arcy of the Fourth Form shook his noble head seriously.

"It does mattah this time, deah boy," he explained. "Kildare has been askin' aftah him."

"Oh!" said Tom.

"As Cardew is a distant welation of mine, it is wathah wotten for me to have his disgwacin' the Form by slackin'," said Arthur Augustus. "Do you think it would do any good to give him a feahful thwashin'?"

Tom Merry laughed.

"Well, it wouldn't do him any harm," he admitted. "Better than frowsting in a study and smoking on a glorious afternoon like this."

"Yaas, wathah! I weally think——"

"Hallo! Look out for your scalp, Tom," said Monty Lowther, coming up with Manners of the Shell.

"You are intewwuptin' me, Lowthah," remarked Arthur Augustus, with calm dignity.

"Can't be helped, old top! Life's too short to wait for you to finish. Kildare's on your track, Tom!"

"What have I done now?" asked Tom, with a smile.

"It's about the slackers," explained Lowther. "Our jolly old captain has missed Cardew from the field, and he's missed him before, and before that. He's going to scalp somebody, and I think that somebody's you."

"Oh, my hat!" said Tom.

"Here he comes!" murmured Manners.

"Bai Jove, old Kildare looks quite watty!" observed Arthur Augustus D'Arcy. "Looks to me like a case of 'bend ovah.'"

Kildare of the Sixth was frowning as he came up to the group of juniors. As captain of the school, football skipper, and head of the games, Kildare had plenty on his hands, and the junior captain was supposed to relieve him of some of the minor details of his duties. And Tom Merry had a rather guilty feeling that he had been a little remiss. Tom Merry never slacked himself, but he was good-natured to a fault, and was a little too merciful to slackers.

"Merry!" rapped out the Sixth-Former.

"Here!" said Tom.

"I believe you were elected junior captain?"

"I believe I was," assented Tom.

"A junior captain's business isn't entirely swank!" said Kildare.

"I never supposed it was," said Tom, colouring.

"I thought you might have," said Kildare, with sarcasm. "Did you know that this afternoon was compulsory football practice?"

"Of course."

"Did you know that every fellow in the Lower School has to turn up, unless he's fortified behind a medical certificate?"

"Yes," said Tom. "Of course I knew."

"I thought you might have forgotten," said Kildare, still sarcastic. "The prefects have routed Racke and Crooke and Trimble out of their studies. Are you making a habit of leaving your duties to the prefects?"

"N-n-no."

"You don't think that Sixth Form chaps ought to do your job for you because you're so busy in the Shell?"

"Nunno," said Tom, his face crimson.

A couple of score of fellows were standing round grinning, and Tom was not enjoying the interview. It was very seldom that Kildare "slanged" a fellow, but when he did he made his meaning clear.

"Good!" said Kildare. "Of course, if you've a lot to do in the Lower School, there's always a Sixth Form prefect ready to run about for you."

"Um!" said Tom, not knowing what else to say. This vein of heavy sarcasm was rather new in the captain of St. Jim's.

"What does 'um!' mean exactly?" asked Kildare.

"Hem!"

"Bai Jove, Kildare is awf'ly watty!" Arthur Augustus confided to Blake and Herries and Digby, and those three youths nodded and grinned.

"Cardew's not here," went on Kildare. "I dare say you know there's a fellow named Cardew in the Fourth Form— or perhaps you have forgotten it?"

"Yes—no!" stammered Tom.

"Why isn't he here?"

"I—I don't know."

"Is he ill?"

"I—I think not."

"Never mind what you think! Tell me what you know!"

"Well, he isn't ill," said Tom.

"Good! Has he had an accident?"

"Not that I know of."

"Then why isn't he here?"

No answer.

Tom Merry was feeling exceedingly uncomfortable. He knew why Ralph Reckness Cardew was not there; it was because the dandy of the Fourth was slacking in his study. And it could not be denied that it was the junior captain's business to see that any Lower boy did not slack in his study on these occasions.

"Well?" rapped out Kildare. "Why isn't he here, Merry?"

"Hem!"

"Is he slacking?"

"I—I suppose so."

"You mean that you know he is?"

"Well, yes."

"It takes a long time to get what you know out of you, doesn't it?" said the captain of St. Jim's. "Is it your duty, as junior captain, to leave him slacking in his study?"

"Nunno."

"Then you don't consider it necessary to do your duty?"

"Oh, draw it mild, Kildare!" Tom Merry protested at last. "I dare say I've been a bit too easy-going. I'll go and rout him out if you like, and run him down here by the back of his neck."

"I'll do that," said Kildare grimly. "This is the third time I've missed Cardew, and it's going to be the last. As you don't seem equal to your job, I'll do it for you, Merry."

"I—I say——" stammered Tom.

Kildare did not seem to hear him. He walked off the field towards the School House.

Tom Merry turned a flushed face round and met grinning glances on all sides.

"Bai Jove, Kildare did pitch into you, deah boy!" said Arthur Augustus sympathetically. "He was feahfully watty."

"It's rotten," said Levison of the Fourth. "Cardew ought to be here!"

"Yaas, wathah!"

"You'll have to buck up, Tommy," said Figgins of the New House, with a shake of the head. "I always said it was a mistake making a School House chap junior captain!"

"Weally, Figgins——"

"Quite a mistake," said Kerr. "The School House is slack."

"Awfully slack!" said Fatty Wynn.

"Why, you burbling New House chumps——" began Jack Blake in great indignation.

"School House slackers!" roared the New House crowd.

"You don't seem to have much idea of law and order, Cardew," said Kildare, "that's why I have decided not to deal with the matter personally. But you'll have a prefects' licking. Now bend down!" "But," protested Cardew, "I——I appeal to the Housemaster. I believe that a lower boy up before the prefects has a right to appeal to his Housemaster?"
(See page 8.)

"Bai Jove, I——"

"They have to be dragged down to footer," said Figgins, with a grin. "I've heard that they have to be kicked out of bed in the morning by the prefects. Is that so, Blake?"

"You know it isn't, you New House burbler!" roared Blake.

"They never wash, you know," said Redfern of the New House. "They never even wash unless their Housemaster comes round with a cane!"

"Ha, ha, ha!"

"Bai Jove! That is a wotten slandah!" exclaimed Arthur Augustus hotly. "Mop up the gwound with those cheekay New House duffahs, you fellows!"

"Yes, rather!"

"You couldn't mop up a mosquito, you School House chump!" retorted George Figgins derisively. "Oh! Ah! Oh, my hat!"

George Figgins bumped on the ground, in the grasp of two or three exasperated School House juniors. His comrades rushed to the rescue at once. Football was forgotten for the moment.

"Mop them up! Give them jip!"

"Kick 'em off the field!"

"Yah! School House slackers!"

"New House cads!"

Darrell and Langton of the Sixth came striding on the scene. It was high time, for football practice seemed to be turning into a House row of unusual magnitude. The two prefects cuffed right and left, and roared commands, and the fray was stopped.

"We've licked those cheekay New House wottahs," said Arthur Augustus, rubbing his nose—"at least, we should have licked them if the pwefects hadn't interfered. But it's wathah wotten to give those wottahs a handle against us like this. Cardew ought to be wagged."

"He will be!" growled Tom Merry, who was feeling decidedly sore at being called to order before the whole Lower School by the head of the games.

"It's rotten," said Blake. "But there's no doubt there's

a lot of slackness. I always thought that junior captain ought to belong to the Fourth, not the Shell."

"Yaas, wathah! That is quite wight!"

"Fathead!" said Tom Merry.

"Weally, deah boy——"

"I say, where's Cardew after all?" said Monty Lowther. "Kildare doesn't seem to have rounded him up."

"Pewwaps he won't come, even for Kildare," suggested Arthur Augustus. "He is a feahfully weckless young ass."

"Oh, my hat!"

Levison and Clive looked very grave. It was quite on the cards that Ralph Reckness Cardew, in a reckless and obstinate mood, might disregard even the captain of the school. And that way lay serious trouble. They looked anxiously for Cardew to appear.

But he did not appear.

CHAPTER 3.
Cardew's Way!

KILDARE of the Sixth stopped at the door of Study No. 9 in the Fourth, and threw it wide open.

He arrived at a rather unfortunate moment for Cardew.

A third cigarette was smoking in Cardew's mouth, and there was quite a haze in the study.

He did not look round as the door opened, but he addressed the newcomer, without seeing him, from his comfortable place on the sofa.

"Don't come in, whoever you are! Can't you let a fellow have a little quiet? I tell you I'm not comin' down to the footer! I'm fed up with footer! And if Kildare butts in, tell him, from me, that he can go and eat coke! Got that?"

"I've got it!" said Kildare grimly.

He strode into the study as he spoke.

Cardew gave a start, and whirled round on the sofa. Even the cool and reckless Cardew was dismayed for a moment as he realised that he had been addressing the captain of the school. Kildare's stalwart form towered over him.

But Cardew was never at a loss for long. He quite understood that he was in a scrape; but it was his pride to go through any scrape, however serious, without turning a hair. Only for a second did his expression change. Then he gave the captain of St. Jim's a genial nod.

"You, Kildare?" he said lazily. "I thought you were busy with the footer, teachin' the young-idea how to shoot, and all that. How kind of you to give me a look in."

"So I can go and eat coke, can I?" said Kildare, glowering down at the dandy of the Fourth.

"Certainly, old bean, if you like; but I should recommend somethin' a little more edible as a matter of taste."

"I've talked to Tom Merry about letting the slackers frowst in the studies," said Kildare.

"Poor old Tommy! I know you're fairly eloquent when you get goin', old bean," said Cardew. "In fact, I believe you're just preparin' a burst of eloquence for me. I can see it in your eye."

"Get off that sofa!"

Cardew sighed.

"What an extremely unpleasant way of askin' a fellow to shift!" he said. "But I was always obligin'."

He rolled off the sofa, and stood up, and yawned.

"How long will it take you to change?" asked Kildare.

"Say a couple of hours."

"I suppose you think that's funny?" said Kildare, after a pause.

"Not at all. Serious as a jolly old judge."

"I found you smoking," said Kildare.

"You did. I've another cigarette left if you're yearnin' for one."

"You will take five hundred lines for smoking."

"So much as that?"

"Yes!" roared Kildare.

"Very well; I'll take them," murmured Cardew. "I think you're overdoin' it, and you really ought to remember the giddy old adage, be just before you're generous. Anythin' else?"

Kildare looked at his watch.

"It's just a quarter to four," he said. "I'm going down to the door. I shall wait for you two minutes."

"That's awfully good of you!"

"You'll join me then, changed and ready for footer."

"That's cuttin' it rather close, isn't it?"

Kildare left the study without replying. Ralph Reckness Cardew cast a rather curious glance after him. He wondered a little why the head prefect of St. Jim's had taken so much back-chat from him without giving him a beating. Certainly there were few other prefects who would not have told Cardew to bend over a chair, while "six" rewarded him for his impertinence.

But Kildare knew the difference between a slacker like Cardew and a slacker like Racke of the Shell. Racke would have frowsted away his life if he had been allowed; while Cardew was lazy at intervals, and sometimes had fits of great energy, on which occasions he played brilliant football, and as a matter of fact he was always fit. His laziness was as much a pose as anything else. Probably Cardew himself did not know how much was affectation and how much was genuine.

Certainly there was an imp of the perverse in his nature, which made him find entertainment in running counter to any general opinion, and he seldom raised any expectation without disappointing it afterwards.

Cardew watched the senior out of sight, and looked at his watch. A minute of the two allowed had elapsed.

Cardew sauntered out of the study.

He did not head for the changing-room; he had no intention whatever of playing football that afternoon. But he was well aware that if Kildare had to come back to the study for him he would bring an ashplant, and that the ashplant would be given some hefty exercise. Kildare was patient, but his patience had a limit.

The dandy of the Fourth, instead of heading for the stairs, disappeared in the opposite direction.

A minute later Kildare's steps were audible in the passage. He had a cane under his arm and a grim frown on his face as he looked into Study No. 9.

"You've asked for it, Cardew! Now——"

Kildare broke off.

The study was empty. He glanced round it, and shifted the screen that stood in the corner; but Cardew was not in hiding there. With compressed lips and knitted brow Kildare stepped into the passage and looked up and down. The junior was not in sight.

"Cardew!" he called.

There was no answer.

Kildare went down the stairs. It was miles beneath his dignity to search the studies and the box-rooms for an elusive junior who was deliberately dodging him. But his look was very angry as he left the School House. Probably

no junior at St. Jim's, with the exception of Cardew, would have ventured to defy the authority of the captain of the school in this way, and Kildare mentally resolved that the cheeky Fourth-Former should regret it.

He walked back to the football-ground alone. Tom Merry & Co. eyed him as he came—Levison of the Fourth with keen anxiety. But Kildare's look did not invite questions, and no questions were asked.

But all the Lower School of both Houses knew that Cardew was not coming to football practice, and that in staying out he had deliberately set himself in opposition to the head of the games. Nobody wanted to be in Cardew's shoes when the football was over.

Meanwhile, Cardew of the Fourth, from an upper window, had watched Kildare of the Sixth depart, with a smile on his face. In his way he liked Kildare, and he respected him, as all the St. Jim's fellows did. Yet, from sheer idleness and perverseness he had set himself up against the captain of the school—a reed against an oak.

Perhaps for a moment or two Cardew regretted his perverse folly, and thought of changing rapidly and cutting down to the footer field. But, if so, he dismissed the thought. He had told Tom Merry and his study-mates that he was not playing football that afternoon, and he would not be rounded up, like a Trimble or a Crooke, and forced to eat his vainglorious words.

Yet, as he knew perfectly well, the contest was an impossible one. He could not stand against authority. When Kildare was at leisure again he would be sent for, and he would be thrashed. That would be a rather inglorious ending to his declaration of independence.

It was perhaps fortunate for Ralph Reckness Cardew—and perhaps it was unfortunate—that he had a quickness of wit unusual in the Fourth, and that he was seldom landed in a scrape by his folly, without finding a way out by his cleverness. He knew that he was up against it now, and he lighted and smoked his last cigarette while he thought out the problem.

Then, with a cheery smile on his face, he strolled away to the masters' studies, and tapped at the door of Monsieur Morny.

"Entrez!"

The French master was seated by the window reading a two-days-old copy of a Paris paper, deep in the problem of the Ruhr. But he looked up and gave Cardew a kind nod. Cardew was not a promising pupil in the French class; he was given to ragging, and he was careless, and inattentive. But he was clever, and he had a knowledge of French that was far and away beyond that of any other junior at St. Jim's. French lesson-books he detested; but there were a dozen French volumes in Study No. 9 that he read for pleasure, and that was a sure passport to the esteem of a French master who had the weary task of driving a faint knowledge of his beautiful language into thick and unwilling heads in a lower Form.

"Entrez, mon garcon," said the French gentleman kindly. "Zere is somezing zat I can do for you, hein?"

"I'm afraid I'm interrupting you, sir——"

"Pas du tout! Vat is it?"

"I've been reading 'Zaire,' sir?" said Cardew. "I wondered whether you would mind helping me with a rather difficult passage?"

Monsieur Morny beamed.

Here was a Fourth-Former who borrowed Voltaire from the school library, and read it without being compelled to do so! No wonder the French master beamed!

"Mon cher garcon, I shall be delight!" he exclaimed.

"It's a shame to take up your time, sir," said Cardew.

"Du tout!" declared Monsieur Morny. "It is one pleasure. I am delight! To find a boy who shall take pleasure in to read ze poetry of ze grand Voltaire! Ah, zat is one delight zat do not often happen to a French master, n'est-ce-pas? Give me zat volume on ze shelf. Point out ze place."

Master and pupil were soon deep in "Zaire." But Cardew had no intention of passing the afternoon in the perusal of the stately and somewhat ponderous poetry of the "grand Voltaire." He would have preferred even football to that. Taking advantage of a pause, he landed Mossoo on the subject of the news from Paris and the Ruhr. On that subject Monsieur Morny was inexhaustibly eloquent. In the masters' Common-room he had bored the whole staff of St. Jim's almost to tears on that topic. Once he was started, Mossoo was lost to all considerations of time and space.

Cardew leaned back in his chair. Voltaire lay unheeded on the table. Monsieur Morny held forth in an incessant flow of eloquence on the subject of "ces sales Boches." Cardew shifted a little to turn his face away, and dozed comfortably while Monsieur Morny ran on inexhaustibly.

It was not till five o'clock sounded from the clock-tower that Cardew made a move. Then he rose, and thanked the French master profoundly.

"Rien, rien!" said Monsieur Morny, with a gracious wave

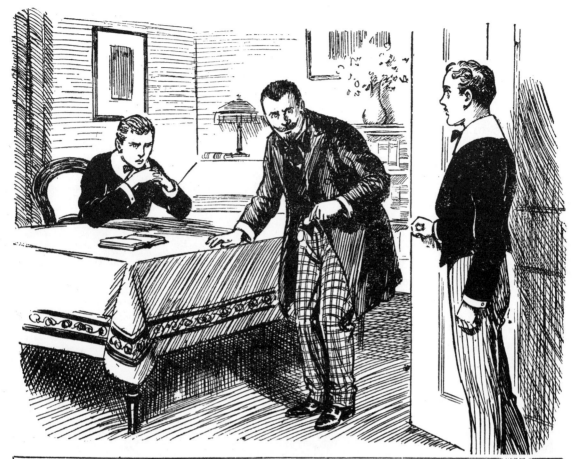

A glint came into Cardew's eyes as the captain of the Shell entered the study of the French master. "Excuse me, Monsieur Morny," said Tom Merry politely, "but Cardew is wanted." "Helas!" said Monsieur Morny. "Zat is too bad, Cardew, vhen we get on so vell viz ze grand Voltaire, but——" "Not at all, sir," said Cardew. "I'm not wanted, and I'm not goin'!" *(See page 12.)*

of the hand. "Alvays I am please to see so clevair a pupil—one so interested in ze language French."

"You are very kind, sir!" murmured Cardew.

"Du tout—du tout."

Cardew turned to the door. As if struck by an afterthought he turned back.

"By the way, sir——"

"Comment?"

"I remember now, sir, that it's compulsory football this afternoon," said Cardew. "We're not allowed to cut it for anything except extra toot. Would you mind, sir, giving me a note to show my Housemaster, so that he will know I've had extra tuition this afternoon."

"Mais certainement," said the unsuspicious Mossoo.

He wrote the note at once, and handed it to Cardew. That glib youth thanked him effusively, and left the study. He smiled as he walked down the passage.

CHAPTER 4.
Up Before the Prefects.

TOM MERRY & CO. came in, in a cheery crowd, in the falling dusk. There was a buzz of voices in the changing-room, and the chief topic was Cardew of the Fourth, and what was likely to happen to him. Football practice on Little Side had passed off without Cardew putting in an appearance—after the captain of the school had specially ordered him there. Such an act of defiance was amazing, unheard-of. That Kildare had not forgotten, and that he would make an example of the cheeky rebel, could not be doubted. The only question was, what form Cardew's exemplary punishment would take.

"Six, at least!" said Jack Blake.

"Likely enough a prefects' licking!" said Gore.

"Or a report to the Housemaster," said Talbot of the Shell. "Cardew must be an ass to ask for trouble like this."

"Yaas, wathah!"

"What the thump is his object?" said Racke of the Shell. "He knows jolly well that a chap can't stand up against the prefects. I jolly well would if I could!"

"Sheer obstinacy," said Wildrake. "I guess Cardew's looking for trouble because he's fond of it."

"He won't be happy till he gets it," chuckled Monty Lowther, "and I've a sort of idea that he won't be happy then."

"Well, he wants a licking," said Tom Merry.

"Yaas, wathah! It's weally your fault, of course, Tom Mewwy——"

"What?" howled Tom.

"Pway don't woar at a fellow, Tom Mewwy! You know I dislike bein' woared at!"

"What do you mean, ass?" demanded Tom. "How is it my fault?"

"Weally, Tom Mewwy, you had that fwom Kildare. You are too easy-goin' with the slackahs."

"Oh, rats!" grunted Tom.

"If you had made Cardew toe the line befoah, he would not have kicked ovah the twaces, you know," said Arthur Augustus, with an air of wisdom. "You are wathah slack, old bean."

"Br-r-r-r-r!" said Tom.

"That is not an intelligible wemark, Tom Mewwy. You often let that wottah Wacke sneak out of football——"

"Eh, what?" interjected Aubrey Racke. "Are you calling me names, D'Arcy?"

Arthur Augustus looked round serenely.

"Did you heah me, Wacke? I was only callin' you a wottah, deah boy. I am suah that that is no news to you."

"Ha, ha, ha!"

"Now, if I were juniah captain," continued Arthur Augustus, unheeding the scowling Racke, "I should wound up the slackahs in gweat style. If you cared to wesign in favah of a bettah captain, Tom Mewwy, I should not hesitate to take on the job."

Tom Merry laughed.

"When St. Jim's wants a captain of a necktie eleven or a top-hat team, Gussy, I'll resign in your favour," he answered.

"Bai Jove!"

The Terrible Three left the changing room together.

As they came upstairs they came on Levison and Clive and Cardew in the Fourth Form passage. Cardew was leaning against the wall, evidently in a state of unruffled serenity. Tom and Manners and Lowther stopped.

"You didn't turn up for footer, Cardew," said Tom.

"Levison and Clive have just mentioned the fact," said Cardew. "But I was already aware of it."

"Kildare told you personally——"

"Yes; he was kind enough to give me his individual attention," said Cardew urbanely. "Awfully kind-hearted chap, Kildare. I like him no end."

"Then why are you setting yourself up against him?" demanded Tom Merry gruffly.

"Anythin' for a new stunt!" yawned Cardew. "It's no end funny to pull the leg of a jolly old Sixth Form prefect."

"You won't find it so funny when you get six!" said Manners.

"But perhaps I sha'n't get six."

"You don't think Kildare will let you off?" exclaimed Lowther.

"Oh, yes!"

"Why should he?" asked Tom, puzzled.

"Well, I've got such nice ways, you know," said Cardew argumentatively. "A really nice and pleasant chap like me——"

"Oh, dry up!" said Tom. "You ought to be licked, and I jolly well hope that Kildare will make it a prefects' licking."

"Thanks so much for your kind wishes!"

The Terrible Three went on their way to Study No. 10 in the Shell. They could not help feeling puzzled by Cardew's serenity, which was obviously genuine. He had committed an act of defiance that could not possibly be passed over, yet he seemed to have no fear whatever of the consequences. Certainly there were plenty of fellows who did not fear a licking, even a prefects' licking, which was quite a severe infliction. But a licking to follow Cardew's insubordination would have spoiled the whole effect, from the rebel's point of view. His defiance became simply ridiculous if he were thrashed for it. But what hope he could have of eluding the thrashing was a problem to Tom Merry & Co.

It was a problem to Levison and Clive as well. They were quite puzzled.

"What about tea?" asked Cardew. "I've laid in some good things to welcome you home after your strenuous exertions on the giddy football-field. Trot along with your uncle!"

"Oh, all right!" said Levison. "You're for it, Cardew. I suppose you'll understand that when you get it?"

"When!" said Cardew. "Let's have tea, anyhow, before the jolly old execution."

The three chums went on to Study No. 9 in the Fourth. Levison and Clive perplexed and a little worried, and Cardew airy and careless. There was quite a good spread in Study No. 9, and the hungry footballers were glad to see it. They had almost finished tea when D'Arcy minor of the Third looked into the study.

"Execution!" he announced. "Cardew's wanted. Better put some exercise-books in your pants, Cardew."

Cardew glanced round lazily.

"Who wants me?"

"Kildare. Prefects' room," said Wally of the Third, with a grin. "All the House prefects are there, sittin' round in a jolly old circle like a family of moulting fowls. It's a prefects' licking, old bean, and you take my tip—put in some exercise-books."

And D'Arcy minor winked and departed.

"I'm sorry for this, Cardew," said Levison.

"Dear man!" said Cardew.

"You've got to go through it now," said Clive. "I must say you deserve it, Cardew. You asked for it."

"We don't get all we ask for in this disappointin' world," said Cardew. "Isn't there an appeal from a prefects' meetin'?"

"You can appeal to the Housemaster if you like, but what good will that do you?"

"Lots, I hope," said Cardew cheerfully. "Come along like good pals and see the fun!"

"Blest if I can make you out!" grunted Clive. "We'll come."

"Oh, do!"

Levison and Clive walked down the passage with the culprit. The news had gone round that Cardew of the Fourth was "up before the prefects," and it excited general interest. A crowd of fellows hailed him on the staircase.

"You're for it, Cardew!"

"And a jolly good thing, too!" hooted Grundy of the Shell.

"Yaas, wathah! I do not sympathise with you in the vewy least, Cardew, though you are a wolation of mine," said Arthur Augustus D'Arcy severely.

"Hold me somebody while I faint!" said Cardew.

"Ha, ha, ha!"

"Weally, you cheekay ass——"

"What on earth are you playing this silly game for, Cardew?" asked Talbot of the Shell.

"Bored, old fellow," answered Cardew affably. "I'm givin' the jolly old prefects a fall, you know, simply by way of entertainment."

"Giving them a fall!" said Talbot, with a stare.

"Just that!"

"How's that?" demanded Blake.

"Follow on and you'll see!"

Ralph Reckness Cardew walked on with his chums. Quite an army of fellows followed him.

The juniors were surprised and keenly interested. The general belief was that Cardew was going to be thrashed, and that he was simply keeping up his swank till the last possible moment. It was, as Manners observed, a case of pride going before destruction, and a haughty spirit before a fall. Yet, in spite of themselves, and the apparent certainty of the affair, the fellows were puzzled. Cardew had started what seemed like a hopeless as well as an unjustifiable contest. Yet it was certain that he would leave no stone unturned to come out ahead, and his cleverness was well known. Half the House followed him to the doorway of the prefects' room, where those great men—the prefects of the Sixth Form—sat in state to deal with the delinquent.

CHAPTER 5.
Before the Housemaster !

KILDARE eyed the dandy of the Fourth grimly as he came in with Levison and Clive. Langton and Rushden, Darrell and North, and the other House prefects, regarded him curiously. Cardew's manner was cool and careless, and he certainly did not look like a fellow who was going to "bend over" and receive an ignominious licking, with a crowd of Lower boys looking on in the open doorway. The door of the prefects' room was left open, in order that Cardew's punishment might be seen, and certainly there were plenty of witnesses. No doubt the prefects considered that the sight of it would have an exemplary effect upon any other reckless juniors who might be inclined to kick over the traces. Kildare waved Levison and Clive back, and they stood in the doorway, with a murmuring crowd surging behind.

"Come here, Cardew!"

"Any old thing," said Cardew, as he lounged forward.

"Cheek won't do you any good, young 'un!" said Darrell.

"Thanks for the tip!" said Cardew imperturbably.

There was a chuckle from the passage outside. Hardly a fellow sympathised with Cardew, who was flagrantly in the wrong all along the line. But there was something entertaining in seeing a Fourth Form fellow bearding the Sixth Form lions in their den in this cool way. Knox of the Sixth scowled round.

"Silence, you fags!"

"You've cut footer practice this afternoon, Cardew," said Kildare. "You did so, though I came to your study personally and ordered you to get on to the ground."

"It was so kind of you," said Cardew.

"I wanted to let you off lightly."

"That's like you, Kildare," said Cardew affably. "You're a good sort. That's why I admire you so much."

Kildare coughed, and some of the prefects grinned, in spite of the seriousness of the occasion. Again there was a chuckle in the crowded passage without, where every word was heard eagerly.

"You don't seem to have much idea of law and order, Cardew," went on the captain of St. Jim's. "That's why I've decided not to deal with the matter personally, but to call a prefects' meeting. I think a prefects' beating may open your eyes a little, and teach you that you can't back up against authority in the school."

"Think so?" said Cardew doubtfully.

"Bend over!"

"I appeal to the Housemaster!"

"What?"

"I appeal to the Housemaster!" repeated Cardew coolly. "Getting deaf in your old age? I believe that a Lower boy up before the prefects has a right to appeal to his Housemaster?"

Kildare stared at him.

"That's true," he said. "But what good will an appeal to Mr. Railton do you? You know very well that he will be more severe on your conduct than I should."

"Nevertheless—that's a good word!—nevertheless, I appeal to the Housemaster," said Cardew calmly. "Got that?"

Kildare paused.

"You know that it means a flogging instead of a prefects' beating?" he said.

"Does it? I'm chancin' that."

"Make him bend over, and give the cheeky young cad the licking of his life," growled Knox.

"He has the right to appeal to the Housemaster if he chooses," said Kildare. "If you are serious, Cardew, I will take you to Mr. Railton."

"Waitin', old man."

"Very well," said Kildare, compressing his lips.

He dropped his hand on Cardew's shoulder and walked him out of the prefects' room. The crowd of juniors made way for them. That august body, the House prefects, looked at one another rather sheepishly. They knew that the juniors were grinning at them. Certainly, the culprit was likely to fare worse at the Housemaster's hands—he had jumped out of the frying-pan into the fire. Nevertheless, he certainly had made the House prefects look rather foolish. They had gathered in state in the prefects' room to judge him and punish him, and they were left sitting there like—as D'Arcy minor irreverently described it—a circle of moulting fowls. Knox jumped up and slammed the door, almost upon a dozen junior noses.

In the midst of a breathless crowd Cardew of the Fourth walked with Kildare to Mr. Railton's quarters. The centre of interest was now shifted from the prefects' room to the Housemaster's study. Kildare would have closed the door as he entered Mr. Railton's presence, but a foot was in the way, and it remained ajar, so that a breathless crowd had full hearing, and a partial view, of the subsequent proceedings.

"Now for the jolly old circus!" whispered Monty Lowther. "Railton will make him hop."

"Yaas, wathah!"

"Levison, old man, as he's your pal, if you have tears prepare to shed them now," murmured Lowther. And there was a subdued chuckle in the corridor.

But the fellows who had a view of Cardew in the study could see him standing before the Housemaster's table, with Kildare at his side, perfectly cool and unconcerned. His manner to the Housemaster was very respectful, but it was confident. Upon what he based his confidence was a mystery to the juniors; but the opinion was growing that Ralph Reckness Cardew had some mysterious card up his sleeve.

Kildare, in a few succinct words, acquainted the Housemaster with Cardew's offence. Mr. Railton fixed a stern glance on the junior.

"You have heard what Kildare says, Cardew?"

"Yes, sir."

"You have chosen to be dealt with by me?"

"Yes, sir."

"Very good!" said Mr. Railton coldly. "Your conduct is utterly inexcusable, Cardew. I cannot pass over such an example of idleness, impertinence, and disregard of authority lightly. I shall report you to the Head for a flogging!"

There was a gasp in the passage from all who heard.

Mr. Railton was bound to uphold the authority of the head prefect, and he had done so, as the juniors expected. Their only doubt had been whether he would cane Cardew himself severely, or report him for a flogging, and he had chosen the more severe course. Evidently he considered that the wayward rebel of the Fourth Form required a lesson that would not be forgotten in a hurry.

Cardew's voice was heard, cool and calm.

"May I speak, sir?"

"You may speak, certainly, if you have anything to say in extenuation of your conduct," said the Housemaster sternly.

"I think I have a great deal, sir," said Cardew urbanely. "I only ask a hearin'."

"You may proceed."

"I was really entitled to cut footer practice this afternoon, sir."

"On what grounds?"

"Extra tuition, sir."

"You are not, so far as I am aware, taking extra tuition in any subject, Cardew."

"No, sir; only Monsieur Morny is sometimes kind enough

to give me extra toot in my French, sir. I understood that when any fellow was with a master for extra tuition he was excused all games practices?"

"That is correct," said Mr. Railton.

Outside in the crowded corridor the juniors simply stared at one another. So this was the mysterious card that Ralph Reckness Cardew had had up his sleeve!

It amazed the juniors. Extra "toot" for Cardew, the laziest slacker in the Fourth, with the exception of Baggy Trimble! Cardew grinding at French on a half-holiday without being driven to it! It was a little too amazing. Not a fellow there believed that Cardew had taken extra lessons in French and given up half-holidays to them. But the keener fellows could guess that he had fixed up a French lesson for that one special afternoon in order to give Kildare of the Sixth a Roland for his Oliver, as it were.

There was a silence in the Housemaster's study. Kildare's look was very peculiar. He waited for Mr. Railton to speak.

"Do you mean to tell me, Cardew, that you were engaged in a French lesson with Monsieur Morny this afternoon?"

"Mossoo gave me a note, sir, as usual, to show to the head of the games if asked for."

"Give me the note."

"Here it is, sir."

Cardew laid the note on the table. It was written in Monsieur Morny's curly Latin script, and in his rather unusual English. It stated plainly enough that R. R. Cardew, Fourth Form, had been taking extra French with him that afternoon till five o'clock.

The Housemaster and the prefect both looked at the note. Then they looked at Cardew.

"Did you tell Kildare you were doing French with Monsieur Morny this afternoon, Cardew?"

"It never crossed my mind, sir. Kildare was with me only a few moments. But I believe it's usual only to show the master's note to the head of the games if asked. Kildare did not ask anythin' about it."

"That is so, sir," said Kildare. "It certainly never occurred to me that Cardew was doing extra French this afternoon."

"I'm goin' in for the special French prize this term, sir," said Cardew calmly. "Monsieur Morny thinks I have a good chance."

Mr. Railton coughed.

He was in a difficult position. Kildare was reddening a little. Outside the study the juniors waited breathlessly. Whatever the Housemaster might think, Tom Merry & Co. knew perfectly well that Cardew was in the wrong—that the extra French lesson was an afterthought, a trick to defeat punishment.

"You should have told Kildare that you were taking extra French with Monsieur Morny," said Mr. Railton at last.

"He did not ask me, sir."

"You should have told him, nevertheless."

"Very well, sir; on another occasion I shall be careful to remember that," said Cardew meekly.

Mr. Railton coughed again.

He looked at Kildare. The prefect was puzzled and disturbed. He could not help suspecting that Cardew was somehow tricking him; but Kildare was too generous to condemn on suspicion. If Cardew had had an extra French lesson fixed for that afternoon, he was entitled to cut games practice, and he was not strictly bound to tell Kildare so unless asked, and Kildare had not asked that question.

"Well, Kildare?" said Mr. Railton at length.

"I—I am afraid, sir, that Cardew has been trying to make a fool of me," said Kildare—"what the juniors would call pulling my leg. There would have been no trouble at all if he had told me in the first place that he was taking extra French with Monsieur Morny."

"Quite so."

"All the same, sir, he was not bound to tell me unless I asked him, and I did not ask him. I simply ordered him to change and go down to the ground."

THE GEM LIBRARY.—No. 824.

Mr. Railton fixed his eyes on Cardew.

"I fear, Cardew, that your line of conduct was dictated by a desire to be impertinent to a prefect," he said.

"Oh, sir!" murmured Cardew.

"You could have made your present statement to the prefects, when called before them, without referring the matter to me."

"Could I, sir?"

"Certainly you could."

"I thought a fellow had a right to appeal to his Housemaster, sir, when he was suffering under injustice."

"That is correct; but——"

Mr. Railton paused again. The incident was becoming slightly ridiculous. Cardew could scarcely be punished for having acted as he had a right to act.

"I—I think, sir, I will ask you to let the matter drop," said Kildare. "I'm sorry I've wasted your time."

"You have not wasted my time, Kildare; but Cardew has certainly done so. Cardew, listen to me. I cannot help thinking that this whole business is an impertinent jest on your part, designed to show your contempt for authority, and to make a sort of hero of yourself in the eyes of the other Lower boys."

"Oh, sir!"

"I will not condemn you on bare suspicion, though that is my impression," said the Housemaster sternly. "On this occasion, as Kildare suggests it, I will give you the benefit of the doubt. You may go."

"Thank you, sir!" said Cardew demurely.

And he went.

CHAPTER 6.
Cardew's Triumph !

A CROWD of fellows walked with Cardew of the Fourth into the junior Common-room, after he had left the Housemaster's study. Cardew was cool and nonchalant, and seemed rather bored with the whole affair; most of the juniors were grinning. It was obvious to them that the cool-headed dandy of the Fourth had scored over the prefects, and even over the Housemaster—a very unusual exploit, yet in this case a successful one. He had disobeyed the head-prefect, he had cut games practice against orders, he had cheeked a prefects' meeting, he had pulled the Housemaster's leg, and he walked off, after all these exploits, unpunished and smiling. Any Lower boy who scored off authority in this way was sure of getting his meed of admiration, and even fellows who were down on Cardew could not help admiring his nerve, and chuckling over his success.

"It was great!" said Lumley-Lumley of the Fourth. "It really was great!"

"Fancy giving Kildare a fall!" chuckled Racke.

"Kildare's a bit of an ass," said Herries. "He might have known that Cardew had something up his sleeve."

"It was cheek!" said Tom Merry abruptly. "If Cardew was fixed for a French lesson when Kildare told him to go down to the field he ought to have said so."

"But I wasn't!" said Cardew.

"What?" exclaimed Tom.

"The French lesson was a giddy after-thought," explained Cardew airily. "Mossoo is an innocent old duck. I let him bore me, and got that note out of him. But when Kildare talked to me in my study I hadn't any idea of extra toot. I thought of it afterwards."

"Oh, my hat!"

"Ha, ha, ha!" roared Racke.

"If Kildare knew that!" exclaimed Manners.

"Luckily he didn't know," drawled Cardew. "Isn't he a jolly old ass?"

"Then you're not taking extra French at all?" exclaimed Blake.

"No jolly fear, old bean—only on special occasions, when it comes in useful to make Kildare look an ass!"

"Ha, ha, ha!"

Tom Merry frowned.

"Then you've simply made a fool of Kildare," he said.

"Just that!"

"And of Railton, too?" said Digby.

"Railton, too!" agreed Cardew.

"And suppose it occurs to either of them to inquire just when that extra toot was fixed up, and they find out that it wasn't arranged till after Kildare had ordered you down to football?"

Cardew shrugged his shoulders.

"I had to take that chance," he yawned. "But it wasn't likely. The matter's closed now, and they won't reopen it."

"That's so," said Tom. "But——"

"But what, old bean?"

"It's a rotten trick to pull Kildare's leg like that. You couldn't have taken in Knox or Monteith in the same way."

You're taking advantage of Kildare being an unsuspicious chap with a sense of fair play."

"Am I?" drawled Cardew.

"Yes, you are!" said Tom sharply.

"Perhaps so. Let it go at that."

"Well, I think that's rather rotten," said Tom.

"So glad to hear your opinion," said Cardew affably. "It's really a benefit to us chaps to have a big authority like Thomas to refer to, when there's any doubt about the moral aspect of a matter. It must be due to the careful way Miss Priscilla brought him up. I never had a dear old governess when I was a little chap."

"Ha, ha, ha!"

"Oh, cheese it!" growled Tom.

"I am boring Thomas," said Cardew. "But tit for tat is fair play. Think of the number of times you've bored me, Thomas."

Tom Merry turned away, half-angry. For a long time there was laughter in the junior Common-room over Cardew's exploit, and there was no doubt that his nerve was a good deal admired. From sheer idleness he had entered upon a contest with authority, and from sheer audacity he had carried it through successfully. That he was in the wrong was a trifling circumstance almost lost sight of in the light of his success.

But when Cardew went to Study No. 9 in the Fourth for prep he found his study-mates with grave faces. He gave them a comical look.

"Funny, wasn't it?" he asked.

"Very!" said Levison dryly.

"Doesn't it amuse you?"

"Not very much," said Levison. "And it's pretty certain, now you've swanked about it to the whole House, that Kildare will get to know, sooner or later, that you fooled him."

"Oh, he won't rake it up again!" said Cardew easily. "Old Kildare won't bear malice. Besides, with all the Lower School laughing at him, he will want to get the whole bizney forgotten as soon as possible."

"That's very likely," said Clive. "But——"

"Well?" said Cardew.

"Oh, nothing!"

Cardew sighed.

"A prophet is never without honour except in his own country," he remarked. "Here's the whole House chortlin', and in my own study there isn't even a smile. This is the only junior study that has ever scored off the Sixth."

"You came jolly near getting a Head's flogging."

"A miss is as good as a mile."

"And you ought to have had it, too."

"What a life if we all got what we ought to get!" smiled Cardew. "As jolly old Shakespeare remarks, who would escape whipping?"

"Oh, bosh! Aren't you going to do your prep?"

"I think I prefer the armchair and a novel. If Mr. Lathom is crusty in the morning, I can easily explain that my extra French studies have taken all my time."

"Oh, my hat!"

Cardew read a novel while his companions worked. In the Fourth Form room the following morning he was called on to construe. All the Fourth watched him as he rose to answer Mr. Lathom.

"I'm sorry, sir," said Cardew. "I feel that I ought to apologise, Mr. Lathom."

"What—what?" ejaculated the master of the Fourth.

"I am bound to confess, sir, that I did no preparation last evening," said Cardew. "I know that I ought not to allow my extra French study to take up the time given to other work, sir, and it shall not occur again."

Mr. Lathom gave him quite a benevolent look over his spectacles.

"If you are working hard at French, Cardew, I will excuse you on this occasion. Monsieur Morny has spoken to me of your great progress in his language. But you must remember, Cardew, that the regular Form work must not be neglected."

"I will, sir," said Cardew respectfully.

And Cardew did not construe. The Fourth Form manfully suppressed their chuckles. Only Arthur Augustus D'Arcy gave the dandy of the Fourth a severe look of reprehension, to which Cardew responded by a playful wink.

CHAPTER 7.
Tom Merry Puts His Foot Down !

T OM MERRY tapped at the door of Kildare's study after lessons that day, and entered, in a very uncomfortable frame of mind. Kildare had sent for him, and Tom could not help suspecting that he was wanted in connection with the affair of Cardew. He found the captain of St. Jim's standing by the study window with a frown on his brow.

"You've heard about Cardew, I suppose?" was Kildare's first remark.

Cardew's struggles were of no avail. Tom Merry & Co. seized him, and he was swung off his feet. Struggling in the grasp of the footballers he was carried along the passage. Suddenly Mr. Railton came out of his study, and signed to the party to stop. "What does this mean, Merry?" asked the Housemaster. "We're taking Cardew down to footer, sir!" answered the junior captain. (*See page 13.*)

"What about Cardew?" asked Tom, to gain time.

"I'm not asking you to tell me anything," said the captain of St. Jim's gruffly. "The story is going the round of the House, and I understand that it is causing great entertainment in junior studies. I was made a fool of yesterday."

"Oh!" said Tom.

"It seems that Cardew was lying—or something very near it—in making out that he had extra French lessons at the time. It seems that he fixed up the French lesson with Mossoo simply in order to have a yarn to spin, after appealing to the Housemaster."

"Oh!" said Tom again. He hardly knew what to say.

"The story has come to me unofficially, of course," went on Kildare. "I can't take any official notice of it. I was bound to hear it sooner or later, and I've no doubt that Cardew is pluming himself considerably. You've heard how the matter stands, of course, though you needn't tell me so. This won't do, Tom Merry."

"No!" said Tom.

"I told you yesterday on the football ground, that a junior captain has duties," said Kildare. "I don't say you're slack—you're not that. But you're too easy with other fellows who slack. If you'd seen that all the Lower boys were on the field yesterday I shouldn't have had to take the matter into my own hands and give that cheeky young sweep a chance of playing off his impertinence."

Tom coloured.

"I know!" he murmured.

"The Housemaster leaves certain matters in my hands, and I leave certain matters in yours," said Kildare. "You've no right to leave your work undone."

"I—I know!"

"If you want to take an easier time, it's easy enough to resign your place. Do you want to do that?"

"Well, not exactly!" said Tom Merry.

"Then you will have to buck up. As the matter stands, a slacker has openly refused to obey the rules, and when called to account he has held authority up to ridicule. It may seem very funny in the junior studies, but it won't do. I won't say anything more at present, Merry, but you know you are expected to play up a little more efficiently. Otherwise, we must think about a new junior captain for the House, if not for the school. That's all."

Tom Merry left the captain's study with a flushed face and a feeling of great discomfort. He was in Kildare's bad books for once, and he had an uneasy feeling that he deserved it. Easy-going good-nature was very well in its way, but there was a limit. At the end of the corridor he passed a group of Fifth-Formers—Cutts, and Prye, and St. Leger. They were talking and laughing, and Tom caught the words "That ass Kildare!" as he passed.

Tom Merry was unusually thoughtful at tea in Study No. 10 in the Shell. Monty Lowther regarded him rather comically, and Manners was a little amused. After tea Monty remarked that there was time to get on with the "St. Jim's News."

"I think I'd better see Cardew," said Tom Merry thoughtfully. And he left the study.

Lowther gave Manners a grin.

"Old Tommy is up against it," he remarked. "I wonder if he will get any change out of Cardew! That fellow's got a nerve."

"Too much!" said Manners.

Tom Merry looked in at Study No. 9 in the Fourth. Levison and Clive were not there, but Ralph Reckness Cardew was stretched in an easy attitude on his handsome new sofa. He gave the captain of the Shell an affable nod.

"Come in!" he said. "I was just gettin' bored with my own company. Let me be bored with yours for a change."

"I'll try not to bore you," said Tom. "You're no-end of a funny merchant in your way, Cardew, but you've gone too far. You've got me into a row."

"Sorry!" said Cardew politely, though his expression did not hint that his sorrow was very deep.

"Kildare has been slanging me, and the trouble is that he's right," said Tom. "I've been slack."

"Thomas has been slack!" said Cardew, addressing space in a tone of wonder. "No wonder common mortals like little me get a little slack at time if the strenuous Thomas has been slack."

"You're turning up for games practice every day till further orders," said Tom.

"Am I?"

"Yes!"

"You think so?" asked Cardew, with an irritating smile.

"Yes!"

"It looks to me as if you're mistaken."

"I think not," said Tom quietly. "I've got my duty to do, and I'm going to do it."

"The call of duty!" sighed Cardew. "What a bore! But when duty calls to brazen walls, how base the slave that flinches!"

"You've cut games practice a lot lately, and I've let you do it," went on Tom. "I've been ragged for it, and it served me right. Now you're going to make up for lost time, see?"

"I don't quite see."

"Games practice is compulsory twice a week in the footer season. You're going in for it every day to make up for the days you've slacked."

"I think not!"

"I shall expect you on Little Side at three to-morrow," said Tom, turning away.

"Isn't there class at three to-morrow?"

"There isn't! It's off for games!"

"What a bore! I'd rather have class, I think! Anyhow, I'm not turning up for games! Not even on the next compulsory date," said Cardew coolly. "I'm fixing up extra French or extra maths—any old thing!"

"You're not!" said Tom grimly.

"Who's to prevent me?"

"Little me! Your extra toot is a fraud! I know exactly how much French you did with Mossoo yesterday."

Cardew laughed.

"But it washes!" he said.

"It won't wash any more! Little Side at three to-morrow!" said Tom, and he went to the door.

"Don't expect me!" called out Cardew.

"I shall expect you!"

"I sha'n't come."

"Then you'll be fetched."

"What?"

"Fetched!" said Tom. And with that he left Study No. 9 in the Fourth, leaving Ralph Reckness Cardew with a rather startled look on his face.

When Levison and Clive came into the study later, Cardew regarded them with a rather droll look.

"Thomas has got his back up," he said.

"Time, too!" grunted Clive.

"I'm down for games practice every day for a week."

"Good!"

"But I'm not going."

"You'll have to," said Levison.

Cardew shook his head.

"You see, my back is up, too," he said. "I never could stand gettin' orders from anybody. If I didn't knuckle under to Kildare of the Sixth, I'm not likely to be ordered about by a Shell fellow."

"Tom Merry is junior captain."

"That for junior captain!" said Cardew, snapping his fingers. "I'm goin' to make the junior captain look as silly as the senior captain. I'm fixin' up extra French for the off hour to-morrow afternoon."

Levison shrugged his shoulders.

"Law and custom will be on my side," argued Cardew.

"A lot you care for law and custom!" said Clive.

"Nothin' at all—exceptin' when they come in useful on my side. But Thomas has to bow to the law."

"On this occasion I fancy he won't," said Levison.

"Nous verrons!" said Cardew.

"Yes—we shall see—and I fancy you will see that you can't slack around on pretence of extra toot, when Tommy has his back up," said Clive.

"And that's all the support I get in my own study!" sighed Cardew.

"And all you deserve."

"Dear man!" smiled Cardew.

And the subject dropped in Study No. 9. But in other studies it was discussed with keen interest, when it leaked out that Cardew was down for games practice every day for a week—and that he did not intend to obey the behest of the junior captain. Cardew had scored off Kildare of the Sixth—it remained to be seen whether he would score off Tom Merry—and all the fellows were keen to see what would happen on Little Side at three o'clock on the morrow.

CHAPTER 8.
Brought to Book !

"CARDEW here?"

"No!"

Tom Merry glanced round Little Side, crowded with junior footballers in the keen autumn afternoon. There was expectancy in every face. Ralph Reckness Cardew had failed to turn up, and it was left for Tom Merry to deal with the revolt.

"Where is Cardew, Levison?" asked Tom quietly.

"I think he is in Monsieur Morny's study," said Levison reluctantly. "I—I think he's fixed up regular extra toot with Mossoo."

"I understand. Lowther, Manners, Blake, and Wildrake, come along with me," said Tom. "You, too, Gussy."

"Yaas, wathah!"

The fellows named followed Tom Merry back to the School House, the rest being left in a buzz of excited discussion. Tom Merry's face was not angry; but it was set and determined. The head of the games had left to him the task of bringing Cardew into line; and Tom Merry was going to perform that task. His companions asked him no questions, but they were fully prepared to carry out Tom's instructions, whatever those instructions might be.

Tom looked into Study No. 9 in the Fourth first of all, but Cardew was not there. The rebel slacker had entered with careless audacity upon the contest with the junior captain, but he had realised that Tom Merry was a hard nut to crack, and he had taken his measures. If Tom intended to force him down to Little Side, he had to tackle him in the presence of the French master.

From Study No. 9 Tom Merry led the way to Monsieur Morny's study. He tapped at the door.

"Entrez!"

Tom Merry entered the study. Cardew was there, and the kind little French gentleman was expounding to him a passage from "Merope." Cardew had not, on this occasion, switched Mossoo on to the Ruhr; he considered it judicious to have genuine work going on, if Tom looked for him there. A glint came into his eyes as the captain of the Shell entered, and the other fellows lined up in the doorway.

"Excuse me, Monsieur Morny," said Tom Merry politely, "Cardew is wanted."

"Helas!" said Monsieur Morny. "Zat is too bad, Cardew, when ve get on so vell viz ze grand Voltaire. But if you are wanted it needs zat you must go."

"Not at all, sir," said Cardew. "I'm not wanted, and I'm not goin'."

"Mon Dieu!" said Mossoo, greatly puzzled.

"Come on, Cardew," said Tom.

"I'm not comin'."

"Do you want to walk, or to be carried?" asked Tom.

Cardew's eyes glittered. All the obstinacy in his nature was roused now, and there was a great deal of it. But he preserved a manner of polite calm.

"I hardly think you'll begin fag horseplay in a master's study," he said. "You will not allow a rag here, Monsieur Morny."

"Mais certainement non," said Monsieur Morny. "I do not comprehend zis. Vat is it all?"

"Cardew's dodging games," explained Tom Merry. "We want him."

"Yaas, wathah!"

"A fellow is allowed to cut games practice for extra toot, sir," said Cardew. "Merry knows that."

The French master looked puzzled.

"I am acting under the authority of the head prefect of the House, sir," said Tom respectfully. "I'm bound to make Cardew come. But if he is not satisfied, he can appeal to the Housemaster."

"A favourite dodge of yours, Cardew!" grinned Blake.

"Yaas, wathah!" chuckled Arthur Augustus.

Cardew bit his lip. He knew that an appeal to the Housemaster would not serve him now. Mr. Railton was not to be deceived twice, and he would know perfectly well why Cardew had planted himself in the French master's study that afternoon.

"Mon Dieu, je ne sais pas!" said Monsieur Morny. "Zese disputes—I do not know. But if you like, Cardew, I comes viz you to see Mr. Railton, and he shall be ask."

"Thank you, sir, I won't trouble you to do that," said Cardew politely. "Perhaps I'd better go."

He left the French master's study calm and cool, but with bitter resentment in his breast. It was better than being dragged out by main force under Mossoo's astonished eyes; and he could see that Tom Merry was prepared to go to that length. Tom closed the study door; he was glad that he had not been driven to drastic measures in a master's study.

In the corridor Cardew was walking away, when Blake caught him by the arm. Cardew gave him a fierce look.

"Let go!" he said, between his teeth.

"What's the orders, Tommy?" asked Blake, unheeding.

"Bring him down to the footer."

"I'm not comin'!" hissed Cardew.

"Bring him along!"

Cardew struck Blake on the chest, sending him reeling back. Then he dashed along the corridor.

"Bai Jove! Aftah him!"

Tom Merry's grasp was on the fugitive before he reached the corner. Cardew turned on him, closed, and struggled savagely. In a moment more all the party had seized him, and he was swung off his feet.

"Are you walking to Little Side?" asked Tom calmly.

"No!" roared Cardew.

"Carry on!" said Tom.

"Yaas, wathah!"

Struggling in the grasp of the juniors, Cardew was carried along. Mr. Railton came out of his study, and signed to the party to stop. Cardew was dropped on his feet.

"What does this mean, Merry?" asked the Housemaster.

"Cardew's going down to the footer, sir."

"Oh, I see!" Mr. Railton fixed his eyes on Cardew's flushed, furious face. "I had occasion to speak to you very severely yesterday, Cardew. I warn you that you had better take care."

An impertinent answer trembled on Cardew's lips, but fortunately he restrained it.

"I was doing extra French with Monsieur Morny, sir," he said. "Fellows are allowed to cut games practice for extra tuition."

"Quite so, unless that is merely a pretext for slacking," said Mr. Railton. "In my judgment, it is nothing more than that in your case. You have taken advantage of Monsieur Morny's kindness in order to gain your own wilful way, I think."

Cardew looked sullen, but did not answer.

"I have my eye on you, Cardew," said Mr. Railton severely. "You appear to have set yourself up against authority in this House. That is a very dangerous game for a Lower boy to play. It might lead to your expulsion from the school if you should prove too intractable. You will go down to games practice with the rest."

"It's not compulsory to-day, sir."

"In this instance I shall leave that to the judgment of your junior captain, and Merry will decide."

With that Mr. Railton went back into his study. Cardew walked out of the corridor with the juniors into the changing-room.

"Get into your footer things!" said Tom.

"I won't!"

"What's the good of playing the fool?" urged Blake.

"Mind your own business!"

"Orders, skipper?" grinned Lowther.

"Change him!" said Tom.

Cardew struggled furiously. In about two minutes he was stripped, somewhat to the detriment of his exceedingly well-cut clothes.

"Are you getting into your footer rig?" asked Tom.

"No!" yelled Cardew.

"Put him in!"

"First time I've ever helped to dress a baby!" remarked Blake.

Cardew was put into his footer things, or the nearest footer things that came handy. There was a good deal of communism on that subject in the changing-room. Then he was led out of the House.

He walked down to the footer-ground in the midst of Tom Merry & Co., simmering with fury.

A roar greeted his arrival.

"Here he comes!"

"What-ho, slacker!" shouted Figgins.

"Play up, old fellow!" said Levison anxiously.

Cardew gave his chum a furious look. He was not feeling chummy at that moment.

"I'm not goin' to play!"

"Look here, Cardew!" said Tom Merry quietly. "You know I'm doing my duty, but I suppose that doesn't appeal to you. If you were junior captain you wouldn't be cheeked like this. To put it plain, you've got to toe the line!"

"I won't!"

"I think you will! Levison and Clive, as you're his pals, you needn't take a hand in this. Every other fellow here is to kick Cardew whenever he sees him slacking."

"Yaas, wathah!"

"Hear, hear!"

"Now pick up sides," said Tom.

Cardew stood breathing fury in the midst of the footballers. This was the end of his campaign. He had set out to pit himself against forces that were arrayed overwhelmingly against him, hoping to carry his campaign through by sheer audacity and "neck." And this was the end of it—kicked into the game like a lazy fag. It was a terrible fall for Cardew's pride, and even yet he was thinking of resistance. But resistance was not possible.

The following quarter of an hour was a hard time for the rebellious slacker. Thrice he attempted to scud off the field, and was collared and hauled back by laughing footballers. After that he refused to move, but hefty drives from football-boots moved him fast enough. At last he played up in sheer self-defence, and fellows, who had seemed to find more entertainment in kicking Cardew than in kicking the ball, had to turn to the ball again.

When the practice was over Cardew looked for Tom Merry. He expected to hear something from the junior captain, but Tom seemed to have forgotten his existence. Tom Merry walked off the field with his friends, without a glance at Cardew. The dandy of the Fourth cast a bitter glance after him.

"Come in and change, old chap!" said Levison, touching Cardew on the arm.

Cardew shook off his hand and walked away by himself.

CHAPTER 9.

"Six" and the Result!

THE next day there was considerable curiosity in the School House as to what Cardew would do. It was known that the junior captain had directed him to turn up for games practice regularly every day for a week, as he was fully entitled to do. Only school work could save Cardew from having to obey, and his trick of fixing up extra lessons was played out. As Blake remarked in Study No. 6, that was a chicken that would no longer fight. Refusal to turn up meant being taken down to Little Side by force and kicked into toeing the line, a humiliating process for Cardew—much more humiliating, in fact, than a frank abandonment of the position he had so wilfully taken up. But it was not like Cardew to surrender if he could help it. And the fellows wondered what he would do.

When the Fourth and the Shell were dismissed at three-thirty that day a good crowd went down to Little Side. It was not a compulsory day, excepting for Cardew, but a good crowd turned up. Ralph Reckness Cardew was not among them.

Tom Merry & Co. proceeded to look for him.

For ten minutes they hunted for the absentee, but they did not find him. Evidently Cardew of the Fourth was lying very low.

Tom Merry & Co. returned to the football-ground without him. It was, as Trimble remarked, one point in the game to Cardew. He had refused obedience, and he had not joined up for games practice as ordered to do. Now it remained to be seen what steps Tom Merry would take next in dealing with the rebel.

When classes were resumed in the Fourth Form room for last lesson Cardew came in with the rest. Apparently he had not been very far away, though he had kept well out of sight. As a matter of fact, he had been reading and smoking cigarettes in a remote box-room.

Mr. Lathom dismissed the Fourth, and Cardew left the Form-room with Clive and Levison. Both the latter were uneasy and worried, but Cardew seemed cool and unconcerned.

"You cut practice to-day, Cardew," Levison remarked.

"I'm goin' to every day!"

"Tom Merry won't stand it!" said Clive.

"He's got to!"

"My dear chap," said Levison patiently, "what are you keeping up this mug's game for? You're really keen on footer, and you're giving it up, or trying to, just to defy a fellow you really like, and who's only doing his duty. Why not chuck it?"

"I'm not givin' in!"

"Oh, you're an ass!"

Levison and Clive were very nearly out of patience with their wayward chum. Cardew, however, seemed to be quite keen on the peculiar contest he had marked out for himself. After lessons Study No. 9 expected to hear from Tom Merry, but the junior captain took no steps. It was scarcely possible that he intended to allow the incident to pass unnoticed; that would have meant triumph for the rebel. At tea in Study No. 9 Trimble of the Fourth looked in, with a grin on his fat face.

"They're at it!" he announced.

"Who are at what?" grunted Levison.

"Meeting in Tom Merry's study in the Shell. Games committee of the Lower School," said Trimble. "They're discussing Cardew. I happened to hear——"

"Oh, get out!"

Levison picked up a loaf and took aim, and Trimble got out promptly. Cardew smiled.

"Then we shall hear from Thomas, after all?" he said.

"I knew we should," said Clive. "He's bound to deal with you if he's not to come up against Kildare. If he lets you defy all the rules, Kildare will ask the Housemaster to

(*Continued on page 16.*)

GRAND NEW "Football"

| First Prize, **£100** | **30 MAGNIFICENT "JAMES" MOTOR-CYCLES** (Complete with Lamp, Horn, and Licence-holder.) |

20 GRAMOPHONES.   **40 FOOTBALL OUTFITS** (Boots, Stockings, Shorts, and Shirt).

50 Pairs of BOXING GLOVES.   100 Pairs of ROLLER SKATES.

RULES AND CONDITIONS
which must be strictly adhered to.

1.—The First Prize of £100 in cash will be awarded to the competitor who sends in the correct, or most nearly correct, solution of all eight sets of the pictures according to the Editor's official solution.

2.—The Second Prize of £50, and the others in the splendid variety of prizes will be awarded in order of merit.

3.—All the prizes will be awarded. If two or more competitors tie, however, the prize or prizes, or their value, will be divided, and the Editor reserves full rights in this respect.

4.—No solutions may be sent in until all the sets of the pictures and the necessary coupon have been published. Full directions will then be given.

5.—The names under the pictures must be written IN INK.

6.—Employees of the proprietors of this journal are not eligible to compete.

7.—Entry to this competition is on the full understanding that the Editor's decision is final and legally binding throughout.

YOU'VE SOLVED THIS SET? GOOD! NOW LO[

COMPETITION!

"...rs' Names!"

100 SPLENDID "JAMES" COMET BICYCLES (Complete with Lamp, Bell, etc.)

Second Prize, £50

Valve Sets and Other Prizes.

6 "RILEY" BILLIARDS TABLES.   100 FISHING RODS.
100 MATCH FOOTBALLS.   20 MODEL STEAM LOCOMOTIVES (With Rails).

MORE SETS TO COME!

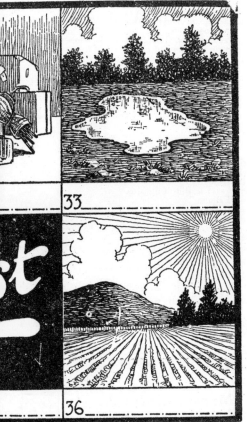

33

36

ALL YOU HAVE TO DO

is to write IN INK in the allotted space under each of the puzzle-pictures the name of the footballer which you think the picture represents. Surely a simple enough task—only six names to discover each week!

In all there will be EIGHT SETS OF PICTURES, so keep your solutions until the other sets appear.

DO NOT SEND YOUR ENTRIES YET.

To help you still further, we have published on cover 2 of this issue a list of footballers' names, which contains the actual names of the footballers represented by all the pictures appearing in this competition.

New readers desirous of entering this contest can do so by obtaining the LAST TWO numbers of the GEM, Nos. 822 and 823, which, between them, contained all the previous sets of pictures. Back numbers of those issues can be obtained on application to the "Back Numbers Dept.," Bear Alley, Farringdon Street, E.C.4. For each single number required twopence in stamps should be forwarded, also one penny stamp to cover postage. The postal rate for additional copies is an extra halfpenny per copy.

Readers of the "Champion," "Boys' Realm," "Union Jack," "Boys' Friend," "Pluck," "Boys' Cinema," "Young Britain," "Popular," "Magnet," "Rocket," and "Nelson Lee Library" are also taking part in the Contest, so that additional attempts may be made with the pictures from these allied journals.

LOOK OUT FOR SET NO. 7—APPEARS NEXT WEEK!

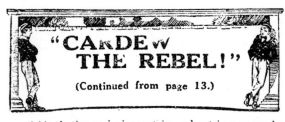

"CARDEW THE REBEL!"

(Continued from page 13.)

cancel his election as junior captain, and get in a man who can handle cheeky kids."

"I suppose so," smiled Cardew. "Rather a joke to see the strenuous Thomas turned out to graze, and a new junior skipper elected."

"It won't come to that, I think."

"What will jolly old Thomas do, then?" asked Cardew lazily.

"Make you toe the line."

Cardew laughed contemptuously.

It was some time after tea that there was a tramp of feet in the Fourth Form passage that stopped at Study No. 9. The door was thrown open and Tom Merry appeared. Behind him came Lowther, Blake, Talbot, and D'Arcy. They were all looking serious. Tom Merry had a cricket-stump under his arm—and Cardew's eyes glittered as he noticed it.

"Oh, you're here, Cardew!" said Tom.

"Adsum!" said Cardew, as if he were answering to his name at calling-over. But no one smiled.

"You cut games practice to-day."

"Guilty, my lord."

"Any excuse?"

"None."

"Very well. The games committee have decided to give you six. Bend over."

Cardew rose to his feet, his eyes burning, though he remained calm. A prefects' beating would have humiliated the lofty spirit of Ralph Reckness Cardew; but a beating from a party of juniors was ever so much more humiliating. He could scarcely believe that Tom was in earnest.

"You hear?" said Tom quietly.

"I hear," said Cardew mockingly. "But in this jolly old instance, to hear is not to obey. Might a fellow request you to go and be funny in some other study?"

"Put out a chair," said Tom.

"Yaas, wathah!"

"We're sorry for this, Cardew," said Talbot of the Shell as he placed a chair in position. "But you've asked for it."

Cardew breathed hard and deep.

"If you're not satisfied with the line I'm takin', Tom Merry, I'm prepared to step into the gym and meet you with or without gloves," he said.

"I'll meet you in the gym any time you please, and knock some of the conceit out of you," said Tom Merry calmly. "But just at present you're dealing not with me personally, but with the junior captain of St. Jim's, and you're going to have six for failing to turn up to games practice this afternoon."

"I fancy not."

"Put him over the chair!"

Cardew jumped back and put up his hands.

He was promptly collared and bent over the chair in a suitable attitude for receiving "six."

He struggled furiously.

In the passage Trimble's fat chuckle was heard, and then his excited shout:

"Roll up, you fellows! Cardew's getting six!"

There was a rush of feet, a buzz of voices, and a ripple of laughter. Cardew's face burned with shame. He struggled madly in the grasp of the representatives of the junior games committee, but he was held face down over the chair in spite of his efforts. He shouted furiously to his study-mates.

"Levison! Clive! Back me up, you rotters!"

Levison and Clive did not stir.

"Back up, you cads!" yelled Cardew.

"You're getting what you've asked for," said Levison. "You're disgracing this study by slacking and frowsting, and that's enough. I've a jolly good mind to give you the six myself!"

"You rotter!"

Tom Merry handed the stump to Blake.

"Go ahead!"

Whack! Whack! Whack!

Cardew made one more struggle, and then remained quiescent. The whacks were hefty ones, but no sound of pain came from his tightly-closed lips.

Whack! Whack! Whack!

The six had been duly delivered, and every one of the six rang through the study like a pistol-shot and echoed in the passage, where a crowd of fellows listened.

"That's done!" said Blake.

Ralph Reckness Cardew was released. He stood up, his face white and his eyes burning.

Without a word to him Tom Merry & Co. left Study No. 9. The delinquent had been dealt with and the incident was closed—until the morrow, when it was obvious that a similar delinquency would be dealt with in a similar manner. It was dawning even upon the obstinate and wilful mind of Ralph Reckness Cardew that he had bitten off more than he could chew.

Levison and Clive left the study. They felt for the humiliation of their chum, though they could scarcely sympathise with him.

Cardew was left alone with his thoughts. And, while the effect of the six still lingered, Ralph Reckness Cardew did some very serious thinking.

. . . .

Many glances were turned on Cardew of the Fourth when he came into the junior Common-room that evening and crossed over towards the fireplace, where the Terrible Three stood chatting.

That he had come in to hunt for trouble was the conclusion of every fellow in the room, and he was watched on all sides as he approached Tom Merry.

Levison made a step towards him and then stopped. He knew that Cardew would not listen to him.

"Practice as usual to-morrow, Tom Merry?" asked Cardew lazily.

Tom looked at him.

"Yes," he said.

"You're not lettin' me off?"

"No."

"Doesn't it sort of seem to you that you're rather over-strainin' the giddy authority of a jolly old junior captain?"

"I don't think so."

"Odd!" said Cardew. "I quite agree with you. I never thought you had so much beef in you, Thomas. You've surprised me."

Tom Merry laughed involuntarily.

"Why not chuck up playing the goat?" he suggested. "You're a good footballer, and you like the game. You don't really want to frowst about, getting slack and unhealthy—it's only your rot! Why not chuck it up?"

"I'm goin' to."

"Good!" said Tom heartily. "I'm glad to hear it!"

"But that isn't all," said Cardew. "You're not goin' to let me be a slacker—you're not goin' to let me kick over the traces. My jolly old liberty is goin' to be curtailed. Now, as I've got to toe the line, I'm goin' to toe it hard. I'm goin' in for football hot and strong. I'm also goin' in for the job of junior captain!"

"What?"

"I'm goin' to replace you, dear man—take your job away," said Cardew easily. "Like the prospect?"

Tom laughed again.

"If the fellows want you for skipper instead of me, they're welcome," he said.

"Wubbish!" said Arthur Augustus.

"Rats!" said Blake.

"Bosh!" said Levison.

Cardew smiled.

"That doesn't sound like an outburst of enthusiastic support," he remarked. "But I mean it! You've put it up to me now, Tom Merry, and I'm going for the bone like a jolly old bulldog. I'm goin' in for the junior captaincy, and I'm goin' to push you out and bag the job. That's a warnin'."

"Thanks!" said Tom, laughing.

Cardew strolled out of the Common-room, and a loud laugh followed him as he went. Nobody was taking him seriously—so far. But, as it happened, Ralph Reckness Cardew was in deadly earnest, as Tom Merry & Co. were soon to discover. But what the result of the struggle would be was on the knees of the gods.

THE END.

Sam Jennings gets more than his share of hard luck, but he faces it all with a brave heart!

On the Stroke of Time!

This thrilling story of football and adventure relates how Sam Jennings' brilliant display as deputy saves his side and brings about the termination of his run of ill-luck.

CHAPTER 1.
At Sea!

HERE'S a story which begins, properly speaking, in the middle of the Pacific Ocean, if there be such a spot, and ends, as all proper tales should end, in the middle of a football-field.

Sam Jennings would have been surprised that day, in the middle of the Pacific, if he could have foreseen the afternoon to come a long way off on the football-field. In fact, he would not have thought it possible, but then truth is ever stranger than fiction.

It was a question of the last place in a boat.

He was the boy in the schooner Nigger, and he should have taken his place, as they pushed off from the sinking ship, allowing the captain and a few last hands to make the best of their way on a rough raft they had lashed together, since the leaking, aged schooner had tried to see what the top of an uncharted coral reef did with the doubtful bottoms of aged hookers.

In fact, he was already in the boat, when suddenly he caught sight of Bill Harding on the deck of the schooner. Good old Bill, who had been such a chum, although several years his senior, and who had taken a real delight in seeing that the youngster was not unduly knocked about by his mates.

It had been only the previous evening that Bill had been telling Sam about the young wife he had just married, and who was waiting for him at home in Portsmouth. Sam, being a lad, hadn't quite followed his friend's enthusiasm, but he had gathered that Bill's wife was the prettiest and best girl in the world, and would be mighty glad when her husband left such an adventurous life as the sea.

But then those who follow the sea do so for more than love of woman. It is for love of adventure, for the sensation of salt upon their lips, the long look across acres of water, without land in sight, and a good breeze filling the billowing sails, listening to the man at the wheel, who sings to himself, as ever they make westing—westing.

And now here was Bill Harding on the deck, with the captain, who was a brute, and a couple of dago officers, whom the lad had not liked.

Why, Bill was the whitest man in the crew.

The lad was on the deck in a second. He understood the possibilities of it all.

Those who took the boat, overcrowded as she was now, at least stood a chance. She had a sail, water, biscuits, and a compass. There was land within five hundred miles, and they might make it. If the wind held in the same quarter they certainly would make it. The Nigger had chosen, conveniently and considerately enough, to strike her coral reef in good weather. Yes, those who took their places in the boat would have a chance, and it had only been the absolute folly of risking another man that had stopped the captain jumping in himself.

And now the lad stood at Bill's side, tugging at his hand.

"All right, Bill, you take my place!"

The big fellow stared down at him.

"Don't be a fool, kid!"

"Come on, Bill," roared someone in the boat, also devoted to Harding. "The kid's right. You've got a wife at home, and he's only a kid. Married men first in this sort of thing. Come on!"

Bill pushed Sam across the slanting deck.

"Back you go, youngster!"

"No, Bill; think of your wife. You remember what you were telling me last night. You didn't know what would happen to her if anything ever happened to you. Go on, Bill! I don't care. Why, I haven't got anyone in the world to worry about me!"

But Bill Harding was made of sterner stuff than that.

"I'm not going to take a boy's place!" he cried, as someone in the boat cursed them both, and said they were going to push off.

Then suddenly there was a shout which went up surely to Heaven—a shout which was sincerely meant:

"Ship ahoy!"

They were saved.

CHAPTER 2.
Down and Out!

THERE comes into the life of every man, and in the boyhood of us all, a time when things go bad. Life would be dull and intolerable otherwise. Of course, it is very difficult to appreciate this at the time. It seems as though all the luck is against

us, and we are apt to forget the good times which have gone before. And yet a stiff upper lip is all that is needed, and it was a stiff upper lip that Sam Jennings was trying to keep these days, and no mistake!

He had left the sea.

Not that he was a coward, but the shipwreck in the middle of the Pacific, and following this the six months on the South Atlantic whaler which had rescued them, had sickened him of a seafaring life for many a long day.

There might be a deal of romance about it, but there was also a great deal of quite unromantic hardship, and when at last a British consul had shipped him back to Liverpool, he had gone ashore in the big port determined to stick to dry land in future, or, in the parlance of the sea, to buy a farm and leave the sea.

Being a friendless and a penniless lad, however, things had been difficult, and never so difficult as of late.

He had found a job in the big factory of "Greyson," in the midland town of Hintoning, and had been content enough at his work, especially when he had discovered that he was not the worst centre-forward in the town.

Then—and this was two years ago now—had commenced the happiest period of the lad's life. At sixteen he had suddenly taken his place in the local League team, and had performed wonders. His enemies said that it was a flash in the pan, and those who really liked him had said it was natural genius.

And now, this year, it seemed as though his enemies had been right, because he simply could do nothing right.

It was just one of those seasons when everything went badly.

He missed opening after opening, and luck was always against him.

The crowd, ever quick to change, had lifted him down from his pedestal, and had already placed him in the ruck. Those who had cheered him most loudly were now amongst the most quick to decry him.

Being an honest, simple lad, he had said little and had done his best. In his heart he had known that the skill was still in him, and that he had only struck a bad patch, like everyone does sooner or later, and that he would soon be all right again. But it was a bad time, and then, when things began to go badly at the factory, he tasted again all the troubles of being down and out.

Old Greyson had always seemed to like him, but there had been several rather

THE GEM LIBRARY.—No. 824.

serious mistakes in the shop in which he worked lately, and as, with the bad times, it was an open secret that the factory was not making money, Sam had been given the tip several times by the foreman not to make any more mistakes.

No use for him to explain that he was not responsible for what had happened. It was not the sort of place where they took arguments well!

And now he stood in front of old Greyson.

"I'm not going to have this sort of thing, Jennings," he said. "It is the third time I've spoken about it. I have given instructions for you to draw your money at the end of the week!"

Sam stood in front of the head of the firm, dumb. It was like him to be dumb. He was not a lad of words. He knew that an injustice was being done to him, but he did not know how he could explain it. It would be a terrifically long story. It would involve many of his pals, it would delve into the system in the factory, it would involve the foreman, it would show old Greyson that he was using inferior material—— Oh, a lad couldn't go into all that sort of thing with the head of his firm, even if he had the words—which Sam hadn't.

"All right—go, Jennings. I'm sorry. But, as you know, these are hard times. We are working at a loss. I'm knocking hands off every day, and, naturally, the ones who make mistakes must pay for those mistakes. It's life."

Sam went.

He felt no resentment, but only rotten. What was going to happen he didn't know. The only cheerful aspect of the business was that he had no one but himself to think about.

At any rate, he had the football.

Perhaps they would take him on at the club now. He had always refused to turn professional. They had made him a jolly good offer two years ago. It had been renewed again and again, and the lad had always refused it. This year it had not been renewed; but until this moment he had never regretted not having ceased to be an amateur.

Yes, he would go along and see old White, the trainer. He was a good friend, and he would give him the best advice he could.

He drew his pay, said good-bye to his chums, and started off at once towards the club ground.

He found old White there, seated on a roller smoking a time-worn pipe, and considering the position of Hintoning in the League with woe on his sunburned face.

"Hallo!" he said.

"White, I've been sacked!"

"Whole bloomin' team ought to be sacked," the old fellow said.

The youngster shook his head.

"I don't mean that, White," he said. "Greyson has turned me off. I'm out of a job!"

The old trainer took his pipe from his mouth and regarded the lad with concern. He was a very good-hearted old fellow, and was a friend to all the lads in the team, even if their display this year had been a thing, as he said, to make a real footballer turn in his grave.

"I say, lad," he exclaimed, "I'm downright sorry to hear you say that! That's bad. How did it happen?"

Sam told his story, and the old trainer listened, full of concern. Then he drew in a great cloud of smoke and blew it heavenwards.

"That's bad, lad," he said. "That's very bad. What are you going to do?"

Sam looked at him quickly.

"I was wondering, White," he said,

"if you think the directors still want to have me on their professional list?"

White started.

"Eh?"

The lad repeated the question.

The old man took his pipe from his mouth, and suddenly looked very serious.

"Lad," he exclaimed, "I'm sorry to talk so gravely to you, but I think you have struck a bad patch. You'll get through it, all right, because you are made of the right stuff. I have watched you, and I know it; but—well, lad, the truth of the matter is, I don't think they will take you on, because—well, Sam, you know that you have not been doing too much this year—eh?"

Sam was white. He nodded.

"I've been rotten!" he admitted.

"Yes; and the fact of the matter is that I think the directors have got some idea of bringing new blood into the team!"

Sam looked at the old trainer a little timidly.

"New blood?" he exclaimed.

The trainer looked him in the eyes.

"Sam, you'd better know the truth, as the directors want to see you this evening. They are going to play a new fellow from Portsmouth next Saturday in your place!"

Sam's heart seemed to stop beating for a moment.

"Oh!"

"Yes," said White, whose long suit had never been conversation, putting his pipe back in his mouth.

"Do you know his name, White?"

The trainer shook his head.

"No," he said, "I don't. I—I only know that—that they told me they were negotiating for a chap. They're paying for him, too. But I believe he is a sudden find from a small club. You'd better see them to-night, lad, and good luck go with you. You have struck a bad patch, but—well, there it is. You'll come through, and when it is all over you'll wonder why you were ever blue!"

Sam tried to feel this enthusiasm for the future, and he spent a useful hour or so at practice. The most aggravating part of the whole business was that when he was not playing in an actual match he seemed better than ever. It was that which made him certain that bad luck was having more to do with his bad play than anything else, and if only he could have got through these bad days he was certain that he would come into his own again. But what a chance now?

Yes, the directors wanted to see him, he was told when he went to the office a little later; and that evening he went in to see the mighty men, and there found old Greyson, who had sacked him earlier in the day, the managing director of the club, looking very serious.

He was a decent old fellow, and he felt his position. The lad would be almost justified in thinking, after this, that he, Greyson, had a down on him, which was absurd. But he hated to have to treat a lad like this.

"Good-evening, Jennings!" he said. "We wanted to see you. Sit down!"

The lad took a chair.

"You've never signed professional forms, Jennings?" Greyson asked, as though he were not very well aware of the fact.

"No, sir," the lad exclaimed, hope suddenly jumping into his heart. Perhaps they were going to give him a chance, after all?

"Umph!" the managing-director nodded. "Well, we sent for you to thank you for all you have done for the team. You haven't been really on the mark this season—eh?"

"No, sir. But I think I shall get into my stride soon. I've had a deal of bad luck!"

One of the other directors gave a nasty grunt. He had never been one of the lad's admirers.

"Well, bad luck looks like getting us kicked out of the League, Jennings," he said. "Unless we win this match against Bottlebury next Saturday, down and out we go for sure."

"Yes, sir," said Sam, feeling very bad.

Greyson cleared his throat.

"The fact of the matter is," he said, "we have a new centre-forward coming from the South to play next Saturday, and—well, my lad, as you are an amateur, we thought it only fair to send for you and let you know that we shouldn't probably be utilising you much in the future. The fact of the matter is, Jennings, if you care to find another club we feel that you have every right to do so!"

The lad closed his eyes for a second, and then looked at Greyson. The managing-director was regarding him as kindly as he could.

"Then, sir, there is no good in my asking you gentlemen if you would think of giving me a place on your professional list!"

Greyson started, and looked at the lad. He understood, and, to do him justice, he felt an absolute brute.

"I'm afraid not, Jennings," he answered. "It is full, and we are paying a good deal for this new man. However, it is not quite certain whether he will be here in time to play on Saturday, so, if you don't mind, perhaps you will keep in training until then, and not make any other engagement."

Sam thought this rather calm, but he was always a good sport, and he understood that the only thing that mattered at all was that the game should be won. So, though he was feeling as though his luck was out for good, and he would never gain favour again, he said that he would be at their disposal if they wanted him. Then he went out into the dismal night, feeling as though he didn't care what happened.

CHAPTER 3.
An Old Friend!

THEY were hard days for the lad. He was out of a job, and he knew that it was almost useless trying to get other work. But it was not like Sam to take a hiding lying down, and so he went all over the town looking for work, and always meeting with the same answer—they were knocking hands off, not taking new hands on.

At last Friday came, and on the morrow there would be the great match with Bottlebury, and all thought of his own troubles were gradually dissipated in the thought of whether he would play, and what the morning would bring forth.

He went to the ground to have a bit of practice, and try to hear what old White had to say.

There had been a good deal of mystery about the new centre-forward who was coming from Portsmouth, and no one had seemed to know his name. The fact of the matter seemed to be that it was not certain whether the transfer was going to be brought off.

And now, as the lad came out on to the field to have a kick about, he saw a tall, rather lusty figure potting away at goal, like a cannon suddenly losing its temper.

He stared, and then ran forward.

At the same moment the new centre-

Tricking three opponents, Sam Jennings headed straight for goal. He was just steadying himself for a shot when a terrific charge in the back brought him crashing down inside the penalty area. "Foul!" A terrific roar rent the air, and the referee's whistle shrilled loudly.

forward turned, and they looked into one another's eyes.

Sam gave a gasp, and was the first to speak.

"Bill Harding !" he cried.

"Why—Sam !"

They shook hands, and stood staring at one another in that speechless pleasure which only comes to two good friends, who have not seen one another for a long time, and are very glad in the meeting.

Then suddenly Bill gave a great whoop of joy.

"My dear boy," he cried, "this is great ! I've often wondered what became of you. What are you doing here ? Do you play for this club ?"

"Yes, Bill ; and what are you doing here ?"

Bill grinned.

"I'm the centre-forward they've brought up from Portsmouth, lad !"

Sam smiled heartily.

"My word, Bill, that's grand ! I never knew that you played Soccer !"

"Nor did I till I got back from that voyage, and decided that I must take to something a little less exciting than a life on the sea."

"Same here !" said the lad.

There was a moment's silence, during which Bill sent in a really splendid shot that defeated the goalie easily.

"But this is good, Sam !" he said. "I was rather fed up at leaving the old club. It was only quite a small one, but we were at the head of our little league, and it was good fun. But it will be great playing with you. I've never forgotten what you did—or what you wanted to do for me that day, lad !"

"Oh, that was nothing !"

Bill grinned.

"Well, I think it was a good deal," he said, "considering that it was my life that you were trying to save, my lad. And my missus has always wanted to see you and thank you yourself !"

Sam said nothing.

"By the way, Sam, where do you play ?"

Sam turned red.

"Play ?" he asked quietly.

"What's your place in the team, Sam —back—what ?"

Sam coughed.

"Er—centre-forward," he said.

Bill stared at him, and his face showed a worried look. He put out a great, kindly hand, and rested it on Sam's shoulder.

"Oh, Sam," he said, in a quiet, manly tone, "this is rotten luck for us both ! You are the chap I'm doing out of a job—eh ?"

Sam looked away, and then, after a moment's emotion, he pushed all thought of self away from him.

"Don't talk rot, Bill !" he said. "I've been playing absolute tripe the whole season. I'm no good. And besides, I'm only an amateur. I've never signed forms. The great thing is to win this match on Saturday, and I'm as pleased as Punch that you have come along to help do the trick !"

Bill looked at him, and was evidently contented with what the youngster said, for he slapped him heartily on the back.

"Oh, all right, youngster !" he said. "All right ! Glad that it is no worse than that—very glad ! We'll pull the team round, and if I have anything to say to it, we'll try you at inside-right or left, and we'll soon run you into form again !"

The two parted on the best of terms, after agreeing to spend Sunday together to talk about the old days when they had been sailors together.

But as he left the ground that evening Bill found himself side by side with old White, the trainer.

"You knew young Jennings, then ?" the old fellow asked.

Bill nodded.

"Yes, I did ! We were before the mast together. He's a fine young chap !"

White agreed, with a characteristic grunt.

"Yes," he said ; "none finer. He's a good lad, and no mistake ! And I'm downright sorry for him !"

Bill started.

"Why ?" he asked.

White gave the other a sidelong look, as though trying to make up his mind whether he would speak or not, and then evidently he decided that he would.

"Well," he began, "he has struck a bad patch this season, and no mistake. Never seen such a thing in all my life. You would have thought from the way in which he played two years ago when he started with us, that he would finish up by playing for England. But he's gone off, and this year he hasn't been able to do any good, and there is no getting away from the fact that he has demoralised the team, and let us down !"

Bill nodded.

"We all strike bad patches," he said quietly.

"That's right !" said White quickly. "And it never rains but it snows. That poor kid ! He got the sack from his job the other day at Greyson's where he worked, and they say that it was not his fault, but that he was too good a sport to say anything about it, because it would have got other people into trouble !"

Bill gave a sharp exclamation.

"I quite believe that," he said.

"Well," the other man went on, "the poor kid came along to me to ask me whether I thought they would sign him on as a professional, and I had to tell him they were getting you up to play to-morrow. A bit rough !"

Bill Harding walked on quickly.

He seemed to be standing again on a

slanting deck, to see the vast stretch of friendless waters about him, hear the angry cries of the men in the boat, the cries of men who are fighting for their lives, and then from out of it all he heard the words of a lad who sprang to his side and offered him his place —that was the sort of stuff Sam Jennings was made of. And now here was he, Bill Harding, the unconscious weapon with which the lad was being knocked over the head!

"Bad luck!" murmured White, the trainer, into the night.

"Rotten!" said Bill.

CHAPTER 4.
The Game.

SATURDAY morning, the day of the great match, saw Sam on the football-field early.

He wanted to show everyone that there was not a bit of bad feeling in him, and that the only wish that he had in all the world was that the old team should win.

He went into the dressing-room, however, to see the boys, and was soon pounced upon by White.

"Here you are!" cried the trainer. "Where have you been all morning?"

"Looking for work," said Sam.

White groaned.

"That's what I told Greyson, sacking a good kid like you. Looking for work! How do they think that you are going to do yourself justice when you have been looking for work all morning? How do they think that you are going to win the match for them this afternoon?"

Sam stared at the old chap in surprise.

"Look here, White," he said, "have you taken leave of your senses, or what?"

"Haven't you heard? No, of course, you haven't, or you would have been here. Harding has sprained his ankle, and can't play until next Saturday. Come on; you get undressed, and I'll give you a rub down. You've got to play this afternoon, and you've got to win this match, or there will be a riot!"

There was almost a riot when the locals saw that the great Bill Harding was not taking the field. Word went round the crowd like wildfire, and the moan of disgust that went up when they saw the young amateur come out to play centre-forward was not very sporting, and certainly did not tend to make Sam feel that he must play the game of his life.

But Sam was determined to play that game. Bottlebury, however, were going to be a hard nut to crack.

They were not very skilful, perhaps, but they had a nasty, rough knack of maiming half the other side, and then scoring at their leisure. Referees cursed, and players were warned on but still things did not improve.

The game started, and almost at the first moment the ball came to Sam, and he made a mess of it.

A roar of disgust went up immediately, as the other line got away to attack fiercely.

"Throw him off! Hang him!" they cried; and a hiss went round the ground.

Then, from a sudden, strange silence which had gone up across the field, Sam heard a booming voice he knew of old —for at sea, amidst wind and storm, greater than all the voices of all the men in the world, he had heard Bill Harding crying a cheery word as they hung on by teeth and nails and hands and legs, to a mad, jumping, plunging stay:

"All right, Sam! Play up, lad!"

It was Bill Harding. He was somewhere in the crowd, and, big-hearted, splendid fellow that he was, he was wishing the other good luck. Sam did not pause to consider it rather strange that Bill was here at all with his badly-damaged ankle.

The Bottlebury attack had now been beaten off, and the ball came flying along to him. He trapped it neatly, tricked a half-back who lounged down on him, and then got quickly away.

"Pass! Pass!" roared the crowd. "Don't fall over it, Sam! Look out, mate, it'll bite!"

Sam listened to nothing of this. Sudden confidence had come to him.

He felt the old feeling of glory in the game again. His feet flew over the turf. This was the stuff. A back came for him, and very calmly, and just when the crowd thought he had hung on too long, he tapped it out to his right-hand man, and a moment later a stinging shot had been sent in, which gave the Bottlebury custodian all he knew to beat away.

The game was very fast now.

In a few minutes the crowd had realised that Sam had regained the old form of two seasons back, and he was at once lifted, with all the inconsistency of a crowd, to a dizzy height of favour again.

"Go it, Sam boy—good old Sam! That's the stuff! One, two, three, and at 'em, Sam!"

THE BIG NOISE!

Forgetting his injuries for the moment, Sam tore towards the goal, then steadying himself, he shot very low and fast into the corner of the net. "Goal!" The roar went up from twenty thousand throats. Then came a breathless hush, as Jennings was seen to stagger and fall!

The lad was certainly playing a splendid game. He was coolness itself, and nothing would stop him. The team were responding grandly, and time and again he would lead a gallant attack, which was only beaten off by sheer good luck.

Half-time came, and there was no score, but the home team had certainly been doing all the attacking.

There was a broad grin on old Greyson's face as he came into the dressing-room and took the lad by the hand.

"My boy," he said, "you are great! Keep it up, and we will be a long way ahead at the end. You've run right into form, eh?"

"Bit better, sir," said Sam modestly.

"It's grand football!" said old White. And praise from him was praise indeed.

The game started again, and immediately Sam got away. He was being marked now, and he could not get the ball out to anyone, in addition to which his movement had been so quick, and so unexpectedly clever that there was no one to help him. Instead, he had to make his own way. He tricked three opponents, however, and then, just as he was steadying himself for a shot, he was brought crashing down inside the area.

"Foul!"

There was a roar from twenty thousand throats, and the whistle was blown as Sam picked himself up. He was limping, for he had been badly kicked.

"Take it, Sam?" asked his skipper.

Sam shook his head.

"Sorry; but I've got a packet," he said, turning rather pale.

It was certainly so. He was in great pain.

However, for a moment Sam said nothing. There was a very much bigger issue on hand, and he stood still until the captain of the team had taken the kick.

He made an appalling hash of it, and Sam saw the ball go flying over the cross-bar.

For the rest of the game Sam knew he was going to be a passenger, and in a few minutes it was apparent to the whole crowd.

He did his best, but he simply could not move, and he ought by rights to have left the field; but he couldn't do that. Without much effort he could have sat down in the middle of the pitch and cursed or wept at the folly of it all—to be hurt at a moment like this! But he could do nothing else for the moment but limp about and try to help.

Still, luck was a good deal with the home team, for now they suddenly went to pieces, thanks to the fact that they did not have Sam at their head, and again and again their goal had an almost miraculous squeak.

There was less than five minutes to go now, and still no score.

Sam suddenly saw the leather coming in his direction. It had been cleared from a fight about his own goal, out of which he had wisely kept.

He caught the leather with his toe, and then suddenly started down the field. People gasped to see his effort. He thought that he was making it without limping at all; but actually he was limping terribly, and yet moving at a terrific speed.

A back came for him, and Sam seemed to fling himself into the air. It was a grand charge. The kind of charge that professionals these days immediately claim as a foul. Indeed, a shout went up, but the referee had his own ideas about what charging was, and he did nothing; but Sam was now away, with only the open goal in front of him.

He came as close as he could, steadied himself, felt someone charging down on him, and then shot very low and fast into the right-hand corner of the net.

"Goal!"

The word went up in a mighty roar from twenty thousand throats.

Sam had won the match. And then suddenly he collapsed in a faint from

sheer pain. At the same moment the referee blew his whistle for "Time!"

It was Sunday, and although he had heard nothing from Bill he went to keep the appointment. He was a good deal of a cripple, but he could walk with a stick, and the doctor had said that the best thing he could possibly do would be to walk.

And now at last he came to the place where he and Bill had agreed to meet, and there he saw a smiling giant who came towards him with his hand held out.

"But, Bill, Bill!" the youngster cried. "I thought your ankle was busted!"

Bill shook his head.

"No, boy," he said; "but my heart would have been busted if I had done you out of your place in the team yesterday. Bravo, Sam! You were great! How's the leg?"

Sam grinned from ear to ear. It's wonderful how the result of a match makes all the difference in the world as to how a leg feels.

"Fine!" he said. "Fine! Never felt better in my life! Fact of the matter is, Bill, I've got a lot to thank you for. I've got my job back at the factory, and I'm going to sign professional forms, and—and old Greyson says they are going to try me at inside-right, as soon as I am fit. Hope I can play there."

Bill put out a hand.

"Play there, Sam," he said. "You bet your life you can! Play there, kid. I'll be centre-forward, and between us we will make things hum—you see!"

And they did!

THE END.

(*Something special, boys! Look out for another side-splitting yarn of that most amusing character, Mike McAndrew, in next week's* GEM. *Note its title, please:* "MIKE MAKES A WIRELESS SET!" *It's one long laugh from beginning to end.*)

Full of Exciting Situations!   *You won't Skip a Line of this!*

THE TRIERS

BY JACK CRICHTON

A faithful band of stalwart sportsmen gathers to the support of Jack Morton in his brave effort to "keep his end up" against the unscrupulous George Clifton.

A Surprise for Clifton!

IT was at nine o'clock that the directors of the Boltwich F.C. were to meet, and one of the matters which were to come up for consideration was the disgraceful scene which had taken place when the Triers had played Boltwich Reserves.

It had, indeed, been brought up at a special meeting, convened shortly after the match; but that had proved so rowdy that it had had to be adjourned. But now the Football Association had asked for a report on the business, and George Clifton had been compelled to call another meeting.

He was strolling about in the dark outside the pavilion, rather thoughtfully, before the meeting, his hands deep in his pockets, and his thoughts perhaps not as full of satisfaction as they should have been, when suddenly he heard a light step on the gravel round the ground, and looked up.

A stalwart form approached him.

"That you, Atkins?" he said, in a low voice.

"Yes, sir!" came the answer.

"Ah! Glad you turned up. Wanted to have a word with you before the meeting. You will have to appear, you know."

Bill Atkins gave a grin in the dark.

"Yes, sir!"

"Well, there may be one or two awkward questions, but don't worry! I shall stand by you absolutely!"

"Of course you will!" said Mr. William Atkins, in a knowing voice, and this time forgetting the "sir."

The change of tone was not lost on the other, but he only flushed in the dark, and did not say a word as to it.

"Well, the reason I wanted to speak to you, Atkins, before you came before us, is this—I understand that some of these idiots are suggesting that you hurt young Morton on purpose."

"Not me, sir!" said Bill indignantly.

There was a moment's silence.

"Well, anyhow, there it is. It is Mr. Graham who is behind this, you know, and I understand that he has got hold of some cock-and-bull story that I wanted you to hurt young Morton."

"You, sir!"

If it had not been dark the men could

have looked into one another's eyes, and have understood one another perfectly. As a matter of fact, the wish that Jack Morton be badly hurt had been conveyed to Bill Atkins by hints, and never by words, as far as George Clifton was concerned, and his understanding had been suitably rewarded by a mysterious fiver, which had suddenly appeared from the blue in the midst of his post.

They understood one another.

"You leave it to me, sir!" said Atkins, quickly and quietly, as the sound of voices approached.

"Right!"

George Clifton went along then. He was in no good humour. Everything was happening to annoy him. His grandfather's original will had turned out to be a much more complicated document than had been supposed at first. He had seen old Mr. Brown, his solicitor, that afternoon, and, to his immense fury and disgust, the old lawyer had hinted that it would possibly be necessary to go to law before they could decide with regard to certain of the provisions in the will. Clifton had expressed his feelings as to lawyers, and had departed in a white fury.

This delay was getting too much for his nerves.

Then the inquiry which he would have to hold to-night into that game with the Triers.

He knew several of the directors of the Boltwich F.C. would welcome a chance to have a dig at him. Fortunately, he held such a large block of shares that he could keep them all quiet, but it was annoying that these things should all come together.

There was this fellow Graham, a junior director, and an upright and decent fellow. For weeks now he had never stopped doing his best to annoy George Clifton.

It was Graham who met Clifton as the latter entered the directors' room.

"Hallo, Graham!" Clifton exclaimed. "What's this I hear? Going to accuse me of bribing Atkins to maim young Morton the other week?"

Graham looked surprised at the directness of the attack.

"Really, Clifton," he said, "I was going to cross-examine Atkins pretty strongly as to his play; but I understand that we have something else to consider to-night before we open the inquiry."

Clifton started.

"What's that?"

"I understand the shareholders in the club have called an emergency meeting, and we must, of course, hear them."

Clifton stared at him.

"Are you mad? Shareholders! We, the directors, are the shareholders! Why, I—I myself hold—hold——"

He paused, and a grim smile came to Graham's lips.

"You don't hold a predominating share of the club's shares, do you, Clifton?"

"No, but—but no one does!"

"Yes, I think a predominating proportion has been recently acquired."

"What!"

"The holders are here. I think I had better show them in, don't you, Clifton? I have spoken to the other directors, and they agree that it is our duty always to listen to the shareholders. After all, we are their servants!"

Clifton bit his lip furiously.

"This is a put-up job! There is a catch here! It's not straight!" he exclaimed.

"Oh," said Graham, "I think it is straight enough, Clifton!"

George Clifton made a great effort. As yet he had not the most shadowy idea of what was happening. He bent his head grimly.

"Oh, by all means let them talk!" he said, seating himself at the head of the table. "I—I am ready for 'em all!"

"Right!"

Graham went to the door and spoke a word, and a moment later Laurie Robson entered.

Clifton leapt to his feet.

"Who are you?" he roared.

"I'm the jolly old shareholders, gentlemen," said the youngster, quietly and modestly, screwing his eyeglass farther and

WHAT HAS GONE BEFORE!

For the sake of his invalid mother, Jack Morton, a lad of seventeen, calls upon his grandfather, Sir Jasper Clifton, for aid. It was by no means a pleasant undertaking for Jack, for his mother, much against her father's wishes, had married a worker in Sir Jasper's mill, who was now dead. Sir Jasper, however, is taken up with the lad straight away, saying that he will alter his will and make him co-heir with George Clifton, another grandson, and Jack's cousin, and whose great interest in life is the Boltwich Football Club. In high spirits, Jack gives up his old job to take up work at Cliftons'. But Sir Jasper dies that night. Thinking only of his mother, Jack goes to George Clifton, but his appeal proves futile, Clifton telling him that the will is unaltered, and that he is not wanted. Jack's anger is aroused, and, meeting Ronnie Stevens, whom George Clifton had deemed it wise to sack, the two lads, former players of Boltwich F.C., determine to fight Clifton.

"We'll get a team that won't be beat," said Stevens, "and call them the Triers."

The team shows great promise, much to the annoyance of Clifton. Seeking revenge, the crafty Clifton approaches Harry Turner, for whom Jack Morton is now working. Offering a handsome price, Clifton buys up the business, immediately ordering Jack's dismissal from the firm. Grasping the situation, Laurie Robson prepares a surprise for Clifton by buying up the bulk of the shares in the Boltwich F.C.

(Now read on.)

farther into his eye. "I hold a great majority of the shares of the Boltwich Football Club, and with your permission I'd like to have a few words with you. I think there are one or two things that ought to be looked into, don't you know!"

GEORGE CLIFTON simply gaped at Laurie Robson without speaking. He could not for the moment understand what Laurie had stated.

"You are what?" he roared.

"I happen to hold a majority of the shares in the Boltwich Football Club, Mr. George Clifton, and I think that therefore I have a perfect right to ask for an inquiry into some of the things which have been happening lately."

Clifton looked quickly round the room, and suddenly realised that on every side of him was antagonism. He was not exactly a coward, and he would have liked to put up a fight. Indeed, he did not give in at once.

"Look here!" he cried. "I don't know so much about this. I'm managing director——"

"That can soon be altered," said Mr. Graham, the one director who for some time had stood up against him.

"Hear, hear!"

Then Clifton realised that he was merely wasting his time, and that as far as the club was concerned his day was done.

He faced them angrily, with a sneer on his lips.

"Oh, very well," he said. "I—I am sorry you don't seem to have any more use for me. It's grateful of you, I must say, after all I have done for the club. I dare say, though, that after a few weeks you will come round to me, asking this and that favour; but I shall not be in. I' will leave you to deal with this young whippersnapper." He turned on Laurie. "He will no doubt play for Boltwich himself now, with some of his out-of-work friends. I'm finished!"

He picked up his hat, and, without another word, went out of the room.

Outside he bumped into Bill Atkins, who was waiting to give evidence.

"Hallo!" exclaimed that individual. "Want me?"

Clifton made a nasty grimace.

"No, not yet! Someone else is in the saddle in there. I have quit——"

"Eh?"

Clifton bent low.

"I am throwing up my connection with the club, Atkins, but not with you!"

The red-headed fellow flushed.

"I get you!"

"To be frank, Atkins," Clifton went on, "I don't suppose you'll keep your place in the team very long now. There is going to be new blood, and you know you have not been at the top of your form this season. Young Laurie Robson is going to be the big noise in the affairs of the club now, and you can imagine who he'll bring back into the team!"

An evil light came into Atkins' eyes.

"Ay! Steve Logan and young Ronnie Stevens—eh?"

Clifton nodded.

"Yes, not to mention a certain Jack Morton!"

Atkins whistled.

"I get you, Mr. Clifton! No, I don't suppose they would keep me long. It's a nice state of affairs, I must admit! All right, you leave it to me. I'll come along and see you one day soon, shall I?"

"Do!"

They nodded to one another and parted.

Meanwhile Laurie Robson, with all the uprightness in the world, had taken possession of the committee meeting of directors.

"I fear," he said, "that I owe you gentlemen an apology for what has happened, but something had to be done to save the Boltwich team. There is no doubt that under the management of George Clifton things were going from bad to worse. Good players were driven from the club. There is not another full-back in the town like Steve Logan, nor a half-back like Ronnie Stevens, and yet Clifton kicked them out."

"That's right!"

"Well, gentlemen, I've bought the majority of the shares in the club, but that does not mean that I want to run things like Mr. Clifton did. I was only interested in getting

him out of the club, and now I have succeeded, I leave the working of the club in your hands!"

"We shall have to elect another managing director," said one of the directors present. "I propose Mr. Robson. He is young, but it seems to me that we need young blood!"

Laurie quickly shook his head.

"No, thanks," he said. "I don't want the job. I'm too young, and the town would not have confidence in me. I'll become a director, if you'll elect me, but I propose Mr. Graham here as managing director!"

This was carried, and for several hours that evening the directors really got down to business. By the time that they departed, having given Bill Atkins a real piece of their minds, Laurie had the satisfaction of knowing that he had started the Boltwich team on the right road again, and, what was more, he had invitations for Steve and Ronnie and Jack to turn out for the first team on the following Saturday.

He himself had been asked whether he would like to play at outside-right, but he had again refused. The team had a capital right-winger, and the youngster was determined that nothing he was doing should possibly be construed as having personal glorification as its basis.

It was far too late that evening for him to see any of the lads and give them his news, but it would keep until the morning.

Jack Morton had left his house that same evening, and had returned to his mother and his own home, as the old lady had been getting very worried about him.

So it was that early the next morning Laurie went round to Jack's cottage home, and, as it happened, found that young man talking over the front gate with no less a person than Steve Logan himself.

"Hallo!" he said, screwing his glass into his eye, and regarding them with a grin. "I've got news for you fellows!"

"Eh?" they cried together.

"I've got jobs for you both!"

Steve flushed with emotion. Things had been very bad for him since Clifton had had him dismissed from his job at the garage, and as he was a married man it had been doubly difficult to endure it all.

"I say," he now exclaimed, "that's good news, I must say. What is it, Laurie?"

"You are both going to be signed on by the Boltwich Football Club!"

"What!"

Laurie laughed, and then slowly and surely went through the whole story of the previous night's proceedings. The other two listened open-mouthed, and when he was finished two hands were held out to him.

"Robson," said Jack, "you are a good fellow. This is the work of a real sport; but"—he suddenly frowned—"it means the end of the Triers."

"Ah, yes!" exclaimed Steve.

But Laurie Robson shook his head.

"By no means," he said. "It means, rather, that the Triers are going to be used for a bigger and a better purpose than we first intended. Our original idea, the only thing, indeed, which bound us together, was a common feud against that king of rotters, George Clifton. But now we have given him one in the jolly old eye to go along with, the best thing we can do, my lads, is to use the Triers to bring Boltwich right to the top of the League!"

"Sure," cried Steve, "and we will!"

Laurie glanced at Jack.

"Why so serious, Jack?" he asked.

The lad smiled, but still seriously.

"Well, to tell you the truth," he said. "I was being rather selfish for the moment. It's fine, this. It was always the ambition of my life to play for Boltwich, and now it is coming about, but I could not help thinking at that moment that as you have succeeded in kicking Clifton out of the club, he will turn his hate and anger on to me, and I shall have rather a more cheery time than ever!"

Laurie laughed in reply.

"Funking it?" he asked.

"Gracious, no! I'm more determined." Jack drew himself up. "I am more determined, Laurie, than ever to get at the bottom of all his rotten tricks, and to find out the truth about my grandfather's will, and I am going to do it or die!"

Laurie placed a hand on his pal's shoulder.

"That's the spirit, old chap," he said. "That is the stuff to give 'em! Stick to it, and know you've always got me behind you. We have kicked Clifton out of the club, and before we are finished we are going to kick him out of the town!"

"Sure!" agreed Jack; and a few moments later went in to see his old mother, and to tell her the news.

He bent and kissed the rather bowed white head very tenderly. The old lady looked up with a start.

"Well, dear," she asked, "any news?"

"Rather!" said Jack brightly. "I should jolly well think I have got some news, mother. I have got a good job, and I am going to stick to it until I have got our rights out of George Clifton!"

In spite of the pain from his ankle, Jack Morton leaped to his feet, then flashing out his right, he sent Atkins flying backwards to land on the turf with a thud.

When Thieves Fall Out!

"MAY I have a word with you?" George Clifton looked up with a start. He was sitting in the library of the Old Hall, an evening or two later, writing some letters, and as he looked up he saw Graves, the butler, standing in the doorway.

"Is that the way to speak to me, man?" he snapped, rising to his feet.

The butler came into the middle of the room. He was a large, old man, with a rugged, rather evil face, and a good deal of grim determination about the jaw.

"I want to have a word with you, Mr. George," he said, "and I am not going to mince matters. Things aren't going satisfactorily for me!"

"What?"

There was an angry light in Clifton's face, but his voice was calmer.

"You know what I mean, Mr. George," Graves went on. "We are in this will business together."

"S-s-h, you old fool!" cried Clifton, and looked quickly about him, as though dreadfully fearing eavesdroppers.

Graves gave a sniggering laugh.

"Oh, there is no one likely to hear us, Mr. George," he said. "Don't keep putting me off. As I say, we are in this will business together, and I want some money!"

Clifton moved about uncomfortably.

"Well, you are getting a thousand pounds out of my grandfather's original will, aren't you, you old miser?"

Graves nodded.

"Getting! Yes, that's the right word. When is it coming along?"

"Well, I don't know, man. I am as anxious for money as you are yourself, but one can't hasten these brutes of lawyers up any more than I have done. As it is, I have rather overdone it. I'm not myself, of course, actually pushed for money, and they must have thought it rather queer of me being in such a hurry. We don't want to let them think that there was another will, and that we are afraid of it appearing suddenly, do we?"

Graves gave a peculiar smile.

"Oh, you're very clever at trying to change the subject, Mr. George," he said; "but I mean business. Of course, we don't want them to know that there was a later will which disappeared in a mysterious way, and that you and I did nothing about it, or said nothing about it. But the point is, you offered me a thousand on your own account if I stood by you by the first will, and as I have been hard pressed for money lately, I can do with a bit of it!"

George flushed.

"Well, I'm pressed myself, man," he said. "You can get money."

"I can't!"

The old butler shook his head, almost, it would have seemed, more in sorrow than in anger.

"I am afraid it's no good talking to me like that, Mr. George. It does not go down with me. I bought those shares you told me about, after Sir Jasper died, and, as you know, there is another call on them. I've got to have five hundred, and you have got to get it for me. Come, sir, be reasonable. I have stood by you, and I mean to, but I want my rights!"

But George Clifton again shook his head.

"I'm in a deuce of a mess myself, man!" he cried. "I could not let you have fifty——"

"You can sell a picture."

"What!"

"You don't want me to spread the yarn about that there was another will." The old fellow gave a rather significant look at the other. "Enough people seem to have got hold of some sort of yarn like that already! Suppose that second will was to turn up, Mr. George!"

"What! That can't happen! My grandfather must have changed his mind that last night; he must have destroyed it."

"I'm not so sure!"

There was a strange significance in the man's voice, and suddenly George Clifton realised it.

In a flash he had lost control of himself, and, leaping across at the old fellow, he had caught him by the throat in a brutal, dreadful way.

"You old fiend!" he snarled. "You know something about it. You've got it up your

sleeve all the time. Don't you lie to me! You know you have! I can see it in your lying eyes. Down you go!"

He forced him down on to his knees.

"I've had enough of your impertinence!" he cried angrily. "This is the finish! I will not stand it another hour. I want to know about that will, or, by Harry, I'll strangle the breath out of you!"

For a moment or so a desperate struggle followed, and then suddenly Clifton seemed to come to his senses. At any rate, he dropped his hands suddenly, and the old fellow sank limply to the ground.

"Weil?" snarled Clifton.

Graves picked himself up slowly. He was trembling and frightened for the moment.

"No, no!" he said. "You have got hold of the wrong end of the stick, sir. I know nothing about any other will. Only I am in a big mess with those shares, and you ought to help me, sir!"

Clifton pointed to the door.

"Get out, and keep out, you old idiot," he said. "You stand to win a thousand pounds by my grandfather's first will, and if you are fool enough to throw that away, then I'm fool enough to risk you double-crossing me. I can't let you have any of the other thousand yet. But I shall not fail you, I will pay you in due course. Now get out!"

Graves, shaken and very much afraid for his own skin, turned and went quickly from the room.

He knew that Clifton was bluffing, but he himself was bluffing, too, as he was no more anxious than Clifton for the second will to see the light of day.

But later that evening, as he walked from the Old Hall down to his own cottage some little way from the Hall, muttering dreadful threats to himself, he tried to work out in his evil old way how best he could get the better of Clifton, without losing thereby himself.

"Good-night, Mr. Graves!" said a cheery young voice suddenly, as he went along.

Graves started.

"Hallo!" he snapped. "Who's that?"

"Me," said Ronnie Stevens. "I heard you muttering away to yourself, Mr. Graves, as though you weren't too happy!"

Old Graves swore under his breath.

"Well, I'm not!" he growled. "I'd like to throttle that young cub!"

And he put a tender finger to his very sore throat.

Ronnie started and laughed. In the old days, when he had been a footman at the Hall, he had, of course, known that Graves and George Clifton were hand-in-glove together, and if they had fallen out, it was certainly rather interesting. He had never forgotten that old Graves had been the other witness when Sir Jasper had called him in to witness a document the night he died.

"Hallo!" he exclaimed. "Not so fond of Mr. George as you were, Mr. Graves!"

"He's a hound, that's what he is!"

"Just found that out?"

"Yes!"

Ronnie laughed.

"Well, we all found it out long ago, Mr. Graves. He is a rotter. And as you are coming round to our way of thinking about him, you'll not be sorry to hear that he has been kicked out of the control of the football club in Boltwich, and young Mr. Robson did that. He's a sport. The club is going to be run on decent lines now. Steve Logan and I, and young Jack Morton, are going to play for them; and you mark my words, the day will come when Mr. George Clifton is shown up before the whole world."

Old Graves gave a quick grunt.

"Yes," he muttered. "I shouldn't be surprised if it did. I could show him up, if I wanted to, and if I have much more nonsense from him, my lad, I'll surprise you all!"

"Eh? How's that?"

But the old fellow shook his head.

"That would be telling, Ronnie," he said. "Well, glad to meet you, my lad. Hope you are getting on all right. Good-night, and come and see us sometimes!"

So saying, he shook hands with the astonished lad, and turned away into the night.

Ronnie watched him go. Then, suddenly, as if remembering something, he started to run, and he did not stop until he had reached Jack Morton's cottage. He knocked loudly on the door, and then burst into the room with a shout.

"Jack," he said, glowing with his news,

"I have got something to tell you and Mrs. Morton. I've been having a few words with old Graves, the butler. He's fallen out with Clifton, and he is threatening dreadful things against him. I could not get any more out of him, but I'm sure he knows something about that second will, and I believe that if you play your cards properly, it will be from old Graves that you'll learn the truth, and come into your own!"

Arrested!

THERE was joy in Boltwich the following Saturday.

Not only were two popular favourites, in Steve Logan and Ronnie Stevens, coming back into the team, but the entrance to the ground had been lowered. And as the leaders of the League were the guests of Boltwich, there was a record gate.

Jack was very nervous. It was enough to turn the head of any youngster; but as he sat, changed, and waiting for the word, he couldn't help wondering whether the occasion would not be too big a one for him. He had, of course, never played in football of this class before, and he realised that it was a good deal of an experiment, and that the club was trying to please Laurie Robson.

Old Blake, the trainer of the team, saw him after a few minutes, and crossed over to him.

"Wind up, lad?" he asked.

Jack smiled.

"A bit!"

"That's all right," he said. "It'll pass off! The only thing you want to do is to forget that it is a League game, and that a lot depends on it for you. Just play your own natural game, and it will be all right!"

"I'm going to try," said Jack.

The old fellow bent close.

"I'm sorry," he said, "they are playing Atkins!"

Jack started, and flushed.

"I mean it," said the trainer. "It's not a happy combination, you and he."

Jack shook his head.

"I know what you mean," he said, "after the way he knocked me about in that reserve match; but I am glad he has not been dropped to-day. In fact, I asked Laurie Robson to try and play him, if he could."

"You did?"

"Yes," the lad exclaimed, "because I didn't want folks to say that he was kicked out of the team on my account. I don't want anyone to say that!"

"Well, have a care, lad!"

Jack stared.

"Well, I don't know what harm he can do me, do you?"

The old trainer nodded, and lowered his voice, for Bill Atkins himself was in the dressing-room.

"He can hold you up all he can, lad," he said, "and he is the sort to do it. But what is more, he can give you a sly one, if there is ever any rough play about goal, or something like that. I've got an idea that he doesn't mean any good, so I thought I would just warn you to be careful. Good luck, lad, and don't worry!"

"Thanks!"

The team went out on to the pitch then, and the roar that went up for the three lads from the Triers was the biggest heard that year on Boltwich ground.

It was good to hear, and Jack grimly determined that he would not disappoint his friends.

It was a terrific strain for a youngster to play centre-forward for the first time against the leaders of the League, and, try as he could, Jack could not run into his proper form at first.

Several times he was given an opening, Ronnie feeding him carefully; but as often as the ball came to him he would fumble with it, and finally lose it.

At last a groan of desperation went up from the crowd.

He had let the other side away, and a moment or so later the first goal had been scored against Boltwich.

"Send him back to his mother!" roared a great voice, which Jack recognised as belonging to the Babe, and a laugh went up.

Jack flushed and bit his lip, and Steve Logan, who was at his side at the moment, patted him on the shoulder.

"Take it quietly, lad," he said; "you'll run into form in a minute."

"Yes," smiled Jack, "when they have scored about ten!"

"Never mind!"

But worse was to happen.

He was given yet another splendid opening by Ronnie five minutes later, and this time he got away without any difficulty, neatly side-stepped an opposing back, and had a clear run for goal. He went right in, and as Boltwich held its breath in agonised expectation, he shot; but the leather went soaring wildly over the bar.

A groan went up, and yells of anger. It might almost have been done on purpose.

George Clifton was in the stands, and he looked towards Laurie Robson in the directors' box.

"Great find of yours, Robson!" he cried, and Laurie had to look away.

All this time Bill Atkins at inside-left was not doing anything to help. It was all done so cleverly, too, that it would have been impossible to accuse him of any wrong doing. But Jack realised full well that he was playing all the time to make it difficult for him to regain the ground he had already lost.

If he got the ball, and was attacked, he passed anywhere except to Jack, and once or twice he actually got in the lad's way. But it was all done so cleverly that it was impossible to be certain that he meant it.

Then suddenly he went too far.

There was a scrimmage in front of the home goal, and they were in the middle of it, and quite deliberately, but out of the sight of the crowd, Atkins gave the lad a brutal kick on the ankle.

With a yell of pain Jack went to the ground, but in another moment he had leaped to his feet, and, with a beautiful right, had sent Atkins flying.

It was pandemonium then in a second. The game was stopped, and the referee rushed up.

"Are you mad?" he cried to Jack. "Off the field at once!"

"But he kicked me deliberately," protested Jack.

"I didn't touch him!" cried Atkins.

"I saw him do it," said a voice calmly, and Jack, turning, found himself backed up by the skipper of the opposing side, an International, and a man of undoubted honesty. "I saw it, and it was the dirtiest thing I ever saw done on a football field! Atkins deserved what he got!"

The referee looked puzzled. This altered the position, and for a moment he did not know what to do. The crowd was yelling like mad now.

"Well, I'll report the whole thing," he said quickly. "Get on with the game in the meantime, and no more of that, either of you!"

The game restarted. Jack was in dreadful pain, but unwittingly Atkins had done the one thing to pull him together. So angry was he at this unsporting trick that he forgot entirely the bigness of the occasion.

He was limping badly, but he limped through the trouble, and suddenly from a miskick he got possession, and was off down the field like a flash of lightning.

Several men tackled him, but without success. An International could not have done it more neatly. He lurched from one side to the other, feinted, and was through on his own.

"Good old Jack!" roared the crowd, as Jack raced on.

One of the opposing full-backs had stuck to him, and he had no time to get in as close as he would like, and he had to shoot while warding off the heavy attentions of his opponent.

But shoot he did, a real beauty, which rattled, as it were, through the air, to land in the net clean out of the goalie's reach.

It was the proudest moment in Jack's life. He had scored for Boltwich! How the crowd cheered, how they yelled!

It might have been a Cup Final for the row they made, and when, ten minutes later, out of a fight in front of goal, Jack got his head to the ball, and scored a second, and, as it turned out, a winning goal, he was made for life in the hearts of the Boltwich fans.

And it seemed that wonders were never to cease that day, for when he got home—and he went quickly back so that his mother should have news of his first game for Boltwich—there was a letter waiting for him.

"It came while you were out, Jack," his mother said. "It's from the Hall!"

Jack stared. On the back of the envelope were the words: "The Old Hall," and after a moment he looked up at his mother's anxious eyes.

"Yes," he said; "I believe that it is from Clifton."

"Read it, dear!"

He tore it open, and in another moment had given a sharp exclamation of surprise.

"My dear Morton," it said, and he read it out aloud: "I have been thinking things over, and I would like to have a word with you. Kindly come and see me, if convenient to yourself, at nine o'clock this evening!

"Yours sincerely,
"GEORGE CLIFTON."

He looked at his mother.

"What do you think of that, mother?" he cried.

The old lady shook her head.

"I am sure I don't know, dear," she said. "It is certainly very surprising. I—I suppose—perhaps—he has relented!"

Jack bit his lip.

"I hate to go!" he said.

"My dear!" exclaimed the old lady, in sudden alarm.

"I hate to take anything from that brute now, mother!" Jack exclaimed. "I would like to make him cough up everything that is yours, but not to accept a thing from him; but"—and, going to her, he laughed gently and kissed her white head—"of course I am going to do it, for your sake, so don't look so down on your luck!"

"My dear boy!"

Jack said no more, but seeing that his mother was eager

for him to go, forgot his own disinclination, and at nine o'clock sharp that evening he presented himself once again at the Old Hall.

Graves, the butler, viewed him with his customary surprise as he saw him.

"Hallo!" he exclaimed. "What do you want?"

"Mr. Clifton wrote and told me to come and see him at nine o'clock this evening," said Jack stoutly, "so here I am!"

"He did?"

"Yes. I should not be here if he hadn't."

Graves gave a grunt.

"All right," he said. "Come in, and I'll see what he says."

He went away, and found Clifton writing in the library.

"There's that young Jack Morton here, sir," he said; they were better friends, for George Clifton had managed to find a little money for the old fellow, as it happened. "He says that you wrote and told him to come and see you at nine o'clock this evening."

"What!"

"He says so, sir!"

Clifton rose to his feet, with all the appearance of a very angry man.

"I did nothing of the sort, Graves!" he cried. "The less I see of him the better. Send him about his business. No—stay. He says I wrote. There is something funny here. I'll see him. Show him in. I'm going to get to the bottom of this sort of thing!"

"Very good, sir!"

A few moments later Jack was being shown into the room, and Clifton awaited him in chilly silence.

"Well?"

The door closed behind Jack.

"I've come!" he said.

"So I see. Why?"

"Why," exclaimed the lad, "didn't you write to me?"

"I certainly did nothing of the sort!" said Clifton.

There was a moment's pause, while Jack stared at the other, wondering what devilry he was up to this time; and then suddenly the thought came to him that there must be some mistake.

He pulled the letter from his pocket, glad that he had brought it with him.

"Didn't you write that?"

Clifton started, took the letter, and then shook his head.

"I am sorry," he said, "I am afraid that someone has been playing a practical joke on you, Morton. This all comes from you spreading the absurd story about Boltwich that I owe you something. This is not my writing. It's not unlike it, and it's infernal cheek on someone's part, but I certainly had nothing to do with it!"

For once Jack was really taken in by the fellow. He accepted his word for what had happened, and for the moment stood raking his brain in trying to think who could have done it.

"I am sorry I came!" he said, flushing.

"There is nothing I have to see you about," returned Clifton.

A moment passed. Jack started towards the door, then, on the sudden inspiration of a moment, paused.

"I say!"

"Well?" exclaimed Clifton, looking surprised at the lad's tone.

"Are you still as pleased with the way things are going as you have always been?"

Clifton started and stared at the lad.

"Why, what do you mean?"

"Well, I should have thought that you were rather fed-up about the way in which you have been kicked out of the Boltwich Club?"

Clifton grew red with anger.

"I'll kick you out of my house, young man," he cried, "if you aren't careful!"

Jack held up a hand.

"No," he exclaimed, "don't start like that, Clifton. I don't want to have words with you. It only occurred to me that, as I have come here by mistake, it might be as well for me to make one more appeal to you. I always seem to be doing so. Why don't you do the decent thing by me and my mother? It would make you popular in the town——"

"You seem to fancy yourself, young man!"

"I don't know about that," said Jack; "but if I manage to do fairly well for Boltwich, I dare say I sha'n't be so unpopular in the town as I might be!"

It was a shrewd thrust, and it went right home. The man paled for a moment, and then snapped his lips angrily.

"You get out of this house!" he said. "I don't want to hear of you or your old fool of a mother again!"

"I'm going!" said Jack, breaking in. "And I don't come back, George Clifton, until I come back master of this house!"

And without giving the somewhat surprised Clifton an opportunity to reply, he hurried out of the room, slamming the door behind him.

He was furious with himself now for having come. As he went down the drive he felt in his pocket for the letter which had taken him on such a fool's errand. He had been mad to go! Then he realised that he had left the letter with his cousin. Well, it didn't matter. He had gone, and he had looked a fool; but never again would he have anything to do with George Clifton. He was through—for good and all.

His mother was waiting up for him, and as he came into the little room of the cottage he caught sight of her dear white head, bent, as though in sleep.

He gave a start, and tiptoed across to her. She had fallen asleep waiting for him, poor old soul, and now when he awakened her it would be to give her bad news.

For a moment he stood and took an oath there, his hand on the back of his mother's chair.

"One day, George Clifton," he muttered to himself, "you shall pay for all this!"

His mother awakened at that moment with a start.

"Why, Jack dear," she exclaimed, "you back already! I must have fallen asleep as soon as you went. What happened, dear boy? Did he do anything for us?"

Jack had to shake his head.

"No, dear—nothing!"

There were tears in his eyes, and the old woman realised how he felt, and so, reaching up with her hand, she drew him down, and told him not to care. But there was bitterness in the heart of Jack Morton such as there had never been before, and he swore to himself in that moment more dreadfully than ever before that he would take his revenge one day.

*   *   *   *   *

He was down early next morning, for he was in strict training now for the club. The Cupties would be soon commencing, and he was anxious to give of his best.

He had started the fire going, and was making a cup of tea to take up to his mother, when suddenly there came a knock on the door.

He started, surprised that anyone should have come to see them so early.

"Hallo!" he exclaimed, and went to the door.

Without he found a police-sergeant and a detective. He knew them both well by sight, and his heart seemed to stop beating for a second as he found himself staring at them.

"Ah, there you are, young fellow!" said the sergeant. "We want a word with you."

"With me?"

"Yes, with you, Jack Morton," said the detective, as they came into the little kitchen. "It's my duty, of course, to warn you that anything you say may be used against you, and you haven't got to answer questions unless you like. But I may as well tell you that there is a charge against you of having stolen a pocket-book containing notes to the value of fifty pounds from Mr. George Clifton when you saw him last night at the Old Hall!"

"What!" cried Jack furiously. "It's a lie! I never touched a thing! I——"

Suddenly there came an exclamation from the sergeant of police, who had already started rummaging about the room.

"Then how do you account for this, young man?" he said, and held up a brown leather pocket-case. "How do you account for this being in your overcoat-pocket, eh?"

(Is this another foul move on the part of George Clifton? Be sure you read next week's instalment of this grand serial.)

THE GEM LIBRARY.—No. 824.

Printed and published every Wednesday by the Proprietors, The Amalgamated Press (1922), Ltd., The Fleetway House, Farringdon Street, London, E.C.4. Advertisement offices: The Fleetway House, Farringdon Street, London, E.C.4. Registered for transmission by Canadian Magazine Post. Subscription rates: Inland and Abroad, 11s. per annum; 5s. 6d. for six months. Sole agents for South Africa: The Central News Agency, Ltd. Sole agents for Australia and New Zealand: Messrs. Gordon & Gotch, Ltd.; and for Canada, The Imperial News Co., Ltd. (Canada).—Saturday, Nov. 24th, 1923.
NN

My Readers' Own Corner.

Tuck Hampers and Money Prizes Awarded for Interesting Paragraphs.

(If You Do Not Win a Prize This Week—You May Next!)

All Efforts in this Competition should be Addressed to : The GEM LIBRARY, "My Readers' Own Corner," Gough House, Gough Square, London, E.C.4.

DONCASTER READER WINS TUCK HAMPER!

CUTE!

The outside-right of the village team sped down the field, and when about three yards from the corner flag sent in a perfect centre. The centre-forward, who had a bald head, jumped up and headed the ball, but, to the dismay of the spectators, the leather glanced off his head and went over the crossbar. "Hey!" shouted a disappointed supporter from behind the goal. "Just chalk your cue next time!"—A Tuck Hamper filled with delicious Tuck has been awarded to H. White, 33, Broughton Avenue, Bentley Road, Doncaster.

RATHER SARCASTIC!

A weary traveller addressed the conductor of a train while he was punching his ticket. "Does this railway company allow passengers to give advice, if they do so in a respectful manner?" he asked. "Er—yes!" grunted the conductor. "Well," went on the traveller, "it occurred to me that it would be better to detach the cowcatcher from the front of the engine, and hitch it to the rear of the train. For, you see, we are not liable to overtake a cow; but what's to prevent a cow strolling after us, getting into the car, and biting a passenger?"—Half-a-crown has been awarded to E. Babington, 11, Cromwell Street, Gainsborough, Lincolnshire.

ROUGH ON SAMMY!

The screams which were issuing from the house were awful. It seemed as if a terrible tragedy was in progress. An anxious knot of people gathered outside, and wondered why someone had not the courage to enter and rescue the victim. At last an unconcerned youth came out of the front door, whistling. One of the spectators promptly buttonholed him. "What's going on in your house?" he asked. "What's the meaning of those fearful screams?" "Eh?" said the youth, as another wail came from within. "Oh, that's Sammy! You see, while he was at the pantry this morning a jar of treacle fell on to his head, and now mother's trying to comb his hair!"—Half-a-crown has been awarded to Roy Hudson, 123, Fitzgerald Street, Bradford, Yorks.

PROVING IT!

"When I was in India," said the club bore, "I saw a tiger come to the river where some women were washing clothes. It was a fierce tiger, and was about to attack them when one woman, with great presence of mind, splashed some water in the brute's face, and it slunk away." "Gentlemen," said one of the club's leading members, "I can vouch for the truth of this story. Some minutes after this incident occurred I was coming down to the river. I met this tiger, and, as was my usual custom, stroked its whiskers. Gentlemen, those whiskers were wet!"—Half-a-crown has been awarded to J. T. Greene, 109, Belmont Road, Anfield, Liverpool.

BEATEN!

Two amateur gardeners were talking about large vegetables. One said that he new someone who grew a pumpkin so large that his two children had half each for a cradle. "Pooh! That's nothing!" replied the other. "In this town four policemen sleep on one beat (beet)!"—Half-a-crown has been awarded to Laurence Mortimer, Clover Greaves, Calverley, near Leeds, Yorkshire.

TUCK HAMPER COUPON.

The GEM LIBRARY.

No attempt will be considered unless accompanied by one of these Coupons.

He could not *buy* them so he built them

Boys build your own Models

WITH Meccano you can build hundreds of working models that you could not buy anywhere. For instance, where could you buy a working model of Eiffel Tower like the one shown here—or a Drop Hammer, a Loom, or a Revolving Crane?

Even models of Cranes, Bridges, Towers, and Motor Wagons, that you can buy anywhere, are not so good as the shining steel and brass models you can build with Meccano.

And the crane you buy is *always* a crane, whereas the crane you build with Meccano can be taken to pieces and the same parts used to build something else.

Every Outfit is complete—nothing further to buy.

EIFFEL TOWER.

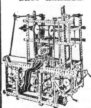

DROP HAMMER.

GRAND PRIZE CONTEST

This is a model-building Competition that brings golden opportunities to brainy, inventive boys. This year we offer splendid Cups and Medals to the value of £250 for the best Meccano models. Write us for full particulars or ask your dealer for an entry form.

OUTFITS from 3/6 to 370/-

LOOM.

MECCANO

ENGINEERING FOR BOYS

FREE TO BOYS

A splendid New Meccano Book

This is a new and splendidly illustrated book, that tells of all the good things that come from Meccanoland, where the best toys are manufactured. No boy should be without this wonderful book.

How to get a Free Copy

Just show this advertisement to three chums and send us their names and addresses with your own. Put No. 36 after your name for reference.

MECCANO LTD : BINNS RD : LIVERPOOL

SPLENDID STORIES AND HUGE COMPETITION!

830 Valuable Prizes
Must be Won!

EVERY WEDNESDAY.

The GEM 2d

LIBRARY of SCHOOL and SPORTING STORIES

No. 825.
Vol. XXIV.
December 1st, 1923.

THE FIGHT IN THE CHANGING-ROOM!

Tom Merry, the junior football captain, loses his temper with Ralph Reckness Cardew. (A lively incident from the splendid long complete school story in this issue.)

YOUR EDITOR CHATS ABOUT NEXT WEEK'S "GEM."

My dear Chums,—Next week's issue of the "Gem" will contain the eighth and final set of puzzle-pictures in the great Footballers' Names Competition. There is not a minute to lose if you want to see your name in the list of winners of some of the magnificent prizes. There still is time.

"CAPTAIN CARDEW!"
By Martin Clifford.

There are big events recorded in the grand St. Jim's yarn for next week. Keen and clever as he may be, Cardew has taken on rather a lot. The struggle between him and Tom Merry for supremacy has culminated exactly as Cardew's supporters wished; but there is a hitch, all the same, and there are doubters abroad. How long will matters rest as they are?

THE "HOLIDAY ANNUAL."

Christmas is coming, and no finer or more companionable gift could be imagined than a copy of the "Holiday Annual." It is the book that pleases all and sundry. It is a splendid pick-me-up. If you leave a volume unattended for half a minute you are bound to find somebody is deep in it while your back is turned. The magnificent "Holiday Annual" is still to be obtained. It's a yearly treat not to be missed.

"THE RED IMAGE!"
By Cecil Fanshaw.

Tales about India are always welcome. The finest romance of the great Eastern Empire ever written will be found in next Wednesday's "Gem." It tells of the thrilling experience of a plucky Britisher named Paul Mannering. You will be entranced by his adventure in the mystic shades of the Temple of Delhi, where the secrets of thousands of years are locked away. I am not going to drop a hint as to the weird mystery of the Red Image, nor the amazing discovery so providentially made by Mannering during his sojourn in the shades of the ancient sanctuary.

"THE TRIERS!"
By Jack Crichton.

You will find grip and heaps of drama in next week's instalment of this fine serial. Jack Morton springs a mighty big surprise on George Clifton. We get a tremendous situation on the footer-field, and it all goes to show that where there's a will there's a way.

"JUNGLE JINKS."

That is the title of my new Companion Paper for the younger chums. It is out on December 6th, and you would be sorry to miss it, for the fact of the matter is that "Jungle Jinks" will please everybody, young or old, with its rare budget of stories, jokes, competitions (with money prizes), tales from the Zoo, and, in short, all the fun of the fair!

Last, but not by any means least, with every copy of "Jungle Jinks" there will be given away

A FREE PACKET OF TOFFEE

Now, drop in the nearest newsagent's, and order a copy of this delightful new paper for your young brother or sister!

Your Editor.

TOM MERRY'S RIVAL !

A Splendid, New, Long Complete Story of St. Jim's, telling of the crafty Ralph Reckness Cardew's bold bid for the captiancy of St. Jim's.

By Martin Clifford.

CHAPTER 1.
Cardew's Programme !

"WHICH are you?"

Ralph Reckness Cardew of the Fourth Form at St. Jim's asked that question. He addressed Tom Merry.

"Eh, what?" ejaculated Tom.

"Which are you?" repeated Cardew.

Cardew asked that question with perfect gravity. His study-mates, Levison and Clive, stared at him, wondering what he was driving at; but Cardew did not seem to notice it.

Tom Merry had dropped into Study No. 9 in the Fourth, with something to say on the subject of football and House matches. That subject was always interesting enough to Levison and Clive; and of late it had seemed an interesting subject to Cardew. Tom Merry, as junior captain of St. Jim's, was an important person in football matters, though there never was a trace of "swank" about him.

Ralph Reckness Cardew interrupted the football talk by asking his rather remarkable question. He was sprawled at ease in the armchair, with his feet resting on another chair, and his hands clasped behind his head. He looked a picture of lazy slackness as he sprawled.

"Is that a joke, Cardew?" asked Tom Merry, after a pause. "If it is, I don't quite see where it comes in. Now, Levison——"

"It isn't a joke."

"Well, never mind. Levison, on Saturday——"

"Dear man," said Cardew, interrupting again with quiet persistence. "Won't you answer a little innocent and harmless question? I really want to know."

Tom looked slightly impatient.

"What do you want to know?" he demanded.

"Which are you?"

"Oh, don't be an ass!"

"Let me elucidate," went on Cardew. "I'll try to put it simply, in the words of one syllable, suitable to the undeveloped intellect of the Shell. You are junior captain of St. Jim's."

"I think that's fairly well known," assented Tom.

"You are also junior House captain of the School House."

"Quite so!"

"Likewise you are captain of the Shell."

"What about it?"

"Well, you seem to be three captains rolled into one," said Cardew. "What I was askin' is this; which are you at the present moment? In which of your many characters have you honoured this study with a visit?"

Tom Merry laughed.

"I suppose I've come here as junior captain of the school, as it's about the football," he said.

"Weren't you discussin' a House match with the New House?"

"Yes."

"Then surely you were speakin' as junior House captain?"

"Eh? Yes, I suppose I was," assented Tom Merry. "What the merry thump does it matter?"

"What are you getting at, Cardew?" asked Levison. "You're wasting time, you know!"

"As per usual!" remarked Sidney Clive.

Cardew shook his head.

"Not at all," he answered. "I only want to get things exact. That's what the study of mathematics is for—the jolly old maths master will tell you any day that it trains its victims into intellectual exactitude. I'm a whale on maths, as you know——"

"Oh, my hat!"

"So I want to get this thing fair and square," continued Cardew, with great gravity. "I am keenly interested in Thomas and the many parts he plays. Shakespeare has remarked——"

"Give Shakespeare a rest, for goodness' sake!"

"He has remarked that one man in his time plays many parts. The same applies to nippers like Tom Merry, apparently. As junior captain of the school, he leads us forth to victory over the Grammarians, and Rookwood, and Greyfriars, and, in fact, over all the barbarians who inhabit the unexplored regions outside the gates of St. Jim's——"

"Fathead!"

"As junior House captain, he guides our faltering steps to conquest over the New House of St. Jim's——"

"Cut it short!"

"As captain of the Shell, he commands the heroes of the Middle School when they play the Fourth. It must be a strenuous life, and I wonder sometimes that Thomas doesn't forget which he is at any given moment."

"Is that all?" asked Tom.

"No; that's only the prelude. A short time ago I was slackin' at footer, and you rooted me out and made me play up. In revenge I told you that I was goin' to make things hum at football, and boost you out of your job as captain."

"Did you?" yawned Tom.

"Don't you remember?"

"I believe you did talk some rot of the kind," admitted Tom, "But you talk such an awful lot of rot, you know, Cardew! You can't expect a chap to remember it all."

Levison and Clive grinned.

"A hit—a very palpable hit!" said Cardew calmly. "Well, among the rest of the rot I talked, there was that little bit which I happened to mean seriously. I'm goin' to boost you out of the captaincy."

"Go ahead!" said Tom, with a laugh.

"I'm goin'!"

"Don't be an ass, Cardew!" suggested Clive.

"Asses are born, not made, old man! What you ask is beyond my power to grant," answered Cardew.

"Fathead!"

"Well, about the House match——" said Levison.

"Let the House match rest for a minute or two," persisted Cardew. "You see, Thomas, when I undertook to boost you out of the captaincy, I forgot for the moment how many captains you were. It seems that I've let myself in for more than one job. I've decided to boost you out of one captaincy to begin with, and leave you the others as a sort of consolation prize."

"Thanks!"

"Not at all. You can keep the captaincy of the Shell—it's no use to me as I'm in the Fourth. That's one job! Now, I'm goin' in first for House captain."

"That's all rot!" said Tom. "House captain is always captain of the school at St. Jim's. Kildare is senior House captain, and he is captain of St. Jim's."

"That's a custom, but not a rule," said Cardew. "I've been lookin' into the giddy history of St. Jim's. At times there have been two captains—one of the House, and one of the school. Generally the two jobs go together—but not always. Captain of the school has to be elected by all St. Jim's—both Houses. House captain has to be elected only by his own House. Figgins is junior House captain in the New House. I'm goin' to be junior House captain in the School House—leavin' you out in the cold."

"Ass!"

"It's a bit complicated," went on Cardew. "Quite a strain on the intellect to work it out. House captain is not always football captain, though they generally go together. Lots of complications and disputes are saved, Thomas, by you uniting all these important offices in your single person. You're football captain, too—that's a fourth captaincy you hold. You really ought to be called a field-marshal, or a general at least."

"Aren't you tired yet, Cardew?" asked Tom Merry. "You're giving your chin a lot of work!"

"Ha, ha, ha!"

"It's simply dazzling, all these high offices that you hold, Thomas," went on Cardew, unheeding. "It reminds a chap of Gilbert and Sullivan. That man Pooh-Bah, you know, who was Lord High Everything-Else. Well, I don't feel hefty enough to go for all these jobs and take them on in a bunch. I shall be satisfied with the House captaincy. After I've held that for a time I may annex the rest of your jobs one by one. Are you thinkin' of resignin' the House captaincy?"

"Hardly!"

"You don't want to give me a chance?"

"How many votes do you think you would get?" asked Tom with an amused smile.

"Lots, I hope. Here's Levison and Clive simply yearnin' to back me up to begin with."

"I'm afraid we couldn't have all the bother of a House election to entertain you in your idle moments, Cardew."

"In short, you won't resign and stand for re-election?"

"No."

Cardew sighed.

"Then I shall have to make you," he said.

"And how will you do that?" asked the Shell fellow.

"If as many as one-third of the House at any time express dissatisfaction with the House captain, and demand a new election, it's bound to take place."

"Is it?"

"Quite so. I seem to know the rules better than you do," yawned Cardew. "I suppose you haven't time to read 'em up, with all those jolly old captaincies to fill? Now, I'm suggestin' that it would be a graceful act on your part to stand down and fix a new election, and give me my chance of gettin' in."

"Rats!"

"It would save me a lot of trouble in electioneerin' and stirrin' up strife," said Cardew.

"Go ahead with your electioneering," said Tom Merry. "I think you're a silly ass, Cardew, and you haven't the remotest chance of bagging the House captaincy; and you couldn't handle it if you bagged it. House captains have to do something more than sprawl in armchairs and talk piffle. Now give us a rest while I speak to Levison."

"I'm done! I was only warnin' you."

Cardew collapsed lazily into the armchair and watched the three juniors, with a smile, while they discussed the coming House match. When Tom Merry left the study Levison and Clive turned to the dandy of the Fourth.

"I suppose you were only pulling Tom's leg?" said Ernest Levison.

"Not at all."

"You're not seriously thinking of standing for School House junior captain?" hooted Clive.

"Quite seriously."

"Then you're an ass!"

"Thanks. You're backing me up, of course?"

"Rats!"

"And you, Levison?"

"Rot!"

Levison and Clive strolled out of the study. Cardew smiled.

He was quite determined upon this new stunt, and with all his laziness Cardew had an iron determination when his mind was made up. He had resolved to give Tom Merry a fall, but he realised that the task he had set himself was not an easy one. To obtain the House captaincy he had first to bring about a new election, and then to obtain a majority of the junior votes. And at the present moment he could count with certainty upon only one supporter—and that was Ralph Reckness Cardew himself.

The Gem Library.—No. 825.

CHAPTER 2.
Grundy Is Not Pleased !

"THAT ass!"

"Looks like it!"

"That slacker!"

Grundy of the Shell was wrathful. The rugged face of George Alfred Grundy was, in fact, crimson with wrath.

He was standing before the notice-board, with his chums Wilkins and Gunn. On the board was a list of the House junior footballers selected to play the New House on Saturday afternoon. Grundy's name did not appear there. Grundy of the Shell haunted the notice-boards, in the hope of some day finding the name of G. A. Grundy down for something. He never found it. He was accustomed to reading down the lists, and snorting contemptuously over nearly every name there. But on this occasion Grundy's snorts were more contemptuous than ever. For in the list, on this occasion, appeared the name of R. R. Cardew.

"That slacking nincompoop!" said Grundy of the Shell. "That dummy! That—that necktie merchant! That piffler in silk socks! He's down for the House match! And I—I'm left out!"

"You're left out, old chap," assented Wilkins. "No doubt about that." And he bestowed a wink on Gunn.

"You're down, Wilkins."

"Seems so."

"That crass ass, Tom Merry, seems to think you can play football better than I can."

"He seems to," assented Wilkins.

"My hat! He'll be playing Gunny next."

"Why shouldn't he?" demanded Cuthbert Gunn warmly.

Grundy snorted.

"No reason why he shouldn't, old chap, as he knows nothing about a footballer's form."

"Look here, Grundy——"

"But this is the limit," said George Alfred excitedly. "This is the outside edge—the very rim! That ass D'Arcy is down to play. But we're used to that. But ain't one tailor's dummy in a team enough? Now Cardew——"

"Weally, Gwunday——"

Arthur Augustus D'Arcy of the Fourth had come along to look at the list. He was pleased to find his own aristocratic name on it, but he was not pleased by Grundy's comments thereon.

"Well, you know you're a tailor's dummy, I suppose?" said Grundy. "But I admit you ain't such a slacking ass as Cardew. What has Tom Merry put him in the team for?"

"Cardew has been playin' up wathah well lately," said Arthur Augustus. "I have heard Tom Mewwy say that it is time he had a chance in a House match."

"Rot!"

"Weally, Gwunday!"

"And that's the fellow who's swankin' about turning Merry out of the House captaincy!" said Grundy. "Looks to me as if Tom Merry is afraid of him, and this is a sop to Hercules."

"A what?" ejaculated Wilkins.

"A sop to Hercules."

"Do you mean a sop to Cerberus?" asked Gunn politely.

"I don't care whether it's Cerberus or Hercules. That's what it is, a sop, because Cardew's making out he's going to boost him. Just to keep him quiet! Why, Cardew would stop in the middle of the game if he got a spot of mud on his clothes," snorted Grundy. "My opinion is that it's time we had a new captain!"

"Then you'd better vote for Cardew when he puts up!" grinned Wilkins.

"Rats! I'm jolly well going to speak to Tom Merry about this! Anybody know where he is?"

"Asking after little me?" queried a cheery voice, as Tom Merry came along with Manners and Lowther of the Shell.

Grundy whirled round.

"Yes. Are you afraid of what Cardew says he is going to do?"

"Not very."

"Then why are you shoving that slacker into the House team?"

"Couldn't possibly explain," answered Tom.

"Why not?" roared Grundy.

"I should have to deal with football matters, and that's a subject beyond the grasp of your intellect, Grundy."

"Ha, ha, ha!"

George Alfred Grundy spluttered with wrath.

"Ask me anything you like about marbles or hop-scotch," said Tom Merry blandly. "You can discuss things like that. But keep off the subject of football, Grundy. It's out of your depth."

And the Terrible Three walked on, leaving Grundy spluttering and the other fellows laughing.

"The—the—the cheeky cad!" gasped Grundy. "Out of my depth—and me the only real footballer at St. Jim's!"

"Ha, ha, ha!"

"Bai Jove! If you are a good footballah, Gwunday, I

George Alfred Grundy rushed after the Terrible Three. He was wrathy; and when Grundy was wrathy, he was reckless. He overtook the chums of the Shell, and threw his arm round Tom Merry's neck. "Now, you cheeky rotter!" Crash! "Ow!" roared Tom, as he toppled backwards in Grundy's grasp. (See this page.)

should weally like to see a bad one," chuckled Arthur Augustus.

"I'll show him!" roared Grundy.

He rushed after the Terrible Three. Grundy was wrathy, and when Grundy was wrathy he was reckless. He overtook the chums of the Shell, and threw his arm round Tom Merry's neck.

"Now, you cheeky rotter——"

Crash!

"Ow!" roared Tom.

He went bumping to the floor in Grundy's grasp. Grundy rolled over him.

"Oh! Ow! Oh!" gasped Tom Merry. "What——"

"Now, you silly cad——" hooted Grundy.

Tom Merry scrambled up. Grundy scrambled up, too, and put up his hands in a hurry. All his defence was needed. The captain of the Shell was coming at him like a whirlwind.

The next few minutes were wild and whirling ones. Grundy was a hefty youth, and a great fighting-man. But Tom Merry's rushing attack carried all before it. Grundy was driven along the corridor under the rain of blows, and he collapsed at last in a gasping heap.

"There, you cheeky chump!" gasped Tom.

"Ow, ow, ow!" gasped Grundy dazedly.

"Better come and bathe your nose, Tom," chuckled Manners.

"Wow, wow, wow!"

The Terrible Three walked away, and Grundy sat up dazedly as they turned the corner. He mopped his nose and rubbed his eyes, and spluttered breathlessly.

"I—I—I'll——" He scrambled up. "I—I'll smash him——"

"I say, hold on!" exclaimed Wilkins.

But Grundy of the Shell did not hold on. His cup of wrath was full to overflowing. He rushed down the corridor after the chums of the Shell, and went round the corner like a whirlwind. There was a terrific crash.

"Now," gasped Grundy, "you—— Oh crumbs! Mr. Railton!"

The Housemaster had reached the corner from another direction as Grundy arrived there. Mr. Railton felt as if a battering-ram had smitten him as he encountered Grundy's frantic rush. He staggered against the wall, and Grundy sat down from the shock.

"What—what——" stuttered Mr. Railton.

"Ow, ow! I——"

"Grundy! How dare you rush round corners in that manner!" exclaimed the Housemaster. "Are you out of your senses?"

"I—I—— Groogh!"

"Come with me, you foolish and thoughtless boy. I shall cane you severely!"

"Ow! I—I——"

"Not a word! Come!"

Mr. Railton grasped Grundy by the collar, and jerked him to his feet. Spluttering and gasping, George Alfred Grundy was hustled away to the Housemaster's study. There Mr. Railton's cane came into play.

After the Housemaster had finished with him Grundy limped from the study, feeling as if life were not worth living. He did not seek Tom Merry. He did not feel equal to any more trouble just then. He limped away in a collapsed state, and for quite a long time afterwards his remarks were chiefly:

"Ow, ow, ow! Wow, wow, wow!"

CHAPTER 3.
The House Match!

THERE was a touch of frost in the air, and it was cold. Fellows who gathered on Little Side to watch the House game thought it cold enough. They stamped their feet and thumped their chests to keep warm. But the footballers found their work warm, very warm indeed.

House games at St. Jim's were generally keenly contested, and this especial match was quite up to the average.

Tom Merry's team was not at its strongest. Talbot of the Shell had been unable to play, and Kangaroo was off colour and standing out. Blake of the Fourth had a damaged ankle and had had to be omitted from the list; it was, in fact, in Blake's place that Ralph Reckness Cardew had been included in the junior School House team. As an all-round player, Cardew could not be considered Blake's equal—Jack Blake was not often brilliant, but he was steady and reliable, and seldom played anything but a very good game. Cardew was good in patches, so to speak. At his best, he was one of the finest junior footballers in the House; at his worst, he was very nearly useless to his side. And nobody ever felt very certain whether Cardew would show up at his best or his worst.

Tom Merry had considered the matter very carefully before he decided to give Cardew a chance. Cardew's new campaign for the House captaincy did not affect his judgment one way or the other. Tom was too good and loyal a football skipper to allow personal considerations to influence him.

In point of fact, Cardew's new stunt irritated him a little. All the more for that reason, Tom weighed the matter carefully, to give Cardew full justice.

Only a couple of weeks before, Cardew had been unmercifully ragged for slacking at games. But since then there was no doubt that he had played up wonderfully, and shown great form.

In the pick-ups Cardew had never lost a chance, and he had played in a Form match—Fourth against Shell—and made a good display. Tom Merry decided that he was worth his place in the junior House team, and so he gave him his chance.

It surprised Cardew a little.

He was now "up against" Tom Merry, and he did not expect Tom to give him a chance in the football if he could help it. A good game on his part would undoubtedly help in his new campaign, and if he succeeded in shining in the House match it would be a great help—and Cardew was determined to do his very best. He reflected rather cynically that Tom Merry was giving away a point in the contest by playing him—and no doubt that was the case, though Tom did not think or care about it. It was not as though Cardew's claim was a recognised one, which the junior captain would have found it difficult to ignore. That was not the case at all. Tom was much more criticised for playing Cardew than for leaving him out.

It was Tom's sense of fair play and the fitness of things that made him act as he did. Cardew had earned his chance, and he should have it, regardless of other considerations.

Cardew grimly resolved to make the most of it. If his rival chose to give away chances, that was his look-out.

So the dandy of the Fourth lined up with the School House team, and threw himself heart and soul into the game.

Figgins & Co. of the New House were in great form. Quite early in the game Kerr gave Figgins a pass from which Figgy scored, and the School House attack was baffled for a long time by Fatty Wynn in the New House citadel. Herries was keeping goal for the School House; but though he was a good custodian, it could not be said that he was anywhere near the form of Fatty Wynn. Arthur Augustus D'Arcy, in the School House front line, very nearly got the ball in, but David Llewellyn Wynn's fat fist drove it out again, and again he defeated a near thing from Levison of the Fourth. At half-time the New House were one up, and both teams were looking ruddy and well exercised. Cardew had played a good forward game, but nothing remarkable about it had so far struck the onlookers.

"Lot of good playing that slacker!" Grundy of the Shell remarked to Gunn at half-time. "What's the good of him?"

"He doesn't seem to be slacking now," said Gunn mildly.

"Not much worse than the rest, perhaps," admitted Grundy. "They're a lot of fumblers, if you ask me!"

Gunn hadn't asked him, but that was only Grundy's way of putting it. Grundy never waited to be asked before he stated his opinion.

"Wilkins is the only decent player in the team," added Grundy, "and he owes that to the tips I've given him on the game."

"Oh, my hat!" murmured Gunn.

"They're off again!" observed Racke of the Shell. Racke and Crooke had strolled down to look on for a few minutes. The black sheep of the School House weren't interested in footer; but they had a bet on the result of the match with Clampe of the New House; hence their unaccustomed presence on Little Side.

"Looks to me like a New House win!" grunted Crooke.

"Lot you care!" snorted Grundy.

"Well, I care," said Racke. "I've put a quid on the School House side, and I don't want to lose it."

"You're a gambling blackguard!" said Grundy.

"Thanks!"

"There they go!" exclaimed Crooke. "By gad, I fancy they'll get through this time!"

Soon after the whistle, the School House attack came up the field against the wind, and the New House forwards were left nowhere. Arthur Augustus D'Arcy had the ball on the left wing; he sent it to Levison, as a New House half charged him over, and Levison centred to Tom Merry at the right moment. Tom Merry came to grief against Redfern of New House, but he had passed the ball out to Monty Lowther on the right wing, quite near to the destination. Owen laid Monty Lowther low, but the ball went to Cardew on the right, and Cardew ran it on in great style and kicked for goal.

Fatty Wynn met the ball with a ready foot, and it whizzed out again, and Cardew's eyes flashed. It had been a near thing, but it had not come off.

But Tom Merry was racing up, and he drove the ball in again. Again the fat custodian dealt with it, fisting it out; and the New House defenders were closing up now. A kick from a rather hurried back dropped the ball at Cardew's feet.

"Pass!" shouted Tom Merry; for two New House men were rushing Cardew down, and he did not seem to have the ghost of a chance, while Tom had almost an open goal before him, with only the custodian to beat.

Cardew did not seem to hear Tom Merry shout. If he did he totally ignored it.

He kicked for goal.

The next instant he was sprawling on the ground, with a New House half sprawling over him, and a New House back staggering across his legs.

But from the watching crowd there came a roar.

"Goal!"

"Hurrah!"

"School House! School House!"

Fatty Wynn had been caught napping. It was small blame to him; for, as a matter of fact, Cardew ought not to have kicked for goal—it was the wildest fluke. But a fluke that lands in the net covers a multitude of sins. And the leather was in the net, and Fatty Wynn stared at it rather blankly.

Cardew picked himself up dazedly.

"You ass!" muttered Levison, who had run across to give him a hand.

"Missed it?" yawned Cardew.

"No; it's a goal."

"Then what's the matter?"

"You know as well as I do!" grunted Levison.

Cardew laughed.

"Line up!" snapped Tom Merry.

The score was level; and Racke and Crooke, among the onlookers, were more cheerful. Their "quids" seemed to be safer now. Grundy was pleased to give an approving grunt.

"Not so bad for a slacker like Cardew!" he said.

"Not so bad?" said Jack Blake, who was standing by. "You born ass! If I were skipper I'd kick Cardew out of the team for that!"

"For taking the only goal?" jeered Grundy.

"For disobeying orders and chancing a fluke!" growled Blake. "It was just a miracle that that goal came off, and it would have been practically a sure thing if he'd let Tom have the ball."

"Well, a goal's a goal!" said Grundy.

"Yes; a goal's a goal," remarked Gunn. "School House was in need of that goal, anyhow, Blake."

Blake sniffed. Nothing succeeds like success, and as Cardew had actually captured the goal, his recklessness was overlooked by most of the fellows. Blake knew better; but most of the fellows were willing to believe that Cardew had seen a good chance and taken it; the success of the goal counted as proof that he had judged well.

The game went on, hot and strong; but the School House did not get through again. All they could do was to defeat the attacks of the New House, and that they did effectually.

After a rather gruelling game the House match ended in a draw, one goal each, and the players came off breathing hard and deep.

CHAPTER 4.
Trouble !

"BAI Jove, you know, we ought to have beaten them!"

Thus Arthur Augustus D'Arcy, in the changing-room in the School House, after the match.

"Well, they sent back as good as we gave," remarked Levison of the Fourth. "I dare say Figgins & Co. are saying just now that they ought to have beaten us."

"Yaas, wathah, that's so! Nevahtheless, we ought to have beaten the boundahs!" declared the swell of St. Jim's.

"Howevah, I suppose we were lucky to get off with a dwaw, considewin', Cardew's fluke saved us fwom a defeat, weally."

"Fluke!" repeated Cardew.

"Yaas."

"Pass!" shouted Tom Merry as the New House fellow left him unmarked to rush down upon Ralph Reckness Cardew who, with the ball at his feet, was closing in upon the goal. "Pass!" Cardew ignored his captain's cry and kicked for goal. By the merest fluke—for the shot was an almost impossible one—the ball shot into the net. It was a goal!
(See page 6.)

"Was my goal a fluke?"

"Don't you know it was, deah boy?" asked Arthur Augustus innocently.

"Time you learned something about football, Cardew, if you're going to play in House matches," remarked Monty Lowther.

"High time," observed Digby of the Fourth.

"Yaas, wathah!"

Cardew yawned.

"Isn't it rather a pity some of you fellows couldn't fluke in the same way?" he asked. "Another fluke like mine would have made it a win for the School House."

"Yaas, but——"

Tom Merry came over to the Fourth-Formers. His face was rather serious.

"That kind of thing won't do, Cardew!" he said abruptly.

Cardew smiled at him cheerily.

"What kind of thing, old bean?"

"Selfish play never does any good to a side. It may come off every now and then, but the game's the thing," said Tom. "You know very well that you ought not to have pitched in the ball from the right-wing, with everything against you, when the centre was clear, and your captain called to you to pass."

"Did you call?"

"Well, if you didn't hear me——" said Tom.

Cardew hesitated a moment.

"I did hear you," he said, after that brief hesitation.

Tom flushed.

"And you took no notice?"

"You remember the jolly old dying gladiator in Byron?" asked Cardew affably—"the chap who heard it, but he heeded not, you know! I was understudyin' the jolly old gladiator."

"Is that your idea of playing your part in a football side?" asked Tom, with dangerous calm.

"Well, you see, I bagged the goal," said Cardew calmly. "You might have bagged it. That's a possibility that never can be proved now. But in actual fact I did bag it. What more do you want?"

"I want you to play the game, if you play for the House," said Tom. "It was the wildest chance that the ball got in."

"Do you think so?"

"I don't think it—I know it. And so does every fellow who saw it, if he knows anything about soccer."

"I don't agree."

"You don't agree?" exclaimed Tom, his colour rising. "Do you set yourself up to know more about the game than your skipper, and to follow your own nose against orders?"

"Well, a goal is a goal, you know," reminded Cardew. "And, with all your superior knowledge of the game, old bean, I didn't notice you puttin' the ball in to any great extent."

There was a laugh from some of the fellows in the changing-room.

"That's enough!" said Tom, biting his lip. "You're dropped out of the House team for the rest of the season. Cardew. That's all."

"Dear me!" said Cardew. "Then I sha'n't play again till I'm House captain—what?"

"Ha, ha, ha!"

"Oh, dry up that rot!" snapped Tom, and he turned away.

"Alas!" sighed Cardew. "How does a fellow get on with Thomas? A couple of weeks ago he was raggin' me baldheaded for shirkin' games. Now he's raggin' me baldheaded for takin' goals! It's really a bit difficult to know what Thomas really wants."

"Weally, Cardew——"

"Well, I only want to know how I've offended," said Cardew. "If it's a sin to take goals when the jolly old captain can't take any, I plead guilty. If it's a sin to put Thomas in the shade, I have to own up that I have sinned."

Tom Merry swung round.

"It's not that, and you know it, Cardew," he said between his teeth. "You know perfectly well that I should have been glad to see you score for the House."

"You didn't seem glad when I did it. You don't seem really glad now."

"Ha, ha, ha!"

"Shut up, Cardew!" muttered Levison uneasily.

"Why should I shut up?" asked Cardew. "I didn't begin this argument; Thomas began it. He turns me out of the team for takin' goals. If he'll play me again I'll promise not to take any more goals."

"Ha, ha, ha!"

"I'll undertake to stand still in my place and gaze at him with speechless admiration, if that's what he wants," went on Cardew. "Is that what you want, Thomas? Just say so."

"Weally, Cardew, you ass——"

"I don't want any more of your cheek, at all events, Cardew," said Tom Merry, his eyes flashing. "And if you call me 'Thomas' again I'll punch you!"

"My dear Thomas——"

Tom Merry came straight at Cardew on that. It did not occur to Tom at the moment that that was exactly what Cardew wanted. Trouble with Tom Merry over that disputed goal exactly suited Cardew's book, and Tom fell blindly into the trap.

Cardew sprang back and put up his hands.

"Tom!" exclaimed Lowther.

"Weally, you fellows——"

"Stop them!" shouted Wildrake.

But there was no stopping them. Tom Merry was really angry, and Cardew, though not in the least angry, was bent on trouble. They were fighting in a moment more, and the crowd of fellows in the changing-room gathered round to look on.

Cardew, with all his black ways, was as hard as nails, and a good fighting-man. But he was no match for the captain of the Shell.

He put up a good fight, however, and seemed to be holding his own.

But a fight in the changing-room was not likely to pass without interruption. It was not the spot to select for a fight to a finish, as Ralph Reckness Cardew knew very well.

Kildare and Darrell of the Sixth came in with several other seniors, and Kildare shouted across to the juniors at once.

"What's that? Stop that!"

And as the fight did not stop Kildare came over, with a frowning brow, and grasped Cardew and Tom Merry, one in either hand, and fairly wrenched them apart.

"Let me go!" panted Tom.

"What?"

"Look here, Kildare——"

"Stand back!" snapped the captain of St. Jim's. "You ought to know better than this, Tom Merry! Stand back, Cardew!"

"I'm standin' back, Kildare," said Cardew meekly. "I'm not in the least keen on fightin' Thomas. He's too hefty for me."

"Let there be no more of this," said Kildare, with a rather grim look at Tom; and the captain of the school went back to his companions.

Tom Merry breathed hard.

"Is the circus over?" asked Cardew urbanely. "If so, I'll get on with changin'. You interrupted me, Thomas."

"If you want this to go farther I'll meet you in the gym after tea, Cardew," said Tom quietly.

"But I don't," smiled Cardew. "As I remarked to Kildare, you are too hefty for me, Thomas. When I'm huntin' for trouble I'll pick a row with Trimble or Mellish or somebody. I'm all for an easy life."

Tom Merry turned his back on the dandy of the Fourth.

The trouble was over; though it was to have its results. Cardew finished changing and strolled out of the room with Clive and Levison. Both the latter were looking serious, but Cardew seemed to be in the best of spirits.

Racke of the Shell met the three on the staircase.

"Hold on, Cardew!" he called out.

"Oh, come on!" muttered Levison.

"Wait a minute, Racke's speakin'," said Cardew. "What is it, Racke?"

"If you're going out for givin' Tom Merry a fall, I'm backin' you up, that's all," said Racke; "and I've got a good few friends who will stand in with me."

"Thanks, old man! I'll be jolly glad of your support!" answered Cardew.

"Then you mean business?"

"Real business."

"Good!" said Racke heartily. "I'm for you, and I fancy I can rally round at least seven or eight fellows."

THE GEM LIBRARY.—No. 825.

"Many thanks, old bean!"

Levison & Co. went on to Study No. 9 in the Fourth. Ralph Reckness Cardew wore a cheery smile.

"Gettin' on!" he remarked, as he sank into the armchair in the study. "Things are movin', old beanlets! I fancy I shall be able to get together the necessary number to call for a new election of junior House captain—what?"

"Fellows like Racke and Crooke and Mellish," said Levison bitterly. "Fellows that no decent chap speaks to!"

"But they have votes," smiled Cardew.

"I wouldn't touch their votes with a barge-pole!" snapped Sidney Clive.

"You're not standin' for election. I am."

"Look here, Cardew," exclaimed Ernest Levison abruptly, "you're not going on with this rot!"

"I jolly well am!"

"You know very well you were wrong about that goal, and you know that you deliberately provoked Tom Merry in the changing-room!" exclaimed Levison angrily.

Cardew nodded.

"Must get on with it somehow," he said. "Thomas is rather a simple old duck—it's child's play to pull his leg and make him hop. I'm rather enjoyin' it. Of course, you fellows are goin' to back up a chum in your own study?"

Levison and Clive made no answer to that.

"Think of Study No. 9 providin' a House captain!" urged Cardew. "It will be no end of a leg-up for our study—what?"

"There's something in that," admitted Levison. "But—but——"

"Well, then, back up!"

"You're not going the right way to work, Cardew," said Clive. "If you played a straight game——"

"Would a straight game down the esteemed Thomas?"

"Well, no."

"Well, I'm out to down him, and so I'm goin' to play any kind of game that's necessary for the purpose," said Cardew coolly. "To be quite candid, my goal this afternoon was a rotten fluke, and I took the chance because I was up against Thomas. But it came off, and so it counts. Nine-tenths of the fellows will look at it like this—I bagged the goal, and Thomas was ratty about it to the extent of punchin' me in the changin'-room. That helps me a lot."

"Don't you call that unscrupulous?" asked Clive.

"I'm an unscrupulous chap when my dander is up!" explained Cardew.

"You won't get any support from me on those lines."

"Nor from me," said Levison.

Cardew shrugged his shoulders.

"I'll try to do without it," he said; and he moved to the door.

"Aren't you going to have tea?" asked Levison.

"I'm goin' to stand tea to some of my supporters. If you change your minds, and decide to back up your old pal, come along to the club-room. You'll find a feast of the gods goin' on."

And Cardew walked away.

Levison and Clive did not change their minds, and they did not follow him. But their faces were rather gloomy as they sat down to tea in Study No. 9. It had often happened that there was a rift in the lute in Study No. 9, and it seemed that history was to repeat itself once more. But whether his chums were for him or against him, it was clear that Ralph Reckness Cardew meant to go his own wilful way.

CHAPTER 5.
Electioneering !

"YOU'RE an ass, Tom!"

"Really an ass!"

Manners and Lowther delivered their chummy opinion in Study No. 10 in the Shell, a few days after the House match.

Tom Merry smiled faintly.

"How's that?" he asked.

"You're giving everything away to Cardew."

"Bless Cardew!"

"Bless him black and blue!" said Monty Lowther. "He's nobody, and worth nothing; but he's dangerous."

"Bosh!" said Tom cheerily.

"He's working hard," said Manners. "The fact is, Tom, it looks pretty certain that there will have to be a new election for House captain."

"You think so?"

"It's almost a cert. While you're turning up your nose at Cardew and anything he can do, he is leaving no stone unturned."

Tom Merry's lip curled.

"Let him rip," he answered. "Do you think I'm going to worry about a fellow like Cardew? No jolly fear!"

"That's all very well," said Lowther; "but if he should get in as House captain he could give you no end of trouble. House captain and school captain here are generally the same chap; but the jobs have been divided before, and may be

divided again. And the two would have to pull together
jolly well to keep from trouble. And you can guess how
you'd pull with Cardew."

"I'm not bothering about it."

"Cardew is. Of course, his game is to give all the trouble
he can," said Lowther. "He doesn't care a twopenny rap
for the House or the school, if you come to that; he's just up
to mischief. And he's not very particular about his methods.
Racke and his gang are backing him up through thick and
thin."

"Let them! I'd be jolly well ashamed to be backed up
by Racke and his gang!" said Tom contemptuously.

"Their votes count, all the same. Every black sheep in
the House is naturally up against you," said Monty.
"Naturally they're rallying round your enemy."

"Oh, Cardew isn't my enemy!" said Tom cheerily.

"Your rival, at least. He's got Baggy Trimble——"

Tom Merry laughed.

"And Mulvaney minor, and other fellows of that kidney,"
said Lowther. "You know he's got plenty of money, and
he's been standing spreads in the club-room, and every fellow
like Baggy Trimble is backing him up for the sake of the
grub."

"There aren't many fellows at St. Jim's like Baggy
Trimble, thank goodness!" said Tom Merry.

"There's a good many who are glad to be chummy with
Cardew, a rich chap and a lord's grandson," said Manners.
"I know he's asked some fellows home to Reckness Towers
for the hols. He's got all the blackguards, all the grub-
hunters, and all the snobs."

"Oh, my hat! What a crew!"

"I know; but their votes count. And there's a lot of
fellows, too, who'd like a change, just for the sake of a change.
Fellows who think they haven't had their proper chances in
matches, and all that. And there's Grundy of the Shell——"

"Is Grundy backing him up?" said Tom, laughing. "He's
welcome."

"I know Grundy is a born idiot," said Manners. "He's up
against you all the more for that reason. He thinks he ought
to play for House and School, though he can't play footer for
toffee. He thinks he will have a better chance under a new
captain."

"Cardew wouldn't play him if he was captain of footer.
He's got more sense than that."

"I'm afraid he isn't above letting Grundy fancy that he
would play him," answered Manners.

"That's a pretty rotten deception."

"Well, Cardew's ways aren't your ways, old chap. That's
why you've got to be on your guard."

"Oh, bother!" said Tom.

"Grundy certainly fancies that he will get a chance under
Cardew, for he is backing him up no end," said Monty
Lowther. "Wilkins and Gunn will follow his lead, or Grundy
will rag them in the study. That's three votes."

Tom Merry laughed carelessly.

"So I've got against me all the blackguards, all the grub-
hunters, all the snobs, and all the fatheads!" he exclaimed.
"I really don't think it's a very dangerous combination."

"There are others, too," said Lowther. "Better fellows,
too. I'm not sure Study No. 6 in the Fourth are reliable."

"They wouldn't back up Cardew."

"No; but you know Study No. 6 thinks that junior captain
ought to be in the Fourth, not the Shell. Rot, of course;
but they're bound to think so in the Fourth. I've got an
idea that a third candidate will butt in from Study No. 6—
Blake or D'Arcy."

"What a storm in a teacup!" yawned Tom Merry.

"Well, you really ought to buck up, and see to things,"
urged Manners. "This study doesn't want a change of
captain."

There was a thump at the door, and George Gore of the
Shell looked into Study No. 10. He gave Tom Merry an
affable, friendly, but somewhat patronising nod. Gore's
manner was that of a fellow who meant to be kind, and
meant to have it understood that he was being kind.

"Looking around for supporters—what?" asked Gore
breezily.

"Who? I!"

"Yes, you. I suppose you've got an eye on what's going
on?" said Gore.

"More or less," assented Tom.

"You've got plenty of backers," said Gore reassuringly.
"As a Shell fellow, I'm not going to see a Fourth Form kid
get in as House captain. I don't say I'm wholly satisfied
with you."

"No?" said Tom, with a smile.

"I'm a candid chap," said Gore. "I speak as I think.
You don't come up to the mark in my opinion. But you're
better than Cardew. Anyhow, you're in the Shell. I'm going
to see you through. You can rely on me to help."

"Thanks!"

"But you'll have to get a bit of a move on," said Gore.
"Your supporters will expect you to hustle a bit."

"Will they?" murmured Tom.

"Of course. What about a meeting in the club-room and
a speech or two? I'm willing to take the chair."

"I don't think I'm going to hold any meetings," said
Tom. "You see, if the fellows don't want me for captain,
I haven't the slightest desire to hang on."

"Oh, utter rot!" said Gore. "When a chap's captain, he
naturally wants to hang on. I know I should."

"Tastes may differ," suggested Tom Merry.

"That's all bosh! I can tell you that the fellows will
expect you to value their support, if they support you," said
Gore warmly. "You'll be expected to go round being a bit
civil, and doing a bit of electioneering, and all that."

"Too jolly busy for electioneering," smiled Tom; "and I
believe I'm always fairly civil. Certainly I shouldn't dream
of putting on any extra civility at election-time."

Gore stared.

"Is that the way you expect to win an election?" he
asked.

"Why not?" answered Tom Merry. "If the fellows want
me to skipper them, I'm ready. If they don't, I'm prepared
to stand down. Do you think a House captain at St. Jim's
ought to go in for electioneering and wire-pulling, and bam-
boozling, like a sneaking politician? That's not quite good
enough for this study."

Gore sniffed.

"You'll get left, at that rate," he said.

"Well, I'm not afraid of getting left," answered Tom. "If
the Lower School wants Cardew, let the Lower School have
Cardew. If they want me, they can have me. There it is
in a nutshell."

"And you're not going to be civil to a fellow because he's
got a vote?"

"No jolly fear! I don't want any fellow to vote for me if
he thinks Cardew the better man."

"Well, Cardew's got a lot more sense than you have, in
some ways," snapped Gore. "He's talked to me for half an
hour, trying to get me round on his side."

"My hat!"

"And you haven't a civil word to say," said Gore. "I
can jolly well tell you, Tom Merry, that you're not going the
right way to work to bag my vote."

"No?" said Tom.

"No! You're going the right way to work to lose it."

"Right-ho!"

Gore flushed angrily. He had come to Study No. 10 to
be kind and friendly, in a rather lofty way—the loftiness
being inspired by the knowledge of his value as a voter.
But evidently Tom Merry had no use for loftiness or patron-
age, even at election-time.

"You don't care, what?" he exclaimed.

"Not a rap!" said Tom coolly. "It's your duty to vote in
the election, if it comes off, for the candidate you believe
to be the better man. You can do that without being soft-
sawdered, I suppose."

"So that's your way of looking at it?"

"Just that!"

"You won't even take the trouble to ask me to vote for
you, I suppose?" sneered Gore, with angry sarcasm.

"Not in the least!"

"Well," said Gore, "I meant to back you up. But if
that's your style, don't count on me."

"Right-ho! I won't," assented Tom.

"And that's all you've got to say?"

"What else is there to say?"

"Oh, rats!"

Gore departed from Study No. 10 in high dudgeon, slamming the door after him. Manners and Lowther looked at
one another comically, and then at Tom Merry.

"Is that your electioneering style, Tommy?" asked
Lowther.

"That's it," said Tom.

"You've lost Gore's vote."

"Cardew's welcome to it."

"Tom, old man——" urged Manners.

"Look here," said Tom quietly. "Do you think I'm the
chap to talk to Gore as if butter wouldn't melt in my mouth,

as he says Cardew's done? I don't like Gore much—we've never been friends. It's his duty to vote for me if he thinks me the best man for the job. If he doesn't choose to do his duty, let him go and eat coke. I'm not asking favours of any man at St. Jim's."

"How many chaps, do you think, would get elected to the House of Commons on those lines?" asked Manners.

Tom shrugged his shoulders.

"I don't know, and don't care! I know that if I ever vote in an election, I shall vote for the man I think the best man, and I shall distrust any candidate who comes sneaking round asking for votes," he answered. "Anyhow, there you are!"

"Dear man," said Monty Lowther affectionately, "I wonder what it will be like with Cardew as House captain!"

"You think he'll get in?"

"Certainly—with your support!" said Lowther.

"My support?" exclaimed Tom.

"Yes, old chap! With your methods, it won't be necessary for Cardew to do any electioneering—you're doing it for him."

Tom Merry laughed.

"Let it go at that, then," he said.

And it was let go at that.

CHAPTER 6.
Moving!

K ILDARE of the Sixth frowned over a paper that lay on his study table. It was a sheet of impot paper, that bore a large number of signatures. The captain of St. Jim's looked up from it, as a tap came at the study door.

"Come in!"

Tom Merry entered the study.

It was some days since Gore's visit to Study No. 10, when Tom Merry had lost the support of George Gore by his reception of that youth. During those days things had been moving in the School House at St. Jim's.

Fellows had expected Tom Merry to be disturbed about the new proceedings; at least, to be keen in his own defence. They had been disappointed.

Certainly, Tom's own friends understood him, and backed him up without hesitation. But there were others.

Apart from Racke & Co., and Trimble and Grundy and fellows of like sort, there were many fellows who felt aggrieved at the indifference displayed by the junior captain. As Smith minor remarked, if a fellow's vote was worth having, it was worth asking for. It was only at election-times that the common member of the rank and file had any importance. At such times he expected his importance to be recognised a little.

Tom seemed quite indifferent.

He was not, as a matter of fact, indifferent. But nothing would have induced him to compete with Cardew on Cardew's own lines.

Not only would he do no electioneering, but he would not deign even to ask a fellow for his vote. If a fellow did not want to support him, Tom Merry did not want his support. That was a method that appealed to the more thoughtful fellows, and to Tom's own friends. But it was not a method by which the thoughtless majority could be won.

Many fellows regarded Tom Merry's attitude as disdainful, and certainly it was in strong contrast to Cardew's attitude. Cardew was exactly the fellow to win an election; he had something gratifying to say to every fellow who had a vote, and a clever way of raising vague hopes which—after the election—were never to be realised. Cardew would not have made false promises; he would never had descended quite to that. But certainly many fellows were expecting advantages from his election. Grundy had the idea fixed in his mind that Cardew's chief object was to back up his—Grundy's—claims to be played in the junior eleven. Racke & Co. believed that under Cardew as House Captain compulsory games practice would be almost a thing of the past. Baggy Trimble was assured that if he voted for Cardew he would always be able to drop into Study No. 9 in the Fourth to tea. Cardew had not said anything of the sort, but his propitiatory manner led his backers to believe in their own hopes.

Cardew, in fact, was following the methods generally followed at elections; and, like the wire-pulling politicians, he despised in his heart those whom he gulled, or who gulled themselves.

Tom Merry would not have descended to such methods to save his captaincy, or to save his life, for that matter.

The junior captain had been called to Kildare's study by a message brought by Wally of the Third, and he came to see Kildare, wondering what was wanted. The grave expression of the captain of the school showed that something was "up."

Kildare tapped the paper on the table before him.

"I suppose you know about this, Merry," he said.

"No, Kildare! What is it?"

THE GEM LIBRARY.—No. 825.

"You know the rule that a new election for House captain can be called for, if a certain number of the House ask for it."

"Oh, yes!" said Tom.

"Well, that's it. This is a list of the junior members of the School House who ask for a new election for junior captain."

"I see," said Tom

"I've seen that something's been going on for some time past," said Kildare. "I can't quite make out why so many fellows are dissatisfied with you."

Tom did not answer that.

"There are other juniors in the House who can fill your place," went on Kildare. "Talbot, of your Form, would make a good captain; Noble, or perhaps Blake, would fill your place fairly well. But I don't see their names in this list."

"No," said Tom.

"This paper has been handed to me by Cardew of the Fourth," went on the captain of St. Jim's. "I think I am right in supposing that Cardew is setting up as your rival."

"That's correct."

"I'm bound to act on this; but if you have any objection to raise, the matter will be referred to the Housemaster. Do you prefer Mr. Railton to deal with it?"

"Oh, no!"

"You've no objection to a new election being held?"

"None at all."

"That's all I wanted to know," said Kildare. "I shall be sorry if you lose the captaincy; you're the best man for the job, I think, excepting perhaps Talbot."

"Thank you," said Tom.

"If you prefer the matter to go before the Housemaster, it is likely enough that he will use his authority to quash the whole thing," said Kildare.

"I don't!" said Tom. "If the fellows want a new election, let them have it."

"Then I've only to fix the date."

"Yes."

"Very well. I'll put a notice on the board this evening."

"That's all right!" said Tom.

And he quitted the study, leaving the captain of the school still frowning thoughtfully.

Tom Merry returned to Study No. 10 in the Shell. The message from Kildare had interrupted tea in that study. Manners and Lowther regarded him rather anxiously as he came in.

"Well?" they asked simultaneously.

Tom smiled.

"There's to be a new election," he said.

"Cardew's got that far, then?"

"It seems so."

"When?" asked Manners.

"Kildare's fixing a date. Saturday, most likely, I should think," said Tom. "Pass the marmalade."

"Well, you don't seem much worried about it, anyway."

"I'm not worried."

"We've time to do some electioneering, anyhow," said Monty Lowther.

"Cut that out!" said Tom.

"Fathead! If you won't lift a finger for yourself, we're jolly well going to wire in and save the situation."

"Rot!"

"Now, look here, Tom——"

"Bosh!" said Tom Merry. "Cardew won't bag a majority of votes when it comes to the test."

"He might!"

"Well, if he does, let him. Don't I keep on telling you that I don't want to keep the captaincy unless I'm wanted to keep it?"

"We want you to keep it!" said Manners warmly. "You're not going to be boosted for a cad like Cardew."

"He isn't exactly a cad," said Tom mildly. "He seems to me to be more a mischievous monkey than anything else. Besides, I dare say he would make a good House captain. He's got his good qualities."

"Oh, you're hopeless!" said Lowther. "You can do as you like, Tom, but I can tell you that we're going in for electioneering hot and strong."

"Don't!" said Tom quietly. "What have you got to tell the fellows that they don't know already?"

"Oh, you're an ass!" said Lowther. "Leave it to us."

"I'd rather you didn't!"

"We're going to save you from yourself, old chap," said Manners kindly. "You can't win an election by standing on your dignity. If the other side tout for votes, you've got to tout for votes."

"I sha'n't do anything of the kind."

"Then we'll do your touting."

"Look here, you fellows——"

"Rats!"

Manners and Lowther left their tea unfinished; they felt that there was no time to lose. Five minutes later there was

There was a roar as Tom Merry, hoisted on the shoulders of his loyal followers, was carried into the crowded club-room.   "Here he comes!"   "Bravo!"   "Tom Merry!   Tom Merry!"   Dishevelled, red, and breathless, the junior captain of St. Jim's was carried to the speaker's platform   (*See page 12.*)

a hurriedly-written notice on the board, announcing that a meeting of Tom Merry's supporters would be held in the club-room at seven o'clock. It appeared beside a notice in Kildare's hand, which announced that the election for junior House captain would take place on Saturday afternoon at three. Ralph Reckness Cardew strolled along with Levison and Clive and read both notices, and smiled genially.

"Things are movin'!" he remarked.

His comrades did not speak.

"The giddy enemy are gettin' a move on, too, you see," added Cardew. "I think I shall hold a rival meetin'. You fellows comin'?"

"I'm going to Tom Merry's meeting," said Levison grimly.

"Supportin' him?"

"Yes."

"And you, Clive?"

"Same as Levison."

"Such is friendship," sighed Cardew. "Why, if either of you fellows put up for anythin', I'd support you through thick and thin."

"Well, you oughtn't to, unless you thought we were doing right," said Sidney Clive bluntly.

Cardew made a grimace.

"That's the higher morality, isn't it?" he asked. "Considerin' what a juicy old reputation you used to have, Levison, you're improvin' wonderfully."

Ernest Levison flushed.

"As for Clive, I believe he was born good," went on Cardew. "What beats me is why either of you two thoroughly good and decent chaps keeps on speakin' terms with me? It isn't because you want me to ask you to Reckness Towers for the hols; you've both refused to come. And you don't want to borrow any money from me. Why do you do it?"

"Ass!" said Levison.

"I wish you'd chuck this, Cardew," said Clive.

What—when the fun's just beginnin'? No fear! Look

here, won't you fellows vote for me if I get you a long stay next vac with my noble grandfather?"

"Cheese it!"

Levison and Clive walked away, leaving Cardew laughing.

CHAPTER 7.
The Meeting!

"TOM MERRY!"

"Where's Tom Merry?"

Two or three score of voices demanded Tom Merry, in the club-room soon after seven.

The meeting was crowded.

With all Cardew's manœuvres, he had certainly not succeeded in getting anything like a majority on his side. He had a powerful minority backing him; but a majority was quite another matter. Tom Merry was popular, undoubtedly very much more popular than Cardew was ever likely to be. The club-room was swarming with juniors, of the Shell, the Fourth, and the Third. And at least two-thirds of the crowd had come there to support Tom Merry.

Manners and Lowther were very satisfied as they looked over the meeting, to begin with. All Tom's best friends had turned up. Talbot of the Shell was prominent; Kangaroo and Glyn and Dane were there. Wildrake of the Fourth was conspicuous as a supporter of the Merry party, and a good many more of the Fourth. Blake & Co. had come in, though it was rather uncertain what line they intended to take. Grundy was extremely prominent on Cardew's side. Cardew had shepherded all his backers into the club-room, with the intention of disturbing the meeting as much as possible, and of swaying it against Tom if he could. Both parties were rather surprised by Tom's own failure to appear.

Monty Lowther had started by addressing the meeting, and Tom Merry's name was cheered again and again. If the same enthusiasm lasted over Saturday, Tom's re-election seemed a certainty. But Cardew had his own ideas about that.

The cry for Tom Merry to appear was started by Cardew's faction. It was taken up by the other side.

"Tom Merry!"

"Where's Tom? Why isn't he here?"

"Is Tom Merry afraid to show up?" roared Grundy of the Shell.

"Shut up, Grundy!" shouted Kangaroo.

"Why doesn't he show up?" retorted Grundy.

"He's afraid to face the meeting, you fellows!" squeaked Trimble.

"He knows he's going to be bunked!" hooted Aubrey Racke.

There was a roar.

"Tom Merry!"

George Gore jumped on a chair.

"Gentlemen——"

"Shut up, Gore! Get down!"

"Gentlemen!" roared Gore. "I call on Tom Merry to show up! If he's afraid to face this meeting of the House, he's not the man to stand for election as House captain on Saturday."

"Hear, hear!"

"Rats!"

"Dash it all, Tom ought to come!" said Bernard Glyn. "Why isn't he here, Lowther?"

"He won't come!"

"That's rot! Doesn't he want to be elected on Saturday?"

"Well, he won't come!"

"Bosh! He's got to come!" said Glyn. "He's got to address the meeting. Some of you fellows come with me, and we'll fetch him."

"Tom Merry's turning up his nose at this meeting!" shouted Crooke. "He thinks we're all his slaves, and bound to vote for him whether we like it or not."

"Bai Jove! I weally think Tom Mewwy might honah us with his pwesence!" said Arthur Augustus D'Arcy seriously. "I am not suah whethah I am goin' to back him up, but weally he ought to be heah!"

"You're goin' to back me up, old top—what?" said Cardew.

Arthur Augustus turned his celebrated eyeglass severely upon the dandy of the Fourth.

"Certainly not, Cardew! If there is an election, aftah all, my ideah is that a candidate ought to stand fwom Study No. 6—eithah Blake or myself!"

"Good man!" said Cardew cordially. "Jolly good idea!"

"Bai Jove! I think it is wathah a good ideah, Cardew, but I weally did not expect you to see it in the same light, you know!"

"Ass!" said Dick Julian. "Cardew wants to split the vote."

"Bai Jove! I nevah thought of that!"

"You wouldn't!" grunted Lumley-Lumley.

"Weally, dear boy——"

"Tom Merry! Where's Tom Merry?" roared the meeting.

Glyn and Kangaroo and Talbot, and several other fellows had hurriedly left the club-room to seek the captain of the Shell. They found Tom Merry in his study, beginning his prep.

"You're wanted, Tom, old chap!" said Talbot.

"What is it?"

"Meeting of your supporters."

Tom Merry shook his head.

"I'm not coming!"

"Now, don't be an ass, old chap!" said Kangaroo. "The fellows expect you to put in a word for yourself. If you don't turn up it's as likely as not that Cardew will get the meeting over to his side."

"Oh, bosh!" said Tom cheerily.

"Some of them are saying that you're afraid to face the meeting," urged Glyn.

Tom Merry flushed.

"They know that's all piffle!" he said.

"Well, come along and prove that it's piffle."

"It's not worth the trouble. I'm not going to tout for votes," said Tom. "I don't want any fellow to back me up unless he's thought the matter out and thinks he ought to do it."

"As if a voter ever thinks!" grunted Glyn. "Come on! Look here, if you won't walk, we shall carry you."

"Rats!"

"Collar him!" said Kangaroo.

"Look here——" roared Tom, jumping up.

Four or five pairs of hands were laid upon him; and Tom Merry, struggling, was whirled into the passage. There he was hoisted on the shoulders of his loyal followers, and carried bodily down to the club-room.

There was a roar as Talbot & Co. appeared in the crowded room, with Tom Merry on their shoulders.

"Here he comes!"

"Bravo!"

"Tom Merry—Tom Merry!"

Tom was carried to the speakers' platform, and there set down, very dishevelled and red and breathless. Manners and Lowther gave him almost imploring looks.

"Play up, Tom!" whispered Monty.

"Oh, rot!"

"Speech! Speech!" roared the meeting.

"Now then, Tom!"

"Speech! Speech!"

"You've got to speak, Tom!" implored Manners. "For goodness' sake, stop playing the goat, and put in something nice and pleasant! Go it! My hat, I'll jolly well punch your nose if you don't make a speech!"

"I'll speak!"

"Good!"

Monty Lowther shouted for silence, and Tom Merry stood up to speak.

CHAPTER 8.
The Rivals!

TOM MERRY stood facing the meeting, his face flushed and his eyes sparkling. His loyal backers had insisted upon his coming—insisted most emphatically; but they had not stopped to reflect that although a horse could be brought to the water, it could not be made to drink. Tom Merry had never had any intention of electioneering, and he had no such intention now. As he was there, and called upon to speak, he simply intended to tell the electors so. That was all. His speech was not precisely what his comrades had expected to hear.

"Gentlemen——" began Tom Merry.

"Hear, hear!"

"Go it!"

There were groans from the Cardewites, but they were drowned by the cheers of the majority.

"Gentlemen, I have nothing whatever to say——".

"What!"

"So I will say it in as few words as possible."

"Ha, ha, ha!"

"Hear, hear!"

"You all know me," continued Tom Merry. "I'm junior captain, and I've done my best in the job. If I keep the job, I mean to go on doing my best."

"Bravo!"

"There's to be a new election on Saturday. I shall stand for re-election."

"Hurrah!"

"I understand that Cardew of the Fourth will be standing against me. Let the best man win!"

"Hear, hear!"

"If any fellow here thinks I ought to keep the job, he ought to vote for me. If he thinks Cardew will do better, he ought to vote for Cardew, and I hope he will do so."

"Oh, my hat!"

"Bai Jove! This is somethin' wathah new in election speechifyin'!" Arthur Augustus D'Arcy remarked to Blake.

"Something jolly new!" grinned Blake. "Not exactly the style for an election meeting."

"I believe it's possible that a third candidate may come forward," went on Tom Merry. "If any junior in the House thinks he's fit for the job, and able to handle it, let him stand. I myself think that Talbot of the Shell would make as good a captain as I myself."

"What rot!" exclaimed Talbot.

"Blake of the Fourth would make a good skipper, too," said Tom Merry. "So would Kangaroo. You've got plenty of good men to choose from, if you want a change. If a new man is elected, I shall back him up, as I expect to be backed up myself while I hold the captaincy. Cardew, in my opinion, would not make a good captain, and I should be sorry to see him elected. But, as I've said, any man who thinks that Cardew's the best man for the job ought to back him up!"

"Cardew gets goals, anyhow!" roared Racke.

"And somebody else rags him for gettin' them!" howled Crooke.

"Silence!"

"Order!"

"Go it, Tom Merry!" shouted Wildrake.

"I've about finished," said Tom. "I've told my friends that I'm not going to do any electioneering. They insist upon my speaking here, so I've spoken. I'm not asking any chap for his vote. The way a fellow votes is a matter for him to settle with his own judgment and conscience. If he's too lazy to think the matter out for himself, he ought not to vote at all."

"Oh, my hat!"

"Don't you want our votes?" shouted Mulvaney indignantly.

"Only on the lines I've explained," answered Tom Merry.

"I am not asking for votes, and I don't intend to ask for them. The fellows know my record, such as it is, and can judge for themselves."

"Do you think you'll get what you're too jolly uppish to ask for?" hooted Mellish.

"Up with Cardew!" shouted Grundy.

"Boo! Boo! Boo!"

Tom Merry turned to walk away. Monty Lowther caught him by the arm.

"Tom, for goodness' sake——"

"I've finished," said Tom.

"Put in a little soft sawder, for goodness' sake—just a word or two!" whispered Lowther. "Something about thanking fellows for rallying round, and loyal support, and all that!"

"Not a giddy syllable!" said Tom.

"Cardew, Cardew!" roared a score of voices; and Ralph Reckness Cardew jumped on a chair to speak.

"Go it, Cardew!"

"Speak up!"

"Chuck it!"

"Order!"

"Gentlemen——" began Cardew in his silkiest tones.

"Boo! Go home!"

"Keep on!"

"Gentlemen, you have listened to the address of our esteemed friend and captain, Thomas."

"Ha, ha, ha!"

"Far be it from me to pick faults in the election address of my esteemed rival. In fact, I regard Thomas as one of my most strenuous supporters. He has done more for me than I could possibly have done for myself."

"Ha, ha, ha!"

"He tells you," continued Cardew, "that he doesn't care a hang which way you vote—for that's what it amounts to. Thomas appears to think that he reigns in the School House by right divine, like one of the jolly old Stuarts. Well—he doesn't!"

"Hear, hear!"

"It's for the honourable electors of this House to decide who shall hold the captaincy. Thomas is above asking you for your votes. I am not above it. I think that you have a right to be consulted, and to be considered."

"Hear, hear!"

"Bravo!"

"We all admire our Thomas," continued Cardew. "He's a straight chap. We all know how carefully he was brought up by his old governess, Miss Priscilla—a lady whom I can never mention without respect, and, indeed, awe."

"Ha, ha, ha!"

"But——" went on Cardew.

He did not get any farther. Tom Merry walked across to him, took him by the collar, and shook him. There was a roar from the meeting.

"Hands off!"

"Don't interrupt!"

"Fair play!"

"Hands off, you cad!" yelled Cardew, struggling in Tom's powerful grasp, his cool insouciance deserting him, and his face red with rage.

"Ha, ha, ha!"

"You rotter!" said Tom, his eyes blazing. "You can be as funny as you like about me, and welcome; but you will not speak disrespectfully of Miss Fawcett! Do you hear?"

"Let go!" shrieked Cardew, struggling furiously.

Tom Merry, with a swing of his arm, sent Cardew whirling across the platform. The dandy of the Fourth sprawled breathless, and Tom walked out of the room, amid a hubbub of voices.

CHAPTER 9.
The Election!

MANNERS and Lowther looked rather gloomy when they came back to Study No. 10 in the Shell after the meeting. Tom Merry was at work on his prep; but he looked up with a cheery smile as his chums came in. He had recovered the usual serenity of his sunny temper by this time.

"You're a bit late for prep," he remarked.

"Blow prep!" growled Lowther.

"You're an awful ass, Tom, old man!" groaned Manners. "You fairly mucked up our meeting!"

"Why, what did I do?" asked Tom.

"Your speech——"

"What was the matter with it?"

"What wasn't the matter with it?" grunted Monty Lowther. "And then handling Cardew before all the fellows——"

Tom Merry flushed.

"You know why I handled him, Monty."

"I know. His silly joke about Miss Priscilla was in rotten bad taste. He said it to make the fellows laugh. You

(Continued on page 16.)

THE BIG NOISE!

GRAND NEW "Footbal

| First Prize, **£100** | **30 MAGNIFICENT "JAMES" MOTOR-CYCLES** (Complete with Lamp, Horn, and Licence-holder.) | 10 Wi |

20 GRAMOPHONES. **40 FOOTBALL OUTFITS** (Boots, Stockings, Shorts, and Shirt).

50 Pairs of BOXING GLOVES. **100 Pairs of ROLLER SKATES**

250

RULES AND CONDITIONS

which must be strictly adhered to.

1.—The First Prize of £100 in cash will be awarded to the competitor who sends in the correct, or most nearly correct, solution of all eight sets of the pictures according to the Editor's official solution.

2.—The Second Prize of £50, and the others in the splendid variety of prizes will be awarded in order of merit.

3.—All the prizes will be awarded. If two or more competitors tie, however, the prize or prizes, or their value, will be divided, and the Editor reserves full rights in this respect.

4.—No solutions may be sent in until all the sets of the pictures and the necessary coupon have been published. Full directions will then be given.

5.—The names under the pictures must be written IN INK.

6.—Employees of the proprietors of this journal are not eligible to compete.

7.—Entry to this competition is on the full understanding that the Editor's decision is final and legally binding throughout.

SET No. 7.

37

38

40

41

YOU'VE SOLVED THIS SET? GOOD! NOW LOOK

COMPETITION!

"_'s' Names!"_

ngland

100 SPLENDID "JAMES" COMET BICYCLES (Complete with Lamp, Bell, etc.)

alve Sets

| Second Prize, £50 |

d Other rizes.

6 "RILEY" BILLIARDS TABLES. 100 FISHING RODS.
100 MATCH FOOTBALLS. 20 MODEL STEAM LOCOMOTIVES (With Rails).

MORE SET TO COME!

ALL YOU HAVE TO DO

is to write IN INK in the allotted space under each of the puzzle-pictures the name of the footballer which you think the picture represents. Surely a simple enough task—only six names to discover each week!

In all there will be EIGHT SETS OF PICTURES, so keep your solutions until the final set appears next week.

DO NOT SEND YOUR ENTRIES YET.

To help you still further, we have published in the preceding issues of the GEM a list of footballers' names, which contains the actual names of the footballers represented by all the pictures appearing in this competition.

New readers desirous of entering this contest can do so by obtaining the LAST THREE numbers of the GEM Nos. 822, 823, and 824, which, between them, contained all the previous sets of pictures. Back numbers of those issues can be obtained on application to the "Back Numbers Dept.," Bear Alley, Farringdon Street, E.C.4. For each single number required twopence in stamps should be forwarded, also one penny stamp to cover postage. The postal rate for additional copies is an extra halfpenny per copy.

There is still time for newcomers to take part in this great contest.

Readers of the "Champion," "Boys' Realm," "Union Jack," "Boys' Friend," "Pluck," "Boys' Cinema," "Young Britain," "Popular," "Magnet," "Rocket," and "Nelson Lee Library" are also taking part in the Contest, so that additional attempts may be made with the pictures from these allied journals.

OR THE LAST SET WHICH APPEARS NEXT WEEK!

"TOM MERRY'S RIVAL!"

(Continued from page 13.)

old ass, Tom; if you can make the other candidate look ridiculous, it's half-winning the battle! That was his game."

"Well, I stopped him."

"That wasn't the way. You ought to have made a rejoinder, holding him up to ridicule. There was plenty of material——"

"Oh, rot!" said Tom. "That may be good electioneering, but it isn't good enough for me."

"Well, it's done now," said Manners. "Do you want to know what happened after you left the meeting?"

"I'm not curious," said Tom, with a smile. "I gave it to them straight; and it's for the fellows to think it out."

"Think it out!" snorted Manners. "Catch them thinking! Cardew made his speech all right after you were gone —leaving the field open to him. He soon had all the fellows yelling with laughter. More than that, he's made most of them believe that you think yourself a sort of tin god, above appealing to them; and lots of them, I know, have made up their minds to show you that they're jolly well to be reckoned with, whether you choose to think so or not."

"Let 'em!" said Tom.

"He's holding another meeting, in the Third Form-room, after prep," said Lowther—"addressing the fags specially. You've got more friends in the Third than he has—Levison minor, and young Manners, and Wally—they'll back you up no end. But, after flattering them and pulling their legs, Cardew will have more backers in the Third than you will have, unless you take a leaf out of his book."

Tom Merry's lip curled.

"Catch me flattering them and pulling their legs!" he said. "It's not in my line, old man."

"Well, your goose is cooked," said Monty Lowther. "You make me tired, Tom! Let's get on to prep."

The Terrible Three settled down to work, and the discussion ceased. When they came down to the Common-room after prep a great many fellows looked curiously at Tom Merry. From the talk in the Common-room it was easy to tell that Cardew's party had greatly strengthened. Racke & Co. were looking jubilant. Trimble was grinning. Grundy appeared very satisfied. Many fellows who had intended to back up Tom Merry had changed their minds now—partly owing to Cardew's electioneering devices, and partly from a desire to show Tom Merry that he was not a little tin god, as Manners had put it.

Clarence York Tompkins was heard to remark that he wasn't going to give his vote to a fellow who was too proud to ask for it, and Tompkins was far from being alone in that view. Tom Merry, as a matter of fact, was the very last fellow in the world to contest an election on the usual lines. Cardew, on the other hand, revelled in all the trickery of electioneering; instead of despising such methods, he despised the fellows who were influenced by them. That was the difference between his nature and Tom Merry's.

But Cardew could speak cheerily, with a smile on his face, to a fellow whom he disliked and despised; and Tom Merry could not. If Racke of the Shell had offered Tom his support, the offer would have been rejected without ceremony. Cardew was "out" for all the support he could get, and his manner to Racke was honeyed, and he treated even Baggy Trimble with studied politeness.

When Saturday came round there was considerable excitement in the School House of St. Jim's.

Cardew and his supporters were counting their numbers again and again, and Tom Merry did not even trouble to make a list of his party. If a fellow wanted to come in and vote for him—well, he could do it; that was Tom's view. Cardew, on the other hand, was busy that Saturday. Even in class in the morning he was eager and whispering.

On one point, at least, Cardew had failed—no third candidate appeared on Saturday. Talbot of the Shell was Tom's firmest supporter. And Blake of the Fourth, after long hesitation, had decided not to split the vote by putting himself forward. Study No. 6 were convinced that a member of that celebrated study would make a first-class House captain. But they realised that if they drew a party to themselves, it would thin out Tom Merry's party, and make Cardew's success almost a certainty. So Study No. 6 nobly stood down and threw their weight into Tom Merry's scale.

At three o'clock on Saturday afternoon the lecture-room in the School House was crowded. Almost every junior of that house was present. The New House, of course, had nothing to do with the affair. It was a House matter.

Kildare and Darrell of the Sixth came in to conduct the

election. Junior elections always required the presence of a couple of prefects, otherwise the excitement was liable to get out of hand. There was a cheer for Kildare as he came in.

Tom Merry was present with his friends, and Cardew stood in the midst of a crowd. There was a cool and confident smile on Cardew's face. He nodded across to Levison and Clive, who were with Tom Merry.

The proceedings started without delay. Kildare stated— what everybody present already knew—that this meeting of the Lower School House was held for the election of a junior House captain. Talbot of the Shell proposed Tom Merry and was seconded by Manners. Kildare called for a show of hands, and there was a goodly show. Arthur Augustus D'Arcy, in his excitement, held up both hands till he was called to order. Cardew shook his head sorrowfully at Levison and Clive as they put up their hands for Tom Merry.

The show of hands for Cardew certainly looked as numerous as that for Tom Merry. A count was called for, and Kildare and Darrell proceeded patiently to count.

There was a buzz of excitement in the room as the count proceeded.

Cardew, with all his cool self-confidence, looked a trifle anxious and eager now. He could not bear the thought of failure, and he realised that he would look more than a little ridiculous if he failed, after his herculean efforts to rally a party round himself and "give Tom Merry a fall."

The two prefects compared notes when they had finished the count, and eager eyes watched them on all sides.

"Bai Jove! I weally wish they would buck up!" murmured Arthur Augustus D'Arcy to his chums. "I am weally on tentahooks, you know. It will be feahfully wotten if Cardew gets in!"

"It will be a near thing, anyhow," grunted Blake. "Blessed if I quite know how Cardew's done it; but he's got a big party."

"It's wathah wemarkable, as Cardew isn't weally populah," said Arthur Augustus, shaking his head. "Only a few days ago Gwunday of the Shell was wagin' with w'ath about Cardew bein' played in the House match, and now he's backin' him up like anythin'. Of course, Gwunday is a sillay ass!"

"Silence!"

Kildare was about to announce the result. His face was grave.

"Tom Merry—seventy votes."

"Bai Jove! That's not bad! Have you any ideah how many fellows there are in the House, Blake?"

"Hush!"

"Weally, Blake——"

"Silence!"

"Ralph Reckness Cardew, seventy-seven votes. Cardew of the Fourth Form is duly elected junior House captain of the School House."

There was silence for the moment. Most eyes turned upon Tom Merry. He did not flinch.

Then Racke gave a yell.

"Three cheers for Cardew!"

And there was a roar. Loud boos and catcalls came from the opposite party, and for some moments Kildare shouted in vain for silence. But silence was restored at last.

"Cardew of the Fourth becomes junior House captain," said Kildare. "Tom Merry, of course, remains junior captain of the school. This election does not affect that. Generally, House captain and school captain have been the same man, though not always. Before this meeting breaks up, I should like to point out that unless House captain and school captain pull well together, the result is likely to be bad for the House, and bad for the school."

"I shall do my best, Kildare," said Tom Merry.

Cardew smiled.

"I hope I can be relied upon to play up," he said. His eyes rested on Tom Merry's face, as he spoke, with a mocking expression.

Tom Merry set his lips. He knew that there was trouble to come—that Cardew would give him all the trouble he could, and in his new position the trouble he could give was very great.

"Bai Jove!" remarked Arthur Augustus. "I wegard the wesult of this election as wotten!"

"Thanks!" said Cardew.

"I mean it, Cardew! Although you are a distant welation of mine, I am vewy sowwy to see you elected House captain. Howevah, I twust you will play up, and pull with Tom Mewwy for the good of the House."

Cardew laughed.

"My dear chap," he said, "I can promise you, at least, that Tom Merry is goin' to have a high old time."

And Cardew walked away with his friends, leaving Arthur Augustus shaking his noble head seriously.

THE END.

(Cardew has scored his first success against Tom Merry. What will happen next? Look out for "CAPTAIN CARDEW!"—the next of this splendid series of school stories by Martin Clifford.)

17

Who Says A Good Laugh ?   Mike McAndrew Meets With More Misfortune !

MIKE MAKES A WIRELESS SET

A Screamingly Funny Yarn of Mirthful Mike, Bright Billy Burton, and Mischievous Marmaduke.

By ELMER K. ARTER.

CHAPTER 1.
A Terrible Tangle !

"I'M going to make a wireless set," said Michael McAndrew to his friend Billy Burton.

"I don't think !" scoffed Billy, from the garden wall. "You don't know anything about it !"

"I've been reading and studying," returned Mike, climbing up on to the wall that separated the two gardens. "It seems simple enough. All you've got to do is to get a lot of wire——"

"I thought you said it was wireless," interrupted his friend, squinting along the model boat he was carving.

"So it is when you've got it made. All you do is to wrap a lot of wire round a cardboard tube, and then you find the sensitive spot, or something, and slide along it and adjust the crystal which can be either a cat's whisper or crystalite, and zincyite, or borneite, or a variometer."

"Help !" cried Billy, holding his hands to his ears. "I know you've got it all wrong. I know enough about wireless to tell you that a cat's whisker is used, not a cat's whisper——"

"Our cat's got some lovely whiskers," piped Marmaduke, Mike's young brother, who had been listening with open mouth.

"You shut up !" said Mike rudely.

"Our wireless hasn't got any cat's whiskers," said Billy, "and it's more complicated than you seem to think, and it hasn't got any crystalites and zincyites and things. When you switch on it lights up, and you sometimes get a noise like a cat——"

"That's the cat's whisper," interrupted Mike.

"There is no cat's whisper," argued Billy. "Nor a cat's whisker. Our's is a three valve set."

"I don't know anything about valves. This book says you need not have valves."

"Oh, all right, have it your own way ! If you don't have valves, you don't get any light."

"What do I want light for ?"

"I don't know. All I know is that if we don't get a light, we don't get any music. Our set cost twenty pounds, and if you think you can do the same as we do with a bit of wire and a cat's whisker, do it. It doesn't sound very exciting to me. All the same, if you want to come and have a look at dad's set, I'll show

you. There'll be no one in the conservatory at dinner-time."

"I've seen it often enough," replied Mike. "It's a box if tricks. My set will be simple. This book says any fool can make one."

"Then make one. Marmaduke will help you. I'm tired of kids' games."

It was clear that Billy was not interested; but later that day when he called round to borrow a book, his attention was attracted by the state of the kitchen in which Mike was busy at work. Making a wireless set seemed to offer possibilities.

Mike was surrounded with wire of various kinds ; there were tools on every piece of furniture, including the gas stove. Dotted about were bright brass terminals and screws, and last, but not least, on one corner of the table, in a small bag, there was something that resembled toffee. Apparently Marmaduke had noticed the toffee-like substance, for he kept walking past it to examine the packet without touching it. It certainly did look like toffee, he thought, but after a second or third look he was undecided whether it was not ginger-snap.

Mike, his tongue between his teeth, was carefully winding purple-coloured wire around a cardboard tube. It was astonishing how much wire it took and how slow was his progress.

"That's funny wire," commented Billy, his nose over the work, and obstructing Mike's view.

"It's enamelled," explained the prospective wireless expert. "When the job's finished, you scrape it off."

"Then why do they put it on ?"

"To keep it from rusting, I suppose."

"Copper doesn't rust."

"Well, it does something !" snapped Mike bad-temperedly. His fingers were getting quite sore and his arms were aching.

Just then, Marmaduke, in investigating the contents of the paper bag, tripped over the enamelled wire, which, unwinding from its reel, was describing many circles on the kitchen floor.

"Look out, clumsy !" cried Mike, in alarm.

Poor Marmaduke tried to avoid the circles of spinning copper, but it was no good. While he was trying to balance on one foot, he found loops of wire on the foot raised in the air, and when he tried to lift the other foot, more coils had wrapped round it. He could not raise both feet at once. Perhaps he tried; anyhow, he finished up in the coal-bucket with the wire decorating the airing rack overhead.

Mike, his hands gripping his half-finished coil, was helpless to assist his brother, but Billy, anxious to help, dived to the rescue across the wire entanglement. His feet also gathered up loops of the wire, and he fell on the fender.

This was too much for Mike. He could see his beautiful kinkless wire becoming so much scrap, so he placed his coil on the side table to free his hands. As he released it, it seemed to jump like a released clock spring. He made a grab to stay its course, but he must have missed, for he, too, found himself wrapped in wire.

"Keep cool !" he shouted to the yelling Marmaduke and the squirming Billy. "Keep cool, stay where you are, and I'll wind it up."

But Mike could not expect his brother to remain with his head in the coal-bucket, and Billy was none too comfortable with one leg through the fender. No doubt Mike could have retrieved the wire in time, but just then the maid decided to enter in a hurry. She had a tray in her hand, and could not see where she was walking. The crash she made as she fell among the wire was heard in the dining-room, and Mr. McAndrew came along to investigate its cause.

"What are you doing ?" he asked, taking care not to step into the danger zone. "What on earth are you doing ?"

Mr. McAndrew was an engineer, but it took all his engineering skill to unravel the puzzle in front of him. Each of the prisoners tried to free himself, but only to get more entangled.

"Don't kink it, pa !" pleaded Mike, anxious for his wire.

"I've got some coal in my mouth !" spluttered Marmaduke.

Billy was silent, but Mary, seeing a mouse scurry along the skirting-board,

THE GEM LIBRARY.—No. 825.

screamed and completely tied herself in a knot in trying to rise to her feet.

Mr. McAndrew could see that things were getting serious. On the table where Mike had been working there was a pair of nippers. He called to Mike to pass them to him, but Mike guessed that this meant ruination to his beautiful wire.

"No, pa, don't cut it!" he cried.

But his father, stepping on to the table and reached for the tool. His first task was to cut Mary loose; the girl seemed in danger of going into hysterics, so he lay on the table and extended his arms towards him. He forgot that the table had an extension which had no supporting leg; the next moment he had dived headfirst into the wire.

This was not the worst; his foot, in describing an arc overhead caught the gas-pendant.

Smash went the globe and the mantle, and darkness fell upon the scene.

At this moment, Mrs McAndrew, hearing the uproar, decided to visit the centre of tumult. She walked clean into the wire; it wrapped around her ankles. For a few seconds she struggled to maintain her equilibrium, then fell upon her husband and the maid.

Mr. McAndrew was a powerful man, so, wire or no wire, he was soon on his feet. Then out of the kitchen he strode, trailing the stuff after him, and tightening the bonds that held the others.

He was still grasping the nippers, and in a few moments he had freed himself by the light in the hall; in another minute he had a candle upon the scene, and one by one he rescued the members of his family, and soon poor Mike's wire was in many pieces.

By the time the gas had been put in order, and Mike had collected all his paraphernalia, it was time for bed, and everyone had decided that "wireless" was not the proper name for such apparatus as he was trying to make.

CHAPTER 2.
First Aid!

IMMEDIATELY Mike had finished his home lessons the next evening he again laid out his materials in the kitchen, hoping that Marmaduke would find something else with which to interest himself.

He was doomed to disappointment, for hardly had he got half the coil completed before his small brother again joined him, and Billy, too, came in to help.

"You must keep your feet in your pockets," said Mike to Marmaduke. "It was all your fault last night. Get a chair, and play with those screws and things."

"Was your father cross?" asked Billy anxiously.

"I don't know," answered Mike. "We went to bed in a hurry."

Assisted by his chum, Mike slowly wound his wire round the cardboard tube, and Marmaduke, tired of playing with the screws and terminals, cast around for the mysterious packet of toffee stuff he had seen the night before. He found it. It certainly did look like toffee. He wondered what it was. Was it toffee? If so, why didn't Mike have some? But, of course, Mike was busy, and had even refused a chocolate offered him by the maid.

It was either toffee or ginger-snap, Marmaduke decided. It was very tempting, and he was inclined to think that Mike was selfish in not offering him some. Surely it would not matter if he took just a little bit!

He glanced at Mike and Billy, who

were bending their heads over the coil, and his hand crept into the bag. He placed a handful in his mouth; but just then Mike looked up, and Marmaduke closed his lips, and again entertained himself with the screws.

"Don't you lose any of those," said Mike.

Marmaduke, unable to speak, nodded that he would not lose the screws, but he was really more concerned about the stuff in his mouth. It was not a bit like toffee. It was quite nasty, and it caused him to puff out his cheeks.

"What are you blowing about?" asked Billy.

Marmaduke was no ventriloquist, and what he said without opening his lips was not clear, but to Mike it looked like a man he had once seen on an excursion steamer in a rough sea.

"What's the matter with you?" Mike demanded.

"Mur-mur-mur——" mumbled Marmaduke, and his effort evidently caused him to swallow some of the stuff, for the next moment he appeared to explode.

The boys thought that the youngster was choking, so they dropped the coil and rushed to his aid; but Marmaduke had left the chair, and was grovelling about under the table, coughing, and making weird noises.

"Oh!" he groaned, crawling out into the open.

"What's the matter?"

"Oh, oh!" gasped Marmaduke, pointing an accusing finger at the packet on the table.

"Have you been eating that?" gasped Mike.

"Oh, oh!" was Marmaduke's only reply.

"That's shellac."

"Is it poison?" whispered Billy, greatly concerned.

"I don't know!" groaned Mike, looking round helplessly.

His mother and father were out, and the maid had gone to the post. He would have to decide things for himself. He had heard that mustard-and-water was good for poisons, and the mustard-jar was near at hand. He emptied it into a basin, ran to the tap, and mixed enough to supply a dozen large restaurants.

"What do you do with it?" asked Billy.

"Haven't you heard of mustard-plasters?"

"I don't want a poultice," whined Marmaduke.

"Grab hold of him," Mike ordered; and Billy caught the youngster, while the self-appointed doctor proceeded to lay out the yellow mixture on a handkerchief.

"Where does it hurt?" he asked his brother.

"It doesn't hurt."

"It will perhaps."

"It tastes nasty in my throat."

"Dab it on his throat," suggested Billy, holding the younger boy between his knees and forcing the curly head backwards.

Without more ado, and in spite of all opposition, Mike slapped the mustard-plaster on Marmaduke's throat and covered it with a towel.

"Is that better?" he asked, after a minute's silence, watching for signs of result.

"Yes—no! Oh, it's starting to burn—it's burning!" screamed Marmaduke, trying to tear the towel from his neck.

But he was no match for the two elder boys, who held him tight.

Marmaduke's cries could be heard a mile away.

Fortunately for Marmaduke, the maid

returned; and, on ascertaining the cause of the uproar, put an end to Mike's drastic treatment by removing the mustard-plaster and giving the patient a glass of milk.

When Mike went back to his coil he found that it had again unwound itself, and the job had to be started again.

With Billy's help the cardboard tube was eventually covered until it looked as neat as a huge reel of silk.

He was holding it up to examine it with admiring eyes when his face fell. He placed the coil on the table, and sat down, holding his head. On his face there was an expression of despair.

"What's up?" inquired Billy.

"I forgot to shellac the tube first," he said.

"Does it matter?"

"I don't know; but if it doesn't matter, why does the book say it should be done, and why have I spent a shilling in shellac and methylated spirits?"

Billy could not answer this question.

And so it had to be done all over again.

After this the work proceeded apace. The finished coil was fixed between two pieces of wood, which were bridged by a slide-rod and a slider. The terminals were screwed into the board, and altogether the apparatus was beginning to look like a wireless set such as are to be seen in dealers' windows.

"Now for the cat's whisker," said Mike, very satisfied with his work.

With heads together Billy and Mike pored over the handbook to obtain knowledge of crystals and cat's whiskers.

"I don't know how it works," said Billy; "but it seems easy enough to make. All you do is to get a bit of zincite in a crystal cup——"

"It's made of brass."

"Who said it wasn't?"

"You said a crystal cup. I see, a cup for the crystal."

"You get the cup and half fill it with solder, and then run in some Wood's metal. Have you got any Wood's metal?"

"Yes."

"Then when the Wood's metal is nearly cold——"

"How do you find out whether it is nearly cold?"

"By your fingers, I suppose."

"It may be very hot."

"You can wet your finger. Anyway, when the Wood's metal is nearly cold you place the zincite in. Got any zincite?"

"Yes; it's that bit of shiny stuff in the pill-box. What else?"

"Having placed the zincite flat in the Wood's metal," Billy read on, "this part of the work may be considered finished. To find the sensitive point——"

"That'll do for the present. Let's do the Wood's metal and stuff."

Before the boys had finished this small job, which meant filling a thimble with solder, the gas-stove and the floor of the scullery were literally treated with flat discs of solder. Mike had burned fingers and thumbs on both hands, and Billy had burned a hole in his trousers. But the job was well done, and they were proud when they fixed it on the base board.

Then Mike discovered that he had lost the cat's whisker.

Marmaduke was at once interrogated. He had not seen it, but he hastened to remedy the loss.

The cat was in the drawing-room, there were a pair of scissors in his mother's sewing-box. Without a word he left the others to apply this knowledge to the benefit of all concerned. He found the scissors, and he found the cat, but Tabby was not to yield up its whiskers, or even one whisker, without a struggle, and it was some time before the youngster emerged from the struggle with victory illuminating his scratched face. He re-entered the kitchen with arms up-raised, the scissors in one hand and the cat's whisker in the other.

"I've got one, Mike!" he cried triumphantly.

Mike was on his hands and knees under the table searching for the missing item.

"Got what?" he asked.

"A cat's whisker. I cut off the longest," replied his brother.

"You clown!" said Mike, in disgust. "It's not a real cat's whisker we want ! It's a bit of wire coiled like a spring."

Considering the trouble Marmaduke had gone to in order to supply his brother's requirements, there was small return for his labour. His face fell, and then just as suddenly brightened. He felt in the pocket of his tunic, and after many contortions withdrew a hairlike piece of brass.

"Is that it, Mike?" he asked.

Mike abandoned politeness, and made a grab at the wire.

"Of course it is ! Why can't you leave things alone?"

"I didn't know it was a cat's whisker," whimpered Marmaduke. "What a silly name to give a bit of wire !"

Mike and Billy carefully studied the handbook, and fixed the whisker in position, and spent the rest of the evening sitting looking at the apparatus, admiring their handiwork, and silently imagining the delights of listening-in.

"To-morrow we rig up the aerial," said Mike finally. "There's a scaffolding pole at the bottom of the garden, and we can run the wire from that to the attic window."

"Will it have to have trapezes in it?" asked Billy, referring to the crossbars on his father's aerial.

"No; the book says a long single wire is best."

"What about the licence?"

"No one will know."

"They'll see the aerial."

"We can take it down each night. No one will see it in the dark."

"But the pole?"

"People will think it's a flag-pole."

CHAPTER 3.
Erecting the Aerial !

MR. McANDREW was very pleased with Mike's workmanship. He liked to encourage his son to study mechanics, and gave him every assistance, so he bought Mike a pair of headphones, which the young wireless expert promptly carried off to show his friend.

"They're four thousand ohms !" he announced.

"Four thousand whats?" asked the puzzled Billy.

"No, not watts. Watt is another electric thing. Ohms are a sort of—kind of—well, you know. They say a motor-bike is so many horse-power. The one in pa's garage is two and a quarter horse-power, but you couldn't harness two horses and a quarter of a horse——"

"That would be a donkey——"

"But you know what I mean."

"Then what's a watt?"

"It's a kind of a—sort of a therm that the gasworks sell."

"Go on. A therm is an insect !"

"Well, if it is," answered Mike, uncertain himself, "a watt isn't, neither is a volt."

"Help ! Don't say any more of them. You'll dream of them. Watts and therms and ohms and volts. You've been reading too much. We don't want any therms and insects like that to put up a flag-pole."

As the prisoners were making frantic efforts to extricate themselves from the encircling wire entanglement, the kitchen door opened, and Mr. McAndrew looked into the room. "What on earth are you doing ? " he asked, taking care not to step into the danger zone.

"But aren't they splendid—these headphones?"

"Yes; but we've got a loud speaker, and everyone can hear." Billy did not mean Mike to have a monopoly in wireless.

"You can't have a loud speaker with a crystal set, in any case. I don't like loud speakers; they are no better than a gramophone. I think headphones look much more like wireless."

Mike strutted about with the phones on his head, and imagined himself a wireless operator.

That day they started on the erection of the mast for the aerial. They found the scaffolding pole; and, deciding that the best position would be at the bottom of the garden near the greenhouse, they commenced to dig.

It was hard work. The ground was firm and apparently had been the burial-ground of a number of brick-ends, so Billy and Mike had not got very far down at the conclusion of the evening's labour.

With tired limbs and blistered hands they went to bed, and next day being Saturday they had plenty of time available. They worked hard, but to get down deep enough it was necessary to enlarge the hole, and it was then that the gardener advised them not to.

"That is where we buried Fido," he said.

Naturally, Mike did not want to disturb the remains of his departed pet,

and reluctantly they filled in the hole and cast around for another site.

Work was proceeding very satisfactorily when Mr. McAndrew interrupted the excavations.

"Don't dig there, my boy," he said. "That is where we buried Fido."

Poor Mike subsided on to the cucumber-frame, and Billy dropped helplessly to the ground.

"But, pa, Jenks said he buried Fido over there," said Mike, pointing to the refilled hole.

"No, my boy; it was just where you are digging," returned his father. "If you want to dig a hole for your aerial mast, there is that bare patch behind Fido's old kennel."

So back into the hole went the soil they had removed so energetically, and another day's work was done.

It was a week before they could get going again. The short evenings made after-school labour impossible, but everything comes to an end, including seven days' waiting for Saturday. Anyhow, it gave their blistered hands a much-needed rest.

Then they started all over again. Despite cramped quarters, they made good progress, and had decided that they had gone deep enough, when the gardener next door popped his head over the wall.

"What are you doing, young gentlemen?" he croaked.

"Discovering Australia," replied THE GEM LIBRARY.—No. 825.

Mike, with a smile that prevented the remark from being rudeness.

"I shouldn't dig just there if I were you," the old man went on.

Mike threw down his spade and faced the major's servant with arms akimbo. His attitude was one of defiance.

"You see, Master Michael," the gardener squeaked—"you see, Mr. Jenks buried your little dog just there."

Mike clasped his hands to his head.

Billy, looking at the blisters on his hands, seemed glad of a respite. But Marmaduke without further ado started to shovel the soil back into the hole.

"I wonder where Fido was buried?" said the puzzled Mike.

A little dazed, he went in search of Jenks, and found that individual tending his plants in the greenhouse.

"Here, Jenks," he said, "where was Fido buried? Wilks, next door, says you buried him behind the kennel."

The old gardener ambled out of the greenhouse, and for some time stood rubbing his brow as if to stimulate his memory.

"Of course, I may be a little mixed," he said finally, staring first at the original site for the mast and then at the second mound. "You see," he went on, "your mother told me to bury him there "—pointing to the spot where operations had been started—"and then your father instructed me to plant him over there. Mr. Wilks said he thought behind the kennel would be best, and I'm blest if I can remember now."

A new thought illuminated his wrinkled face.

"I know," he said. "Mr. Brown, the chauffeur, helped me. He will know."

The chauffeur was in the garage cleaning the car, and to him went Mike, Billy, and Mr. Jenks.

"Mr. Brown," wheezed the old gardener, "where did we bury Fido?"

"He wasn't buried," replied Brown. "If you remember, we placed him in an old sack, and when we had dug the hole we found that the sack had been stolen

by that rag and bone merchant who came mooching about."

"Ah!" cried Jenks. "I remember now, you see, Master Michael——"

But Mike wanted to know nothing more.

"Carry on!" he cried.

And the two boys raced back to the hole, only to find that Marmaduke had worked very hard and nearly completed filling it in.

"Br-r-r-r-r!" cried Mike. And poor Marmaduke went off to tell his mother.

However, the soil was soft, and did not take Mike and Billy very long to remove it, and the work of placing the pole in position began.

A scaffolding-pole is not light. It is not an easy thing to handle; in fact, it is extremely difficult to up-end such a long and weighty piece of wood.

There were several things to do before tackling this job, however, and they set to work in earnest. On the thin end of the pole they fixed a small pulley, in which they threaded the clothes-line. Half-way along it they fixed a band for three ropes to act as guys. Then the pole was ready for placing in the hole.

With Jenks' help they got it to the hole, but the gardener disclaims all responsibility for the glass that was broken in the greenhouse.

Mike was engineer in chief, so he placed a man at each guy-rope—Billy, Jenks, and Marmaduke—and, taking the thin end of the pole, raised it from the ground. His plan was to walk along with the pole on his shoulder, and so gradually raise it to the perpendicular. He was surprised to find that every step he took the pole got heavier, and he had it raised quite a height when the others thought they would help with the ropes. Next moment the pole was swinging round, first towards the greenhouse and then towards the major's wall. It ended up on the wall.

Although it was Saturday, the major's servant had been having a wash-day, and the end of the pole rested just beneath the array of the major's underwear.

Mike rearranged his forces, and gave the order to pull. The pole moved, turning to the right and then to the left, and, unknown to the boys, collected a

great deal of the washing from the next garden in the process.

Puffing and panting, the boys got the pole nearly upright, with the major's garments flying from it like the signals of a ship in distress.

When Mike saw the waving linen overhead he let go in surprise. Billy, too, let go, and bang went the pole, to rest upon the wall that separated the garden from the street beyond.

"Pull!" shouted Mike, throwing his weight upon the ropes.

And when finally the pole was raised again there was nothing but the ropes upon it. The major's underwear was in the street.

While Jenks, Billy, and Marmaduke held the ropes, Billy started to shovel in the soil around the base of the pole.

"Those clothes, Mike!" said Billy in a hoarse whisper.

"Shut up!" Mike growled. "They'll think the wind has done it."

"There isn't any wind, Master Michael," said old Jenks.

"Well, we can't let go now to hunt for that stuff!" panted the young contractor.

CHAPTER 4.
The Major is Wrathy !

WHEN finally the pole was fixed, the boys climbed on the cucumber-frame to look over the wall into the street. They were just in time to see a clergyman and his wife disappear round the corner with the major's linen in their arms.

"What have you done with Major Clinton's clothes?" a shrill voice cried from over the garden wall.

The boys wheeled suddenly, to see the major's housekeeper glaring at them.

Mike tried to speak, but he did not know what to say. Marmaduke and Billy disappeared behind the greenhouse, and after another fruitless effort to answer the major's servant, Mike followed them.

"You naughty boys! You naughty boys!" shrieked the woman.

But the wireless experts were crouching low, Billy with his handkerchief stuffed in his mouth and Marmaduke looking very scared.

Jenks had returned hurriedly to his work, and was very deaf indeed that afternoon.

"We'll put the aerial up to-night," announced Mike, when the housekeeper had finally gone back to the house, and they parted company for tea.

But the aerial was not fixed that night. Just as the brothers were leaving the table after tea the front door bell rang violently, and the maid came in to announce that Major Clinton wished to speak to Mr. McAndrew.

Mike and Marmaduke exchanged glances. Several thoughts flashed through their minds, but their retreat was cut off. To reach the stairs, the kitchen, or the garden they would have to pass through the hall. Now, if their father took the major into the drawing-room they might escape, but from the noise made by the major in the hall, there was little chance of this happening.

Mrs. McAndrew left the table to ascertain what was disturbing their neighbour, and this gave the boys an opportunity to crawl under the table.

"It is an outrage!" they heard the major bawl. "An outrage, sir! My housekeeper saw those young rascals reach for the laundry with a pole, and deliberately deposit it in the back street. Unfor—— Fortunately the Rev. Shepley

Held securely between his knees, Billy forced the squirming young Marmaduke's head backwards, while Mike clapped the mustard plaster on the youngster's throat.

and his wife discovered them, and very kindly brought them to me. I repeat, sir, it's an outrage, and I demand that you chastise them!"

"I will interrogate them," Mr. McAndrew was heard to say. "And if I am satisfied that they deserve it, they shall be punished."

"The old crank!" muttered Mike.

Marmaduke began to whimper, which gave away their whereabouts to their mother who peered into the room.

"Michael!" she said severely. "Come here!"

Mike emerged from beneath the table, looking very sheepish.

"Did you have anything to do with the major's washing?" she asked.

"Well, you see, mother——" Michael commenced.

"Come here, Michael!" called his father.

Mike slowly went to the door.

"Did you hear Major Clinton's indictment?" Mr. McAndrew solemnly questioned him.

"I heard his voice," faltered Mike.

"Michael. That is being rude," warned his mother.

Poor Mike looked puzzled.

"Did you, or did you not interfere with the laundry next door?"

"I didn't know the major had a laundry," answered Mike stubbornly.

"My washing, you young rascal!" shouted the infuriated major.

Mike looked round helplessly for a way of escape.

"It—it—— They were only old things!" he stammered. "They were all patched and holey."

"Michael!" cried his mother.

"Br-r-r-r-r!" spluttered the major.

"Go to your room!" said his father calmly.

And Michael went, expecting a visit from his parent later on.

When Billy called for him to continue the work, he saw his chum at his bedroom window.

"Clear off!" whispered Mike, in a hoarse stage whisper. "The major is in the house!"

That night Mike heard his mother and father enjoying a good joke at someone's expense, and after a while he felt convinced that it was not at himself they were laughing.

Next day was Sunday, and throughout the bright, sunny day the boys sauntered about with envious eyes on the aerial mast. Darkness came at last. Mr. and Mrs. McAndrew then went out, and Mike and Billy got busy with their coil of aerial wire.

Whispering and moving about the garden like burglars, they fixed one end of the wire to the line on the pole, and the other to a length of rope lowered from the attic window. The aerial wire had been prepared beforehand, and after several stealthy trips down the garden to disconnect it from bushes and tree branches, they finally got it up, and out of sight in the darkness overhead.

Then upstairs they went to connect it to the wireless set.

Mike, complete with head-phones, started to tune in. Up and down the coil he slid the slider, but nothing happened.

"I suppose there is a concert?" queried Billy, impatiently waiting to try the head-phones.

"Yes—8-30 to 10-30. I've seen it in the Sunday papers," replied Mike, staring at the cat's whisker. "You can't expect too much at first. I don't know whether the cat's whisker has a sensitive spot."

"You mean whether it is on the sensitive spot," corrected Billy, who remembered the context of the book better than his chum.

"Hush!" whispered Mike. "I heard something!" "What?" "A clicking noise!" "That would be ships signalling," suggested Billy. The two boys listened intently, unaware of the fact that the wire was disconnected and that young Marmaduke was amusing himself by tapping the two ends of it together.

"Perhaps so," returned Mike, resuming his painstaking task of discovering the particular pin's point on the crystal which would transmit sound.

For quite an hour Mike tried, and then for half an hour Billy manipulated the little wire on the zincite.

"Let me have another go," said Mike, taking the head-phones from his chum and refitting them on his own head.

After five minutes' earnest research work, Mike suddenly stiffened.

"Hush!" he whispered. "I heard something!"

"What?"

"A clicking noise."

"That would be ships signalling," suggested Billy, who had heard Morse on his uncle's wireless. Marmaduke was seated on the floor behind Mike's seat, playing with the ends of two pieces of wire.

"I heard it again!" whispered Mike.

"Let me hear," pleaded Billy, and reluctantly Mike passed the head-phones.

"I know," he said. "We can unscrew one of the phones and then we can both hear."

This was accordingly done, and presently both boys could hear the clicking sound referred to by Mike.

"That's Morse right enough," said Billy, as if he were accustomed to hearing Morse every day.

"Let's take it down."

"Dot, dot, dot, dot, dot, dot, dot, dot, dot, dot!" called Billy, making signs on a piece of paper.

"Well, what does it mean?"

"It sounds like the S O S. There's a ship in distress somewhere."

"I think," said Marmaduke, assuming a knowing tone—"I think, Mike, you ought to connect these wires with the set."

Mike looked down and staggered back with surprise, pulling the head-phone off Billy's head in doing so.

"You—you—— What are you doing with those?" he gasped.

For Marmaduke was playing with the telephone wires, and the Morse messages they had been hearing were of his making.

"You clown!" he snorted, snatching the wires from the youngster's hands.

"We haven't been listening to wireless at all. We haven't been connected up!"

It did not take long to remedy this small fault, and after a little more adjusting of the crystal, and a little more sliding the slider, their operations were abruptly stopped by a well-known voice bawling in their ears.

"Yes," it said, "the boys of Mr. McAndrew. Proper nuisance, sir! But now you have a chance to prosecute! At this moment, sir, they are tampering with my telephone wires. They have a wire across it, and for half an hour or more they have been trying to break down the telephone wire which is Government property. I demand, sir, that you send a policeman at once. Are you there? Confound you, sir! Miss! Exchange! We have been cut off!"

Billy and Mike knew very little about wireless; they thought they knew less about ordinary telephony, but now they knew enough to realise that their aerial was fouling the major's telephone wire.

The boys read each other's thoughts. Billy snatched the lead-in off the set, and threw it out of the window. Mike let go the line that held the aerial, and they both ran downstairs.

In another minute it had been lowered from the mast, and the wire coiled up.

Then the whole lot—wire, set, and odds and ends that were evidence of their activity, was rammed into a box which was hidden under Mike's bed.

When Mr. and Mrs. McAndrew returned from their evening walk, Mike and Marmaduke were in bed, a most unusual happening, since they had not been ordered to go.

Events, however, passed in favour of Mike and Billy, and the whole business was soon forgotten.

⁂

Mike has now got his wireless set in working order, but, like many other things he possesses, he has tired of it, and now he is engaged in making something else.

THE END.

(Look out for a splendid story of thrilling adventure in India next week, boys: "THE RED IMAGE!" You will vote it ripping.)

THE TRIERS

By JACK CRICHTON

A victim of Fate, Jack Morton, with the assistance of his stalwart followers, fights valiantly against his rascally cousin, George Clifton, for the rights of which he has been deprived.

Clifton's Treachery!

JACK didn't answer at once. He was simply too flabbergasted for words. With his own eyes he saw the sergeant of police take the missing pocket-book out of his own overcoat pocket. He rubbed his eyes, as though to make quite certain that he was not dreaming.

"Well?" asked the detective. "What now?"

The lad made a great effort.

"Well," he replied in the same tone, "the fact of the matter is that I haven't worn that overcoat for several weeks, and that I did not wear it last night when I went to see Mr. Clifton!"

The two policemen exchanged an incredulous smile.

"Well, you know," said the sergeant, "you had better not say anything more without understanding that we shall use it against you!"

"Against me!" cried Jack. "All right, go ahead, but you can't do anything. I know nothing about that pocket-book. I don't even know how it got there!"

"Fairies put it there," sneered the detective after the manner of his kind.

"Well," exclaimed the lad stoutly, "Mr. George Clifton can tell you that I had no overcoat last night!"

"Will he?" said the detective.

And suddenly the lad's heart seemed to stop beating, and he stared at them with fresh horror in his eyes. He seemed to understand. He was in a trap. He didn't, of course, for one moment believe that these two men were in it against him, but there it was, a trap, and one from which escape began to look very doubtful. Of course, that miserable cousin of his would

THE GEM LIBRARY.—No. 825.

not dream of speaking a single word to help him!

"Can you explain how it got there?" asked the detective harshly.

"No, I can't!"

"Well, it can't have walked there, or flown there, so the best thing you can do is to come along with us."

"What?"

The sergeant smiled grimly.

"There are notes for fifty pounds in here, young man," he explained. "You don't suppose that sort of thing can be looked over, do you?"

Jack caught his breath. He needed all his pluck now, all his presence of mind. For two pins he would have made a fight of it, as mad as that would have been. But the unfairness of it all seemed so outrageous. Every moment brought with it the growing feeling that this was George Clifton's dirty work, and that somehow he had been trapped like this by his cousin's machinations.

"My mother——" he said.

"Oh," sneered the detective, "we've all got mothers my lad, and if we let everyone go who happened to have a mother, we should soon be in a fine state. Now, come along like a sensible lad, and we'll try to make the best of it for you. Dare say it was sudden temptation——"

"It was sudden nothing, you idiot!" Jack exclaimed, unable to endure the insults any longer, "and I am going to have a word with my mother!"

"No you are not!" cried the sergeant, putting a hand on the lad's shoulder.

Jack drew himself up.

"Look here," he said, "I don't blame you two for this. You have both got to do your duty, but the fact of the matter is—my mother is very, very ill. If she hears of this it might kill her. Let me go up and have a word with her. I'll tell her something——"

"Yes, and slip out of the back window!" said the detective.

"I give you my word of honour that I will be back in five minutes," said the lad. "Oh, please be kind about this. You have both had mothers of your own!"

The two men exchanged another glance.

"All right," said the sergeant. "Only if you are more than five minutes we'll be after you, and don't you try any tricks! I shall watch the back of the house!"

"Thank you!" said Jack, and he hurried away.

He knocked on his mother's door, and went quickly in when the old lady replied.

She was in bed, of course, looking very sweet and frail, and for a moment or two the lad knelt down at her side and pressed his lips to her forehead.

"Early, dear?" she said.

Jack nodded.

"Mother," he whispered, "I am very sorry to wake you up so early like this, but I've got to go out early to-day. I sha'n't be back for a few days. We are going down to London for a special match, and then into training by the sea on the South Coast—Brighton, you know. I am sorry, but I have to go now I belong to the club!"

The old lady gave him a brave smile.

"Yes, dear," she said, "I understand perfectly. Be happy. I am proud of you!"

WHAT HAS GONE BEFORE!

For the sake of his invalid mother, Jack Morton, a lad of seventeen, calls upon his grandfather, Sir Jasper Clifton, for aid. It was by no means a pleasant undertaking for Jack, for his mother, much against her father's wishes, had married a worker in Sir Jasper's mill, who was now dead. Sir Jasper, however, is taken up with the lad straight away, saying that he will alter his will and make him co-heir with George Clifton, another grandson, and Jack's cousin, whose great interest in life is the Boltwich Football Club. In high spirits, Jack gives up his old job to take up work at Cliftons'. But Sir Jasper dies that night. Thinking only of his mother, Jack goes to George Clifton, but his appeal proves futile, Clifton telling him that the will is unaltered, and that he is not wanted. Jack's anger is aroused, and, meeting Ronnie Stevens, whom George Clifton had deemed it wise to sack, the two lads, former players of Boltwich F.C., determine to fight Clifton. "We'll get a team that won't be beat," said Stevens, "and call them the Triers." The team shows great promise, much to the annoyance of Clifton, who, scheming to get Morton hounded out of Boltwich, makes a spoof appointment with the lad. Unsuspiciously Jack falls into the trap when calling upon Clifton, who denies knowledge of the letter. Later, to Jack's surprise, he is arrested and accused of the theft of fifty pounds from Clifton. Jack pleads not guilty, but a close search reveals Clifton's missing case in his overcoat pocket.

Come back quickly, but do not worry about me!"

"And you'll be all right?"

The old lady nodded bravely.

"Yes, yes, dear!" she answered. "I'll get someone to come in and help me. Now run along, if you must, and take care of yourself!"

"You bet I will!" said the lad.

The smile he gave his mother then cost Jack more than a smile had ever cost him in his life, and then he was gone from her.

The two men downstairs were evidently surprised to see him return so quickly.

"I am at your service," said Jack.

"That's right!" grunted the detective. "No good kicking up rough at these times, my lad!"

"Well, I'm ready!"

They left the cottage.

It was early yet, and there were not many people about; but now and again they would run into someone, and Jack realised that before many hours were out the news would go through Boltwich that Jack Morton, the new centre-forward of the club, had been taken in charge for something.

At the station they were not unkind to him, but they were not very sympathetic.

The inspector questioned him stoutly, for the lad still insisted on sticking to his story that he knew nothing about all that had happened.

"You say that Mr. Clifton sent you a letter to go and see him?" he asked after a little while. "Got the letter?"

Jack started.

"No!"

"Ah," said the inspector grimly, "and where may it be?"

"I left it with Mr. Clifton."

"What?"

"He said it was not his letter, that he had not sent for me at all, and asked me to show him the letter. I did, and he forgot to hand it back to me. That's the truth, and if you ask Mr. Clifton he will tell you that it is!"

The man nodded.

"Yes, we had better have Mr. Clifton. Take him along to the cells, Smith, and I will telephone to Mr. Clifton, and ask him whether he will come along. We won't charge him till then, as Mr. Clifton may, of course, clear him!"

So Jack found himself in a cell, alone with all his miserable thoughts. Yet he was not entirely downhearted. Things were bad. They had, of course, never been nearly so bad before, but he was not despairing. Had this been something unconnected with George Clifton he would have felt like despairing. But he realised now very well that it was all his cousin's doings, all part of the fight which was being waged between him, and, after all, he must not expect in that fight that everything would go his way. There must be ups and downs, and he had no doubt that in a little while he would come through this very successfully.

Half an hour later he was taken before the inspector again, and there he found his cousin waiting.

"Well, I'm very sorry about this, Morton," said George Clifton—"more sorry than I can possibly say. Why on earth didn't you tell me that you wanted money?"

Jack could do nothing but stare.

The cool cheek of it was more than he could swallow, and it rendered him speechless.

"You'd better let me do the talking, Mr. Clifton," said the inspector of police. "Oh, yes, certainly!"

The inspector turned to the lad.

"Now, you understand, young man," he said, "you are in a very serious position. You look like being charged with stealing a pocket-book containing fifty pounds belonging to Mr. George Clifton from the Old Hall last night, and I have to warn you that anything you now say will be taken down and used as evidence against you!"

Jack squared his shoulders.

"I understand," he said.

"Did you steal that pocket-book?"

"No, I did not!"

"Why did you go to see Mr. Clifton?"

"Because I received a letter asking me to go and see him!"

"Got the letter?" asked the inspector for a second time.

"No. I told you I haven't. I handed it to Mr. Clifton!"

There was a moment's pause, and all eyes were turned on Clifton. He looked merely pained.

"Know anything about this letter, Mr. Clifton?"

To Jack's horror, the man shook his head, and burst out:

"No, of course I don't. But, I say, inspector, I hate this sort of thing. Can't something be done?"

"Not now, sir," said the inspector, who had the reputation of being a brute.

He turned to Jack Morton again.

"Now, you hear that, Morton," he said sternly. "Mr. Clifton knows absolutely nothing about that letter. So that is that——"

"He is lying!"

"How dare you!" cried Clifton, springing forward.

The sergeant of police rested a hand on his arm.

"Steady, sir!"

"I beg your pardon," said Clifton. "But it is abominable to have a whippersnapper like this give one the lie direct. He—he knows perfectly well that I wrote no letter, and that he gave me none!"

Jack said nothing.

"Well, young man, anything else?" asked the inspector.

Jack drew himself up, and instead of speaking to the inspector, he turned and faced his cousin.

"You know perfectly well that this is your doing, George Clifton," he said. "You have been trying to get me down, and you have nearly succeeded. But you won't! You have robbed me of my grandfather's money, you leave my poor old mother to starve, and now you have worked up this plot to get me put away in prison. But I'm not afraid of you, not in a million years; and the time will come soon when I shall show to the whole of Boltwich that you are a thief and a scoundrel—and perhaps worse!"

The Escape !

THINGS were not going quite so smoothly for the renovated Boltwich Club as might have been expected now that George Clifton was out of the saddle.

The trouble was with some of the players.

It had been apparent enough on the previous Saturday against the League leaders—who had indeed been beaten—that the whole team was not pulling together, and had it not been for Jack Morton's supreme efforts there was little doubt that the home lads would have had a very nasty smack in the eye.

And now the directors, with Laurie in their midst, confident, inspiring, and amazingly self-assured, were facing something which looked like nothing more nor less than open rebellion.

Old Blake, the trainer, had been the first to bring the news to the directors. It had come about through trouble with Bill Atkins, owing to the way in which he had behaved on the previous Saturday.

There had been a short and sharp inquiry into the trouble between himself and Jack Morton, and during it Atkins had lost his temper, had told the directors what he thought of them, and had as good as admitted that he had done his best to maim Jack.

There had been nothing left for the directors to do but to stand Atkins down.

He had been too secure in his place, and there were several youngsters fighting for it, and so after a short deliberation the directors had informed him that he would not be needed in the club again. Indeed, it was the sack complete.

He could not have taken it with a worse grace, cursing and threatening as he did, and now Blake had come to the

Suddenly darting in, Jack Morton caught the burly Bolton by the wrist. In another moment, with a swift clever movement, he had caused the bully to sling his stick aside. "Now fight like a man!" he roared.

directors and had informed them that several other members of the team had sworn that until Atkins was reinstated Boltwich should not gain another point.

"Talking about putting through their own goal, one or two of them," Blake had said; and the position, with a match coming on every week, looked serious.

Besides, to-day their brilliant new centre-forward had been arrested and thrown into prison.

No wonder, then, that the group of men round the table looked serious, and that only Laurie Robson, screwing his eyeglass farther and farther into his eye showed the slightest sign of light-heartedness.

"It's a nasty, sticky mess," he agreed, "but at the same time, I'm all for fighting the blighters. Who are they, Blake?"

The old trainer told them.

"Hunter, the goalie, sir," he said. "Tomkins, left-half, and Jevings, inside-right!"

Laurie nodded.

"Are they here?"

"Yes, sir."

Laurie looked round at his fellow-directors.

"It's a serious position," he said, "and it calls for a serious remedy. One can do nothing by gentle means in a thing like this. I suggest that we call these three men before us, tell them that we didn't think much of the way they played last Saturday, and let them understand that we suspect their game, and then if they do not play up on Saturday we will out them!"

One of the directors gave a bit of a gasp.

"Wait a minute, young man," he said. "Aren't you going rather fast?"

Laurie smiled.

"I always do. It saves time."

"But what is going to become of Boltwich Club? Our centre-forward seems to be rather a doubtful character——"

"Excuse me," said Laurie, flushing hotly. "I will speak for Jack Morton. He is under suspicion, but it is up to us to believe in him, gentlemen; and I will pledge you my personal word of honour that he is not capable of doing a dirty trick to any man. It is all the handiwork of that fellow Clifton, and I should not be surprised if this trouble in the team was also his handiwork!"

"Nor I!" agreed Mr. Graham, the managing-director.

There was a short silence, and then it was agreed that Laurie's way was a good one, and the three players were sent for.

They came in together, looking sulky and angry, three great, hulking fellows, who were obviously in no mood to do themselves justice or to listen to reason.

"Sit down," said Mr. Graham, and they sat down opposite the directors rather like a trio of truants at school.

"We have sent for you men," the managing-director began, "to have a friendly talk with you. We were not satisfied with the way you shaped last Saturday, although we won the match, and we are not entirely satisfied that you put in all you knew. Mind you, we do not make any direct accusation, but the fact of the matter is, we thought it most fair to send for you and tell you quite plainly that you must give a better show this coming Saturday!"

There was a short silence.

"If not," said Mr. Graham, "we may have to do something else!"

Tomkins, the left-half, looked up.

"Is that all, sir?" he said.

"Yes, Tomkins; but if you have got anything to say, say it, and don't be afraid. We only wish to be fair!"

Tomkins gave a bit of a sneer.

"The team's upset, sir!" he said.

"Eh?"

"Well, sir, it's not for us to criticise, but you can't be surprised, with the changes that there have been. First of all you bring in a kid to play centre-forward——"

"What," asked Laurie Robson quickly, screwing his glass into his eye—"what was wrong with his play last Saturday, my dear fellow?"

Tomkins gave a grunt.

"Stunts!" he said.

Laurie started.

"Very useful stunts, as it turned out!"

"Hear, hear!"

Tomkins looked up quickly, and there was a patch of red on his cheek which showed he was angry. As a matter of fact, he was a great personal friend of Bill Atkins, and he had always hated Mr. Graham and Blake, the trainer, and now, egged on by Atkins, and, unwittingly by George Clifton, he was all for trouble.

"Then, sir," he said, "it hasn't made a nice impression in the team the way poor Bill Atkins was turned down. After all, he has been a faithful servant to the club for a long time, and that business last week was six of one to half a dozen of the other!"

Mr. Graham snapped his lips together.

"Look here, Tomkins," he said, "we want to be just to you; but do you really think you are in a better position to judge as to this than we are?"

Tomkins nodded.

"Yes, sir!"

"What?"

"I was in the middle of it all, and young Morton was to blame, and, anyhow, sir, to get down to business, we three are not happy. Of course, we are always going to do our best for the club, but we think the team would work better together with Atkins in his old place, and if we were not asked to play with a fellow who seems to spend most of his time in prison!"

This was too much for Laurie.

He jumped to his feet.

"Look here, Tomkins," he said; "you—you can't say that sort of thing about a pal of mine. All Boltwich knows that George Clifton is after Jack Morton's blood, and you can take it from me that in some dirty way or other George Clifton has now managed to get him put away in prison!"

Mr. Graham rose to his feet.

"Excuse me, Robson!"

"Sorry!"

"We won't go into that, if you don't mind. We will stick to points. Do you three men mean to play properly next Saturday?"

The three men looked at one another, and for a few seconds there was a deadly silence in the room.

Then Tomkins looked up again.

"We don't feel we can do much good if that fellow Morton is centre-forward, sir!"

"It's open rebellion, then?"

"I don't know about that, sir——"

"Yes, it is!" cried Mr. Graham. "And it is now the moment to nip it in the bud. If Jack Morton is available he will, after his brilliant display last Saturday, play for us! Well?"

Tomkins stood sullen and furious.

"It's not for me to say what will happen, sir," he replied.

Graham looked round at his fellow-directors.

From them all came a nod. He turned to the three men again.

"Are you all of one mind?"

"Yes, sir!" said Hunter.

"Yes!" said the third.

There was a pause.

"Very well," said Mr. Graham, "then you are all placed on the transfer-list, and we shall not play you again!"

A gasp ran round the room. The three men had evidently not expected such strong methods. They had hoped to be bargained with, and this was a bit strong.

"But you'll not get a team out, sir!" exclaimed Hunter, the goalie.

Laurie laughed.

"Oh, yes, Hunter," he said. "There is a certain Mr. Harry Turner, you may have heard of, the amateur boxer. He is the finest goalkeeper in this town, and I think he will help us in a pinch!"

"That's all," said Graham then, and the three men went slowly and sorrowfully from the room.

A short silence followed their departure.

"Well," said Laurie brightly, "we've done it; and now we can really start and build up our team!"

One of the directors, who had always been rather disposed to look down upon Laurie and his opinions on account of his youth, gave a short grunt.

"Well," he said, "I only hope we can get a team on to the ground next Saturday. We have no centre-forward to speak of now."

Laurie held up a hand.

"Wait a minute, gentlemen," he said. "I'll manage to get young Morton to the game——"

"Eh?"

"And I'll arrange with Turner, if you will fill the other two vacancies!"

Graham smiled.

"You certainly have a way of doing things, young man," he said.

Laurie nodded.

"I'm one of the Triers, sir," he said. "And it takes more than a smack in the eye to stop us. I will promise you here and now that before the end of the season the Triers have raised Boltwich very near to the top of the League, and, mayhap, they will have done sturdy things in the Cup. Are you willing, then, to leave Morton and Turner to me?"

"We are!"

"I thank you, gentlemen!"

•   •   •   •   •   •   •   •   •

On the following Friday Jack was to be brought up before the court on the charge of having stolen fifty pounds from his cousin, and he was not feeling exactly merry and bright about the business as he waited in his lonely cell.

Indeed, nothing had happened to make him feel at all hopeful that he was going to get off.

The dice were too heavily weighted against him.

He tried to believe that something would turn up, and when Laurie had engaged an eminent lawyer to defend him, he had been quite hopeful.

But after he had spent half an hour telling all his story to the eminent lawyer, and then had realised that the eminent prig had regarded him as a confounded young liar, his spirit fell heavily again.

The cell door opened suddenly, and a constable appeared.

"Come along, lad," he ordered.

Jack rose and followed the man out to the waiting van which was to take him to the court.

He entered it, and sat there alone, as miserable as he had ever been.

Suddenly he realised that the constable was speaking to him.

"Pity you can't go over to Crewbridge with the team to-morrow, lad!"

"It is!"

"I'd like to see our lads beat them Crewbridge boys!"

Jack nodded. But he was not very interested in Soccer at the moment. He was too downhearted. Still, he understood well enough what the other man meant. Crewbridge was a neighbouring town, and the rivalry between them and Boltwich had been keen for generations.

"Pity you can't manage it," said the constable, and looked at Jack meaningly.

Then quite deliberately he walked away from the door of the van.

Jack gave a gasp.

He looked about. Not a soul was in sight. It was a terrible temptation. He ought, of course, to stay and face the music. That would be the wise thing to do. But the temptation was terrible. He seemed to have so little chance of getting off,

and if he were sent to prison, what earthly chance would he have to follow up all the clues against George Clifton? What chance would he have to get the rights for his darling old mother?

Besides, if he could play to-morrow! Of course, the mere thought was insane, but if he could, how foolish Clifton would look?

In a flash he jumped to the ground, and in another moment he was scudding round a corner, and safe for the time being.

A Chase and After!

JACK did not make for home His instinct was to do so, but after the first few seconds of freedom he found his mind working very clearly.

He made for Laurie's house, and then, instead of going up to the house and asking for that young man, he hung about, hidden, until he saw him coming along by himself. And then, with a yell of delight, he sprang forward to meet his pal.

"Laurie!"

The young man dropped his eyeglass, with a gulp.

"Golly, dear lad," he cried, "you nearly made me swallow the jolly old thing! So there you are. My word, but you are giving me a bit of trouble, young fellow m'lad. I have had to promise that policeman a life job on the estate after he gets the sack for letting you escape this morning. And even then he would not have done it had it not been for the fact that he would give his right hand to see us beat Crewbridge to-morrow!"

Jack caught his breath.

"Crewbridge," he cried. "Are you mad? I can't turn out for Crewbridge —against them, I mean!"

"Why not?"

"Great Scott, they will nab me!"

"Nothing of the sort," said Laurie. "You leave that to me. And the great thing now is not to get nabbed before you turn out to-morrow. Come along with me. I am going to fix you up in a spare room in the house, and bring you your grub myself. No one in the house shall know how you are about. That is best, isn't it?"

"Sure!"

Rather like one in a dream, the lad went along, listening to all that Laurie had to tell him. And as soon as he heard how a minor rebellion had broken out in the team on his account, as it were, he became more and more keen to turn out the next day and to give of his best.

How this was going to be done he did not know, and Laurie Robson was mildly mysterious about it.

They got into the house all right, and for the rest of the morning the lad sat about in his room, reading and waiting.

After lunch Laurie came to him.

"My word," he said, with a laugh, "there is an ado in the town to-day about your escape. The police are raising Cain, and George Clifton, they say, is almost off his nut with anger. Now, my gay lad, don't you think that you ought to kick a football about this afternoon?"

Jack started.

"I am sure I should!"

SPECIAL NOTICES.

Would Miss M. Ravelle, of Liverpool, who wrote to the Editor in May, 1922, and whose Correspondence Notice appeared in the "Gem" Library dated January 5th, 1923, kindly communicate with the Editor again?

"Right. Here are some togs. I'll go and change, and we will slip back on to one of our meadows, and we will soon see whether you are in good trim."

Jack changed, marvelling at it all, and wondering what the end of all this weird business was going to be, but for the moment content to leave everything in the hands of his pal.

Half an hour later his troubles were forgotten as he slipped about with Laurie, exalting in the fresh air, his freedom, and the glory of having a football at the end of his toe.

"This is fine!" he said. "I don't ever want to go to prison again!"

Laurie laughed.

At that moment Jack turned with the ball, but it was too late.

He gave a shout.

"Look out, Laurie!"

But his warning shout came too late.

Babe Bolton had approached Laurie from behind, and even as Jack shouted be brought down the stout stick he carried with a brutal thud upon the lad's head, and in another moment Laurie had fallen to the ground.

"You brute!" cried Jack, springing forward.

"I'll show you!" muttered the Babe. "You gaolbird—I'll show you! There'll be a nice little reward for this job!"

Jack was at a sore disadvantage. The fellow was coming at him now with murder in his eyes, and there was no doubt that he meant mischief. The trouble was that he carried that wicked-looking weapon.

As he struck at the lad Jack dodged; but he realised even as he did so that he was in a bad way. It could not last long, and perhaps the best thing was to take to flight.

But that was not Jack Morton's way. Suddenly darting in, he caught the bully by the wrist, and in another moment, with a swift, clever movement, he had caused Bolton to fling the stick aside, with a scream of pain.

"I'll show you!"

"Then fight like a man!" roared Jack, springing at the burly Bolton.

It was a goodly fight, witnessed by no one, and for a long time it went in Jack's favour, for the professional was so furious that he had thrown his undoubted science and experience to the winds, and was fighting madly.

But although Jack got home some shrewd blows, he didn't manage to down his man, and after a few minutes the Babe began to fight his own battle.

A right-hook caught Jack unawares, and he went down.

A brutal kick followed, and he lay groaning on the ground, with the Babe gloating over him.

"Now you'll come along with me, you young brute," he muttered. "This'll teach you. This—"

Jack had darted to his feet.

There was no time to waste.

The Babe grabbed at him, and he dodged, and in another moment anyone looking into that meadow would have seen the somewhat amazing sight of the centre-forward of Boltwich Association Football Club, in full Soccer togs, pursued by a very heavy, angry, and slow professional boxer, a young gentleman in footer togs slowly getting to his feet, and a football sitting up and wondering why it was so neglected.

The Babe was no match now for Jack. He was slow and heavy, and within a few minutes he was a long way behind his man, and before he had covered half a mile he had stopped altogether, and was merely shaking his great fist after the lad.

"I'll get you!"

In the fight he had dropped his cap, and now he went back for it. He stopped suddenly as he saw Laurie Robson, still dizzy with pain, coming towards him.

They met and regarded one another.

"Ah," exclaimed Laurie, "the playful Babe, is it? And I suppose it was you who hit me so considerably on the back of the head!"

"Yus—it was!"

"I sha'n't forget!"

The Babe grinned.

"I don't want you to forget, young fellow," he said. "And I ain't going to forget, neither. I sha'n't forget that you were playing football in this 'ere meadow with that gaolbird. I am going straight to the police now, and I dare say you'll be under lock and key yourself in half an hour!"

Laurie drew a deep breath.

"I see," he said. "Well, I can't stop you doing that, if you mean to, Bolton, but you are being rather an idiot!"

"What?"

"Don't you think you are backing the wrong horse, man!"

"I don't back horses!"

"Oh, come, Bolton, I know that you bruisers are all half-witted, but you know what I mean. Don't you think you are a fool to throw in your lot with George Clifton? Take my advice and leave the Triers and Jack Morton alone. We are going to beat George Clifton, and if—if, when we have done so, we have to make certain inquiries into your private history, I fancy you will be sorry. Take my advice. I will forgive this whack on the head. Keep your silly mouth shut, and don't get me up against you! I'm as rich as Clifton—and I happen to keep my word. Make a friend of me, man, not an enemy!"

(Whether Bolton takes Laurie's hint remains to be seen. Anyway, look out for some startling situations in next week's grand long instalment of this powerful serial.)

Printed and published every Wednesday by the Proprietors, The Amalgamated Press (1922), Ltd., The Fleetway House, Farringdon Street, London, E.C.4. Advertisement offices: The Fleetway House, Farringdon Street, London, E.C.4. Registered for transmission by Canadian Magazine Post. Subscription rates: Inland and Abroad, 11s. per annum; 5s. 6d. for six months. Sole agents for South Africa: The Central News Agency, Ltd. Sole agents for Australia and New Zealand: Messrs. Gordon & Gotch, Ltd.; and for Canada, The Imperial News Co., Ltd. (Canada).—Saturday, December 1st, 1923.
NN

My Readers' Own Corner.

Tuck Hampers and Money Prizes Awarded for Interesting Paragraphs.

(If You Do Not Win a Prize This Week—You May Next!)

All Efforts in this Competition should be Addressed to : The GEM LIBRARY, "My Readers' Own Corner," Gough House, Gough Square, London, E.C.4.

TUCK FOR MANCHESTER!

"SOME" COFEEE!

After a strenuous football-match two of the footballers entered a coffee-shop for a cup of coffee. After being served, one of them was heard to remark : "This coffee tastes like mud." "Well," chimed in the shopkeeper, overhearing the remark, "it was only ' ground ' this morning, sir !"—A Tuck Hamper filled with delicious Tuck has been awarded to H. Davies, 58, Cromwell Avenue, Whalley Range, Manchester.

KINDNESS NOT APPRECIATED !

The furniture-van blocked the way in a suburban thoroughfare, and a little boy was standing by the horse, giving it some bread to eat. The driver looked on approvingly. "That's right," he said to the young benefactor : "always be kind to dumb animals. Look how the horse enjoys it. But does your mother generally give you big hunks of bread like that?" "No," replied the youngster. "I found it in the van." "What !" yelled the carrier. "Why, you young imp, that was my breakfast !"—Half-a-crown has been awarded to Miss May Paget, 33, Coombe Road, Gravesend, Kent.

HARD ON THE PIG !

The twenty-fifth anniversary of two dear old villagers, Jarge and Ann, was drawing nigh, but it was Ann who first spoke about it. "Dost know, Jarge," she said, "it be our silver wedding next week? We ought to have a celebration o' sorts that day. Shall us kill the pig?" Jarge grunted. "Woman," he said, "whoi murder an innocent pig for what 'appened twenty-foive year agone?"—Half-a-crown has been awarded to H. Hanmer, 1, Scott Avenue, Chorlton-cum-Hardy, Manchester.

THEN HE FLED !

"In vain—in vain !" cried the young man distractedly. His face was deathly white, and his damp hair hung in wisps about his forehead. A crowd gathered. "In vain—in vain !" he cried again, wringing his hands and gnashing his teeth. "What?" cried the curious crowd. "What is in vain ?" "The letter ' V ' !" cried the young man, jumping on a passing omnibus.—Half-a-crown has been awarded to Edward Welch, 6, Derwentwater Road, Acton, W. 3.

SARCASM !

A very stout man mounted the scales and dropped a penny in the slot. After a furious clanking and rattling, the pointer finally came to rest not far from the twenty-five stone mark. There was an unseen witness to the ceremony, and as the big man contemplated the result, the voice of a small boy piped from behind him : "Say, mister, how many times did it go round?"—Half-a-crown has been awarded to E. V. Barwood, 41, Marlborough Road, Tue Brook, Liverpool.

SURE PROOF !

Mrs. Greene : "I hear that Mrs. Newlywed simply worships her husband." Mrs. White : "Yes : she places burnt offerings before him three times a day !"—Half-a-crown has been awarded to Miss A. Wenninger, 389, Chester Road, Old Trafford, Manchester.

This clock stands 6 feet high, keeps perfect time and is made entirely of MECCANO

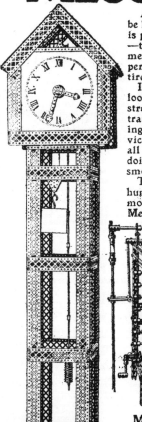

Anything that works may be built with Meccano. Here is proof in the form of a clock —that most delicate piece of mechanism—which keeps perfect time and is made entirely of Meccano.

It stands 6ft. in height and looks a realistic and beautiful structure. Look at the illustrations carefully. Note the ingenious "escapement" device, the pendulum, the gears all working correctly, each doing its work efficiently and smoothly.

This is only one of the hundreds of shining steel models that may be built with Meccano.

Wouldn't you like to build such a clock as this—or a fine steel Crane — a Tower — a Bridge, or anything you like? Ask your father for Meccano. Ask him to-day.

Enlarged Section Showing Portion of Mechanism

MECCANO PRICES :

No. 00 Outfit	3/6	No. 5 Outfit	55/-	(Carton)
No. 0	5/-	No. 5	85/-	(Oak Cabinet)
No. 1	8/6	No. 6	105/-	(Carton)
No. 2	15/-	No. 6	140/-	(Oak Cabinet)
No. 3	22/6			
No. 4	40/-			
No. 7 Outfit	370/-			
(Oak Cabinet with lock and key.)				

FREE TO BOYS

A Splendid New Meccano Book

This is a new and splendidly illustrated book that tells of all the good things that come from Meccanoland, where the best toys are manufactured. No boy should be without this wonderful book.

How to get a Free Copy

Just show this advertisment to three chums and send us their names and addresses with your own. Put No. 36 after your name for reference.

MECCANO

ENGINEERING FOR BOYS

GRAND PRIZE CONTEST

This is a model-building Competition that brings golden opportunities to brainy, inventive boys. This year we offer splendid Cups and Medals to the value of £250 for the best Meccano models. Write us for full particulars or ask your dealer for an entry form

MECCANO LTD : BINNS ROAD : LIVERPOOL

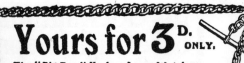

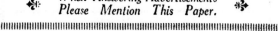

EVERY WEDNESDAY.

The GEM 2d

LIBRARY of SCHOOL and SPORTING STORIES

No. 826.
Vol. XXIV.
December 8th, 1923.

HARD LUCK FOR CARDEW!

The new junior captain, a fraction too hasty, hits the bar and fails to score! (An exciting incident from the grand school story of St. Jim's contained in this issue.)

OF INTEREST TO YOU!

My dear Chums.—It is absolutely the last chance this week to enter the grand Footballers' Names Competition. Time has been skimming along at its usual record rate, and now we are at the final opportunity. Mind nobody misses that opportunity!

"SKIPPER AND SLACKER!"
By Martin Clifford.

In next week's stirring St. Jim's yarn we see what success will do for a fellow. It is not always a desirable thing to win a position, not unless there is a grim determination to do the best possible once the goal is attained. Circumstances alter cases, as the cat said when she jumped upon the printer's frames. Cardew was keen as mustard, but once he has the captaincy in his grasp he shows a tendency to slack. Just like Cardew, that! The new skipper is not on the spot when St. Jim's is meeting the Rookwood team. He turns up late. There is trouble, of course. It is a great yarn with the real ring in it.

"THE COINERS!"
By Roland Spencer.

For next Wednesday, too, we have a treat in this exciting tale of River-wise Ned and his staunch chums, Tony Parr and Jim Cartwright. The chums knock up against some yachtsmen, and after that wonder is piled on wonder, culminating in a breathless wind up, to say nothing of a surprise for Ned and his friends, for the innocent-looking yachtsmen are not what they seem.

"THE TRIERS!"

Jack Crichton carries forward the interest in grand style next week. This writer goes all in to fascinate his readers, and there is a splendid lesson to be drawn from the fight of the fellow who, though under-dog, is set on victory.

OUR CHRISTMAS NUMBER!

This will be in your hands in a fortnight's time. It will put all former bumper numbers in the shade. It is full of star turns.

Your Editor.

Keen and clever as he may be, Cardew
has shouldered a big responsbility.

Will he justify
his position?

CAPTAIN CARDEW !

A Splendid, New, Extra-Long
Complete School Story of St.
Jim's, featuring Ralph Reckness
Cardew, the slacker of the
Fourth Form, in a new light.

BY

Martin Clifford.

CHAPTER 1.
Trimble Has to Go!

"TRIMBLE!"

"Hallo!"

"Turn out!"

"Sha'n't!"

"Wha-a-a-t!" ejaculated Tom Merry.

Trimble of the Fourth grinned. He stretched himself a
little more at ease in the armchair in his study, and repeated,
with relish:

"Sha'n't!"

Tom Merry looked at him expressively. He was standing
in the doorway of Study No. 2, in the Fourth, with a coat
on over his football clothes. He had dropped in for Trimble
on his way down to Little Side.

"I thought you'd be frowsting here, Trimble," said Tom
mildly. "I'm bound to rout you out. Come on!"

"Sha'n't!"

"Don't you know you mustn't say ' sha'n't ' to the junior
captain of St. Jim's?" asked Tom.

"Rats!"

Baggy Trimble seemed to be enjoying himself. It was the
first time he had ventured to "cheek" Tom Merry, and
apparently he felt quite safe in doing so on this occasion.

Tom stepped into the study.

He did not understand in the least upon what Baggy
Trimble's amazingly bold defiance was founded. But he
knew that he was due upon Little Side, and that Baggy had
to turn up there for games practice. Tom Merry had been
called over the coals more than once by Kildare of the Sixth
for going too easy with the slackers. And although Baggy
Trimble was as clumsy and useless at football as at everything else, it was certainly for Baggy's good that he should
go down to footer practice, instead of "frowsting" in the
study on a keen, frosty afternoon.

"Get a move on!" said Tom.

"Sha'n't!"

"Do you want me to roll you out of that chair?"

"Rats!"

"Look here, Trimble——"

"Mind your own business!"

"But this is my business," urged Tom good-naturedly;
"and it's ever so much better for you, Trimble."

"Yah!"

Tom Merry felt that he had exhausted his patience.

"Are you coming?" he demanded.

"No."

Tom Merry took a grip on the back of the chair, to tilt
the fat Fourth-Former out. Trimble gave a yell.

"Look here, you rotter—— Yarooch!"

The armchair was tilted up, and Baggy Trimble was shot
out on to the hearthrug with a heavy bump.

He sat there and roared.

"Now come on!" said Tom sharply. "I've got no time
to waste on a lazy, fat slacker."

"I won't!" roared Trimble.

"Look here, do you want me to boot you down the
stairs?" demanded Tom angrily.

"I'm not coming!" howled Trimble, glaring up at the
junior captain of St. Jim's from the hearthrug. "I'm let
off this afternoon."

"Who's let you off—Kildare?"

"Blow Kildare! No."

"The Housemaster?"

"Blow Railton! No."

"Well, nobody else can let you off," said Tom. "I suppose
the Head hasn't specially chipped in to let you slack?"

"Blow the Head! Cardew's let me off."

"Cardew!" exclaimed Tom.

Trimble sneered.

"You seem to have forgotten that Cardew of the Fourth
is junior House captain now," he said. "Wasn't he elected
the other day—junior captain of the School House? House
captain has power to let any fellow off games practice if he
chooses."

Tom Merry paused.

More than once, since Ralph Reckness Cardew had been
elected junior House captain in the School House of St.
Jim's, Tom Merry had found that Cardew's new powers
interfered with his own.

The dividing line, indeed, was not clearly marked.

Certainly it was Tom Merry's duty, as junior captain of
the school, to round up the slackers on the days when games
practice was compulsory. He was answerable to Kildare,
senior captain, for that, and Kildare expected him to do his
duty.

Nevertheless, it was undoubtedly within the power of
junior House captain to let a fellow off, subject to the
approval of the captain of the school—Kildare, of the Sixth.

In the New House Figgins was House captain of the
juniors, and Tom Merry never, as a matter of fact, intervened in that House. Figgy could be relied upon to do his
duty.

With Cardew it was a different matter.

There was a pause, and Baggy Trimble, still sitting on the
hearthrug, blinked triumphantly at Tom Merry.

"Cardew can let any fellow off that he chooses," he went
on. "Only Kildare of the Sixth can stop him. And Kildare
never interferes, as you know jolly well. Cardew's given me
leave to cut football practice this afternoon."

"Has he?" said Tom slowly. "For what reason?"

"I'm not bound to tell you that," jeered Trimble. "Still,
I don't mind mentioning that I've got a pain."

"Where have you got the pain?" asked Tom.

"In my—my—my back."

"Do you want another in your ear?"

"Eh?"

"Because if you don't you'd better get a move on," said
Tom. "You're coming down to footer practice, Trimble."

"Cardew says——"

"Never mind what Cardew says," said Tom Merry quietly.
"It's what I say that matters just now. Get a move on!"

"Look here——"

THE GEM LIBRARY.—No. 826.

"Are you coming?"

"No!" yelled Trimble desperately.

Tom Merry stooped and took the fat junior by the collar. With a swing of his powerful arm, he rolled Baggy out into the passage. Then, with the help of his football boots, he dribbled Baggy along to the stairs, to the accompaniment of a series of fiendish yells from Baggy Trimble.

"Yow-ow-ow-ow-ow!"

"Bai Jove!" Arthur Augustus D'Arcy came out of Study No. 6. "What's the feahful wow, deah boy?"

"Help!" roared Trimble.

"Baggy thinks he going to frowst, and I think he isn't!" explained Tom Merry.

"Yarooh!" roared Trimble. "I've got leave from the junior House captain, D'Arcy. Honour bright. I'm ill, you know. Tom Merry's got no right to interfere with me. He can ask Cardew. Yaroooh!"

"I'm not likely to ask Cardew anything," said Tom. "Roll on, or I'll roll you!"

"Bai Jove! I weally think, Tom Mewwy, that you had bettah go slow, you know," said Arthur Augustus D'Arcy thoughtfully. "Cardew is only actin' within his powahs in lettin' Twimble off."

"Rot!"

"You can weport the mattah to the captain of the school, and head of the games, if you are not satisfied, you know," said Arthur Augustus. "I believe that is the wule."

"No time to bother," said Tom. "Get on, Trimble!"

"I weally considah, Tom Mewwy——"

"Oh, bow-wow!"

Tom Merry's boot came into contact with Baggy Trimble's fat person again, and Baggy roared and bolted down the stairs. Tom Merry followed him grimly.

"I give you two minutes to change," he said.

Baggy changed in a very few minutes. He had had enough of football boots applied to his person. He had relied upon the protection of the junior House captain, but Ralph Reckness Cardew was not there to protect him now. Baggy rolled out of the School House with a furious fat face, and Tom Merry walked after him, to see him safely down to Little Side.

Arthur Augustus D'Arcy followed on, shaking his noble head seriously. Arthur Augustus, who was a fellow of tact and judgment, had foreseen trouble when Cardew "wedged" in as junior House captain in the House; and the trouble, which had already threatened more than once, was evidently at hand now. And Arthur Augustus wondered what would come of it.

CHAPTER 2.
Face to Face!

RALPH RECKNESS CARDEW smiled.

It was not a pleasant smile.

He looked very handsome, and very fit, as he stood on the junior football ground in shorts and jersey. Certainly, since Cardew of the Fourth had thrown himself keenly into St. Jim's junior football, he looked a good deal changed from his old lazy, loafing self. Since he had been elected House captain nobody could have complained of Cardew as a slacker.

Indeed, many fellows suspected that he regarded the House captaincy as only a step, and that his real aim was the junior captaincy of the School, now held by Tom Merry.

Tom had held both posts, and filled them well, and it was very probable that Cardew aimed at following in his footsteps in that direction. And Tom, excellent footballer and excellent skipper as he was, was not exactly the fellow to hold his own against the wiles of an insidious enemy.

Levison and Clive, Cardew's chums, had not backed him in his campaign against Tom Merry. But now he was junior House captain they gave him their support. They were not insensible to the honour of having the House captain chosen from their study and from their Form. And indeed, most of the Fourth had veered round to the side of Cardew now that he had proved himself keen and dutiful. Jack Blake had long maintained that the Fourth ought to have a better show in things generally. Herries and Dig and D'Arcy agreed with him, and as Cardew was in the Fourth they felt that he was entitled to their support so long as he played up for the House. Had Cardew kept up his old slacking ways they would have been down on him fast enough. But Cardew seemed to have turned over a new leaf in that respect, and Study No. 6 was not disposed to hunt for faults.

Levison and Clive were on Little Side with their chum. They noted that peculiar smile on Cardew's face, and followed his glance, to discover the cause. And they sighted Baggy Trimble, rolling unwillingly down to the football ground with Tom Merry walking after him, and Arthur Augustus D'Arcy bringing up the rear.

"That fat slacker's been routed out," said Clive with a laugh. "You ought to have done that, Cardew."

"I!" repeated Cardew.

"Certainly! It's compulsory games practice to-day. Now you're junior House captain you mustn't overlook these things, you know."

"Or leave them to Tom Merry," added Levison. "Of course, he has to see to it if you don't, but it's really up to you now."

Cardew looked whimsically at his chums.

"You see, I'd let Trimble off," he said.

"Let him off?"

"Yes. The poor fellow had a pain, and wasn't fit for footer to-day. So I excused him from games practice."

Ernest Levison looked very grave.

"Did you mention that to Tom Merry?" he asked.

"Why should I?"

"Trimble was pulling your leg," said Sidney Clive abruptly. "He's always got some sneaking excuse for cutting games."

Cardew laughed.

"I'm bound to take a fellow's word," he answered.

"Not Trimble's."

"Well, even Trimble is entitled to be believed, unless he's proved to be a liar," said Cardew. "I took his word."

Sidney Clive looked hard at him. The quiet, straightforward South African junior was unlike Cardew in most ways, and he did not always find it easy to understand his chum.

"I suppose you knew Tom Merry would make the rounds and rout him out?" he remarked.

"Thomas is so dutiful!" sighed Cardew.

"Dash it all, Cardew! A suspicious fellow might think that you'd wangled this with Trimble, for the sake of picking trouble with Tom Merry!" exclaimed Clive.

"Dear me!" exclaimed Cardew. "Surely there aren't any fellows at St. Jim's so suspicious as that?"

"Well, I must say it might look like it."

"I hope not," said Cardew gravely.

Levison looked troubled. He was far keener than the straightforward, unsuspicious Clive, and he was perfectly well aware, on the spot, that Cardew was seeking trouble with the junior captain, on a matter where it was possible to place Tom in the wrong.

"Cardew!" yelled Trimble, as he came breathlessly up.

"Hallo, fat old bean! Is your pain any better?" asked Cardew.

"Ow! No."

"But you've come down to footer," said Cardew. "I suppose you feel fit, or you wouldn't have come?"

"I didn't want to come!" shrieked Trimble. "Look here, Cardew, I've been kicked——"

"Hard, I hope!" interjected Monty Lowther.

"You're likely to be kicked again if you don't stop yowling like a tom cat on the tiles," exclaimed Manners.

"Yah! I say, Cardew, I'm let off, ain't I?"

"Certainly!"

"You hear that, Tom Merry?" yelled Trimble.

"You're not let off," said Tom Merry decidedly. "I've told you that, Trimble. You've got to play up!"

"I won't!"

"You will!"

"Excuse me," interrupted Cardew in his silkiest tone. "Trimble informed me that he wasn't fit for footer to-day, and I let him off, Merry."

Tom looked at Cardew steadily.

"Trimble should have told you that," added Cardew. "But it's all right, now I've mentioned it, isn't it? You can cut off, Trimble."

"Stay where you are, Trimble!" said Tom Merry.

Trimble blinked from one to the other. His terror of Tom Merry was great, and he was not quite sure of Cardew's power to protect him. He stood irresolute.

The junior footballers gathered round, some of them with very serious faces. The tug-of-war between the rivals of the School House was evidently beginning.

"I don't want a row about this, Merry," said Cardew, urbane as ever. "But I'm afraid I must insist upon Trimble goin'."

"I insist upon his staying!"

"Let it drop, Cardew!" muttered Levison.

"Can't be done; it's a matter of principle," said Cardew calmly. "You know how hefty you are on principle, Ernest, old bean. Don't advise me to go back on my principles."

Levison shrugged his shoulders helplessly. He was aware that Ralph Reckness Cardew was out for mischief, and that there was no stopping him.

"Trimble will leave the field," went on Cardew. "As junior House captain, I have accepted his word that he is seedy to-day, and unfit for games practice."

"You know that that is only a lying excuse," said Tom Merry contemptuously.

"I don't know anythin' of the kind," said Cardew coolly. "Last practice Blake told me his ankle was crocked, and

"Pick up for sides, you fellows!" said Tom Merry. "Trimble, you are to line up with the rest." "I say he is not to!" said Cardew, and he slipped his arm through the fat junior's. "I will see you safe off the field." Tom Merry stepped in the way. "Stand away from Trimble, Cardew," he said between his teeth, "or I shall knock you away!"
(See this page.)

he never turned up. Ought I to have told Blake he was a liar?"

"That's quite a different matter. Blake isn't a slacker, like Trimble, and can be trusted."

"Perhaps I'm of so trustin' a nature that I feel I can trust Trimble," smiled Cardew. "Anyhow, I have the authority, as junior House captain, to accept his excuse. If you are not satisfied, you have to report the matter to the head of the games. That's Kildare of the Sixth."

Tom Merry breathed hard.

Cardew was right, technically; but in actual practice it was quite impossible for every trifling dispute to be reported to the captain of the school for judgment. To avoid endless disputes and recriminations, it was necessary for House captain and school captain to pull together in trifling matters at least; and Cardew made it quite plain that he did not intend to pull with Tom Merry. Certainly the senior captain would soon have become "fed-up" if two junior captains had incessantly brought trifles light as air before his judgment-seat. The fellows looked on silently.

Even Manners and Lowther had nothing to say; they felt that Cardew had succeeded in placing Tom in a false position. He could scarcely give way; and yet Cardew was technically right in standing to his point.

"I'm perfectly willin' to refer the matter to Kildare," said Cardew blandly. "In the meantime, Trimble clears off."

"Trimble does not clear off," said Tom.

"My dear fellow——" urged Cardew.

"We'd better have this out plain, Cardew," said Tom Merry quietly. "I haven't your way of beating about the bush, and laying little traps for more straightforward fellows to fall into. Let's put it into plain English. You know that Trimble is slacking, and you pretend to believe his excuses, simply to take a rise out of me. Isn't that it?"

"You can tell Kildare you think so, if you choose," yawned Cardew. "I hope I may be able to make my case good."

"The matter is not going before Kildare. I've brought Trimble down here for games practice, and that ends it."

"It doesn't end it. I say he's excused."

"I say he is not."

"Weally, you fellows——" murmured Arthur Augustus D'Arcy, in distress.

The rivals of the School House were facing one another now, both of them looking rather grim, though Cardew still kept a smile on his face. Trimble edged nearer and nearer to his protector.

Cardew raised his hand.

"Cut off, Trimble."

"Pick up sides, you fellows," said Tom Merry. "Trimble, you are to line up with the rest."

"I will see you safe off the field, Trimble," said Cardew, and he slipped his arm through the fat junior's.

Tom Merry stepped in the way.

"Stand away from Trimble, Cardew," he said, between his teeth.

"Sorry, can't be done."

"I shall knock you away, if you don't!"

"Dear me!"

"Tom——" murmured Monty Lowther.

Tom Merry did not heed. It was not often that he was angry; but he was angry now, and his blue eyes were blazing.

"You hear me, Cardew?"

"I'm not deaf, dear man."

"Stand aside."

Cardew shrugged his shoulders, and did not move. Tom Merry advanced on him, and there was a buzz among the footballers.

"Tom!" called out Talbot of the Shell.

Cardew stood like a rock, and Tom Merry came at him. The dandy of the Fourth put his hands up just in time.

"You will have it, then," said Tom.

The next moment they were fighting. Games practice was quite forgotten now, as the junior footballers gathered round eagerly to stare at the fight.

CHAPTER 3.
Tom Merry Resigns !

"BAI Jove! This is weally wotten!" murmured Arthur Augustus D'Arcy.

Tramp, tramp, tramp!

Crash !

Cardew of the Fourth went heavily to the ground. There was a crimson stream from his nose, as he lay there.

He lay panting for some moments.

Tom Merry stood and looked at him grimly, waiting for him to rise. Blake of the Fourth called out suddenly:

"Here comes Kildare!"

Kildare of the Sixth was on Big Side with a number of seniors at football practice. Evidently he had seen the startling occurrence on Little Side, for he had left his companions, and he came striding over to the junior ground with a deep frown on his brow.

Cardew staggered to his feet and dabbed his streaming nose. He gave Tom Merry a bitter, evil look.

It was a galling reflection to Cardew that it was only in cunning and clever trickery that he was the master of his rival. When it came to blows, he had to take the second place.

The crowd of juniors opened for Kildare to reach the spot.

Kildare gave the combatants a grim look.

"Is this games practice?" he demanded.

"Yaas, Kildare!" murmured Arthur Augustus.

"Who's in charge here?"

"I am," said Tom.

"And you are fighting with Cardew?"

"Yes."

"Very well! I want to know what the trouble is," said the captain of St. Jim's. "This won't do, Tom Merry."

Tom was silent.

"It's a dispute between House captain and junior captain," said Talbot of the Shell. "It's really nothing, Kildare."

"House captain and junior captain can't fight out their disputes on the football field," said Kildare. "The point in dispute should have been referred to me as head of the games. You know that, I suppose, Cardew?"

"Of course, Kildare."

"Then why didn't you——"

"Merry refused."

"Oh!" said Kildare, rather taken aback. "And what was the point in dispute?"

Tom Merry did not speak. He was deeply incensed, and he disdained to enter into a wrangle, justifying himself. But Ralph Reckness Cardew had no such objection. Tom Merry had, in fact, played into his hands by the line he had taken, and Cardew intended to take full advantage of the fact.

"Trimble informed me that he was seedy and unable to join in games practice to-day, Kildare. As junior House captain, I let him off."

"The slacker was very likely pulling your leg," said Kildare, with a glance of strong disfavour at Baggy.

"Well, I felt bound to take his word," said Cardew. "He looked rather seedy, I thought."

"And then Tom Merry kicked me out and bundled me down here, and I've got an awful pain!" said Trimble pathetically.

"You should have told Merry you were let off."

"I did!"

"Oh!" said Kildare, again taken aback. "And why did you bundle him down here, then, Merry?"

"I knew he was lying," said Tom scornfully. "I knew, too, that Cardew knew he was lying."

"I don't think you have a right to assume that," said Kildare tartly. "But any dispute between junior captains has to be referred to the head of the games for decision. You know that?"

"Yes."

"Well, then——"

"Oh, I'm in the wrong!" said Tom bitterly. "I'm in the wrong for not referring the matter to you, and I should have been in the wrong if I'd let Trimble frowst in his study all the afternoon, and I should be in the wrong if I came to you every half-hour with a complaint about Cardew interfering with me. I don't claim to be able to keep my end up against a treacherous cad who is trying to trip me."

"Hear, hear!" murmured Kangaroo.

Cardew crimsoned.

To do him justice, he did not realise how his line of action must look to a plain, direct fellow like Tom Merry; and Tom's description of it startled him a little.

Kildare knitted his brows.

"That's not the way to talk, Merry!" he rapped out. "It seems to me that you are stepping over into Cardew's province, and taking his duties on your own shoulders."

"I suppose you think so," said Tom. "I know I'm not going to argue about it."

"What?"

"This isn't the beginning, and it won't be the end!" said Tom Merry. "If Cardew remains junior House captain, and I remain junior school captain, something like this will happen every day. I shall be in the right, and Cardew will make it appear that I am in the wrong. It will be a rotten thing for the House. The two jobs ought to be held by the same man."

"I don't see that. Figgins is junior House captain in the New House, and no trouble has come of it."

"Cardew's rather different from Figgins. I have had plenty of rows with Figgins, but he's an honourable chap and would be ashamed to take mean advantages."

"And I'm not?" exclaimed Cardew.

Tom looked at him steadily.

"No; you're not," he answered. "You don't care what happens to the House, or to the school, so long as you score a point over a fellow you've made your enemy. You'd be willing to see St. Jim's lose every match this season to gain some mean little advantage for yourself!"

Cardew winced.

"Dash it all, that's a bit too strong!" exclaimed Clive angrily. "That sort of talk won't do any good, Tom Merry."

"Weally, Tom Mewwy, you know——"

"That's enough!" rapped out Kildare. "I think I had better warn you, Merry——"

"No need," said Tom coolly. "I can see as well as you that this won't do. The next trouble will be about the House matches, with Cardew pulling one way and myself pulling another. Then the school matches and the rest of it. The sooner it stops the better, and there only one way. I resign the junior captaincy!"

"Tom!" shouted Lowther.

"If you mean that, Merry——" began Kildare.

"I do mean it, and I sha'n't stand for re-election. The fellows have chosen Cardew for House captain, and we can't pull together. They can e.ect him junior captain of the school, and things can't go much worse. Anyhow, I stand out."

"If you are determined not to pull with Cardew, perhaps that's about the best thing you can do," said Kildare rather gruffly. "Anyhow, I'll leave it till this evening before I accept your resignation and put up the notice."

"No need to leave it a minute; I mean what I say."

"Very well."

With that Kildare turned and walked away, leaving the juniors in a buzz of excitement.

Tom Merry's friends gathered round him in great dismay. His resolve had come as a surprise and a shock to all of them.

"You ass, Tom!" muttered Manners. "You've played right into Cardew's hands now."

"It was the best thing to do," said Tom briefly. "Let's get on with the footer!"

Cardew smiled.

"Trimble!" he called out.

"Yes, Cardew?"

"Cut off!"

Baggy Trimble gladly rolled off the field. There was no one now to say him nay.

Ralph Reckness Cardew assumed the direction of the football practice. When Darrell of the Sixth came on to Little Side to take charge, he found more talking than football going on, however. After it was over Cardew walked back to the School House with Levison and Clive, with a smile on his face.

His victory had come suddenly, unexpectedly.

He had looked for a long struggle that would have called for all his cleverness, all his cunning, all his artifice. And, instead of that, his rival had thrown the victory into his hands.

Cardew could scarcely understand it.

But he rejoiced in his success, and he intended to push it on to the limit. He was House captain already, and if Tom Merry kept his word and stood out of the election, Cardew had no doubt whatever that he would be elected junior captain. It was all that he had aimed at—all that he had dreamed of—to drive out Tom Merry and take his place, and attain the highest position that a Lower boy could obtain in the school.

"Dear old Thomas!" he remarked. "He's disappointed me

"You know, Tom Merry," said Kildare tartly, **"that any dispute between junior captains has to be referred to the head of the games for decision. I think I had better warn you that——"** **"No need,"** said Tom Merry coolly. **"There's only one thing I can do, and that is to resign the junior captaincy, and you can accept my resignation now !"** *(See page 6.)*

a little. I never thought he would give in so easily. A victory is better than a fight, I suppose, but it's not so excitin'."

"You'll be putting up for the place?" asked Clive.

"Well, just a few."

"I dare say you'll get in," said Levison.

"You're backin' me?"

"Not if Tom Merry puts up again," said Levison.

"He says he won't!"

"If he doesn't I shall back you. I believe you'd make a good junior captain—if you tried!"

"Oh, I'll try!" said Cardew.

"It's not an easy job. There's not much room for slacking in a man taking Tom Merry's place."

"Have I been slackin' lately?"

"Well, not lately," admitted Levison, "but a fellow never knows how long you will stick to a thing, Cardew. You'll simply have to live and breathe football this season. I suppose you know that the junior captain is always junior football captain. We shall have you captaining the team in House and School matches; the football committee are bound to follow the usual rule."

"Then there'll always be two places in the team for you and Clive," said Cardew.

"Only on our form, I hope," said Sidney Clive quietly.

"How jolly particular we are!" smiled Cardew. "Now, I believe with jolly old Themistocles—was it Themistocles?—that a man in power ought always to remember his friends."

"Rot!" broke in the voice of Grundy of the Shell, who was following the three into the changing-room. "You ought to play a man on his form, Cardew, or not at all."

Cardew glanced round.

"You'd like to be played on your form, and nothin' else, Grundy?" he asked, smiling.

"Yes, rather!" answered George Alfred Grundy emphatically.

"I'll remember that when it comes to handing out places in the eleven."

"Do!" said Grundy.

Cardew laughed, and went in to change. The room was in a buzz of discussion, and the one topic was Tom Merry's resignation, and the possibilities it opened to his ambitious rival.

CHAPTER 4.
Victory!

"TOM, old man——"

Monty Lowther spoke in a tone more of sorrow than of anger. Tom looked up with a smile as Monty came into Study No. 10 with Manners.

"I must say you're an awful ass, Tom," said Lowther.

"Frightful!" assented Manners.

"How do you make that out?" asked the captain of the Shell.

"You've played into Cardew's hands."

"I know."

"Oh, you know!" exclaimed Lowther.

"Yes." Tom Merry spoke quietly. "I know what Cardew was playing for, and I've let the thing go. It was for the best. When he got in as House captain he got enough power in his hands to muck up everything for the House, and he would have stopped at nothing. He will do less harm as junior captain than as House captain trying all the time to muck things up and make trouble. I suppose even Cardew will have the decency to do his best for the House, when he's got what he wants."

"So you chucked in your resignation for the sake of the House!" said Manners.

"Yes."

"Well, you're an old ass, Tom," said Lowther. "I'd have fought Cardew tooth and nail, and if the House went to pot in the process, the House could thank itself."

"You wouldn't, old fellow," said Tom, with a smile. "The House comes first; and Cardew mayn't make a bad captain of the House and the school. Luckily, there will always be the senior captain over him. But he's a good footballer when he chooses, and he's got an eye for a fellow's form. He ought to be able to win matches."

"But if you don't play in his team——"

"I hardly think Cardew will carry the feud as far as that. Besides, the football committee would have something to say to leaving me out."

"I don't mean that! I—I thought that you wouldn't care to play under Cardew's captaincy."

"Rot!" said Tom. "I shall play if I am asked. My personal feelings towards Cardew haven't anything to do with the footer, I suppose?"

"Well, no; but——"

Monty Lowther paused, and gave his chum rather a queer look.

"Do you know what you're doing?" he asked. "If you play up and get your friends to play up, you'll make Cardew's captaincy a success, after he's ousted you."

"Well, I want to make it a success."

"You want to?" yelled Lowther.

"Of course," said Tom, "if Cardew fails to pull the fellows together, we shall have a pretty rotten season. We don't want to lose House matches to the New House, and, above all, we don't want to lose School matches to the Grammarians, and Rookwood, and Highcliffe, and the rest. And we don't want the fellows at loggerheads, do we?"

"If Cardew were in your place he would think of nothing but mucking up things for the fellow who ousted him."

"Possibly. But I hope I sha'n't think of anything of the kind. If Cardew makes a good captain, he can rely on me to play up."

"Tommy, old man, you're a bit too good for this world," said Manners. "I shall expect to see you sprouting wings shortly."

"Fathead!" said Tom, laughing.

And the subject dropped in Study No. 10, and the Terrible Three of the Shell gave their attention to prep. Prep was interrupted a little later, however, by the arrival of Arthur Augustus D'Arcy. His noble face looked in at the doorway.

"You fellows know?" he asked.

"Who, what, and which?" inquired Lowther.

"The notice is up on the board. Election for juniah captain on Wednesday," said Arthur Augustus. "I heah that there is feahful excitement in the New House."

"There would be!" agreed Lowther.

"The New House boundahs are goin' in for it—they hope to get in Figgins as juniah captain of St. Jim's," said Arthur Augustus. "Of course, we can't have that. It would be a feahful disastah to have a New House wottah ovah us."

"Figgins would make a good captain," said Tom Merry.

"I twust you have some House patwiotism, Tom Mewwy," said the swell of the School House, with dignity.

"Figgins won't get in," said Manners. "As soon as there's a New House candidate in the field, the School House will stand together as one man, to make sure of the House candidate."

"Yaas, wathah! Are you puttin' up again, Tom Mewwy?"

"No."

"Suah of that, deah boy?"

"Quite sure."

"Cardew is up, of course," said Arthur Augustus. "I was thinkin' of puttin' up myself; but Cardew wefuses to withdwaw in my favah. I think it is wathah selfish of him, but there you are! As he will not back me up, I shall back him up, to make suah of keepin' the New House man out."

"Good man!" said Lowther. "I'd rather vote even for Cardew than for a New House outsider. After all, he's a School House chap."

"Yaas, wathah!"

Arthur Augustus retired, to give as much of his time to prep as he could spare for such trifles, in the present exciting state of affairs.

Levison of the Fourth looked in after prep.

"You're standing down in the election, Merry?" he asked.

"Yes."

"If you put up, I'm backing you."

"Thanks; I'm not putting up."

"Then I'm for Cardew. We've got to keep out the New House man."

After Levison had gone, Tom Merry went into Talbot's study, where he found Talbot and Gore and Skimpole. Gore was talking—in a loud and positive voice, as usual.

"You've got to back up Cardew, Talbot! I tell you you've got to. Do you want to risk a New House man getting in?"

"I'm not backing Cardew," said Talbot quietly. He nodded to Tom Merry in the doorway. "I wish you'd put up again, Tom."

"I came here to say the same to you," said Tom Merry, with a smile.

"To me!" exclaimed Talbot.

"That's it! I'm conceited enough to think that I made a fairly good captain——"

"The best," said Talbot.

"But I think you're as good a man, and I'd like to see you get in, Talbot. You might be able to pull with Cardew better than I did—you've got a lot more tact than I have," said Tom, rather ruefully, "and Cardew isn't up against you personally, as he is against me."

Talbot shook his head.

"It's a good idea, Talbot!" exclaimed George Gore eagerly. "I'll back you. You'd knock Cardew out—you're awfully popular, even in the New House."

"I'm not going to stand," said Talbot briefly, "and if Tom does not put up, I shall not vote."

"Then it's Cardew," said Gore. "We've got to keep the New House out."

"There is one solution of this somewhat abstruse problem that does not seem to have occurred to you, my friends," said Skimpole, blinking at the juniors through his spectacles.

"And what's that?" snapped Gore.

"Too much attention, I think, is bestowed upon mere trifling games such as football and cricket, and so forth," said the learned Skimpole seriously. "A fellow of a more scientific turn of mind would, in my estimation, make a superior junior captain. I was reflecting upon the possibility of offering myself as a candidate."

"Ha, ha, ha!" roared Gore.

"My dear Gore, I see no occasion for that outbreak of risibility in my observation," said Skimpole, in surprise.

"Ha, ha, ha!"

Tom Merry smiled as he left the study. Herbert Skimpole was not likely to be taken seriously as a candidate. As Tom walked down the passage, several voices hailed him, to inquire whether he was, after all, putting up for re-election on Wednesday. The reply being in the negative, there was an evidently unanimous decision to vote for Cardew. On one point, at least, the School House fellows were united—a New House bounder wasn't going to get in as junior captain of St. Jim's if they could help it. As the School House was, numerically, by far the larger House, there was no doubt that they could help it if they stood together.

So willy-nilly, as it were, all the Lower School boys in the School House were turned into Cardewites. A rival School House candidate would simply have split the House vote, and given the New House man a chance of slipping in. So the bare idea of a rival candidate was frowned upon on all sides; and even Tom Merry, after reflection, decided to vote for Cardew when the poll was taken.

Over in the New House, Figgins & Co. were hoping to hear of division in the opposite camp. But they did not hear of it; the School House stood together.

The result was a foregone conclusion.

On Wednesday, when the election was held, there were only two candidates for the junior captaincy—Cardew, School House, and George Figgins, New House. It was turned into a purely House contest; every School House voter rolled up for Cardew, and every New House man held up his hand for Figgins. After which, it only remained for Kildare to announce that Ralph Reckness Cardew, of the Fourth Form, was elected junior captain of St. Jim's by a bumping majority.

CHAPTER 5.

Not G. A. Grundy!

"GOOD!" said Grundy of the Shell.

Grundy of the Shell was satisfied.

He looked satisfied.

Wilkins and Gunn, his study-mates, glanced at him and smiled. They were wondering just how long Grundy's satisfaction would last.

Grundy of the Shell, the worst footballer that ever was, had had a perennial source of complaint in the circumstance that Tom Merry never would play him either for House or School—not even in a Form match.

Grundy's complaints had reached all ears, and caused laughter on many an occasion. In football matters at St. Jim's it was Grundy who furnished the comic relief.

Grundy had backed up Cardew of the Fourth through thick and thin, first in the election for House captain, secondly in the election of junior captain of the school. He had voted for Cardew; he had threatened his pals with the direst penalties if they did not vote for Cardew; he had left no stone unturned to get Cardew in.

Now Cardew was in, and Grundy was satisfied. Now that there was a new junior captain, Grundy's claims were going to be recognised at last—according to Grundy.

"It's good!" said Grundy. "Jolly good! Last Wednesday's election was the best thing that ever happened at St. Jim's."

"Was it?" murmured Wilkins.

"Yes. Now, to-day's Friday," said Grundy. "The list

will be up for the match with the Grammar School soon. It's to-morrow, you know."

"We know," assented Gunn.

"For the first time, St. Jim's will see the name of its really finest footballer in the list!" said Grundy impressively.

"Tom Merry generally plays, doesn't he?" murmured Wilkins.

"I'm not alluding to Tom Merry."

"Oh! You mean Talbot——"

"I don't mean Talbot!" roared Grundy.

"Blake?" said Wilkins, persisting in misunderstanding. "Well, Blake's a good man for the Fourth, but I should hardly call him the finest footballer at St. Jim's."

"Not Blake, you thundering ass!"

"Figgins?" asked Wilkins. Wilkins' misunderstanding was really inexcusable. "Well, I think Figgins——"

"You're a crass ass, Wilkins. If you knew anything about football, you'd know that the finest footballer at St. Jim's is to be found in this study!" snorted Grundy.

"You flatter me, old chap!" murmured Wilkins modestly.

"You!" yelled Grundy.

"Don't you mean me?"

"Of course I don't!"

"I mean me!" shrieked Grundy.

"Oh, my hat! Do you?"

"Yes, I do!" roared Grundy. "And if I have any more funny back-chat, George Wilkins, I'm prepared to mop up the carpet with your face!"

Grundy jumped to his feet in great excitement. Wilkins soothed him with a gesture, as if he were a baby.

"All serene, old man! All right. You're the finest footballer at St. Jim's, not excepting any of the Fifth or Sixth."

"I suppose you mean that to be funny; but, as a matter of fact, you've got it," said Grundy. "I should like to see the fellow in the Fifth or Sixth who plays football as I do."

"There isn't one!" said Gunn, with a private wink at Wilkins.

"I know there isn't," said Grundy. "I'm not a fellow, I hope, to brag——"

"Oh gum!" ejaculated Wilkins involuntarily.

"Bragging isn't in my line," said Grundy, with a ferocious glare at his chums. "But I don't believe in false modesty. I state the facts. I happen to be the finest footballer that St. Jim's ever turned out, and I see no harm in saying so. And now Tom Merry's laid on the shelf, where he ought to have been long ago, I'm coming into my right—like the king in the song, you know, coming into his own."

"Oh, yes! Oh—hem!" gasped Wilkins. "Just like that. I see!"

"Cardew's a cheeky sort of cad and a dashed slacker, and I don't say that I approve of him," went on Grundy. "But Cardew's got this quality, he's got an eye to a fellow's form at games. Now that Cardew is junior captain, I shall be down to play in matches."

"Oh, will you?"

"That's arranged."

"Phew! Better not say so outside this study," said Gunn. "It would look a good bit like bribery and corruption at elections."

"Don't be a silly owl, Gunny! I don't mean that Cardew has offered me a place in the eleven as the price of my support. I should punch any fellow's head who made such an offer, as you know jolly well. What I mean to say is, that at last we've got a junior captain who knows a fellow's form. That's all that's needed."

"Oh! So you think Cardew will play you, Grundy?"

"Naturally! In fact, he's as good as said so. He said distinctly that when it came to handing out places in the eleven he would remember a hint I gave him, that a fellow ought to be played on his form, and nothing else. See?"

Wilkins and Gunn gazed at Grundy. It could hardly be

said that Cardew had deceived him, to obtain his support in the election. Grundy had been so ready to deceive himself that there was no need for Cardew to deceive. Certainly, Cardew had allowed him to deceive himself to the top of his bent. No doubt he had been laughing in his sleeve all the time at the egregious Grundy. Grundy's belief that he could play football, and that he was certain of a place in the eleven if only he got justice, was really almost pathetic. Cardew had undertaken to give him justice; that was all. Grundy did not yet know the kind of justice he was going to get.

Wilkins and Gunn could guess. They knew that a football captain who began by playing fellows like Grundy would not keep his post long. In fact, it was absolutely certain that Cardew had no more idea of putting Grundy into the team than of putting in Baggy Trimble or Taggles the porter.

Grundy's chums wondered what would happen when this knowledge dawned upon the powerful brain of George Alfred.

Grundy strolled to the door of the study. He was in an eminently satisfied mood. Already, in his mind's eye, he saw the name of G. A. Grundy figuring in the football-list. It really was unfortunate that he was never likely to see it with any other eye.

"I—I say, old chap," murmured Wilkins, "I—I wouldn't make too sure of it, if I were you."

Wilkins really felt a touch of compassion in advance for Grundy's inevitable disappointment.

"Oh, you're an ass, Wilkins, old man! Come along and see the list, and you'll see my name there," said Grundy.

And he walked out of the study.

Wilkins and Gunn exchanged glances and followed him. They did not expect in the least to find Grundy's name in the list, but they were curious to know what would happen when Grundy failed to find it there.

Quite a little crowd was gathered before the notice-board when the three Shell fellows arrived there.

The list for the Grammar School match was Cardew's first official step since he had taken over Tom Merry's post. Naturally, it created a great deal of interest.

Many fellows who would have expected to play under Tom's leadership were doubtful whether Cardew would acknowledge their claims. It was not likely that the new captain would see eye to eye with the old. And it was certain that all Cardew's backers would feel that they had a claim on him, and it was difficult to see how Cardew could elude them.

The list came rather as a surprise, and as a relief to most of the junior footballers. Cardew was beginning cautiously. If he meant to make changes, he was in no hurry to make them. Tom Merry's name was conspicuous in the list as centre-forward. Some of the fellows wondered that Tom consented to play under his supplanter—others wondered that Cardew was willing to play him. But there was the name, and all the footballers were glad to see it there. A St. Jim's junior team with Tom Merry missing would have been a good deal like "Hamlet" with the Prince of Denmark left out.

The noble name of Arthur Augustus D'Arcy was there. Blake's name was there. Talbot, of course, was there, and Figgins of the New House. Fatty Wynn was down to keep goal. Ernest Levison was there, and Sidney Clive as centre-half. They were Cardew's chums, but Tom Merry had played Levison often enough, and Clive had figured several times in matches, so there could be no suspicion of favouritism. Lowther, Kangaroo, and Cardew himself made up the rest.

Only two of the men belonged to the New House—a circumstance that might cause a little soreness "over the way." But that circumstance rather won approval in the School House. One or two of the men were given changes in position, but really that was all there was to distinguish the team from a team picked out by Tom Merry himself.

Certainly the name of G. A. Grundy was nowhere to be found.

Grundy read the list twice carefully, with puckered brows and a very puzzled expression. Wilkins and Gunn smiled at one another. The crowd of fellows before the board commented freely on the list, and generally the comments were favourable.

"Might have put Herries in goal," remarked Jack Blake. "But Fatty Wynn is all right, though he's a New House bounder."

"Yaas, wathah!" concurred Arthur Augustus. "It weally would not do to make it wholly a House team to play a School match."

"They'll be grousing in the New House," remarked Digby. "They think Redfern ought to have a show."

"Well, Reddy's a good man," said Blake. "Might have given him Clive's place; but, after all, Clive's all right."

"Fellow must stand by his friends!" remarked Racke of the Shell.

"Oh, rot! Not in footer!" said Blake.

"Wathah not! I weally should have liked to see one or two more New House men in the eleven."

"Easy enough!" sneered Racke. "Get out of it, and let Kerr or Reddy have your place."

"I wegard that suggestion, Wacke, as uttah wot, and only displayin' your uttah ignowance of football!"

"This is jolly queer!" said Grundy.

"I don't see that!" said Talbot of the Shell. "I must say it's a good list, and better than I looked for."

"My name isn't there."

"Your name!" ejaculated Talbot.

"Yes, mine!"

Talbot smiled, and some of the fellows chuckled.

"You see, Grundy, this is a football match!" said Kangaroo. "I'm sure Cardew would have put your name down it it had been marbles or hopscotch! But it's footer!"

"Ha, ha, ha!"

"I'm going to see Cardew about this," said Grundy, unheeding. "I suppose it's only a mistake, but it's a mistake that's got to be set right!"

And George Alfred Grundy, with a knitted brow, started for Study No. 9 in the Fourth to have that mistake set right, leaving the crowd of juniors chortling.

CHAPTER 6.
Alas for Grundy !

RALPH RECKNESS CARDEW was toying with prep in Study No. 9, while Clive and Levison were working. Prep always bored Cardew more or less; of late it bored him more than ever. Undoubtedly since Cardew had entered upon his contest with Tom Merry, he had given up slacking at games. He had compensated himself, as it were, by slacking at work. Mr. Lathom, the master of the Fourth, was growing to regard him with a severe eye, and he was beginning to reap a harvest of lines and detentions. It was Cardew's way never to be keen on more than one thing at a time; he followed his latest wayward fancy where ever it led him, and let other matters "slide."

As a matter of fact, he was booked for detention on Saturday afternoon, when the Grammar School match was due to be played. That circumstance did not seem to worry Cardew in the least. Mr. Lathom was a kind gentleman, who could generally be relied upon not to let fixtures be interfered with if it could be helped. Cardew had little doubt that he would get leave on acquainting Mr. Lathom with the circumstances of the case. The doubt would certainly have worried Tom Merry, in Cardew's place. It did not worry Cardew.

There was a heavy tramp in the passage, and the door of Study No. 9 opened to admit George Alfred Grundy.

Grundy's rugged face was flushed, and his eyes were sparkling. But he was trying to keep his temper. If the new captain had made a mistake, Grundy was willing to give him a chance to set it right.

"Trot in, old bean!" said Cardew cordially. "Awfully glad to see you, Grundy!"

"That's all very well!" grunted Clive. "But we're trying to work."

Grundy's face cleared.

"I won't keep you a minute," he said. "It's only about a mistake in the football list, Cardew."

Levison and Clive smiled. Cardew assumed an expression of interest.

"My little list—my first humble essay as junior captain!" he said. "I hoped you'd approve of it, Grundy."

Grundy looked quite genial. It was always easy to pull Grundy's egregious leg.

"Well, it's a good list," he said, "but there's one name left out, you know."

"Oh gad! I'm really new to the business, you know,"

said Cardew. "Give a chap time to settle down. Have I really put up a list with only ten names in it?"

"I don't mean that. There's eleven names, right enough."

Cardew looked perplexed.

"Didn't you say there was a name left out?"

"Yes, I did."

"I admit I'm a child in these matters," said Cardew blandly. "Is there a new rule in Association football that I haven't heard of? Are they playing twelve men a side this season, Levison?"

Levison laughed.

"If they are, St. Jim's will have to come into line, I suppose," continued Cardew gravely. "I must look out for a twelfth man."

"Oh, don't be a goat!" said Grundy. "That isn't what I mean. You really seem awfully ignorant of football, Cardew."

"I'm willin' to learn!" said Cardew meekly.

"What I mean is you've made up a list without putting my name in it," explained Grundy.

"Yes, that's right!"

"Right!" ejaculated Grundy.

"Yes; you remember you asked me to leave you out."

"Asked you!" yelled Grundy.

"Just so. These fellows were witnesses."

"Well, I'm blessed if I remember asking you to leave me out!" said Grundy blankly. "You must have misunderstood me, Cardew!"

"I think not. I believe I remember your exact words," said Cardew, with great gravity. "You said that I ought to play a man on his form, or not at all. I said I'd remember that when it came to handing out places in the junior eleven. Isn't that clear?"

Levison and Clive chuckled, and Grundy stared uncomprehendingly at the new captain. The powerful brain of George Alfred worked slowly.

"Well, I want you to play me on my form," said Grundy at last.

"But you haven't any football form, old chap!"

"What!"

"You see, you can't play footer!"

"Wha-a-a-t!"

"I'd play you on your form like a shot, if you had any," explained Cardew. "But as you haven't——"

"Look here——" bawled Grundy.

"How can I play you on form you haven't got?" asked Cardew, in a tone of patient remonstrance.

George Alfred Grundy breathed hard.

"I feel bound to keep my word to you," went on Cardew. "I said I'd only play a fellow on his form. I'm sticking to that. If I played a fellow for his good looks or his nice manners or his gentle voice, of course, I should slam you in at once."

"Ha, ha, ha!" yelled Levison and Clive.

"But on your football form I couldn't play you," said Cardew. "Some day, when we play the Third, I might shove you in as back, if you'd make a solemn promise to stand quite still and not move all through the game. We'll think that over later."

"You cheeky ass!" yelled Grundy.

Cardew looked pained.

"I don't think you ought to slang a man for keepin' his plighted word to you," he said reproachfully.

"What do you think I've been backing you for in the elections?" demanded Grundy.

"Because I'm so nice, I suppose."

"Ha, ha, ha!"

"I thought you had sense enough to improve on that dummy Tom Merry, and put me in the team."

"I should have to get insured first," said Cardew thoughtfully.

"Insured!"

"Yes. The fellows would lynch me, you know."

"I've had enough of your funny talk!" roared Grundy. "What I want to know is, am I playing against the Grammar School to-morrow?"

"As they say in the House of Chinwag, the answer is in the negative."

"Not?" exclaimed Grundy.

"Not!" assented Cardew.

"You've taken me in."

"Well, if I've taken you in I'm prepared to put you out!" yawned Cardew. "Will that set it right?"

Grundy did not answer that question. Whether Cardew had taken him in, or whether the egregious Grundy had taken himself in, did not really matter very much. It was clear that he was to be no better off under the new regime than under the old regime. All his herculean efforts to get Cardew elected had left him precisely where he was.

That was such an exasperating reflection to Grundy that it was not surprising that he lost his temper—never very reliable.

Tom Merry's quick eye saw where his best chance lay. He passed the ball back to Cardew at the psychological moment, and it was Cardew who drove it true and hard into the goal. The Grammarian custodian, whose eyes had been glued on Tom Merry, clutched at it too late, and there was a roar as the leather entered the net. (See page 10.)

He rushed at the new captain with his hands up.

Cardew whipped out of his chair in a twinkling, and stepped round the table.

"Dear man——" he began.

"Let me get at you!" roared Grundy.

Levison and Clive jumped up. Grundy had his own lofty ideas on the subject; but it was obvious to everyone else that a football captain could not be expected to fight every fellow he failed to select for a football team. Grundy was collared at once.

"Let me go!" roared Grundy. "I'm going to smash him!"

Cardew eyed him coolly.

"Let him go, you fellows," he said. "He's a bit hefty for me, but I think I can manage him."

"Don't be an ass!" retorted Levison. "Lend us a hand to bump him down the passage."

"Anythin' to oblige."

Three pairs of hands propelled Grundy from the study. Hefty as he was, Grundy had no chance against the three.

In the passage he smote the floor with a loud concussion.

Bump!

"Hallo! What's the row?" asked Blake, coming along.

"Grundy wants to pitch into Cardew for leaving him out of the eleven," explained Clive.

"Ha, ha, ha!" roared Blake.

"Lend a hand!"

"Yes, rather!"

Several more fellows came along to lend a hand. It was felt that George Alfred Grundy required to learn that his high-handed methods were off-side, as it were. The hapless Grundy was bumped along the Fourth Form passage, bumped along the Shell passage, and bumped into his own study, where he was deposited in a breathless and dusty heap. And for quite a long time afterwards Grundy had no leisure to think of his wrongs and grievances. He was too busy thinking of his damages. And the name of G. A. Grundy did not appear in the football list.

CHAPTER 7.
Tom Merry to the Rescue!

"CERTAINLY not!"

Mr. Lathom spoke very sharply.

It was Saturday afternoon, and Cardew of the Fourth had presented himself in his Form master's study, to beg off detention for the afternoon. Cardew was looking as meek as possible, but Mr. Lathom looked cross, and not without reason.

"You see, sir——" murmured Cardew.

"For some time past, Cardew, you have been the very worst boy in my Form," said Mr. Lathom. "You have consistently neglected your preparation, your construe has been as bad as Trimble's, and you have been careless and inattentive, and you have failed to hand in your impositions."

"I've been working very hard——"

"Nonsense!"

"At football, sir."

"Indeed! I believe that a short time ago there was some trouble because you attempted to elude the compulsory games practice."

"That was some time ago, sir. Since then——"

"Nonsense!"

"The fellows want me this afternoon, sir."

"You may explain to them that your detention is due to your own idleness and carelessness and disrespect."

Cardew's eyes glittered. Mr. Lathom's statement was perfectly correct. Cardew had absolutely no claim what ever to be let off. It looked now as if he had counted too much on the easy-going good nature of his Form master.

But to be detained on the occasion of the first match since the election was not to be thought of. It would be a blow from which he could scarcely recover.

If the match took place without Cardew, and his absence was due to his own idle recklessness, it would be about as bad a start as he could possibly have made as junior captain of St. Jim's. He realised, too, that he would have to ask Tom Merry to captain the side. He would prefer, no doubt, to ask Levison or Clive, but public opinion would be too strong for that. He would have to ask Tom.

It was not as if Mr. Lathom was a hard master, like Mr. Ratcliff, for instance, who might detain a fellow from sheer crossness of temper. It was well known that no fellow need ever be detained by Mr. Lathom unless he fairly asked for it.

The Fourth Form master made a gesture of dismissal. He regarded the matter as closed.

"You may go, Cardew!" he said, in a tone of finality.

"But, sir——"

"I have no more to say."

"It's an important football match, sir."

"Possibly. I should be the last man to interfere with a match which the boys regard as important," said Mr. Lathom. "If it were Blake or D'Arcy or Levison—— But I cannot believe, Cardew, that your presence is very important, since only a few weeks ago you were in trouble for slacking at games. You may go."

"I assure you, sir——"

"Enough!"

Mr. Lathom waved his hand to the door, and Cardew understood that it was useless to say anything further. He left the study, his eyes gleaming and his teeth set.

It was a heavy blow. Cardew would not have hesitated for a second about "cutting" detention had the match been at the Grammar School. But the game was to be played on the St. Jim's ground, almost in sight of Mr. Lathom's study window. Obviously he could not play in those circumstances. Before the game had been ten minutes old he would have been called off the field.

Cardew went slowly down the passage, his handsome face almost white with rage. This was how he was starting his captaincy—writing out an imposition in the Form-room, while his supplanted rival captained the side! At the corner of the passage he came on the Terrible Three of the Shell, chatting at the big window. Cardew gave them an evil look. He could imagine how Tom Merry and his friends would smile when they learned how he was starting his new career as junior captain.

"About time you got changed, Merry, if you're playin'!" snapped Cardew, in a mood to say something unpleasant.

Tom looked at him.

"The match isn't till half-past two," he answered. "It's barely two now."

Monty Lowther chimed in:

"What I like about Shakespeare," he said, "is the way he hits off a chap. Remember the lines:

"'Man, vain man,
Dressed in a little brief authority,
Plays such fantastic tricks before high heaven
As make the angels weep!'"

Manners chuckled, and Tom Merry smiled. Cardew grew crimson. To do him justice, he was not a fellow to use a "little brief authority" in such a manner as to make the angels weep. It was his anger and annoyance after the interview with Mr. Lathom that had led him to speak to Tom as he had.

He strode on, leaving the Terrible Three smiling; but he turned back again.

"The laugh's on your side!" he said bitterly. "I may as well tell you now. I'm detained this afternoon."

Tom Merry whistled.

"Won't Lathom let you off?"

"I've asked him. No."

"And that's how you start?" exclaimed Manners indignantly. "You've played no end of tricks to bag the captaincy, and that's how you handle it when you've got it!"

"I'm goin' to ask Levison to captain the side!" said Cardew savagely.

"You're jolly well not!" bawled Lowther. "If you're detained, and can't show up, it's up to Tom Merry!"

"Who's captain?" sneered Cardew.

"You are, at present; but I can jolly well tell you that you won't keep it long at this rate!"

"And I can tell you that Levison will refuse," said Manners. "All the fellows will expect Tom to act, and Levison isn't fool enough to set himself up against the whole lot of us just to please your malice."

Cardew bit his lips hard. It dawned upon him that Manners was right, and that Ernest Levison certainly would refuse to be used in such a way.

"Why not ask Grundy?" said Monty Lowther satirically. "You seem to have led Grundy to believe that you'd play him. Ask him to skipper the team."

"I would if I dashed well chose!" snapped Cardew. "By gad, I've a jolly good mind to, to show you your place!"

Tom Merry laughed contemptuously.

"I believe you're reckless fool enough," he said. "But if you play Grundy there will be no match. Every other fellow will resign from the team, and I shall be the first!"

"And I the second!" said Monty Lowther.

Cardew looked at them evilly. He knew that if he was kept off the field, Tom Merry had to take his place. It would be an utterly ridiculous climax to his campaign against Tom Merry; but there seemed no help for it.

"You ought never to have got detained," went on Tom coldly, "and Mr. Lathom would let you off for a match if you hadn't put his back up by lazy slacking. That's clear enough."

"When I want a sermon I'll ask for one!" snapped Cardew.

"Well, I won't give you one now," said Tom. "The question is, what's going to be done?"

"I suppose I'm goin' to be done," said Cardew, with a gleam of his old sardonic humour. "It's a regular catch for you, Tom Merry, and you can make the most of it."

Tom Merry shook his head.

"I don't suppose you'll understand it, Cardew, but I'm not keen on making the most of it, or in making you look like a slacking fool before all the fellows. Have you put it to Lathom——"

"Oh, I've tried that. Nothin' doin'!"

"Would you like me to try?"

Cardew stared at him.

"You! Do you think Lathom would listen to you?"

"He might."

"Oh gad!" said Cardew. "You're a queer customer, Tom Merry. Go and beard the lion in his den, if you like."

Tom Merry walked along the passage to Mr. Lathom's study, and tapped at the door. The Fourth Form master gave him a genial nod as he entered.

"Well, Merry?"

"May I speak about Cardew, sir?" asked Tom respectfully. "He's detained this afternoon, and he's wanted for a school match."

Mr. Lathom frowned.

"Cardew should have thought of that earlier, Merry."

"I know, sir. But he's been elected captain, and it's awkward if the match has to be played without him. We should all feel it a favour, sir, if you——"

Mr. Lathom blinked at Tom rather curiously over his glasses.

"I understood that you were junior captain, Merry."

Tom smiled faintly. The exciting affairs of the Lower School evidently had had no echo in the scholastic quiet of Mr. Lathom's study. He had not even noticed the election.

"Cardew is captain now, sir. There has been a new election. I—I know it's rather a cheek to ask you to let him off, but as there's an important match on, and Cardew is captain, I thought you wouldn't mind Cardew being detained Wednesday instead of to-day."

The Form master gave Tom a very benevolent blink.

"I understand, Merry! If you, whom I certainly trust, assure me that Cardew's presence is necessary, I shall accede to your request."

"It is necessary from our point of view, sir," said Tom. "Of course, the match could be played without him; but that's very awkward, as he is captain. It's his first match, too, since he got the captaincy."

"Very well, Merry; you may tell Cardew that his detention may stand over till Wednesday afternoon."

"Thank you, sir!" said Tom.

"Not at all, my boy," said the Fourth Form master very kindly. And Tom left the study.

"Bitten your napper off?" asked Cardew, as Tom Merry rejoined the juniors at the corner of the corridor.

"No," said Tom, with a smile; "your detention's off till Wednesday, and you can play in the match to-day, Cardew."

"My only hat!" Cardew stared at Tom. "You mean that?"

"Yes. It's a message from Lathom. Official," said Tom.

"Thanks!" said Cardew, and he walked away.

Monty Lowther and Manners looked at their chum with somewhat uncertain expressions.

"Well, you're the limit, Tom!" said Manners at last.

"How's that?"

"You'd have captained the team if Cardew hadn't played, and he'd have looked the biggest ass at St. Jim's, in the circumstances."

Tom Merry laughed.

"I'm not out to score over Cardew," he said. "I'm thinking chiefly of beating the Grammarians."

"We could have beaten them without Cardew."

"Very likely; but now Cardew's got the job, I don't want to butt into it. I'd much rather not, in fact! Besides, why shouldn't he have a chance of showing what he can do?"

"Well, I've heard of turning the other cheek to the smiter," said Monty Lowther, "but you're the first chap I've ever heard of putting that jolly old maxim into practice."

Tom Merry flushed a little.

"I'm bound to back up my captain or get out of the team," he said. "That's how I look at it."

"Is that how Cardew looked at it when you were captain?"

"Well, no. But I suppose I'm not called on to follow a rotten bad example?"

"All serene, old bean," said Lowther. "You're right, Tom, of course, only precious few fellows would look at it as you do. Let's go and get changed."

When the St. Jim's footballers gathered on Little Side for the match with the Grammarians, Cardew was in his place, looking very fit and cheerful. He gave Tom Merry a pleasant nod. Cardew did not wholly understand Tom's nature, any more than Tom understood Cardew's. As a matter of fact, their ways were as far as the poles asunder. But Cardew could, as least, respect a high principle which he hardly understood and did not share.

That Tom Merry, after being supplanted, was willing to back him up loyally, was a puzzle to Cardew. Yet he could see that it was the case. Tom had simply put his personal feelings aside for the sake of the House and the game. It would have been easy for him to make a division, and to form an opposition party to give Cardew trouble. And the thought of it never even crossed his mind.

Cardew of the Fourth was one person; Cardew, the junior captain of St. Jim's, was another. In the former person, Tom Merry did not vare to speak to him if he could help it; in the latter capacity, he was prepared to back him up with steady loyalty. And that was the distinction which Ralph Reckness Cardew was perplexed to comprehend.

However, there it was, and Cardew was glad of it. Without Tom Merry to head it, there was no opposition for him to look for, and his captaincy started under the very best auspices. And Cardew quite realised how much that meant in the first school match in which he was to figure as captain.

CHAPTER 8.
The Winning Goal!

"GOAL!"

The ball went into the net from the foot of Gordon Gay, of the Grammar School. And fifty Grammarians who had followed their team over to St. Jim's burst into a roar.

"Goal!"

It was first blood to the Grammarians. For twenty minutes of the first half the game had been ding-dong, and Gay was the first to break the ice.

Cardew's face was a little set as he lined up his men after the goal.

He wanted to win—almost passionately he wanted to win that match. He wanted his rule to start with a football victory; in fact, a victory was needed to clinch the matter. Only too well Cardew knew the talk that would go on in the studies and the changing-room if the first match after the ousting of Tom Merry was lost to the old rivals of St. Jim's.

He had picked out a winning team, and Tom Merry's loyalty enabled him to play the best junior footballer in the school. If he had made a mistake in giving Clive the place many of the fellows thought should have gone to Redfern of the New House, it was a slight one. Clive was certainly good at centre-half. In order to place himself, with Levison, in the front line, Cardew had had to make some changes in position, but every man was good in the place that was given him.

Nevertheless, the team did not seem to be pulling together so well as of old. Cardew, at inside right, did not seem to hold it together as Tom Merry had been use to holding it. It was a team that was, at least, equal to the Grammarian crowd, and if defeat came, it was pretty certain that the defeat would be attributed to the change in the captaincy, and the other changes caused by it. That verdict might be unjust; but it was fairly certain to be given.

Cardew played up, personally, at his very best; he was playing the game of his life. No one who saw him now would have dreamed of calling him a slacker. Fellows who were looking on found it hard to remember that only a few weeks before Cardew had been given a beating by the games committee for slacking at footer.

But fortune did not smile on Cardew. Half-time came with the score unchanged, the Grammarians one up.

"May as well call it a goner," said Grundy of the Shell, behind the goal to Wilkins and Gunn. "That is what comes of leaving out good men."

Wilkins, for once, was disposed to agree with his great chief. On this occasion Wilkins had been left out.

But the game was not a "goner" yet. Early in the second half Levison gave Tom Merry a pass, from which the former captain scored, and the goal was greeted with deafening cheers by the St. Jim's crowd.

It was a relief to Cardew, yet he was not wholly pleased. It was his old rival who had taken the goal. Cardew had not even helped; he had been laid on his back by a Grammarian charge just before Tom Merry found the net.

"Goal! Goal! Good old Tommy! Goal!" roared the St. Jim's crowd; and that roar was not music to Cardew's ears.

"Good old Tommy!" murmured Monty Lowther, as they walked back to the centre of the field. "I suppose you know what the fellows would say about Cardew, Tom, if he lost this match."

"Haven't thought about it," answered Tom.

"You wouldn't, old buck! But you're going to save his bacon for him if you can—what?"

"I'm going to beat the Grammarians if I can."

"Right-ho! In your place, Cardew would be thinking of beating his own captain."

"Oh, rot!" said Tom.

"If he begins with a victory over the jolly old Grammarians he will be pretty firmly seated in the saddle," said Lowther. "Nothing could be much more popular than that."

"And we're going to beat them," said Tom cheerily.

"Hear, hear!" grinned Lowther.

The sides lined up, and the Grammarians started in with a hot attack. Again and again they came down on the St. Jim's goal. But Fatty Wynn, between the posts, was in great form, and he drove the leather out again and again. Kangaroo cleared to midfield, and the game swayed away towards the Grammar School end.

"On the ball!" roared Grundy. "Can't you get hold of the ball? My hat! What a game!"

"Dry up, you ass!" said Wilkins. "Cardew's got the ball."

Snort from Grundy.

"How long will he keep it? Look at him making a present of it to that back—that ass Carboy."

But the great Grundy was mistaken—as he so frequently was in football matters. So far from making Carboy of the Grammar School a present of the ball, Cardew wound round Carboy and ran for goal. There was no St. Jim's forward up to take a pass, and Cardew ran for goal and kicked.

The Grammarian goalkeeper swung to face him, and slipped and sat down. There was a buzz of excitement as Cardew kicked, over a sitting goalkeeper.

Perhaps Cardew was a fraction too hasty. The ball struck the crossbar and bounced back. The next second Frank Monk was on it, and had cleared it, and Lane sent it past the half-way line with a mighty kick.

Cardew gritted his teeth. His face was almost white with disappointment and suppressed rage. It had been a glorious chance, and it had failed. The chance was utterly gone now, play and players swayed away into the home field.

"What a kick!" said Grundy derisively. "Some captain—I don't think."

"Might happen to anybody!" said Gunn tolerantly.

"It wouldn't have happen if I'd been there," said Grundy. "You've never seen me hit the crossbar."

"Never seen you hit anything within a mile of it," assured Gunn; and even then Grundy did not seem satisfied. Indeed, Gunn strolled away to a different part of the field to escape Grundy's further observations, which were entirely of a personal nature.

"Hard luck, old chap," said Levison, as Cardew passed him, and the new captain nodded without speaking; his feelings were too bitter just then for speech.

"Ten minutes to play," remarked Wally of the Third, laying down the law to a group of fags. "Looks to me like a draw."

"Well, my brother's there!" observed Levison minor.

"So's mine," said Wally. "But I think it will be a draw all the same. Your major doesn't seem to be setting the Thames on fire, young Levison."

"Bow-wow!" said Frank Levison cheerily. His eyes were on Levison of the Fourth; evidently in his opinion Ernest Levison was the principal person concerned in the Grammarian match.

"Five minutes to play!" said Reggie Manners. "What they really want is some of the Third in the team."

"Now you're talking sense!" said Wally approvingly. "There's your major on his back, Frank. Is that how you generally play football in the Levison family?"

"Oh, rats!" said Frank quite crossly. "He's up again!"

(Continued on page 16.)

GRAND "FOOTER" COMPETITION!

The Opportunity of a Lifetime!

FOOTBALLERS' NAMES
COMPETITION

First Prize £100	30 MAGNIFICENT "JAMES" MOTOR-BIKES. (Complete with Lamp, Horn, and Licence-holder.)	Second Prize £50

100 SPLENDID "JAMES" COMET CYCLES. (Complete with Lamp, Bell, etc.)

20 GRAMOPHONES.

40 FOOTBALL OUTFITS (Boots, Stockings, Shorts & Shirt).

50 Pairs of BOXING GLOVES.

100 Pairs of ROLLER SKATES.

10 Two-Valve Wireless Sets.

250 BOOKS and other Consolation Prizes

6 "RILEY" BILLIARDS TABLES.

20 MODEL STEAM LOCOMOTIVES (With Rails).

100 MATCH FOOTBALLS.

100 FISHING RODS.

ALL YOU HAVE TO DO is to write IN INK in the allotted space under each of the puzzle-pictures the name of the footballer which you think the picture represents. You will find on pages 15 and 25 the full list of names used throughout the competition, so that you have only to fit the correct name to each picture. Having done this, fill in the coupon under this picture-set and cut out the whole tablet—DO NOT CUT THE PICTURES AND COUPON APART. Next collect the other seven sets, see that you have filled in your answers properly in all the spaces, remembering, too, that only one name may be written in each space, then pin them together and post to :

FOOTBALLERS' NAMES CONTEST,
c/o "GEM,"
Gough House,
Gough Square,
London, E.C.4;
so as to reach that address not later than Tuesday, Dec. 18th.

LAST WEEK.   FINAL SET.

43___   44   45

46___   47   48

In entering "FOOTBALLERS' NAMES" competition, I agree to accept the Editor's decision as absolutely final and binding.

NAME ....

ADDRESS ....

Closing Date, Tuesday, December 18th.   G.

RULES AND CONDITIONS
which must be strictly adhered to.

—:*:—

1.—The First Prize of £100 in cash will be awarded to the competitor who sends in the correct, or most nearly correct, solution of all eight sets of the pictures according to the Editor's official solution.

2.—The Second Prize of £50, and the others in the splendid variety of prizes, will be awarded in order of merit.

3.—All the prizes will be awarded. If two or more competitors tie, however, the prize or prizes, or their value, will be divided, and the Editor reserves full rights in this respect.

4.—Any number of entries may be made, but in each case only the complete series of eight picture-sets (pictures Nos. 1 to 48, that is to say) will be admissible. No responsibility will be accepted for any communication lost or delayed in the post. Any entry arriving after the closing date, Tuesday, December 18th, will be disqualified.

The first seven sets of pictures are reproduced on pages 15 & 25 for the benefit of GEM readers who missed the previous issues.

WRITE YOUR NAME AND ADDRESS CLEARLY!

5.—The names under the pictures must be written IN INK.

6.—Employees of the proprietors of this journal are not eligible to compete.

7.—Entry to this competition is on the full understanding that the Editor's decision is final and legally binding throughout.

Readers of "The Champion," "Boys' Realm," "Union Jack," "Boys' Friend," "Pluck," "Boys' Cinema," "Young Britain," "Magnet," "The Popular," "The Rocket," and "Nelson Lee Library" are also taking part in the Contest, so that additional attempts may be made with the pictures from these allied journals.

FOOTBALLERS' NAMES.

The following list contains the actual names of the footballers represented by the puzzle-pictures:

Ashurst, Anderson, Armstrong, Aitken, Adams, Amos, Alderson, Allen, Armitage, Archibald, Ashmore.

Brett, Broadhead, Blyth, Boreham, Blackburn, Bradford, Bassnett, Brittan, Blair, Ball, Barkas, Birrell, Bradley, Barnes, Bulling, Burton, Branston, Buchan, Blake, Bowser, Bishop, Barras, Braithwaite, Bullock, Bliss, Bateman, Best, Bagge, Barson, Broadhurst, Broad, Bolam, Brelsford, Blenkinsopp, Beedie, Birch, Bellamy, Bainbridge, Bowen, Burnham, Boyle, Blackwell, Bennie, Ballantyre, Buchanan, Bamber, Byers, Banks, Brooks, Blood, Baker, Bird, Bromilow.

(*Continued on page 25.*)

No. 1 SET.

No. 2 SET.

No. 3 SET.

No. 4 SET.

No. 5 SET.

No. 6 SET.

YOU WILL FIND No. 7 SET ON PAGE 25, BOYS!

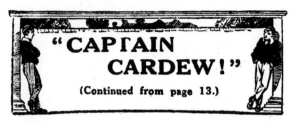

"CAPTAIN CARDEW!"

(Continued from page 13.)

"Looks rather at sea, doesn't he?" remarked Wally. "Sort of sleepy, what?"

"No!" roared Frank.

Wally chuckled.

"He's got the ball!" exclaimed Levison minor a minute later. "Hurrah! Go it, Ernie!"

"Too late for Ernie to do anything!" grinned Wally of the Third. "Even jolly old Ernie—— Hallo, he's down again! You Levisons seem fond of taking little naps on the football-field."

"Fathead!"

"Look here, young Levison——"

"Cardew's got it!" shouted Frank. "Ernie gave him the ball! You don't often see a chap pass like that!"

"Go it, Cardew!"

"Hurrah!"

Levison of the Fourth had been charged over, but Cardew had trapped the ball. Four of the St. Jim's forwards were rushing up the field. Cardew was stopped, but he centred to Tom Merry, though even in the rush and excitement of the moment he felt a pang at parting with the ball to his rival. Tom had the ball, and drew the defence—but he did not kick for goal. His quick eye saw where the best chance lay, and he was not thinking of kudos for himself. He sent the ball back to Cardew at the psychological moment, and it was Cardew who drove it into goal.

The Grammarian custodian, whose eyes were glued on Tom Merry, clutched at it too late. There was a roar from the St. Jim's crowd as it landed in the net.

"Goal!"

"Cardew—Cardew!"

"Goal! Goal! Goal!"

The Grammarian goalkeeper grunted and tossed out the ball. It had been a near thing—a very near thing for the first match Cardew played as junior captain of St. Jim's. But it was a win—on the very stroke of time the winning goal had been captured—and captured by Ralph Reckness Cardew.

"Goal—goal!" the St. Jim's crowd were shouting. "Hurrah! St. Jim's wins! Goal!"

"Oh gad!" murmured Cardew. "It's a win after all!" He walked over to Tom Merry. "Your goal, Merry!"

"Yours," said Tom, with a smile.

Cardew's features seemed to twitch for a moment. It was this fellow whom he had supplanted—whom he had "downed" by the use of every trick his clever brain could think of; and this was the fellow who had made him a present of the winning goal. Cardew could not help thinking of what his own action would have been in Tom Merry's place, and the colour came into his cheeks.

"Well, we've won!" he said. "We've beaten them! I— I say, Tom Merry—I'm sorry—for a lot of things——"

He broke off abruptly, and walked off the field with Levison and Clive. Tom Merry looked after him, a rather curious expression on his face.

"Bai Jove! We've beaten the boundahs!" said Arthur Augustus D'Arcy, with great satisfaction. "I weally thought it was goin' to be a dwaw, you know—but a miss is as good as a mile. Cardew makes a pwetty good captain. I think I could name a fellow in the Fourth who would do bettah, pewwaps; but weally I must say that Cardew is quite good."

"Good enough!" agreed Blake.

"Certainly that was a wippin' goal!" continued Arthur Augustus. "Cardew was on it like a flash when you gave him the chance, Tom Mewwy!"

SPECIAL NOTE.

"He was!" agreed Tom.

"But in your place, deah boy, I think I should have kicked," said Arthur Augustus sagely. "In my opinion, you should have kicked for goal then instead of passin'!"

"My faulty judgment, perhaps!" said Tom, with a laugh.

"Yaas; howevah, it turned out all wight," said Arthur Augustus. "I am glad you agwee with me."

"But I don't," answered Tom cheerfully. "I thought Cardew had a better chance of putting the ball in, you see—and it seems to have worked!"

Arthur Augustus shook his head.

"In your place I should have kicked myself," he said.

"You would have kicked yourself!" ejaculated Monty Lowther. "Well, old bean, if I kick you instead, will that make it right?"

"You uttah ass!" roared Arthur Augustus.

"Ha, ha, ha!"

"Bai Jove! If you think that funnay, Lowthah——"

"Good game—what?" said Figgins, interrupting Arthur Augustus. "Cardew's not a bad skipper. He made a mistake in putting so many School House chaps into the team, but, on the whole, I must say that he's started well."

It was the general opinion that Cardew had started well. His team had beaten the Grammarians, and it was Cardew himself who had kicked the winning goal. Much more than that could scarcely have been expected of the new captain. Ralph Reckness Cardew left the football ground with his blushing honours thick upon him.

.   .   .   .   .   .

That evening Tom Merry and Manners and Lowther, as they sat in Study No. 10, preparing Milton and eating baked chestnuts, were rather surprised to receive a visit from Cardew of the Fourth.

Cardew strolled into the study, his manner quite as easy as if he supposed himself to be a specially welcome guest there.

Tom gave him a nod; Manners and Lowther regarded him rather grimly. Tom Merry's chums, at least, could not forget that Cardew had supplanted Tom Merry, and that he had succeeded in doing so by methods that Tom would have disdained to use either in attack or in defence. Manners and Lowther were ready to follow Tom's lead in giving Cardew the support he was entitled to as junior captain; but they were not ready to give him any cordiality over and above.

Cardew seemed unaware of the freezing atmosphere of the study. He sat on a corner of the table, swung his elegant legs, and regarded the Terrible Three with a smiling face.

"Mugging up jolly old Milton?" he asked.

"Yes; Sunday prep," said Manners very briefly.

"Interestin' old johnny, what?"

"More or less."

"But I haven't come here to discuss the beauties of Milton," added Cardew.

"No," said Tom.

"What have you come for?" asked Monty Lowther bluntly. "You're no fool, Cardew, and you know jolly well what we think of you in this study."

"Quite! Just a word with Thomas."

"Well, what is it?" asked Tom, rather restively. "The fact is, Cardew, the less we see of one another the better."

"Candid, at least," said Cardew cheerily. "I downed you, Tom Merry, just as I said I would. I bagged the post of House captain, and then that of junior captain, by a series of knavish tricks, which you look upon with just disdain. Am I right?"

"Not far from it," assented Tom.

"And I'm unrepentant," said Cardew. "That's my way —pretty Fanny's way, you know. But, instead of yearnin' for revenge, and goin' for me hot and strong, as I should in your place, you heap giddy coals of fire on my unfortunate head. You won my first match for me to-day. I don't know why you did it, but you did."

"Oh, rot!" said Tom.

"I've come to make you an offer."

"You needn't."

"I'll make it, all the same. If you want the captaincy back, you can have it."

"What!"

"Surprised you?" smiled Cardew. "Well, I mean it! What do you say?"

"Rot!"

"Better catch me while I'm in the mood. It's an offer that we can't afford to repeat, as they say at the shop sales."

"Rubbish!" said Tom.

Cardew slipped from the table.

"Well, I've made the offer," he said; and he sauntered out of the study, leaving the chums of the Shell staring.

THE END.

(Look out for another ripping yarn of Tom Merry & Co. next week, in "SKIPPER AND SLACKER." You will vote it as being one of the finest yarns you have ever read.)

Plucky Paul Mannering's adventure in the
mystic shades of the Temple of Delhi—

—leads to an amazing
discovery !

THE RED IMAGE

A Topping Tale of Indian Adventure.
By
CECIL FANSHAW.

CHAPTER 1.
A Villainous Plot Afoot !

"INDIA'S supposed to be a land of adventure and romance ! But I'm hanged if I can see anything romantic in sitting on an office stool all day totting up figures in a book ! Well, I'll go and have a good look round that quaint old temple I discovered last week."

Thus spoke Paul Mannering, who had only been in India six months, as he ran down the steps from the veranda of his bungalow and seized the bicycle he had flung against the trunk of a tall mango-tree on his return from the bank where he worked. The next moment Paul shot out of the dusty little compound, or garden, that surrounded the old mud-walled, thatched bungalow he shared with a couple of office chums, and pedalled away as hard as possible to get clear of the precincts of Delhi city while there yet remained a few hours of day-light.

Frequently, in the cool, dry evenings that are experienced in Northern India, as autumn draws on, Paul used to ride out to the ancient tombs and temples that abound round Delhi, India's capital, and spend the few hours of daylight available wandering amongst the ruins, whose history so deeply interested him, and in which he was fairly well versed.

Paul was rather a solitary youth of an inquiring nature, and he had the lean, dark face of a deep thinker ; but he was no book-worm for all that. On the contrary, he was a very active young fellow who would have given anything to be in the Indian Police. But financial difficulties at home had prevented the lad from getting into the police—every white man in the Indian Service being a commissioned officer—so he had had, perforce, to be content to come out to the romantic East as a junior clerk in a branch of one of the biggest European banks in India. But the confined life far from satisfied Paul's adventurous character.

For about half an hour the lad pedalled along a white, dusty road, flanked on each side by tall mango and peepul trees, and the low mud walls that encircled the gardens and bungalows of English residents. Then he reached the native bazaar, and was forced to slacken speed,

for his way now led through narrow, twisting, evil-smelling streets, shut in on either side by overhanging, picturesque white buildings—a rather dirty white in most cases.

A few of these buildings were gaudy, modern temples, plastered with queer images of Hindu gods ; but most were shops owned by native merchants, who sat cross-legged all day amongst the wares heaped up in the open shop-fronts. . Until he was clear of the restless, shifting natives who thronged the bazaar streets, their bright-hued raiments lending vivid splashes of colour to the otherwise dingy scene, Paul was obliged to proceed slowly, ringing his bell incessantly. But once he was out on the open road again, he hit up a good speed.

Now the scene was flat and monotonous, mile after mile of black cotton soil, studded with the stunted cotton bushes themselves, stretched away into the distance on either hand, broken only by occasional groves of mango-trees. A marauding kite swooped down within a few inches of Paul's face, and a "brain-fever " bird piped harshly in one of the tall groves as the lad sped by.

But Paul was not interested in the scenery ; he was thinking of the ancient temple he was heading for, and which he had only recently discovered about five miles out of Delhi. The place was in a remarkably good state of preservation, and he was anxious to explore it thoroughly.

As the young fellow pedalled onwards, the wheels of his machine making a faint swish and raising little spurts of dust, he reflected on the wonderful history of India and also the present condition of the country—the general unrest, principally fostered by paid agitators. There was even a rumour, Paul remembered, of a plot afoot to murder the Viceroy, who had just come down from the Himalayan heights with his staff, to spend the winter in Delhi. But this rumour Paul rather scoffed at, for the plot seemed so pointless and absurd—a new Viceroy would be appointed immediately, while, in any case, the assassination would be a very difficult matter. But Paul had not had much experience of India, or Indian fanatics.

Anyway, the lad reflected, it was none of his business, and he had no intention

of poking his nose into other people's affairs—he was not in the Indian Police, however greatly he wished he was !

An hour after leaving his bungalow Paul found himself nearing the small tract of jungle, mostly palm-trees, that surrounded the temple he wished to explore. Dismounting, and leaving the road, he pushed his bicycle, the wheels of which moved heavily in the deep sand, between the trunks of the tall, nodding palm-trees. On his right there suddenly appeared a sheet of water, an artificial pond, whose banks were formed of ancient crumbling brick-work. Numerous small monkeys scampered away at the lad's approach and fled, shrieking and chattering, to the tops of the palm-trees.

Taking no notice of these sole inhabitants of the vicinity of the temple, Paul continued to trundle his machine forward in the direction of a square, stone gateway that lay in front of him, a couple of small shrines on its left.

Passing through the archway, the lad found himself in a large, derelict court-yard, flagged with great stones, encircled by a high wall. Directly in front of him was the temple he had come to explore, a large square building with a queer conical roof and a grim, dark, open portal, about eight feet high. Paul had been into the courtyard before, but he had never entered the temple, and this he proposed to do now.

The mouldering old place seemed entirely deserted, and a dead silence reigned, broken only by the whisper of gently-stirring palm-leaves or the scamper of a squirrel across the cracked flags as the youthful explorer stowed his bicycle away behind some enormous tombstones, and crossed over to the temple entrance. There was very little risk of the bicycle being stolen in such a lonely spot, but Paul thought it as well to be careful.

Without hesitation the lad mounted the crumbling steps that led up to the gloomy doorway, and his footfalls rang out harshly in the brooding silence. At the top of the little flight of steps he paused, weighted down by the solitude and uncanny atmosphere of the place, then he pulled himself together and entered the temple.

At first the air within struck cold, and Paul could scarcely see anything by the dim light of the setting sun whose slanting rays filtered down through tiny apertures high up in the walls. Then, his eyes becoming accustomed to the gloom, the lad recognised that he was standing in a bare, vaulted chamber, the walls of which were of pure white marble. On the farther side of this first chamber was a narrow, arched doorway, and to this he crossed over, his footsteps echoing eerily.

Beyond lay another high-roofed room, and yet another doorway, but everywhere was cold, white marble and grim silence. The dust of ages lay thick upon the flagged floor.

Paul wandered on, finding nothing but a series of desolate, gloomy vaults, then, somewhat disgusted, he returned to the outer chamber.

"I must be getting back soon," he muttered to himself. "It's jolly nearly pitch dark. But I guess I'll rest a bit first."

So saying, the lad seated himself on a marble ledge in a corner and closed his eyes.

"It's a disappointing hole," he thought. "Must be centuries old, but for all that there is to see I might as well have stayed away."

These were Paul's last thoughts, for, thoroughly tired out after a long day, he quickly dropped off to sleep.

How long the young fellow slept he was unaware; but he woke up suddenly, stiff and cold, and with a chilly sensation of fear trickling down his spine. And at the same time the hair on his scalp rose, for he sensed that he was no longer alone. It was dark, quite dark, but not quite silent. Something warned Paul to keep still, and, scarcely daring to breathe, he listened with straining ears.

Surely he had heard a sound! No, it was the heavy pounding of his own heart, or else nothing but overwrought imagination. Yet he felt that he was not alone!

Yes, there it was again—a soft, sliding footfall that had just paused on the steps outside. Now it was coming nearer. Now a dim figure was standing in the temple doorway, blocking out the faint light of the twinkling stars. It was a shapeless figure, about the height of a man, and Paul caught his breath.

No one had entered the abandoned temple for centuries, the age-old dust on the temple floor had borne no footprints when Paul had entered. Yet there was someone or something coming silently.

While Paul clutched at the cold edge of the marble ledge on which he sat, staring intently and aghast, the shapeless figure suddenly moved forward. It crossed the chamber swiftly and noiselessly, then vanished through the black archway in the farther wall.

Beads of cold sweat stood out on Paul's forehead. He was in Asia, not in Europe, seated at night in a long-abandoned Hindu temple which might once have been the scene of unheard-of orgies. Local natives shunned the place by day and night; the weird visitor could scarcely have been human. What could a man have come for? The inner chambers were all bare and empty, as Paul knew for a fact.

Shaking off the unreasoning dread that gripped him in the foreboding silence, the youngster half rose to his feet; then he sank down again. A second figure stood in the doorway! After an instant's seeming hesitation it vanished noiselessly in the direction taken by the first.

Paul strained his ears to catch any sound of a voice, but there was nothing, no sound at all. The strange figures had appeared, crossed the outer chamber, and the blackness had swallowed them up. The lad made up his mind to leave the haunted place without delay. There was nothing to be gained by staying. But before he could get to his feet the pale glimmer of the stars was once again blotted out by a shrouded figure in the outer archway. Then, at short intervals, came a fourth and a fifth apparition, and all disappeared in the same direction.

Five awesome beings had appeared and vanished, and Paul, stupefied, sat still, with eyes glued on the shadowy outline of the entrance wondering how many more would come. But none came; instead, a sound broke on the lad's ear which was such a relief to his tense nerves that he could scarcely choke back a cry of joy.

From one of the tomb-like inner chambers had come the sound of a human voice; and though the voice spoke in Hindustani the youngster understood. If Paul had been still before, he was now absolutely rigid as he strained his ears to catch what was said.

"Brothers," said the voice. "Children of Vishnu! The hour has come to strike a deadly blow at the hated white race who oppress our land of Ind! Out of many faithful I have chosen you four to assist me in this deed; for, though unknown to each other, ye are each known to me. And since ye have each answered my summons to meet me in this ancient temple of Vishnu, where there is no danger of prying eyes, ye are all, therefore, pledged and bound to carry out my bidding. Is that so?"

"Ay, High Priest of Vishnu! It is so. Command us!" came a low murmur of voices in Hindustani.

Paul gasped, wondering what villainous plot he had stumbled across. He was soon to learn.

"Brothers," droned on the voice, "tomorrow is the feast day of our god, as is well known, and, according to custom, all Hindus in the city of Delhi will parade the streets, some bearing images. Shortly after noon the chief of the oppressors, he who is called the Viceroy, and who represents the white King across the Black Water, will ride down the street of the silver merchants, the Chandni Chowk. That much is certain. But you and I, my brothers, will also be amongst the joyful crowd, and we also will bear our image of Vishnu; but it shall be a red image, not white like the others. And the red image of Vishnu will contain a bomb—it is even now prepared. You, my most trusted followers, shall assist me to approach this Viceroy. Then shall I launch our image at him and hasten both him and his chief men to perdition. The death of the tyrant will be the signal for general rebellion throughout the whole land of Ind, nor will it be long before we return to our ancient greatness and once more have our own kings."

The speaker hissed out his last words with vehement energy, and with all the concentrated hatred of a fanatic.

Paul instantly grasped the situation. The ancient, unused temple of Vishnu that he had come to explore, had been selected by the high priest of the god as a safe place in which to meet his most trusted followers and unfold his villainous design.

Each man had evidently received instructions to arrive at the temple at a slightly different time, and each had covered his head and turban with a sort of hood, in order, doubtless, to scare off any superstitious native villagers who might be lurking around. Not that the plotters were likely to be disturbed—the local natives shunned the old temple like the plague. But what Paul realised was that the plot to murder the Viceroy, at the rumour of which he had scoffed, was no fiction. The assassination was to be

With slow, noiseless footsteps the Hindu ruffians came creeping across the dark chamber. Paul Mannering stood stock-still, trying to locate the position of the conspirators by the sound of their breathing.

attempted the very next day, and he alone knew of it. Holding his breath, the youngster sat still, determined to slip away at the first opportunity, but anxious to learn all that was possible before leaving.

However, suddenly the voices, which had sunk to a whisper, ceased altogether. Then one by one the conspirators filed out of the inner vault, passed through the pitch-dark chamber in which sat the English lad, then shuffled down the broken steps outside. Paul breathed more easily. In a couple of minutes he would be scorching away to hand his vital information to the nearest white police officer.

Then, out in the courtyard, the stillness of the Indian night was suddenly broken by a loud metallic crash. And instantly, in Hindustani, arose a cry of "Spy!" followed by a rush of feet up the temple steps. One of the plotters, searching the courtyard to make sure they had not been observed, had stumbled over Paul's bicycle.

With a gasp of dismay, the English lad sprang to his feet. Then, within the darkness of the temple, awaited the coming attack with clenched fists. The next instant the furious Hindus, snarling out the most blood-curdling threats, stormed in through the entrance.

CHAPTER 2.
A Race Against Time !

ON the threshold of the temple entrance the scoundrels halted, unable to see. Then the leader of the gang, he who had been doing all the talking, rapped out swift commands in Hindustani.

"Stay by the entrance, Franji!" he barked. "Let none pass. You others join me in a thorough search within. Would that we had a light!"

Paul was unarmed, but had no doubt that the conspirators bore knives. And he knew his one chance of escape was to break through forward. There was no way out of the back of the temple, and ultimate discovery was inevitable.

It was a ghastly situation. With slow, noiseless footsteps the Hindu ruffians came creeping across the dark chamber, determined to discover the owner of the bicycle and kill him on the spot. Paul stood stock still, not daring to move, trying to locate the position of his opponents in the Stygian darkness by the sound of their breathing.

Seconds passed—tense seconds fraught with destiny. Paul wondered how long his keyed-up nerves would stand the racking strain. A slight shuffle sounded a foot away from him, and a hissing breath came almost direct in his face, accompanied by a strong odour of garlic and betel-nut. Paul sank his nails deep into his palms in his violent effort to repress a sudden cry. Then, a moment later, the lad realised that he had been missed by a miracle—the Hindus had passed on in their search into the inner chamber!

A sigh of intense relief escaped Paul's lips, then he sprang like a tiger at the fellow on guard in the doorway. As he sprang, the young Englishman let drive with his right fist, putting all his weight behind the blow. He could just make out the figure of the Hindu, but the latter had no notion of the coming attack from the dark till struck. Then, caught full on the jaw, without time to cry out, the ruffian reeled over backwards, landing on his head with a crash.

Paul lost not a second in following up his advantage, and dashed down the broken steps of the temple in great bounds. The pale glimmer of the tropical stars barely illuminated the

Suddenly the scarlet image, already swaying dangerously, toppled off its pedestal and crashed to the ground, landing right in the midst of its raging supporters. There was a deafening explosion, accompanied by a blinding, vivid flash.

walled-in courtyard, but this meagre light was sufficient for the English lad to discern the tomb by which he had left his bicycle. Racing over, the youngster grasped the machine which had betrayed him, then thrust it before him in a headlong dash for the outer gate.

Panting for breath, Paul gained the stone archway, placed one foot on the near pedal of his bicycle, and was about to leap on, when he felt a man's arms close about him. Twisting round, the lad gazed into the evil face of yet another scoundrel, a man left to guard the exit from the courtyard itself. Truly the conspirators were leaving no loophole of escape.

It was Paul's dread that his new assailant would cry out and give the alarm, for evidently the men within the temple had not heard the knock-out blow which had been delivered to the guardian of the steps. Therefore the lad released his machine, and fought with desperate fury to escape from the iron bands which pinioned him.

The struggle was fought in grim silence, the Hindu seeming unwilling to risk attracting a chance passer-by; and therein lay Paul's hope of escape. His arms secured, the young fellow could only employ his legs, but these he used to great advantage. Bending his right knee, he drove upwards with a swift, sudden blow, planting his kneecap in the pit of his assailant's stomach, wringing forth a deep groan. But the man was powerful, and held on. Moreover, he drove his hard head into Paul's face.

Half dazed, the youngster thrust up mightily again with his bended knee, and this time the other's hold was loosened.

Following up the second blow with a twisting wrench, Paul sent the ruffian staggering back to the archway; but at that instant came a sudden cry from the top of the temple steps. Dismayed, Paul spun round, only to see the remainder of the conspirators come charging down the crumbling stairway. They had found nothing inside the old building, but without they had discovered the prone body of their comrade.

A swift glance at the gateway told Paul his retreat was cut off. The fellow he had flung aside had recovered, and was about to make another spring. But to escape with his news was of vital import, so the lad swung round and dashed away across the dim courtyard, seeking another way out. Hot on his heels came the fanatical pursuers, now—with their quarry in sight—grimly intent on slaughter.

Leaping over broken masonry, dodging round tree trunks, Paul ran a race for his life in the semi-darkness. He could hear the swift patter of feet close behind him. They were catching him up—and men pledged to kill a Viceroy would not hesitate to slay an unknown lad who had discovered their plans.

At the high wall Paul shot a glance of despair, but there was no escape that way. The thing was unclimbable. So, flashing off at a tangent, Paul raced round to the back of the temple; but he was like a rat in a trap—the courtyard wall penned him in all round.

With a sudden sprint one tall man burst forth from amongst the pursuers, closed up to the youngster, and laid a hand on his shoulder. Paul swung round, dashed his fist into the fellow's face, then turned and ran on again, his breath coming in deep sobs.

At top speed Paul rounded one corner of the temple, then hope almost left him. He was running full-tilt into a ruffian coming round in the opposite direction! A hoarse chuckle, the first human sound in all that grim race, broke from a man at the lad's heels; then Paul lowered his head and charged straight into the new opponent in front.

Then something descended with fearful force on to the youngster's head, a red mist swam before his eyes, and he plunged headlong into black oblivion.

For hours Paul must have laid senseless, being restored to consciousness by the grilling rays of the sun. His head was racked with agony, and a feeling of impending calamity numbed his brain.

"Where am I?" he gasped, sitting up. "How did I get into this place?"

The lad's gaze wandered round the ancient courtyard, which was bathed in sunshine, but he could remember nothing.

The wind rustled gently in the palm leaves, and a bird piped harshly on the temple's queer dome, but Paul stared at the unwonted scene with vacant eyes. Presently, to ease the pain, he clapped a hand to his tortured forehead, and drew it away again stiff with congealed blood. Then he stared at his fingers in horror, and slowly memory returned.

Little by little, striving to collect his wits, Paul began to piece together the previous day's happenings. First he had left his bungalow on his bicycle, meaning to explore an ancient temple. Yes, here was the temple all right, but why had he not returned home?

Then he recollected that he had gone into the temple, had found nothing in the echoing chambers, and had returned to the outer one to rest. He had fallen asleep, and had been awakened by strange figures that entered mysteriously. And—yes, the apparitions had proved to be men! What had they talked about? Hadn't they hunted him through a dim courtyard, in silence, lit only by stars? Why had he been hunted?

Then suddenly full realisation beat in upon the lad's brain.

"Great Scott!" he cried, leaping to his feet. "How could I have forgotten? Those blackguards in the temple were Hindus, plotting to murder the Viceroy! And they were to do it at the feast of Vishnu! To-day, by heck! A bomb was to be in a red image—and no one knows of it but me! What's the time? Heavens, my watch has stopped! I suppose I was left for dead. Well, I'm very much alive, and half an hour will see me in Delhi. Guess I'll frustrate those plans!"

Paul clenched his teeth with sudden determination, snatched up his smashed hat, which lay on the ground beside him, then dashed across the sun-steeped courtyard, one side of which lay in black shadow, making for the great archway where he remembered dropping his machine in the struggle.

In the shadow of the court entrance the lad halted abruptly, and the chill hand of fear clutched at his heart, for the bicycle had gone!

"Ten miles from Delhi!" he gasped. "And the outrage will be attempted at mid-day! How the deuce can I get there in time?"

Utterly dismayed, Paul spun round and commenced a frenzied search throughout the ruinous precincts of the temple. But he found nothing. The invaluable machine had completely

vanished, removed, doubtless, by the men who had struck him down.

Here and there the young fellow hunted, high and low, searching every nook and cranny in which the bicycle might have been hidden. Finally, wet with perspiration, he gave up his useless quest and tore out of the desolate courtyard.

Once again in the sparse jungle, Paul glanced hastily around under the nodding palm-trees, but there was no sign of what he sought; then, with blazing eyes and clenched jaws, he dashed down towards the main road.

Past the ancient artificial pond he sped as fast as he could put one foot in front of the other, sending shrieking monkeys fleeing before his wild approach. But Paul no longer had eyes for anything. He was determined to run the whole way to Delhi, and that in a desperate race against time. And every moment the scorching rays of the tropical sun were growing stronger and stronger.

Out of the jungle on to the white, glaring ribbon of road that stretched straight to Delhi the distraught youngster shot at his best speed.

Paul had no clear plan in his mind. There would be no time now to discover and warn a white police officer. There remained only a vague idea of dashing into the city and intercepting the Viceroy as he rode through. Could the lad be in time to reach the fatal spot in the Silver Bazaar before India's ruler was blown to pieces? For on the speed of Paul's legs depended whether the Festival of Vishnu would be remembered in history as the day of a black, outrageous crime. Nay, more—the assassination of the Viceroy would be the signal for a rebellion and bloodthirsty mutiny throughout the Indian Empire. Thus one English lad, perhaps, carried the fate of millions in his hand.

Very soon Paul realised that he could not last long at such a speed, and he settled down to a steady run, blinded by the sun's glare and half choked by the rising columns of white dust, for the unmetalled road was soft, and every puff of hot wind was dust-laden and stifling.

The lad's long, wiry legs did him good service, but he gradually tired, though he forced himself onward with aching calves and bursting lungs. The issue at stake was far too great to permit of any rest or much slackening of speed.

Native peasants and chance wayfarers, clad in the brightest colours, gaped amazed at the dishevelled white lad who raced past. Then, thinking that the Englishman must be mad, they shouldered their burdens and trudged forward again. But Paul took no notice of foot passengers or slow-moving ox-carts; he was straining his eyes in vain for a glimpse of some Englishman's motor-car. And how he wished that he had told his chums about the temple he had been making for.

Paul reeled as he topped a last rise, and his breath sobbed in his labouring lungs; but the sight that he saw spurred him on again. Not a mile ahead, at the end of the white ribbon of road, lay the glittering roofs of Delhi city, shimmering in the fierce noon-day sun. Then, borne on the breeze came a sound that struck chill into the lad's heart; the rising and falling clamour of a vast crowd of natives. The festival of Vishnu had begun! Tomtoms throbbed and drummed, and the people howled in religious frenzy. The narrow streets of Delhi must be thronged with

humanity, packed with wandering beggars, vagabonds, and priests gathered in from miles around. Had they come to honour Vishnu or to witness a fearsome tragedy?

Paul redoubled his efforts, and raced on; but he was racing against time, and Heaven alone knew how much time!

CHAPTER 3.
A Close Shave!

EXHAUSTED by his punishing run and want of food, suffering tortures from the blow he had received on his head, Paul at length reeled into the hot, shut-in, narrow streets of Delhi bazaar. The back ways of the city were packed with natives in gorgeous gala dress, all pressing forward in the direction of the Chandni Chowk, the place of the Silver Merchants. The bright-hued crowd was yelling in honour of their god Vishnu, and some bore strange banners, and others white images of their heathen deity.

The air was thick and heavy, and the smell of the Indian crowd was mingled with the odour of incense and spices. Drums throbbed, cymbals clashed, and trumpets blared; a perfect pandemonium of discord—the vast throng of Asiatics was delirious with religious frenzy.

Well-nigh finished, Paul was swept forward by the surging multitude, and a great dread seized him that he might be too late.

"Has the Viceroy yet entered the Chandni Chowk?" the lad bawled out in Hindustani to a grey-bearded old native who was pressed up against him.

"Nay, sahib," was the reply; "I think not. But what manner of sahib art thou to mingle thus in a native crowd? And why art thou so dishevelled?"

Gasping out a sigh of relief, not stopping to give explanations, Paul struggled mightily to get forward. But as he neared the centre of the city the crush grew denser and denser and the din more intense.

Up the packed back streets the lad gradually fought his way, and his look was wild and his clothes were all torn. Fifty more yards, and he would strike into the centre of the Silver Bazaar.

Finally, almost at his last gasp, Paul broke through into the middle of the Chandni Chowk. Already native policemen, under their white officers, were clearing the centre of the famous street to make a way for the Viceroy who was about to pass by. The English lad thrust forward. He had but a few seconds in which to avert an unparalleled catastrophe. Could he reach one of those white officers? Could he, moreover, convince him before it was too late after all?

The yelling but good-tempered crowd, bearing aloft their white images of Vishnu, were giving way before the police on each side of the street. But Paul felt as if in a nightmare; his feet were clogged, and his bursting lungs refused to let him speak.

Then the lad reached the side of a mounted British officer, and, clutching the horse's bridle, he shrieked out:

"Send word to stop the Viceroy! And look out for a red image! There's a desperate plot to assassinate——"

Angrily the harassed officer reined his horse back, and looked down at Paul's white face and dishevelled appearance.

"What do you mean?" he barked. "Let go my horse at once! Are you

Reaching the side of the mounted British officer, Paul clutched at his horse's bridle. "Send word to the Viceroy ! And look out for the red image ! There's a desperate plot afoot to assassinate him ! "

raving mad? There are no red images in this mob!"

Paul opened his mouth to explain, but the words died in his throat, for, at that instant, with a jingle of bridles and clattering of horses' hoofs, the Viceroy and all his staff came riding up the famous street.

Tragedy was imminent!

"Stop him!" yelled Paul.

But the officer wheeled his horse to one side, shouting to the lad to get out of the way, almost dragging him off his feet.

Then, above the already terrific din, rose a new shrieking note. Paul glanced in its direction, and quailed, for from the top end of the Chandni Chowk came surging down a fresh crowd of fanatics, who had just swung in, and they were blowing wind instruments and howling like Dervishes. High up above their midst, on a little platform, they bore an image of Vishnu—and this image was flaming scarlet!

"There you are!" shrieked Paul. "Oh, it'll be too late!"

And, indeed, it seemed as though the lad's words must prove right.

With a searing oath, the officer plunged spurs into his horse and darted forward, intending to turn aside these latest arrivals. But as though forced on with irresistible might, the bearers of the red image surged round and past him.

Paul had not waited. As the mounted officer, shouting to his men, dashed forward, the lad, passing between the ranks of bewildered native policemen, raced headlong down the street. But the Hindus with the red image, more than one of whom recognised Paul, surged forward again with angry cries. Before them ran the English lad whom they thought lay dead in the temple courtyard, and they understood his intention and bellowed with rage.

But Paul had a good start, and he dashed on, blindly intent on stopping the approaching cavalcade.

The Viceroy, clad in ordinary civilian attire, was riding steadily up the street at the head of his staff. Nor did he heed the uproar farther up the Chandni Chowk, deeming it to be part of the usual demonstration always made by an Indian crowd on a feast day—a mere ebullition of fanaticism. The distraught white youth, who was racing down towards him, he regarded curiously, but did not draw rein.

Summoning up his last energies, Paul dashed up to the ruler of British India, and he halted with hands outstretched. A hundred yards behind him roared the bearers of the Red Image, and that idol rocked above the heads of its supporters like a small boat in an angry sea.

"Stop, sir!" shouted the exhausted lad. "The red image contains a bomb! Turn——"

The Viceroy reined up, but Paul got no further, he had expended all his strength; a mist swam before the lad's eyes, and he pitched forward into the white dust. One of the Viceroy's staff, utterly perplexed, rode forward to pick him up. But at that moment events happening at the top of the street drew all eyes in that direction.

Shouted at by the mounted officer, who had grasped Paul's meaning when it was too late, the native constables on each side of the road hurled themselves forward in a converging wave. Then they drew their truncheons, and shouted out to the oncoming gang who bore the scarlet Vishnu, ordering them to halt.

Police and conspirators, the latter seeming now to number about fifty, met with a violent impact, and yells of warning and shrieks of dismay rose high above the indescribable clamour and confusion.

Bamboo sticks and truncheons rose and fell, and members of the hemmed-in crowd fought madly to get clear of the scrimmage. Then suddenly the scarlet image, already swaying dangerously, toppled off its pedestal and crashed to the ground, landing right in the midst of its raving supporters.

Followed instantly a deafening explosion, accompanied by a blinding, vivid flash. And dismembered bodies, torn clothes, and smashed flagstones shot up heavenwards. If the scene before had been wild, it was now appalling, and the groans and cries of the wounded added to the general din.

The shock of the explosion stove in the front of the nearest flimsy houses, and they came crashing down with a roar like thunder, sending up clouds of red-brown dust. The affrighted horses of the Viceroy's party reared and plunged in their terror.

Then gradually the dust-clouds began to clear, and the police, those that were uninjured, began to push the mob back, warily skirting a great hole blown in the road. The surviving conspirators fled, yelling, leaving their dead and dying to take care of themselves.

Very shortly the street was cleared, and the Viceroy's party began to move forward again, but at the yawning gap the horses shied, leaping away from other bloodstained things.

"That was a close shave!" exclaimed one of the Viceroy's staff, mopping his brow; and the Viceroy himself nodded. Then he turned in his saddle, and ordered that the young Englishman, who had rushed down with the warning, should be brought before him as soon as he had recovered.

* * * * *

Some hours later, Paul came to his senses in the hospital to which he had been immediately taken. And the Viceroy's summons surprised as well as delighted him, but he lost no time in obeying.

Arrived at the Viceregal Lodge, the lad found himself in the presence of a tall, distinguished-looking Englishman, who questioned him carefully as to how he had stumbled on the plot.

Briefly Paul related his experiences, laying stress on the fact that he had had no intention of prying into matters that did not concern him. Nevertheless, the lad gave voice to his desire to enter the Indian Police Service. Ultimately he was dismissed, but first received a firm handshake from the Viceroy and a promise that his wishes would not be forgotten.

So Paul returned to his clerking. But a week later, to his unbounded delight, he was appointed to the Indian Police, a career after his own heart, which offered to give him all the romance and adventure he could wish for.

However, whatever the future might hold, it was very unlikely that Paul would ever forget his grim experiences in a certain temple, one dreadful night before the annual festival of Vishnu.

THE END.

(Another exciting yarn of River-wise Ned and his staunch chums of the London barge, Estuary Belle, in next week's GEM, entitled : " THE COINERS ! " Look out for it.)

Jack Morton springs a big surprise on George Clifton —

—who is besieged by the angry football crowd.

THE TRIERS

BY JACK CRICHTON

Jack Morton, with the assistance of his faithful band of stalwart sportsmen, strives hard to checkmate his rascally cousin and win the rights which are his due.

A Strange Game !

THERE was no possible question as to the rivalry between Boltwich and Crewbridge, and the two towns were so close to one another that whenever the two teams met in League or Cup games thousands merely tramped from Boltwich to Crewbridge, or vice versa.

This Saturday it was a question of the good folks of Boltwich making the journey to Crewbridge, and this they were doing with somewhat mixed feelings.

Boltwich was beginning to get annoyed.

Things were not right with the team, and the news that three more of the old players had been placed on the transfer list did not do anything to improve the ruffled feelings, coming so quickly after the news that their new idol, Jack Morton, had been arrested, and would be unable to turn out for the team.

And, strangely enough, the feeling of the crowd was all with Jack and the new directors. Indeed, things were blamed at the door of George Clifton which were not his fault, and there was no question that the thousands of sturdy fans who made the journey this Saturday afternoon to Crewbridge were ready for anything—the more exciting the better.

"If young Jack Morton could turn out," was the feeling, "we'd show them !"

"George Clifton's put him away !"

"Yes, and now the lad's escaped !"

"Good luck to him !"

"I'd like to see him turn up."

"Ay, lad; and if he does he shall have a fair chance to play !"

Such were the expressions of opinion which could have been heard on every side of the road as the crowd made its way to the ground.

In the meantime Jack Morton had entered the ground very quietly, with Laurie Robson, who had acquired a moustache and a large pair of horn-rimmed spectacles during the night, and THE GEM LIBRARY.—No. 826.

was changing in a quiet shed far from the madding crowd and the police.

After Jack had escaped from the Babe he had been taken by remorse as soon as he realised that the Babe had turned back and was not following him. The last he had seen of Laurie was on the ground, unconscious, and now he was suddenly afraid to leave him to the tender mercies of that brute.

So he hurried back, throwing his own safety to the winds, and had the satisfaction, from behind a hedge, of seeing Laurie and the Babe parting. Five minutes later the youngsters were together again and discussing a plan of campaign.

Laurie thought he had frightened the Babe, but he was not certain.

WHAT HAS GONE BEFORE !

For the sake of his invalid mother, Jack Morton, a lad of seventeen, calls upon his grandfather, Sir Jasper Clifton, for aid. It was by no means a pleasant undertaking for Jack, for his mother, much against her father's wishes, had married a worker in Sir Jasper's mill, who was now dead. Sir Jasper, however, is taken up with the lad straight away, saying that he will alter his will and make him co-heir with George Clifton, another grandson, and Jack's cousin, and whose great interest in life is the Boltwich Football Club. In high spirits, Jack gives up his old job to take up work at Cliftons'. But Sir Jasper dies that night. Thinking only of his mother, Jack goes to George Clifton, but his appeal proves futile, Clifton telling him that the will is unaltered, and that he is not wanted. Jack's anger is aroused, and, meeting Ronnie Stevens, whom George Clifton had deemed it wise to sack, the two lads, former players of Boltwich F.C., determine to fight Clifton.

"We'll get a team that won't be beat," said Stevens, "and call them the Triers."

The team shows great promise, much to the annoyance of Clifton, who, scheming to get Morton hounded out of Boltwich, makes a spoof appointment with the lad. Unsuspiciously Jack falls into the trap when calling upon Clifton, who denies knowledge of the letter. Later, to Jack's surprise, he is arrested and accused of the theft of fifty pounds. However, through Laurie Robson, holder of the bulk of the Boltwich F.C. shares, Jack is able to effect an escape on the eve of the great match with Crewbridge.

"Can't ever tell with a customer like that," he said.

"No, by Jove !"

"But, at the same time," Laurie went on, "I think he will keep his tongue between his teeth. But we will hide you more carefully."

So Jack had spent a night in a very secret cellar in Laurie's domain, and when the morning came he was glad to hear that so far no word had come to Laurie from the police.

Now the question was to get him on to the pitch and to let him play undisturbed.

Laurie had done his work well.

Dressed with a long overcoat and a pair of greasy flannel bags over his soccer gear, the lad strolled with Laurie towards the dressing-room.

On the ground the excitement was intense. There was something electric in the air, as though everyone expected something amazing to happen. Slowly the clock crept round towards the time appointed for the kick-off. The two sets of supporters yelled furiously at one another, and, curiously enough, Boltwich seemed every bit as confident as the home team.

At last !

Here they come !

A shout went up, and suddenly Jack, handing his coat to Laurie, and slipping out of his flannel bags, bounded on to the pitch after his own team.

What a roar went to the skies! It was a splendid moment and an amazing one. First that roar, then suddenly a sob of silence.

What would happen?

Some fool yelled at the top of his voice:

"It's Jack Morton! Our Jack turned out, after all !"

"Jack, Jack, Jack, boy !" yelled the mob.

Even as the roar of the multitude died away into a murmur a shrill, piercing cry rang out from the direction of the grand-stand. It came from George Clifton.

"It's Jack Morton! It's the boy who escaped from prison yesterday. They want him! Arrest him! Arrest him——"

He got no further, for at that moment a couple of policemen had started towards the pitch. It was an amazing sight.

Within a second twenty stalwart Boltwich fans pounced on them, and they were gently but firmly forced back to their former positions on the ring-side.

"Arrest him!" shouted George Clifton wildly.

"Shut up, you!" cried a Crewbridge fan, knocking Clifton's hat over his eyes. "Haven't you got any sport in you? Let the lad play, anyhow!"

"But he's a thief!"

"So are you probably!" cried someone else, and the crowd began to laugh.

Meanwhile, on the pitch, an extraordinary state of affairs had taken place. A pompous inspector of police had gathered together his men and had started again towards the lad; but in a second they were surrounded by a thousand Boltwich fans and gently but firmly pushed back.

"Let him play! Sport's sport! Give Jack a chance!"

And so the crowd took charge of the game.

The Crewbridge fans were with the Boltwich lads, too. And suddenly the referee, who was very much in the dark about it all, blew his whistle, and the game started, with a dozen stalwart Crewbridge policemen very closely guarded.

Never in his life had Jack felt so keen to do his best; never had he felt so inspired, so capable.

The ground was a bit heavy, but he seemed to get through it like a fish in water.

Within the first few seconds of the game he was away. He simply trifled with opponents. He dashed right down the field, tricking men right and left, and then sent in a long, low, groundshot, which the opposing goalie only just managed to save by conceding a corner.

It was a brilliant start, and it put the crowd on very good terms with Jack.

"Good old Jack! Give it 'em, boy! We'll look after you, lad!"

And they did, while the lad played the game of his life.

Nothing could stop him.

He had confidence to-day in the men about him. New blood had been imported, but he had old friends behind him. There was Ronnie, Steve, and Harry Turner in goal. He felt that he could take risks with those three behind him; they would never concede a single point.

And so it happened.

He had no fear, and, fearing nothing, he did things which he would not have dared to do ordinarily, and within ten minutes he had scored a brilliant opening goal and had the Crewbridge team obviously rattled.

It was a long time since such a brilliant display as this had been seen on the Crewbridge ground, and the dramatic nature of the game had fairly taken the crowd's imagination.

After that first goal all was plain sailing.

The Crewbridge team played hard, but they simply could not cope with Jack in this mood.

He marshalled his men cleverly; he was not selfish, and yet he was obviously the predominating figure in the field.

Once, indeed, the Crewbridge forward-line attacked. It came from a miskick by Steve Logan—a thing that happened about once a year, and which invariably sent up a groan of horror from his host of faithful admirers.

Still, the greatest of players have moments of fallibility, and within a flash the home line were swarming about the Boltwich goal, and Harry Turner was performing every sort of wonder and miracle.

Again and again the ball missed the goal by inches. Once it hit the cross-bar and rebounded into play, was sent back flashing against the right-hand post, back to the cross-bar again, and then into a mob of players.

Then suddenly Jack arrived on the scene.

He could mix it when needed. Not roughly or unfairly, after the Bill Atkins fashion; but he could give and take a hearty charge when there was need. And now, indeed, there was need as he barged into that surging mass of players and insisted, as it were, on relieving the situation.

And he did!

He got the ball, cleverly tricked his opponent, and then suddenly was away.

A shout went up:

"Come on, Jack!"

A back and a goalkeeper were in front of him.

He started off like lightning. He did not even try to dodge the back, simply depending on his speed. He came up to him, punted, and raced after the leather, leaving the other simply standing.

And now for goal. He swerved right in. The goalie came out to meet him. He had already seen too much of Jack's shooting to wish to stand and suffer. He rushed out, and as he reached Jack the lad side-stepped, and a moment later had scored a second brilliant goal.

A mighty yell went up, and Crewbridge itself congratulated him. This was brilliant stuff, and no real man who liked to see a good sporting effort could do otherwise than admire it.

So half-time came, and with it the strangest sight surely ever seen on a football-field. A crowd surged out and surrounded Jack, while the police were kept very much to their own quarters.

In the stand George Clifton was expressing his feelings somewhat freely.

"A nice state of things, I must say!" he said to a man close to him. "You haven't enough police in Crewbridge to stop a gaolbird playing like this! You ought to see if there are any ex-convicts who want a game in your side!"

The man stared at him.

"You're George Clifton, aren't you?" he said.

"I am!"

"Well, we've heard about you in Crewbridge!" said the man. "If you don't want a thick ear you had better keep your mouth shut! You ought to be pleased to see the lad play like that for you!"

Clifton said no more, but moved away. He was white with anger, and already he was cursing himself for having wasted so much time. He went quickly from the stand. He would soon put a spoke in the wheel of his cousin, he thought.

But even as he went to telephone the

Immediately the whistle sounded for half-time the crowd surged upon the playing field and surrounded Jack Morton, at the same time keeping the police well out of the lad's reach.

amazing news to the police in Boltwich he was seen, and Laurie Robson followed him.

The End and After!

FOUR goals did Boltwich score against Crewbridge, and each one of them came from the toe of Jack Morton, the centre-forward. It is doubtful whether there were enough police in the country to have arrested Jack after the game; it is certain there were not enough on the ground or even in Boltwich. Military would have been needed on that amazing occasion to have arrested the youngster.

Even as the final whistle went Laurie Robson rushed on to the pitch, followed by an enormous crowd.

"The police from Boltwich are outside!" he cried excitedly. "Give him a chance to get away, boys!"

The boys needed no second bidding.

A battle royal ensued. The police were now reinforced by men from Boltwich, and they surged towards the players. But a coat was flung about Jack, he was pushed from hand to hand, and within a few minutes he was indeed lost by himself—while the battle still raged within—in Crewbridge.

Laurie Robson had prepared for all this, and within a few more minutes Jack saw a car waiting for him at the end of a quiet street. He bounded towards it.

Laurie was waiting for him.

"Jump in, lad!" he said.

Jack wasted no time.

It wasn't safe for them to return to Boltwich that night, so they drove in the opposite direction, and before long had come to a neighbouring town, where they felt they would be safe for some days, at any rate.

"And now," said Laurie, as they sat down to a very welcome supper, "we have got to review the situation, my lad! I don't really know if I have done you a lot of good! You certainly can't go back to Boltwich for a bit!"

Jack smiled.

"Nor can you, can you, Laurie?"

Laurie laughed.

"I guess not!" he answered. "Well, then, what are we to do? It's this fellow Clifton every time! My word, Jack, I would like to down him! I tell you what. You stay here, hiding, a few days, and I will go back. I think I shall be able to keep out of their touch. After all, they can't very well do anything to me. If they try to they must arrest all the directors; no one can actually prove that I had anything more to do with you playing than any-one else. It simply looked as though the crowd took the matter into their own hands. I'm going back, and, now we have a few days to spare I am going to find out if I can whether we cannot discover what is at the bottom of this charge of stealing fifty quid!"

Jack put a hand out.

"You are a real pal, Laurie!" he said.

"Oh, I'm just a Trier!" Laurie laughed. "And I shall never quit trying until I have downed that brute Clifton! You ought to have seen him

---

---

to-day! I'll slip back to-morrow morning!"

Gripping Jack's hand, Laurie hurried away.

Those were hard days for Jack Morton.

He felt that he could have endured anything better than simply sitting still and doing nothing. But that was what he had to do.

He saw by the papers that there was a hue-and-cry all over the place for him.

His game at Crewbridge had done the trick.

There was real trouble now for the directors, and there was no knowing where it was going to end. The police were angry.

Happily, Boltwich was behind the directors to a man, and that made all the difference; but Jack realised that he must lay very low indeed, and that it would be simply madness for him to attempt to go back to the old town.

Still, it was hard.

Nothing was being done about the will, nothing was being done to exonerate him from the charge of being a thief, and he did not know how his old mother was getting along.

At last he could stand it no longer. He must return.

He knew that to a certain extent he was letting Laurie down, but he had to see his mother. The police would probably be watching the cottage night and day.

He travelled by night, and it was after midnight when at last he carefully approached the little home.

So far he had not seen a single sign of anyone hanging about, but he knew that the police would probably not be hanging about with a brass band in attendance.

He did not, of course, approach by the front. Instead, as soon as he entered the street he slipped into another gateway, round to the back of the cottage, and then he started a long, crawling, climbing journey over fences.

On and on he went until at last he found himself in his own back garden. No one was about; a deathly silence prevailed, broken only after a little while by the sudden clanging of the church clock.

He tiptoed up to the back door and idly tried the handle. To his surprise, it came open, and he went in. Already he had a feeling within him that all was not well, but he could not turn back now. On and on he went—up into his mother's room, breathing softly, and hoping against hope that everything was all right.

Then he spoke:

"Mother!"

There came no answer.

"Mother!"

Casting caution to the winds, he turned on the light. The room was empty. His mother was not here. Suddenly his heart seemed to stand cold within him, and he turned quickly away.

What had happened to his mother? He tried to think.

Supposing she was ill? Supposing she was dead? He felt his heart stop beating for one second. If she had died wanting him—then Heaven help George Clifton!

He had grown careless now, and he moved downstairs as though there was no danger at all. And even as he entered the little kitchen again the light from a policeman's lantern was flashed into his startled face, and a harsh voice cried:

"Hands up, Jack Morton! It's a fair cop!"

In the Nick of Time!

JACK had grown used by this time to acting on the spur of the moment.

As he recognised the voice of the detective who had originally arrested him his hand came into contact with the top of a chair.

With one swift movement he picked it up and let fly.

A cry followed as the chair found a billet, and the light crashed to the ground. The man made a dive for Jack, but missed him by inches. In another moment the lad was out in the night again.

Pandemonium was let loose in the quiet street then.

The detective rushed after Jack, blowing his whistle for all he was worth and yelling like a maniac, and as the lad dashed up the street, windows were thrown open and shouts followed him.

But Jack had a good start, and he was in the pink of condition. The detective really had no more chance of catching him than Babe Bolton had had a week before, and within a few minutes the lad stopped to take a breather, safe behind a hedge, with the dark mantle of the night to hide him.

But there was no time to waste.

He must get back again. But could he? Suddenly he paused, and asked himself a question. What had happened to his old mother? Would it not be better to go and give himself up to the police, so that he might have the answer to that question?

Still, the instinct of freedom is, perhaps, the strongest in the world, and the lad moved on and on into the night, back in the direction of the town he had left earlier in the evening. There would be no train until the early morning, and it would not do for him to board one anywhere near Boltwich.

He had just reached a small wooden bridge over the River Bolt, from which the town took its name, when suddenly the sound of a motor approaching made him dive down quickly into the ditch which ran at the side of the road.

"That was a narrow squeak!" he muttered to himself.

But even as he spoke he jumped to his feet, with a shout, for the car had suddenly skidded on the sticky surface of the road, and even as it was about to cross the bridge had plunged into the wooden railing which protected the path at the side of it.

There was a crash, a roaring of the engine, and in another moment, above it all, there came the sound of a woman's scream.

"Great Scott!" muttered Jack, dashing forward.

His natural thought had been that the car belonged to the police, and that this was the beginning of his pursuit in earnest. But now he knew otherwise.

He dashed down the side of the river bank, and in another moment was up to his waist in the rather swift-running water. The car had turned a complete somersault, and he could tell at a glance that it was touch and go. Pinned in the car were some people, doubtless. At any rate, not a sign of life came to greet him in that weird moment.

It needed terrific strength, but he had it—inspired, too, as he was, by the horror of it all—and in a few moments he had opened the door of the car beneath the water. He thrust a hand in, and a moment later a hand had caught his wrist. It was rather a ghastly feeling. There was madness about that (Continued on page 26.)

FOOTBALLERS' NAMES.

(Continued from page 15 *)*

Cockle, Crosbie, Cross, Clennell, Cameron, Chedgzoy, Cock, Chadwick, Clough, Curry, Cookson, Cope, Cook, Crilly, Chaplin, Collier, Crockford, Campbell, Crown, Chance, Chipperfield, Crompton, Charlton, Conner, Craig, Cosgrove, Cherrett, Crossley, Carter, Clarke, Cotton, Cunningham, Cairns, Clunas, Connolly, Cassidy, Carr, Cowan, Chapman, Chambers, Clay, Cresswell.

Dunn, Dickson, Dorrell, Dawson, Davies, Donaldson, Dinsdale, Dimmock, Duckett, Duncan, Dominy, Davison, Duckworth, Dockray, Danskin, Dreyer, Denoon, Denyer, Duffus, Dunlop, Dixon, Doyle, Doran, Dale.

Emerson, Evans, Ellerington, England, Ellis, Edelston, Edgley, Eggo, Elliott, Edge, Edwards, Emmett, Ewart.

French, Ferguson, Ford, Forshaw, Fletcher, Flood, Flint, Feebury, Fleming, Fleetwood, Flynn, Fox, Foxall, Fort, Forbes, Fowler, Fazackerley, Findlay, Featherstone, Forsythe, Frame, Fyfe, Finney, Forster, Fitton, Fairclough, Fern.

Grimshaw, Gill, Gilchrist, Gough, Gillespie, Grimsdell, Gittins, Gibson, Graham, Goldthorpe, Grundy, Gallogley, Gibbon, Gomm, Gregory, George, Getwood, Groves, Greig, Gardner, Gallagher, Glancy, Greenshields, Gourlay, Goodchild.

Howarth, Haworth, Hampton, Harrow, Harland, Hopkin, Hudspeth, Harris, Ramill, Hill, Hardy, Hamilton, Hawes, Handley, Hufton, Hine, Hughes, Heap, Higginbotham, Hoddinott, Hebden, Hilditch, Howson, Hunter, Hayes, Hutchins, Hannaford, Harrold, Howie, Henshall, Hodges, Halstead, Hugall, Hogg, Henderson, Harper, Hulton, Hillhouse, Hair, Hart, Haines, Hole.

Irvine, Islip, Iremonger, Irwin.

Jennings, Jack, Jackson, Johnson.

Kirton, Kelly, Kneeshaw, Keenor, Kay, Knowles, Kane, Keenlyside, Kidd, Kilpatrick, Kean.

Linfoot, Longworth, Low, Lindsay, Little, Lonsdale, Lockhead, Longmuir, Lea, Lievesley, Lane, Lockett, Legge, Lofthouse, Lenny, Lyner, Lawson, Lambie, Lacey.

Moss, Mort, Mosscrop, Meehan, Maitland, Mitchell, Murphy, Morgan, Milton, Mercer, Marshall, Magee, Moore, Martin, Mills, Mason, Mew, Matthews, Moule, Myers, Marsden, Middleton, Maidment, Mehaffy, Mee, Moody, Musgrove, Malcolm, Morton, Manderson, Meiklejohn, Muirhead, Moffat, Mutch, Meredith, Marriott, Mackie, Menlove, Mitton, Marks, Marsh, M'Intyre, M'Neil, M'Kinlay, M'Nabb, M'Intosh, M'Donald, M'Call, M'Grory, M'Cluggage, M'Lean, M'Candless, M'Coll, M'Lacklan, M'Stey, M'Alpine, M'Kenna, M'Inally, M'Nair, M'Minn. McBain, McCracken.

Nuttall, Neesam, Neil, Needham, Nash, Nisbet, Nelson.

Osborne, Ormston, Orr, O'Hare.

Pym, Pringle, Price, Parker, Poole, Paterson, Pearson, Penn, Plum, Page, Preston, Probert, Pagnam, Peel, Potts, Palmer, Prouse, Puddefoot, Pender, Pape, Peacock, Pantling, Partridge, Peers.

Quantrill, Quinn.

Robson, Rollo, Raitt, Richardson, Rawlings, Ruffell, Robbie, Rigg, Radford, Ridley, Reay, Ramsay, Robb, Ritchie, Ranskin, Reed, Rooke, Roe.

Spiers, Smart, Stephenson, Seddon, Sewell, Smelt, Smith, Scott, Slade, Spencer, Seymour, Spaven, Sampy, Seed, Storer, Stage, Shea, Steele, Simms, Smailes, Symes, Sturgess, Sayles, Spottiswood, Scattergood, Sinclair, Stuart, Sayer, Sutcliffe, Salt, Summerfield, Shaw, Sillito, Sneddon, Somerville, Shone, Streets, Sampey, Stannard, Skinner, Sage.

Townrow, Turnbull, Tremelling, Thain, Troup, Tunstall, Tresadern, Tonner, Thoms, Torrance, Tompkin, Titmuss, Tempest, Timmins, Thorpe, Templeton, Townsley, Toner.

Urwin.

Voysey, Vizard, Vallis, Volsey, Vigrass.

Womack, Walsh, Weaver, Wilding, Whitton, Wadsworth, Woosnam, Woodhouse, Walters, Walden, Watson, Wainscoat, Wood, Williams, Winship, Wolfe, Whitehouse, Whalley, Whipp, Wolstenholme, Waterall, Worrall, Williamson, Weston, Wigglesworth, Ward, Webster, Whitehurst, Waddell, Wright, Wilson, Wren, Widdowson, Wylie, White, Welsh, Walker.

York.

No. 7 SET.

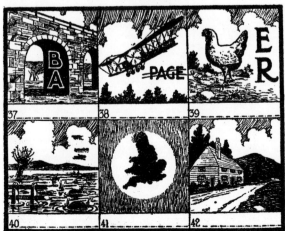

Don't Delay with Your Entries!

Build this fine Crane for Yourself

these Letter Scales for Father

this Wool Winder for Mother

this Doll's Pram for Sister

" THE TRIERS ! "
(Continued from page 24.)

hand which clutched at him. He could imagine it dragging him down and down to death. But it did not do so, and a minute later he sank exhausted to the dark side of the river with a young lady in his arms.

He made a great effort, and, bending over her, tried to get her to speak.

"Anyone else?" he roared.

She shook her head, then again closed her eyes.

And so they rested for, perhaps, five minutes.

At last the girl sat up.

"You saved my life!" she said.

Jack gave a grunt.

"Well, I dare say I did!" he exclaimed. "But I always said that that bridge is a scandal, and so it jolly well is! There ought to be a row about it! And your car—look at it!"

The girl gave a nod. In the darkness Jack could not see her face, but she had a pleasant voice.

"Yes—and my father only gave it to me a little while ago for my birthday! It's a shame——"

Jack started.

"I say, do I know you?" he asked, forgetting that it was not very wise for Jack Morton to know anyone at this moment.

"I am Gracie Grayes."

"What?" exclaimed Jack. "You are the daughter of old Graves, up at the Old Hall?"

"Yes."

"I'm Jack Morton!"

It was the girl's turn to start now, and a moment or so later, while she sat and stared at him, the lad realised what had happened.

"Jack Morton!" she murmured. "Oh, you poor soul! You must have been having an awful time lately! I have been hoping and praying they would never get you! I never believed you stole that fifty pounds! I always believed that it was a wicked plot——"

"It was!"

"I know! And here you are still!

THE GEM LIBRARY.—No. 826.

I hoped you were miles away, and now you have saved my life, and I shall not be able to tell all the world!"

Jack started violently.

"No, for goodness' sake, Miss Graves, don't say anything about me! But perhaps you can do me one good turn?"

"Anything!" said the girl. "You saved my life!"

"Oh, I simply did what anyone would have done! Do you know what has happened to my mother?"

The girl nodded in the dark.

"Yes. I heard that she had gone to live with some friends," she said. "But, if you like, to-morrow I will go and see her, and give her your love and any message you like."

Jack breathed hard.

"Would you?"

"Of course I would!"

"It would make me your slave for life!" he said.

"It would be a very slight way of repaying all you have done for me," the girl went on.

Jack smiled.

"Well, would you just tell her that I am all right, and that I am going to prove that I am innocent, and that I am still going to get our rights out of George Clifton?"

The girl bent her head.

"Very well," she said. "And please believe, Mr. Morton, that there is one more person in Boltwich who believes in you. I think nearly all Boltwich does believe in you, and it will not be long before you are free to do what you want!"

She rose.

"Hurt anywhere?" asked Jack.

The girl smiled and shook her head.

"No—except I am horribly wet!"

"I know! You'd better hurry back to Boltwich and get help!" he smiled, as he held out a hand. "You will not think it feeble of me to desert you now?"

"I think you have been splendid!" said the girl, as they parted.

A Bad Business !

THERE was, of course, no possible question now of Jack turning out for Boltwich again.

There had been too much trouble about the game against Crewbridge, and the directors had received a very sharp message from the F.A. that the lad was not to appear again.

Besides, the police had no intention of being caught napping a second time.

A large force had been drafted into the town, for all sorts of rumours had been put about to the effect that Jack was going to play, that a thousand fans were going to march to the ground with him, and that the military were going to be called out.

Actually, nothing of the sort was even in contemplation.

The only person besides Jack himself who had even dreamed of such madness was Laurie Robson, and he had soon given way to calmer reason.

No; Jack was safely in hiding fifty miles from the old town, and the team turned out without him.

However, the result of it all was quite electric.

The gate was a record one, and the number of police on the ground was enormous. Indeed, until the game started the crowd amused itself by counting them and gibing at them; but

serious trouble did not arise, and the game started without undue incident.

The change in the Boltwich team was apparent at once, and was quite remarkable.

They seemed like a team without a leader—as, indeed, they were. A very decent player had taken Jack's place, but he was not able to do much.

Again and again Ronnie would give him his chance; but he was overawed, it would seem, by the occasion, and he never got his forward-line properly under control. Before half-time the home team was two goals to the bad.

This would have been serious enough, but the crowd had suddenly taken it nastily.

"It's George Clifton's doing!" someone shouted; and the cry was taken up until it went round and round the ground like a song.

"We want George Clifton! We want Clifton!"

Actually, Clifton was seated in the stand, looking on at the game with a grim, set look.

He had not been very happy lately. Things simply did not go right for him. Long before this he had expected that Jack would be safe under lock and key. And he was still free. Also, old Graves, the butler, Babe Bolton, Bill Atkins, and others of his hirelings were demanding more and more money as the price of their silence.

That would not have mattered so much, for Clifton was very rich, but the wretched will was being held up in the most ridiculous way. He could almost have sworn that old Brown, the solicitor, was doing this on purpose, although young Clifford, the other partner, declared that this was not so.

Still, it was terribly annoying. And now suddenly, as he listened and his ears caught the refrain which was going round and round the ground: "We want George Clifton!" his heart stood still.

Was this a sign of the beginning of the end?

"Of course not!"

Laurie came suddenly towards him.

"Hallo, Clifton!" he said.

"What do you want?"

Laurie regarded his enemy with a sort of benign friendliness and superiority.

"Well, I only wanted to say," he began, "if you would give a chap a chance to speak to you civilly, that you are a bit foolish to be here."

Clifton started.

"Indeed?" he said.

Laurie yawned.

"Of course," he said, "there are some people who cannot see in front of them, but if the crowd gets to know you are here it might go badly for you."

Clifton sneered.

"Oh, I know that some of your gaol-birds don't care for me, Robson, but I do not happen to care a hang! In fact, I should be much obliged if you would mind your own business and would leave me to mind mine!"

Laurie flushed. He had really spoken out of decent feeling. He hated Clifton heartily enough, but he realised that there was actual danger for him here, and he didn't want to see the fellow made a mess of.

"All right!" he said, turning away. "Go your own way, then!"

It was not long before George Clifton was bitterly regretting that he had ignored Laurie's warning!

(Look out for another full-of-thrill instalment of this powerful serial next week, boys.)

Printed and published every Wednesday by the Proprietors, The Amalgamated Press (1922), Ltd., The Fleetway House, Farringdon Street, London, E.C.4. Advertisement offices: The Fleetway House, Farringdon Street, London, E.C.4. Registered for transmission by Canadian Magazine Post. Subscription rates: Inland and Abroad, 11s. per annum; 5s. 6d. for six months. Sole agents for South Africa: The Central News Agency, Ltd. Sole agents for Australia and New Zealand: Messrs. Gordon & Gotch, Ltd.; and for Canada, The Imperial News Co., Ltd. (Canada).—Saturday, Dec. 8th, 1923.
NN

My Readers' Own Corner

Tuck Hampers and Money Prizes Awarded for Interesting Paragraphs.

(If You Do Not Win a Prize This Week—You May Next!)

All Efforts in this Competition should be Addressed to: The GEM LIBRARY, "My Readers' Own Corner," Gough House, Gough Square, London, E.C.4.

GLOUCESTER TAKES THE TUCK HAMPER.
NO SUCH THING!

An enthusiastic grocer had, the other day, printed in large letters on a board placed over the shop door the following words: "Mr. Gladstone said jam is a good substitute for butter. Try our home-made jam." A woman entered his shop, bought two pots of jam and carried them off. In a few days she returned, laid one pot of jam on the counter, and with an indignant air, exclaimed: "I've been brought up to believe that everything Mr. Gladstone spoke was truth. I'll never believe another word!" "Indeed, madam, why not?" inquired the bewildered grocer. "Why," said the indignant woman, "because he said jam was the best substitute for butter. It is not. It won't fry my fish."—A Tuck Hamper filled with delicious tuck has been awarded to Frampton E. H. Stoke, 21, All Saints Road, Gloucester.

NOT QUITE KINDNESS!

Tony was a boy Scout, and one night he awoke full of terrible remorse, for he had not performed his two acts of kindness. Suddenly he heard the click of the mousetrap. He got up and let the mouse away—that was one act of kindness. In the morning he told his father about it. "Yes, my boy, but what was your second act of kindness after liberating the mouse?" "Oh, I gave it to the cat," answered Tony quite unconcerned.—Half-a-crown has been awarded to W. Hare, 3, Clifton Terrace, Portobello, Scotland.

NOT WHAT HE MEANT, EXACTLY!

The "Reds" goalkeeper and centre-forward were discussing the manners of their corpulent left-back, and from high words they got to blows, and were both engaged in a hot fight when the left-back appeared on the scene. "What's the meaning of all this?" he said. "Oh," said the goalie, "I was only sticking up for you." "Sticking up for me! What do you mean?" asked the corpulent back. "Well, Brown said you were not fit to live with a pig." "Oh, did he! And what did you say?" "I said you were!"—Half-a-crown has been awarded to A. Yelland, 69, Broadfield Road, Sheffield.

WRONG END UP!

A construction gang were working on a section of the railroad, where the mud was excessively deep. The foreman was resting in a shanty nearby, when suddenly he heard a workman—a foreigner—shout: "Queek, queek, bringa da peek, bringa da shovel! Antonio stuck in da mud!" The boss, making a megaphone of his hands, shouted back: "How far in?" "Up to hees knees!" was the excited reply. "Well, then, let him walk out!" the boss replied disgustedly. Back came the unexpected answer. "Oh, but he canna no walk, he wronga end up!"—Half-a-crown has been awarded to A. May, 36, St. John's Road, Balby, Doncaster.

TUCK HAMPER COUPON.
The GEM LIBRARY.
No attempt will be considered unless accompanied by one of these Coupons.

The Book for Every "Gem" Reader.

THE "HOLIDAY ANNUAL."—GET IT TO-DAY!

EVERY WEDNESDAY.

The GEM 2ᴰ

No. 827.
Vol. XXIV.
December 15th,
1923.

LIBRARY
OF
SCHOOL AND SPORTING STORIES

TURNED BACK FROM THE TEAM!

Ralph Reckness Cardew, the junior football skipper of St. Jim's, is ordered back to detention on the day of the Rookwood match! (A startling incident from the long complete school story of Tom Merry & Co., in this issue.)

Your Editor Chats With His Readers.

Address all letters: The Editor, The "Gem" Library, The Fleetway House, Farringdon Street, London, E.C.4. Write me, you can be sure of an answer in return.

My dear Chums,—Our Grand Christmas Number of the "Gem" will be on sale next week. That is the leading item of intelligence I have to impart on this occasion. It seems to me that it is just one of the jolly things that really matter. I have had plenty of letters suggesting this thing and that for our Christmas "Special." When you have the issue in your hands next Wednesday I know one thing—you will admit that it is the finest, most seasonable, and varied number of the "Gem" ever put on the market. Christmas brings no end of cheery reminders, and new ideas come in with a rush at the end of December, when the old year starts packing up its bag ready for departure. You know how it is. You want to get busy about crowds of things—really important matters—and you want the old friends to remember the season in the usual manner. Well, the "Gem" can put in a claim for being a very old friend, a true friend, a chum who has stood the test of years. And it is not going to disappoint you. Not likely!

" D'ARCY'S CHRISTMAS PARTY!"
By Martin Clifford.

Our St. Jim's yarn is a nailer. You will like it, boys. It shows how the feud between Cardew and Tom Merry is still at fever-heat. Of course, there can be no question of putting this fine story in a nutshell. It cannot be done. There is too much in it to grip the attention, with the brilliant scene at the mansion of Lord Eastwood, where the festive season is being spent, and with Cardew nursing bad feelings, whatever Tom Merry does. There is a lot more to it. The tale has a sting in it; also the spirit of something which may be called life music, for there are other influences working for peace in the grand old home of D'Arcy. It is a real, proper sort of Christmas yarn, this—drama, wit, sparkle, and heaps of good cheer!

THE "HOLIDAY ANNUAL."

Enough has been said to show that no Christmas can be considered complete without the Special Number of the "Gem." But the "Holiday Annual" fits in here like a glove as well. It is the merriest and most fascinating book for the holidays, or any other old time, on the market.

THE "ST. JIM'S NEWS."

And now here's a positive treat! Circumstances have compelled our Supplement to go on short commons of late. Compensation for this fact will be found in the "Gem" Christmas Number. The "St. Jim's News" for next Wednesday will be found to be the brightest, smartest, and most captivating ever printed.

FREE TUCK !

Apply to the "Gem" for this. Our Tuck-Hamper Competition is romping along in great style. If you like tuck, just enter our easy competition. Besides the substantial Tuck-Hamper, which finds its way to some reader's address each week, there are extra prizes of nimble half-crowns.

"THE GHOST OF GREYMINSTER CASTLE !"
By Vincent Owen.

Do you ever have daydreams? They are immensely popular. It is enormously attractive to weave a genial little plot about how a fortune of the extra-large kind drops in unexpectedly, say, about Christmas-time. But in this splendid Christmas story the chief character, Dick Baker, comes in for the glorious experience without dreaming about it. This is a wonderful story, with a legend thrown in concerning the mysterious disappearance of the heir to the grand old castle and the wealth of Sir John de Coverley. It is packed with thrills, for Greyminster's ghost is one calculated to strike terror into the pluckiest. Whatever you do, don't miss this splendid treat for next week.

WHAT'S TO COME ?

That is always the question. It is reasonable enough. We all have to look forward and prepare for the future. On the other side of next week's superlatively excellent issue of the "Gem" there are plenty of big happenings. Just ahead of us we descry the lights of the New Year of 1924, and it will be all clear ahead for our favourite paper, with new triumphs for it on every hand. I have, as a beginning, made arrangements for a particularly powerful new serial. This story will soon be starting, so look out for further details next week.

THE WINNING "GEM" !

Of course, I get criticisms from loyal supporters. I must just mention a hint from the Potteries. "Potter" says there is too much D'Arcy, and too little Monty Lowther, Tom Merry, and Fatty Wynn. Well, wrinkles are ever as welcome as the flowers in May, but half a minute, please! What would be said to me if good old Gussy took a back seat I tremble to think. When the noble scion of Eastwood is left out there are grumbles. Still, for all that, no reason why Fatty Wynn and the others should not have their innings. Martin Clifford will attend to that part, safe as houses!

Your Editor.

SKIPPER AND SLACKER!

A Grand New Extra - Long Complete School Story of St. Jim's, recording the amazing exploits of Ralph Reckness Cardew as junior skipper of St. Jim's. A Sensational Yarn

By

Martin Clifford.

CHAPTER 1.
Bucking up Cardew!

"FINISHED?"

Levison of the Fourth asked the question, as he came into Study No. 9.

Ralph Reckness Cardew certainly looked like a fellow who had finished his occupation, whatever that might have been.

He was reclining in the study armchair, with his feet on the fender, and a cigarette in his mouth.

A blue spiral of smoke floated upward.

Levison stared at him. Sidney Clive, who had followed Levison in, frowned at him.

Cardew turned his head lazily.

"Oh! You fellows?" he said.

He yawned.

"I thought you were on the footer-ground," added Cardew.

"We've done footer practice," said Levison curtly. "And as you happen to be junior captain of St. Jim's now, Cardew, it would have been just as well if you had turned up."

"Just as well!" said Clive. "In fact, better!"

Cardew shook his head gravely.

"There are many responsibilities attached to the job of junior captain," he answered. "You fellows—the rank and file—only have to use brawn. Your skipper has to use brain as well."

"Is that how you use your brains—slacking before a fire and smoking like a frowsy fag?" asked Clive.

Cardew seemed to remember suddenly that he had a cigarette in his mouth. He removed it and tossed it into the glowing coals.

"My mistake," he said. "Old habits, you know."

"It was understood that you gave up that foolery when you were elected captain in Tom Merry's place," grunted Clive.

"Quite so. Merely an old bad habit," said Cardew gracefully.

"Well, have you finished?" asked Levison again.

"Finished what?"

"Weren't you going over the football list for the Rookwood match?"

"Eh! Oh, yes."

"As the match takes place to-morrow, it might be as well to give the matter a little thought, now you're captain," said Clive.

"Don't give me any sarc, old chap!" urged Cardew. "I'm beginnin' to think that I made a mistake in buttin' in and baggin' the junior captaincy. It isn't all beer and skittles, I can tell you. It was rather a jest downin' Tom Merry. But is the game worth the candle? Now that I've shown that I could do it, I feel that it wasn't worth while to do it at all. A captain's job is a bore, like everythin' else."

"Look here——"

"Comin' to think of it, I really believe that true happiness is found in the humble and happy state of a subordinate," said Cardew. "I suppose that's why so few men get on in life. They find it easier to keep in second or third place. Anythin's better than work."

"It's a bit too late to think of that," said Levison quietly. "You've upset the whole show, and bagged the captaincy from Tom Merry. You did it against our advice."

"If you'd advised me to do it, old bean, I mightn't have done it," remarked Cardew. "Good advice always has these rotten results. Whatever a fellow does, he should never give good advice. Bad habit."

"Have you finished the list?"

"What list? Oh, the Rookwood bizney! Is there any hurry?"

"It's got to be posted on the board. All the fellows are keen to see it."

"Well, I started it," said Cardew. "Then my thoughts wandered, and I put on a cigarette to think it over. And then I began to think about the Christmas holidays."

"Plow the holidays!"

"But they're quite near at hand, old man. You don't want the school to break up and find us unprepared for the hols, do you? Be prepared, you know—that's a motto or somethin'——"

"Where's the list?"

"On the table."

Ernest Levison looked over the table. Cardew settled down at ease in the chair again.

For several weeks Cardew of the Fourth had been leading quite a strenuous life.

He had contested the junior captaincy with Tom Merry, and he had won. He had shown up brilliantly as a footballer. He had made his chums, Levison and Clive, hope and almost believe that a permanent change had taken place in him, and that his idle slacking was a thing of the past.

Now, however, the old Cardew was coming to the surface again.

He had triumphed, and for a time triumph had been sweet. But it seemed to have turned, at last, to dust and ashes in his mouth.

A junior captain had plenty of duties on his shoulders. Tom Merry had always performed his duties quietly, without ostentation, but very efficiently. He had not given satisfaction all round, because that was not within the bounds of possibility. But he had been unanimously acknowledged to be a good skipper, and, at all events, it was known that he did his best.

Cardew might have made as good a captain, with the same steady sense of loyalty to duty.

But that was where Cardew differed from Tom Merry. An exciting election, a brilliant football match, called forth all Cardew's powers. But for the steady, humdrum doing of plain duty he had no taste or inclination.

Having gained all that he had aspired to, he tired of it as he tired of everything else in the long run.

Among other duties of a junior captain, was the duty of seeing that slackers did not shirk games practice. And already Cardew had begun to shirk games practice himself.

The coming match with Rookwood School filled all the junior footballers at St. Jim's with excitement and anticipation—excepting Cardew. Ralph Reckness Cardew was beginning to find it difficult not to yawn when the Rookwood match was mentioned.

He stared at the fire, while Levison picked up a sheet of paper from the table and looked at it, and then held it up for Clive to look at.

On the paper were written three names in Cardew's elegant caligraphy. The names were Cardew, Levison, Clive.

"Is this the paper?" asked Levison.

Cardew made an effort and glanced round.

"Yes."

"You've got three names down."

"Have I?"

"Yes!" roared Levison.

"Right-ho!" said Cardew pacifically. "I've got three names down. That's a beginnin', isn't it?"

"You slacking ass!"

"Heigh-ho! I say, old chap, you know lots about football and footballers," said Cardew. "Help me."

"I'm willing to do that, of course."

"There's a pal! I think there's a pen on the table. Finish the list for me."

"What?"

"And then Clive will go and stick it on the board, like a good chap," said Cardew.

"You don't want to look at it first?" asked Levison sarcastically.

"Not at all. I'm relyin' on your judgment, old bean."

"And that's how you're going to carry on as junior captain of St. Jim's."

"That's it," assented Cardew lazily.

"Do you think it's good enough?"

"Quite!"

"Well, I don't," said Levison grimly. "You've got the job now, Cardew, and you've got to play up. You're not going to let this study down by playing the goat after you've turned Tom Merry out of his job and bagged it. You're going to get a move on."

"Dear me!" said Cardew.

"You're going to be ragged when you shirk your duty."

"Oh gad!"

"Collar him, Clive."

"You bet!" grinned Clive.

"Here, hold on!" yelled Cardew, losing his easy nonchalance all of a sudden, as the two juniors seized him over the back of the armchair.

"Bump him!"

"Oh crumbs!"

Cardew was yanked bodily over the back of the armchair. The chair rolled over, and Cardew sprawled on the study carpet with a roar.

Bump!

"I say——"

Bump!

"I—I—I——"

"There!" gasped Levison. "I hope that's woke you up! Now get on with your job, Cardew, or we'll come back and give you some more."

Levison and Clive walked out of the study. Cardew sat on the carpet, gasping, and staring after them blankly.

"Oh gad!" he gasped.

He rose rather slowly and painfully to his feet. The energetic measures of his study-mates had certainly awakened him effectually.

"Oh gad!" he murmured. "I'm beginnin' really to think that I made a bad break in baggin' the captaincy! Oh gad! Ow!"

CHAPTER 2.
Manners is Satisfied !

TOM MERRY stopped and looked at the notice-board. Manners and Lowther stopped, too, and followed his glance. There were a good many notices on the board; but among them there was no paper in the hand of Ralph Reckness Cardew.

"Not up yet," remarked Tom.

"About time," said Manners.

"Possibly Cardew's forgotten that there's a football match with Rookwood to-morrow?" suggested Monty Lowther satirically.

Tom Merry laughed.

"Well, he could hardly have forgotten it," he said, "but it's high time the list was up. Fellows want to know whether they're playing or not."

"Yaas, wathah!" observed Arthur Augustus D'Arcy of the Fourth, who had strolled elegantly along to look at the board. "I feah that Cardew is gettin' a little slack, you know."

"Oh, give him time!" said Tom good-naturedly.

"Yaas; but if I am not playin' Wookwood to-mowwow, you kn w, I want to take a little wun out of 'gates," said Arthur Augustus. "A fellow is entitled to know. Of course, I suppose I can take it for gwanted that I am playin'. Cardew wants to win the match. Nevahtheless, a fellow wants to know."

The Terrible Three of the Shell chuckled.

"I see nothin' to cackle at in that wemark, you fellows. I think I had bettah speak to Cardew! Anybody know where he is?"

"He, he, he!"

That unmusical cachinnation came from Baggy Trimble of the Fourth. Arthur Augustus adjusted his celebrated eye-glass in his noble eye, and turned it inquiringly upon Baggy.

"I've just seen him," grinned Trimble. "Levison and Clive have been ragging him in his study."

"Ragging Cardew?" said Tom Merry.

"He, he, he! Yes! He hasn't settled the eleven yet, and they bumped him for slacking!"

Tom Merry looked grave.

"Cardew ought to have made up his mind by this time," he said. "I dare say he wants time to think it out, as he's new to the job. But——"

"But——" said Manners.

"He wants time to smoke a cigarette, you mean!" chuckled Trimble.

"Oh, dry up!" snapped Tom. "Cardew's given up that rot."

"He hadn't ten minutes ago," said Trimble, grinning.

"Bai Jove! This won't do, you fellows, you know," remarked Arthur Augustus, shaking his head seriously. "This won't do for St. Jim's."

"St. Jim's should have stuck to a good skipper when they had one," said Monty Lowther.

"Yaas, but——"

"Oh, rot!" said Tom. "Anyhow, it's not for us to interfere with Cardew. Let's get on to prep!"

The Terrible Three walked away. But Tom Merry's face was very thoughtful. Since Cardew had captured the junior captaincy Tom Merry had backed him up loyally, for the sake of the House and the School. But he knew the slacker of the Fourth too well to trust him, and he did not expect Cardew to make a good or efficient skipper.

And the Rookwood match was a serious matter. It was one of the big junior fixtures, and St. Jim's needed to put their b st team into the field to beat Jimmy Silver & Co., of Rookwood. Certainly it was not a time for the junior captain to be slacking.

On such occasions Tom Merry had always given a great deal of anxious thought to the selection of the eleven. That, apparently, was not Cardew's method.

It was not, however, for Tom Merry to intervene. The new captain had not asked assistance from the old captain, and certainly it could not be offered unasked.

But as it happened, the Terrible Three met Cardew on their way to Study No. 10 in the Shell. Cardew was looking a little flushed, and they wondered whether Trimble's story of the ragging was true.

"Hold on a minute, Cardew," said Manners.

Cardew politely stopped.

"You haven't posted up the list yet."

"No!" said Cardew, with great seriousness. "You see, I'm givin' that matter a lot of thinkin'."

"That's right," said Tom.

"I'm glad you approve, dear man. You see, there's the rival claims of the Fourth and the Shell to be considered,

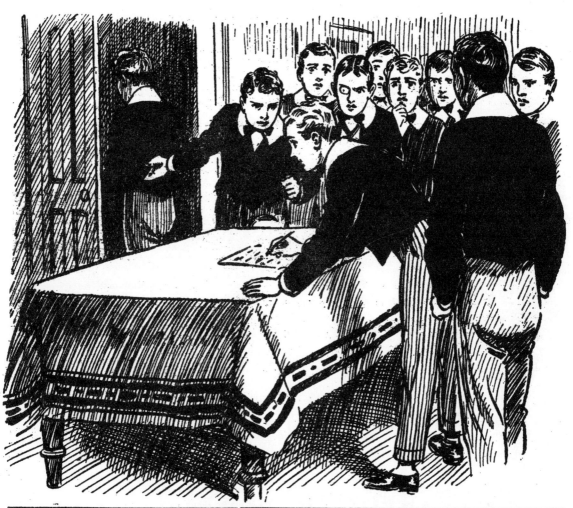

"If it wasn't for deserting the side," said Tom Merry, "I'd resign at once from the eleven." "Don't let that worry you," said Cardew, coolly, "I could fill your place quite easily." Tom Merry's eyes glinted. "Fill it, then!" he said, and he walked out of the study. Without replying, Cardew crossed out Tom Merry's name in the list. (*See page 10.*)

and then the proportion of New House men to School House men in the team, an' all that. I've nearly brought on a brain-storm, thinkin' it out."

Tom Merry looked at him rather suspiciously. He was not of a suspicious nature, but he could not help guessing that Cardew's seriousness of manner was assumed, and that the dandy of the Fourth was laughing in his sleeve.

"It's rather an important matter, Cardew," said Tom.

"I'm aware of that! In fact, its importance could scarcely be over-estimated, in my opinion."

Tom compressed his lips a little, and moved on.

"Hold on," said Cardew. "I'm puttin' your names down. Merry, Manners, Lowther—that's three."

Manners looked pleased. Manners was a better scholar and mathematician and photographer than footballer, and though he frequently figured in House matches, it was but seldom that he had a chance in a school match, where the captain had both Houses of St. Jim's to select his players from. Tom Merry was his best chum, but Tom had always placed football before friendship on such occasions, and Manners had cheerfully acquiesced.

But certainly he was pleased at being picked out by the new captain. Manners had always acquiesced in Tom's decision without thinking of grousing. Nevertheless, he had nourished a secret conviction that he was, for school matches, a really useful man.

Cardew appeared to hold the same opinion, and naturally Manners felt a little flattered. His estimation of Cardew as a captain rose considerably.

"Good man," he said. "I'll play up, you can depend on that."

"I'm sure you will," said Cardew.

The Terrible Three walked on to their study. Lowther was smiling, and Tom looking very grave. In the study, as they sorted out their books for prep, Manners gave his chum a quick look.

"You don't care for Cardew's selection, Tom?"

"It's not for me to criticise it, old chap."

"I think I shall do pretty well."

"I hope so."

"But you don't think so?" asked Manners, rather tartly.

"Why not?" asked Tom. "Let's pile in. We've left prep a bit late."

"I'd rather you gave me a direct answer," said Manners, with growing tartness.

Tom looked at him steadily.

"You wouldn't have played me if you'd still been captain?" said Manners.

"Not in the Rookwood match, old chap."

"Cardew seems to think I'm good enough."

"You're good enough, old fellow; but with both Houses to select from, you know——"

"So you think Cardew's made a mistake?"

"Yes."

"Well, we shall see," said Manners, with unaccustomed acerbity. "I never groused when you left me out, did I? I don't see why you should grouse when I'm put in."

"But I haven't groused. I answered your question," said Tom mildly.

Manners gave a grunt.

"I fancy Cardew's a pretty good captain," he said. "I think it's a good idea to try some new blood in School matches."

"I hope so. Don't let's argue about it."

"Well, I think you might be pleased to see me play for St. Jim's, though you never thought me good enough."

A sharp reply rose to Tom Merry's lips, but he suppressed it. Manners was being a little unreasonable, and at such times, among friends, silence is golden.

But there was rather a strained and uncomfortable atmosphere in Study No. 10 when the Terrible Three sat down to prep.

CHAPTER 3.
Pleasing all Parties!

"CARDEW, deah boy!"

Ralph Reckness Cardew suppressed a groan and smiled politely as he met Arthur Augustus D'Arcy in the passage.

"Yes, old bean?" he said.

"The footah list isn't up yet. Of course, I wouldn't think of huwwyin' you," said Arthur Augustus graciously. "If you wequiah any advice in makin' up the list I should be only too happy to assist, as a fellow of tact and judgment, you know."

"Thanks, no end!"

"Not at all, deah boy. Twot into my study, and let's talk it ovah," said Arthur Augustus encouragingly.

"I've just got to see a fellow," explained Cardew. "Later. Of course, your name is goin' down."

"Good! I admit, deah boy, that I had some doubts at first, but I am weally glad to see you turnin' out a good and efficient skippah," said Arthur Augustus "Are Blake and Hewwies and Dig playin', too?"

"Certainly!"

"May I tell them so?"

"Please, do!"

"Wight-ho!" said Arthur Augustus cheerfully, and he trotted away to Study No. 6, to impart the glad news to his chums.

But the news, when he imparted it to Blake & Co., did not have a whole gladdening effect.

"Us four are down for the Wookwood match," Arthur Augustus announced.

"Good!" said Digby.

"Then I suppose I'm keeping goal, instead of Fatty Wynn of the New House!" exclaimed Herries brightly.

"Yaas, I pwesume so, Hewwies."

"Jolly good!"

Jack Blake looked very grave.

"You fellows know that I like to see this study to the fore in footer," he said. "But, dash it all, if Wynn's in form he ought to be keeping goal against Rookwood to-morrow."

"Can't I keep goal?" demanded Herries warmly.

"Yes; but you're not Fatty's form."

"Rot! I think it's jolly sensible of Cardew to put a School House chap in goal instead of that New House bounder!"

"That's all very well," said Blake. "But Houses don't matter when it's a School match. We want to beat Rookwood."

Herries reddened.

"Do you think I'm going to let them win?" he asked.

"It's no good making out that you keep goal like Fatty Wynn, Herries, because you jolly well don't!" said Blake testily.

"That may be your opinion!" snapped Herries.

"I fancy it's the opinion of every fellow in St. Jim's. I can't make out what Cardew's driving at."

"Well, he's playing you," said Herries crossly. "That may show that he's a bit of an ass."

"Oh, don't be a chump, Herries!"

"Weally, you fellows——"

"What am I put down for, Gussy?" asked Dig, who was looking very pleased. "Forward, of course? I never knew Cardew had specially noticed my form. He sees more than a fellow supposes."

"Less, I should say!" growled Blake. "You're my pal, Dig, old man, and I'm glad to see you have a chance; but it's sheer rot to say that a better man couldn't be found for the front line. Cardew must be going off his rocker!"

Digby gave his study-mate a glare.

"Where's the better man?" he demanded, in a tone that could be heard at the end of the Fourth Form passage.

"Weally, you fellows, don't wag about it!" urged Arthur Augustus. "It's wathah wippin' for the whole study to show up in a big School match."

"That's so," said Blake. "But——"

"But Blake thinks he's the only fellow in this study who can play football!" sneered Dig.

"Weally, Dig——"

"What's the good of jaw?" said Blake. "A skipper who knew his business would find better men. I could name them. I fancy the school will soon be jolly sorry that Cardew was elected captain."

"Weally, Blake——"

"Swank!" said Dig.

"Cheek!" said Herries.

Blake grunted and sat down again to his prep. In Study No. 6, as with the Terrible Three, prep went on that evening in a rather electric atmosphere.

Meanwhile, Ralph Reckness Cardew, having got rid of Arthur Augustus by the simple process of granting all he asked, had turned into the Shell passage, and entered Study

No. 7, which belonged to Racke and Crooke, the black sheep of the House.

Racke and Crooke were not at prep. They were smoking cigarettes, and they nodded and grinned to Cardew when he came in.

"You're rather late," observed Racke.

"Lot of borin' fellows would talk to me," said Cardew. "But better late than never."

"Oh, yes! Lock the door, Crooke."

Crooke locked the door, and Aubrey Racke produced a pack of cards from the table drawer. The three young rascals sat down round the table to play banker.

Three cigarettes thickened the atmosphere of the study. Racke burst into a sudden chuckle.

"I say, Cardew, what would the fellows say if they could see you now?" he asked.

Cardew winced.

To do him justice, he was not without shame for the slackness and self-indulgence which had followed his energetic campaign against Tom Merry. He did not choose to pull up, but he had the grace to be a little ashamed of himself.

"My hat! There would be a shindy!" said Crooke, with a whistle. "This isn't the way Tom Merry used to get ready for a football fixture. Ha, ha, ha!"

"Ha, ha, ha!" roared Racke.

"You fellows must have your merry little jest," said Cardew, with a yawn. "Anybody got a match?"

"Hark!" whispered Crooke.

A voice was heard in the passage outside, the voice of Gore of the Shell.

"Anybody seen Cardew?"

"I haven't, for one," answered the voice of Grundy.

"Where's the blessed ass got to?" exclaimed Gore angrily. "I want to know about the footer to-morrow."

"So do a lot of fellows!" snorted Grundy. "I fancy the list won't be up to-night."

"It's always posted over-night," shouted Gore, "and I jolly well want to know! Hi, Trimble! Seen Cardew?"

"He, he, he!"

"What are you he-he-heing about, you fat dummy?"

"He, he, he! He's in Racke's study."

"What the thump is he doing in Racke's study?" George Gore thumped at the door. "You here, Cardew?"

Gore turned the handle. The door did not open, and Gore of the Shell thumped again.

Cardew set his lips hard.

"Caught!" murmured Crooke. "Shall I open the door, Cardew?"

Racke chuckled.

"Are you here, Cardew?" roared Gore.

"Yes, dear man."

"Let me in, then!"

"Can't ask you into another fellow's study," said Cardew. "I'm helpin' Racke with his prep, and don't want to be interrupted."

"Oh gad!" murmured Racke.

"Am I down to play to-morrow?" shouted Gore. "That's what I want to know."

"Yes."

"Oh, good!" said Gore, modifying his voice considerably. "Where have you got me down?"

"In the list."

"You ass! I mean on the field?"

"Oh, forward."

"Forward! You know I'm a back!"

"I mean back."

"Good! Left or right?"

"Whichever you like."

"What?" roared Gore.

"I mean left."

"Good!"

George Gore walked away feeling satisfied—one more fellow who came to the conclusion that Cardew was, after all, a pretty good captain. Cardew lighted a fresh cigarette, while Racke and Crooke stared at him.

"I say, is Gore up to the Rookwood match, Cardew?" asked Racke. "I shouldn't have thought so."

"Let's hope for the best," said Cardew.

"Oh, my hat! Is that how you look at it?"

"Just that."

"Phew! Some skipper!" grinned Racke.

And the interrupted game of banker was resumed in Racke's study. When Cardew left he strolled back to Study No. 9 in the Fourth with a rather thoughtful frown on his face.

"Now, how many dashed fellows have I given places in the eleven?" he murmured. "I jolly well wish I could remember. Oh gad!"

He stopped with an exclamation, as four juniors suddenly collared him in the passage. They were Julian, Hammond, Reilly, and Kerruish, of Study No. 5.

"Here he is!" grinned Julian.

"Anythin' wanted, old tops?" asked Cardew blandly.

Quietly and coolly, Cardew drew himself up to the window, and dropped on to the ground outside. A junior who was sauntering along the path stopped and stared at him. "Bai Jove! Cardew——" Cardew did not even look at Arthur Augustus D'Arcy, but scudded away. *(See page 13.)*

"Don't rumple my collar! I'm rather particular about my collar!"

"Yes, places in the eleven to-morrow," said Kerruish. "Are you playing any of us? We want to know."

"Sure, we'll bump you if you say no!" added Reilly.

"Hard!" said Hammond, laughing. "You see, as you don't seem to have made up your mind yet, we're going to help you make it up."

"Bump him anyway!" said Kerruish.

"Hold on!" exclaimed Cardew. "You're all in the list! That's four more! I'm jolly glad to be able to please you fellows like this!"

"Hurrah!"

Cardew walked on—unbumped. He found Levison and Clive at work in Study No. 9 when he entered. They looked up at him rather grimly.

"Finished the list yet?" asked Levison.

"Quite."

"Oh, good!" said Clive. "You've done it at last!"

"I've done it!" assented Cardew. "Indeed, I'm rather beginnin' to think that I've overdone it!"

"What?"

"Oh, nothin'!" yawned Cardew, sinking into the arm-chair. "It's all serene—at least, I hope it is. I'm tryin' to please all parties, an' a fellow can't do more than that, can he?"

"Well, that depends," said Levison. "Aren't you going to do your prep, Cardew?"

"No! The fatiguin' duties of football captain leave me no time for prep on the eve of an important match," said Cardew gravely.

And Cardew did no prep that evening. He wondered a little how many fellows would be counting on places in the junior eleven on the morrow, and whether the number exceeded eleven. That was rather a problem for a football captain, and Cardew treated it as he did most problems that came his way—he gave it up, and turned his thoughts to something else.

CHAPTER 4.
Trouble in the Form-room!

FIGGINS of the Fourth gave Cardew an expressive look when they met in the Fourth Form room the following morning. Kerr and Wynn gave him expressive looks also. So did Redfern and Owen and Pratt and several more of the Fourth Form who belonged to the New House of St. Jim's. In fact, all the New House section of the Fourth seemed to look at Cardew that morning with strong disfavour. Cardew noticed it, and wondered why, though he was too lazy to think the matter out. Also, he did not think that it mattered.

Cardew had plenty of other things to think of that Wednesday morning. There was the journey over to Rookwood to play Jimmy Silver & Co. in the afternoon. There was the composition of his eleven, a matter not yet settled. There was the number of fellows to whom he had awarded places in the team—a number more than sufficient to make up a Rugger team. There was the fact that he had done no prep in the evening, and might be called upon by Mr. Latham to construe, in which case he was certain to make a hash of it and draw upon himself the vials of his Form master's wrath. For Mr. Lathom's wrath in itself Cardew did not care a pin. The fact that Mr. Lathom expected him to work only afforded him a mild amusement. But wrath might be followed by detention, which was a rather serious matter for a football captain on the day of a match. With all these matters to think about Cardew did not care whether Figgins & Co. looked glum or gay, whether they gave him smiles, or whether they gave him truculent scowls. He had troubles enough in the School House without worrying about the New House.

During first lesson George Figgins contrived to pass a note along to Cardew. Cardew looked at it idly. It ran:

"Who's in the eleven?"

Cardew smiled faintly. The eleven ought to have been posted the night before in both Houses. It had not been posted in either. The New House fellows were still quite in the dark.

Figgins looked across at Cardew and signed to him that he wanted an answer to his note. Cardew wrote an answer on the back of the fragment of paper.

"Goodness knows!"

That was Cardew's reply, which was passed along surreptitiously under the desks to Figgins.

Figgins blinked at it.

It was not a reply that Figgy could make anything of. That Cardew was simply being funny on so serious a subject as a School match was almost incredible to Figgins. He tried to catch Cardew's eye again, but failed. Cardew avoided his eye.

Meanwhile Fatty Wynn of the New House had made a discovery. He was near Herries, and Herries had been unable to abstain from letting him know that he—George Herries—was to keep goal in the Rookwood game.

It was surprising news to Fatty Wynn. Even School House fellows admitted freely that St. Jim's had never boasted a junior goalkeeper who was a patch on David Llewellyn Wynn. Herries was good, quite good, and he was improving. He was a hard-working and painstaking fellow. But Fatty had a genius for keeping goal. He was one of those custodians who are born, not made. It was always understood that when a match was important Fatty Wynn kept goal, if Fatty was available. Sometimes—rarely—he was off colour, occasionally he was crocked, but when he was available he was the "goods," so to speak. That he should be set aside in the Rookwood match was a surprise for Wynn, and not a pleasant surprise.

"Gammon!" was his reply to Herries.

"Cardew says so!"

"Then Cardew's a fool!"

Herries shrugged his shoulders. So far from deeming Cardew a fool, his belief was that Cardew's selection, in this instance, showed something very like inspiration.

Fatty Wynn, like Figgins, tried to catch Cardew's eye. Like Figgins, he failed. Cardew wasn't catching an eye that morning if he could help it. Neither was he attending to the class work. He was wondering rather dismally what was going to happen after class. He did not even hear Mr. Lathom when that gentleman called on him.

"Cardew!"

Levison nudged his chum on one side, Clive on the other. Cardew awoke to his surroundings.

"Cardew!" repeated Mr. Lathom, frowning.

"Oh! Yes, sir!"

"You will go on where Blake left off."

Cardew, who had not been listening, had not the faintest idea where Blake had left off.

"Oh! Yes, sir!"

"Well, go on, Cardew!"

"Certainly, sir!"

"Construe!" snapped Mr. Lathom.

Levison made a movement, and Mr. Lathom fixed his eyes on him at once.

"You need not show Cardew the place, Levison."

"Oh! No, sir!" stammered Levison.

"You do not know the place, Cardew?"

There was no help for it. Cardew had to admit the soft impeachment, as it were.

"Sorry, sir—no!"

"You will take a hundred lines, Cardew!"

"Thank you, sir!"

Mr. Lathom's eyes glinted behind his glasses. He was a patient and good-tempered gentleman; but Cardew had tried him severely of late. And the smiling impertinence of the dandy of the Fourth was too much for his patience and good temper now.

"Two hundred lines, Cardew!" he rapped out.

"You're very good, sir!" said Cardew imperturbably.

Some of the Fourth grinned. "Ragging" a Form master was considered amusement in all Form-rooms. And Cardew was a past-master in that art. But there was a limit to what even the kind-tempered Mr. Lathom would stand.

"You are impertinent, Cardew!" he rapped out.

"Oh, sir!"

"Take five hundred lines!"

Cardew did not thank Mr. Lathom this time, or tell him that he was very good. Even Cardew did not want the imposition to grow into a thousand lines.

"You may now show Cardew the place, Levison, and you will construe, Cardew!"

Levison pointed out the place, though he knew it was useless. Cardew had not even looked at the section of the "Æneid" which should have been prepared the previous evening. He had chanced being called on to construe, trusting to luck. He had chanced it once too often.

Cardew stared at the Latin without being able even to begin. Mr. Lathom's brow grew more thunderous as he waited.

"You have not prepared this lesson, Cardew," he said at last.

"Sorry, sir—no! You see, sir, as football captain I've had a lot to see to—there's a big match to-day. So I hope, sir, that you'll excuse me this once," said Cardew.

"If it were this once, Cardew, I should certainly excuse you," said Mr. Lathom grimly. "But it is not this once. You have been consistently slack at your lessons for several weeks, and to slackness and carelessness you have added impertinence. You will be detained the whole of this afternoon, and will write out a whole book of the 'Æneid.'"

"Oh gad!" murmured Cardew.

"You will now go on, Clive, where Blake left off."

Up rose Arthur Augustus D'Arcy.

"Pway excuse me, sir——"

"You may sit down, D'Arcy!"

"Yaas, sir; but I should like to wemark that the Wookwood match takes place this afthnoon, and Cardew is football skippah. We cannot vewy well go ovah to Wookwood without our skippah, sir!"

"That will do, D'Arcy!"

"Certainly, sir! I do not defend Cardew, sir—he is a feahful slackah, and certainly deserves detention," said the swell of St. Jim's. "But I twust, sir, that you will be willin' to detain him next Satahday instead of to-day, so that he can come ovah to Wookwood."

"I shall do nothing of the kind, D'Arcy!"

"Oh, bai Jove!"

"I do not desire to be misunderstood," said Mr. Lathom. "I should accede to such a request in the ordinary way. But only a week or two ago Cardew was released from detention, on the occasion of a match, at the intercession of Tom Merry. I warned him then that such a concession would not be made again, and that he must be careful. He has not chosen to be careful, and so he must take the consequences!"

"But as football skippah, sir——"

"I recommend you to select a football captain who does

not get detained on match days," said Mr. Lathom dryly. "Kindly say no more!"

"Yaas, sir; but——"

"If you say another word, D'Arcy, I shall detain you also."

"Oh, bai Jove!" murmured Arthur Augustus.

He sat down promptly.

Cardew sat and stared at his desk. The thunderbolt had come down on him; he had risked it from sheer carelessness, and now it had fallen. He was detained; the Rookwood match would have to be played without him. He had started his captaincy well—with luck! Now his luck had failed him, and this was how he was carrying it on. And he knew perfectly well that he had only himself to thank—if that was any comfort. Probably it was not.

CHAPTER 5.
A Little Excitement!

TOM MERRY did not learn of Cardew's disaster till after dinner. The captain of the Shell—no longer junior captain of St. Jim's—had made his preparations for the train journey to Rookwood. He took it for granted that he was to play—no official notification having reached him yet. But he was quite prepared to be told at the last moment that he was not wanted. True, Cardew had told the Terrible Three the previous evening that they were to be in the eleven. But it had reached Tom's ears that he had told more than a dozen other fellows the same thing. Nobody could know for certain how the eleven was to be made up till the list was posted; and even yet Cardew had not posted it. Even the junior football committee, who had a voice in the matter, did not know what his intentions were. As a matter of fact,

"Blessed if I can make the fellow out," said Tom. "Is he pulling our legs all round?"

"The Rookwood match isn't exactly a subject for leg-pulling," remarked Lowther.

"Oh, give him a chance!" said Manners. "I dare say Cardew's got his reasons for what he does. I believe in new blood in the team, though I admit it's going too far to put Herries in goal instead of Wynn."

"Hallo, Talbot!" called out Tom, as Talbot of the Shell appeared in sight. "Have you heard whether you're playing this afternoon?"

Talbot halted.

"No, I'm not playing—at least, Cardew hasn't asked me."

Tom breathed hard. He was anxious, very anxious, not to interfere with the new captain. He was aware that such interference would be ascribed to pique—that it would look "rotten." Hitherto Tom had backed up the new captain, and kept his own opinions strictly to himself. But he felt that the limit was reached now.

"Gore's playing," added Talbot.

"Gore?" repeated Tom.

"Yes. He's told me Cardew told him."

"It's impossible!" exclaimed Tom. "There are a dozen backs better than Gore—heaps and miles better."

"I don't quite catch on," confessed Talbot. "Gore says that Cardew told him he could play forward if he liked."

"It's some sort of a jape, I should think," said Tom. "I think I'd better speak to Cardew. We must have this out. Where is he?"

"I hear he's detained this afternoon. Has he said anything to you about the captaincy?"

"I haven't even seen him."

"It's a queer business," said Talbot. "I'm afraid that Cardew isn't taking his new job very seriously. It's a pity."

Cardew did not himself know what his intentions were. Slacking had landed him in a sort of morass from which there seemed no satisfactory way out. Now it seemed that he was barred from the match himself, and that was the climax.

"It's too thick!" exclaimed Tom Merry indignantly, when he heard the news. "The silly ass was detained on the Grammar School match day, and Lathom let him off. He won't do it a second time."

"Not likely!" agreed Manners.

"You'll have to skipper the team, Tom," said Monty Lowther. "All the better, if it comes to that."

Tom Merry frowned.

"It's not all the better," he said. "Cardew bagged my place; but I don't want to bag his! In fact, I won't! The fellows had better ask Talbot to captain the side."

"Talbot doesn't seem to be playing," said Kangaroo of the Shell.

"That's rot! Talbot couldn't be left out!"

"Well, the list isn't posted," said the Australian junior. "But Cardew seems to have told all the fellows who were wanted. He hasn't honoured me, and there doesn't seem to be a single New House fellow in the team at all."

"That will cause trouble between the Houses," said Tom. "There ought to be at least three New House men. He must be going to play Fatty Wynn in goal."

"No; I hear it's Herries for goal."

"Herries is a good man in House matches; but Fatty Wynn is wanted to keep goal for School."

"I fancy all St. Jim's knows that, excepting Cardew and Herries," grinned Kangaroo.

Tom Merry proceeded to look for Cardew, and his comrades went with him. They were irritated and anxious. The time was drawing near for catching the train to Rookwood, and apparently the junior captain had made no arrangements whatever. It was an unprecedented state of affairs in football matters at St. Jim's.

In the changing-room—a general meeting-place for the footballing fraternity—there was a hubbub of voices, and Tom Merry & Co. looked in. Cardew was not there, but a crowd of other fellows were, and many of them seemed excited. Levison and Clive were there, looking worried and anxious. Figgins & Co. had come in full of wrath.

"Not a single New House chap in the team!" Figgins was roaring. "I'll believe that when I see the list! Why isn't the list up?"

"Goodness knows!" said Blake.

"This is what comes of having a School House chap for skipper!" snorted Fatty Wynn.

"Well, Tom Merry was a good enough skipper," said Kerr, in his quiet, judicial way. "But I must say that Cardew is the limit."

"Yaas, wathah! It is all weally vewy queeah!" said Arthur Augustus D'Arcy. "Fortunately, all my study are down to play."

"Herries in goal!" roared Figgins. "What about Wynn?"

"I'm not keen on it," said Fatty Wynn. "Let him chuck me, if he likes. But I want to know why."

"What does Cardew mean by all this, Levison?" asked Tom Merry.

Ernest Levison shrugged his shoulders hopelessly.

"Better ask him. I don't know."

"Oh, give the man a chance !" said Kerruish. "It's the first time I've been asked to play for School, and I back up Cardew."

"You ?" said Tom.

"Yes. All my study, too," said Kerruish.

"How the thump many players has Cardew picked, then ?" demanded Tom Merry. "He told us three, and Study No. 6 are four—that makes seven; Kerruish and his lot make it up to eleven. Then there's Gore, and Levison and Clive, and Cardew himself——"

"That's fifteen," said Lowther. "Does Cardew think we're going over to Rookwood to play Rugger ?"

"I think nobody had better take it for granted till he sees the list," remarked Talbot quietly. "I've heard from two or three other fellows that Cardew has told them they'll be playing."

"I know I'm going to play !" bawled Gore hotly. "My skipper's told me, and that's enough for me. I'm keeping him to it."

"Bai Jove ! It is weally vewy wemarkable," said Arthur Augustus D'Arcy. "The sillay ass seems to have told at least fifteen School House chaps, and he knows that the New House can't be left entirely out of a School match."

"I should jolly well think not !" roared Figgins, in great wrath. "I know we shall all jolly well resign for good if it happens."

"Where's Cardew ?" demanded Kangaroo.

"In the study," said Levison.

"Come on !" exclaimed Tom Merry. "We'd better go and see him, all of us. We shall lose the train, at this rate, and there won't be any match at Rookwood at all."

It was quite an army of excited juniors that marched off to the Fourth Form passage to interview Ralph Reckness Cardew. That nonchalant youth's amazing methods as captain seemed to be bringing a hurricane about his ears.

CHAPTER 6.
The Eleven !

"CARDEW !"

"Cardew, you ass !"

"Cardew, you chump !"

"Trot in, dear men," said Ralph Reckness Cardew. "I've been rather expectin' a call. Roll in your jolly old thousands !"

The juniors crowded into Study No. 9. Study No. 9 would not hold them all, and there was an overflow meeting in the passage. A score of indignant voices called on Cardew to explain himself.

"You ass !"

"You slacking dummy !"

"Where's the list ?"

"Who's playing at Rookwood this afternoon ?"

Cardew smiled sweetly. He held up a sheet of impot paper with a list of names on it, scribbled in pencil.

"There's the list," he said.

"Why wasn't it posted up before ?" demanded Figgins.

"You see, I've been giving this subject a lot of thought," said Cardew gravely. "With so many first-class footballers to choose from, it wasn't an easy matter."

"That's all very well !" snapped Lowther. "Tom Merry never used to leave it till the last minute like this."

"Wathah not."

"But there is only one Thomas," said Cardew. "I'm not claimin' to equal Thomas, though I'm really doin' my humble best to follow in my father's footsteps, as they say in the jolly old song."

"Well, let's see the list," said Blake.

"Fatty Wynn for goal——"

"Good !" said Figgins, mollified at once.

"Eh ? What about me ?" roared Herries, justly incensed.

"You ? Nothin' about you, old bean."

"I understood that I was put in goal."

"Somethin' wrong with your understandin', then."

"Well, where am I put, then ?" demanded Herries. "I'm best in goal, but I can play back all right, and half-back."

"You're not in the team, old man."

"Not ?" bawled Herries.

"Not !" assented Cardew.

"You told D'Arcy all our study was wanted to play." Cardew sighed.

"Did I ?"

"You certainly did, Cardew !" exclaimed Arthur Augustus warmly. "You told me I could tell these fellows."

"Mea culpa !" said Cardew. "But I appeal to all the fellows present—wouldn't a fellow say almost anythin' to stop Gussy when his chin begins to wag ?"

"Ha, ha, ha !"

"You uttah wottah !" roared Arthur Augustus.

"Then you were only pulling my leg !" gasped Herries, purple with wrath.

"Gussy's leg !" corrected Cardew.

"You uttah wapscallion !" howled Arthur Augustus. "I would wefuse to play at all, Cardew, only I cannot afford to wisk the match for St. Jim's."

"That's all right, you're not playin'."

"Not playin' !" stuttered Arthur Augustus, like a fellow in a dream. "Bai Jove !"

"No. Shall I get on with the list ?" asked Cardew.

"Get on !" growled Blake.

"Backs—Kangaroo and Thompson, of the New House."

"Where do I come in ?" howled Gore.

"You don't come in at all !"

"You told me——"

"Did I ?"

"You did !" shrieked Gore.

"You were worryin' me when I was—was helpin' a chap with his maths," said Cardew. "You asked to have your leg pulled, old bean. Here, keep him off !"

Three or four fellows grasped Gore as he was hurling himself on Cardew. Gore was dragged back and ejected from the study. Certainly Gore had been badly treated, but the fellows were so relieved to hear that he was not playing in the Rookwood match that they forgot that circumstance. Gore went into the passage with a bump.

"Halves," went on Cardew imperturbably. "Redfern, Clive, and Kerr !"

"Good !"

"Front line, Talbot, Levison, little me, Figgins, and Tom Merry."

"What about me ?" asked Blake, in a gasping voice.

"Nothin' !"

"And me ?" gasped Digby.

"You don't play in school matches, you know."

"You—you told D'Arcy——"

"I've already explained that," said Cardew cheerily. "Nobody's responsible for what he says to Gussy."

"You cheekay wottah——"

"And I ?" asked Manners very quietly.

Cardew started a little.

"By Jove ! You ! Sorry, but I can't make up an eleven of more than eleven men, can I ?"

Manners gulped. He remembered his hasty words to Tom Merry the previous evening. With a very red face Manners left the study.

"You told me I should be wanted, too," said Lowther.

"Figure of speech, old chap."

"And what about my study ?" began Kerruish.

"Your study can go and eat coke."

Tom Merry fixed his eyes on Cardew.

"You've acted rottenly all round, Cardew," he said. "I don't know why you've done it, but you have. You've treated my friends rottenly, and if I play in your team it's only because I don't think I ought to desert the side. Otherwise, I'd resign at once from the eleven."

"Don't let that worry you," said Cardew coolly. "I could fill your place quite easily."

Tom Merry's eyes glinted.

"Fill it, then," he said; and he walked out of the study.

"Stop, for goodness' sake !" exclaimed Talbot. "Cardew, you can't be ass enough to lose the best forward in the school."

Without replying, Cardew crossed out Tom Merry's name in the list. That proceeding was watched in silence by the crowd of fellows.

"I shall want you, Blake."

Blake gave him a grim look.

"You can want !" he said: and he walked out after Tom.

"Yaas, wathah, and I shall certainly wefuse to play if you ask me now, Cardew."

"Don't worry. I'm not goin to ask you," said Cardew coolly. "I want a man rather useful than ornamental, Gussy."

"I wegard you with contempt, Cardew." And Arthur Augustus D'Arcy walked away with his noble nose in the air.

"Figgins, will you tell Owen that he's wanted for the front line ?" said Cardew.

"I'll tell him," said Figgins slowly. "Another New House chap will strengthen the team, but——"

"That's the lot," said Cardew.

"Not quite," said Talbot. "Have you forgotten that you're detained for the afternoon, Cardew ?"

"Not at all."

"Well, you can't play football at Rookwood if you're detained at St. Jim's, I suppose."

"That is what I call an incontrovertible proposition," said Cardew, smiling. "It follows, then, that as I am goin' to play football at Rookwood I sha'n't be detained at St. Jim's. See ?"

"Does that mean that you're going to try to break detention ?"

"Probably."

"And suppose you don't get clear ?"

"What's the good of supposin' ?" Ralph Reckness Cardew looked at his watch. "Two o'clock, and we're catchin' the

(Continued on page 12.)

THE CHRISTMAS FIRESIDE COMPANION!

The "Holiday Annual," with its coloured plates, its magnificent photogravure pictures of famous schools, its immense budget of school stories, helpful articles, and jolly drawings, is unquestionably THE Christmas book for GEM readers. Its popularity has grown year by year, and the volume for 1924 which is now in evidence everywhere is better than ever. All "Gemites" should make sure of getting this famous book for Christmas. Price only six shillings.

"SKIPPER AND SLACKER!"

(Continued from page 10.)

two twenty-five! I must go an' pack my little bag now that I've settled these matters to the general satisfaction."

Cardew left the study.

There was no more time to be lost, that was certain. The footballers prepared hurriedly for their departure. But throughout the Lower School of St. Jim's reigned dissatisfaction, resentment, and wrath. Cardew had eliminated the second-class players from the team, and that was all to the good from a football point of view, but his treatment of those players had roused their fiercest wrath. To tell a fellow he was wanted to play, and to let him down at the last moment was a kind of procedure never known under Tom Merry's captaincy, and it was a kind of thing that no fellow could be expected to forgive. Cardew, indeed, had not acted from malice or ill-feeling—simply and sheerly from utter carelessness and want of thought; but that did not make the matter any better. An important football fixture was not an affair to be treated in that nonchalant way.

More serious still, the best junior footballer at St. Jim's had been left out, in the person of Tom Merry. And many of the fellows suspected that Tom Merry's hot words, due to his natural resentment at the treatment of his friends, had been seized upon by Cardew as a pretext for dropping the former captain from the team. It weakened the team. Nobody—not even Owen himself—supposed that Owen of the Fourth was anything like Tom's form in the front line, or Blake's, for that matter. It was with unusual misgivings that the St. Jim's footballers prepared to start for Rookwood, and of the fellows who remained behind, to judge by their talk, many were feeling disposed to lynch Ralph Reckness Cardew.

CHAPTER 7.

Tom Merry Joins Up!

"CARDEW!"

Mr. Lathom gasped out the name.

Cardew & Co. were hurrying to the station. The eleven, and four or five fellows who were going over to Rookwood with them, were going down the lane at a trot towards Rylcombe. And after them, with his gown fluttering in the breeze, came Mr. Lathom, the master of the Fourth.

Cardew had coolly left the school with the rest, utterly ignoring his Form master's order to repair to the Form-room for detention at two o'clock. Probably he hoped that the sheer "cheek" and audacity of that proceeding would render it successful. As for the punishment that would follow, Cardew did not give it a thought; the Rookwood match would be over, and that was all he cared about. Not that Cardew was really keen even on the Rookwood match. But he was very keen indeed on retrieving the false position in which he had placed himself, and on disappointing the numerous fellows who were looking for his fall.

But as it happened, Mr. Lathom was not so easily eluded. Before the footballers had been five minutes gone, the Fourth Form master discovered Cardew's absence. Without even stopping to remove his gown, Mr. Lathom hurried after the fugitive. He was breathless with exertion and wrath when he overtook the juniors in Rylcombe Lane.

"Cardew!" he gasped.

Cardew set his lips.

"Put it on, you chaps," he muttered. "We can race Lathom."

Cardew was the only fellow there who felt disposed to "race" Lathom. Defiance of authority to that extent did not appeal to less reckless fellows. Nobody quickened his pace.

Mr. Lathom came up panting, and halted. The juniors stopped also, with glum looks.

Cardew's eyes glittered. He was in a mood for any reckless defiance; but he had no support or sympathy to expect from his companions. His own careless folly had caused the trouble, and they were fed-up with his methods—fed right up to the chin, and even Levison and Clive shared the feelings of the rest. They had hoped, certainly, that in the circumstances, he would elude Mr. Lathom. But now that he was caught, their annoyance was directed towards Cardew himself, not towards the Form master.

"Cardew, return to the school at once!"

Cardew glanced round at the footballers.

THE GEM LIBRARY.—No. 827.

"Get back!" muttered Levison. "Don't be a fool, Cardew!"

"If you fellows back me up——"

"Go back, and don't talk rot!" growled Clive.

"Back you up!" repeated Figgins. "Back up a slacking duffer against our Form master! What did you get detention for?"

"We've got to play Rookwood," said Cardew moodily. "I tell you, I'm comin' to Rookwood with the team."

Mr. Lathom came nearer, and dropped his hand on Cardew's shoulder.

"Come with me," he said.

Cardew breathed hard. It was in his mind to strike the Form master's hand aside, and scud for it. If he refrained, it was not because he cared for the consequences, but because he could see that such a wild act would be futile. Figgins, reading his thoughts in his face, drew closer and clenched his fists. Mr. Lathom was Figgy's Form master as well as Cardew's, and Figgy was prepared to knock Cardew spinning if he raised his hand against the old gentleman.

The wild thought passed—Cardew's face set in cold calmness.

"Very well, sir," he said.

"I am sorry, my boys," said Mr. Lathom kindly, "but I cannot possibly allow a defiance of authority like this to pass unchecked. You must select someone else to play in Cardew's place."

"Yes, sir," said Talbot of the Shell.

Mr. Lathom walked back towards the school with Cardew. With grim faces, the footballers hurried on to the station. They had little time left to catch their train, and if that train was lost, the Rookwood match could not be played that day. Cardew, with a set face, walked back with Mr. Lathom.

That gentleman walked slowly and breathlessly by his side. Mr. Lathom had reached an age when hurried exertion told upon him, and he was panting rather painfully all the way back to St. Jim's. But he was very watchful, prepared for a desperate attempt to bolt on the part of the junior in his charge.

Near the gates of the school three Shell fellows were mounting their bicycles when the Form master and Cardew came up. Tom Merry and Manners and Lowther looked grimly at Cardew and Mr. Lathom.

Lowther and Manners, feeling extremely sore at the way Cardew had treated them over the Rookwood match, were rather inclined to be pleased at seeing Cardew marched home with a hand on his shoulder. Tom Merry could scarcely feel sorry.

Tom was in a deeply troubled frame of mind.

So far as Cardew was concerned, he was glad to be done with him; but he felt that he ought to have played up for the school that day, even at the cost of submitting to Cardew's insolence. He was no longer captain, but he was as keen as ever on seeing St. Jim's send out a winning team. Yet to play under Cardew's lead, after the way Cardew had treated his best friends, would have been bitter enough to Tom. Exactly what he ought to have done, in the circumstances, was rather a puzzle to him; but he was feeling troubled and dissatisfied. The Terrible Three were going out for a cycle spin, to fill up the afternoon which they had expected to spend at Rookwood. Their black looks, as Cardew passed, drew a mocking smile to the face of the dandy of the Fourth.

Tom Merry stepped towards him quickly.

"You're not going to Rookwood after all, then, Cardew?"

"Mr. Lathom says not," smiled Cardew.

"It is impossible, Merry," said Mr. Lathom. "Come, Cardew!"

He drew the junior on.

Tom Merry looked after them as they went in at the gates. Manners and Lowther exchanged glances.

"Some skipper!" said Manners bitterly.

"The fool!" said Lowther. "The dummy! That's how he manages football affairs—slacking and fooling, and then sending off the team without a captain."

Tom Merry put his leg over his bicycle.

"Come on!" he called out.

"What——"

"Quick!"

Tom Merry pedalled away rapidly in the direction of Rylcombe. His chums, not quite understanding, followed him fast.

The Terrible Three fairly raced up the lane towards the village. They reached Rylcombe Station just as the football party were going in. Talbot of the Shell looked round, and called out joyously.

"Tom! Just the man we want."

"Oh, good!" exclaimed Levison, his gloomy face brightening. "Tom Merry! Cardew's been taken back——"

"I know," said Tom. "I came on to ask you fellows if you'd like me to come after all?"

"Oh, good!" said Lowther. "Hallo! There's the train! Give me your bike, Tom! Get a move on!"

Every face in the football crowd brightened. Their skipper was gone—detained by his own folly. They were glad enough to have their old captain back.

Talbot caught Tom Merry's arm, and ran him into the station. The train was in, and the footballers crowded into it, with Tom Merry. Manners and Lowther waved good-bye.

"What ripping luck!" exclaimed Talbot, as the train rolled out of Rylcombe Station. "Tom, old man, you've saved the situation!"

"Hear, hear!" said Figgins heartily.

"Good man!" said Redfern.

Tom glanced round the crowded carriage, his handsome face colouring.

"I saw Mr. Lathom taking Cardew back, and came on," he said. "I thought, in the circumstances, I ought to join up."

"Right as rain!" said Kangaroo.

"Of course, I don't want to butt in," said Tom, his colour deepening. "Cardew is captain! But as he isn't here——"

"As our captain has chosen to get himself marched off like a silly fag, we've got to find another man to fill his place," growled Kangaroo. "I fancy, if we put it to the vote, all the men here will say 'Tom Merry.'"

"Yes, rather!"

"Hear, hear!"

"Of course, it's for this time only," said Tom. "Cardew's out of it, and in any case you'd have to fill his place. If you want me, I'm here. But I'm willing to play under any captain you select."

"You're captain," said Talbot.

"As the matter stands, old man, I'd rather you took it on," said Tom.

Talbot shook his head.

"Rot!" said Figgins decisively. "We're going to play this

match under our old skipper, and that's you, Tom Merry. And I jolly well think there ought to be a new election, with the order of the boot for that slacking chump Cardew!"

"Hear, hear!"

The train rolled on; the footballers changed into the express at Wayland Junction, and rushed on towards Rookwood School.

CHAPTER 8.
Cardew's Way!

MR. LATHOM led Cardew into the Form-room in the School House. The dandy of the Fourth went meekly to his desk.

Outwardly, he was all submission. Inwardly, he was as determined as ever that he would not submit to detention that afternoon, and that he would play in the match at Rookwood. But Mr. Lathom certainly could not guess that from his looks.

"You will remain here until five o'clock, Cardew," said the master of the Fourth.

"Yes, sir!"

"You have an imposition of five hundred lines to write. I shall expect them to be written by five o'clock."

"Very well, sir."

"And as I cannot trust you, Cardew, I shall lock the door and take away the key," said Mr Lathom sternly.

Cardew breathed hard.

Mr. Lathom left the Form-room, and the key clicked in the lock. Cardew did not sit down at his desk.

He stood leaning on the desk, thinking hard, his hands in his pockets. The problem before him was a difficult one, but Cardew was not beaten yet. The door was locked, but there was the window, and then—— Already the train must be gone. Cardew looked at his watch. In those very moments the football party would be changing at Wayland Junction. The express was starting.

Cardew gritted his teeth.

He climbed to the high window of the Form-room and looked out. Mr. Lathom, nothing doubting that the detained junior was secure, locked in the Form-room, had gone back to his study. But there were a good many fellows in the

quadrangle—two or three prefects of the Sixth were in sight. Among them Cardew noticed Rushden of the Sixth, wheeling his motor-bike down to the side gate.

His eyes gleamed.

Quietly and coolly Cardew drew himself up to the window, and dropped out to the ground outside. A junior who was sauntering along the path stopped and stared at him.

"Bai Jove! Cardew!"

Cardew did not even look at Arthur Augustus D'Arcy. He scudded away, and a couple of minutes later was dropping from the school wall, behind the elms, into the road. A dozen fellows had sighted him, and he left them in a buzz of excitement.

Outside the school precincts, Cardew did not head for the station. He knew that that was useless. There was no train to take him to Rookwood in time for the match. He had a vague idea of getting somehow to Wayland and hiring a fast car—he had plenty of money. But the sight of Rushden and his motor-bike had put a new thought into his mind.

A fast car might have done the journey in time, but it was miles to Wayland. Cardew would have tried it as a last resource. But Rushden's motor-bike was a better resource—it was a certainty, if the dandy of the Fourth could get possession of it. And Cardew was absolutely regardless of consequences now.

Rushden was starting up the bike in the road, giving it all his attention. He glanced at Cardew without heeding him; he was not even aware that Cardew was under detention that afternoon.

Cardew stopped, breathing hard, but cool and calm. At any moment, he knew, there might be pursuit. At least a dozen fellows had seen his escape—among them Kildare of the Sixth—and he thought he had seen Mr. Railton, the Housemaster of the School House, in the quad, as he ran. But it was at moments of tense excitement that Cardew's brain was clear and cool and decisive.

"Rushden!" he called out.

"Well?"

"You're wanted—Head's study."

Cardew sauntered on unconcernedly, leaving Rushden staring. The Sixth-Former muttered something below his breath.

Not for an instant did it cross his mind that a junior of the Fourth Form would venture to give him a "spoof" message. Neither could he have imagined any reason why Cardew should do so.

A message from the Head could not be disregarded. If Dr. Holmes had sent for him Rushden of the Sixth had to go.

He secured the motor-bike, and strode—or rather stamped—away to the gate, leaving the machine by the roadside.

Cardew glanced back at a little distance.

He saw Rushden disappear at the gate, and came scudding back. A minute more, and the motor-bike was throbbing again.

"Dear man!" murmured Cardew. "Innocent old duck! I fancy he got a false impression from what I said. I wonder whether a strict moralist would call it an untruth? He's wanted in the Head's study—wanted bad—only he's wanted by me, not by the Head! I dare say he will find that out when he sees the jolly old Head, though."

Cardew mounted Rushden's machine.

He was moving when Kildare of the Sixth came out at the school gates, and stared along the road.

"Cardew!" he shouted.

Cardew smiled, but did not look back. Head prefect and captain of the school mattered nothing to the reckless junior now.

Kildare broke into a run after the motor-bike.

"Cardew!" he roared.

Cardew put on speed. Kildare was a good man on the cinder-path, but he had, of course, no chance of overtaking Cardew unless the latter chose to stop. And he did not choose.

The captain of St. Jim's ran savagely for fifty yards or so, and then halted, setting his lips with anger. Cardew was vanishing round a corner far ahead on the road.

THE GEM LIBRARY.—No. 827.

Kildare turned back. Rushden of the Sixth met him at the gates. Rushden was red with wrath.

"Seen that young villain Cardew?" he exclaimed. "He sent me to the Head's study with a spoof message."

"He's gone—on your bike!"

"On my motor-bike?" yelled Rushden.

"Yes."

"Why, I—I—I—I——" Rushden spluttered. Words failed him.

Kildare went in.

"You have found the boy, Kildare?" called out Mr. Railton.

"No, sir; he's got hold of Rushden's motor-bike and cleared off," answered Kildare.

"Upon my word!"

A few minutes later Mr. Railton, Mr. Lathom, and the Head were in solemn conclave together on the subject of Ralph Reckness Cardew. The decision of the three gentlemen was, that when Cardew returned to St. Jim's, his punishment should be so exemplary that it could scarcely fail to act as a warning to him.

In the meantime Cardew was going strong.

Rushden's motor-bike was a good machine, and in good form. Cardew got the very best out of it.

By road and lane he whizzed on, his face set, staring straight before him, thinking of nothing but of getting to Rookwood in time to captain the St. Jim's side in the football match. Trees and hedges and villages flew by him.

Latcham! He had to slow down in the streets of the town, but on the other side he let the machine out again, and hummed on to Coombe. By the church clock at Coombe he knew that the train was long in. The St. Jim's footballers had already left the station—they were at the school, or near it, by that time. Up the lane from Coombe to Rookwood School Cardew went tearing.

At the gates of Rookwood he halted. One glance at his watch—he was just in time!

CHAPTER 9.

Rival Captains !

JIMMY SILVER & CO., of Rookwood, greeted the footballers from St. Jim's cheerily. Tom Merry & Co. were shown into their dressing-room, and proceeded to change for the match.

Tom, in the hurry of his departure, had not, of course, had time to get his football outfit. But that did not matter, as Levison had Cardew's things in his bag. Cardew's elegant outfit was a size small for Tom, but an exact fit was not wanted on the football field. He changed with the rest, and the St. Jim's team came out.

That Ralph Reckness Cardew could, by any chance, arrive at Rookwood for the match had not crossed Tom's mind; or the mind of any fellow in the team. He was detained at St. Jim's, and the train was lost, anyhow. Cardew's arrival was too impossible to be thought of.

But it was the impossible that happened.

"Levison, old bean !"

Ernest Levison gave a jump.

He spun round, to see Cardew of the Fourth, dusty, but cheerful, with the Rookwood fellows regarding him curiously. Cardew nodded coolly to his amazed chum.

"You brought my things along, of course ?" asked Cardew.

"Eh—what—yes !" stuttered Levison.

"You here !" ejaculated Clive.

Cardew raised his eyebrows.

"Where should I be ? This is Rookwood, isn't it ? And we're due here for football."

"But—but——" gasped Levison.

"You've cut detention !" exclaimed Talbot.

"Guilty !"

"How on earth did you get here ?" exclaimed Levison. "There was no train——"

"Rushden lent me his motor-bike."

"Oh !"

"Without meaning to," added Cardew. "I borrowed it without asking. It's at the porter's lodge here now. I'm glad I'm in time."

A grim silence followed. Cardew's eyes, roving over the footballers, lighted on Tom Merry, and he started.

"Merry here ?" he said.

Tom's face was crimson.

The arrival of Cardew placed him in an utterly false position. He was in Cardew's place, in Cardew's clothes, because it had seemed impossible for Cardew to come. And Cardew had come !

Cardew's eyes glittered like steel.

"Have you been makin' some changes in the team ?" he asked very quietly. "Tom Merry does not belong to this eleven."

"You left us in the lurch," said Figgins hotly. "We were jolly glad to get Tom Merry to take your place."

"I told you I should be here."

THE GEM LIBRARY.—No. 827.

"I know that. But——"

"Tom played up when you had practically deserted us," said Talbot of the Shell quietly. "I vote that Tom Merry captains the side in this match."

"Hear, hear !"

"Tom's the man," said Kangaroo decidedly. "Your motor-bike stunts are a bit superfluous, Cardew ! You're not wanted now."

Jimmy Silver & Co., exchanging glances, drew away, politely appearing oblivious of this strange dispute among the visiting team. It was time for kick-off, and the referee was ready; but the Rookwooders were content to wait a little.

Cardew's face hardened grimly.

"I am captain of this side," he said. "I refuse to allow anybody to take my place."

"You won't be asked," said Kerr. "A football captain isn't supposed to get detained, and to bolt against orders, and to borrow a motor-bike without permission, and turn up on the field, like a character in a film play, at the last moment. It may be dramatic, but it isn't footer."

"Let's get on," said Fatty Wynn. "You can stand around and cheer, Cardew."

Levison and Clive did not speak. They wanted to back up their chum, but it was difficult for them to support Cardew, in the circumstances.

Cardew's teeth came together hard.

The previous day he had displayed an utter disregard of the Rookwood fixture. But circumstances had changed now. All his obstinate determination was roused at the sight of his old rival in his place.

"Tom Merry will stand out of this game," he said.

"He won't !" snapped Talbot.

"I refuse to play him."

"You won't be played yourself. Get on, you fellows !"

"Hold on," said Cardew quietly, with gleaming eyes. "I am your captain, properly elected and appointed. You can't rebel like this on the football-field."

"We can—and shall !" said Figgins.

"Then I shall speak to the referee and the Rookwood skipper, and claim a postponement of the match."

"You cheeky cad——" burst out Figgins.

"Hold on !" said Tom Merry.

So far, Tom had not spoken. In the strange state of affairs, he hardly knew what to do. He had been thinking it out while the other fellows were speaking.

"You've got to play up, Tom," exclaimed Talbot quickly.

Tom shook his head.

"Cardew's captain," he said. "I came because he couldn't come. But he's got here. I'm bound to stand out."

He walked back to the dressing-room. Cardew cast a vaunting look at the gloomy, lowering faces of his team.

Then he followed Tom into the dressing-room.

He came out in a few minutes, clad for football. In grim silence the St. Jim's team went into the field.

The whistle went.

The game had started when Tom Merry came out, dressed in his ordinary clothes, his face a little pale.

He did not stay to watch the game.

While the footballers were busy Tom Merry walked to the station, and took the train home for St. Jim's.

CHAPTER 10.

Nothing Succeeds Like Success !

"ONE up !" growled Kangaroo at half-time.

Rookwood were one up.

The St. Jim's footballers had gone into the game in a mood very different from their usual mood on the football-field. It was not surprising that they had failed to score, and that Rookwood had penetrated their defence.

The team was not the best St. Jim's could have sent out. All the members of it were disturbed by the happenings just before the game. And even Cardew was not at his best—the long and fast run on the motor-bike had told on him. And a captain who had forced himself upon a reluctant team did not seem likely to be a winning captain.

In the interval no man in the team spoke to Cardew, but all of them gave him grim looks.

"We're out for a licking," said Figgins glumly. "For goodness' sake, Fatty, do your best to keep the margin down."

Fatty Wynn nodded gloomily.

"Dear men," said Cardew lightly, "a game isn't lost till it's won—and Rookwood hasn't won yet."

Nobody answered him.

"As your captain," continued Cardew in the same tone, "it's up to me to give you a word of advice. If you go into a football match as if you were going to a funeral, you're asking for a licking. Keep your pecker up."

Grim silence.

Cardew coloured a little.

The ball came in from Levison, and Rawson caught it and drove it out. It came back, and the Rookwood goalie stopped it with his ready hand. At the same moment, Ralph Reckness Cardew came pounding down upon him, and goalkeeper and ball went charging in the net together. "Goal!" It was the winning goal for St. Jim's. _(See this page.)_

"What a jolly crew!" he said, glancing round him. "At any rate, Rookwood will beat us by about a dozen goals, I should say. I'm afraid I shall have to bunk most of you out of the eleven."

Fortunately, the call to play came then, or hot words would have followed.

The sides lined up again.

Jimmy Silver & Co. attacked hotly, and the Rookwooders were soon swarming round the visitors' goal. But Fatty Wynn, between the posts, was a tower of strength. St. Jim's were fortunate in their goalkeeper, if not in their skipper.

The attack did not materialise. Kangaroo cleared to midfield, and the St. Jim's forwards got going at last. And then Cardew was on the ball.

Luck favoured him, that was undoubted; but equally undoubtedly he put in some very fine play. It seemed like magic to the Rookwood crowd, looking on, to see him threading his way through the defence, and they could scarcely believe their eyes when the ball went in.

But it went in, and there was a gasping shout:

"Goal!"

St. Jim's had equalised.

"By Jove!" Jimmy Silver murmured to Arthur Edward Lovell. "They've got a good man there—regular lightning."

The St. Jim's faces were brighter as the sides formed up. There were no more black looks for Cardew, at all events.

As if inspired by Cardew's success, the St. Jim's footballers bore down on the home goal, and after a tough struggle Figgins put the ball in.

With twenty minutes to play, St. Jim's were a goal ahead; and Jimmy Silver & Co. were fighting hard now. For ten minutes the game was ding-dong, and then there was an irresistible attack on the visitors' goal. Fatty Wynn played up magnificently; but even Fatty was only human, and in spite of his defence, the ball found the net.

"Two all!" gasped Kangaroo. "How long to go now?"

"Five minutes."

"Play up, men!" said Cardew. "We'll beat them yet!"

"We'll try jolly hard!" said Levison cheerfully.

"Yes, rather," said Talbot.

Cardew smiled. Success had brought a change of sentiment in the team. Instead of the defeat almost every fellow had expected, the St. Jim's side had done well. Victory was still on the knees of the gods, but certainly their chance was as good as the enemy's now. The fellows seemed to have forgotten all Cardew's offences, for the time at least. The game had atoned for them.

The whistle shrilled, and there was a desperate struggle for victory. Jimmy Silver & Co. came down hotly on the visitors' goal, but the backs cleared, and St. Jim's got away again. In the last few minutes of the match the fight was in front of the home goal, with Rawson of Rookwood between the posts, watchful as a cat. The ball came in from Levison, and Rawson caught and drove it out. It came back, and the Rookwood goalkeeper, stepping out of the goal, stopped it with his ready hands. And at the same instant Ralph Reckness Cardew charged him in, and goalkeeper and ball went headlong into the net together.

"Goal!"

Pheep! went the whistle.

"Goal!"

Rawson staggered up.

It was a goal, and St. Jim's had won! Cardew stood rather unsteadily, gasping for breath. Levison caught his arm.

"Good man! Good man! Goal!"

"Good old man!" gasped Clive, smacking Cardew on the shoulder. "You've done it! Oh, ripping!"

"Hurrah!" panted Figgins.

"That was splendid, Cardew!" said Talbot, in a quiet way.

"Well, we seem to have won," yawned Cardew, and he walked cheerfully off the field with the St. Jim's crowd.

. . . .

It was quite a cheerful party that crowded into the train for St. Jim's later, with Rushden's motor-bike in the guard's van. Cardew was as cheerful as any, though he could scarcely have forgotten what awaited him at St. Jim's.

He had not counted the cost, but the cost had to be paid. But at least he had reinstated himself with the footballers. The winning goal counted for a very great deal.

"You'll have trouble with Rushden when you get in, Cardew," Levison said, when they changed at Wayland.

"I expect so. Sixth Form chaps can't possibly be pleased when a junior bags their motor-bike without permission," assented Cardew, with a cool nod.

"What about Lathom?" asked Figgins.

Cardew laughed.

"I fancy Lathom will be tearing his hair with wrath. I shall have to go before the Head. What a life !"

"All your own fault !" remarked Kangaroo.

"Quite so. That's a comfort, isn't it ?"

"It will mean a flogging," said Clive uneasily.

"If that's all, old bean, I sha'n't worry. But if the jolly old Head bunks me from the school you'll lose your captain. Fancy that ! If you have tears, prepare to shed them now !"

"Well, you're taking it coolly, anyhow," remarked Fatty Wynn.

"What's the good of gettin' into a fluster?" said Cardew lightly.

The returning footballers arrived at St. Jim's. Tom Merry and Manners and Lowther met them at the gates.

"How did it go?" asked Tom, addressing Talbot of the Shell, and taking no notice of Cardew.

"We beat them—three to two."

"Oh, good !"

"Happy news, what?" smiled Cardew. "We've actually beaten Rookwood without any help from Thomas. Quite a record."

"Cheese that, Cardew !" muttered Levison.

"Cardew kicked the winning goal, Tom," said Talbot hastily. "He played up really well."

"I'm afraid that won't please Thomas," murmured Cardew.

Tom fixed his eyes on the dandy of the Fourth. There was a scorn in his look that brought the colour to Cardew's cheeks.

"I'm glad St. Jim's has won," he said. "I never expected it, but I'm jolly glad. But that doesn't alter the fact, Cardew, that you are a rotten bad captain, that you have neglected all your duties, and that you have acted like a slacker and a cad all round."

"Yaas, wathah !" chimed in Arthur Augustus D'Arcy. "I endorse evewy word uttahed by Tom Mewwy."

"Dear me !" said Cardew lightly. "I am condemned by Thomas and condemned by Gussy, the one and only. Take me away somewhere where I can hide my diminished head."

Some of the fellows laughed.

Cardew walked on to the School House. Rushden of the Sixth met him in the doorway, with a grim face.

"Where's my motor-bike?"

"At the station. It's being sent on," said Cardew. "Thanks so much for lending it to me !"

Rushden gave him a look.

"I'd give you the licking of your life," he said. "But you're going to get enough from the Head, I fancy."

"I agree," said Cardew.

"You're to go in to the Head at once, Cardew !" called out Kildare.

"Certainly !"

Cardew walked away airily to Dr. Holmes' study. Mr. Lathom followed him there, and a few minutes later it was noted that Taggles, the porter, was sent for.

"It's a flogging !" said Levison.

"It might have been the sack !" said Clive, with a breath of relief. "I fancy it was touch and go."

Levison nodded.

"After all, he won the match for us," remarked Kangaroo. "He's a queer fish, but he's a footballer. We beat Rookwood."

"Yaas," said Arthur Augustus. "But——"

"Well, we beat Rookwood," said several fellows. It was evident that, in Cardew's case, a winning goal covered a multitude of sins.

Quite a little army of fellows had gathered at the corner of the Head's corridor. They were all anxious to see Cardew.

No sound of a voice came from the Head's study, no sound of a cry. Cardew was as hard as steel. If he was going through it, he was going through it in grim silence. Trimble, venturing nearer the Head's door, brought back the news that he had heard the steady swishing of the birch.

"The Head's laying it on !" grinned Trimble.

But nobody else grinned.

It seemed an age to the juniors before the Head's door opened, and Ralph Reckness Cardew came out. His face was pale, almost white, as he came slowly up the passage.

But he was still cool. He nodded to the crowd of juniors.

"Had it bad?" asked Talbot.

"Well, a little. The Head is really a hefty athlete for a gent of his years," said Cardew. "I never thought he had so much beef in him. My belief is that he's been doing physical jerks this afternoon to get his muscle up for the job."

Levison quietly took Cardew's arm and led him away, and the crowd broke up, some of them grinning. Cardew, whatever his faults and failings—and their name was legion—was game to the backbone, that was certain.

. . . .

Tom Merry did not speak to Cardew again when they met. But with most of the fellows he seemed to have jumped into popularity. He had captained a winning side, after all, and he had reached the football-field by a daring defiance of authority that few fellows would have been capable of, and he had taken his punishment afterwards without a murmur. Pluck and determination, at least, he had in plenty, and they were qualities that put his faults into the shade. He had regained the position he had almost lost. His luck had held good. And before he was put to the test again St. Jim's broke up for the Christmas holidays. But, as it happened, the feud between Cardew and Tom Merry was not destined to sleep during the Christmastide. The end was not yet.

THE END.

(Another splendid story of Tom Merry & Co. will appear in next week's Bumper Christmas Number of the GEM. Make a note of the title, chums : "D'ARCY'S CHRISTMAS PARTY !" by Martin Clifford. You cannot afford to miss this topping yarn.)

Tuck Hampers and Money Prizes Awarded for Interesting Paragraphs.

BRISTOL BAGS THE TUCK HAMPER !
NO FEAR !

Jones entered the office one morning, looking very pale and drawn. "Hallo, you look ill, old chap !" said his friend. "What's the matter?" "Tooth-ache !" groaned Jones. "I haven't had a wink of sleep all night." "Ah !" replied his friend confidingly. "You should try the faith cure. Just repeat to yourself fifty times a day, 'Get behind me, pain !' " "Not likely !" snapped Jones angrily. "Do you think I want lumbago !"—A Tuck Hamper filled with delicious Tuck has been awarded to Ivor Cox, 80, Aubrey Road, Chessels, Bedminster, Bristol.

HE WAS SURE HONEST.

The waiter coughed apologetically. "If you please, sir——" he began. "Well, Benskin," inquired the amiable diner, "what can I do for you?" "Well, sir, I'm going to leave this restaurant, and the boss won't give me a character. I thought perhaps you would say as I was honest. I've always served you here, sir." "But I don't know anything about your honesty," said the diner. "Oh, but I'm awfully honest, sir, really !" "All right, then," said the diner. "I'll say you're honest. Give me a pen and paper !" The deed was soon done. "Oh, thank you, sir !" said Benskin, firmly clutching his character in his hand. Then he bent low, and whispered in his customer's ear: "Come here to-morrow, and I'll wangle you a meal for nothing, sir !"—Half-a-crown has been awarded to D. Finlayson, 4, Wilder Place, Galashiels.

NEW ANTIQUES !

It was in a country cottage, and after the antique dealer was gone it was observed that the old man who owned the cottage was chuckling to himself. "What ever be up with thee, granddad?" asked his granddaughter. "Why, I sold tho old kitchen chair to that chap from Lunnon as a genuine antique, and I can remember me old grandfeyther tellin' me he made it himself !"—Half-a-crown has been awarded to E. T. Willmott, 9, North Street, Wellington, Somerset.

(Continued on page 27.)

River-Wise Ned and his
staunch chums meet—

—thrilling adventure
in every quarter

THE COINERS !

by Roland Spencer

A Thrilling
Story of Amaz-
ing Adventure
aboard the
Thames Barge,
Estuary Belle.

CHAPTER 1.

Up Against It.

THE Estuary Belle, London sailing-barge, commanded and owned by Ned Derry, the ever-cheerful youth who had earned the name of River-wise Ned, owing to his surprisingly extensive knowledge of the great Thames Estuary, was in disgrace.

Owing to the wind having fluked at a critical moment, the barge had stove in the side of a smart eight-ton cutter yacht in the River Medway, and the yachtsmen had had a lot to say about it.

The owner of the yacht, Stockton Burr by name, and his companion, a young fellow called Sanderley had abused Ned and his mates, Tony Parr and Jim Cartwright, in right nautical fashion, and the chums had borne it all quite patiently.

Stockton Burr had suggested twenty pounds as a just compensation for the damage. But Ned would not pay until he had been allowed to go into the yacht's cabin to judge the extent of the damage to interior fittings. This, for some reason, Burr would not agree to.

Names and addresses had been exchanged, and both parties had retired in high dudgeon, the Belle to set off for Harwich, and the yachtsmen to see to repairs to their boat.

"You'll hear from my insurers before long," had been Stockton Burr's parting shot, as the Belle swung down the Medway on the ebb.

It was a few days after the event, and Ned was sorting out the mail.

"Well, here are our letters, you lazy beggars! Nothing from the two nice yachtsmen with whom we scraped such a pleasant acquaintance in the Medway."

The Estuary Belle was at Harwich, having delivered her cargo of linseed-cake to that port from the Medway. Ned had just been ashore on business at the post-office and at the custom-house.

"Wish those Burnham bounders would get on with it," said Tony Parr. "We'll have to pay through the nose, of course. Still, it won't leave us exactly like broken reeds. We've still a bob apiece for the pictures to-night."

"Yes," cut in Ned; "and there's a ripping sea film on that I'd just like to see. It's about a girl who works a square-rigger singlehanded, with dead men all round her or something. It

sounds thrilling. Get your greasy old caps on, chumps, and let's be off!"

The young bargees were soon ashore. They went straight up to the Magnificent Picture Palace, and took their seats in the shilling rows.

"Dolly Farne is starring in the big picture this evening," said Ned, before the lights went out. "Won't it be great when we can see the picture we and the Belle acted in?"

The lads enjoyed the whole programme thoroughly, and when the show was over, walked silently and thoughtfully back to where the barge-boat was moored. The Belle herself was lying some distance below Parkeston Quay.

The chums had just reached the alleyway from which they could get a view of the place where their boat was tied up when Ned suddenly threw up his head and snorted indignantly, like a war-horse scenting battle.

"Look at those youngsters messing about with our boat, chums!" he cried, pointing ahead. "Let's catch 'em and give 'em a good fright!"

The three chums dashed with more speed than wisdom down the narrow alleyway, and hardly had they reached the bottom than they cannoned into two yachtsmen struggling along a lane at right angles, carrying a heavy box of fish between them.

The heavy fish box fell with a thud, the yachtsmen went flying, and Ned and his chums sprawled flat on the ground, Tony Parr ploughing up the dust in the gutter with his chin.

The urchins, who had left the barge-boat, already in flight, stopped and shrieked with laughter. Then they scudded off as Ned and the others picked themselves up.

Some money had been spilt in that little collision. The loose coins in Ned's pockets had clinked and clattered on to the cobbles. When Ned had collected his wits and his cap, he saw one of the yachtsmen already rearranging the fish in the box. The other yachtsman was grabbing at the loose money on the cobbles.

"I beg your pardon," said Ned, as he stooped to pick up some of the money.

There was a lot of it there, but Ned only took what he had had in his pocket—three half-crowns and a few odd pence.

"Gosh!" ejaculated Long Jim. "Mr. Burr and Mr. Sanderley! Fancy meeting you like this! We seem doomed to crash up against you at every turn."

It was a surprising coincidence that they should have again fallen foul of the yachtsmen whose yacht they had damaged in the Medway. Stockton Burr had stepped back in alarmed surprise as he recognised Ned and his chums. Sanderley had collected all the money now, and he turned on Ned.

"I say——" he began. Then: "What, you again? Look here, hand back that money! I dropped it!"

"When a man shoots forward with some force, loose money in his pockets is apt to come out," said Ned. "That's precisely what has happened in my case, sir. I've got my little lot back—seven-and-tenpence. All the rest is yours."

"I'm three half-crowns short!" protested Sanderley.

"Then they'll be on the ground," said Ned, peering about. "Must be."

"They're not! Hand 'em out! This ten-shilling note was yours, perhaps?"

"Not at all. I had no note," replied Ned. "That must be yours. I'm sorry for the accident——"

"Burr, that young rat's trying to steal seven-and-six from me!"

"Here, hold on!" flashed Ned, clenching his fists. "Don't call me a thief, for all the trouble my chums and I have been of late to you two. I've only got the money I had before the accident."

"Your fish isn't damaged," broke in Long Jim, anxious to preserve the peace. "We're sorry we were so careless. Shall we give you a hand with the fish-box?"

"Oh, it's all right, thanks!" replied Burr. "We've been out fishing in the Eileen, and we're taking this box of fish to a friend. Like to buy some?"

Ned and his pals looked at the fish. They were very fresh and tempting.

"Have five bob's worth," said the yachtsman, looking at Ned. "We'll give you a pile of 'em for five shillings."

River-wise Ned shook his head.

"We'd like some, but as a matter of fact we can't afford to pay for fish when we can catch all we want."

THE GEM LIBRARY.—No. 827.

After further talk, when the matter of the accident in the Medway and a sum of seven shillings were discussed, the chums went out to the Belle. When in the cabin, they discussed the yachtmen further.

"Jolly decent of those chaps not to charge us anything for that smash," said Long Jim. "You ought to have given them that seven shillings towing fee, Ned."

"I said I'd send it on, didn't I? We need all the hard cash we've got at the moment."

"You might have given them the money there and then, though," said Tony Parr. "They wanted it, you could see. For all their prosperous-looking rig-outs they may be pretty low as regards ready-money Their wanting to sell us fish would bear that out. Didn't sound gracious to me, saying you'd send on a miserable seven shillings. However, the business is over, anyway, and a good job for us. That smash in the Medway was worrying me."

"Well, worry it out a bit more in your bunk, chum," replied Ned. "Your turn to take in the riding light and make tea in the morning, Jim. If you go on jawing here much longer you won't feel like getting up in the morning, and if I have come to rouse you—well——"

Jim Cartright grunted as he drew his trousers off his long legs.

"Last one undressed blows out the light," continued Ned, a few minutes later, after he had performed operations with his toothbrush. Then: "Goo'-night! Don't be a month turning in, and don't talk!"

Five minutes later the Estuary Belle was wrapped in slumber.

CHAPTER 2
On the Track of Adventure!

THE next morning Ned and his mates went ashore to do a bit of shopping.

"We want some bacon, a quarter of tea, and another pound of sugar, for a kick-off," said Long Jim, as the three walked into Harwich. "Now. what about meat? I vote we have some stewing steak. That won't cost a lot."

"Wish we could afford something special," put in Tony Parr. "But we'll have to be content with a plain diet for a bit, I suppose?"

The lads pushed on, talking about their passage back to Gravesend. They would have to be under way the next day. They had no freight waiting for them. but Ned's opinion was that, with the barge all ready and available at Gravesend, he'd be able to secure a job he had had his eye on for some time—the shifting of a mass of old building materials near the water-front.

They entered the first grocer's shop they saw.

"A quarter of two-and-eightpenny tea, please," said Ned. "Pound of sugar and a pound of bacon—nice streaky stuff."

The grocer busied himself about, preparing the order. When the things were ready Ned paid him with two half-crowns. The grocer chinked the coins on the counter as he opened the till drawer. Then he chinked them again and examined them closely.

At last he looked up.

"Bad!" he said. "Both these half-crowns are bad!"

Ned held out his hand for them, tested them, and came to the conclusion that they were bad. The young bargee looked meaningly at his pals.

"Remember the mix-up of money with those two beauties last night?" he said.

"Yes, the blighters! And their great efforts to get the half-crowns you had pocketed back, by jingo! It seemed a bit funny at the time—first threatening us, then wanting us to buy fish, then to pay seven shillings towing fee. Gee, it looks suspicious!"

"It does," said Ned. Then, to the grocer, after examining his other half-crown. "I'm sorry, but I have only a few coppers of good money and one good half-crown. Will you give me two-and-fourpenny tea and take away a quarter of the bacon? Then I can do it."

The grocer eyed the chums suspiciously.

"Oi reckon you'll have to account for them bad coins to the police," he said.

The lads became alarmed. That would mean great delay for them. Ned took the bull by the horns and told the grocer the whole story. When he had finished, the portly old Essex tradesman, who had a habit of standing with his hands on his stomach, under his apron, said:

"So you're River-woyse Ned? Oi've read all about you in the papers. Gum, you're on to another adventure, then, looks loike. Well, get to it now, lads, an' tell me the whole yarn nex' toime you're at Harwich, will 'e? I won't say nothing to the police this toime. The papers of the past few weeks have said lots about bad coins bein' circulated in inland towns. That makes me careful."

The chums thanked the old grocer and hurried back to the Belle. In the cabin Ned called a conference.

Unable to check their mad rush Ned and his chums cannoned into the two yachtsmen, sending them toppling backwards. There was a thud as their heavy fish box fell to the ground, followed by a jingling sound as a number of loose coins clinked and clattered on the rough cobbles.

"Look here, you two chumps," he said, "let's put two and two together. We bashed that yacht, the Eileen. The owner, Stockton Burr, generously, wouldn't let us pay."

"Bur-r-r-r!" said Long Jim.

"He rated us for peering into the hole we made in the yacht, and wouldn't let us go into the cabin. We thought it funny at the time. I'll bet those bounders—Burr and Sanderley—are distributors of bad money for some coiners."

"Yes, and that fish episode. There was bad money under the fish, I'll bet my shirt," said Tony Parr excitedly. "The blighters were afraid you'd got hold of a bad coin or two when you picked up the half-crowns, Ned, so tried to get them back, knowing that the discovery of their badness would result in suspicions being directed towards them."

"We're on another rattling mystery, lads!"

Ned suddenly made a leap for the cabin steps as a new thought flashed on his mind.

"Ay!" he called down when his head was above the companionway, "and there's the Eileen hull down on the horizon, just to the south'ard of Landguard Point. Clear decks for action! Shorten in the chain, Tony. Jim, bass line off the mains'l. I'll lower the leeboards."

"Getting after her, Ned?"

"Sure thing. We'll dog her if she goes to the North Pole!"

"Hurrah! Look slippy!" cried Tony Parr, as he sprang forward to the windlass.

"If the Eileen can outsail a London sailing barge she'll be a smart yacht," cried Long Jim, as he tugged at the knot of the grass rope tied round the brailed mainsail.

"We'll find out if those brutes are circulating bad money or not," said Ned, lowering a leeboard in a series of jerks. "Chain short, Tony? Right-ho! I'll stand by the wheel. Draw out the topsail and let go mainsail brail, Jim. Trip anchor, Tony. Freights can wait when the Belle scents an adventure! What-ho!"

By nightfall the Estuary Belle was well to sea, Yarmouth a-beam, the Eileen ahead, leading them north-west along the Would—that is, the deep-water channel past Cromer. The yacht was either desirous of not getting too far to sea, or was bound for the Wash. Otherwise she would have pointed up for the Outer Dowsing Bank.

The yacht, evidently unsuspicious that the barge was dogging her, pointed over the Docking Shoal for Lynn Deeps. The chums could follow her by the light from her cabin door. The Belle herself carried no lights, merely keeping a combination-lamp handy in case any craft should get near them.

Throughout the dark hours the Eileen drew the Belle into what the lads found from the chart was Walbeach Channel, a deep, narrow gut leading up through the Fens. The Eileen had entered, there was no other way out, so the Belle pointed over to Walbeach Channel, found a reedy, deep creek there, secured the barge, and got the mast down flat on the deck just before the grey in the eastward heralded the approach of day.

The light showed the Eileen in her berth, as, apparently the sole occupant of the extensive, barren, and treacherous Walbeach Marshes. But Ned and his mates were watching, and soon they were again hot on the scent, shadowing Burr and Sanderley, again carrying a fish box, over the marsh land towards Long Sutton.

The two men suddenly disappeared from sight, so, stepping warily and silently, Ned and his chums followed up the tracks in the coarse grasses of the marsh, and saw a hole in the ground where the tracks ended.

A stairway led down into the dark hole. It was like a war-time dugout. On the marsh hard by was the "lid" of the hole—a wooden covering with about eighteen inches of turf on top of it.

Ned and his chums realised, as they watched silently and in wonder, that this "lid," when put in place, would completely hide the fact that there was dug-out below.

"Going in?" whispered Tony Parr.

"To get a crack on the head?" asked Ned sarcastically. "Not on your life. We'll lie flat here, watch, and wait. The beggars won't be long, I expect."

Ned surmised correctly, for very soon voices sounded from the dug-out.

convict them. We'll walk the bounders into Long Sutton."

The two men were out of the dugout now, so with a sudden spring, the chums of the Belle leapt at them, and a desperate struggle was soon in progress.

CHAPTER 3.
Bad Luck for the Chums!

THE three young bargees thought they had a soft nut to crack in downing Burr and Sanderley. So they would have had if Long Jim hadn't been knocked out by a terrific blow from Burr, delivered from behind.

With Ned and Long Jim at the wheel the barge breasted the roaring black seas much easier. Burr and Sanderley crouched back in fear as the seething waters washed half over the lee hatch covers.

"Put the letter to Denborough under the weight on the shelf, Sanderley. That's right. Now they'll get their instructions."

"I think you were right, old man," then said Sanderley. "We've used Manchester long enough, and Liverpool's too close to Manchester to do that town yet. A spell with small market towns would be best now. A lot of small money changes hands at cattle markets, and farmers and country tradespeople are not so cute as town folk."

"That's so. If there's much more yap in the papers we'd better clear out in a week or so. Think those young bargee rats were suspicious?"

"Pooh, no! They'll pass the two coins they had somewhere, even if they discover they're bad. Two like that will soon get lost. Come on up, now! Mustn't leave the trapdoor open too long. You never know who'll spot it."

"No, you never know!" breathed Ned, grinning, as he squeezed his chums' arms. "At 'em when they come up. That letter of instructions will

They were thus left two to two, and Ned felt confident of victory even now for the rogues, evidently, were not armed.

Ned took on Burr, and Tony Parr tackled Sanderley. Burr was a scientific boxer, as Ned soon found out, and, under less dramatic circumstances, Ned would have gloried in the struggle for mastery.

Tony was well matched with Sanderley, who was a quick man on his feet. Tony, however, fought warily, without tiring himself too much.

Long Jim had received a complete knock-out. He had not stirred since he went down, so Ned and Tony could hardly hope to receive help from him for some time to come.

Sanderley danced about in front of Tony, stopping now and again, a smashing blow that made him gasp. Ned had lowered his head, and was beginning slogging tactics, for he realised that his man was becoming winded. Sanderley, out of the corner of his eye, realised this, too, so resolved on cunning to win the fight for himself and Burr. The man danced about in front of the dugout hole, then suddenly leapt backwards.

Tony followed up with a heavy lunge forward, put one foot in the hole, overbalanced, and received a stinging blow on the ear from Sanderley's right. He fell sideways, and Sanderley grabbed him by the neck and sent him sprawling, face forwards, into the dugout. Then the man, with a yell, leapt to the aid of his confederate.

In an instant Ned was badly bashed about. Then, he, too, was sent down the dugout steps on top of Tony. Long Jim was dragged over and bundled, doubled up, into the hole, thus preventing Tony and Ned from scrambling out again.

A mocking laugh rang out from above, and the "lid" was lifted and then lowered into place, plunging the dugout into darkness. Ned and Tony soon began to sort themselves out.

They brought Jim round after a bit of trouble and much rubbing of hands and chest. Then they paid attention to the trapdoor of their prison. It was impossible to raise it.

"A catch, or something, is holding it," said Ned. "Well, at the worst, we can dig ourselves out. Let's look for a crowbar or tools of some sort."

An examination of the dugout at the cost of half a box of matches revealed a bare apartment, save for the box the two men had taken down. This box was full of bad half-crowns and florins. There was a shelf at the end of the apartment, and on this a letter under a stone, the latter used as a paper-weight.

Ned read the letter. There was no name, but it was written in someone's handwriting, so would be sufficient to convict the writer. The letter stated:

"Leave Liverpool. Work market towns Derby, Warwick, and Oxford. Circulate amongst country tradesmen and at farm and market auction sales, avoiding big establishments or branches of big establishments. Good luck."

Ned put the letter back in place, and Long Jim struck another match.

"These matches are damp," he said. "Not burning well at all."

"Jingo, no! And I'm not breathing well at all. Golly, chums, this blithering

hole is airtight. We'll suffocate, with the trap closed. Crumbs, we must get out quickly!"

Greatly alarmed, the lads searched round frantically.

"There must be some device for opening the trap!" gasped Ned at last. "It stands to reason that a place like this, made by thorough villains like Burr and Sanderley, is a refuge as well as a depot. Search up the stairway."

The matches burned even less readily on the stairway, but after twenty minutes' search, with only two matches left, Ned found a string. He pulled it gingerly, half fearing a booby-trap, while Tony Parr and Long Jim pressed with their shoulders at the wooden trapdoor above.

The trapdoor yielded, and, once open, the chums thankfully drinking in the pure, fresh, marshland air, they saw that the string operated a spring catch that held the trapdoor down. They also saw that the Belle's mast was raised, and that Burr and Sanderley were struggling towards the barge with a box of something, presumably taken from the yacht.

"After them, chums! But put the trapdoor back into place first. We'll be the ones to report the dugout's existence!" cried Ned. "They're going to put to sea in the Belle, but not if we know it!"

The lads ran rapidly over the marshland towards the Belle. Burr and Sanderley saw them coming, hurried with their work, and were poling the barge down the gut, with, unluckily, just enough water left in it to float the old craft by the time Ned, Tony, and Jim arrived at the point.

Realising that desperate measures alone would now win them through, the lads plunged into the water, and, with heads down, and a powerful trudgeon-stroke, they swam out across the narrowing channel and intercepted the barge, just as the topsail was sheeted home, and the old ship gathered good way.

Scrambling aboard, Ned led a rush at the two rascally counterfeiters, only to be brought up, gasping, with two blue-glinting automatic pistols pointing at them. Behind the pistols a pair of evilly grinning faces looked at them.

"Hands up!" ordered Burr grimly. Then, as the chums complied, having read correctly the expression in Burr's eyes. "So far, so good, my lads! Thanks muchly for delivering yourselves to us! We saw you put the trapdoor over, and thanks again for that! Wish we'd taken these shooters from the yacht when we went to the dugout with the box. However, all's well that ends well—what? While I steer and keep them covered, Sanderley, just go through their pockets and extract that little note we left in the dugout."

The chums were powerless to do anything but keep their hands high above their heads while Sanderley gingerly searched in their wet pockets.

"Lump of marine glue," he said, grinning, when he had taken everything from the lads, "about a fathom of spun-yarn, some tarred serving twine, old shackle, our two pretty half-crowns—art productions as they are—various papers not concerning us, three jack-knives, a pocket compass, and three handkerchiefs. Pretty little collection."

"So they've left the letter in the dugout?" said Burr. "All the better! D. will get his instructions all right next week when he calls there. Not that that matters much to us now. Down below into the fo'c'sle with these rats! We'll live in the cabin. We're going deepwater sailing in the famous Estuary Belle, my lads! We'll scuttle her off some foreign shore, you with her, and you'll be washed up as poor, unfortunate

shipwrecks. All our coining plant is below in the cabin. That can go, too. You three have made us clear out of England only about a fortnight before we meant to, so we bear you no grudge now we've got such a topping old barge to make a safe crossing in. We meant to risk it in the Eileen before. Down below with 'em now, Sanderley, and let go the brail-rope. This nor'-wester will put us well out to sea very quickly."

CHAPTER 4.
The Belle Takes a Hand!

"WELL, Ned, you blithering chump, this is a bit of all right, isn't it?" cried Tony, as the three chums imprisoned in the Belle's cabin, exchanged glances.

"We've been locked up below here before now, haven't we, and we've got out?"

"Yes; but only because we've been carried out. What's going to save us this time?"

"Rough weather, and the old Belle," replied Ned "She's a beast in heavy weather, as is every chine-built barge. If it blows up, and on such a long passage as dead across the North Sea, we're bound to run into dirty weather, those swabs above will miss their self-draining cockpit and a comfortable few hours every now and again hove to. There's no comfort on a barge in bad weather, and the flat type like the Belle won't heave to. Oh, there's going to be some weeping and wailing and gnashing of teeth before this pleasure jaunt is out, and we'll be in great demand to save the barge and her distinguished company from a watery grave. You mark my words. I, who know the Belle so well, have had some. 'It ain't no bobby's job in the North Sea,' as the poet said, and the poet was right."

"Crumbs, yes!" replied Long Jim. "Gosh, I never thought of that! A buster from the nor'-east, or any other quarter for that matter, might be our salvation."

"Then let's have a sleep to be ready for it," put in Tony. "They'll get no sleep above—only two of 'em—as we well know. We're not licked yet."

It was even as Ned had predicted. It piped up from the north-east, and a very heavy sea was running by the evening. The two men above stuck it till midnight, smashing the barge into the teeth of it. But they were used to a deep-keel boat and the washing decks of the Belle, her yawing and lunging frightened them very considerably. The chums chuckled as they felt the fo'c'sle reeling and the smashing and banging of the seas and the booming of the foresail as the helmsmen nervously luffed to each comber.

At last they were released. They swamped down the weather waterway to the wheel, where two white faces greeted them

Ned grinned cheerily.

"The Belle's lovely in a seaway, isn't she, Burr?" he inquired, shouting above the roar of the wind.

"Curse her; she's a pig-headed brute! You've got to sail her."

"Then we must run for home!" shouted Ned. "You're a couple of crack-brained mugs for forcing a flat-bottomed barge to face heavy weather like this! I'm not so sure now that we'll be able to bear away with safety. Running is the only way to save the barge in weather like this."

Burr swore savagely, but he was very frightened, and his pistol shook as he held it.

"Can you save the barge?"

"Dunno, but we'll do our best. Best place for you and your mate is below in the cabin. You brought some bottled courage with you, I noticed."

"Well, stand clear for a minute," quavered Burr. "I'll leave the wheel, Sanderley, and cover them. For Heaven's sake, don't let this brute of a barge come broadside on! These young hounds will take over the deck, and we'll get below."

Ned gripped the wheel, and nodded curtly to Sanderley.

"You can let go now!" he shouted.

The two men crouched near the sliding hatch of the cabin. The barge was smashing and plunging about like a van-horse bogged, but at the feel of the hands of Ned and Long Jim on the wheel she became easier. She now breasted the roaring black seas more tractably, for Ned and Jim were more bold than Burr and Sanderley in their sailing. The latter two crouched together in fear as they saw seething water washing half over the lee hatch-covers.

"Stand by the fores'l halliard and mains'l brail, Tony!" ordered Ned. "When you see us spin the wheel, brail up hard, and put a jerk into it at the brail winch! Let go the fores'l halliard if we broach to."

The two crouching men were quivering with fear and gasping every time a sea swept over them. They saw, with trepidation, Ned and Jim lash themselves to the mizzen mast, and Tony take a turn of the fall of the topsail halliard round himself and the sprit.

"Get into the cabin companion-way, you!" shouted Ned to the cowering men. "We'll be swept fore 'n aft at best. Now then, Jim, that was a big one! Stand by for a 'smooth.'"

What is known as a "smooth" in rough weather is the slight lull between the extra big billows; generally each ninth wave is the biggest, the cause being cross waves in the water mingling themselves with the straight-flowing ones.

Ned judged his time.

"Hellum up!" he roared at last.

Jim strained hard at the spokes, a wave suddenly caught the rudder, and the wheel spun round like a flywheel. When the helm was full over, Ned and Jim threw their weight on the iron circle and held it hard. The Belle roared, spinning round on the crest of a wave, and the next snarling comber caught her on the quarter. She lunged, the water flowed waist high round the chums, and Tony was tugging and jerking at the brail winch.

Another sea burst over the barge's transom, and all but pooped the stout old ship. The foresail, however, tore the gallant old barge forward, and the stern was not forced down sideways into the trough, the danger Ned so feared.

The helm was put amidships, and the old craft swung on rapidly and more easily, pointing back for England.

"It's all right now!" bawled Ned to the heads of Burr and Sanderley. "You can get below! We'll get to some anchorage, with a bit of luck."

They did, the next day, but it was due to a good big slice of luck and the superb seamanship of Ned, Tony, and Jim. Haggard, reeling, hands bleeding, and eyes bloodshot, the chums shot up the Belle, nose into the wind, inside the shell beach at Orford Haven.

Burr himself let go the anchor, then, holding back the chums with their pistols, the two villains made the lads descend to the cabin. The hatch was slid over and secured, and, the barge-

boat having been smashed and washed overboard, Burr and Sanderley sprang into the water and swam ashore.

The barge was visited later in the day, and the exhausted chums released. The coiners' complete plant was found in the cabin, and the lads were marshalled up to the nearest police-station. There, they told the inspector their story. He at once phoned to the north to have the dugout watched. Ned had said that the villains would be sure to make for there, posthaste, to destroy the evidence.

The police were too late, however. The dugout was deserted. The coup was made not far away, however, Burr and Sanderley being captured in King's Lynn, trying to hire a motor-car. The incriminating letter was found on Burr, and a confession was forced, revealing the whole coining organisation.

The bad money was made aboard the yacht Eileen, and sent to various secret depots for distribution, many miles from the east coast. Needless to say, the villainous schemes were stopped, and Ned, Tony, and Jim greatly praised for their smart work.

"Another honour for the Belle, lads." River-wise Ned said, when the whole matter was closed. "Crumbs, the old ship will be all dolled up with thousands of winners flags before she's finished!"

Tony and Jim heartily agreed. It was characteristic of the chums to lay all the credit at the feet of their lady-love, the old barge that had borne them through many adventures to fame and favour.

THE END.

(There's a real treat of a story in next week's grand Christmas Number of the GEM. Note the title: "THE GHOST OF GREYMINSTER CASTLE!" On no account must you miss it.)

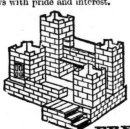

Hard though his
task may be—

—Jack Morton is determined
to win through!

THE TRIERS
BY JACK CRICHTON

A Powerful Story of Plot and Intrigue, telling of
Jack Morton's great fight against his rascally
cousin to regain the rights which are his due.

Light at Last !

THE game started again.
It was a ragged exhibition indeed on Boltwich's part. There was no life, and even Ronnie Stevens and Steve Logan seemed to have lost heart. Harry Turner had not been able to turn out to keep goal, and the newcomer was not a success. Things went from bad to worse.

The referee gave a decision against Boltwich which, to the unprejudiced mind even, seemed very open to question. The temper of the crowd grew nasty indeed, and when at the finish Boltwich had taken a severe beating from an inferior team at home there was no telling what would happen.

The crowd surged towards the stands, and then suddenly, for the first time, George Clifton realised how foolish he had been not to have taken Laurie Robson's advice.

Someone saw him.

"There he is !" came a cry.

Clifton turned and faced them. It was a bad moment. The crowd was yelling and jeering, surging ever towards the stands, and the police were evidently in the mood to get a bit of their own back for the previous Saturday's work at Crewbridge. At all events, they were not displaying their usual gentle methods, and already here and there a free fight had commenced.

"Come on, boys!" someone shouted. "Let's duck George Clifton! Let's show him what we think of him and his dirty ways!"

And at that moment the crowd broke loose. There was a sharp tussle with the police, and then it was too late.

Like maddened men they swarmed towards Clifton.

Realising the little chance of escape he had, he darted along the top of the stands; but his retreat was cut off everywhere. Again and again he darted here and there, but the crowd gave him never a chance. And then suddenly he turned and faced them, more of a man than people had known him to be.

"Come on, you curs !" he cried, squaring up. "I'll face the lot of you —one at a time !"

But they were not coming one at a time; they were coming in their hundreds.

Things certainly looked very bad for George Clifton at the moment, and it would have been a clever man who could have seen how he was to get out of it.

The crowd was surging towards him, and the crowd was in a very nasty mood indeed. It wasn't as though he had been popular to start with. Ever since he had had anything to do with Boltwich he had been overbearing and a bully, and people hated him. And now he had made matters infinitely worse by ruining the team and getting young Jack Morton, their hero, into trouble.

Indeed, it must have gone ill for

WHAT HAS GONE BEFORE !

For the sake of his invalid mother, Jack Morton, a lad of seventeen, calls upon his grandfather, Sir Jasper Clifton, for aid. It was by no means a pleasant undertaking for Jack, for his mother, much against her father's wishes, had married a worker in Sir Jasper's mill, who was now dead. Sir Jasper, however, is taken up with the lad straight away, saying that he will alter his will and make him co-heir with George Clifton, another grandson, and Jack's cousin, whose great interest in life is the Boltwich Football Club. In high spirits, Jack gives up his old job to take up work at Cliftons'. But Sir Jasper dies that night. Thinking only of his mother, Jack goes to George Clifton, but his appeal proves futile, Clifton telling him that the will is unaltered, and that he is not wanted. Jack's anger is aroused, and, meeting Ronnie Stevens, whom George

Clifton had deemed it wise to sack, the two lads, former players of Boltwich F.C., determine to fight Clifton.

"We'll get a team that won't be beat," said Stevens, "and call them the Triers."

The team shows great promise, much to the annoyance of Clifton, who, scheming to get Morton hounded out of Boltwich, makes a spoof appointment with the lad. Unsuspiciously Jack falls into the trap when calling upon Clifton, who denies knowledge of the letter. Later, to Jack's surprise, he is arrested and accused of the theft of fifty pounds. However, through Laurie Robson, holder of the bulk of the Boltwich F.C. shares, Jack is able to effect an escape, and plays in the great match with Crewbridge. He is absent from the next game, however, and the crowd, greatly annoyed, advances threateningly upon Clifton, who ignores Robson's warning to clear.

Clifton at that moment had it not been for Laurie Robson.

That young man had turned away in disgust when Clifton had refused to take his advice and get away from the ground while there was still time. It served the fellow right if he did get half-killed; if they took him, as once they had taken a full back who was seriously suspected of having kicked into his own goal on purpose, and flung him into the River Bolt.

But as Laurie now turned and saw the man's danger, and realised that he was but one against hundreds, his chivalrous nature revolted.

He bolted up towards Clifton, and a moment later was facing the ringleaders of the crowd, his monocle firmly fixed in his eye, and a look of disgust on his face.

He was well known. People were already saying that he had had something to do with the rejuvenation of the Boltwich team; and folks also said that he had been a good pal to Jack Morton. So now the crowd hesitated.

"Stand back, you chaps !" Laurie shouted at the top of his rather high-pitched voice. "It's not sporting to attack him in a mob like this !"

"He's asked for it !" one of the crowd roared.

"I dare say he has," said Laurie, standing himself in front of the angry mob. "But he's not going to get it here on Boltwich Football Ground. It isn't the game, and I'm not going to allow it. You are too many for him !"

"Who are you?" demanded another.

Laurie twisted his monocle into his eye and regarded the speaker with cold contempt.

"If any fighting is necessary," he said, "I am prepared to come and have five roun" with you, sir, whoever you may be; but I am going to see Mr. Clifton off the field!"

Laurie had saved the situation, for the police were now clearing the crowd away, and he was able to turn to George Clifton, an angry gleam in his eye.

"A nice state of things!" muttered Clifton, as soon as the danger began to grow a bit less.

Laurie gave him a look of contempt.

"Oh, clear out while you can, Clifton!" he said. "Another time I might not be able to help you. And don't think you are out of the wood yet by any means!"

"Eh?" snarled Clifton.

Laurie bent close to him.

"Jack Morton and I are going to be even with you yet, old son, and don't you forget it! That is all I have got to say to you! Now, slip along while the going's good!"

And George Clifton slipped along, muttering to himself and swearing awful vengeance; but, probably, deep down in his heart realising that the end of his tether was in sight.

Laurie felt very pleased with the way things had gone, and when he reached home that evening he had reason to feel more pleased. He was just on the point of sitting down to write a line to Jack Morton—to whom he wrote under a different name, of course—when someone was announced.

"Mr. Graves wishes to see you, sir," said his old butler.

Laurie looked up in surprise.

"I don't know any Mr. Graves," he said.

The butler cleared his throat.

"I think it is the butler from Mr. George Clifton's, sir."

Laurie started; this was very strange. He was on the point of saying that he would not have anything to do with anyone who had seemingly come from George Clifton, when he reflected that this was not perhaps the best way in which to repay Jack, and he said nothing.

"He says it is a personal matter and important, sir."

"Oh, all right, bring him in!"

A few moments later old Graves, Clifton's butler, came into the room.

He was obviously in a very excited state of mind, and he could scarcely hold his words back until they were alone together. Then it all came out with a rush.

"Mr. Robson, sir," he exclaimed, "I've come to see you about young Jack Morton! I didn't know who else to see. I had to come to you. I've got to see him, and at once!"

Laurie fixed his eyeglass firmly in his eye.

"Won't you sit down, Mr. Graves?"

"Thank you, sir—thank you!"

He sat down.

"Now, pull your socks up—er—I mean take your time and tell me what it is all about. I may as well inform you that I don't like you!"

The old man started and grinned sheepishly.

"I beg your pardon, sir?"

"On principle!"

"Yes, sir?"

"You see, Mr. Graves, you are butler to Mr. George Clifton; and as I take it you come from him I suspect you and dislike you, for I do not like Mr. George Clifton——"

"Quite, sir, but——"

"And at the same time," the young man continued, "I have it upon the excellent authority of my friend young Stevens, who used to be one of your footmen, and of Jack Morton himself that you are not at all nice to know. So where am I?"

It was not a very pleasing start for the old fellow, but he managed to grin his way through it.

"Well, sir," he said, "the fact of the matter is I—I have not come from Mr. Clifton at all. In fact, I've come with the best intentions."

"Ah!" said Laurie, taking his eyeglass out and polishing it. "You will recall, Mr. Graves, that good intentions are popularly supposed to pave the way to an exceedingly hot quarter of the universe. However, proceed. What can I do for you?"

The old man gave him a quick glance.

"Tell me where I can find Mr. Jack Morton."

Laurie started.

It was surprising to hear the "Mr." He didn't understand it for a moment.

"I—I wouldn't tell you if I knew, Graves," he said.

Graves looked desperate.

"Listen to me, sir," he said, "and then perhaps you will trust me. Jack Morton was close to this town, Boltwich, last night."

Laurie started.

"The deuce he was!"

"Yes, sir, he was. He had come to try and see his old mother."

George Clifton had taken the oath, and was about to speak when Jack Morton suddenly leant forward from the dock.
"One moment, Clifton;" he said. "I accuse you of asking a certain person to destroy my grandfather's will!"

"Ah, yes!" said Laurie, beginning to sit up and take interest.

"He didn't, because—as perhaps you know, Mr. Robson—the old lady has moved to friends since all this trouble with her son started. He had a narrow squeak of being taken by detectives, who were waiting for him in his home and——"

"How do you know this, Graves?" asked Laurie suspiciously.

Graves bent his head.

"I'm coming to that, sir," he said— "I'm coming to that! My dear daughter——"

"Now, look here, Graves, what has your dear daughter to do with it?"

"Everything, sir!"

"What!"

"I worship that girl, Mr. Robson, sir——"

"Oh, come, man, out with it!"

"Well, you see, sir, it was like this. I bought a two-seater for my daughter Gracie not long ago, and she has been a perfect terror for driving it about by herself. Scared me to death. But you couldn't do anything with the girl. And last night quite late she was coming home, when suddenly, at the little wooden bridge outside the town on the London road—you know it, sir——"

"Yes, yes!"

"Well, sir, the bridge broke, or the car skidded, or something went wrong somewhere, because before my poor girl knew where she was she had been flung headlong, with the car, over the bridge into the Bolt; and she would certainly have been drowned if it had not been for Jack Morton, who was close by, and most gallantly saved her!"

"Good for Jack!" said Laurie, in excitement.

The old man nodded quickly.

"Yes, sir!" he exclaimed. "That is what I say! Good for Jack Morton! The one thing I love in this world is that girl; and if anything had happened to her I would have had nothing to live for. And—well—well, sir, I can

THE GEM LIBRARY.—No. 827.

do Jack Morton a real good turn, and I am out to do it!"

Laurie started.

"Tell me!" he said.

But here the old chap shook his head quite firmly.

"No, sir; I'll tell Jack Morton, and no one else!"

"But how do I know," said Laurie Robson gravely, "if I take you to Jack Morton—and I am not sure that I can—but how do I know, if I do, that this is not all a trick of George Clifton's, and that my poor young pal will find himself in the lock-up five minutes after I have kindly taken you to him?"

Graves gave a cry.

"I'm not as bad as that, sir," he said.

"You must be pretty bad, Graves," Laurie said, "if you have had much to do with George Clifton all these years."

The old fellow blinked.

"I promise you, by a father's love, Mr. Robson, that the only desire I have got in this world is to help that young man and put right some of the wrong that has been done to him. I swear to you it is true! He saved the life of my girl, and I am going to pay him back as well as I can!"

For a long time Laurie looked the old fellow in the eye, and then he suddenly took a resolution.

"All right!" he said. "Are you game for a long drive?"

"I'm game for anything if I can repay that brave lad!" said Graves.

"That's the spirit, I must say! All right, I'll join you in a minute."

He got his coat, ordered his car, and made sure as far as he could that old Graves had not got a squad of people outside; and a few minutes later he had rejoined the old butler.

"Come along, you old sinner, I'll risk it!"

He got Graves into the car, and started off. He drove so fast that the old man hung on to the side of the car breathlessly and wondering when his end was coming, and he went in such a

round-about way that it would have been almost impossible for Graves to have the slightest idea where he was going.

They stopped at last on the edge of a big town, almost fifty miles from Boltwich, and Laurie left the car at a small garage.

"Come on, my friend," he said; "we'll soon be with Jack now."

They hurried along up a side street or two, and then at last Laurie dived into a narrow doorway and knocked three times.

In a few moments a man came to the doorway, and when he saw Laurie he touched his forelock at once.

"Upstairs, sir!"

The old man followed him, and they went up the rickety stairs at once. Laurie seemed to know his way, and did not even knock on the door at the top of the stairs.

Jack was writing at a table, but he jumped up with a cry as the door was opened.

"Laurie!" he cried.

"Jack, old man!"

The two chums shook hands, and then suddenly Jack caught sight of the pale face of old Graves behind his pal.

"What on earth——" he began.

But old Graves came forward.

"Mr. Jack," he said, "I—I have come to repay you for saving my daughter's life!"

There was a moment's silence, during which Laurie curiously watched his friend's face, and then he knew that old Graves had not lied.

Jack smiled.

"Oh, it was nothing!" he said. "I—I just did what I could. I am afraid the car was finished, though!"

"The car!" cried the old butler. "Oh, I don't care about that! Besides, it was well insured!" he grinned. "But I have come to thank you, Mr. Jack. That girl was all the world to me; and, thank Heaven, I have got it in my power to repay you for what you did for me!"

Jack stared.

"That's all right, Graves——" he began.

"Nothing is all right," Graves replied, "until I have undone the great wrong which I did. Mr. Jack, do you mind Mr. Robson hearing your private business?"

Jack laughed.

"Well, I guess there is not much of my private business that Mr. Robson does not know already, Graves," he said. "But what, in the name of goodness, are you getting at?"

Graves drew a deep breath, and then leaned forward mysteriously between the two lads.

"Sir," he said, "that George Clifton is a deep-dyed villain!"

Laurie laughed.

"Look here, Graves, my friend," he said, "if you have brought me all this way to tell me that, you are barking up a wrong tree. I want more for the petrol I have used than that!"

"Wait a minute, sir!" exclaimed the old man. "All in good time! I say that George Clifton is a bad egg, sir, and I can prove it! I can help you to send him to prison, and—and I can bring you into your rights, Mr. Jack!"

Jack was pale with excitement.

"Well," he said, "get ahead with it!"

"And I am going to do all this because you saved my girl's life, Mr. Jack. Don't forget that! Whatever you may think of me after you have heard all, don't forget that!"

Jack sighed. He was getting impatient.

"All right, I won't!" he said. "But get on with it!"

"I will!"

"Mr. Graves," said Laurie, "get on with it, or I shall explode, and then you will have to walk back to Boltwich! It is a long way!"

The old fellow nodded.

"That was the wrong will!" he said.

"Ah!" cried Jack. "I knew it!"

Graves started.

"That night when you came to see Sir Jasper—I remember it well, Mr. Jack. I remember you going in to him, and I remember you coming out; and I remember the old gentleman saying that he had made a new will, in which you had been left half. I—I knew, because young Stevens witnessed it, though he didn't know what it was he witnessed; and I had further reason to know all about it soon enough."

He paused, and both of the lads were content now to wait for him to go on, for this was the real thing, and they were getting down to bed-rock.

"The next day he died!"

"Yes?"

"Well," the old man said in little more than a whisper, "poor old Sir Jasper had scarcely breathed his last than Mr. George came to me——"

"Ah!"

"Why?" asked Jack quickly.

"About the second will!"

"Oh!"

"You see, he had been robbed, as he put it, of half, and the reason he came to me was twofold. In the first will I had been left a thousand pounds; and in the second, Sir Jasper had been in too much of a hurry to think of me, I suppose. But, at any rate, I'd been done out of my thousand, and got nothing; and so Mr. George wanted me to help him find the first, which he could not, and destroy the second."

Jack and Laurie stared at the old butler in surprise.

"What happened?" asked Jack in a low tone.

"Mr. George found the first," said old Graves, "and we couldn't ever find the second—at least, we never seemed to find it, because I had it all the time!"

The boy gave a cry.

"Great Scott, Graves, man!" exclaimed Laurie. "What did you do with it? Where is it?"

Graves smiled rather sadly.

"I am afraid, young gentlemen," he said, "that I was rather a bad lot in those days, and I—I was thinking that the time might come when that second will—the real will—would be rather a useful document with which to put the screw on Mr. George. You see that even in those days I didn't trust him, and I didn't believe that I should get all he promised as my share of the dirty work. So when I found the second will I said nothing. And here it is!"

He put the document down on the table in front of Jack.

Eagerly the two boys bent over it. And there, in clear writing, it was stated that Jack Morton was to come into half of everything that Sir Jasper, his grandfather, left.

In a little Laurie looked up.

"Well, Graves"—he held out a hand—"I beg your pardon for doubting you when you turned up earlier. You have done a good thing to-night! And you can take it from me that as far as your share in this bad business is

HORNBY CLOCKWORK TRAINS

THE Hornby Trains are quite different from any other Clockwork Trains, being strongly built in sections and screwed together with nuts and bolts, just like Meccano models. You can take them to pieces, clean them and rebuild them, and if a part becomes lost or damaged you can buy another and fit it yourself quite easily. The clockwork mechanism is strong, does not easily get out of order and gives the train a remarkably long run. Hornby Trains last for ever.

HORNBY CLOCKWORK TRAIN PRICES

No. 1.	No. 2.
Goods Set - 25/6	Goods Set - 45/-
Passenger Set 35/-	Pullman Set 70/-
Hornby Tank Loco 32/6	

ZULU CLOCKWORK TRAIN PRICES

Passenger Set 25/-	Goods Set 18/6
Zulu Tank Loco 12/6	

THE WINDSOR STATION is a thing of beauty—the only British Station obtainable. Its bright colouring and realistic appearance will bring joy to the heart of every boy who sees it. Dimensions:—Length 2ft. 9ins. Breadth 6ins. Height 7ins.

BRAKE VAN

CRANE TRUCK

NEW ACCESSORIES

This year there are new Wagons, Signals, Lamps, Stations, Turntables all built in correct proportion in size, gauge, method of coupling, etc., to the Hornby Trains. Most important of all, they have the uniformly beautiful finish which is the great feature of the Hornby system. To use cheap looking rolling stock or a foreign-looking station with a Hornby Train spoils all the fun. Make sure you buy Hornby Accessories.

MECCANO RAILS, POINTS & CROSSINGS

Meccano Rails, Points, and Crossings are made of the finest materials and hold together rigidly. The extra sleepers give strength and steadiness to the track. Superior in quality and finish. Low in price, and obtainable from all dealers.

FREE TO BOYS

PERFECT MECHANISM
BEAUTIFUL FINISH
STANDARDISED PARTS

A Splendid New Meccano Book

This is a new and splendidly illustrated book that tells of all the good things which come from Meccanoland, where the best toys are manufactured. No boy should be without this wonderful book.

How to get a Free Copy

Just show this advertisement to three chums and send us their names, and addresses with your own. Address your letter to Dept. W.

MECCANO LTD : BINNS RD : LIVERPOOL

concerned, I will move heaven and earth to save you!"

"Yes!" said Jack in a low voice, but he was so excited he could scarcely speak.

"He saved my girl," said the old man. "That is all I care about!"

"Shall we be able to prove this will?" asked Jack.

Laurie laughed.

"You bet your sweet life we shall! I happen to know that George Clifton has never been able to get the other will finally ready for probate, as they call it. Besides, with that and old Graves here to testify, the brute will soon make everything over to you, Jack. Give us your hand, lad! You are a rich man now, and no one is more glad than I!"

Jack was smiling queerly.

"Do you know what I am going to do now?" he said.

"No."

"I am going back to Boltwich, and I am going to give myself up to the police, and risk that fifty pounds business; because now I have got Mr. George Clifton, and I rather fancy he will be sorry he ever did all this dirty work. Here, Laurie, you keep that for me."

And he handed Laurie the will.

The Beginning of the End !

I T was in the middle of the next day that Jack Morton suddenly walked out of the railway-station at Boltwich.

So far he hadn't been seen; but suddenly, as he came into the square, a football fan espied him and set up the shout:

"Good old Jack!"

In a moment a crowd had surrounded him.

"What cheer, Jack! Where are you going? How's your luck?"

He faced them all.

"It's all right, boys!" he said. "I'll play for you next week, see if I don't! I'm just going round to give myself up!"

And so the cheering crowd went along to the police-station with him, and when they reached there and a sergeant came out to see what all the trouble was about he had the surprise of his life as Jack Morton, the lad they had been looking for for such a time, marched up the steps himself and said:

"I have come to give myself up."

The sergeant gave a grunt and jerked his head towards the station.

"All right!" he said. "In you go! We have had enough trouble about you, young man; and now we have got you we'll keep you!"

Jack was taken inside at once and charged, and a few minutes later he was under lock and key in the cells, and this time there was no question of him escaping.

But he was happy now.

He had no fear whatsoever as to the future. He was going to be cleared; and, what was more, he was going to be able to keep his old mother in all the comfort that was necessary.

Still, there was the trouble with regard to the fifty pounds which he was supposed to have stolen from George Clifton, and that was rather worrying.

Nor was George Clifton enjoying himself.

He had settled down to read the THE GEM LIBRARY.—No. 827.

newspaper after lunch that day, when he was informed that he was wanted on the telephone, and he thought that there was rather a curious glint in the eye of old Graves, the butler.

"Who is it?" he asked.

"Police-station, sir!"

The man went pale; then pulled himself together.

"Suppose they have got young Morton," he muttered, and picked up the receiver.

"Hallo!"

"Is that you, sir?" came the voice of the inspector at the other end of the line.

"Yes. What is it? Got young Morton yet?"

"Yes, sir!"

"Ah! Good! Splendid! How did you catch the young brute?"

"He came and gave himself up, sir."

"What?"

Clifton had turned very pale, and he almost dropped the receiver as he heard the words. Jack Morton had given himself up! Why? Well, he pulled himself together. Perhaps it was because he could not keep in hiding any longer. One could not tell.

"I see!" he said into the telephone while these thoughts were racing through his mind. "Suppose he had had enough of it!"

But in answer the police-inspector laughed at the other end.

"Well, no, sir, not exactly. He came here of his own accord. Seems very pleased with himself, and not a bit down in the mouth. And a crowd brought him here. Well, sir, we shall see what we shall to-morrow. You will turn up at the court, sir?"

"Sure!"

"Thank you, sir!"

"And, inspector——"

"Sir?"

"Keep him safe this time!"

The other laughed at this.

"I've got a constable in with him. I don't trust him," came the answer. "And even if I trusted him, I would not trust the town. There is a mob outside the station now, yelling like mad for him. By the way, Mr. Clifton, I don't think that I should go down into the town to-day if I were you, sir!"

"Eh?"

"Might be rather dangerous for you!"

Clifton scowled.

"Oh, all right, inspector!" he said. "I'm not afraid."

But he was very white as he looked up, after putting the receiver back, and found old Graves watching him.

"What do you want, you old fool?" he hissed.

The butler bowed.

"Nothing, sir—nothing!"

"Well, then, don't stand there staring at me as though I were some form of strange beast! Here, Graves," he cried, as the old man started to turn away, "you—you don't ever think of trying to let me down about the thing we are in together, do you?"

Graves raised his thin brows.

"No, sir; of course not!"

Clifton nodded.

"Well, that is just as well for you, Graves, because, don't forget, if you are ever so tempted, that we are in this thing together, and that you would swing just as much as I!"

Graves smiled to himself. Outwardly he was like ice.

"Yes, sir. I am sure that I don't want any trouble "

"That is right."

But Clifton was worried.

He went back to his study and sat down, and tried to think. He could not see any way in which things could have gone wrong. He was a fool to have any fear at all To-morrow young Morton would be sent for trial, and a jolly good job. He would be out of the way.

But he was nervous, nevertheless.

He could not understand why the young brute seemed happy in prison. And why—why had he given himself up? That was the chief thing that worried his guilty conscience now. Jack had seemed well away by this time. True there had been the meeting with the detective in his mother's home, but he had got away, and nothing had been heard of the lad since then.

And here he had come and given himself up, and the mob were yelling for him.

He grinned savagely to himself. It would be very sweet when Jack was in prison. He had had much too much of his own way had that young man so far.

Suddenly he started and listened.

He heard a shout.

"We want George Clifton!"

His blood turned cold within him, and he jumped to his feet. There was a revolver in his desk, and he found it at once. Then he ran quickly upstairs and went to a front window, from which he could look out on to the broad drive leading up to the house.

The crowd had come for him.

His heart almost stopped beating, for he realised what sort of a time he would have if they got him.

He stood shivering there for some moments, not knowing what to do, and then he saw old Graves go out to them.

Why, Graves was speaking to them and they were listening!

If only he could hear. But he couldn't. The window was closed, and he did not dare to open it, for fear of drawing attention to himself.

Yes, and, by Jove, the old fellow seemed to be holding them!

What could he be saying?

Then suddenly they started to move away, the whole surly mob of them, and old Graves came quickly back into the house.

When he was quite sure that the crowd had gone, George Clifton went down into his hall, where he found Graves wiping his brow.

"Great heavens, man!" Clifton cried. "What was that all about?"

"A very nasty crowd, sir!"

"Yes, I saw the fools. The police ought to do their job better. What did they want?"

"You, sir!" said the butler, and seemed to take a delight in saying it.

"I know—I know. But what did you say to send them away, Graves? You were quite successful. What, man?"

Graves gave a grin, and there was something in that grin which, for the first time, told George Clifton that things were going wrong for him.

"I just told them that they ought to wait till to-morrow, sir, and see what happened in the police-court."

"Yes, yes—quite," started George Clifton and then suddenly turned away.

There was something in Graves' eyes that made him wonder.

(Look out for a great surprise in next week's grand long instalment of this powerful serial, chums.)

Printed and published every Wednesday by the Proprietors, The Amalgamated Press (1922), Ltd., The Fleetway House, Farringdon Street, London, E.C.4. Advertisement offices: The Fleetway House, Farringdon Street, London, E.C.4. Registered for transmission by Canadian Magazine Post. Subscription rates: Inland and Abroad, 11s. per annum; 5s. 6d. for six months. Sole agents for South Africa: The Central News Agency, Ltd. Sole agents for Australia and New Zealand: Messrs. Gordon & Gotch, Ltd.; and for Canada, The Imperial News Co., Ltd. (Canada).—Saturday, December 15th, 1923.
NN

"MY READERS' OWN CORNER."

(Continued from page 16.)

NO COMPLAINTS !

"Say, landlord!" a guest shouted. "I want a clean towel. This one is awful!" "Well, that's strange!" said the landlord. "Nearly a hundred men have used that towel, and you're the first to complain!"—Half-a-crown has been awarded to James Dunlop, 11, North Square, Gartsherrie, Coatbridge, Lanarkshire.

AND SO IT APPEARED !

The omnibus, travelling at a good pace, gave a sudden jerk, and the old gentleman having momentarily loosed his hold on the strap-hanger, was flung unceremoniously into the lap of a lady near by. "I beg your pardon, madam——" he began, when the irate spinster cut him short. "How dare you, sir! I warrant you're no Englishman!" "No, madam," he replied. "Unfortunately, I appear to be a Laplander!"—Half-a-crown has been awarded to Horace Whorton, 12, Ivanhoe Street, Scotts Green, Dudley.

NASTY!

The fair visitor had called upon her artist acquaintance. "Yours were the only pictures I could look at at the Academy to-day!" she exclaimed. "Believe me, I appreciate the honour," replied the artist. "Honour!" she echoed in tones of perplexity. "The others, you know, were so surrounded by the crowd!"—Half-a-crown has been awarded to Ernest C. Higgs, Globe Works, Clapton Park, E. 5.

PUTTING MATTERS RIGHT !

A Scottish farmer sold some eggs to the local laird. He discovered later that he had included one egg too many in the consignment and went at once to the laird. "You may be right," said the laird laughingly. "But anyway, have a drink and call it square. What will you take?" "Egg-and-milk!" snapped the Scotsman.—Half-a-crown has been awarded to Jeanne Drover, Brighstone, Mill Hill, Cowes, I. of W.

HIS SUPERIOR KNOWLEDGE !

Two Highlanders, in London for the first time, were greatly amazed at the heavy street traffic. While they were standing, awestruck, on the pavement, a water-cart passed, spraying the dusty streets. "Hey, mon!" yelled Donald, running after the cart. "Ye're losin' a' yer water!" "Come back, ye old fule," called his companion after him. "Dae ye no' ken that's tae keep the bairns frae sittin' on the back o' the cart?"—Half-a-crown has been awarded to Donald Macfarlane, 48, Second Avenue, Clyde Bank, Scotland.

INEXPERIENCED !

A labourer was walking along the road and met a friend who looked down in the "dumps." "'Allo, 'Enry!" he said. "Are you out of work again?" "Yes," came the reply. "I had to resign. They set me to push a wheelbarrow, and what do I know about machinery!"—Half-a-crown has been awarded to Edgar Vincent Barwood, Melita, Thames Ditton, Surrey.

(If You Do Not Win a Prize This Week—You May Next!)

All Efforts in this Competition should be Addressed to: The GEM LIBRARY, "My Readers' Own Corner," Gough House, Gough Square, London, E.C.4.

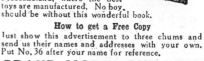

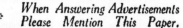

EVERY WEDNESDAY.

The GEM 2ᴰ

LIBRARY OF SCHOOL AND SPORTING STORIES

No. 828.
Vol. XXIV.
December 22nd,
1923.

RATTY IN THE LINE OF FIRE!

The School House invaders find an unexpected target for their snowballs. (An exciting incident from the grand long complete Christmas story of Tom Merry & Co. at St. Jim's contained in this issue.)

" Hi, hi, clear the way,
We've the 'HOLIDAY ANNUAL'
Hip-hip—HOORAY ! "

GREYFRIARS
THE HOLIDAY ANNUAL

The "Holiday Annual," with its coloured plates, its magnificent photogravure pictures of famous schools, its immense budget of school stories, helpful articles, and jolly drawings, is unquestionably *THE* Christmas book for GEM readers. Its popularity has grown year by year and the volume for 1924, which is now on sale everywhere is better than ever. All "Gemites" should make sure of getting this famous book for Christmas. Price only Six Shillings.

The feud between Tom Merry and
Cardew is still at fever heat!

A Splendid Christmas
Yarn This, Boys!

D'ARCY'S CHRISTMAS PARTY!

Ralph Reckness Cardew cannot sink his animosity
towards Tom Merry even though they are guests
of Arthur Augustus D'Arcy at Eastwood House.
A Grand Christmas Story of Tom Merry & Co. of
St. Jim's. By popular

MARTIN CLIFFORD.

CHAPTER 1.
Awkward !

"CHWISTMAS is comin' !"

Arthur Augustus D'Arcy of the Fourth Form confided that circumstance to Blake and Herries and Digby in Study No. 6.

Blake & Co. stared at him.

They were, as a matter of fact, quite aware that Christmas was coming—
especially as they had talked of hardly anything but the Christmas holidays for
some days past.

Arthur Augustus had been sitting in deep thought for some time, and he made
his statement seriously and solemnly, as if it were the outcome of deep reflection.

"You don't mean it ?" asked Blake.

"Christmas generally does come at the end of December," remarked Herries.

"I am quite awah of that, Hewwies. But I am feahfully wowwied."

Arthur Augustus looked worried. There was a deep line in his noble brow,
showing that his powerful intellect had been given some unusual exercise.

Blake & Co., on the other hand, looked anything but worried. They looked
particularly cheerful. The coming of Christmas certainly did not have a
worrying effect on them.

"What's the trouble ?" demanded Blake. "Anything gone wrong at home ?"

"Nothin', deah boy."

"Pater and mater all right ?"

"Wight as wain."

"Has Lord Eastwood changed his mind, and doesn't he think he would like
you to bring three nice chaps home with you for the vac ?"

"Nothin' of the kind."

"Then there's nothing the matter," said Blake. "It's all right, Gussy. Don't
worry."

"But it's not all wight, Blake !"

"Blessed if I see what's wrong, then. Isn't cousin Ethel coming for
Christmas ?"

"Yaas, wathah !"

"Has your tailor sent in a specially big bill ?" asked Digby sympathetically.

"Wats ! I am fwightfully wowwied. You see——"

"I don't !" remarked Blake.

"I have asked Tom Mewwy and Mannahs and Lowthah for Chwistmas——"

"That's all right. They can behave themselves," said Blake. "If they put on
any Shell swank we'll jolly soon take them down a peg."

"Yes, rather !" said Herries and Dig together. "That's all right !"

"But it is not all wight;" said Arthur Augustus distressfully. "Because I
have asked Cardew and Clive and Levison also."

"Oh !" said Blake.

"It was all awwanged long ago," said D'Arcy. "I weally considahed that
it was goin' to be a vewy pleasant Chwistmas-partay. And now Tom Mewwy
and Cardew are at daggahs dwawn."

"Hum !" said Herries thoughtfully.

"Cardew is a distant welation of mine, as you are awah," continued Arthur

Augustus. "The pater expected me to bwing him. When the awwangements were made there had not been any wow. Since then Cardew has bagged Tom Mewwy's place as juniah captain of St. Jim's, and they are on fwightfully bad terms. I must admit that Cardew tweated Tom Mewwy vewy wottenly."

"He did!" grunted Blake. "And he treated this study rottenly, too."

"As a matter of fact, he's a bit of a rotter," said Dig. "That accounts for it."

"I do not appwove of Cardew's conduct," said Arthur Augustus. "His election methods were wathah thick. As juniah captain, he has not played up in a way I can appwove. Tom Mewwy took it vewy well, and backed him up as skippah, and Cardew seems to have gone out of his way to make himself unpleasant to Tommy. At the Wookwood match, f'winstance——"

"We know!" growled Herries. "Cardew made out he was playing me in goal, and let me down at the last minute."

"And dropped Tom from the team!" growled Blake.

"And all of us!" said Dig. "After making out that the whole study would be wanted for the match."

"It was wotten!" said Arthur Augustus. "I don't think Cardew meant any harm, weally; but it was vewy thoughtless and inconsidewate, to say the vewy least."

"The very, very least!" assented Blake.

"Tom Mewwy vewy natuwally wesented his conduct," went on Arthur Augustus. "They do not speak now."

"That's so."

"That is why I am fwightfully wowwied," continued the swell of St. Jim's. "They are booked to spend Chwistmas at Eastwood House with us, and they are not on speakin' terms. It's feahfully awkward."

Blake nodded.

"I suppose it is a bit awkward," he assented. "You had better drop Cardew out, Gussy."

"Imposs, deah boy! Some of his welations will be there— Lord Lilburn, and pewwaps his old gwandfathah. And my patah is a sort of second uncle twice wemoved, or somethin', to Cardew, and he expects to see him at Chwistmas."

"You can't drop Tom Merry."

"Wathah not! Besides, I don't want to! Tom is goin' to bwing ovah his old governess, Miss Fawcett, on Chwistmas Day, and it would be weally imposs to say anythin' to upset that estimable old lady. It is all fixed, and cannot be altahed without makin' a feahful lot of people feel dweadfully awkward and uncomfortable. And yet how can two fellows who are not on speakin' terms stay at the same house?"

Blake grinned.

"They can stay without speaking," he suggested.

"Weally, Blake——"

"After all, Tom Merry isn't so gone on talking as you are, Gussy. He can shut up a bit."

"You uttah ass!"

"And Cardew might be induced to hold his tongue," went on Blake. "They can be civil, I suppose?"

"Yaas; but it is feahfully awkward, and I am howwibly wowwied. Besides, Chwistmas is the time of peace and good will, you know, and fellows ought not to be on bad terms. Cousin Ethel will notice that there is somethin' up, so will Levison's sister, Dowis. And it was awwanged to fix up a football match one day if the weathah permits, and on football mattahs Tom Mewwy and Cardew are vewy likely to get as fah as punchin' noses."

"My hat! What an entertainment for Christmas!" said Blake. "You seem to have landed yourself, Gussy. The only thing I can suggest is that you take them under your wing—Tom Merry under one wing and Cardew under the other—and exercise all your tact and judgment."

"Ha, ha, ha!"

Arthur Augustus rose to his feet, and jammed his celebrated eyeglass into his eye, and regarded his grinning chums more in sorrow than in anger.

"You fellows do not seem to know how to take a sewious mattah sewiously," he said. "It is a fwightful wowwy, and there is only one way out. Tom Mewwy and Cardew must make fwiends befoah Chwistmas."

"Not much time, as we break up to-morrow," remarked Blake.

"I shall twy to do my best as peacemakah," said Arthur Augustus. "Aftah all, a fellow of tact and judgment ought to be able to bwing about a weconciliation."

He moved to the door of Study No. 6.

"Hold on!" exclaimed Blake, in alarm. "Better let them alone, Gussy. You know what an ass you are."

"Weally, Blake——"

"Yes, you ought to know that by this time," assented Herries.

"Weally, Hewwies——"

"They can be civil to one another without speaking," said Blake. "But if you butt in, Gussy, you'll make matters worse."

"Wats!"

Arthur Augustus walked out of the study, evidently bound upon a peace-making mission, with the noble object of bringing about peace and good will between Tom Merry and Cardew—a state of affairs highly desirable at Christmas-time, and indeed at all times.

Blake & Co. looked at one another and grinned.

"Good old Gussy!" sighed Blake. "Always putting his cheery old foot in it!"

"They won't make friends," said Dig.

"Hardly!"

"What do you think will happen, then?"

"A fight, most likely."

"Oh, my hat!"

"Let's hope for the best," said Blake cheerfully. "Let's hope, at least, that Tom Merry and Cardew won't take a black eye each to Eastwood House for Christmas."

And there was a chortle in Study No. 6.

CHAPTER 2.
Follow Your Leader !

CRASH!

"Oh!" gasped Tom Merry.

He sat down suddenly in the snow.

There was snow in the quadrangle of St. Jim's, snow ridged on the old walls and the ancient chimneys. The leafless branches of the elms were gleaming with it. Tom Merry and Manners and Lowther of the Shell came up the path towards the School House, tramping in the newly-fallen carpet of white. And suddenly, from somewhere, a volley of snowballs whizzed, raining on the Terrible Three.

Tom Merry caught one with his nose, one with his chin, and one with each ear. He sat down.

There was a roar of laughter, and a shout in the well-known tones of Figgins of the New House.

"Give 'em socks! Down with the School House!"

Whiz! Whiz! Whiz!

"Look out!" gasped Manners.

Figgins & Co. of the New House rushed from their ambush. There were Figgins, and Kerr, and Fatty Wynn, and Redfern, and a dozen more fellows. They rushed down on the School House trio, hurling snowballs as they came. Figgins & Co., apparently, were bent on winding up the term with a House row.

Tom Merry scrambled up.

"Collar them!" roared Figgins. "Roll 'em in the snow!"

"Give 'em socks!" yelled Fatty Wynn.

"Hook it!" said Tom breathlessly. "They're too many for us!"

The Terrible Three ran for the School House. Behind them came the New House crowd, whooping and whizzing snowballs.

"Rescue, School House!" shouted Tom Merry.

"Back up, School House!" came a roar from a dozen quarters. And School House fellows rushed to the rescue.

From one direction came Levison, Clive, and Cardew of the Fourth; from another, Talbot and Kangaroo of the Shell. Julian and Kerruish, Hammond and Reilly appeared from somewhere and rushed into the fray. The Terrible Three halted and turned on their pursuers.

In a moment a battle was raging.

Snowballs whizzed and crashed, and overturned juniors rolled in the snow and yelled.

Out of the School House a crowd came pouring—Wally of the Third and a crew of fags, Fourth-Formers, and Shell fellows. Blake and Herries and Digby, hearing the alarm in Study No. 6, dashed downstairs, and out into the quad without waiting for caps or coats. In a couple of minutes the odds were against the New House enemy, and Figgins & Co. retreated in their turn.

"After them!" roared Blake.

"Down with the New House!"

"Hurrah!"

Tom Merry led the rush at the enemy. He was manfully backed up by the School House crowd. The air was thick with snowballs, and ringing with yells and howls and cheers.

From the window of his study Dr. Holmes, the Head of St. Jim's, looked out with a smile. Mr. Railton looked out of his window, and laughed. There was no harm in a snow battle between the juniors of the rival Houses, especially at the end of the term, when the bonds of discipline were relaxing. Kildare and Darrell and the other prefects heard the shindy without heeding it. Only one prefect—Knox of the Sixth—who had a genius for interfering where

Cardew stood up grasping his whip. "Stand off!" he shouted angrily. Unheeding, the juniors fairly dragged the horse to the side of the road. The reins were torn away from Cardew, and Tom Merry coolly tied them to a fence. The whip came down with a crash across Tom Merry's shoulder. (*See page 11.*)

interference was not needed—sallied out with an ashplant. And Knox of the Sixth—perhaps by accident—was overwhelmed by a rush of the juniors and rolled in the snow, and trampled over, till he hardly knew whether he was on his head or his heels, and wished from the bottom of his heart that he had stayed in his study. And the snow battle went on vigorously, and Figgins & Co., outnumbered but plucky, were driven back towards their own House, disputing every foot of the way.

"Down with the New House!"

"Yah! School House cads!"

"Give 'em beans!"

"Hurrah!"

Tom Merry led the rush fairly up to the steps of the New House. Under a rain of whizzing snowballs, Figgins & Co. were driven into the shelter of their own House. And then Tom Merry sighted a thin, acid face in the doorway—the face of Horace Ratcliff, Housemaster.

"Hook it!" he called out.

And the attacking party backed. They did not want trouble with a Housemaster.

"Follow on!" shouted Cardew.

"Yah! School House cads!" came a howl from the enemy. "Go home! Funks!"

"Come on!" shouted Cardew. "Follow your leader!"

"Ratty's there!" panted Tom Merry.

"Hang Ratty!"

"Look here, Cardew——"

"Hold your tongue!"

"What?" roared Tom Merry.

Cardew gave him a mocking look.

"You seem to have forgotten that you're not junior captain now, Tom Merry! Allow me to remind you!"

"You cad!" burst out Tom

"That's enough! Back up, School House!" shouted Cardew. "Follow your leader!"

And he led the way in a rush up the New House steps, much to the amazement of Figgins & Co., and still more to the amazement of Mr. Ratcliff, who had expected the mob to melt away at his appearance on the scene.

There was a momentary hesitation in the School House ranks. But Tom Merry did not care to stand back where Cardew went forward. He rushed on, with Manners and Lowther, and Blake & Co. followed, and Levison and Clive and the rest.

They came swarming up the New House steps, and in at the wide open doorway. Snowballs whizzed right into the House.

"Boys!" shouted Mr. Ratcliff furiously.

Mr. Ratcliff was not heeded. Cardew dodged round him, and a rush of his followers sent the Housemaster spinning against the wall. Mr. Ratcliff staggered there and gasped.

"Back up!" roared Figgins.

"Figgins—Merry—boys!" gasped Mr. Ratcliff.

The New House rallied, and met the School House invaders manfully. The last snowballs whizzed, and the rivals of St. Jim's came down to their fists. In the hall of the New House a terrific combat raged, amid tremendous excitement. But in their own domain the New House had the advantage, and the School House were driven out at last, and driven down the steps.

Then Monteith and Baker, and several other New House prefects, came on the scene with their canes, and the School House crowd hurriedly retreated. Even Cardew, reckless as he was, did not seem disposed to enter into combat with prefects of the Sixth Form. As the crowd broke up Mr.

THE GEM LIBRARY.—No. 828.

Ratcliff sallied forth, like a lion from his lair, his eyes glinting with rage. His grasp fell upon Tom Merry's collar.

"You are the ringleader in this," he panted. "I—ow!—I shall see that you are properly punished!"

"Let go!" gasped Tom.

"Come with me!" snapped Mr. Ratcliff.

He fairly dragged Tom Merry into the New House. Properly speaking, Mr. Ratcliff had no right to cane School House juniors; they were under the authority of their own Housemaster. On this occasion Mr. Ratcliff stretched a point. The invasion of his House enraged him, and he supposed—without inquiry—that Tom Merry was the leader in the raid. He propelled the Shell fellow into his study. There he grabbed up a cane.

"Hold out your hand, Merry!" he shouted.

Tom Merry kept his hands down. In the first place, he was not guilty, as Cardew had led the attack on the New House against Tom's judgment; in the second place, Tom had no intention of submitting to any Housemaster but his own.

"Do you hear me?" thundered Mr. Ratcliff.

He did not wait for an answer. He caught Tom by the collar again, and brought down the cane over his shoulders.

"Oh!" roared Tom.

Whack, whack, whack!

Tom Merry tore himself loose, and leaped out of the study.

"Come back!" shouted Mr. Ratcliff.

The Shell fellow did not heed. He scudded for the door, and dodged a clutch made at him by Monteith of the Sixth. A few moments more and he was in the quad, sprinting for his own House. A crowd of fellows in the doorway of the School House greeted him.

"Ratty bagged you, old bean?" asked Blake.

"Yes," gasped Tom.

"Must be an ass," drawled Cardew. And Cardew of the Fourth walked away as Tom turned on him with flashing eyes; and what Tom Merry would have answered remained unuttered.

CHAPTER 3.
Gussy Butts In !

"TOM MEWWY, deah boy!"

The elegant figure of Arthur Augustus D'Arcy appeared in the doorway of Study No. 10 in the Shell. Tom Merry and Manners and Lowther were at tea there—the last study tea of the term. On the morrow St. Jim's was breaking up for Christmas, and the chums of

the Shell were discussing that matter when D'Arcy appeared in the offing.

"Trot in, old man," said Tom. "Just in time. There's some of the cake left."

"Thank you vewy much, deah boy," said Arthur Augustus, coming in. "I have not come to tea, howevah. I have had tea. I suppose you chaps wemembah that Chwistmas is comin'."

"We had a sort of vague idea that it was," said Monty Lowther gravely. "But it's good of you to remind us. We might have forgotten."

"These little things do slip the memory!" remarked Manners, with a nod.

Tom Merry laughed.

"Have you trotted along to remind us that it is Christmas-time, Gussy?" he asked.

"Not entiahly, deah boy. But bein' Chwistmas-time, no doubt you chaps are awah that it is a pwopah time for peace on earth and good will to men, and so forth—what?"

"Peace be with you, Gussy!" said Lowther solemnly.

"Also good will!" added Manners.

"May your shadow never grow whiskers," went on Lowther.

"I am speakin' sewiously, deah boys—especially as wegards Tom Mewwy. I am, in fact, goin' to speak a word in season to Tom Mewwy."

"Little me!" exclaimed Tom in surprise. "My hat! Are you winding up the term with a sermon?"

"Not exactly, Tom Mewwy. But——"

"Keep it for the House supper to-night!" suggested Manners. "You'll have a bigger audience."

"Weally, Mannahs——"

"And the whole House will listen with rapt attention—perhaps!" said Monty Lowther.

"Pway don't wot, deah boys. It's about Cardew, Tom Mewwy."

Tom Merry's brow darkened.

"The less said about Cardew in this study the better, D'Arcy," he answered curtly.

"That is quite a mistake, Tom Mewwy. I have come heah specially to speak about Cardew."

"Then ring off before you get any further," suggested Tom.

"Cardew is not persona grata here," explained Monty Lowther. "Put the brake on the giddy exuberance of your verbosity, old bean."

"Wats! About Cardew, Tom Mewwy——"

"Blow Cardew !"

"I admit that he has acted wottenly."

"He has acted more than rottenly," said Tom, his eyes gleaming. "I want to have nothing to do with him, and nothing to say about him. I know you mean well, Gussy, but don't butt in."

"I am bound to butt in, Tom Mewwy, in the circs," said Arthur Augustus calmly. "I want you to make fwiends with Cardew."

"Rats !"

"Bein' Chwistmas-time——"

"Have you come from Cardew with the olive-branch?"

"Oh, no! I have not spoken to Cardew. I am goin' to."

"Then go and do it," said Tom. "If he wants to make friends with me it's easy enough. He will have to leave off acting like a cad, and he will have to resign the junior captaincy, which he got hold of by treachery, and has abused since he got hold of it. In a word, he will have to become a decent fellow—and as that's impossible for Cardew, it's no good talking."

Tom Merry spoke with unusual heat. Manners and Lowther glanced at him, slightly surprised. It was not like Tom to nourish wrath; but he was angry with Cardew, and he did not feel that he was wrong to be angry. Tom had lost the junior captaincy to his rival, simply because he disdained to combat Cardew with his own weapons. He had backed up the new captain loyally till Cardew made it clear that he was using his new position to humiliate the fellow who had previously held it. The raid on the New House that afternoon had been the finishing touch. Tom Merry was feeling much more inclined to seek Cardew in his study and give him the thrashing of his life than to make friends with him.

Arthur Augustus coughed. He seemed to have started rather badly on his peace-making mission.

"Howevah——" he said.

"Oh, chuck it!" said Tom. "I tell you I want nothing to do with Cardew. Isn't that enough?"

"Yaas; but——"

"Well, chuck it!"

"Weally, Tom Mewwy, I hoped that you would be willin' to come along with me to Cardew's studay, and give him the wight hand of fellowship!"

Tom Merry entered the ball-room with a face that was far from bright, and looked round for Ethel. His brow grew almost black as he saw her in the throng with Cardew. His eyes gleamed as he stood behind a mass of ferns watching. (*See page* 17.)

"I'll come to Cardew's study, if you like——"

"Good!"

"And give him my right hand——"

"Vewy good."

"On his cheeky mouth!" added Tom. "Is that what you want?"

"Oh cwumbs! No! Not at all! Weally, Tom Mewwy, I——"

"If the fellow were a match for me in a fight, I'd go to him and make him put up his hands," added Tom. "But he's not—and that's the only reason why he hasn't seen me already. Let it drop, Gussy."

Arthur Augustus polished his eyeglass thoughtfully. Considering the way in which Ralph Reckness Cardew had won the junior captaincy, and his conduct since to Tom Merry and Tom's best chums, Tom's feelings were not to be wondered at. They were quite natural, in fact. But certainly they were of no use to the self-constituted peacemaker.

"You have disappointed me, Tom Mewwy," said the swell of St. Jim's, at last.

"Sorry!" said Tom. "Have some cake?"

"Thank you, no!" said D'Arcy with dignity. "I did not come heah for cake. I came heah for peace!"

"Piece of cake?" asked Monty Lowther.

"Certainly not, you ass! When I say peace I mean peace, not piece! Pway do not make wotten puns. I twust, Tom Mewwy, that if Cardew should come to you to make it up, you will not wepulse him."

"On the terms I've stated," said Tom, half-laughing, "Cardew isn't likely to play up."

"I am goin' to speak to him vewy sewiously."

"Poor chap!" said Lowther.

"Wats!"

Arthur Augustus walked very thoughtfully out of Study No. 10. Tom Merry went on with his tea, with rather a flushed face. Tom Merry had had his enemies, but he had never been anybody's enemy himself. It was seldom, or never, that he allowed the sun to go down on his wrath. But at the present time, undoubtedly, the mere mention of Ralph Reckness Cardew was enough to rouse his ire.

"It's a bit awkward," Manners remarked after a long pause. "We're meeting Cardew, I understand, at Gussy's place for Christmas."

"I know it's awkward," said Tom. "I've thought of telling Gussy I can't come. But Miss Priscilla would want to know why—and Lord Eastwood, too—and old Conway."

"We sha'n't go if you don't!" said Monty.

"Well, you must go. Your uncle will be there, Monty. And Manners' sisters are coming for Christmas Day. It's awkward all round. But I suppose in such a crowd as there will be I can keep clear of Cardew without anybody noticing anything."

"Will Cardew let you?" said Manners.

Tom breathed hard.

"Well, I suppose Cardew won't want anything like a scene in another fellow's house," he said.

"No, he would draw the line at that. But it would be just his way to provoke you into a scene, if he could."

"I know. I shall take care to keep clear of him. I don't see how I can possibly keep away now—unless Gussy should give me a hint, of course." Tom set his lips. "Besides, I'm not going to allow Cardew to make any difference to my plans. He's given me enough trouble at St. Jim's, with his dirty tricks! I'm not going to let him muck up my Christmas holidays!"

"I say, Tom Merry!" Baggy Trimble put his fat face in at the door of Study No. 10. "I say——"

"Oh, hook it!" snapped Tom. He was not in a humour for Baggy Trimble just then.

"I say, the fellows say that Cardew is going to speechify

at the House supper this evening," said Baggy, blinking at Tom. "Some of the fellows think you ought to do it, as you were captain. Cardew's only been captain a couple of weeks. I hear that Cardew says——"

"Bother what Cardew says!"

"Yes, but he says that if you butt in he will shut you up fast enough," said Baggy, grinning.

Tom Merry crimsoned.

"Shut up, you fat mischief-maker!" growled Manners.

"Well, I'm only putting Tom on his guard," said Trimble. "I say, Merry, what will you do if Cardew shuts you up?"

Tom Merry did not answer the question. He jumped up and caught hold of Baggy Trimble's collar.

"Here, I say——" roared Trimble in alarm.

Bump! Bump! Bump!

Baggy Trimble roared as his bullet head was knocked thrice on the door of Study No. 10.

"Yow-ow-ow! Oooop! Leggo! Oooop!"

SPECIAL CHRISTMAS - WEEK ISSUE OF YOUR OLD FAVOURITE NEXT WEEK, CHUMS—

Tom Merry, with a swing of the arm, pitched Trimble into the passage. Baggy sprawled there with a wild roar.

He seemed disposed to follow the fat junior out and help him along the passage with his boot. But he restrained himself, and closed the study door with a slam.

"Yah!" Trimble's voice came through the keyhole. "I'll tell Cardew! Yah!"

Tom Merry made a movement, but Lowther caught him by the arm.

"Nuff's as good as a feast, old bean!" murmured Monty. "What's the good of taking any notice of a worm like Trimble! Most likely Cardew never said anything of the kind! You know Trimble! He loves making trouble!"

"It's like Cardew!"

"Yes, but——"

"I've a jolly good mind——" Tom paused.

"Don't let's wind up the term with a scrap," urged Manners. "Keep clear of Cardew till school breaks up. It isn't long now."

"You're right," said Tom.

He dropped into his chair again. But his brow was clouded over tea. Tom Merry was angry, and, like the ancient prophet, he felt that he did well to be angry. But it was not a happy or comfortable frame of mind for any fellow to be in.

CHAPTER 4.
Peace-Making Extraordinary!

RALPH RECKNESS CARDEW rose from the tea-table in Study No. 9 in the Fourth, sat down in the arm-chair, and took a gold-tipped cigarette from his pocket. Meeting the rather grim glances of Levison and Clive, he smiled, and tossed the cigarette into the fire.

"Forgettin' again," he remarked.

"It's time you remembered," said Ernest Levison rather gruffly.

"High time!" said Clive.

Cardew nodded agreeably.

"You fellows are always right," he said. "That, I suppose, is why you bore me so." Cardew sighed. "Are you fellows looking forward to Christmas at D'Arcy's place?"

"I am," said Levison.

"It's jolly decent of him to ask us, I think," said Sidney Clive. "I'm glad to go!"

"We shall have to be on our best behaviour," sighed Cardew. "That won't come hard to you fellows, I suppose. Though from what I've heard, Levison, it would have come rather hard to you once upon a time."

"Oh, let that rest!" grunted Levison.

"Tom Merry and his crowd will be there, too," said Cardew, with a mocking gleam in his eyes. "That may turn out entertainin' in some ways. There's such a pleasure in pullin' Thomas' innocent old leg."

"Weally, Cardew!" murmured a voice in the doorway of Study No. 9.

"Dear old Gussy!" said Cardew, turning to smile and nod at the swell of St. Jim's. "How good of you to give us a look in. We were just discussin' your jolly old Christmas

party, and I was warnin' Levison that he must be careful to keep clear of his wild old ways."

Arthur Augustus looked severely at Ralph Reckness Cardew. But Cardew's beaming good-humour was not to be withstood, and D'Arcy's severe expression melted.

"I twust you fellows will find it all wight at my place," he remarked.

"Top-hole, I'm sure!" said Cardew.

"Tom Mewwy will be there."

"Yes, that makes it all the more interestin'. I've such a high opinion of Thomas, though unfortunately we've had our little differences lately," said Cardew gravely.

Arthur Augustus smiled cheerily. He had found Cardew in a more promising mood for peace-making than he had found Tom Merry. At all events, it seemed so to him.

Levison and Clive looked glum. It was all very well to pull Arthur Augustus' leg, but this was neither a proper time nor a proper subject, in their opinion. But Ralph Reckness Cardew was quite indifferent to their disapproval.

"I am vewy glad to heah you speak like that, Cardew!" said D'Arcy.

"Such a pleasure to confer pleasure!" murmured Cardew.

"The fact is, I have come heah in the wole of peace-makah."

"Oh gad! I mean, just so! Fire away!"

"I want you and Tom Mewwy to make fwiends," said Arthur Augustus genially. "It ought to be quite easy, I think."

"You think so?" smiled Cardew.

"Yaas, wathah! You see, all the w'ong is on your side, Cardew, so you have nothin' to forgive."

"Oh, my hat!"

"And Tom Mewwy has weceived all the injuwies, but he is a wathah forgivin' chap," continued Arthur Augustus brightly. "All you have to do is to expwess some wegwet for havin' acted wottenly. See?"

"I—I see!" gasped Cardew, while Levison and Clive stared blankly at the swell of St. Jim's, almost overcome by this sample of tact and judgment.

"I am suah that will set it wight," continued Arthur Augustus. "In fact, I have alweady seen Tom Mewwy, and he actually said that he is willin' to make fwiends if you would leave off actin' like a cad."

"What?" ejaculated Cardew.

"I twust I make myself cleah."

"Oh! Oh, yes! Keep on! You're puttin' it so tactfully!" gasped Cardew.

"Yaas, I wathah pwide myself upon my tact and judgment, you know," said Arthur Augustus modestly. "I have no doubt I shall be able to awwange this little mattah satisfactowily. Tom Mewwy is pwepared to make fwiends if you will be a decent chap, Cardew."

"Is—is he?"

"Yaas. In fact, he said so."

"Oh!"

"He considahs that it is impossible——"

"For me to be a decent chap?" gasped Cardew.

"Yaas. But it is up to you to show him that it is fah fwom impossible," said Arthur Augustus encouragingly.

Cardew sat and stared at the swell of St. Jim's. Gussy had many interesting and curious manners and customs of his own. But this method of peacemaking was amazing.

—FILLED FROM COVER TO COVER WITH GOOD THINGS. IT WILL PLEASE YOU ALL!

"Is it all wight?" asked Arthur Augustus. "Can I go back to Tom Mewwy and tell him that you are pwepared to speak to him?"

Cardew's eyes glittered.

"You can tell him that I shall be in the Common-room presently, and that if he's there I shall be glad to speak to him," he said.

Arthur Augustus' kind face beamed with satisfaction.

"That's wight, deah boy!"

He walked out of Study No. 9. Cardew sat silent, his brow wrinkled in thought. There was an unpleasant gleam in his eyes.

Levison eyed him rather uneasily.

"What are you thinking of, Cardew?" he asked at last.

"Dear old Thomas, and his flatterin' opinion of me," said Cardew, with a smile. "So kind of Gussy to come and tell me how he speaks of me behind my back."

"Gussy meant nothing of the sort."

"I know that—he's an innocent old bird. But he was statin' the facts."

"Rot!" said Clive abruptly. "Tom Merry's said nothing to Gussy that he wouldn't say to you, and you know it."

"I know. That's why I'm goin' to ask him."

"If you mean that you're going to wind up the term with a row with Tom Merry——"

Cardew yawned, and rose from the chair.

"I'm goin' down," he remarked. "No prep this evenin', thank goodness. Let's get down to the Common-room and have a jaw with the fellows."

"Look here, Cardew——"

The dandy of the Fourth left the study. Levison and Clive, with troubled looks, followed him. Obviously, Arthur Augustus, with the best intentions in the world, had not succeeded in pouring oil on the troubled waters. Rather he had added fuel to flame.

There were a good many fellows in the junior Common-room, discussing the House supper or the break-up or the coming holidays. The Terrible Three were not present just then, and Cardew joined in the chat, with a smile on his face that gave no clue to the thoughts in his mind. It was a little later that Tom Merry and Manners and Lowther strolled in, and crossed over to the fireplace, taking no heed of Cardew.

A gleam came into Cardew's eyes, and he followed them. Levison gave him a look, but he did not heed.

Cardew leaned against the mantelpiece, a few feet from the chums of the Shell. Tom Merry glanced at him, but made no sign. He had heard from Arthur Augustus that Cardew was prepared to speak to him, but he was not at all keen on a talk with Cardew. The less they had to say to one another, in Tom's opinion, the better it would be.

Something in Cardew's manner, though he was still smiling, drew a good many eyes upon him. There was something like trouble in the atmosphere of the Common-room just then.

"So you've shown up at last," said Cardew, in quite a pleasant tone.

Tom looked at him again.

"D'Arcy's kindly told me what you were pleased to say about me—in my absence," continued Cardew.

Tom's eyes gleamed.

"I've said nothing in your absence that I'm not prepared to say in your presence, Cardew," he answered. "Do you want me to tell you what I think of you?"

"Well, that would be better than runnin' a chap down behind his back, wouldn't it?" smiled Cardew.

"That's not my way," said Tom, his lip curling. "What I said to D'Arcy I've said before, and I'm ready to say again. I forget the exact words, but my opinion of you is that you are a tricky cad, that you don't even try to be decent, and that a decent fellow naturally would not want to have anything to do with you."

Manners and Lowther chuckled.

"Straight from the shoulder!" said Manners. "Hear, hear!"

"Passed unanimously!" added Lowther.

Cardew still smiled.

"If there's anything else," said Tom Merry, "you've only to remind me, and I'll repeat it fast enough. Yes—I remember I said that you got hold of the junior captaincy by treachery, and that you've made a rotten use of the job since you got hold of it. I said that, and I repeat it. I'll repeat it as often as you like."

"And I'll give you an answer!" said Cardew.

He stepped forward and struck full at Tom Merry's face. Quick as the blow was, Tom's movement was as quick. His arm came up like lightning, sweeping the blow aside. The next second his knuckles rapped on Cardew's nose, and the junior captain of St. Jim's went to the floor with a crash.

In those very moments Arthur Augustus D'Arcy was coming down the passage with Blake and Herries and Digby in a highly satisfied mood.

"It's all wight, you chaps," he was saying. "Quite all wight! They're both in the Common-woom now, and they're goin' to make it up."

"I don't think!" murmured Blake.

"Little mattahs of this kind, deah boy, can always be awwanged by a fellow of tact and judgment," said Arthur Augustus, reassuringly. "Just come in and see—— Oh cwumbs! Bai Jove!"

The chums of Study No. 6 entered the Common-room. Arthur Augustus D'Arcy's eyeglass fell from his eye in his startled amazement. They were just in time to see Ralph Reckness Cardew scramble up furiously from the floor and spring like a tiger at Tom Merry.

CHAPTER 5.
Hand to Hand!

"STOP them!"

"You fellows——"

"A fight! A fight!"

"Bai Jove! This is weally wotten!"

There was a rush of the fellows round the combatants at once. Tom Merry and Ralph Reckness Cardew were fighting fiercely.

Tom's eyes blazed with anger; and it was easy to see, by the look on Cardew's face, that all the evil in his nature was aroused.

There were no rounds and no rests in that sudden fight; it was hammer and tongs all the time.

"Go it, Cardew!" squeaked Baggy Trimble.

"Give him beans, Tommy!" gasped Lowther.

Tramp! Tramp! Tramp!

"Stop it, you fellows!" exclaimed Talbot of the Shell. "Separate them!"

"Rats! Let 'em fight it out!" said Grundy. "It's about time that cheeky cad Cardew had a licking!"

"Hear, hear!" said Kangaroo.

"It was bound to come," said Blake. "Put your beef into it, Tommy!"

"Bai Jove! Weally, you fellows——"

"Cave!" shouted Wildrake from the door. "House-master!"

"Look out!"

But Tom Merry and Cardew were too angry and excited to heed, or even to hear. They were still punching furiously as Mr. Railton, the House-master of the School House, walked into the room.

"Stop that at once!" rapped out the Housemaster.

And he strode at the combatants, grasped one in either hand, and swung them away from one another.

"Good!" gasped Arthur Augustus.

Tom Merry panted for breath. His face was flushed crimson and his eyes flashing. But he made an effort to control himself, as he saw that it was Mr. Railton who had intervened.

Cardew staggered back from the Housemaster's powerful grasp. He found it less easy to control himself. He made as if he would spring at Tom Merry again, and Mr. Railton stepped quickly between them.

"Cardew!" he exclaimed sternly.

Levison caught his chum's arm.

With a great effort Cardew calmed himself.

"Excuse me, sir," he said, "I am afraid I was a little bit excited. Sorry!"

"How dare you fight in the Common-room, either of you?" exclaimed Mr. Railton. "And on the last day before break-up, too! Are you not ashamed of yourselves?"

"I am sorry, Mr. Railton," said Tom, with an effort. "I lost my temper."

"I shall not punish you," said Mr. Railton severely. "But I require you both to promise that this shall not recur."

"Very well, sir," said Tom.

"Certainly, sir!" said Cardew at once.

Mr. Railton eyed the two juniors. Both of them were very flushed, and both bore traces of the encounter, brief as it had been. Cardew's handsome Greek nose did not look quite Greek now. It had, as Monty Lowther whispered to Manners, a list to port.

"I accept your word," said the Housemaster after a pause. "See that there is no more of this."

And he left the Common-room.

"Dear man!" remarked Cardew lightly. "He was bound

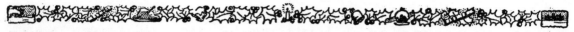

to come buttin' in! I suppose he's saved somebody from a lickin'."

"Not much doubt who the somebody is," said Manners.

"Little me?" smiled Cardew. "I think not! But I suppose we mustn't put the matter to the test, now we've promised our kind master to be good little boys. Still, if you're keen on it, Merry, I'll stretch a point and oblige you."

Tom gave him a scornful look.

"I shall not break my word to Mr. Railton, if that is what you mean, Cardew," he answered.

"High sense of honour, and all that," smiled Cardew. "Very convenient sometimes—what?"

Tom breathed hard.

"Let's get out of this, you fellows!" he said to his chums. "I can't keep my hands off that cad if I stay here."

"Hold on!" said Cardew coolly. "There's somethin' else I've got to say, dear boy. I hear you've been bullyin' Trimble."

"What?"

"Trimble complains that you've banged his head on a study door."

"That's true."

"I'm bound, as junior captain, to put a stop to bullyin'," said Cardew. "Mind you don't do anythin' of the sort again."

"I shall do exactly as I please, without any sort of reference to you, Cardew."

"Then you'll find yourself up against trouble," smiled Cardew. "I don't want to have to report you to the prefects for bullyin', but if you make a habit of it you give me no choice in the matter. I'm just givin' you a friendly warnin'."

Tom Merry's eyes blazed, and he made a stride towards Cardew. Manners and Lowther caught him quickly.

"Come on, Tom!"

"Railton, old chap——"

Tom nodded, and dropped his hands and walked out of the Common-room with his chums. Arthur Augustus called to him as he went, but Tom did not answer. Perhaps he had had enough of Gussy's peace-making.

Cardew remained in possession of the field of battle, so to speak. But what satisfaction he felt vanished when he looked into the glass and saw the dark bruise on his handsome nose—no longer handsome. Blake was watching him, and he grinned.

"You'll have an ornamental boko over the Christmas holidays, Cardew," he remarked.

Without answering, Cardew left the room, evidently to attend at once to the damage, in the hope of reducing it. The dandy of the Fourth was particularly careful about his personal appearance—and a bruised nose was the last thing in the world that he desired to take with him to a Christmas party.

"Bai Jove!" said Arthur Augustus to his chums, in great distress. "This is uttahly wotten!"

"What did you expect, when you butted in?" asked Blake.

"I was goin' to make peace, you know."

"Ha, ha, ha!"

"It is not a laughin' mattah, deah boys. I wegard it as vewy awkward and fwightfully unfortunate."

"Yes, it's a bit awkward and unfortunate, Railton butting in like that," said Blake, with a nod. "Cardew would have had the hiding he's been asking for so long."

"I do not mean that," said Arthur Augustus.

"I do," said Blake.

"In the circs, deah boys, I do not see how I can vewy well do anythin' more! I shall have to let them wip."

"Hear, hear!" said Blake. "That's a jolly good idea of yours, Gussy. Why didn't you think of that sooner?"

To which Arthur Augustus only rejoined:

"Wats!"

CHAPTER 6.
A Row En Route!

"ROTTEN term!" said Monty Lowther.

It was a bright and breezy morning. There were banks of snow along the lane down which the big motor-car rolled from St. Jim's. The old school was breaking up for Christmas, and among the earliest to depart were some of our old friends.

In the big car were packed more fellows than it had ever been designed to hold, large as it was. Tom Merry and Manners and Lowther were there, and Blake and Herries, Digby and D'Arcy. Also there were D'Arcy's young brother, Wally of the Third, and his special pals Manners minor and Levison minor. Wally was in front with the chauffeur, but

the rest were packed somehow into the big car. It was the first contingent of D'Arcy's Christmas party, and the swell of St. Jim's was taking them direct to his home in the family car.

Levison, Clive, and Cardew were to come later. Arthur Augustus could not help feeling glad that they were not coming direct to Eastwood House at break-up. Perhaps the car might have held them, with some skilful packing; but it was a great relief not to have Cardew and Tom Merry travelling together.

D'Arcy's peace-making having proved such a ghastly failure, he had, fortunately, given up any further attempts in that direction. He had left matters worse than he had found them, but no doubt he could have made them worse still by the exercise of a little more of his inestimable gifts of tact and judgment.

But as peace had not been made, and Tom Merry and his rival were on worse terms than ever, it would have been decidedly awkward to pack them in the same car, to arrive on the same day.

By the time they met at Eastwood House Gussy hoped that wrath would have cooled on both sides.

Certainly, Tom Merry looked very bright and cheerful now. He seemed to have forgotten the unpleasant existence of Cardew of the Fourth.

Monty Lowther pronounced that it had been a "rotten" term, and most of his companions agreed with him. Lowther was not thinking of the school work, and the number of marks that might have been gained, and hadn't been gained. He was thinking of the more important matter—from his point of view—of the junior captaincy and the football.

"Rotten!" agreed Manners. "But we'll make a change next term. Of course, there will be a new election."

"Oh, of course!" said Blake.

"I fancy the whole show will be fed up with Cardew," said Manners.

"All the same, a junior captain ought to belong to the Fourth Form," remarked Blake in an argumentative sort of way.

"Yaas, wathah!"

"What utter rot!" observed Manners.

"Piffle!" concurred Lowther.

"Weally, you know——"

"Bosh!" said Wally of the Third decidedly, looking round.

"There!" grinned Lowther. "Out of the mouths of babes and sucklings! Even the Third know that a Fourth Form captain isn't any good."

"That's so," said Wally cheerfully. "What the school really wants is a captain belonging to the Third."

"You cheeky young ass!"

"Weally, Wally!"

"Hear, hear!" chortled Frank Levison and Reggie Manners together.

"Hallo, there's Cardew!" sang out D'Arcy minor. And he yelled: "I say, Cardew, where did you dig up that nose?"

"Ha, ha, ha!"

The car was overtaking a trap, in which sat Cardew, Levison, and Clive. Cardew was driving, and he glanced round at the car. His nose was showing signs of the trouble in the Common-room of the day before—very plain signs. Possibly it was painful; but Cardew cared nothing for the pain. For the appearance of his handsome nose, however, he cared a great deal, and he was not in a good temper.

"Where did you get that boko?" howled Wally, as Cardew glanced round at the car behind.

"Dwy up, Wally!"

"Oh, don't you begin, Gus!" implored Wally of the Third. "You young wapscallion, wemembah that Cardew is our guest for Chwistmas!" said Arthur Augustus severely.

"He isn't our guest till he comes to Eastwood, I suppose?" retorted Wally. "When he's there, I'll tell him his nose would take a prize in a beauty show, if you like. Just at present he's only a measly Fourth Form bounder, and I'm going to chip him, see?"

"You are to dwy up at once!"

"Bow-wow! Are you going to have it amputated, Cardew?" roared Wally.

"Ha, ha, ha!"

Cardew looked straight ahead now, without heeding, though his face was flushed with anger. Levison and Clive smiled. If a fellow chose to butt into unnecessary trouble, and get his nose punched, it was his own lookout if his nose looked ornamental afterwards; that was how Cardew's chums looked at the matter. His deep annoyance on the subject did not win any sympathy from them.

The chauffeur was tooting his horn incessantly for the trap ahead to make room for the car to pass. Cardew kept steadily to the middle of the road, and the car had to slow down. There was no room to pass unless Cardew drew in.

"Clear the road there!" shouted Blake.

"Hallo, Tom Mewwy, old bean!" The two rivals were interrupted by the sudden appearance of Doris Levison and Arthur Augustus D'Arcy. Cardew stopped suddenly and dropped his hands, and stood quivering with passion, while Tom Merry stood motionless. *(See page 17.)*

"Cardew, deah boy, would you mind lettin' us pass?" called out Arthur Augustus politely.

Cardew seemed deaf. Levison touched his arm.

"Let them pass, old fellow," he said.

"Rot!"

"You can't keep them hanging up like that all the way to Wayland," urged Levison.

"Can't I?" grinned Cardew.

Hoot, toot, hoot, snort! came from the motor-horn.

"Drive on, and push 'em out of the way!" shouted Wally in great excitement. "Yah! Road-hog!"

"Pull to one side, Cardew!" shouted Tom Merry. "You know we've got a long run ahead of us."

Cardew drove steadily on. He was driving to Wayland, to take the express at the junction there, while Tom Merry & Co.'s way lay through Wayland for the road to Hampshire. All the crowd in the big car stared after the trap in great exasperation. The trap was going at a fair pace—for a one-horse trap—but it was a crawling pace for the car. Evidently Cardew was pleased that morning to make himself as annoying as he possibly could.

The chauffeur drew close to the right, to make an attempt to pass, but it was impossible. He had to dawdle behind the trap.

"Look here, we're not standing this!" exclaimed Monty Lowther. "It's just Cardew's cheek. Let's shift him!"

"Good egg!"

"Bai Jove, it's weally wotten!"

"Stop, driver," said Tom Merry.

The car stopped and the party turned out. With a rush they came at the trap. Two or three fellows hung on behind, two grasped at the horse, and one or two grasped handfuls of snow, and whizzed snowballs at Ralph Reckness Cardew.

Cardew's hat was knocked off by a well-timed ball, and another crashed in his neck. He stood up, grasping his whip.

"Stand off!" he shouted angrily.

Unheeding that angry shout, the juniors fairly dragged the horse to the side of the road. The reins were torn away from Cardew, and Tom Merry coolly tied them to a fence.

"Now we can pass!" he remarked.

"Ha, ha, ha!"

Cardew brandished the whip.

"Let that horse loose!"

"Rats!"

The whip came down with a crash across Tom Merry's shoulders. The chauffeur was already tooling the car past the trap. Tom Merry sprang away from the horse as the whip lashed at him, and as he did so, Cardew struck again. The next moment Tom, with a furious face, was scrambling into the trap, and a moment more, and he and Cardew were rolling out of it, struggling.

"Bai Jove, this is weally howwid!" gasped Arthur Augustus. "Tom Mewwy—Cardew—weally, deah boys——"

"Punch the cheeky cad!" roared Wally of the Third.

Cardew wrenched himself loose from Tom Merry and sprang back. He was close to the ditch at the side of the road, and as he sprang back he slipped over the edge. There was a crash as he went through frozen rushes and landed in the ditch. A thin crust of ice cracked, and Cardew sat in water and mud.

"Ha, ha, ha!"

There was a yell of laughter from the car party as Cardew sat down, with muddy water and fragments of ice floating round him up to the arm-pits.

The anger faded out of Tom Merry's face, and he chuckled.

"That will do!" he gasped. "All aboard!"

"Ha, ha, ha!"

Tom Merry & Co. took their places in the car again, and the big car rolled onward. Cardew struggled frantically out of the ditch, anxious to get to close quarters with his rival again. Levison and Clive watched him without a helping hand. Squelching out water and mud, Cardew scrambled into the road and gave his comrades a furious look. The car was vanishing in the distance.

"Why didn't you help me out, you grinning fools?" yelled Cardew.

"We've had enough rowing," said Clive coolly. "Better for the other party to get clear, I think."

"Much better," said Levison, with a nod. "You asked for that, Cardew, and now you've got it I hope you like it?"

Cardew stared after the car. It turned a corner and vanished as he stared.

"Better get on," suggested Clive. "You'll want some cleaning before you can take the train, Cardew."

"Oh, go and eat coke!"

"You got what you asked for. What are you grumbling at?" asked Levison.

"Are you fellows my friends or Tom Merry's?" asked Cardew between his teeth.

"Both," said Levison.

"Well, you can't be both. I'm up against him all the time, and all along the line," said Cardew savagely. "If you're not with me you're against me. You can't run with the hare and hunt with the hounds."

"Rats!"

"What?" shouted Cardew.

"Rats! When you're cooler you'll forget all that," said Clive cheerfully. "Look here, are you coming on? We've got a train to catch at Wayland."

Cardew choked down his rage and mounted into the trap again. His face was savagely set as he drove on to Wayland, reeking with mud. There was once more a rift in the lute among Levison & Co. But it was not for the first time, and it was not likely to be the last.

CHAPTER 7.
Gussy's Christmas Party!

TOM MERRY & CO. enjoyed the long run through the frosty air. The encounter on the road was soon forgotten—or, at least, left unmentioned. As Cardew was due at Eastwood House a few days later the situation was rather awkward for Arthur Augustus, and his comrades felt that it was so. D'Arcy minor did not feel the same concern as his noble major. His opinion was that Cardew had asked for, and got it; and the row on the road had had a rather cheering effect on him. Indeed, Wally confided to his Third Form chums that if Cardew put on any "swank" at Eastwood House he would not find all the members of the D'Arcy family so long-suffering as the polite and polished Arthur Augustus. Wally of the Third was prepared to show Cardew of the Fourth who was who, and what was what; at least, he told Levison minor and Reggie Manners so emphatically.

Tom Merry was not feeling wholly comfortable. In so large a party as the gathering at Eastwood House it would be easy enough for two fellows who weren't on good terms to keep out of each other's way. That was Tom's intention. But he doubted very much whether it was Cardew's intention. And Tom realised, rather ruefully, that when it came to trickery he was no match for his rival. He knew very clearly that Cardew would give him all the trouble he could, and he could only resolve to be on his guard.

But he forgot Cardew when the party arrived at Eastwood House. Lord Eastwood and his lady greeted them with urbane hospitality; and they found Lord Conway—Gussy's elder brother—there, and Monty Lowther's uncle and guardian, Mr. Lowther, M.P., J.P., as well as two uncles of Cardew, Lord Lilburn and Commander Durrance. Cousin Ethel had not yet arrived, but was due in a day or two with Aunt Adelina. Arthur Augustus marched his numerous guests off to their rooms, and with great care saw that they were comfortably bestowed. Nothing could have exceeded the polished urbanity of Arthur Augustus. He was an ideal host.

In that respect, his happy minor did not come up to the standard set by the Honourable Arthur Augustus.

Wally of the Third marched his special guests—Frank Levison and Manners minor—off to the stables, to show them round there—that spot being the most interesting part of the Eastwood establishment from Wally's point of view. Moreover, he was anxious to see Pongo. Pongo showed great delight at seeing his master, and clambered over him, and clambered also over Reggie Manners and Frank Levison in the exuberance of his spirits. Frank did not mind, but Reggie Manners did—strongly; and an argument was the result, and before long Wally of the Third and one of his guests were busily engaged in punching one another's noses.

However, they were good friends again when they met at supper. Incidents of that kind were not unusual in Third Form friendships. But Aunt Matilda turned her tortoise-shell glasses on Wally.

"Dear me! What has happened to your nose, Walter?" she inquired.

"Ran it against something in the stables, auntie," answered Wally cheerily.

And Reggie Manners chuckled.

Arthur Augustus turned his eyeglass very severely upon his minor. Wally closed one eye at him.

A couple of days later Levison and Clive arrived. Cardew was expected to arrive with them, but he sent an explanation instead.

Nobody, probably, was disappointed at the postponement of Cardew's arrival.

"Waiting to get his jolly old boko mended before he shows it to the giddy party!" Monty Lowther remarked to Tom Merry and Manners.

That was probably the reason for the delay. Levison's sister Doris came with Levison; and the same day Manners departed, to return, accompanied by three sisters. The next day the Terrible Three motored to Huckleberry Heath to fetch Miss Priscilla Fawcett. That kind old lady and her inseparable Hannah arrived with the three Shell fellows, all smiles, feeling that life was really worth living with her dear Tommy at her side. They reached Eastwood House in time for tea, and found that Cardew was there.

Tom Merry looked at Cardew as he came in, wondering whether the dandy of the Fourth would display any sign of the ill-feeling between them. Cardew was not likely to be guilty of bad form; but Tom did not trust him. He would have been best pleased if Cardew had ignored him and allowed him to return the compliment. Somewhat to his surprise, Cardew made it a point to be very cordial.

The dandy of the Fourth seemed to be in great spirits. He contrived to seat himself next to Miss Priscilla, and looked after that old lady with a kind and gentle attentiveness that quite won her heart. She could not help observing that Cardew's nose showed signs of damage. In spite of the care he had lavished on it, the lapse of time had been too brief. Nobody could look at Cardew without knowing that he had recently been engaged in fisticuffs. Miss Priscilla certainly did not think of fisticuffs; she supposed that there had been some sad accident.

"What a very nice boy!" Miss Priscilla murmured to Tom Merry, while Cardew was gone away with her teacup.

"Mmmmmm!" was Tom's reply.

"Is he a great friend of yours, Tommy?"

"Oh, we—we're in different Forms, you know," said Tom.

"He speaks of you very nicely. He seems to have a great admiration for you."

"Does he?" said Tom grimly.

"I think he would be a very nice friend for you, Tommy. His manners are so kind and gentle, and he seems so open and frank."

"Oh, my hat!"

"He seems to have been hurt in some accident," pursued Miss Priscilla. "Was it at cricket?"

"We're not playing cricket in the winter, you know," said Tom, with a smile.

"Dear me! Of course not! I suppose it was at football. I have heard of dreadful accidents to the wicket-keeper. Does Cardew keep wicket when you play football?"

"Oh! Ah! No! Not quite!" gasped Tom.

Cardew came back with the teacup. He gave Tom Merry a curious look, as he received a sweet smile from Miss Priscilla. He had evidently heard some of the old lady's remarks.

"I hope you've not let out that I got this nose fightin', old bean," he remarked.

"Dear me!" said Miss Priscilla, shocked. "My dear, dear little boy, surely—surely——"

"Not my fault, madam," said Cardew. "I'm the most peaceable fellow at the school, as Tommy—dear Tommy—can tell you. But as it happens, I came up against a very ruffianly chap."

"How very horrid!" said Miss Priscilla.

"A perfect beast," went on Cardew. "I felt bound to lick him, as he had been bullying a fellow—chap named Trimble. I simply had to do it. I hope you don't blame me, madam."

"My dear boy, it was brave, noble of you!" said Miss Priscilla, without noticing the expression on Tom's face, which was rather extraordinary at that moment. "It is just like what we read of in those nice books for young people. I hope you defeated that dreadful bully."

"Well, I should have given him the licking of his life only a master came in and he sort of skulked behind him," said Cardew. "But he had enough, I think."

Tom Merry felt like choking.

"Was not that very noble of Cardew, my dearest Tommy?" said Miss Priscilla.

"Oh! Ah! Yes! Very!"

Tom Merry moved away and went to talk to Manners' sisters. He felt that if he had any more of Cardew, there was danger of his punching Cardew's nose again, in the presence of the distinguished company assembled for tea in Lady Eastwood's drawing-room. Which certainly would never have done.

CHAPTER 8.
Cardew's Little Game!

"COUSIN ETHEL is comin' this aftahnoon." Arthur Augustus made that remark to the Terrible Three the next day. He was looking a little thoughtful.

"If you fellows would like a little wun——" he went on.

"Yes, rather!" said Tom Merry, with a smile.

"Count us in!" said Manners.

"Ethel awwives at Easthorpe Station with Aunt Adelina at two-thirty," said Arthur Augustus. "Of course, a cab will be sent to meet them. If you fellows cared to go in the cab——"

"Hear, hear!"

"That's awwanged, then," said Arthur Augustus, with satisfaction.

The Terrible Three were quite pleased at the idea of meeting cousin Ethel at the station and escorting that popular young lady to Eastwood House. Moreover, Tom Merry had fallen into the way of concurring with every suggestion made by Arthur Augustus. Gussy, with deep diplomacy, was labouring to keep the rivals of St. Jim's as far apart as possible, and had not the slightest suspicion that his little manœuvres were perfectly palpable to both parties.

Having arranged with Tom Merry & Co. to use up that afternoon looking after cousin Ethel, and having already arranged that Cardew was going on a motor-drive with Levison and Clive, Arthur Augustus felt that he had been very diplomatic indeed.

Of course, he felt that he could rely upon the good manners of his two guests. Nevertheless, it was only tactful to keep them out of each other's way as much as possible.

After lunch that day, the Terrible Three joined a party skating on the frozen lake, till it was time to start for the station. Blake and Herries and Digby seemed to find plenty of entertainment in leading Manners' three sisters through the mazes of skating, and Sidney Clive was equally occupied in looking after Doris Levison. Cardew was strolling by the lake, not skating, and the Terrible Three passed him when they left.

He gave them a curious look and smile when they passed, which Tom Merry remembered later.

"Levison, old bean!" called out Cardew.

Levison came off the ice. Clive looked round, but shook his head with a smile. Apparently he preferred skating to motoring that afternoon, possibly because Doris Levison was skating.

"I suppose you're comin'?" said Cardew.

"Right-ho!" said Levison. "Leave Clive to it—he wants to stay."

"That's all right."

"They've lent us a four-seater," said Cardew, as the two juniors walked to the garage. "It would hold five all right——"

"Are you taking some of the other fellows?"

"Oh, no!" said Cardew, with a smile. "I was just thinkin'. As Clive's standin' out there will be plenty of room."

"Lots, I should think, for two."

"Might pick up some passengers," said Cardew carelessly.

Levison looked puzzled. They were soon in the car, which the chauffeur tooled down the drive to the gates. The other car, in which the Terrible Three were going to the station, stood waiting. Cardew glanced back at it and smiled.

"The dear boys are indoors, puttin' on their best bibs and tuckers," he remarked.

"Yes; they're meeting cousin Ethel at the station," said Levison.

"Are they?"

"Gussy said so."

"Let her out," said Cardew to the chauffeur, and the four-seater began to hum.

In a few minutes the car was through Easthorpe, and keeping on towards Redmay, the next village.

"Where are we going?" asked Levison.

"Redmay."

"No farther than that?"

"There's a station there," said Cardew.

"My hat! We're not motoring out to look at a country railway-station, are we?" asked the perplexed Levison.

"Why not? The two-thirty at Easthorpe stops there for three minutes, at two-twenty."

"Does it?"

"It's the station before Easthorpe, you know," said Cardew. "I've looked it all out in the jolly old time-table."

"What on earth for?"

"My dear chap, you know my thirst for knowledge. No end of information to be extracted from a railway time-table."

"Fathead!" said Levison, and he gave it up. He knew that Cardew had something "on," and he knew, too, that Cardew did not intend to tell him what it was, yet.

The car ate up the distance between Easthorpe and Redmay. The chauffeur drew up at the little station. Cardew alighted.

"Going in there?" asked Levison, in surprise.

"Yes; only a few minutes. Wait in the car, old bean!"

"All right!"

Cardew disappeared into the station, followed by Levison's puzzled glance. Levison looked at his watch: it was a quarter-past two. It came into his mind that Cardew was there to see cousin Ethel in the train, which stopped at Redmay. But why?

Cardew strolled on the platform, with a smile on his face. His cheeks were ruddy from the rapid run through frosty air, and he looked very handsome, save for the disfiguring mark on his nose. A few minutes later a train came in and stopped.

One glance along the carriages, and then Cardew stopped at a window and raised his hat to Ethel Cleveland and Aunt Adelina.

"How do you do, Miss Cleveland? How do you do, madam?" Cardew opened the carriage door. "The car's waitin' outside."

"Dear me! Are we at Easthorpe already?" asked Aunt Adelina, giving Cardew a gracious nod and smile.

"No; this is only Redmay," said Ethel. "Has Arthur sent the car to this station?" She looked at Cardew.

"Car's outside," said Cardew easily. "Did you expect to be met at Easthorpe?"

"Yes. But——"

"Dear me! If the car is here, we had better get out." said Aunt Adelina, gathering up her muff and other articles, of which the good lady carried a goodly number. "Dear me!"

Cardew politely relieved the old lady of most of her impedimenta. Cousin Ethel alighted from the train without a suspicion. It was rather unusual for a guest at Eastwood House to be met at Redmay; but she supposed that there was some reason for the arrangement.

Levison, waiting in the car outside, started, as Cardew issued from the station, with Miss Cleveland on one side of him and Aunt Adelina on the other, and a porter following carrying several bags.

Levison was so astonished that he almost forgot to raise his hat. But he jumped from the car and saluted the ladies.

"You know Levison, of course," said Cardew. "Put the bags here, porter. I hope you'll find the car comfortable, madam—that's a nice cushion—and I had a hassock put in for you—yes, there it is!"

Aunt Adelina had an impression that Cardew was an exceedingly nice boy. Certainly he made the old lady very comfortable in the car, without failing in attentions to cousin Ethel. Levison hardly spoke a word—he just looked on blankly.

He knew that, by this time, Tom Merry & Co. would be waiting at Easthorpe Station for cousin Ethel. He understood, at last, what Cardew had planned; but he could say nothing. His look, for a moment, showed Cardew what he thought of his trick; but it was impossible to speak out in Ethel's presence. Moreover, it was quite certain that nothing would have made Cardew give up his little scheme.

(Continued on page 16.)

Here's a Feast of Fun— **—and Frolic for you, chums!**

The St. Jim's News
BUMPER CHRISTMAS ISSUE.

EDITORIAL.
By TOM MERRY.

It is with a keen thrill of pleasure that I wish all my reader-chums, near and far, a Merry Christmas! It is an old, old wish, oft-expressed, but it comes from my heart.

Christmas is the most glowing and glorious festival of the year. What a dreary world it would be without the Christmas dinner, and the Christmas greetings, and the Christmas carols—to say nothing of the Christmas ghost!

And what a sin of omission it would be if the "St. Jim's News" didn't bob up with an extra-special number to celebrate this festive season!

As soon as Christmas began to loom on the horizon, I instructed my contributors to get busy. They have risen to the occasion in grand style. My friend Talbot—possibly the most popular fellow at St. Jim's—has served up a thrilling and exciting Christmas story. Baggy Trimble has also given us a story, and you will all agree that our plump Falstaff is an expert at "telling the tale!" Dick Redfern has blossomed forth into poetry, and the mirth-making Monty Lowther contributes some "Christmas Chatter."

Of course, all the St. Jim's fellows are on holiday at this merry season. The old school stands silent and deserted, and no sounds of happy schoolboy laughter echo down its corridors. But at Eastwood House, the home of Arthur Augustus D'Arcy, a goodly company of guests has assembled, and all is merry and bright. We are devoting our time to footer, skating, gorging, pulling crackers—also Gussy's leg—dancing, and other delights too numerous to mention.

Our one hope is that all our readers will have as good a time as we are now having.

Before I close, Baggy Trimble wishes me to issue a word of warning to all my chums. Baggy says: "Tell them not to eat too much Christmas dinner, or they will know all about it on Boxing Day! And tell them to spare a kind thought for a poor, famished fellow who never gets enough grub to keep body and soul together!"

I have informed Baggy that our readers are well able to look after themselves, and that the only person likely to make a beast of himself on Christmas Day—if he gets the chance—is Bagley Trimble.

My last word to you all must be the time-honoured wish: "A Merry, Merry Christmas and a Happy New Year!"

TOM MERRY.

THE GEM LIBRARY.—No. 828.

THE GHOST of TRIMBLE HALL!
BY DICK REDFERN.

I am the Ghost of Trimble Hall—
Tremble!
And I am feared by great and small—
Tremble!
I'm mantled in a shroud of white,
I wander in the pale moonlight,
And make weird wails at dead of night!
Tremble!

When I go gliding through the gloom—
Tremble!
I enter Baggy Trimble's room—
Tremble!
I stand just where the moonbeams fall,
And in a fearsome voice I call:
"I am the Ghost of Trimble Hall!
Tremble!"

I hear a movement from the bed—
Tremble!
My victim wakes, with yelps of dread—
Tremble!
I utter deep and dismal groans
That freeze the marrow in his bones;
Then croak in terrifying tones:
"Tremble!"

His hair is standing up on end—
Tremble!
A sleepless night he now will spend—
Tremble!
And even when I disappear,
The wretched Trimble seems to hear
My distant echo, faint but clear:
"Tremble!"

CHRISTMAS CHATTER.
By Monty Lowther.

BAGGY TRIMBLE bitterly derides the time-honoured custom of hanging up a stocking on Christmas Eve. He intends to hang up an empty coalsack! Baggy assures us that he's not greedy, but he likes a lot!

* * *

FATTY WYNN found the following couplet in a Christmas cracker:
"At Christmas-time, a good tuck-in
Delights the heart of David Wynn!"

* * *

Everybody seems extra polite at Christmas-time. We hear of people "saluting" the happy morn, and in the hall at Eastwood House I actually saw the "mistletoe bough!"

* * *

The sour, ill-tempered Mr. Ratcliff wishes all the St. Jim's fellows a "snappy" Christmas!

My CHRISTMAS DINNER.
BY BAGGY TRIMBLE

I found myself, dear readers, in a large banquetting-hall. Fat, well-fed butlers were gliding to and fro with laden trays. An orkestra was playing at the end of the hall, and a grate company of people was gathered together to enjoy the finest funkshun of the year—the Christmas Dinner!

I had a table all to myself. Three butlers had been specially told off to wait on me. And I kept them jolly busy, I can tell you! I had been starving myself for this big event, so that I should be able to do full justiss to it when it arrived.

It was a twenty-corse dinner. Space will not allow me to tell you what all the corses konsisted of; but I will deskribe a few of them.

To kick off with, we had mock turtle soop. Personally, I never "mock" turtle soop. I'm always very civil to it, bekawse it's jolly delishus!

Then we had some fish. By my halibut, but it was lovely! I enjoyed it so much that I made one of the butlers bring me three more helpings.

Oh, I forgot to mention that before we had the fish, they served a mixed sort of dish, called "horse doovers." It's a French dish, I beleeve. They evidently eat horses in France, as well as snails and frogs; and I must admit that the "horse doovers" were very tasty and pallatable.

After the fish, they served what they call an "ong-tray." Then came several more corses, followed at length by the roast turkey and stuffing. I did the "stuffing" myself!

No words of mine, dear readers, can deskribe the delights of that divine Christmas Dinner. Perhaps the plum-pooding was the best part of all, for, instead of kontaining threepenny-peaces it was full of half-sovverins! I kollected all those that I didn't happen to axxidentally swallow; and I became rich in about five minnits!

To finish up with, there were jellies and blommanges and all that sort of thing; and at last I had to stick a placard on my chest, like they stick on the London busses:
"FULL INSIDE!"

I was sitting back in my chair, with my hands crossed in the region of my lowest wasteccoat button, when a loud gong boomed through the banquetting-hall.

BOOM!

. . . .

I awoke with a start, to find that it was all a dream. I had been taking forty winks on the sofa at my Aunt Agatha's, where I was spending the Christmas vack.

A Christmas Eve Adventure!

By Reginald Talbot.

'TWAS Christmas Eve, and Arthur Augustus D'Arcy, of St. Jim's, was swinging gaily along the road, in the direction of Eastwood House, his father's stately mansion, at which a whole crowd of St. Jim's fellows were spending the vacation.

Gussy was walking on a carpet of snow. It was a couple of inches thick on the road, but it was hard and firm, for which the swell of St. Jim's was thankful. Soft, melting snow would have taken the lustre from his patent-leather shoes.

Gussy hummed a merry tune as he strode along. There was joy in his heart, for this was to be a gala night at Eastwood House.

Whiz!

Suddenly, from somewhere, came a snowball. It was aimed with deadly accuracy, for it removed Gussy's "topper" as clean as a whistle, and sent it spinning.

"Bai Jove!"

Arthur Augustus stopped short in his stride, and spun round. Like Moses of old he looked this way and that way, and there was no man.

Whiz!

Another snowball zipped through the air, and crashed upon Gussy's aristocratic nose. Then another, which crashed upon his aristocratic chin. Then a whole volley of snowballs was fired from some mysterious ambush. It seemed, in fact, to be raining snowballs!

"Yawooooop!" yelled Arthur Augustus, dancing wildly to and fro, and gouging snow from his eyes and mouth. "You awful wottahs! If only I get hold of you I will administah a feahful thwashin'!"

"Ha, ha, ha!"

A merry peal of laughter came from behind the hedge. Gussy recognised the shrill laugh of his minor, Wally, and the somewhat coarser laugh of two village boys—the brothers Binks.

Arthur Augustus frowned. He was annoyed. Not mildly or slightly annoyed, but very considerably annoyed. His wrath was kindled against Wally.

It was bad enough to be snowballed by a younger brother; but when that younger brother had been solemnly ordered not to mix with the scamps of the village, and when he openly defied that order—why, it was almost a crime!

"Wally, you young wascal!" shouted Arthur Augustus, making a sudden dart towards a gap in the hedge. "I will thwash you most severely for defyin' my ordahs!"

"You've got to catch me first, Gussy!" came the cheery reply.

And that was where Arthur Augustus found himself in a fix. For Wally and the two scapegraces of the village had taken to their heels. They declined to be caught.

Gussy abandoned the hopeless pursuit. He picked up his "topper," and brushed his clothes with his hands, and went on his way to the House. But he no longer hummed a merry tune. His brow was dark and stormy.

Wally D'Arcy had escaped a "feahful thwashin'"; but only for a time. He would not be able to keep out of the way of his incensed major for ever.

As a matter of fact, Wally was fairly caught at tea-time. When he entered the hall at Eastwood House, it was to find Arthur Augustus waiting for him, with a malacca cane in his hand, and a frown on his brow.

"Come heah, Wally!" commanded Gussy sternly. "I pwopose to thwash you for settin' my ordahs at defiance, an' for snow-ballin' me in the lane!"

With a gasp of alarm, Wally turned to flee. He saw that his major was in deadly earnest, and he had no wish to get within range of that malacca-cane.

Wally darted through the doorway of the dining-room, with Gussy hard on his heels. Panting and breathless, Wally D'Arcy dodged round and round the table, with Gussy gaining on him rapidly. Presently Wally felt an iron grip on his collar, and then the malacca-cane came into play.

Swish, swish, swish!

"Yarooooh!" yelled Wally, at the top of his lungs. "Give over, you beast! If the pater comes in and catches you bullying me you'll get it in the neck! Ow-ow-ow!"

Arthur Augustus desisted at last, and Wally, his face very white, his eyes gleaming defiantly, walked rather unsteadily from the room.

It didn't take very long for Gussy's anger to simmer down. His wrath endured, but as the twinkling of an eye. Late that night, when he tossed sleeplessly on his bed, listening to the mellow Christmas chimes which sounded from the church tower in the village, he began to regret having been so heavy-handed with Wally. True, the youngster had kicked over the traces; but, dash it all, it was Christmas-time, when allowances ought to be made for the misdoings of young brothers.

After a good deal of reflection Arthur Augustus slipped out of bed, and put on his clothes.

"I'll go along to Wally's woom an' make it up!" he murmured. "I'll tell him I'm feahfully sowwy I lammed him so hard. Then we'll shake hands, an' be good fwiends again, an' all enjoy a weally mewwy Chwistmas togethah!"

But when Gussy reached his minor's room, behold, there was no Wally. The bed showed signs of recent occupation, but it was not occupied now.

"Bai Jove!" murmured the swell of St. Jim's, in astonishment. "What's become of Wally, I wondah?"

For a moment he stood blinking at the empty bed. A clock downstairs chimed the midnight hour, and then it dawned upon Gussy in a flash where his minor had gone. He had stated his intention of taking part in a midnight adventure with the brothers Binks. They were going tobogganing on the Downs, by moonlight.

Arthur Augustus had warned Wally not to go; but the foolhardy youngster, more defiant than ever after the thrashing he had received, had once again set his major's orders at defiance.

"The silly young duffah!" muttered Gussy. "He'll be bweakin' his neck if he's not careful! I don't twust those village scamps. They are leadin' Wally astway. I'd bettah wake Tom Mewwy an' the othahs, an' we'll go an' find him."

He did so, and the juniors set off together.

It did not take them long to reach the Downs. They ascended by a steep and winding path, until they reached the summit. But the side they ascended was not nearly so steep as the far side, where there was no path at all, and where accidents might easily happen.

From time to time the juniors raised a shout, but there was no response.

It was snowing hard, and the night was bitterly cold. But the members of the search-party were warm as toast, owing to their exertions.

"Fancy those silly young sweeps being out on a night like this!" said Tom Merry.

"And tobogganing down the steepest slope they could find!" said Lowther. "It's madness!"

At long last, the searchers were rewarded. They came upon the brothers Binks, who stood, white-faced and shivering, on one of the highest points of the Downs.

"Where is my minah?" was Gussy's first question—or, rather, demand.

"He—he's come a cropper!" faltered one of the village scamps. "He went whizzin' down in his toboggan, an' he never come up again!"

"Down where?" asked Tom Merry quickly. The elder Binks pointed rather vaguely towards the gloomy abyss below.

"He's down there somewhere," he said. "He ain't broke his neck, 'cos he keeps hollerin' for help. Listen!"

From far below came a muffled cry.

"Help! Help!"

Arthur Augustus turned quickly to Tom Merry.

"Tie the wope wound my waist, deah boy," he said "an' lowah me down!"

This manœuvre took some little time, but eventually the would-be rescuer was lowered down the steep slope. He was able to obtain a foothold here and there; all the same, it was a perilous descent, and Gussy reflected that his minor must indeed have been mad to undertake it in a toboggan.

At length, guided by the shouts from below, Arthur Augustus found his brother.

The unfortunate Wally was half-buried in a snowdrift at the foot of the Downs. He was numbed with cold, and he could not possibly have held out much longer. He uttered a sobbing cry of relief as Arthur Augustus approached him.

"Gussy!"

"Wally, deah boy! Are you hurt?" asked Arthur Augustus anxiously.

D'Arcy landed at the foot of the hill, where he found Wally.

"No; but I'm pretty nearly perished with the cold."

"Let me fix this rope wound your waist. Then I'll give the signal for the fellows to haul you up."

The rescue was accomplished without mishap. First Wally and then Arthur Augustus was hauled to the summit, and the party hurried back with all speed to Eastwood House, for Wally was in grave danger of contracting a chill.

On reaching home the foolhardy youngster was wrapped in warm blankets, and laid before a blazing log-fire. He was also regaled with hot cocoa, and his spirits quickly revived.

Tom Merry & Co. went back to bed, leaving the brothers together. Nobody ever knew what passed between them; but it was observed that they were on the most affectionate terms with each other next day. The breach had been healed, and the guests at Eastwood House revelled in a right Merry Christmas!

THE END.

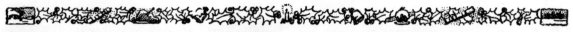

"D'ARCY'S CHRISTMAS PARTY!"

(Continued from page 13.)

"Jump in, Ernest, old bean," said Cardew lightly.

Levison followed the others into the car.

The engine throbbed, and the four-seater moved off. The chauffeur had already had his instructions from Cardew, and he took a roundabout way back to Eastwood. Aunt Adelina settled down comfortably in her furs and wraps among the cushions. Ethel looked out of the car rather curiously. Cardew understood her look and answered it.

"It's such a rippin' afternoon, I thought you'd like to run round the country for a few miles before gettin' in," he said. "Say the word, of course, and I'll tell the chauffeur to head right home at once. Otherwise we're gettin' in for tea."

"Oh, I shall like it!" said Ethel, with a smile. "Do you mind, auntie?"

"Not at all, my dear!"

Cardew chatted cheerily while the car ran on, eating up the miles. Levison sat almost silent, and must have seemed rather dull beside his lively companion. Cardew could be very entertaining when he liked, and cousin Ethel was soon laughing merrily at his drollery, and Aunt Adelina smiling sweetly. The minutes flew by, and it was half-past four when the four-seater turned in at last at the gates of Eastwood House.

At the door Arthur Augustus was standing, to meet the new arrivals. He ran down to the car.

"Bai Jove, I'm jolly glad to see you!" he exclaimed. "I was afwaid somethin' must have happened!"

"Why, what could have happened?" asked Ethel.

"It is weally vewy puzzlin'. You must have left the twain befoah weachin' Easthorpe—that is the only way of accountin' for it!" said the perplexed swell of St. Jim's. "Did you happen to meet Cardew?"

"Did you not send the car to Redmay for us?" asked Ethel, equally perplexed.

"Eh! Tom Mewwy is in the othah cab, at Easthorpe, waitin' for you now!"

"Then—I do not understand——"

"Come, my dear, the wind is very cold," said Aunt Adelina gently, and explanations had to be postponed.

Levison gave Cardew a grim look when they were alone. Cardew gave him a cheery smile in return.

"Dear old Thomas—still hangin' up at the station!" he murmured. "What a life!"

"Do you call this playing the game, Cardew?" asked Levison after a pause.

Cardew nodded.

"Yes—my game!" he answered, and he walked away cheerily.

CHAPTER 9.
Coming to a Crisis!

TOM MERRY was feeling puzzled and rather worried. The two-thirty at Easthorpe had come and gone without landing cousin Ethel and Aunt Adelina. The Terrible Three decided that the newcomers had lost their train, and would come by the next. The next was due in an hour, and the chums of the Shell walked about the village for an hour, and returned to the station in good time for the train. It came in without bringing the expected guests.

"It's jolly odd!" said Tom Merry. "It's not like cousin Ethel to lose trains. I wonder if Gussy made a mistake about the time?"

"Just like Gussy!" remarked Lowther.

"I think I'd better telephone."

Tom Merry called up Eastwood House on the telephone from the station. Arthur Augustus came to the phone, and could only say that he was quite sure of the train Ethel had been coming by, and that he couldn't account for the delay.

"All serene!" said Tom. "We'll hang on, then!"

And the three Shell fellows "hung on" and waited for the next train, which was at four-thirty. That train also came in without the expected guests.

"Well, this is a jolly afternoon!" said Manners. "Is it any good kicking our heels about here any longer?"

Tom Merry knitted his brows.

"We can't hear of any accident on the line," he said. "They may be coming down by car, after all, and there's some mistake somewhere. Hallo, this Johnny wants to speak to us!"

The rubicund station-master of Easthorpe came out and came over to the car, by which the juniors were standing.

"Call from Eastwood House, sir!" he said. "Master Arthur's sent a message."

"Oh, good!"

"He's asked me to tell you that the ladies have arrived at Eastwood House, sir."

"Oh! Thanks!"

In a puzzled and perhaps slightly exasperated frame of mind the Terrible Three got into the car and drove back to Eastwood House. They arrived there, and Arthur Augustus met them in the hall with a slightly distressed expression on his noble face.

"It's weally too bad, you fellows——" he began.

"All serene, if it's all right," said Tom. "I suppose they came down by car—what?"

"Oh, no! It is vewy perplexin'," said Arthur Augustus. "They got out of the twain at Wedmay, befoah weachin' Easthorpe, you know."

"What on earth for?" asked Manners.

"Cardew was out in a cab, and he met them there and bwought them home," said Arthur Augustus.

"Cardew!"

"Yaas, wathah! It seems that he was unawah that it was awwanged for you fellows to meet them at Easthorpe."

"He was not aware of it?" said Tom Merry quietly. "He knew it perfectly well!"

Arthur Augustus looked more distressed than ever.

"It's wathah wotten," he said. "Cardew seems to have acted in good faith—at least, I twust so. Of course, he ought to have known that a cab would be sent to the station for cousin Ethel and Aunt Adelina. It does not seem to have occurred to him. I must say it was fwightfully thoughtless of Cardew!"

Tom Merry compressed his lips.

"But it's not a long run from Redmay," he said. "They should have been here long before three o'clock, and you could have let us know."

"It's fwightfully unfortunate. Cardew had the idea of takin' them for a wun wound the countwy, and gettin' in to tea, you know. So, weally, they have only just awwived."

"So as to leave us kicking our heels in Easthorpe, waiting for nothing!" remarked Manners.

"Bai Jove! Do you weally think so, Mannahs?"

Manners grunted. Cardew's scheme was clear enough to him, and, indeed, to Arthur Augustus too, only the swell of St. Jim's hated to realise it or admit it to himself.

"I can only apologise, you fellows," said Arthur Augustus after a long and painful pause. "It is fwightfully wotten!"

"All right, old man," said Tom. "It's not your fault. Anyhow, there's no harm done."

"Not at all," said Monty Lowther.

The Terrible Three got away to their quarters, having made as light of the incident as possible, in order to soothe the troubled spirits of their host. In Tom Merry's room, however, they looked at one another grimly.

"Cardew's keeping up the feud—here, in Gussy's house, under Lord Eastwood's roof!" said Tom Merry. "This is going to be a merry Christmas, if this goes on."

"I suppose we can't punch him here?" said Manners.

Tom Merry laughed.

"Hardly! And we can't go. I couldn't possibly give Miss Priscilla any reason."

"And my sisters," said Manners.

"And my jolly old uncle," said Lowther ruefully. "It seems to me that Cardew has us in a cleft stick, and can do as he jolly well likes. We'll take it out of him next term at St. Jim's."

"Let's get down to tea!"

The Terrible Three found all the party assembled when they came down to tea. They were rather late. Cardew made it a point to address some cheery and cordial remarks to them, apparently oblivious of the fact that the Shell fellows were yearning to take him by the scruff of the neck. It was not even possible to avoid Cardew. He persisted in being agreeable, and, with cousin Ethel and Doris Levison and others within hearing, it was impossible for the Terrible Three to answer him as they would have liked to answer. The mocking gleam in Cardew's eyes showed that he read their thoughts clearly and thoroughly enjoyed their discomfiture.

Arthur Augustus glanced at them once or twice anxiously. With all his diplomacy, and all his tact and judgment, Arthur Augustus could not help feeling that matters were getting strained.

Arthur Augustus felt that it was decidedly "wotten," for he had, as a matter of fact, other and more important matters on his noble mind that day. For it was Christmas Eve, and there was to be a dance that evening, and on such occasions Gussy, as the best-dressed fellow at St. Jim's, felt it his duty to turn out looking a thing of beauty and a joy for ever.

With such tremendous considerations to be pondered over and determined, it was really hard lines for Gussy's attention to be drawn away to more trifling matters.

But it couldn't be helped. In the midst of weighing the pros and cons, the rival claims of the pearl and ruby studs, Arthur Augustus found himself wondering whether there would be open trouble between Tom Merry and Ralph Reckness Cardew before his Christmas-party came to an end. He shuddered at the thought and almost forgot the important subject of his appearance at the dance—but not quite !

— — —

CHAPTER 10.
The Limit !

"MY dance, I think ?"

A string band discoursed sweet music. In the ball-room at Eastwood House all was merry and bright. Light feet glided to merry music; bright and happy faces exchanged glances and smiles.

Cardew, very handsome in his evening clothes, his good looks marred only by that unforgotten mark on his nose, bowed gracefully to cousin Ethel. Ethel glanced at her programme.

"No; this is Tom's dance," she said.

Cardew smiled.

"In me you behold an unworthy substitute," he said. "Tom Merry has been called away."

Ethel raised her eyebrows.

"I heard him asking Gussy to make his excuses," smiled Cardew, "so I came first to avoid the crush, if you'll excuse the expression. There'll be a rush when it gets out that you've got this dance free."

"You're sure that Tom——"

"A message came in for him," explained Cardew. "He didn't confide the matter to me——"

Arthur Augustus slid gracefully up.

"Ethel, deah gal, Tom Mewwy is feahfully cut up, but——"

"I've just explained to Miss Cleveland," said Cardew airily. "She is givin' me the dance."

Ethel hesitated a moment, and then inclined her head. A moment more and Ethel and Cardew were gliding with the dancers. Arthur Augustus jammed his eyeglass a little more firmly into his eye and gazed after them. Then he shook his head thoughtfully and glided away to seek his own partner.

A good many admiring eyes rested on Cardew and cousin Ethel. There was no doubt that Cardew was an excellent dancer. He excelled Tom Merry in that respect. Ethel liked dancing, and a partner like Cardew made a dance very enjoyable. Her face was bright. Tom Merry came back into the ball-room with a face that was far from bright, and looked round for Ethel. His brow grew almost black as he saw her in the throng with Cardew.

A surprised glance from Lowther, who passed him with Doris, recalled him to himself, and he remembered that a Christmas Eve dance was no time or place for black looks. He composed his face, and stood back behind a mass of ferns, watching. His eyes gleamed as he watched.

The dance ended, and Cardew led cousin Ethel back to her seat between Aunt Matilda and Miss Priscilla. Tom Merry joined them, and Cardew gave him a cheery smile.

"Cussy told you——" Tom began, speaking to Ethel, without looking at Cardew.

"Yes," said Ethel.

"I had a message from Lord Eastwood, asking me to come to the library at once and speak to him," said Tom. "I hoped I should get back in time for our dance. I wasn't more than a minute——"

"I—I didn't understand——"

Cardew, with a cheery smile on his face, bowed to Ethel and retired, as her next partner came to claim her. Tom Merry stood for a moment or two, and then followed Cardew.

Lord Eastwood, after opening the dance, had retired from the ball-room, and Tom, receiving that unexpected message, had supposed that something was "up," and obeyed the message at once.

He joined Cardew, and slipped his arm through that of the dandy of the Fourth. Cardew stared at him.

"What's this game ?" he asked.

"I want to speak to you," said Tom, in a choking voice.

"Not here, I think."

"Will you come along, then ?"

"No. Let go my arm."

"I'll speak here, or in private, as you choose," said Tom Merry with a blaze in his eyes.

Cardew breathed hard. He made a motion with his head of assent, and they passed through the ferns, and then through french windows to the terrace.

"Now, will you let go my arm, or do you want a hooligan row in D'Arcy's house ?" asked Cardew in suppressed tones.

Tom released his arm and faced him.

"A servant brought me a message," he said.

"I know."

"I went to the library, and found Lord Eastwood there. He told me he had sent no message."

"Indeed !"

"It was a spoof message, to dish me and make me lose my dance with cousin Ethel."

"Surely a servant here would not play such a trick ?" said Cardew airily.

"Not unless he was put up to it by a treacherous cad," said Tom.

"Dear me ! I advise reporting the bad man to his employer."

"Never mind the footman," said Tom. "You may have deceived him, or bribed him—I don't know and don't care which. My quarrel isn't with him."

"I !" said Cardew. "What have I to do with it ?"

"Do you deny it, then ?"

Cardew shrugged his shoulders.

"Will you give me your word that you had nothing to do with it ?"

"I decline to say anything about it."

"That's good enough," said Tom. "You've got to the limit, Cardew, and you've got to stop. Any decent fellow would have chucked rowing, when we're both Gussy's guests. You've kept it up all the time, and in a way I can't deal with without making a scene."

"You are rather handicapped in the way of brains, aren't you ?" assented Cardew.

"It's got to stop !" said Tom between his teeth.

"Didn't you tell Gussy that it was impossible for me to be decent ?" grinned Cardew. "What's the good of askin', then ?"

"I'm not standing any more," said Tom in a choking voice. "If we were at St. Jim's, now, I'd knock you spinning for your dirty tricks !"

"But we're not at St. Jim's—we're at Eastwood House," said Cardew, laughing. "And you've got to stand it, dear man, unless you'd like to vary the entertainment at Gussy's Christmas Eve dance with a scrap ?"

And Cardew laughed mockingly.

Smack !

Tom Merry's open hand struck him across the face, and Cardew's laughter died away suddenly.

He staggered back.

"What—you—you——" he panted.

There were steps on the terrace, and a well-known voice was heard.

"Yaas, it is wathah warm ; pway walk on the tewwace for a few minutes, Miss Dowis. Hallo, Tom Mewwy, old bean !"

Cardew was springing forward with clenched fists and blazing eyes. He stopped suddenly and dropped his hands, and stood quivering with passion.

Arthur Augustus turned his eyeglass upon them alternately, and there was a curious expression on Doris Levison's face. Tom Merry muttered something indistinctly and walked away to the ball-room. Arthur Augustus gave Cardew a look, and walked on with Doris.

Cardew remained alone. His face was white, save for a deep red mark on one cheek. He was still standing there, motionless, when Arthur Augustus and Doris repassed. He did not seem to see them ; but Arthur Augustus glanced at him, and the look on Cardew's face haunted the swell of St. Jim's the rest of the evening.

. . . .

Christmas Day dawned upon the party at Eastwood House, the day of peace and good will and happy faces. Tom Merry and Cardew met at the breakfast table, and Tom carefully avoided looking at his enemy ; but Cardew's glance rested on Tom with a look that was calm, smiling, and implacable. But that day, at least, there was no hostility between the rivals of St. Jim's, and it was, after all, a merry Christmas.

THE END.

(Look out for " THE VENGEANCE OF CARDEW !"
in our great Christmas-Week issue of the GEM.)
THE GEM LIBRARY.—No. 828.

Little did Dick Baker, of no-where, realise the fortune—

—which awaited him until he impersonated Guy Derrington!

THE GHOST OF GREYMINSTER CASTLE

A Tale of Christmas Mystery and Thrilling Adventure.

By VINCENT OWEN.

CHAPTER 1.
A Strange Request!

DICK BAKER stood on the corner of Berners Street, in Oxford Street, wistfully watching the bustling throng of Christmas shoppers. It was Christmas Eve, and all the great shops in London's busy thoroughfares were radiant with light, and noisy with the chatter and laughter and shuffling of feet of countless people.

"Christmas to-morrow!" muttered Dick, digging his hands deeper into the rather thin pockets of his overcoat. "Wonder where I shall be spending it, anyway?"

This thought fetched a frown to his young, handsome face.

Dick was "roughing it," like many thousands of others in the empire's great capital. He had no friends, no relations whom he could visit for the Christmas. Yesterday he had been "sacked" from his job as mechanic and motor-driver to a small firm at King's Cross. He had done nothing wrong, but the manager of the firm had said that there was not enough work for him to do, and it would not pay the firm to keep him on. So he had had to go. It was one of those cruel strokes of misfortune to which he had by now become accustomed. Still, it seemed very hard to be turned away on the eve of Christmas.

Dick could have made a living—and a good living—had he chosen to follow his father's profession. But Dick's father was a thief and head of a desperate East End gang of criminals, and Dick preferred to "rough it" honestly, rather than become a crook.

Two years ago he had run away from the Limehouse eating-house that served as the headquarters of his father's circle of accomplices. Life there had become intolerable to a lad with scruples. Dick had read well, and was as plucky and able a youngster as one could wish to find; but, with friends and relations he was ashamed to own, he had found life a hard struggle.

He was standing there in the glare of the shop lights, musing on things in general, when he felt a tap on his arm. Turning round, he gave a start, for he found himself staring at a young fellow who, despite his immaculate dress, bore a remarkable likeness to himself.

"I say, old chap, I'd like a few words with you!" said the stranger, with a pleasant smile. "It isn't often one meets one's double, anyway, is it? Are you in a hurry?"

"No," replied Dick.

"Then come into the Cosy Cafe here; we can get a corner to ourselves and have a jaw."

Seated at a small table in a corner of the cafe, the two regarded each other curiously.

"Well, we are alike, aren't we?" said Dick, with a laugh.

"Yes, rather! That's just why I asked you to come in here and talk with me," came the quick, eager reply. "I'll introduce myself first. My name is Guy Derrington. I'm just up on the Christmas vac, from Telby College. Who are you?"

"Dick Baker, of nowhere; and I'm just roaming the streets and watching the people do their Christmas shopping, and wondering what on earth is to become of me," replied Dick. "I've just lost my job, you see."

"Hard lines!" said Derrington. "Through no fault of your own, I'll bet my boots! You look a jolly decent sort, and I'll confide in you. First of all, though, are you willing to impersonate me during the Christmas holidays? I'll pay you a hundred quid if the thing works, and I can assure you that you'll have plenty of everything where you go."

Dick gave a look of surprise.

"Impersonate you!" he exclaimed. "Where? What for?"

"I'll tell you the whole tale from beginning to end," said the other. "The Derringtons, I must explain, are related to the ancient family of De Coverley. The home of the De Coverleys is at Greyminster Castle, in Kent, a fine old Norman building that has been held by the family since Richard I. There are no De Coverleys now. The last of the line was Sir John de Coverley, who died some sixteen years ago without leaving an heir to assume the title. Sir John made a will before he died, leaving the castle to his old friend and physician, Jasper Oldacre, and his money to the Derringtons, who were his only near relations. But he made a special and, to my mind, a foolish stipulation in his will.

"He demanded that all members of the Derrington family benefiting under the will should meet at the castle every

Christmas, and spend Christmas there together in the old home of the De Coverleys, and that the villagers of Coverdale should be invited to the festivities. Any member of the family failing to turn up for the Christmas reunion forfeits the remainder of his heirloom, which then is divided among the others. Funny sort of stipulation to make in a will, wasn't it?"

"Well, it shows that Sir John was proud of his family; and the Christmas reunion at Greyminster Castle is quite a good idea, I think," said Dick Baker, with a smile.

"Yes, the spirit of the thing is all right; but—well, Christmas at Greyminster Castle isn't exactly a pleasant affair!" said Derrington, with a grimace. "The old place gives me the creeps, and so does Jasper Oldacre, who lives there. There are only three of the family left to turn up at Greyminster Castle this year—myself, my brother Lionel, and Ralph Tredegar. Lionel is rather an invalid, and he lives at Greyminster Castle with Oldacre. Jasper is a clever physician, and he is looking after my brother, you see. Lionel will be there this year, and so will cousin Ralph—trust Ralph for that! I ought to be there, but—well, to tell you the truth, old man, I'd rather be anywhere this Christmas than at Greyminster Castle.

"Some college chums of mine have asked me to spend Christmas with them, and I very badly want to. But I don't come into my own money until next year, so that I cannot afford not to turn up at the family reunion, such as it is. Now, perhaps, you can see what I am driving at? I was in the dickens of a quandary until I spotted you in Oxford Street just now!"

"You want me to attend the Christmas reunion at Greyminster Castle, posing as yourself, and thus save you from being cut off without a shilling?" said Dick Baker, with a whimsical smile.

"That's it!" said Guy Derrington eagerly. "Now, the question is—will you? I'll tell you everything about the castle and the people and myself. You can take my bags and luggage. I'll give you more than enough money for what you'll need. You speak well, although you're down and out. You'll do it, Baker? It's a chance you can't afford to miss."

"No, I can't afford to miss it," replied Dick. "I'll do it, Derrington."

CHAPTER 2.
A Miraculous Escape!

SEATED alone in a corner of the first-class compartment of the 8.15 p.m. train from Charing Cross, Dick Baker had ample time to muse on the unexpected stroke of Fate that had given him a destination for Christmas.

Dressed in Derrington's clothes, he looked more remarkably like the other. He had spent a long time in conversation with Derrington, and felt confident of being able to carry out the masquerade successfully.

"So long as I don't forget that my name is Guy Derrington, everything should be fine!" He laughed to himself as he turned over the pages of his favourite motoring journal. "This is rather an adventure, besides being a jolly good stroke of luck for me. Here's wishing a Happy Christmas to both Guy Derringtons!"

The train roared on through the darkness. Snow was falling out in the open country, and, peering into the semi-darkness through the train window, Dick could see that the countryside was laden with a white mantle of snow.

He had to change at Ledbury Junction, and catch a slow local train for Coverdale. Ledbury was bustling with happy crowds and the noise of Christmas holiday traffic. The Coverdale train left at last, and Dick could not repress a certain amount of thrilled excitement on contemplating his journey's end.

Snow everywhere as he looked from the train window. The train churned up the stiff gradients of the Kentish hills, stopping at each small station. Looking at the map, Dick saw that Coverdale was now only two stations ahead. He was about to sit down again, when the train stopped with a jerk. He opened the window and looked out, and saw the guard walking in the snow along the line. When the guard came back Dick asked him what was wrong.

"Snowbound!" grunted the guard. "Big fall of snow on the line ahead. We shall probably be stuck here for a few hours yet."

"Br-r-r-r-r!" said Dick, shivering at the prospect. "Then I'm not staying!"

He gathered up his two suitcases and jumped down from the train. Crossing the other line, he slid down the railway embankment, and struck out across some fields towards a farmhouse, the lights of which he had seen twinkling in the darkness.

There was no telephone at the farmhouse, but the farmer directed him to an inn lower down the country road. Dick found the inn, and used the telephone there to ring up Greyminster Castle. He informed them that it was Guy speaking, and told them what had happened, requesting that a car be sent along to pick him up. He was told to wait at the inn, and that his cousin Ralph would be along as soon as possible in his car.

Dick sat in front of the fire in the parlour of the inn until, after nearly an hour's wait, he heard a car draw up outside, and heard his name—or, rather, the name he had assumed—being called.

He turned, to see a tall, dark, small-featured man of thirty years of age or thereabouts enter the parlour. He immediately recognised Ralph Tredegar from Derrington's description of him.

"Hallo, Ralph!" he exclaimed, rising and taking the proffered hand. "I'm glad you came! How's everything?"

Tredegar looked at him rather curiously, Dick thought, but it was apparent that his identity was not suspected. Dick carried on the conversation in a free and easy manner, but found Tredegar somewhat reserved and taciturn.

They entered the rather old four-seater car that was waiting outside, and Ralph Tredegar drove it away.

No conversation passed between the two until, having left a small village behind, Tredegar turned to Dick.

"You can drive, can't you?" he asked.

"Rather!" said Dick promptly.

"Would you like me to take the wheel for a bit?"

"I want you to drive on alone to the castle," said Tredegar. "I'm stopping here to make a call, and sha'n't be back till late. You go on in the car—you can't miss the way. Keep straight ahead on this road and turn to the left after you pass the railway-crossing. That brings you to the castle."

Dick assented, noticing a strange uneasiness in Tredegar's manner. Tredegar put the gear-lever into the neutral position, and allowed the car to draw slowly to a standstill. Then he jumped out of the car, and Dick took the wheel.

He changed up the gears quickly, and soon had the car humming along the road at a good pace. He came at length to where the road ran steeply downhill to the railway level-crossing at the bottom. As the car gained speed down the hill, Dick, in attempting to ease her pace, suddenly made a dramatic discovery.

The brakes would not act!

"Oh, good heavens!" he gasped, wrenching vainly at the hand-brake lever. "I can't stop, and——"

He broke off with a thrill of horror, for he saw the light on the crossing-gate at the bottom turn from green to red. The gates had closed, indicating that a train was coming! He realised that this was the main line to the coast over which the fast expresses travelled.

The car was hurtling down the hill at unchecked speed now. Dick closed the throttle and thrust home the low gear—that was all he could do. But the car did not stop. It dashed downward to the level-crossing.

Dick's grip on the steering-wheel tightened; his teeth came tight together. As the crossing-gates loomed up, he decided on a daring plan of action—his only alternative to crashing into the wall at the other side of the line. Not far away came the sound of an approaching train.

Crash! The flimsy wooden gate buckled like matchwood under the impact of the runaway car. In the same instant Dick wrenched round the steering-wheel. The car lurched drunkenly round, and then took a course along the railway-line, its pace easing as it bumped over the sleepers.

Dick flung a look behind him, and saw the headlights and the glare of the approaching express. The train would not be able to slow up in time, and unless he acted quickly the car would be run down.

Dick put the car into top gear, and drove his foot down hard on the accelerator. The car bounded forward along the permanent-way. The train behind roared closer and closer!

Dick timed himself to a nicety. Just when it seemed inevitable that the train would crash into the car, he jerked at the steering-wheel, and turned the car on to the opposite line. Next minute the express thundered by and disappeared, glaring, into the darkness.

"Whew! A close shave that!" muttered Dick, as the car stopped of its own accord on the level railway-line. "I wonder whether Tredegar knew that the brakes wouldn't act when he sent me on alone? He knew about the hill, and the railway-crossing, and he seemed to be pretty nervous and restive. No wonder he never used the brakes to stop the car when he got out. He knew that they wouldn't work! The rascal meant me to be injured, or killed!"

His thrilling experience over, Dick got the car round and drove back to the level-crossing. He explained matters to the scared signalman, and, having left the car in a shed at a farmhouse, he set out on foot for the castle.

CHAPTER 3.
The Truth Revealed!

GREYMINSTER CASTLE was a grand, greystoned pile, bearing with its four towers and the battlements on the walls, all the grandeur of the Middle Ages.

Dick was shown into the castle through the main door, and he found himself in the Knights' Hall. All around him in this lofty hall were links of the past glory of the castle. Large oil paintings hung from the oak-panelled walls, the windows were of stained glass, many suits of armour stood about the hall, and on the walls, too, were spears, and daggers, and weapons of all kinds, while the tattered and stained banners of past De Coverleys hung from the wall over the large open fireplace.

"Master Guy!"

A cracked, wheezing voice broke into the lad's meditations, and, looking round, he saw a short, wizened old man regarding him from a doorway on the left. It was Jasper Oldacre, the present occupant of the castle. Oldacre's looks were of incredulous amazement. His eyes, as he approached Dick, seemed to glint maliciously.

"Hallo, Jasper!" said Dick. "You seem surprised to see me!"

"No, Master Guy, not surprised, but glad!" croaked the old man. "A merry Christmas to ye! Ah, here is Lionel!"

A pale, delicate-looking young man walked in. On seeing Dick his listless eyes brightened, and he hurried over and grasped the lad's hand.

"So you have come, Guy!" he said fervently. "I was wondering whether you would come. I—I somehow had a feeling that you wouldn't."

Dick laughed as easily as he was able. Talking to Lionel, he kept his eyes on Jasper Oldacre, and saw that the old man was watching him furtively. He took an instant dislike to Oldacre.

Dick carried out his part well. There was something strange and repelling in the atmosphere of the castle, but Dick felt convinced that all believed him to be Guy Derrington.

Ralph Tredegar did not arrive until after supper. Dick saw him give a guilty start on seeing him.

"So you—you got here all right, Guy!" stammered Tredegar.

"Yes—after being nearly killed in that car of yours!" rapped Dick sharply. "Did you know that the brakes were useless, Ralph?"

The other licked his dry lips, and a hunted look came into his small, beady eyes.

"The brakes were useless?" he muttered. "I—I didn't know. Of course, the car is rather old, and all sorts of things are liable to go wrong——"

"Yes, of course!" said Dick meaningly. "How fortunate for you, Ralph, that you had to make that call! You THE GEM LIBRARY.—No. 828.

missed a thrill that was worthy of a screen serial!"

The main hall of the castle had been gaily decorated for the Christmas festivities on the morrow, when prominent local residents and the villagers would gather at the ancestral home of the De Coverleys and join together in celebrating Yuletide, in accordance with the wishes of the late Sir John.

Dick wandered alone about the old corridors and the musty rooms of the castle before retiring to bed. The old-world place fascinated him and stirred his imagination, conjuring up visions of the romantic past.

Traditions and superstitions were associated with Greyminster Castle, as with every old building in the country. The most popular superstition was that the spirit of Sir Roger de Coverley, the first of the line, walked abroad in the picture gallery every Christmas at midnight. The villagers of Coverdale were convinced of the truth of this, and several of them who had been servants at the castle swore that they had actually seen the ghost with their own eyes.

Dick retired to bed at last. His was a large, old-fashioned bed-room, oak-panelled, and containing antique furniture. Midnight had struck from a distant church before he blew out the light and settled down to go to sleep.

He was awakened from his sleep, however, by a mysterious tapping on the wall. It was pitch-black in the room, and not a sound disturbed the night silence until the tapping sounded again.

His nerves tensed, Dick found the matches and lit the candle. There was nobody else in the room. Yet again there came that strange tap, tap, tap! on the wall.

Dick sprang out of bed and put on his slippers. He was not a believer in ghosts, being too matter-of-fact and clear-headed a lad for that. He was resolved to discover the origin of the mysterious tapping and what it meant. He examined the oak panels carefully where he judged the tapping to have come from. Several minutes passed, and then a loud shriek of terror rang out through the night stillness.

Dick ran from the room and entered the room next to his, where Lionel Derrington slept.

Huddled up on the floor in front of a large mirror was Lionel Derrington. He was writhing and moaning like one demented. With one spring Dick reached his side.

"What is the matter?" he demanded. "What has happened?"

The other was inarticulate with horror. His face was blanched, and he looked into the mirror with large, dilated eyes. Then, shuddering, he turned his face away and pointed into the mirror.

What had Lionel seen in the mirror that had sent him into such a helpless state of terror? Looking into the mirror, Dick saw that directly opposite it stood a large, carved oak chest. And as he looked his quick eyes detected a slight, almost imperceptible movement of the lid.

Waiting first to give Lionel a drink of water, he sprang over to the chest and grasped the lid. It would not come open.

Dick snapped his teeth down hard.

"The lid moved two minutes ago, I could swear to that!" he muttered. "I mean to discover what this means!"

Finding it impossible to raise the lid, he grasped the chest and swung it over on its side. Then an exclamation of amazement broke from his lips. The bottom of the chest was false. The edges of a sliding panel could be seen.

Dick swung the panel open and saw that the chest was empty.

Instinctively his eyes turned to the floor where the chest had stood. He went down on hands and knees and examined the oak boards. And, as he had expected, he discovered a sliding panel there immediately underneath the secret panel in the base of the oak chest. He found the spring, and pressed it. A square section of the floor swung inwards, revealing a black, open cavity beneath.

Dick flung a look at Lionel.

"Go on, go on!" hoarsed the other. "Find out what it means! I shall be all right now. A form appeared out of the trunk; it was that that frightened me. Now I know that it was a trick, and not supernatural, I shall not be frightened. Go on down and see what it means."

Dick took a lighted candle and lowered himself through the hole in the floor. He found himself in a narrow tunnel, which led upwards, it seemed, between two walls. Dick traversed this, and guessed that he was walking behind the panelled wall of his own bed-room.

"The fellow who frightened Lionel must have been the one who tried to frighten me by tapping at the wall," he mused, as he passed. "I wonder if Ralph or Jasper are at the bottom of this?"

He passed on until he reached a flight of stone steps. Clambering up these, he came to another narrow, tunnel-like passage. This ended abruptly in a stone wall. But Dick soon discovered that, by shifting one of the stone slabs, he could get through. The keen night air swept in through the aperture.

Climbing through it, Dick found himself at the top of the west tower. Looking through the wide battlements, he saw the dark, snow-clad countryside for miles around.

Then a stealthy footstep behind caused him to turn. Hardly had he done so than he found himself assailed by a tall figure clad in a flowing white robe. Dick grappled with his assailant, and the pair rocked to and fro at the top of the tower, fighting desperately.

"I planned death for you, but you shall die now!" hissed the other, dragging him with demoniacal strength towards the low-built battlements. "You shall go over, to fall into the moat below; and people will think that you walked in your sleep——"

Dick gripped the man's throat and forced him back. They were rolling together between the battlements now at the top of the tower.

Looking down, Dick saw that to fall from there would mean certain death.

He smashed a terrific right-hander on his assailant's chest that sent him reeling back. Suddenly there was a shriek, and Dick saw the other topple off the stonework and disappear over the other side.

With blanched face and heart beating fast he looked over, and then drew a deep breath of relief. His assailant was clinging to the ivy that grew on the walls. He had saved himself in the nick of time.

"Save me!" panted the man below.

Crash! The flimsy wooden gate buckled like matchwood under the impact of the runaway car. Dick saw the approaching express!

"Do not leave me here! For mercy's sake, get me up!"

Dick gritted his teeth and swung himself over the battlements. He clambered down the ivy till he reached the other.

"Hang on to me with one hand, and on to the ivy with the other!" he cried. "When we reach the top I'll help you over."

It was a terribly difficult task for Dick, for the man was almost helpless with fear. But at last, by dint of great risk to himself, Dick managed to get him back to safety at the top of the tower.

"I thank you!" muttered the other. "You have saved me when I tried to murder you. Come with me. I will tell you all."

Dick followed the white-clad figure through the gap in the tower wall left by the removed stone. The stone was put back into place, and Dick was taken along the tunnel he had traversed until another tunnel was reached. This eventually gave access to a small stone-walled room. It was furnished comfortably, and a large oak bedstead stood in one corner.

"This is where I live," said the old man, removing the white shroud. "Look at me. Whom do you think I am?"

Dick looked at the handsome, pallid face that was lined with the furrows of care. He gave a start. He had seen a portrait of this man in the castle picture-gallery.

"Sir John de Coverley!" he cried, reeling back.

"Yes, I am your uncle!" said the other. "Do not be afraid. You know that I am not a ghost, although I have been masquerading as one. That terrible experience I have just had at the top of the tower seems to have cleared my brain and brought a return of reason. For sixteen years I have been a madman, hiding here in secret, awaiting the culmination of my revenge."

"Then the report of your death was false!" ejaculated Dick.

"Yes. There was a mock burial in the grounds of this castle. I was not dead. I lived—in secret—to attain my revenge."

"On whom?" demanded Dick. "For what?"

"On your family—the Derringtons!" came the fierce reply. "I craved revenge on them for stealing my infant son—the son who was heir to my title. It was one of the Derringtons who took away my son. I received proof that the baby had died. And then I decided to die, too—and to get my revenge. My son stood between the Derringtons and my fortune, because he was my heir. With the heir to Greyminster out of the way, the Derringtons knew that they would inherit. I let them inherit, but made the stipulation in the will that they should meet at the castle here once a year—at Christmas time. Every Christmas for sixteen years the Derringtons have met here—and there have been deaths—numerous deaths. I and old Jasper between us achieved those deaths. We selected our victim, and on Christmas Eve Jasper had a draught put into his drink—a draught that weakened the heart. Then, at night, I would appear as a ghost, and the fright killed my victim—his heart was weak, and he died of shock. That was my revenge on the Derringtons. It was a Derrington who sent my family into oblivion by killing my son. And I swore to obliterate the Derrington family as the De Coverleys have been obliterated."

Dick Baker listened to this impassioned speech in amazement. He looked at the old man before him, and saw that he was in earnest. Tears glistened in the shrunken eyes.

"I realise my madness now!" said Sir John, quietly. "Jasper Oldacre kept

alive the fires of my hatred and urged me on to get rid of all the Derringtons. I can see his motive now. With all the Derringtons gone, he would inherit everything, under the terms of my will."

Dick nodded.

"I see," he said. "You are sorry now, that you have kept on with this awful campaign against innocent members of the Derrington family?"

"Yes, I am sorry. It was madness. The whole business has been madness—the mock burial and my living in hiding here for sixteen years with only Jasper knowing my secret. But what had I to live for? My son was gone—stolen away and killed by an accursed Derrington who——"

The old man broke off, and Dick saw that he was looking at him with dilated eyes. The other came towards him, slowly, and pulled aside the torn sleeve of Dick's pyjama jacket. The tear had been made during the fight on the tower, and Dick's bare arm was showing.

"That mark—that birthmark on your arm—do you know anything of it?" cried Sir John, hoarsely.

Dick looked down at the birthmark on his arm that was shaped somewhat like a heart.

"I've always known the mark was there, of course," he said. "But I know nothing special about it——"

"But it's the birthmark of my own son!" came the quick, eager response. "Every De Coverley had a mark like that on his arm at birth! Boy, you are not a Derrington at all!"

"I know that," said Dick, with a chuckle. "I'm an impostor. The real Guy Derrington met me and was struck by my likeness to him——"

"Of course there is a likeness! You two are cousins! You are my son! But—but I cannot realise it. Go on—tell me your story."

Dick told Sir Roger frankly all about himself, how he had never known his mother and how he had been brought up among thieves in Limehouse until his better self had asserted itself, and he ran away.

"I am convinced that you are my son!" cried the old man, when Dick had finished his story. "An amazing coincidence sent you here this Christmas! But if only I could get proof——"

Dick had been thinking hard, and he suddenly burst out with:

"I have an idea! To-morrow night the villagers will be here for the Christmas festivities. At midnight the ghost is supposed to walk. This Christmas the ghost will walk and——"

He talked earnestly with Sir John, who listened with hands clenched and eyes gleaming. Dick laughed softly as he left the secret room, having been told the way back to Lionel's room.

"Oldacre will have a surprise to-morrow," he muttered. "The old rogue was in the conspiracy with the Derringtons who made off with the infant heir to Greyminster—myself, if what Sir John says is true. Gee, but this seems all so unreal—more like a story than real actuality! There will be stirring happenings at midnight to-morrow, or I'm a Dutchman!"

THE GEM LIBRARY.—No. 828.

Dick Baker smashed a terrific right-hander on his ghostlike assailant's chest and sent him reeling backwards. Then followed a sudden shriek, and Dick saw the other topple off the stonework and disappear over the side of the tower.

CHAPTER 4.
A Rude Awakening!

NEITHER Jasper Oldacre nor Ralph Tredegar had heard the commotion during the night. Dick shrewdly suspected that they had put themselves well out of ear-shot. That Ralph was in league with old Jasper he felt convinced, for they both evinced disappointment in the morning on finding Lionel still alive.

"Oldacre has been doping Lionel—making his heart weak so that he wouldn't be able to stand a fright!" muttered Dick to himself. "The old villain! He and Ralph are as thick as thieves. I shouldn't be surprised if they weren't planning to get the three of us out of the way—Lionel, myself, and then Sir John. But I'll give 'em a surprise to-night."

Dick announced that, as a further attraction for the Christmas revellers that would be at the castle, he proposed "laying the ghost" in the picture gallery. Old Jasper did not dissuade him from the idea, but Ralph appeared nervous.

When the lad had gone out, the two met in the Knights' Hall.

"Supposing Sir John does venture out to play ghost to-night, Jasper?" said Ralph Tredegar. "That kid is cute, and he may discover the truth—and then our game will be up!"

"Listen!" chuckled Oldacre, his eyes glinting like a monster's. "To-night Sir John will play ghost. I will see him and persuade him to—he does all I tell him. As soon as he appears there will probably be a panic. You will sham fright, pull out your revolver and shoot the 'ghost'—shoot him dead. It will be believed that you did it in fright, not knowing that the 'ghost' was really a human being. That will put Sir John out of the way, and put you and I into the chance of getting the entire fortune for ourselves. We shall easily be able to dispose of Lionel and young Guy."

"But won't it come out that you——" faltered Ralph.

"Nothing will come out about me!" rapped Jasper. "It will be thought that Sir John has been living here unbeknown to anybody. I will disclaim any knowledge of the affair. We shall be safe if you keep your nerve, Ralph—and shoot."

Ralph Tredegar nodded.

"I'll do it, Jasper," he muttered. "But mind, if there's a hitch, you'll get into trouble with me!"

Dick did not put in an appearance until dinner-time. He did not satisfy Oldacre's demands to know where he had been. The Christmas dinner was a gloomy affair, but later on the villagers began to arrive, and the real spirit of Christmas pervaded the old castle.

The rafters rang with sounds of music and laughter. Christmas at Greyminster Castle was an event that was made the most of by the people of Coverdale. Feasting and merrymaking was the order of the day.

A dance was in progress in the ancient ball-room when Dick announced that at midnight the ghost was supposed to walk, and he invited all who were bold enough to turn up at the picture gallery in order to "lay" the ghost.

This announcement was greeted with cheers, and there was no lack of volunteers. The village doctor, and the grocer, and the constable, and a dozen others all announced their willingness to help in snaring the ghost.

Night drew on; the castle was gaily lit, and the Christmas revelry reached concert pitch. Nobody thought of returning home until the small hours of the morning.

As midnight approached, Dick summoned all the volunteers to the picture gallery. Ralph and old Jasper accompanied them.

There was silence and darkness in the long, lofty picture gallery. On either side of the panelled walls hung large portraits of past De Coverleys. At one end was a handsome stained-glass window, and priceless tapestries adorned the walls on either side. A door that gave access to the main corridor was at the other end, screened with curtains.

All lay in hiding behind the massive curtains and waited breathlessly.

Midnight! Hearts beat fast as the last reverberating note of a distant clock died away. Then, out of the tense silence that followed came the sound of soft footsteps in the picture gallery.

Dick, Ralph, Oldacre, and the villagers looked from behind the curtain and saw a dim figure, dressed in the picturesque garb of a courtier of the Middle Ages, walking slowly along the picture gallery in the darkness.

Cries of amazement arose from the watching villagers, several of whom evinced fear.

Oldacre nudged Ralph.

"Shoot!" he muttered.

Tredegar whipped out his revolver with a cry and took aim at the moving, ghost-like figure in the picture gallery. In the same instant as the spiteful crack of his revolver sounded there was a blinding flash of light that lit the gallery from end to end and then it plunged back again into darkness.

Dick's voice rang out above the cries of the frightened village people.

"You rascal, Tredegar! You knew it wasn't a ghost! You shot on purpose—you and Oldacre planned it between you!"

The lad flung himself on Tredegar and wrenched the revolver from his grasp as he swung, snarling, towards him.

Oldacre snapped on the light and ran to the figure that lay huddled on the gallery floor. He turned it over and the face was revealed.

Then Oldacre recoiled from the victim of his plot in horror, a shrill cry escaping his lips.

"Seth Baker!"

The man who had masqueraded as a ghost moved. His eyes opened and he groaned. Then, on seeing Oldacre, he gave a hoarse cry and started up.

"Seth Baker!" shrilled Jasper Oldacre, his shrivelled face going livid. "You—here!"

"Yes, Seth Baker is here, to confront you with your villainy!" cried Dick, stepping forward with Ralph's revolver in his hand. "This is a surprise I planned for you, Jasper. Look!"

One of the pictures in the gallery swung suddenly outwards, revealing a cavity through which stepped two figures.

One was Sir John de Coverley, and the other Guy Derrington.

Shouts of fear and amazement arose from the villagers, who believed the late owner of Greyminster Castle to be dead.

"Oldacre, you miscreant, Seth Baker has told me all!" exclaimed Sir John, in a ringing voice. "My son Richard planned this surprise on you. His idea was to have the people of the village here as witnesses."

"Your son!" almost screeched Jasper Oldacre. "What do you mean!"

"He means that I am really his son, stolen by you from this place when I was a kid and put into Seth Baker's hands to be brought up as his son!" cut in Dick laconically. "I met my father, you see, last night, and he recognised me by the birthmark on my arm as his son. But we wanted proof. So this morning I hired a car from Coverdale and drove to London, taking with me two friends. I visited Seth Baker, my supposed father, at Limehouse, and told him that unless he made a confession of the truth about my parentage I would give information to the police about himself and his gang. That frightened him, and he told me all. He returned here with me and I hid him where Sir John, my father, has been hiding for sixteen years, a victim of your malicious influence, Jasper. Then I rang up the real Guy Derrington and told him to come here—and this is the surprise we planned for you! So you intended that Ralph should kill my father. No wonder you came up to him this afternoon and threatened him with exposure if he did not play ghost to-night. You wanted to decoy him out here to be shot. But, you see, I got some magnesium flash-powder and made Seth Baker play ghost—just to give you a surprise!"

Oldacre and Ralph Tredegar recoiled in horror and fear.

Seth Baker, lying wounded on the floor of the picture gallery, then gasped out his confession. The villagers listened in amazement.

Dick turned to Oldacre again.

"Now, you rascal, what have you to say?"

Oldacre collapsed at Sir John's feet, whining for mercy. The doctor attended to Baker's wound, and announced that it was not fatal. Baker was taken away to the village hospital, while Ralph Tredegar and old Jasper were made captives by the villagers and locked in a lower room.

Then all returned to the ball-room, where Sir John de Coverley amazed the revellers by revealing himself, and telling them the whole story. Tears streamed down his pallid face as he introduced Dick as his son, and heir to the title and estates.

Never before had there been such Christmas revels at the old castle as those which followed. Guy Derrington confessed to Dick that he was "knocked flat" by the revelations.

"It seems like a magazine yarn to me, Dick," he said. "What a stroke of fortune, though, that I spotted you in Oxford Street last night and sent you here to impersonate me!"

"It was!" said Dick fervently. "But I made you turn up for the family reunion after all, and my father is sticking to the terms of his will. You'll get your money for this year, and then——"

"And then I shall come into my own, so I don't care!" laughed Guy Derrington. "I'm jolly glad all this happened, Dick. As for that old rogue Jasper, and my precious cousin Ralph——"

"My father will let them go, provided they leave the country," said Dick.

THE END.

(Be sure you read " The Stolen Pie !" a magnificent story, featuring old-time favourites, Gan Waga, Ching Lung, Rupert Thurston & Co. in next week's Special Bumper Number of the GEM Library.)

Faced without a friend
in the world—

—George Clifton deems
it wise to confess!

THE TRIERS

BY JACK CRICHTON

A Powerfully Written Story telling how plucky
Jack Morton wrings the truth from his rascally
cousin and brings about the rights which are
his due.

In the Court.

IN all the history of Boltwich it was
by far the most amazing day.

Certainly, since Jack Morton had
become so dear to the hearts of the
Boltwich fans, he had been making
history, and many strange things had
happened; but there was no getting over
the fact that the crowd which now stood
outside the police-court was one of the
greatest and worst-tempered that had
ever collected in the town.

The police, however, on this occasion,
had not been taken unawares, and they
had drafted in great squads of police
from other towns, so that there was little
risk of real trouble, and getting into the
court itself was a matter of no small skill.

George Clifton had fortified himself
with some little refreshment before he
had left home, and he had walked down
towards the court feeling quite certain
that everything was going to go all
right.

And then, when he suddenly got close
to the court itself and heard the crowd
yelling and cheering, singing songs, and
again and again demanding his blood, he
realised that he could not possibly get to
the court as he was.

What was he to do?

It was somewhat against his dignity,
but he was passing by a barber's shop
at the moment, in which reposed a false
beard, and so he entered in and, much
to the man's surprise, bought it. A
moment later he bought a pair of
spectacles, and then, with his coat-collar
turned up about his neck, he approached
the police-court.

But here again he was handicapped.

At last he found a policeman, and,
slipping a pound into his hand, he whispered his name.

The policeman started, grinned, and
gave him a quick glance of surprise.

"What's the game?" he asked.

"I could not get through otherwise,"
Clifton whispered, in reply. "The fools
want me!"

Again the policeman grinned.

"Yes, they do," he said. "All right,
sir; you come along with me. I'll get
you in."

And so, pushing and shoving, during
the process of which Clifton's false beard
very nearly came to a sad and a bad end,
he was pushed into the police-court, and
it was only as he entered the court itself
that he slipped the beard into his pocket
and took off the glasses.

The inspector came up to him at once.

"Had rather a bad time getting here,
didn't you, sir?"

Clifton nodded angrily.

"I did. It's a disgrace. When are
you people going to get this mob into
order?"

The inspector looked serious about it.

"Don't ask me, sir," he said. "The
trouble is that they are so fond of him.
Anyhow, it looks as though we have got
him this time; but I don't know what is
going to happen if he gets sent for trial.
All the magistrates have had threatening
letters, and it looks nasty. We've got a
lot of police, but it is altogether a nasty
show!"

George Clifton gave a grunt of disgust.

"A nasty show!" he ejaculated. "Do
you know that I had a raging, tearing
mob of them up at my place last night?"

"I heard something about it, sir.
You'll have to look out!"

Clifton started angrily.

"Look out! Do you think I'm going
to clear out of my own home for a
whipper-snapper like that, and a lot of
roughs? I tell you, inspector, it seems to
me that you are the person who is to
blame."

"I, sir?"

"Certainly! Respectable citizens
should be looked after better than this,
and I shall certainly go up to London
to-morrow and have a word with the
commissioner!"

The inspector said nothing aloud, but
he said a good deal under his breath, and
it seemed to be to the effect that he
hoped that Mr. George Clifton would
stay up in London when he got there.

Suddenly there was a silence in court
and the magistrates entered.

There was an electric atmosphere about
the place, and it was clear that it had

spread to the magistrates themselves, for
they took their seats looking very serious.

There was silence for a moment, and
then the chairman of the Bench began
to speak.

"I—I want to say, before we take the
first case, that the Bench is very much
disturbed by the state of affairs which
seems to exist in our town. It is not a
credit to Boltwich, and we hope very
sincerely that there will soon be an end
to it. And I have one thing further to
say. It would be idle for us not to
confess that we know about the case
which is causing so much excitement;
but we have to put it on record at once
that none of the letters of a threatening
nature we have received, will stop us
doing our duty, and, further, if we discover the writers of these letters, which
are most improper, we shall not hesitate
to take the gravest steps. Now, call the
first case!"

"Jack Morton!"

There was a great silence, and then
a buzzing as Jack entered the court.

He glanced quickly round, and in the
front row of the court he saw the Triers.
One and all they were there, and their
cheery smiles did him good.

He was charged and, having pleaded
not guilty, the first witness was called. It
was the police-sergeant to whom he had
given himself up.

He was soon done with, and then the
name of George Clifton was called in
court.

He had been sitting with the solicitors,
talking hard to young Clifford, and he
rose with a jerk and went to the witness-
box very pale. Every eye was upon him
as he moved, and as he passed Jack in
the dock he raised his eyes, and for one
moment the two looked at one another.

Clifton took the oath, and was about
to speak when Jack suddenly leaned forward from the dock.

"One moment, Mr. Clifton," he said,
pointing to that worthy. "Before you
start, I just want to say that my defence
is that you know all about that fifty
pounds, and that, further, you know
very well that you asked a certain
person to destroy my grandfather's will."

THE GEM LIBRARY.—No. 828.

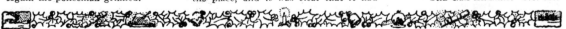

The Truth Comes Out !

THERE was indeed silence in court. Then the Chairman of the Bench turned quickly to Jack.

"Look here, young man," he said, "you can't behave like that in this court. You must wait; a proper time will come for you to have your say. Wait until that time comes!"

"I am sorry; but——"

All eyes, however, were upon George Clifton by this time.

An amazing change had come over him. As he had entered the box he had seemed confident and insolent almost in his bearing; but now as he stood there he was holding to the edge of the box as though in physical pain, and his face was a ghastly white.

"It's ridiculous—a fairy tale!" he stammered; but the voice was the voice of a man who knew he was doomed, and the effect upon everyone in that court was electric.

The Chairman of the Bench turned to him.

"You need take no notice of anything that the lad said, Mr. Clifton," he said; "it is quite irrelevant to this charge. Kindly proceed with your evidence."

"Yes."

George Clifton made an effort.

He drew himself up in the box and squared his shoulders. He looked about the court, and then suddenly his jaw dropped again.

At that moment he had caught sight of old Graves, the butler, staring at him from across the court.

He started to speak.

"I—I——"

He got no further, but suddenly he raised his hand, which was shaking like a leaf in the wind, and, pointing at Graves, cried in a hysterical voice:

"What are you doing here? What are you doing here?"

And with those words he pitched forward to the ground in a dead faint.

It was an amazing moment. People rushed to his assistance, there was confusion in court, and for some minutes it was quite impossible for anyone to make themselves heard.

They carried him outside, and then silence was ordered once again.

The chairman looked curiously at the lad in the dock.

"The question now is what to do with you?" he said.

At that moment a wild cheering broke out in the square without, and for a minute or so it was impossible to transact any further business in the court. In fact, it was not until the chairman had threatened to have the court cleared that he could make himself heard again—though it was difficult to see how he could have it cleared at all, for at that moment there was a wild mob fighting round the door for admission, all yelling like mad for Jack Morton.

At that moment a police-sergeant came hurrying into court, and as he was one of the people who had taken Clifton out when he had fainted, there was immediate silence.

"Mr. Clifton wants to withdraw the charge, sir!" he said.

"What——"

That was as far as the magistrate got, for now there was no holding the crowd. Men jumped over seats, sweeping the police on one side as they struggled and fought to get to Jack and shake him by the hand.

But the lad kept his head.

He was still a prisoner, and he wasn't so foolish as to try to leave the dock until he was told that he could go.

There was a consultation during the turmoil, and when something like order had been restored the chairman turned once again to the hero of Boltwich.

"Well, Morton," he said, "this has been a very strange morning, and not, I am afraid, a very creditable one for any of us. But as the charge has been withdrawn there is nothing for it but to discharge you!"

It was not very gracefully said. In fact, the chairman was not in a good temper at all. He was a friend of Clifton's; but, even more than that, he was a great believer in good order, and it made him furiously angry to see all this disorder in his native town, and, rightly or wrongly, he blamed Jack for it.

"Go on!" said the police-sergeant to Jack, as the lad still lingered in the dock; "you can go."

But Jack drew himself up proudly, and looked the chairman in the eye.

"I don't understand quite, sir," he said. "Do I leave here without a stain on my character?"

And while the chairman hesitated for one fraction of a moment, a mighty cheer went up in the court.

"Of course you do, boy! Good old Jack!"

That was answer enough for Jack. As a matter of fact, except for the chairman, he saw that he had the Bench with him; and so he turned, having bowed to the magistrates, and tried to get down into the court.

It was not too easily done. People were pressing about him, and for a few moments he felt himself absolutely lost in the midst of the press.

But suddenly a cheerful sound came to his ears.

"Come on, the Triers!"

Such a scene had never, of course, been seen in the court before, and probably will never be seen again. The Triers, arm-in-arm, soon cleared a path to him; and while the Chairman of the Bench shouted for order, and finally told his clerk that the sitting would be adjourned until the afternoon, they gathered round their pal and shook him heartily by the hand.

They were all there, and there were tears in Jack's eyes by the time he had shaken hands with them all.

Then they cleared a way again, and got him outside into the lobby of the Court House.

A pompous police-inspector came up to Ronnie, who was running the show.

"He'd better go out by the back entrance," he said.

"Why?"

The answer came in a moment.

"We want Jack Morton!"

It was shouted by thousands of voices, like the roll of thunder, and Ronnie smiled as he heard it.

"All right, old friend," he said to the inspector; "you go out by the back door yourself, if you like. We are going to take Jack out this way, and if you don't like it you can lump it. But you are rather foolish to stop us, if you can, because once we get him out into the square the crowd will soon clear off!"

The inspector evidently saw the sense of this, for he said no more, and did nothing to try and stop the Triers as they dragged their hero along towards the door of the Court House.

Suddenly in the square there was silence.

It was certainly one of the proudest moments in Jack's life, and although he felt that he had done little enough to call for all this, he would have been little short of human if he had not been intensely happy at the cheer that went up a few moments later, as the crowd saw who it was.

In a little while they were silent again, and Ronnie, waving his cap in the air, yelled:

"Acquitted, without a stain on his character!"

The air was rent with another terrific cheer, and then they started to call for a speech from Jack, and nothing would satisfy them until he had spoken.

He hated doing it.

In the first place, he felt that altogether too much of a fuss was being made of him, and in the second place he felt that it was scarcely his place—a youngster and a newcomer to the Boltwich team—to make public speeches.

But he had to do it, and so they lifted him on some stalwart shoulders, and he thanked them in a few simple words.

"It's very kind of you to take such an interest in me," he said. "Of course, I had nothing to do with the thing of which I was accused, and if I have deserved this kindness from you, I will try in the future to deserve it still more by scoring lots of goals in our games!"

How they cheered! It was not a long or a very brilliant speech, but it was what they wanted. And then came the question of getting Jack away.

Here the Triers came to his rescue again, and a few minutes later they had carried him down into the square, and, literally fighting a way through the mob, escorted him from the scene of his triumphs.

Another moment, and, by a clever ruse, Laurie Robson had managed to sneak him into his two-seater, and they were spinning away out of Boltwich for Robson's house.

They scarcely spoke until they reached the place and were safely inside Laurie's library.

Then Jack held out his hand.

"I've really got you to thank for this, Laurie," he said.

But young Robson shook his head.

"No, my lad. You have got yourself to thank, because you have always played the game. That is why you are out of the mess now. But did you ever see such a cur as that cousin of yours? He has not even the courage to carry out his own rascality to a successful conclusion!"

Laurie laughed as he spoke, but there was a serious light in his eyes.

"As a matter of fact," he continued, "it's rather a funny position. What about the will, Jack?"

Jack nodded.

"I meant to confront him with the whole thing in court!"

Laurie agreed.

"Yes, I know; and you told him about it; but I don't think that many people understood to what you were referring."

Jack shook his head.

"No. But he understood all right. That is why he fainted."

"And what now?"

Jack considered for a moment or two, puckering up his brow.

"Well, to tell you the truth, Laurie," he said, "I would rather go and see my old mother than anything else in the world; but I think I ought to finish this business first with Mr. George Clifton, for her sake as much as for anything else.

There is no telling what the fellow will get up to now that he is frightened!"

"You are right there," said Laurie. "He is frightened to death. We ought to get after him!"

As he spoke the telephone-bell rang, and he picked up the receiver.

"Yes?"

There was a pause, and as Jack watched he saw the look of surprise come to Laurie's face as he spoke through the transmitter.

"Yes, yes. All right. He's here with me now, inspector. All right. I'll see what he says. Hold on a minute!"

Laurie put down the receiver and turned to Jack.

"Jack, guess what has happened?"

"What?"

"Clifton went home, feeling pretty rotten. Some of the crowd saw him going, and now half Boltwich is outside the house, trying to break in, and declaring that they are going to have his blood.

George Clifton gave a hoarse cry as he found himself face to face with his cousin. "You!" he cried. "What are you doing here?" Like a flash Laurie sprang upon him.

That's the inspector. He says that he has not got enough police to deal with the situation, and he thinks that you ought to go along and try to quieten them."

Jack jumped to his feet.

"It means saving the skin of George Clifton!" said Laurie.

Jack answered with a nod and smile.

"After all," he said, "we are not cannibals, Laurie. Say I will come straight along!"

Laurie went to the telephone and gave Jack's message, and then turned back to his pal.

"I must say, Jack," he exclaimed, "that I don't think that I, personally, would move a hand to save a hound like that!"

Jack shook his head.

"Yes, you would, Laurie," he said. "you know perfectly well that you would!"

"Well, do you want me to run you over there, young fellow m'lad?"

Jack blushed.

"You are being very good to me, Laurie!"

"Shut up! Come along!"

So once again the two lads bundled into Laurie's two-seater, and were soon hurrying towards the home which should have been Jack's.

As they neared the place they heard the shouts and roars of anger which were going up from all round it, and when the car swung through the lodge gates and they could see the house itself, they were met with a really remarkable sight.

A sort of pitched battle was going on there in front of the fine old house between the mob, police, and Clifton's servants, and it was clear that the mob would soon get the upper hand.

Laurie laughed as he stopped the car some way from the fray, and tried to hide it behind some trees, in case the mob turned their kindly attentions to it.

"I should think you'll owe me a new car this time to-morrow, Jack," he smiled.

"All right," said Jack; "you shall have it!" They both ran forward.

The fight was getting along very nicely as they rushed upon the scene, but suddenly someone saw Jack Morton, and a shout went up, and it was really remarkable the effect that it had upon the townspeople.

Like magic the fight stopped. But the crowd was in a nasty mood, and Jack realised that it would take more than this to quieten them.

"Say, chaps," he cried, standing upon the steps which led up to the house, "this isn't the game! You are robbing me of a bit of sport!"

"What's up, Jack?" some of them cried. "We want to get at George Clifton!"

"I know you do. So do I!"

They roared at that.

"Look here, chaps! Give me a chance," he said. "I am going in now to have a few words with Clifton, and I am taking a few of these policemen along with me. You clear off, and leave him to me, and I promise you that you will all be satisfied at what I do with him!"

For a moment or two it did not look as though the crowd were going to listen to their young hero this time, but at last wiser counsels seemed to prevail, and perhaps the fact that a fresh lot of police were arriving, helped them to make up their minds.

"All right, Jack," one of their leaders said, "we will leave him to you. But give it to him good and strong!"

Jack laughed.

"You bet I will," he said. "You bet!"

They started to clear off, and a police inspector came hurrying up to thank Jack.

"Look here, inspector," the lad said, "I am going in to see Mr. Clifton——"

"But——"

"I am going in, and I want you to come with me, and make a note of all that is said. If you don't let me get in, or don't make them let me in, then I shall be forced much against my peace-loving nature to get those chaps back to help me get in to him!"

The inspector grinned. He happened to be a great football fan himself, and he was all with Jack.

"All right," he said, "I haven't got any objection to you going in, Jack. I only want to see this town settle down again. We are going to hear too much about this as it is. Come along with me. We'll see Mr. Clifton together!"

The Confession.

OLD GRAVES greeted them as they knocked at the front door, and let them in at once.

Laurie went in with Jack and the inspector and also a sergeant of police.

"Where is he?" asked Jack at once.

Graves grinned.

"He is in a terrible state. He has locked himself in the smoking-room. There used to be a story, sir, about a secret panel in one of the walls and he's been knocking round the walls for a long time. He's half mad with fear. Never knew such an exhibition in my life. You'd better be careful, sir, he's armed to the teeth!"

The inspector gave a grunt.

"Show me which room, Mr. Graves," he said.

"Yes."

They crossed the hall. Now that the shouting of the crowd had died away the hall was strangely quiet, and except for the whispering of excited and

frightened maid-servants who hung about and peered over the banisters, there was scarcely a sound as they reached the smoking-room.

Certainly the man within was being quiet for the time being. Perhaps it was that he, too, had heard the shouts of rage die down. At any rate, all was silent when the inspector of police knocked boldly on the thick door.

There was a moment's silence, and then there came a reply from within.

"Who's that?"

The inspector nodded to Graves.

"Tell him I am here!"

"Yes."

Graves went close to the door.

"It's the inspector, sir. He has cleared them off and now wants a word with you."

"Sure they have gone, Graves?"

"Yes, sir; sure."

Another moment passed, while George Clifton was obviously making up his mind within. Then he said:

"All right, I'll see you, inspector, but I have had about enough of this disgraceful business. I—I—I—"

He started to unlock the door. It was clear that it took an effort on his part, and that his hand was trembling.

But at last he threw the door open and stepped out, and then a hoarse cry came to his lips as he found himself face to face with his cousin.

"You!" he cried. "What are you doing here?"

He carried a revolver in his hand, and as he spoke he started to raise it, but like a flash Laurie had jumped forward and had knocked the weapon out of his hand.

The inspector bent down and picked it up.

"I'll keep this, sir," he said. "We don't want any accidents. And now that the mob has cleared off I dare say we shall be able to settle up any little difference we have between us without resource to this sort of thing, Mr. Clifton."

Clifton was deathly white again. Indeed, much as he hated him, Jack could not help at that moment feeling a little sorry for the fellow.

He looked an awful sight.

He was dishevelled, white, ill, and he was now trembling violently, but for all this he had resource in bombastic methods.

"I should like to know what this insult means?" he asked.

The inspector told him.

"Mr. Morton here has a charge to

make against you, Mr. Clifton, and he asked me to come in with him while he made it."

Clifton sneered.

"Am I bound to be insulted in my own house in this way?" he asked.

"No, sir," said the inspector. "You are not bound to listen to what Mr. Morton has to say. Personally, I think that you ought to be rather grateful to the young fellow, because if it had not been for his arrival five minutes ago, the crowd would certainly have got in, and I would not have answered for your life then, Mr. Clifton."

George Clifton bit his lip, but suddenly an idea came to him, and he gave a quick, inquiring glance at his cousin. There was just, perhaps, one flickering ray of hope for him. If he could get on the better side of young Morton he might still get away with it.

He looked long at Jack, as though trying to read what was in the youngster's mind, but Jack's face was like a mask. He had never looked half so calm, even when about to shoot one of his coolest goals.

"I'll speak to Morton alone," Clifton said in a moment, "if that is what he wants."

Jack laughed.

"It is not," he said.

"Eh?"

"I want all these gentlemen to hear everything that I have got to say to you, George Clifton," the youngster said, "especially Graves there. He has quite a lot to do with it."

Clifton grasped the situation in a flash. He realised that the business about the two wills had been given away, and he lost his head to the extent that, without in the least thinking what he was going to do if he got away, he suddenly dived through them, and tried to make a dash for his liberty.

Laurie Robson merely put out one foot, and the terrified fellow came hurtling to the ground.

Laurie stood over him, grinning, as he picked himself up.

"You know, Clifton," he said, "if you want to stand a dog's earthly, you had better hear what Morton has got to say. We are five to one, and we are not going to let you go. There has been too much dirty work going on, and I am going to see that you listen to Jack."

Jack went up to Clifton.

"Come on, my good cousin," he said, "let us get this over. I don't like it any more than you. We'll go in here. It will do as well as anywhere else."

He took Clifton by the arm, Laurie took him by the other, and so the strange group entered the smoking-room, from which Clifton had just emerged.

The door was then closed, and the police-sergeant stationed himself in front of it. Clifton was at bay.

And now he made a better showing than he had done before. He squared his shoulders, faced them all, and seemed to indicate that even if he knew he must sink, he was going down with a smile on his lips.

"What is it?" he said.

Jack turned to Graves.

"Graves, here, has a somewhat strange story to tell, Clifton, about a will."

"What?"

Graves came forward, but at the same moment the inspector held up his hand.

"This looks like developing into a pretty serious matter," he said. "I think that I had better take notes!"

He sat down at a desk and picked up a pen and paper, then he looked up at Graves seriously.

"Of course, Mr. Graves," he said, "I do not know what you are going to say. But you know, don't you, that you have no need to say anything which could possibly be used against you at any future time? This is in no way an official inquiry. We are merely here because we have been asked to stay by Mr. Morton."

Graves nodded.

"I understand all that, inspector," he said. "And I dare say that I shall get into serious trouble for what I am going to say; but it is gospel truth, and I am speaking out now because it is time that justice was done to this young man, Jack Morton—Jack Morton, who saved my daughter's life!"

"What?" cried Clifton.

Graves turned on the man.

"That is another story," he said; "and I will not waste time with it now. But it is more than you would ever have done for anyone, George Clifton!"

So the old fellow told his tale. He left nothing out; and as he came to an end—to the point where he had told George Clifton he had destroyed the second will—Clifton jumped forward and shook his fist in his face.

"It's a dirty lie!" he said. "And you shall go to prison for this, you dog! You cannot say this sort of thing with impunity, and I will teach you that you can't! My word is as good as yours; and you cannot prove a word that you have said!"

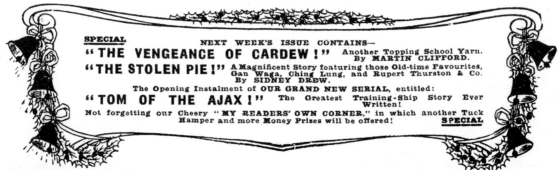
THE GEM LIBRARY.—No. 828.

Printed and published every Wednesday by the Proprietors, The Amalgamated Press (1922), Ltd., The Fleetway House, Farringdon Street, London, E.C.4. Advertisement offices: The Fleetway House, Farringdon Street, London, E.C.4. Registered for transmission by Canadian Magazine Post. Subscription rates: Inland and Abroad, 11s. per annum; 5s. 6d. for six months. Sole agents for South Africa: The Central News Agency, Ltd. Sole agents for Australia and New Zealand: Messrs. Gordon & Gotch, Ltd.; and for Canada, The Imperial News Co., Ltd. (Canada).—Saturday, December 22nd, 1923. **DN**

"I can!"

"How?"

"There is the second will," said Graves, and he took something from an inner pocket and handed it to the inspector. "You had better keep it, inspector. And what I have said is the truth, and nothing but the truth!"

A deadly silence followed his words. Both Jack and Laurie were staring at Clifton, wondering what he was going to do, what he was going to say. And suddenly they had the surprise of their lives.

He did just what they had not expected him to do.

"All right," he said. "I give in!"

"What?"

He turned to Jack.

"Morton," he said, "I am beaten! How are you going to treat me?"

Jack felt his heart swell within him. For a moment or so he did not know what to say. He just stood staring at the other rather helplessly; and then, to their fresh amazement, Clifton confessed everything.

"I admit the truth of what has been said," he told them. "I lost my head that night. After all, you must surely all agree that it was a terrible blow between the eyes, after I had been brought up all my life to consider that I was going to be my grandfather's sole heir, to be suddenly faced with the fact that I had been, as I considered it, rightly or wrongly, robbed of half my inheritance.

"The result of the matter was that I—I fell to the temptation of trying to do away with the second will. I imagined that Graves had done so, and—— Well, Morton, I put it to you like this. You will have to contest the first will. The whole thing is going to take time and money. And even if you get me put in prison, is it worth it? Won't you let bygones be bygones, and be satisfied if I sign a document to the effect that I am content with the second will, and that I personally know that it is the right document?"

They all looked at Jack.

It was a difficult moment, but the youngster dealt with it in his usually calm way.

"Sign such a document, and I will think matters over, Clifton."

"Right!"

Clifton rushed to the desk, and a moment later he had signed the document and had handed it to Jack.

The youngster took it and read it, and then he handed it to Laurie, whom he trusted more than he trusted himself in these matters.

"What about it, Laurie?" he asked.

Laurie screwed his eyeglass into his eye.

"It seems all right," he said. "But it seems rather a shame not to see the handcuffs on a beast like this!"

Here the inspector broke in.

"I'm not sure, sir," he said, "whether I could arrest this man at the moment. There would have to be a more formal charge made——"

Jack held up a hand.

"I'll think it over," he said. "But all I want to do now is to get back to my mother and let her know that everything is all right."

He turned to Clifton.

"You have done us all some pretty bad turns, George Clifton," he said. "If you want to have any mercy shown to you, you will keep very low and quiet during the next few days."

(To be concluded.)

A FEW SEASONABLE WORDS
TO MY READERS!

My Dear Chums,—It is a tip-top issue of the good old GEM which is in your hands to-day. My heartiest Christmas greeting to you all go with it. A Merry Christmas and a Happy New Year to everyone! May this jolly season bring along tons of happiness, with rare good luck to everybody in the coming year of 1924.

OUR CHRISTMAS NUMBER.

You will be pleased with the grand yarn of St. Jim's this week. It carries on the superb traditions of the old school, and does Mr. Martin Clifford immense credit. The author has surpassed himself. The story carries on the famous dingdong struggle between Tom Merry, the stalwart young skipper of St. Jim's, and Ralph Reckness Cardew, his sworn rival. This yarn will rank among the best ever printed.

" THE VENGEANCE OF CARDEW ! "
By Martin Clifford.

Now, what of next week's treat? The title tells a lot. Martin Clifford handles a big theme in masterly and trenchant style. Cardew has been swept along by a strong tide of personal ambition. He sees things at a wrong angle. It is often like that in the case of a fellow with a marked personality. Cardew has a tremendous belief in himself, and for some reason he has come to regard Tom Merry as an enemy. The two have often been pals. It is not so now. There is deadly rivalry, and you will be carried away by the grippiness of it all, and the thorough-going intensity with which Mr. Clifford has worked out his plot. Ernest Levison figures also very prominently in next week's story. You will come to like him better. What's more, your admiration for Tom Merry will be increased considerably. Feelings will be mixed as regards Cardew. Without a doubt, there will be plenty of argument amongst GEM

readers concerning next Wednesday's tale. It raises a whole heap of questions connected with St. Jim's, and the captaincy, likewise the strange contradictoriness of Cardew. I want you to make sure of your copy of the GEM next week. There is bound to be a rush. And just tell your chums about the wonderful yarn in store.

THE " HOLIDAY ANNUAL ! "

No better treat for a winter evening can be found than a copy of the "Holiday Annual." Let the icy blast blow as it may, and whistle round the house; you can forget all the discomforts of winter when you sink into a cosy chair

by a jolly fire and open the "Annual." The budget of stories it contains meets all tastes. Do you like school yarns best? The "Holiday Annual" gives them in plenty. Or, maybe, you are keen on adventure in the trackless wilds, or on romance. You will find such fiction in the prize book which is the best of all.

"THE STOLEN PIE!"
By Sidney Drew.

Our old favourite, Sidney Drew, will contribute a most seasonable story for next Wednesday's GEM. It introduces the amusing Eskimo, Gan Waga, and Rupert Thurston & Co. Sidney Drew is, so to speak, a Pasha of many tales, but in all his brilliant record I do not think he has ever turned out anything more humorous or out and out interesting than this splendid yarn of the pie which vanished.

"TOM OF THE AJAX!"
By Roland Spencer.

Mr. Spencer, the author of our magnificent new sea serial, is the writer of the "River-wise Ned" stories, which everybody liked. I cannot say enough for the dash and excitement which characterises the great nautical romance just starting. It has the real atmosphere of the sea. The author knows the briny well, and he describes the life of a training-ship in first-class style. The story starts with a bang, but there is still better stuff to come. Mention the matter to non-readers. They will thank you. It is a tip worth having, for there is real life in this romance of the deep, and thousands of my friends are casting longing eyes to a career on the water. You are plunged right into the thick of things, and you meet sundry characters who will be remembered for long. Look out for a certain adventurer of a novel type, a man who fears nothing in the world, and is always ready to face the worst danger.

ONE MORE WISH.

In bidding you farewell till next week, just let me repeat my wish that this season may be the jolliest ever. May Christmas be full of good cheer, and may there be lots of sunshine in the New Year, whose footstep we can hear at the door!

YOUR EDITOR.

My Readers' Own Corner

Tuck Hampers and Money Prizes Awarded for Interesting Paragraphs.

THE POSTMAN'S PONDERINGS !

Old lady (to postman): "Do you know, my good man, that during all the years you have been coming to this house I have wondered, as I have watched you making your daily rounds in the heat of summer and the rigours of winter, just what you are thinking about? You always seem to be philosophising as you plod along in silence, apparently buried in sober reflection and at peace with the world. Do you ever let your thoughts roam at will through that bag and play among its contents—missives wet with tears, messages of joy, tender words of love, shattered hopes, and high ambitions realised? Tell me, upon what do you ponder? What do you think of day after day, hour after hour, step after step?" Postman: "My poor feet."—A Tuck Hamper filled with delicious tuck has been awarded to Michael Adams, Reama, Climsland Road, Paignton, South Devon.

A QUAINT SENSE OF HUMOUR !

A costermonger met his friend the other day. The friend was convulsed with laughter, and it was some time before anything could be drawn from him. At last he explained the case of merriment. "You would have laughed! I've just been round to see old Bill 'Iggins. When I got there 'is 'ouse was all alight. 'E lives in one of them there tenement 'ouses—six floors. 'E's on the third flood. There 'e was dancin' about on the window-sill in his nightshirt. We 'ollers up to him: 'Jump, Bill! We've got a tarpaulin to catch ye!' But 'e 'adn't the pluck to jump. Instead, he runs up to the next floor, and there 'e dances about again. We shouts up to him to jump again. But, no, up 'e goes as the flames mount higher, until he gets to the roof. There 'e

is dancin' about as we 'ollers up again: 'Jump, Bill! We've got a tarpaulin to catch yer!' And he jumps." Here the story-teller was overcome with laughter, but at last managed to gurgle: "And the funny part about it was we 'adn't no tarpaulin!"—Half-a-crown has been awarded to Roy Hudson, 123, Fitzgerald Street, Bradford, Yorks.

LOCAL COLOUR !

"I want my photograph taken," said the man as he came into the studio. "Certainly, sir," said the knight of the camera, as he sat the victim down in a chair. "Would you like a carte or a cabinet?" The prospective customer glanced at a full-length picture of Wilson, the Wednesday International, and wriggled uneasily. "It doesn't matter much whether there's a cart or a cab in it," he said; "but if you can put a railway touch in it it'll be all right, 'cause I'm a guard."—Half-a-crown has been awarded to A. Yelland, 69, Broadfield Road, Sheffield.

A "TACKLESS" REPLY !

The old Scottish butcher noticed that one of his customers had not been visiting his shop lately, so he made up his mind to ask her the reason for her falling off when he next saw her. "Why do ye no' buy your meat off me noo?" he asked when he met her a few days later. "Weel," replied the old woman, "the last I got frae ye I could hae soled my buits wi' it." "And why did ye no', then?" asked the other sarcastically. "So I wud if I could hae got the tacks to go through it!" was the sharp reply.—Half-a-crown has been awarded to I. Macdougall, 21, Crawford Road, Edinburgh.

(If You Do Not Win a Prize This Week—You May Next !)

All Efforts in this Competition should be Addressed to: The GEM LIBRARY, "My Readers' Own Corner," Gough House Gough Square, London, E.C.4

TUCK HAMPER COUPON.

The GEM LIBRARY.

No attempt will be considered unless accompanied by one of these Coupons.

"TOM OF THE AJAX!"

Great New Training-ship Story Starts in This Issue!

EVERY WEDNESDAY.

THE GEM 2ᵈ

LIBRARY

SCHOOL and SPORTING STORIES

No. 829.
Vol. XXIV.
December 29th,
1923.

CARDEW'S VENGEANCE!

Returning from their ramble in the snow Wally & Co., of the Third Form, find Ernest Levison lying in the snow, the victim of a dastardly outrage. (A dramatic incident from the grand long complete story of Tom Merry & Co. contained in this issue.)

A FEW SEASONABLE WORDS TO MY READERS!

MY DEAR CHUMS,—A Happy and Prosperous New Year to you all! Of course, the start of a new year sets everyone thinking. There comes the question as to the headway that is being made. But the best thing about such a time is that there comes a bigger determination than ever to do better. I hope all my friends will discover that 1924 has heaps of the pleasantest surprises for them. And, talking of surprises, you will see crowds of these during the months ahead in the pages of the good old GEM.

"TOM MERRY'S FOE."
By Martin Clifford.

Next week's programme is immense. We get away with a rattling story of St. Jim's, in which the great feud between Tom Merry and Cardew is carried forward another stage. Cardew, like many another fellow placed in temporary authority, takes his position far too seriously. He has had a rough-and-tumble with Cutts of the Fifth at an earlier period of his career. The dramatic happenings related in next week's fine yarn go further. The part played by Tom Merry in a situation which has its tragic side is more than noteworthy.

NEW FEATURES.

The year of 1924 will be full of good things, and the GEM can be relied upon to come up smiling with a full share of brilliant novelties and happy notions making for enhanced popularity. I have been making arrangements for the grandest serials and most gripping complete stories on record. Just mention what the GEM is doing in this line to a non-reading pal. I shall take such genial recommendation as a kindly New Year offering from true chums.

NOTE THIS!

There will be a topping issue of the "St. Jim's News" next Wednesday. There have been grumbles because the amusing Supplement has of late been left out in the cold. It could not be helped. Next week's number is devoted to "Adventure." They know plenty about adventure at St. Jim's, and the scope of the subject will have generous justice done to it.

THAT REMINDS ME!

A moment ago I pointed out that there had been grousing because the Supplement had been given a miss. All that shows interest, and I should take it as a favour if you would let me have a line on a handy postcard to let me know just what special topic you would like to have handled in the "St. Jim's News." I shall try and oblige.

A CIGARETTE CARD CLUB.

Collecting cigarette cards is a hobby which never palls, and Jack Hall, 248, Stafford Road, Lichfield, Staffs, has met a real want by his Cigarette Card Club for the exchange of cigarette pictures. All those interested should write to him at the address given.

"GAN WAGA'S HUNTING."
By Sidney Drew.

Among the treats for the next number of the GEM you will find this thoroughly typical, rollicking, and sporting story of the amusing Eskimo. Many of Mr. Sidney Drew's most successful tales have been written round the rotund Northerner with his liking for blubber and his quaint mannerisms. You cannot afford to miss this great yarn, chums all. Next week. Dinna forget—as they put it north of the Tweed.

A TALE OF THE TALLANTYRE.

What is the Tallantyre? It is the name of a ship which figures prominently in the rousing new sea serial you will find in the "Boys' Friend." This magnificent romance is the work of David Goodwin, the celebrated author whose name is venerated by everybody. Mr. David Goodwin was too busy fighting in the North Sea as a naval officer during the war. This new story of his—by name, "Topsail Tony"—is his first since the Peace. It is the real goods.

A ST. JIM'S "WHO'S WHO"?

A reader at Pendlebury says it is high time we had a new "Who's Who?" for St. Jim's in the GEM, as lots of new characters have come in since the last was given. This suggestion is under consideration.

RIGHT ON THE SPOT.

A cheery word of encouragement reaches me from Chelmsford. "You seem to know exactly when to give us Mike McAndrews," says this correspondent. "Mike is welcome. As to school stories, these always retain their popularity, possibly because school life offers a greater range for originality." True enough. But there is more in it even than that. I shall have further to say about school yarns shortly.

"TOM OF THE AJAX!"

Tom Gale, the plucky young hero of our wonderful serial, goes through much trouble in next week's thrilling instalment. We see the brute, Stoniky Burr, in his true and most unpleasant colours. The yarn fairly swoops ahead.

THE TUCK HAMPER.

Naturally the splendid Tuck Hamper feature will remain a leading attraction during the New Year. Send in your brightest yarnlet. It is always wise to have a shot at winning something really worth while, and that description fits a Tuck Hamper like the proverbial glove.

YOUR EDITOR.

The Greatest Training-Ship Story Ever Written!

STARTS TO-DAY!

TOM of the AJAX

by ROLAND SPENCER

The Opening Instalment of a Powerful Yarn of the Sea.

CHAPTER 1.
The Bully of the Ajax!

CHIEF PETTY OFFICER Tom Gale chuckled.

"Well, of all the luck!" he said. "Hanged if this doesn't take the jumping biscuit!"

His chum—a cheery-looking, stocky youngster with bright red hair—grunted.

"I should say it does take the biscuit—and a whole shopful of buns as well! I was hoping they'd put you and me down as hares, Tom; and, instead of that, hanged if they've not put you and old Stoniky Burr together! That's a good one!"

The two youngsters in the smart blue uniform of the training-ship Ajax were looking at the green baize notice-board on the mess-deck. Several notices were pinned here. But the one on which their eyes were fixed announced the details of the cross-country hare-and-hounds that was to take place that afternoon.

And though Tom Gale laughed good-humouredly, his chum, Dicky West, was still grumbling as they turned towards the ladderway that led down to the orlop deck.

Not that that meant anything. Dicky West was as cheery a youngster as could be found in the starboard watch, but he always grumbled—it was just his way.

"Oh, chuck grousing," grinned Tom. "Stoniky Burr mayn't be the ideal companion for a run, but it'll be worth while just to see his face."

Stoniky Burr, also a chief petty officer of the starboard watch, though in another division, was commonly known on the training-ship among the youngsters as the bully of the Ajax—a title he had done everything to deserve. As chief petty officer of the Blake division, he had a good deal of opportunities for his favourite pastime—that of making things hot for boys smaller than himself. That was why he was known as "Stoniky."—stoniky being slang on board the Ajax for a rope's end, which was one of his favourite weapons when there was no ship's officer about. And Stoniky Burr and Tom Gale, who was of the Hood division, had had more than one little argument on the subject of bullying.

In consequence, Stoniky Burr hated Tom Gale, and Tom knew it. Tom was still chuckling as he descended into the orlop deck at the thought that he and his sworn enemy were to run together that afternoon as the two hares.

In that section of the orlop deck—the lowest deck in the ship, just above the stores—that was apportioned to the Hood division, a group of laughing, talking youngsters were already changing into their running togs.

"Seen who you're running with, Gale?" called one of the division.

Tom nodded and grinned.

"I should say so!" he said. "I'm just going along to break the glad news gently to old Stoniky."

The Blake division was some way down the deck, and together the two chums strolled towards it. Stoniky Burr was already changing, and he looked up with a scowl as Tom hailed him.

"What-ho, Stoniky! Seen the board?"

"Of course I have!" growled Stoniky. "Dashed bad luck for me, too, put in with a wet like you! Think you can last the run?" he sneered.

Tom smiled more broadly. Slim and athletic, he knew that he could outrun Stoniky, who, though a good long-distance man, was too big and heavy to touch the Hood youngster. And the sight of Tom's laughing face, with its fair hair and merry blue eyes, made Burr growl again as he turned away.

Already the orlop deck was a medley of voices as the youngsters of the various divisions—each named after a famous British admiral, and consisting of about thirty boys, with one chief petty officer and two petty officers—poured down from the upper decks to change into their running togs.

Tom returned, grinning, to the Hood division. Ever since he had been a "newjee" he had made friends, and now that he was a "mower," as an old hand is called aboard the training-ship, and had been promoted to the position of chief petty officer, he was one of the most popular youngsters of the starboard watch—or of the whole ship, for that matter. Like a great number of the training-ship boys, Tom had been a waif before he had been drafted from a charity school on to the Ajax, and knew nothing of his birth or parentage. He had been named Gale simply because he had been found in a gale of wind—a brain-wave on someone's part! His earliest recollection was of a crèche in the Walworth Road. Not that his origin worried him—he had grown so used to the idea of being alone in the world as far as relations were concerned.

The Ajax was moored on the southern bank of the River Thames, a quarter of a mile down the river from Fleethithe. She was a fine big vessel, built for the purpose, after the style of an old-time battleship, the "wooden walls of Old England," as they were called in Nelson's day. A fair stretch of water separated the training-ship from the stone causeway opposite, with its wooden jetty and hutments at the shore end.

"Now for it!" remarked Tom Gale a quarter of an hour later, as he and Stoniky Burr landed from the gig that had rowed them across to the jetty. "We've got to show a clean pair of heels, and no mistake!"

Without waiting an instant he led the way at a swift trot along the sea-wall that fronted the river at that part, his haversack of "scent" bobbing at his side. Stoniky followed, a sullen scowl still on his face. He was none too

THE GEM LIBRARY.—No. 829.

(Copyright in the United States of America.)

pleased at having Tom for a companion, and he did not mean to let Tom forget the fact.

A broad stretch of undulating country lay at their disposal, with plenty of cover. Before plunging down a winding, hedge-bordered lane that came down to the water just opposite the training-ship, Tom glanced back. Already, with a splash of oars and the water creaming from their bows, half a dozen cutters had put off from the Ajax in swift pursuit, lashing the water to foam with their oars in their efforts to minimise the lead that the hares had already got.

Pulling fiercely, the cutters came shooting up to the jetty, and the swarm of hounds scrambled out, some leaping on shore when the boats' noses were still more than a yard from the wooden staging. Dicky West, Tom's chum, was among the first to pour into the lane after those two white figures ahead, already swallowed up several minutes ago among the trees.

But already Tom Gale and the bully of the Ajax had sprinted through a gap in the hedge at the side of the road, and had cut across a short field to the cover of a wooded hill. Swiftly Tom laid a false trail towards the main road, then they doubled back and plunged down towards the second copse below them. The hares were well away!

Tom was a fine runner; it was chiefly through his powers in that direction that one of the many challenge cups and shields owned by the Hood division had been carried off in triumph. The Hoods considered themselves the crack division of the Ajax, and had some grounds for doing so.

Though sailors in the making, the boys of the Ajax were well up to the mark where land sports were concerned. They were as proficient at football and cricket and running as they were at their own pet sports of swimming and sailing. So, although it was a stiff course that the hounds had to follow in pursuit of Tom Gale and Burr, they raced over the uneven country in fine style. At the end of an hour the majority were still going as strongly as ever.

But where the two hares were concerned, one, at any rate, had bellows to mend. Stoniky Burr was finding the pace a bit too warm, for he was out of condition, largely due to the "drags" he was partial to when a chance came. Drags—or fags, as a land youngster would call them—were rather a hobby of Burr's.

"Come on, for the love of Mike!" urged Tom good-humouredly, when he found that Burr was beginning to lag.

They had come round in a huge semicircle, so that now they were back near the river once more. Beyond a line of trees they could see the broad waters of the Thames ebbing swiftly to the sea. The sun played on the water and on the brown sails of the barges that were driving seawards before a good capful of wind; but, though it was a fine sight, Tom and Burr were too busy just then to pause and admire the view.

"I can't come on any quicker, blow you!" snarled Burr.

Tom said nothing; but ran on, slowing his pace slightly to suit Burr's lagging steps.

They were running along a rough valley studded with bushes, but without sufficient cover to hide them if the hounds should appear on the higher ground behind them, as they might do at any moment. They had risked the open stretch in order to gain the thick

cover beyond, where the ground was broken into craggy hillocks and dips that would be a fine place for throwing the hounds off the scent again. But if Burr was going to give in before that cover was reached——

Tom glanced round. A swift exclamation escaped him, and he gripped Burr's arm.

"Look! There they are!"

A scattered group of white figures had appeared on the hill behind them, running steadily in pursuit. So far, it seemed to Tom, they had not been seen. But there were still a couple of hundred yards or more for the hares to cross before they again reached cover, and unless luck were with them they would be spotted at any moment now.

"Get a move on!" cried Tom. "Can't you sprint this last bit?"

Burr couldn't—or wouldn't. And a far-off shout told the two youngsters that the hounds had seen them. There were some strong runners on their track—already they were near enough for Tom to distinguish the flaming red hair of Dicky West for one—and now that the hounds were no longer hampered by having to look out for scent it was touch-and-go with Tom and Burr.

Again Tom urged on his companion. A snarl was his only answer. Burr was in a bad temper, and his face showed it.

But at last they plunged in among the gullies ahead, though the hounds were pouring after them in a long line, with the leading man scarcely five hundred yards behind. Something had to be done, and done quickly.

"We've got to throw 'em off the track; we're dished otherwise as sure as eggs!" panted Tom. "There's just time—only just! I'll lay a false scent down this gully here, you lay another into those trees! Then double back here like mad, and we'll get away round to the left."

It was the best scheme under the circumstances, and Burr knew it. But he snarled:

"Who do you think you are—giving orders? Just because you're a chief petty officer now, you needn't stick on side, hang you! I'm a chief P. O., too, so—"

Tom ground his teeth, and his strong, determined mouth closed tightly. His eyes met Burr's, and he read there the sullen bad temper of his companion. With a shrug, Tom swung on his heel.

"Right-ho!" he said shortly. "If you can't play the game, I suppose you can't! I'm laying a false trail here, though, and you can do as you like!"

Burr's eyes were alight with an ugly gleam. All his old hatred of Tom was coming to the surface. But he said nothing, and Tom got on with the job on hand. Returning to Burr, he raced off without a word by the bully's side.

The gully they had taken opened out into a damp, marshy stretch by the side of a narrow creek, called the Fleet, that ran down to the river, emptying its muddy waters into the mother stream near the Ajax. A couple of planks spanned it at this narrow part, where the sluice and dam gates were, and together they raced on to them. Cover in plenty—trees and rising ground—lay on the farther side, and so far their pursuers were not in sight again. Hope revived in Tom. Perhaps they could get back to the jetty, after all!

His feet padded softly on the plank bridge, scarcely three feet wide. Burr's laboured breathing sounded in his ear, and at that moment a sudden impulse seized the bully of the Ajax.

To Tom it was all so sudden and unexpected that he had no chance of

keeping his balance. Burr lurched heavily into him. The next instant, with fingers clutching the air, and a startled exclamation breaking from him, Chief Petty Officer Tom Gale of the Hoods had gone crashing into the dark water of the creek with a mighty splash!

Chapter 2.
The Man with Green Spectacles!

BURR stood on the narrow plank bridge looking down at Tom, with a queer gleam in his little eyes.

For the moment he seemed almost frightened at the success of his caddish act. Then he saw Tom rise to the surface and spit out the dirty water as he struck strongly for the bank.

But the banks above the dam were high and slippery with thick, black mud. Burr offered Tom no help, but stood watching savagely as the other tried to scramble up. His lips were curled in a sneer, his hands clenched.

But at last, covered with mud, his clothes running with water, Tom managed to gain the top of the bank. Then only did Burr step back off the planks, as if in sudden alarm. But if he had expected Tom to go for him there and then he was mistaken.

Tom's first natural impulse had been to do so. But, though he was burning with rage, he was first and foremost a sportsman. He had others to consider just then, and he did not mean to let his own feelings stand in the way of the enjoyment of the others, the hounds. His voice was quite quiet—dangerously quiet—as he said curtly:

"Stoniky, you're about as low a cad as I've had the bad luck to run across. But I'm not going to muck up this run because of you. We've got the other chaps to think of. But when we're back aboard the Ajax I'll give you about the soundest thrashing you've ever had! See?"

Already Tom could hear the distant shouts of their pursuers as the hounds came across the false scent. Tom, without another word, turned to run on. But Stoniky Burr stood his ground.

"I always knew you were a coward, Gale," he sneered. "Afraid to fight, eh? Well, I'm not surprised."

Tom came to a standstill. His eyes and cheeks were burning, his fists clenched. He longed at that moment, above all things, to throw down the bag of scent—dripping water like a sponge now—and go for Burr. But still he kept control of himself.

"Don't talk like a fool!" he said, coolly enough. "You know that's a codge up—just a rotten lie. I'll have you out right enough when we get back, but now we've got to play the game by the others."

He was standing close to Burr, whose face was thrust forward aggressively. The contemptuous look on Tom's face stung the bully beyond endurance. The next instant Stoniky Burr had lifted a clenched fist and driven it straight between Tom's eyes.

The youngster staggered back, blinded. He heard Burr's harsh laugh, and then Tom saw red. He had controlled himself to the limit, human nature could stand no more. Forgetting everything for the moment, he flung off his haversack of scent and raised his fists, in spite of the mists that were still swimming before his eyes as a result of that cowardly blow.

"Put 'em up!" he cried between clenched teeth.

Burr put up his fists readily enough. An inch taller than Tom, and longer in the reach, with muscles that could find no match on board the training-ship, the bully had no doubts as to his ability to lick the Hood fellow. He advanced threateningly, and in a moment the two were at it hammer and tongs.

But Tom, slim of build though he was, had muscles of steel. He had a far quicker brain than Burr, and was more nimble. He fought with his head and feet as much as with his fists, and this time Burr found in a very short time that he had met his match.

It was an unpleasant surprise to Stoniky Burr when he felt Tom's fist, hard as iron, crash into his ribs, driving him back. The next instant Tom had followed up with a straight left to the chin that sent Burr reeling.

With a cry of rage Burr flung himself forward. He got to his opponent's chest, but he could not reach Tom's face. Try as he might, Burr always found Tom's head jerked aside in just the right fraction of a second, and his blows, for the most part, fell on air.

Tom was smiling as he fought—a smile that his chum Dicky West knew of old as a danger signal. When Tom Gale wore his fighting smile it meant trouble hot and strong for someone, and in this case it was Burr who learnt that painful lesson.

Again Tom's fist crashed into the other's ribs, and Burr's answering blow struck air as the Hood fellow stepped aside like a streak of light. Again and again. Burr panted for breath, his guard running wild. And then Tom put all his lithe strength into a straight left that smashed home on Burr's mouth. Burr tottered where he stood, and then fell with a crash, just as the foremost of the hounds came running into sight at the end of the gully.

Burr lay where he had fallen. He had learnt his lesson—a lesson richly deserved if ever one was. But black rage filled his heart, hatred deep and bitter for the youngster who now stood looking down upon him with relaxed fists. Tom knew that he had ended the fight with that final flashing blow.

There was a shout of amazement from the leading hounds as they came racing over the bridge. The hares were caught right enough, and Tom felt sick that a fine run had been ruined in such a way. He turned away with tight lips, and at that moment Dicky West came panting up.

"What the policeman!" panted Dick in amazement. He scratched his red head in perplexity as he stared at Burr, now struggling slowly to his feet. "What's happened, Tom?"

Tom sucked his hand where the skin had been cut by Burr's teeth.

"We've had a scrap, that's all, Dicky."

Dicky grinned.

"You don't say so, old son! Shouldn't have thought it," he said with deep sarcasm. Then he chuckled. "Seems to me you've given Burr a jolly good licking, too! Jove, isn't his face a treat? This is first-rate! But what's it all about?"

Briefly Tom explained. The others were crowding up now as the stragglers came in by twos and threes. It was obvious that everyone was glad to see that Burr had taken a good licking, and that fact did not escape the bully of the Ajax. He stood apart, sullen and savage, and wiped his crimson mouth.

There was a sudden scream of terror, and the next instant a dark figure was hurtling downwards. Stoniky Burr was crashing down to the very fate he had meant for Tom Gale!

A dozen questions were showered upon Tom, but he was in no mood to answer them. Together with Dicky West, he set off at a jog trot in an attempt to warm himself, for the air was cutting coldly through his soaking clothes. Tom did not mean to get laid up in the sanatorium with a bad chill on account of Stoniky Burr.

The others followed. About sixty youngsters had taken part in the run, and not one of those sixty stayed with the unpopular chief petty officer of the Blakes. He was left alone to attend to his battered features, his eyes dark and brooding.

"I hate him! I'll get my own back on Gale!" he muttered savagely to himself, as his eyes followed the retreating figures.

And then suddenly he swung round with a start as he heard footsteps on the grass behind him. A swift exclamation escaped Stoniky Burr.

A man had appeared from the bushes behind him, a tall, lean figure with pointed black beard and dark, sallow features. A high forehead showing beneath the black felt hat made the face appear peculiarly long and thin. But what caused Burr's exclamation of startled amazement was the strange appearance of the man, caused by a pair of spectacles, worn evidently as a protection to the eyes—spectacles dark green in colour, that glistened in the sunlight like cat's eyes.

As if instinctively, Burr started back. There was something queer and sinister in the man's appearance—this man, who had appeared as if from nowhere with noiseless, cat-like footsteps. Those queer green circles of glass stared down at Burr like blind eyes.

"Who was that boy—the boy you fought with?"

The voice was cold and harsh, with a slight accent that was un-English. For a moment Burr did not reply. Then he muttered:

"That? Oh, his name's Gale. I—I——"

"Gale—they call him, do they?" White teeth gleamed as a sudden strange smile appeared on the man's face. "Gale! And you do not like this boy Gale?"

The tall figure stood there watching Burr keenly with his unseen eyes. Again the sunlight caught the glass of his spectacles, and they seemed suddenly like flames of green fire.

There was something repelling about that sinister figure, but at the man's words Burr forgot everything but the

hatred that was burning within him. Again he dabbed at his bleeding lips.

"Not like Gale?" echoed Burr, and his voice was like a snarl. "I—I hate him!"

Again the man smiled, a smile hard and cold as his voice. He glanced round. There was no one in sight. The last of the runners had disappeared among the distant trees.

"Then let me introduce myself," he purred softly. "My name is Kalche, and I do not like him, either. We should be friends, eh?"

There was something in that soft voice that caused Burr to step back a pace. The man in green spectacles bent forward, a sallow hand held out towards Burr. The long, sinewy neck was outstretched like a vulture's, and again the lips curled back in that smile that was colder than ice.

As if half-hypnotised, Burr held out his hand almost against his will. Those long fingers grasped it. Then the man who called himself Kalche nodded.

"We should be friends!" he repeated. "Good friends! Your name? Burr? Good! I have something I would say to you, Burr, my young friend!"

And Tom Gale, running on with Dicky West towards the Ajax, little dreamed of the amazing, far-reaching results that were to come from that queer paper-chase—little dreamed that even now the weaving of the web had begun—that web that was soon to ensnare him in its cruel, relentless clutch.

CHAPTER 3.
At the Yardarm Tip.

THERE was lively discussion on the mess-deck of the Ajax that afternoon when the youngsters gathered there for tea.

At the Hood tables, Tom, under pressure, was recounting his story of the run. Burr had returned to the ship rather late, but had escaped questions by the officer of the watch. He sat at his own table, scowling and friendless, but for a crony of his named Hemming—a lanky, ferret-faced fellow, who toadied up to Burr. Otherwise, even in the Blake division,

Burr received no honour, chief petty officer though he was.

Dicky West was elaborating Tom's account of the fight, his red head bobbing from side to side in his excitement as he talked. There was much laughter at the Hood tables, and turning of heads to stare at Stoniky Burr.

An under-sized and over-daring boy named Pole at Tom's table shouted for attention, then cried in a voice loud enough for Burr and his companions to hear:

"Say, I reckon Stoniky didn't do so bad out of the business. He must have found a purse, or a quid note, or something. I saw him when he came aboard and his pockets were bulging with tuck. When he was changing from his running-togs, I saw him slip a couple of boxes of drags into his trousers, too!"

Burr looked over at these words with a deeper scowl than ever, and Pole's neighbour at the mess-table kicked the youngster on the shin.

"Shut up, you crow! You're lappin' out for a touch o' the stoniky!"

But Pole only laughed, and shouted:

"I'll watch it! Stoniky can have me out, if he likes. But I reckon we ought to 'ave an unofficial tosh out wi' Stoniky!"

This remark brought forth yells of approval from the boys of all tables. "Tosh out" is training-ship slang for turning out one's pockets and lockers, and Stoniky Burr rose in some alarm.

"You let me alone!" he roared, glaring round. There was a queer look in his eyes as he stammered: "What if I did find half a quid? There's them as can't see further'n their noses, and you mokes must have passed it yourselves on the way back to the jetty. Here you are, anyway. I'll tosh out right enough."

Burr dived his hand defiantly into his pocket and produced a few articles that brought exclamations of astonishment and envy from the staring boys.

"A watch! Oh crumbs, we've a jumping millionaire aboard!"

"Three slabs o' toffee!"

"And bars o' milk chocolate!"

Such a wealth of property had never before been enjoyed by a boy on the Ajax within the memory of any present on the mess-deck. The boys gaped with surprise, and many envied Burr his luck in having found a ten-shilling note—for no one doubted the bully's words, that he had found the money on his way back to the training-ship after the fight with Tom. How else could Stoniky have become the sudden possessor of that wealth of chocolates, toffee, and forbidden cigarettes—his own speciality—not to mention a real watch that was ticking quite healthily?

Before darkness closed in the training-ship boys were allowed the run of the upper deck and the rigging. The Ajax was jury-rigged as a barquentine—that is, she had three masts with yards on the foremost mast. The boys of the Ajax thought nothing of shinning up the rat-lines to the tops, and some of the more daring worked their way out on to the yards and stood up at the yardarm, with a hand grasping the "lift," as the rope there is called.

Tom and Dicky West were among the first to make a charge at the shrouds of the foremast. Laughing and shouting to each other, they swarmed up to the fore-top, thirty feet above the deck below, and nearly seventy from the surface of the water. There they paused, panting and joking, watching the stream of youngsters following them up the rigging.

"I'll race you out to the yardarm,

Tom!" cried Dicky West, before the other boys had mounted to the futtock-rigging under the platform, or "top," on which the pair were standing. "You take the starboard, and I'll take the port!"

"Right-ho! I'll give the word. Ready?"

Both got their feet on the footrope under the sling of the yard, their stomachs pressing on the great round spar itself, and, arms extended, ready to work their way along to the outermost tip.

"Ay, ay, I'm ready!" replied Dick.

Tom gave the word, and the footropes swayed and jerked as the two daring youngsters wriggled along the yard, a dizzy height above the water. Each was so intent on the race that neither noticed that the first boy to reach the foretop after them was Stoniky Burr.

For a moment the bully of the Ajax glanced down furtively. There was a queer gleam in his eyes as the heavily built, broad-shouldered figure at once began to work his way out along the yard, out to starboard, following Tom Gale.

"Come on, fellows!" roared Stoniky suddenly; "as many on the yard as we can get! Every other chap to starboard! follow me, Hemming!"

Tom was still too intent to notice what was happening. And when he reached the yardarm tip and turned to see how Dicky West was getting on, he was rather taken aback to see the sneering, unpleasant face of Burr not far behind. The others, with much laughter and shouting, were still working their way out along the footropes. However, it was no new game, this crowding out on the yard, so Tom thought little of it. He rose to his full height, hand on the lift, to find that Dick was just completing his passage along the third quarter of the yard, and had not yet reached the part known as the yardarm.

"Licked you, Dicky!" he shouted.

Boys were crowding along the port side of the yard, in the wake of Dick, and by the time Tom's chum had risen to an upright position, like Tom, the spar was thick with boys from the sling outwards, clinging like flies at what would seem to a landsman a terrifying height.

Tom looked round, and his eyes met Burr's. And there was something in those eyes that Tom did not like.

Burr had worked his way close to Tom, and though the young leader of the Hoods was not afraid of Stoniky, he felt that he would be more comfortable lying across the yard than standing with his toes on the spar and his hand on the lift. So he lightly lowered himself on to his stomach and groped about with his heels for the footrope.

There was an ugly grin on Burr's face now. He edged nearer.

"Closer, boys!" he yelled. "Git another two on to the yard! See if we can get more on our side than them on the port!"

The boys on the port side took up the challenge, and there was much good-natured shouting and chaff as they shuffled still closer towards the yardarm tip. Tom felt Burr crushing close against him, and the press behind the bully forced the young chief petty officer of the Hoods right out on the yardarm tip, where there was no grip on the footrope, and where the yard itself had thinned down to about six inches in diameter.

"What's the game, Burr?" said Tom angrily. "Shove back—you'll have me off!"

Tom Gale uttered a sudden cry and staggered back as the stem of a huge, red-rusty steamer came crashing through into the deck of the Ajax!

Tom was clinging to the yard with both hands, his feet sliding inwards on the footrope. Burr, perfectly safe himself, chuckled.

"Got the wind up?" he jeered. "You're no better'n a 'sos,' Gale! Frightened because you're the outermost on the yardarm! Yah!"

As he spoke, Burr gave a furtive hack at Tom's ankle with his boot. Tom's lips were tight. It was impossible for him to retaliate. All his efforts were needed for clinging on.

Training-ship boys are well used to being reliant on a slender spar at dizzy heights above the water. But a sudden instinct warned Tom that Burr meant mischief.

He drew a sharp breath. Could it be possible? Was Burr actually trying to make him fall? Tom glanced down at the curdling, muddy water far below him; and then his eyes met Burr's again. He read there something that made even the plucky youngster that Tom was go suddenly cold.

Again Burr hacked furtively at Tom's shin, and the youngster on the yardarm tip winced with pain.

There was only one thing to be done, terrible though the risk was. Swift as light, Tom let go his hold with one hand and gripped Burr's shoulder like a vice.

"Hang you, Burr!" gritted out the young officer of the Hoods. "If you make him fall off the yardarm, you'll come, too!"

Burr laughed harshly, though a sudden look of fear had leapt into his eyes. Savagely he tried to fling off Tom's hand. Interlocked, the two swayed together in a desperate trial of strength.

And then a sudden scream of terror cut the keen upper air like a knife. There was a wild scraping of finger-nails on the polished paintwork of the yard, worn smooth with use. The next instant a dark figure was hurtling downwards, hands clutching wildly in the empty air.

But it was not Tom Gale. The bully of the Ajax was crashing down to the very fate he had meant for his enemy!

**CHAPTER 4.
Disaster!**

TOM hung from the footrope, which he had caught, like a spider from its thread, horrified, as he saw Burr disappear below. The youngster twisted his head downwards and followed the lightning-like descent of the heavily built bully.

The hurtling form struck the edge of the life-net. Then, with another shriek that froze the blood in the veins of the watchers, Burr was flung off the edge of the net. By a hairbreadth he escaped smashing on the high rail of the bulwarks of the ship, to fall into the water with a terrible splash.

Tom Gale, by a gigantic effort that nearly sent him after Burr, hauled himself to safety. He lay on the yard, scarcely breathing, his face as white as paper, waiting for Burr's head to reappear on the surface.

Already the officer of the watch was bawling to the boys on boat duty in the jollyboat that had been plying between the ship and the causeway. The shouting orders had just died away when Burr appeared, a tiny spot on the dark water, it seemed to Tom from his great height. Then a gasp of horror came up from those who crowded the bulwarks. Burr was unconscious, and the ebb-tide was carrying him swiftly away from the Ajax. It looked as though he must drown inevitably before help could reach him.

Tom saw Burr sink again. And then a desperate scheme flashed into Tom's brain.

Swiftly his eyes measured the intervening distance. Never before had the height from the yardarm tip to the water seemed so great to Tom Gale. But already his mind was made up, and, without waiting another instant, he drew himself up with lithe agility till he was standing on the yard.

Dicky West, as though reading Tom's daring purpose, gave a wild shout from the port side of the yardarm. Tom stood there like a statue, white and motionless, and all eyes were turned in his direction. A gasp of wondering amazement came from the startled lips of those watching. The youngster was standing on the six-inches' thick yardarm tip without holding the lift!

Vaguely Tom heard the shouting die away as a terrible hush seized those on board the Ajax. He stood there, perfectly balanced, his eyes on the water. And slowly his hands went up above his head.

From somewhere on the deck far below an inarticulate cry rang out from someone, and was choked back. Dicky

West seemed frozen to the other end of the yard, his face as white as chalk. The red-headed youngster saw Tom shoot suddenly forward, his arms poised—then curve downwards in the most perfect swallow dive that any aboard the Ajax had ever witnessed.

The curdling water seemed to rush up towards the plucky young leader of the Hoods. Tom just had time to wonder how he would meet the uninviting depths, when the crash came. The water sang about his ears, his head seemed to have burst open. His senses reeled—And then Tom found himself striking out mechanically for the surface, heard the wild cheer that went up as he took a life-giving breath of pure, sweet air.

He was conscious that his head was aching horribly. Then, bending his head to his own particular, powerful side-stroke, Tom struck out for where he knew Stoniky Burr would again reappear for the last time.

Tom saw him, but he was four yards ahead. The young leader of the Hoods changed to a rapid over-arm stroke, but he swam right over the spot where Burr had been. However, Tom grasped at a last chance. He dived, and went full tilt into a soft form below the water. He gripped hard and kicked out with his legs towards the surface.

It seemed to Tom an age before he felt the wind cold on his face. But after a long, gasping breath the lad got a firmer hold of Burr's collar, and drew the bully's head above the surface. Then he trod water, supporting Burr the while. His strength was almost exhausted. Could he hang on till help came?

Again his senses reeled; a mist came before his eyes—and then out of the mist the jollyboat came leaping towards them.

Tom drew a deep breath. Just in time!

. . . . .

"But how on earth did Stoniky come to fall off the yard?" asked Dicky West. "Hang it all, it's not as though he's a newjee!"

It was late that night. Tom and Dick were lying in their hammocks on the orlop deck. Tom, like Burr, had soon pulled round after his terrible ordeal, though his head was still aching a little.

Burr was also lying wakeful in his hammock in the Blake division. He was thinking of all that had passed between him and the man named Kalche that afternoon, and of Tom Gale. He felt no gratitude to Tom for having saved his life. When the Hood youngster had spoken to him after the accident—that accident that had so nearly ended in tragedy—he had simply snarled, and turned away.

Dicky West, his hammock slung next to Tom's, repeated his question in a low voice. For a moment Tom lay staring before him in the darkness. Then, the snores around them convincing him that the rest of the Hood division were sleeping, he answered in a low tone:

"Dicky, no one saw it, luckily for Burr; but he meant to have had me off that yard! Only he fell himself! I can't understand it, Dick. I know he hates me, but not enough to want to kill me, I feel convinced. I've been wondering about it; there's something fishy afoot. I don't see how there can be any connection between the two things, but how is it Burr has got all this boodle to chuck about?"

"Says he found half-a-quid," answered Dick, in the same low tone.

"Yes; he says so. That doesn't mean it's true—not from Stoniky!" Tom broke off, to add slowly: "I wish I knew what it all meant. Of course, as I say, I know he was down on me; but when it comes to downright attempted murder, Dick—and that's what it was, right enough—there's no other name for it! I can't doubt it, after seeing his face up on that yard when he was edging me out on to the tip! But why—why? Why should the navy-neck want to do for me?"

Dicky shook his head in the darkness, yawning sleepily.

"Ask me another, Tom! Why? Not just because you licked him. It beats me, and I'm too tired to think, so g'-night!"

Dicky dropped off to sleep first, then Tom, and, down in the Blake division, Burr fell asleep. But if they considered the events of that adventurous four-and-twenty hours at an end, they were sadly mistaken. Had they known it, a creeping, blanketing, thick London fog was crawling silently from the south-west to take the river and its numerous throbbing hearts of shipping in its dreaded grip.

Soon the sirens of the steamers were hooting their melancholy notes, muffled by the thick atmosphere. The last of the outward-bounders from up-river were coming down on the falling ebb tide. The roar of anchor cables was heard from here and there, as ships brought up to wait for the weather to clear.

The officer of the watch, stumping about near the gangway, while the ship's searchlight bit into the ever-thickening fog, shivered, and buttoned his coat more closely round him.

"There'll be a ship or two take the mud on the Ness to-night, maybe," he said to himself, as he listened to the sirens, shouts, and other sounds from the thick mists towards the west.

The double-flash of the Ness light was shining very dimly in the murk, and at last the fog got so thick that even that became invisible. The searchlight of the Ajax would pierce no more than fifty yards of fog.

Sensing the danger from downward-bound craft, the officer of the watch passed over to the starboard side of the training-ship. He stood there, peering into the white blanket of fog, and at last cocked his ear alertly as the booming notes of a big steamer came to his ears. He could hear the throb of the ship's engines. She was forging ahead a bit so that her great bulk could withstand the kick of the tide from the bend in the river just above the Ajax.

"The fools!" muttered the officer of the watch. "Why don't they come to anchor till it clears, and they can see a thing or two?"

Meanwhile, the sleeping youngsters on the orlop deck were in blissful ignorance of the change in the weather. Dicky West was sleeping the untroubled sleep of a clear conscience, Tom Gale was a trifle restless, probably dreaming of falls from yardarms on to broad iron bulwark rails, while Stoniky Burr was snoring in his own sweet way.

But suddenly the sound of the tide swirling against the side of the ship on that low deck changed its note. A big hump of water struck it with a splash. Then there was an alarmed shout above, that broke the muffled silence of the Ajax like a knife.

Started into abrupt wakefulness, Tom Gale heard an order shrieked through a megaphone, heard the clatter of sea-boots on iron decks. And then, above it all, there came a rending crash, and the Ajax quivered from stem to stern.

Tom was flung violently from his hammock. He scrambled to his feet, to find the arms of Dicky West round him, clutching frantically in the darkness. A cold draught of air whipped across the boys' faces. Then the electric lights suddenly blazed forth, bathing the orlop deck in the brilliant glare.

The next instant Tom uttered a startled cry, and staggered back. Scarcely a yard from where he stood, a jagged hole had appeared in the ship's plates, torn like paper by the stem of a huge, red-rusty steamer that was crashing through with its giant strength into the orlop deck of the Ajax!

———

(The interesting chapters of this splendid new serial, which will appear in next week's issue of "The Gem" Library, tell you more about the mysterious, sinister man with the green spectacles. This man, who plays such an amazing part in Tom Gale's life, has his knife in the lad. Why? That is a question that will be answered for you if you Order your "Gem" NOW!)

For Next Week.

"TOM MERRY'S FOE!"
A topping yarn of St. Jim's, by Martin Clifford.
Another thrilling instalment of our Grand New Serial.

"TOM OF THE 'AJAX'!"
An Extra Splendid Edition of the "St. Jim's News."

"GAN WAGA'S HUNTING!"
An amusing story of Gan Waga, the Eskimo, and Rupert Thurston & Co.

And further awards of a Tuck Hamper and Money Prizes in "MY READERS' OWN CORNER."

THE VENGEANCE OF CARDEW

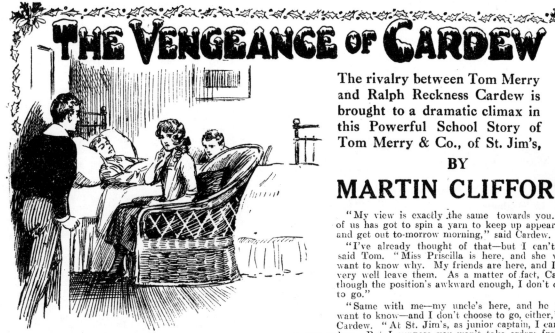

The rivalry between Tom Merry
and Ralph Reckness Cardew is
brought to a dramatic climax in
this Powerful School Story of
Tom Merry & Co., of St. Jim's,

BY

MARTIN CLIFFORD.

"My view is exactly the same towards you. One
of us has got to spin a yarn to keep up appearances,
and get out to-morrow morning," said Cardew.

"I've already thought of that—but I can't go,"
said Tom. "Miss Priscilla is here, and she would
want to know why. My friends are here, and I can't
very well leave them. As a matter of fact, Cardew,
though the position's awkward enough, I don't choose
to go."

"Same with me—my uncle's here, and he would
want to know—and I don't choose to go, either," said
Cardew. "At St. Jim's, as junior captain, I can give
you orders. But I suppose you won't take orders from me
here?"

"Hardly," said Tom, laughing.

"Well, we've got to settle it, here and now," said Cardew.
"That's why I've come to speak to you."

Tom Merry turned to the glass again, and proceeded with
his tie. There was a contempt in his manner that brought
a gleam to the eyes of Ralph Reckness Cardew.

"I've got a sportin' proposition to make," continued
Cardew. "The situation's too awkward to last—and neither
of us chooses to go, and leave the enemy in possession of the
field. I'm willin' to toss up for it."

"What?" ejaculated Tom.

"Heads you go, tails I go," said Cardew. "Here's a
half-crown. Are you agreeable?"

Tom shook his head.

"You refuse?"

"Yes."

"It's a fair offer," said Cardew.

"I dare say it is, in its way," said Tom. "But I can't leave
Eastwood House now, and I'm not going to. There was no
need for us to have any trouble here, if you'd chosen to
keep the peace. I wanted to keep it, and I want to keep it
now."

"You should have thought of that before you laid hands
on me last evening," said Cardew.

Tom coloured a little.

"I lost my temper—and I'm sorry I did," he answered.
"But you fairly drove me into it, Cardew. You've played
rotten trickery on me ever since we've been here, and last
evening you bagged my dance with cousin Ethel by a sneaking trick. You couldn't expect a fellow to put up with that
kind of thing for ever."

Having finished his tie to his satisfaction, Tom Merry put
on his dinner-jacket. Cardew stood with his back to the
door, watching him, his eyes gleaming.

"I'm givin' you a chance," he said. "We can't fight in
Lord Eastwood's house. It would be fairly bad form to turn
up at Christmas dinner with a black eye apiece."

"Well, rather," agreed Tom.

"But I hardly suppose you imagine I'm the kind of fellow
to take a blow quietly, lyin' down," said Cardew.

"Not at all. I'll meet you, with or without gloves, on the
first day of term at St. Jim's."

"That's not good enough—if you stay here. If you go,
well and good."

"I'm not going."

Cardew drew a deep breath.

"Then I'm afraid that good form will have to be thrown to

CHAPTER 1.
At Eastwood House!

"TROT in!" called out Tom Merry cheerily, as a tap
came at the door of his room at Eastwood House.

Tom Merry was standing before the glass, arranging his tie to his satisfaction.

Tom was not, as a rule, very particular about his tie. But
dinner at Eastwood House, on Christmas Day, was a rather
special occasion.

"That you, Gussy?" asked Tom, without looking round, as
the door opened.

"No."

Tom turned quickly.

It was Ralph Reckness Cardew, of the Fourth Form at St.
Jim's, who had entered.

Cardew closed the door, and stood looking at Tom Merry,
with a smile on his face. The dandy of the Fourth had
already dressed for dinner, and he looked very handsome in
his evening clothes.

The cheery expression faded from Tom Merry's face.
Cardew of the Fourth was the last fellow he would have
expected to drop into his room, and certainly the last fellow
he would have wished to see there. The rivals of St. Jim's
were both members of Arthur Augustus D'Arcy's Christmas
party at Eastwood House; and Cardew, at least, had not
allowed the feud to sleep.

"Well?" said Tom curtly.

"Am I interruptin' you?" drawled Cardew.

"Well, yes."

"Sorry! I've been lookin' for a chance to speak to you,"
said Cardew. "With so many people buzzin' about all day
it's rather difficult—so here I am."

"I can't see that you've got anything to say to me," said
Tom coldly. "If you've come here to quarrel, Cardew,
you've come for nothing. I don't intend to row in D'Arcy's
house."

"Isn't it a little too late to think of that?" smiled Cardew.
"We were enemies at St. Jim's, and we're enemies here."

"I never wanted to be," said Tom; "and on Christmas
Day, at least, you might give the subject a rest, Cardew.
Plenty of time for rowing when we get back to St. Jim's
next term."

"You should have thought of that sooner. It's an unlucky
thing that we're both D'Arcy's guests for Christmas. But
there it is. One of us will have to go."

Tom smiled slightly.

"I've no objection to your going," he said. "The sooner
the better, so far as I'm concerned."

the giddy winds, and that I shall have to give you your blow back with interest, without waitin' till next term," he said.

He came towards Tom Merry as he spoke.

Tom backed away.

"Are you off your rocker, Cardew?" he exclaimed. "Haven't you the least sense of decency? We can't fight here."

"I'm not insistin' on it—if you choose to take back the smack in the face you gave me, without puttin' up your hands."

"Oh, don't be a fool."

"You want it all your own way, old bean," said Cardew. "I'm afraid there's nothin' doin'. You're takin' the smack, anyhow, and you can please yourself about fightin' afterwards."

CHAPTER 2.
By the Strong Hand !

TOM MERRY'S eyes blazed.

He leaped back as Cardew came at him. But as the Fourth-Former came on, Tom Merry closed with him and grasped him. Cardew was by no means a weakling; he was slim and elegant, but he was sturdy, and he was known at St. Jim's as a good fighting-man. But as soon as Tom's sinewy grasp closed on him, Cardew realised that he had taken on too large an order. Tom's grasp slid to his wrists, and he held Cardew's slim wrists in a grip of iron, and the dandy of the Fourth struggled in vain to release them.

For a full minute he wrenched and struggled, to the detriment of his immaculate shirt-cuffs—no longer spotless. They were decidedly crumpled by that silent, furious struggle. Tom Merry did not speak; and Cardew was silent, save for his hurried, furious breathing. But Tom's grasp did not relax.

Cardew broke the tense silence at last.

"Will you let go my hands?"

"No!"

"You rotter! You coward!"

"I think you're out of your senses," said Tom coldly and quietly. "You provoked me yesterday till I lost my temper. You did it intentionally. I shall not lose my temper again. You're not worth it. But I'm not going to fight you here. You must be mad to think of such a thing. In Lord Eastwood's house——"

"Let go my hands!"

"We're both D'Arcy's guests. We've got to face a crowd of people this evening—girls among them. What would they think of us?"

"Let go!"

"And you such a stickler for good form!" said Tom contemptuously. "You want to act like a hooligan! Well, I'm not playing up! As soon as we're out of D'Arcy's house I'll fight you as quickly as you like. Not here."

"Will you release me?" hissed Cardew.

"Not till you give me your word to let this drop till after we're both gone from Eastwood."

"I won't!"

"You will!"

Tom Merry spoke calmly, quietly, but resolutely. His grip on Cardew's slim wrists was like the grip of a steel vice. Cardew struggled again—silently, persistently, savagely. But he could not release his wrists. He was in the grasp of a fellow stronger than himself, and quite as determined.

He stood panting at last, white with rage and humiliation. There was a tap at the door.

Some other member of the party was calling on Tom Merry. The strange scene was interrupted.

"Let go!" breathed Cardew.

"Will you promise?"

No reply.

Tom Merry compressed his grip on the slim wrists as the door opened. Manners and Lowther, his chums in the Shell at St. Jim's, came into the room.

"Ready, old bean!" said Monty Lowther. "Hallo! What——"

"Cardew here!" exclaimed Manners. "My hat! What's the game?"

The two Shell fellows stared blankly.

"Cardew's looking for trouble," explained Tom Merry. "I'm trying to persuade him to keep the peace."

"Looking for a row—in D'Arcy's house!" said Manners contemptuously. "Even you ought to know a bit better than that, Cardew."

Cardew writhed with rage.

"You're stronger than I am, Tom Merry," he said in a low, choking voice. "I have to admit that."

"I'm sorry to use my strength like this," said Tom. "But if you were cool, you'd understand that we cannot make a scene in another fellow's house; and if you're bent on it, I must stop you."

"I should jolly well think so!" exclaimed Monty Lowther.

There were footsteps and voices in the corridor outside Tom Merry's room. Blake and Herries, Digby and D'Arcy were there, apparently about to go down. Levison's voice was heard:

"Seen Cardew, you fellows?"

"I think he went along to Tom Mewwy," came the voice of Arthur Augustus D'Arcy.

Monty Lowther softly backed to the door and planted his heel against it. Arthur Augustus was not wanted on the scene just then. There was a tap at the door.

"Cardew heah, Tom Mewwy?" called out Arthur Augustus cheerily.

"Yes," called back Tom.

"You fellows comin' down?"

"Yes."

"Wight-ho!"

Cardew breathed harder. The vice-like grip was still on his slim wrists, and at any moment the St. Jim's fellows might come in. He looked at Tom Merry's face and read inflexible determination there.

"Let go!" he breathed. "You've got the better of me this time. I—I promise not to touch you."

Tom Merry released him at once.

"I only want you to keep clear of me while we're both staying here," he said. "I shall keep clear of you, if you'll let me."

Cardew rubbed his wrists. There were dark marks on the white skins, and the bones ached. It had not been a gentle grip that Tom had laid on him; but a gentle grip would not have controlled him. Cardew had had what he asked for.

The door opened.

Arthur Augustus, in evening clothes, a thing of beauty and a joy for ever, stood in the doorway, and nodded and smiled to his guests.

"You fellows havin' a chat?" he asked.

"Just that," said Cardew, with a smile. He drove his hands deep into his pockets.

A minute before his face had been almost convulsed with rage. Now it was calm, smiling, cheery. It was a startling change, and it made the Terrible Three stare. In spite of his recent conduct, it was clear that Ralph Reckness Cardew desired to keep up appearances, and to prevent his host, Arthur Augustus, from discovering that he had come to Tom's room with hostile intentions.

"Just goin' down," added Cardew; and he gave the Terrible Three a cheery nod and strolled to the door.

"Well, my hat!" murmured Manners.

Arthur Augustus remained to exchange a few words with the Terrible Three. Cardew joined Levison and Clive in the corridor. Ernest Levison gave him a quick, searching look.

"Anything up?" he muttered.

Cardew raised his eyebrows.

"Up? What could be up?" he drawled.

"I was afraid you'd gone looking for trouble," said Levison curtly.

"What rot, old chap," said Sidney Clive. "I suppose Cardew isn't capable of kicking up a shindy while he's a guest here, is he?"

Cardew laughed.

"Why not?" he said. "Old Ernest knows me better than you do, Clivey."

"You don't mean to say you've been rowing with Tom Merry—here!" exclaimed Clive, quite aghast.

"Dear man, so far from rowing, I've given him my word not to touch him so long as we're D'Arcy's guests."

Sidney Clive looked relieved.

"That's good," he said. "Blessed if I see at all why you're so up against the chap, Cardew. You bagged the junior captaincy from him at St. Jim's, and it's up for him to feel ratty, if for anybody, I should think."

"Don't you remember what the jolly old poet says," grinned Cardew:

"'Forgiveness to the injured does belong:
But they ne'er pardon who have done the wrong.'"

"Oh, rot!" said Clive.

"Well, let's get down," said Levison uneasily. There was a look in Cardew's eyes that Levison of the Fourth did not like.

"I've got to change my shirt," smiled Cardew. "I've got these cuffs a bit rumpled. Dear old Thomas has been showin' me some wrestlin' tricks, and he's got a rather heavy hand."

"Cardew!"

The dandy of the Fourth sauntered away to his room.

" Careful, sir ! " said the poacher hurriedly, as he caught sight of Wally D'Arcy staring into the summer-house: Cardew looked round. " What the thump ! " he exclaimed, with an angry look at the fag. Wally eyed him. " I'm looking for Pongo," he explained. " Have you seen anything of him ? "   (See page 12.)

Levison and Clive looked at one another very uneasily, but they did not speak. They waited, however, till Cardew joined them before they went downstairs. And they were glad to get him into the drawing-room, where the presence of cousin Ethel and Doris Levison and Manners' sisters and the other ladies of the party made " trouble " impossible.

Tom Merry came down soon afterwards, with Manners and Lowther. Arthur Augustus D'Arcy moved among his guests with a bright and beaming countenance, evidently utterly oblivious of any recent trouble between two of the party. Indeed, Arthur Augustus remarked to Jack Blake that it was " vewy decent " of both Tom Merry and Cardew to bury the hatchet so thoroughly, and forget their old differences during the Christmas holidays—a remark at which Blake smiled, without making any comment.

At the dinner-table, under the shaded lights, Tom Merry glanced once at Cardew.

Cardew's face was cheery and smiling, and he chatted to cousin Ethel, at his side, like a fellow who had not a care in the world.

Seemingly, he had forgotten the scene in Tom Merry's room.

Tom Merry was glad of it.

He knew that Cardew was not a fellow to forget or to forgive; but he knew, too, that Cardew was a fellow of his word. The promise he had given, he would keep.

That was good enough: and the Christmas festivities at Eastwood House would not be marred by any further trouble. Tom Merry was not the fellow to guess the deep, black, bitter rancour that lay under the smiling exterior of the dandy of the Fourth; and he would have been startled, had he been able to read the thoughts that were passing through Cardew's mind, even while he smiled and chatted so cheerily.

CHAPTER 3.
Wally butts In !

" WALLY, you ass——"

" Wally, you dummy !"

Reggie Manners and Frank Levison spoke simultaneously, with emphasis.

" Oh, dry up !" grunted D'Arcy minor.

It was Boxing Day, and the dusk was falling thickly. The snow was falling more thickly than the dusk.

The three Third-Formers of St. Jim's were tramping through a " ride " in Eastwood Park, thick with snow, swept by the wind. The snow had started suddenly, and it was coming down almost in masses, and the wind dashed it in the faces of the three fags.

" Look here, I'm fed-up !" exclaimed Manners minor.

" Same here !" said Frank Levison.

Snort from Wally of the Third.

" We've got to find Pongo !" he said.

" Blow Pongo !"

" Who's afraid of a little snow ?" demanded Wally.

" Fathead ! Call this a little."

" I'm hungry, too."

" Oh, rats !" said Wally crossly.

Levison minor and Reggie Manners were the guests of Walter Adolphus D'Arcy for Christmas. But manners were not polished in the Third Form at St. Jim's. Host and guests generally forgot that they were not in the old Form-room, when they addressed one another. And in the Third Form room at St. Jim's, language was very plain.

" Pongo's got off his chain," said Wally. " He's gone wandering. I'm bound to find him. You asses said you would come."

"We've been searching for the brute for two hours," said Reggie sulkily, "I can tell you I'm fed up with Pongo, Wally."

"Rats!"

"I'm jolly well going in!" roared Reggie.

"Sooner the better," said D'Arcy minor. "You can't stand a little snow and wind. You're rather soft."

"Oh, go and eat coke."

Reggie Manners tramped off in the direction of Eastwood House. Frank Levison looked as if he would like to follow. But he hesitated.

"You backing out?" demanded Wally crossly.

"Nunno! But what's the good of looking for Pongo in this snow-storm?" argued Frank. "We'll never find him."

"Well, you wouldn't," agreed Wally. "You haven't much sense. I'm going to find him somehow."

"You're an ass, Wally."

"You're another."

"Look here——"

"Bow-wow!"

"I'll jolly well leave you to it, then."

"Do! Make the job easier if you don't help."

"Br-r-r-r-r!" said Levison minor. And he started off in the tracks left behind him by Reggie Manners.

Wally of the Third was left alone, looking and feeling cross. He was very much concerned about Pongo, his favourite mongrel. Nobody but Wally of the Third was able to discern any lovable qualities in Pongo—but Wally's fixed belief was that there never had been such a dog as Pongo. Pongo had gone wandering, and Wally was determined to find him, somehow. How, was rather a problem.

"Pongo! Pongo! Pong! Pong!"

If Pongo was within hearing he did not listen to the voice of the charmer. At all events, no answering bark or whine came.

Wally tramped on doggedly.

He knew that he would be late for tea, and that after tea there were going to be great festivities, participated in with keen enjoyment by the younger members of the Christmas party, and with cheerful tolerance by the elders. But tea and festivities failed to appeal to Wally when Pongo was in trouble. Possibly the elusive Pongo was miles away—possibly he had returned to his kennel while his master was hunting for him; but, possibly he was being buried in the snow in the wide bleak park, and frozen—and that possibility kept D'Arcy minor keenly on the search.

In the thickening dust, the St. Jim's fag pursued his quest, determined to keep it up till dark at least. It had come into his mind that perhaps Pongo had taken refuge from the falling snow in the summer-house in the park—an open structure, used only in the summer, open to the winds, but sheltered from falling snow. Wally of the Third tramped up the "ride" to the summer-house.

He came up rather wearily through the thick snow, in the dusk. As he had almost reached the open doorway he was startled by the sound of a voice within.

"You've kept me waitin'."

Wally jumped.

It was the voice of Ralph Reckness Cardew. He wondered what on earth Cardew could be doing there.

A hoarse, husky voice answered:

"Sorry, sir! The snow came on, and——"

"Never mind."

There was the scratch of a match; Cardew was lighting a cigarette. Wally stepped in.

In the light of the match, he saw Cardew's handsome face, and caught a glimpse of the man Cardew was talking with. He knew the man by sight—a disreputable character, well-known to be a poacher and a pilferer, who was generally to be seen at the Spotted Dog in Easthorpe, loafing about the bar or the billiards-room.

Cardew blew out a cloud of smoke.

"Well, look here, Lomax——"

"Careful, sir," said the poacher hurriedly. He had caught sight of the St. Jim's fag.

Cardew stared round.

"What the thump——" he exclaimed, with an angry look at the fag.

Wally eyed him.

"I'm looking for Pongo!" he explained. "Have you seen anything of him?"

"No! Bother your rotten mongrel!"

"You seem to be palling with a mongrel yourself, Cardew," said the fag sarcastically. "Do you know that that man is Mike Lomax, who's been in gaol more times than he can count?"

The poacher gave Wally a savage look, and a thick cudgel, that he carried under his arm, slipped down into his hand. The fag looked at him fearlessly.

Cardew gave the man a warning look, and Lomax muttered something under his breath, and turned away. The match had gone out, and the dusk was deep in the summer-house.

"Your dog isn't here, kid," said Cardew, controlling his annoyance, and speaking civilly. "I've seen nothing of him, and I've been in here ten minutes or more, sheltering from the snow—as this man seems to have done."

"Lomax has no right on my father's land," said Wally. "If a keeper found him here, he would be shifted off fast enough. He's a bad hat, and the less you have to say to him the better."

Cardew gritted his teeth. But he answered cheerily:

"My dear kid, thanks for the tip—it's kind of you fellows in the Third to look after your elders like this."

"Oh, rats!" grunted Wally.

"But I suppose I can wish a merry Christmas, even to a bad hat," went on Cardew, with a laugh.

"You can do anything you jolly well like, so far as I'm concerned," snapped Wally, and he went out again into the snow, to look further for Pongo.

Wally was quite well aware, from the words he had heard accidentally, that Cardew's meeting with the poacher was not by chance.

What Cardew's business could be with such a character was a mystery, but Wally did not think about it. It was no concern of his. Moreover, he was deeply concerned about Pongo just then.

But a few minutes later Wally stopped with a surprised exclamation. Mike Lomax, poacher and pilferer, was a dog-stealer among his other activities. Pongo was missing—and Lomax was on the spot! That Pongo was worth stealing Wally had not the slightest doubt, though Reggie and Frank would have chortled at the idea.

"He's got him!" gasped Wally.

And he turned round and tramped back towards the summer-house. If Mike Lomax had got Pongo, Wally meant to have him back, even at the cost of a battle royal with a six-foot ruffian.

All was dark in the little summer-house now, and Wally wondered whether the poacher was gone. But the husky voice came to his ears.

"I ain't see'd him. How shall I know him, sir?"

"You can see him to-morrow morning." It was Cardew's voice. "He's taking an old lady to see the ruins of the abbey. Just hang round and watch for him there."

"And then——"

"Nothing in the presence of Miss Fawcett, you fool! You'll watch, and get a look at him, so that you will know him again."

"Leave it to me, sir."

D'Arcy minor stood quite still. The words, muttered in low tones, came quite clearly to him, and they amazed him so much that he stood and blinked at the dark summer-house like a fellow in a dream.

"Good enough! I'm going now!"

There was a sound of footsteps. Cardew left the little summer-house by the door on the opposite side. Then Wally heard the heavy steps of the poacher coming out. In the doorway, not six feet from Wally, Mike Lomax stopped to light his pipe and to turn up the collar of his rough coat and to mutter a curse on the snow and the wind. Then he came tramping along, and almost ran into Wally of the Third on the dark path.

"Who's that?" muttered the ruffian.

"Little me," said Wally, recovering himself. "I want to know whether you've got my dog, Lomax?"

"You young fool!"

"Look here——"

The poacher gave him a savage shove, and Wally went sprawling in the snow. Lomax laughed gruffly and tramped on, disappearing into the darkness.

"Ow! My only Aunt Jane! Ow!"

Wally scrambled to his feet. He was greatly inclined to rush after the poacher and take summary vengeance, but he realised that this was a proposition of considerable difficulty. Moreover, he was fairly certain by this time that Lomax had not been there on account of Pongo. There was something between the ruffian and Cardew—something that was odd and underhand—but evidently Pongo was not concerned in the matter. D'Arcy minor shook his fist after Lomax, instead of pursuing him, and then started off on a further search for his valuable mongrel.

Tom Merry jumped to his feet with a laugh and shook the snow from his clothes. " My dearest Tommy ! " ejaculated Miss Priscilla. " It's all right, dear," said Tom hastily. " But," continued Miss Priscilla tenderly, " you will catch cold, darling ! Run in and change your clothes at once ! "   (*See page* 14.)

CHAPTER 4.
Tom Merry's Substitute !

"**B**AI Jove !"
Arthur Augustus D'Arcy jammed his celebrated monocle into his noble eye and gazed at his young brother with horror.

Wally had returned at last.

He was in a parlous state.

"Gweat Scott !" said Arthur Augustus faintly. "Is that weally you, Wally? Or is it some howwid twamp?"

"Oh, come off !" said D'Arcy minor. "I've been looking for Pongo. Has he come in ?"

"Weally, Wally, I take no intewest whatevah in the movements of that howwid mongwel of yours. Pway huwwy up and change your clothes befoah anyone sees you !"

"Bow-wow !"

"You young wapscallion——"

"Pongo's come in, Wally !" shouted Reggie Manners from the distance. "He's in his kennel now."

"Oh, good !" said Wally.

"Come on, old kid—we're doing charades !" shouted Frank.

"Right-ho !"

Wally of the Third tramped away to change his clothes. He was wet to the skin, and smothered with snow and mud. He had searched for Pongo not wisely, but too well.

But he was very bright and cheery when he joined the festive party. Pongo being all right, everything was all right, from D'Arcy minor's point of view.

But during the festivities of that merry evening Wally did not forget the curious incident of the summer-house in the wood.

He found himself thinking of it a great deal, and more than once he glanced curiously at Cardew, who was cheerful and smiling and debonair as usual.

Cardew's secret meeting with Lomax meant mischief of some kind. He had told the poacher where he could see and watch Tom Merry, so that he would know Tom again on another occasion. That it was Tom who was spoken of Wally knew, for he was aware that Tom Merry was to take Miss Priscilla to see the abbey ruins in the morning.

Wally wondered. He could not help wondering.

He knew all about the St. Jim's feud, and he had seen more than one sign during the Christmas holidays that Cardew had not forgotten his enmity.

Some trick was to be played on Tom Merry by means of the poacher—that much was clear to Wally. For that purpose Lomax was to get to know Tom by sight.

That anything worse than a trick was intended did not cross the fag's mind for a moment. Some jape, such as snowballing the Shell fellow from behind a hedge, or something of the kind—that was what Wally considered probable. He was not likely to suspect anything more serious than that.

He wondered whether he ought to speak to Tom on the subject. What he had heard, he had heard by accident—and

THE GEM LIBRARY.—No. 829.

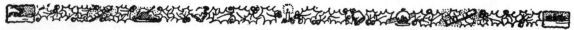

a jape was only a jape, though certainly Eastwood House was not a proper place for japes.

Wally of the Third had not made up his mind on the subject when he went to bed that night, and the next morning Wally was busy. The lake was frozen, and most of the younger members of the Christmas party were going on the ice. Wally and Reggie and Frank were among them, and for the time Wally forgot about Cardew and his schemes. It was not, after all, an important matter—so far as the fag could see, at least—and there was plenty of time to speak to Tom Merry if he decided to do so.

Wally & Co. were among the first on the ice, disporting themselves gleefully, after the manner of the Third Form. Blake & Co. came on, and Manners and Lowther, and Sidney Clive, and cousin Ethel, and Doris, and Manners' sisters. Ralph Reckness Cardew joined them, skating with remarkable skill and grace. Levison of the Fourth had lingered to speak to Tom Merry, who was waiting in the hall for Miss Priscilla to come down for the walk to the abbey.

"I haven't had a chance of speaking to you quietly, Tom," said Levison in a low voice. "I—I hope that there wasn't any trouble when Cardew came to your room Christmas Day?"

Tom Merry looked rather uncomfortable.

"Well, there was a bit of an argument," he said. "But it's all right. Cardew's agreed to a truce while we're here with Gussy."

Levison looked very relieved.

"I'm glad of that," he said. "It would be pretty rotten if there was anything like a scene in D'Arcy's house. I really can't quite understand Cardew lately. I should have thought him the last fellow in the world to make a scene at any time. But I'm afraid he's been rather near it."

"It's all right now," said Tom. "He's given his word to keep clear till we've both left Eastwood House."

"That's good!" said Levison. "If Cardew keeps clear, I know you will, and it's all right!"

"Right as rain!" said Tom, with a smile.

Miss Priscilla Fawcett came down, wrapped in furs, her kind old face looking very frail and delicate under her bonnet.

"My dearest Tommy, have I kept you waiting?"

"Not at all!" said Tom cheerily. "Luckily, the snow's stopped, and it's a lovely morning for a walk."

Levison walked down the drive with Tom and Miss Fawcett. He had his skates under his arm. And then occurred an incident which, trifling as it was, was destined to have strange results. Miss Priscilla dropped her muff, and Tom Merry's foot slipped in the snow as he stooped to pick it up, and he went with a plunge into the drift of snow piled beside the drive.

He jumped up with a laugh and shook the snow from his clothes.

"My dearest Tommy!" ejaculated Miss Priscilla.

"All right, dear!" said Tom hastily.

Miss Priscilla never could quite understand that Tom Merry was no longer the fascinating little baby of years ago. Tom was deeply grateful for her kind affection; but at fifteen he felt a certain discomfort at being coddled, especially before other fellows. But that little incident, trifling to Tom, was of deep import to his kind old friend.

"My darling, you will catch cold," said Miss Priscilla tenderly. "Run in and change your clothes at once."

"I'm not wet——"

"And warm yourself thoroughly before the fire——"

"But——"

"Change down to the skin," said Miss Priscilla. "And, oh, my dearest child, be careful that your things are well aired, and be very careful to put flannel next to your skin, and——"

"I—I——"

"Quick, my dearest boy!"

Levison contrived not to smile. Tom Merry's face was crimson.

"But we're going to the abbey——" gasped Tom.

"That is nothing! We can go another time. Run into the house at once, Tommy—at once!"

"But——" stuttered the hapless Shell fellow.

He broke off. Miss Priscilla was looking deeply distressed, and Tom would not have distressed the kind old lady for worlds.

"All right!" he gasped. "But——"

"Leave it to me, Tom," said Levison. "It will be a pleasure to me to walk to the abbey with Miss Fawcett."

"Thanks, old man! Right-ho!"

"Darling Tommy——"

Levison passed his skates to Tom, and Tom Merry hurried back to the house. Levison of the Fourth, with great politeness, walked on with Miss Priscilla. Tom went into the house, left Levison's skates in Levison's room, and then went to his own room. He did not trouble about changing his clothes; Miss Priscilla's tender fears for her darling's

health were quite unfounded. He had some letters to write —that duty having been rather neglected during the holidays, a not unusual circumstance—and he filled in the next hour with pen and ink.

Meanwhile, Levison of the Fourth walked to the abbey ruins with Miss Priscilla. He showed the old lady round the ruins with indefatigable politeness. A rough-looking man was loafing about the ruins, smoking a pipe, with his hands in the pockets of a frowsy woollen jacket. Levison glanced at him carelessly; but the rough-looking fellow gazed at Levison in a very fixed way. Had Levison taken any heed of him he might have guessed that the man was observing him carefully, fixing his features upon his memory.

After a few minutes the man lounged away, with a grin on his stubbly face.

CHAPTER 5.
Struck Down!

"CARDEW, old man!"

It was the following day, and Ralph Reckness Cardew was lounging in an easy-chair before a log fire in his room at Eastwood House. A spiral of smoke curled up from a cigarette between his slim fingers.

"Hallo! Trot in, Levison!"

Levison came in, and Cardew pointed to a chair. Levison sat down and looked at his chum.

Cardew blew out a cloud of smoke.

"Have a cigarette?" he asked.

"No."

Cardew laughed.

"We're not on duty now," he remarked. "I've sneaked up here for a quiet smoke. Gussy's an ideal host; he lets a fellow do as he likes. Have you come to fetch me for anythin'?"

"I'm a bit worried!" said Levison.

"Reel it off," said Cardew encouragingly. "Confide it to your old pal. Droppin' money on steeplechases?"

"Don't be an ass!" said Levison gruffly. "Look here, Cardew, I'm jolly uneasy about you!"

"About me?" Ralph Reckness Cardew raised his eyebrows. "Dear man, I'm all right—enjoyin' myself at the present moment, in fact. A good smoke, and particularly agreeable company——"

"I thought when we came here for Christmas you were going to leave St. Jim's troubles behind," said Levison.

"But——"

"I've a good memory," said Cardew.

"You seem to me to have set out to provoke Tom Merry in every possible way," said Levison.

"That's so."

"You seem to have depended on his unwillingness to make a scene to keep on worrying him," went on Levison.

"Right!"

"Oh, you admit it?"

"Quite!"

"Isn't that rather rotten, Cardew?"

"I dare say," assented Cardew coolly. "It's my way! I detest the fellow, and I never forget a grudge. Under a jolly old screen of politeness and good manners, I set out to make him writhe. Havin' been endowed by Nature with about ten times as much brains as the excellent Thomas, the task was an easy one."

"It's a risky business," said Levison. "He might lose his temper some time, and then——"

"He lost it on Christmas Eve when I bagged his dance with cousin Ethel," smiled Cardew.

"Was there a row, then?"

"Somethin' like it! He smacked my face."

"Oh!" ejaculated Levison.

"Then, as your charmin' sister appeared in the offing, I couldn't take action," said Cardew, still smiling, but with a deadly gleam in his eyes. "I nursed my injury till a more favourable moment. That's why I looked into his room on Christmas Day—to give him back what he had given me. But, alas! the excellent Thomas is sadly lackin' in brains, but he shines in the muscular line. I was held."

"I guessed something of the kind," said Levison. "I saw the state of your cuffs and your wrists. You must have been mad to act in such a way, Cardew!"

"Think so? Well, nothin' came of it," drawled Cardew. "I was held; and I promised not to touch him again while we were at Eastwood House. I didn't promise that he shouldn't be touched. Only that I wouldn't touch him. There's a distinction there, though it did not dawn on the powerful intellect of Thomas."

"What do you mean?"

"Nothin'!" yawned Cardew. "I never mean anythin'. Shall we go down and play billiards?"

Levison shook his head. He was deeply troubled.

Levison showed Miss Priscilla round the ruins with indefatigable politeness. A rough-looking man was loafin about the ruins smoking a pipe, with his hands in the pockets of a frowsy woollen jacket. Levison glanced at him carelessly, but the rough-looking man gazed at Levison in a very fixed way. (See page 14.)

"What's the worry?" asked Cardew lightly. "I've been smacked and I've been held like a helpless baby and I've been made to toe the line and make a promise. Dear old Thomas triumphs all along the line, and I'm left to swallow my own smoke and grin and bear it. You know my patient, lamb-like nature—how meek I am in endurin' injuries and humiliation."

He threw the stump of the cigarette into the fire. Levison noticed that his hand was shaking.

"What are you thinking of, Cardew?" asked Levison very quietly.

"Nothin'!"

"I know you better than the other fellows do. I knew something must have happened—I knew you were brooding over it. You've let Tom Merry alone the last day or two. Cardew, I know quite well that you've got something in your mind—some silly scheme! What is it?"

"Guess!" said Cardew, smiling.

"I can't guess—I want to know."

"So that you can stop me?" grinned Cardew.

"So that I can save you from making a fool of yourself," said Ernest Levison sternly. "So that I can save you from doing something that you'll be sorry for later, when you're cool."

"Dear man!" said Cardew.

"You won't tell me?"

"No."

"You admit that you've got some scheme in your mind?"

"I don't admit anythin'."

Levison sat in silence for a few minutes. Ralph Reckness Cardew stared at the fire. The forced smile had faded from his face; he looked hard, and bitter, and revengeful. Only too well Levison knew how bitterly Cardew must be resenting his humiliation—how it must have roused everything that was evil in his wayward nature. And Levison's uneasiness intensified. He was oppressed by a fear that the Christmas holidays would not terminate without some

outbreak on Cardew's part, though what form it would take he could not imagine.

"You're a cheery sort of companion," said Cardew, breaking the silence at last. "Are you understudyin' the jolly old Quakers?"

"I'm worried," said Levison. "Cardew, if you can't keep your enmity to Tom Merry in check, wouldn't it be best to leave? Your uncle, Lord Lilburn, is leaving to-day."

"Not till I've finished with Tom Merry."

"But how——"

"Better not ask questions," yawned Cardew. He glanced at the clock. "I'm goin' down to play a hundred up with Clive. Comin'?"

"I'm going down to Easthorpe," said Levison. "Like to come with me?"

"Not in this snow, thanks. You know what a slacker I am."

"You'll keep clear of Tom Merry while I'm gone?"

Cardew laughed.

"My dear chap, haven't I promised not to touch Tom Merry? Isn't my word my bond?"

"Well, yes, I'm sure you'd keep your word," said Levison. "But—but I wish——"

"What's the good of wishin'?"

Levison made an impatient gesture, and left Cardew's room. The dandy of the Fourth shrugged his shoulders. At St. Jim's, Levison of the Fourth had seemed to have a great influence over Cardew, but that influence was quite gone now. Ralph Reckness Cardew was going on his own way, spurred on by the bitterness of his humiliation, which blinded him to all else.

Ernest Levison, muffled up in a thick coat against the falling snow, tramped away by the footpath through the park, a short cut to the village of Easthorpe. He had a purchase to make in the village, and he would have been glad of Cardew's company in the walk to Easthorpe, if only to keep him away from Tom Merry.

But it never occurred to him that there was any danger in that walk in the winter dusk by the woodland footpath.

Once or twice he heard footfalls behind him, faint on the snow, but he did not look round. He was near the spot where the footpath joined the road when the footfalls behind him hurried, and then Levison noted them and glanced round.

A man in a rough coat and cap was close behind him. In the dusk and the falling snow recognition was not easy; but Levison's eyes were keen, and he knew that this was the man he had seen loafing about the ruins on the morning he had walked there with Miss Priscilla. Something in the man's manner warned him of hostility, and he jumped back.

Mike Lomax peered at him sharply.

"You're my bird, I reckon," he said.

Levison backed away.

"What do you mean? Stand back!"

Lomax chuckled hoarsely and made a spring at him. In a moment Levison was struggling in the grasp of the ruffian.

"Help!" shouted Levison.

His voice rang through the park, echoing among the frozen, leafless trees.

But the place was too lonely; there was no help. Mike Lomax had chosen his time well.

His powerful grasp was on the junior; Levison, sturdy as he was, was like an infant in his hands.

But he struggled desperately. He could only suppose that this ruffian, a stranger to him, was a footpad, and designed to rob him.

He freed his right arm and drove his clenched fist full in the ruffian's stubbly face. The blood spurted from Mike Lomax's mouth.

The ruffian panted out a curse.

Levison went to the ground with a crash. His face was driven into the snow, and a savage grip on the back of his neck held it there.

The stick Lomax carried under his arm had dropped to the ground. He picked it up and gripped it savagely.

Lash, lash, lash!

The blows descended like rain on the struggling junior.

Levison struggled, and writhed, and panted. Twice he kicked at the ruffian, and Lomax's howls showed that he was hurt. But the junior's desperate resistance only provoked his savage temper. The blows of the stick descended with more and more savage force.

Lash, lash, lash!

It seemed to Levison that he must be in the grip of a madman. The man, a stranger to him, was not seeking to rob him—he was beating him savagely, brutally. To the last Levison struggled and resisted, but he was powerless in the ruffian's grip. The blows descended harder and faster as the junior writhed with his face in the snow. His struggles ceased suddenly.

Lomax rose, panting.

The junior lay quite still. The ruffian realised that he was insensible.

He looked round quickly, stealthily, and then hurriedly plunged into the wood and disappeared.

On the lonely footpath Levison of St. Jim's lay unconscious, with the snow falling thicker and thicker upon his motionless form.

CHAPTER 6.
Not Tom Merry!

"LOOKING for Tom Merry?"

Ralph Reckness Cardew asked that question in a casual sort of way. Manners and Lowther were standing by a window in the hall, looking out at the falling snow in the thickening December dusk.

"Not yet," said Lowther.

"I dare say this snow's delayed him," remarked Manners. "He may have stayed at Dawes' cottage for shelter."

"I wonder!" said Cardew musingly.

Manners and Lowther glanced at him rather curiously. They did not see why Cardew should be interested in Tom Merry's movements that afternoon.

Cardew strolled away to the billiards-room, where some of the St. Jim's party were amusing themselves by knocking the balls about. Blake was performing a series of cannons, and Arthur Augustus D'Arcy stood watching him, cue in hand. Herries and Digby looked on, and Cardew joined them.

"Good shot!" he remarked, as Jack Blake brought off another cannon.

Then he strolled restlessly away. In a deep window-seat he came on Sidney Clive and Doris Levison, reading a "Holiday Annual" together. Cardew exchanged a few words with them and wandered away.

He seemed strangely restless and ill at ease.

Wally of the Third and Manners minor and Frank Levison came downstairs muffled in coats and scarves.

"Goin' out?" asked Cardew.

"Looks like it, doesn't it?" said Wally cheerily. "We ain't afraid of a little snow in the Third, are we, you fellows?"

"No fear!" said Levison minor.

"Besides, we're taking out Pongo," remarked Reggie Manners with a slightly sarcastic inflection in his voice. "What does the weather matter when we've got Pongo?"

"Look here, young Manners!" began Wally warmly. "If you don't want to come for a run with Pongo——"

"Could a chap like anything better?" demanded Reggie, still sarcastic, and Levison minor chuckled.

"Some chaps might like to have their heads punched!" said Wally darkly.

"Some chaps might be able to punch them!" retorted Reggie. "Not you."

"I'll jolly well——"

"Begad!" It was Lord Conway's voice. "Are you always as polished as this, Walter, in dealing with visitors?"

"Oh, my only Aunt Jane!" ejaculated Wally, and he turned quickly at his eldest brother's voice.

"Oh, it's only Wally's gas!" said Reggie cheerfully. "We just let him run on, don't we, Frank?"

"We do," chuckled Frank.

"Oh, rats!" said Wally. "For goodness sake, get a move on, and don't stand cackling like a lot of old hens. Like to come for a run with Pongo, Conway?"

"At the present moment I beg to be excused," said the viscount, with a smile. "Even the delightful company of Pongo will not tempt me out in this weather."

"You mustn't get soft, you know," warned Wally, and he grinned and walked off with his comrades, leaving the heir of Eastwood staring.

Cardew smiled, and strolled away. He looked into the drawing-room and found Manners' sisters there, trying over things on the piano, with Miss Priscilla and Aunts Adelina and Matilda listening and knitting. Cardew backed out, and moved along to the library. Cousin Ethel was there helping Lord Eastwood with his correspondence, and Cardew did not enter. He went to his own room at last and smoked a cigarette.

But he was too restless to remain there. He came down to the drawing-room again. Miss Priscilla gave him a kind smile.

"Has dear Tommy come in?" she asked.

Cardew started a little. The kind old face seemed to give him a twinge of pain or remorse.

"I—I think not," he stammered.

"Is Tom out?" asked Doris Levison, looking round from the piano. "Perhaps he has met Ernest. Ernest has gone to the village, I think—they may have got shelter from the snow."

"I hope dear Tommy has taken shelter," said Miss Priscilla. "He is so delicate." Doris smiled. "The dear boy has gone to Mrs. Dawes' cottage," said Miss Priscilla. "He has taken the woollen comforter I knitted for her husband, who has rheumatism, or bronchitis, or lumbago, or something—I quite forget which, but I know it is something very unpleasant. It was so kind of Tommy to go; but he is always such a good little boy."

Cardew drifted out again.

Manners and Lowther were sitting by the big fire in the hall, playing chess, now. Cardew glanced at them without speaking. A few minutes later, muffled in a thick coat, Cardew was tramping through the snow and wind, into Eastwood Park. Dusky as it was under the leafless, frozen trees, Cardew tramped on without a pause, and he reached the deserted summer-house in the wood.

From the interior of the little building, open on two sides to the wind, he caught a red glow, which he knew came from the bowl of a pipe. A scent of strong tobacco came to him. He stepped inside, and there was a husky exclamation.

"That you, sir?"

"Yes. Anythin' happened?"

Cardew drawled out the question in his usual lazy tones. But his eyes were keen and anxious as he peered at Mike Lomax in the gloom.

The ruffian chuckled hoarsely.

"Yes, sir! I've carried out your orders."

Cardew drew a quick hard breath.

"Tom Merry——"

"I follered him on the footpath," said Lomax. "He put up a fight—look at my mouth! But I paid 'im!"

"On the footpath?" repeated Cardew, puzzled, "I understood that he was gone to the Dawes' cottage. That's in another direction."

"I was watching on the drive, and saw him start," answered Lomax. "I follered him—I don't know where he was going, but he went by the footpath in the park, and I collared him there."

"What—what did you do?" breathed Cardew.

"What you told me, sir—gave him the hiding of his life," answered Lomax. "I reckoned I've earned that five pun, sir."

Cardew's face was pale now.

"You—you did not go too far?"

Lomax did not answer. Cardew made a step towards the ruffian, and caught him by his sleeve.

"You fool! I told you to thrash him! If you've hurt him—really hurt him—I'll have you landed in prison for it."

"He hit me in the face," muttered the ruffian sullenly. "He kicked and struggled. I gave it to him harder for that."

"Where did you leave him?"

"On the footpath."

"He was unable to get home?"

"I dunno."

"You fool—you brute!" hissed Cardew. "Do you dare to tell me that he was not able to get home?"

"I reckon he's home by this time, or ought to be," muttered Lomax. "He's all right! I reckon he'll bear the marks for a good time to come. That's all. I want my money, sir."

There was a threatening growl in the ruffian's voice.

Cardew stood silent.

"You hear me, sir. I've earned my money, and I shall have to get out of this neighbourhood for a bit—the feller might have knowed my face."

With a gesture of scorn, Cardew flung a five-pound note at the ruffian.

"Get out of my sight," he muttered.

Lomax gave him a savage look, crammed the note into his pocket and slouched away.

Cardew stood motionless after he had gone. For a long time he stood there, forgetful of his surroundings, his heart beating painfully.

What had he done?

The fierce, black, bitter resentment that had spurred him on till that moment seemed to have died away in his breast. His brain seemed to clear — in those moments he saw his conduct as it really was—and it sickened him. He had fallen to this—a depth to which he would never have dreamed of falling! It seemed to him now, as he stood there in the silence and solitude, like some evil dream.

He shook himself at last, as if shaking off troubling thoughts, and left the little building. With his head bent to the wind he tramped back to Eastwood House.

It was done now!

It was done, and could not be undone. He had been insulted, and had had to endure the insult. In revenge his enemy had been beaten by his order. After all, he began to reflect cynically, there was nothing in that to make a bother about. Nothing! Only if the ruffian had gone too far—if he had struck too hard——

Cardew hurried his steps.

He was glad to see the lights of Eastwood House gleaming through the winter dusk and the falling snowflakes. Had Tom Merry come in? Surely he had come in! He could not have been hurt—seriously hurt—surely Lomax could not have been such a fool—such a brute—— Ralph Reckness Cardew's heart was throbbing when he entered the house.

"Hallo! You've been out in the snow?"

Cardew started violently.

It was Tom Merry's voice.

He stared blankly at the Shell fellow. Tom Merry looked ruddy and cheery, and there was no sign of damage about him. With what Mike Lomax had told him fresh in his mind, Cardew stared at Tom like a fellow in a dream, utterly confounded.

His strange expression did not escape Tom Merry's notice, and Cardew saw the wonder in his face, and tried to pull himself together.

"Yes—no——" he stammered. "You've been out? Caught in the snow?"

"Yes, rather," said Tom. "It's pretty thick, isn't it? I stayed at the Dawes' cottage for a bit to see if it would blow over, but it didn't, so I chanced it."

"You got home all right?"

"Eh! Looks like it—here I am," said Tom.

Cardew's brain was in a whirl. Had Lomax lied to him—lied to obtain his bribe unearned? Was that the explanation? It was possible, but Cardew did not believe so. What fearful mistake had the ruffian made?

It seemed to Cardew, for some moments, that the walls were whirling round him. He saw Tom Merry's ruddy face as in a mist. And he saw the wonder growing there.

"Did you meet anybody coming back?"

Cardew knew, vaguely, how incautious such a question was, in the circumstances. But for his life he could not have helped it. He wanted to know—he felt that he must know.

"Meet anybody?" repeated Tom. "No—the lane's pretty lonely. Are any of the fellows out?"

"Oh, yes! Levison's gone to the village," stammered Cardew. "I—I thought you might have met him."

"No, I haven't been near the village."

Cardew moved away. As soon as possible he sought his room, anxious for solitude, to think the thing over. Tom Merry had escaped the designed attack—that was clear now; he had escaped the danger without even knowing that it had threatened. Yet Lomax had carried out his orders—Cardew felt sure of it. What had happened? Had the brutal ruffian, in the winter dusk, made a mistake—attacked some other person in mistake for Tom Merry? Yet how was that possible, when he had watched Tom at the abbey ruins, a few days before, in order to know him again without possibility of mistake?

What had happened?

Cardew hoped—he almost prayed—that Lomax had cheated him—that the ruffian had claimed his wages for a service unperformed. But if it was not that—what had happened?

CHAPTER 7.
By Whose Hand?

"PONGO!"

Pongo did not obey his master's voice.

The little mongrel was scuttling through the snow on the footpath, and the three fags of St. Jim's scuttled after him. The dusk was thickening into darkness, and Wally & Co. felt that it was time to return from their ramble in the snow. But Pongo seemed to have other intentions.

"Pongo!" shouted Wally.

"Stop, you horrid mongrel," yelled Reggie Manners.

"Stop, you beast," shouted Frank Levison.

Pongo scuttled on. Something seemed to have attracted his attention, and he declined to stop.

"Oh, let him rip!" said Reggie crossly. "Let's get back. They'll be having tea."

"Bosh!" said Wally.

A loud, prolonged whine came from Pongo. The dog had stopped of his own accord, and stood over something that was stretched in the snow. Loud and sharp and eerie, in the darkening woods, sounded the whine of the dog.

"He's found something," said D'Arcy minor.

"Rot!" said Reggie.

"You're a silly ass, Reggie!"

"You're a silly chump, Wally!"

"Look here——"

"Oh, cheese it, you two," said Levison minor. "Let's go and see what he's found, and nail him before he can scoot."

The three fags ran on. Pongo, whining over the still form in the snow, showed no desire to "scoot." He whined and whined again as the fags ran up.

"My only Aunt Jane! It's somebody!" exclaimed Wally.

"Phew!" Reggie Manners whistled.

Frank Levison ran quickly forward. He raised the head of the fallen figure in his arms, and a faint moan was heard.

"Strike a match, Wally," said Frank. "Let's see who it is."

Wally fumbled for a match-box. The first match was instantly blown out by the wind; the second Wally sheltered in the cupped palm of his hand, holding it over the white face that was turned from the snow. A loud, terrible cry broke from Frank Levison.

"Ernie!"

"What?" gasped Wally.

"It's my brother."

"Great Scott!"

"Ernie!" panted Frank. "He's hurt—he's hurt! Ernie!"

Levison moaned faintly. His face was white as chalk, his eyes closed. His hands were frozen.

Frank dragged him to his feet. Wally grasped him, and the two fags held Levison between them.

"What—what's the matter with him?" exclaimed Reggie Manners.

"I don't know—he's hurt," sobbed Frank. "Ernie, old man. Can't you speak, Ernie?"

"Something's happened to him," said Wally sagely. "Look here, he's half frozen. We've got to get him up to the house, quick."

"We can carry him somehow," said Reggie. "He ain't a heavy-weight. Take hold, you fellows."

"Can't you speak, Ernie?"

But Ernest Levison could not speak. He was partly conscious, but his lips were frozen and numb. Only a faint moan came from him.

Frank choked back his rising terror. That there was something seriously wrong with his brother was clear, and it was no time for grief and fear; it was a time for rapid action. The three fags lifted Ernest Levison in their arms, and tramped away with him up the snowy path.

It was a good distance to the house—and it seemed like miles to the fags, in the wind and snow, with the weight of Ernest Levison on their arms.

But they tramped on with dogged determination.

Wally led the way by a short cut across the grounds, when the park was left behind, and they came out on the drive near the great portals of Eastwood House.

"Cut ahead and tell them, Reggie," panted D'Arcy minor.

Manners minor shot ahead at a breathless run, and clamoured at the door. Wally and Frank followed, panting, labouring under the weight of their burden.

The great door was wide open when they arrived, with light streaming out into the winter dark.

Reggie had spread the news. A crowd of startled faces greeted the fags as they arrived with their burden.

"It's Levison——"

"What's the trouble?"

"He's ill——"

Lord Conway received Levison from the arms of the fags, and carried him in. Lord Eastwood came hurrying from the library, with a startled face.

"What is it, Conway?"

"Something has happened to Levison, father! Will you telephone for the doctor at once, while I take him to his room?"

"But what——"

"He has been brutally attacked, I think—and has lain in the snow since."

"Good heavens!"

The viscount carried Levison up the stairs. The junior's weight was nothing to him. Frank Levison followed—he did not mean to leave his brother. He did not even think of Doris in those terrible moments.

Lord Eastwood was busy on the telephone. A few minutes more, and a car was grinding away on the snowy drive to fetch the doctor. The Christmas party gathered, discussing

the strange affair in hushed tones. Cardew, shut up in his room, was the only one of the St. Jim's party who did not know what had happened.

Lord Conway carried Levison into his room, switching on the electric light. Frank followed him. Clive had come up, his face pale and startled. With deft, quick hands Lord Conway removed Levison's clothes and put him into bed; and in a few minutes more there were hot-water bottles at his feet, and the blankets were piled on him. The viscount sat by the bed to await the arrival of the medical man. Frank sat down, quietly, his face colourless, to wait, too. Clive sat on the edge of the bed, his face the picture of misery.

Downstairs, Tom Merry & Co. were discussing the occurrence, when a soft hand was laid on Tom's arm. He turned to see Doris Levison.

"What has happened?" whispered the girl.

Tom hesitated.

"My brother——"

"Something's happened to him," said Tom reluctantly. "He—he seems to have been knocked down—somehow—I—I think it's not serious, Miss Doris."

"Where is he?"

"In his room."

The girl ran lightly up the stairs.

The Terrible Three looked up at one another with dismal faces. They knew what a shock this would be to Doris. The three Levisons—the two brothers and the sister—were bound to one another by a strong tie of affection.

"Poor Doris!" muttered Manners.

"But who—who could have done it?" breathed Lowther.

Tom Merry shook his head.

"Some footpad, I suppose—I can't make it out! Poor old Levison!"

"Bai Jove! This is feahful, you fellows," said Arthur Augustus D'Arcy dismally. "Pooah old Levison! What howwid wuffian can have pitched into him."

"It beats me," said Blake. "Hallo! Here's the doctor! Thank goodness for that."

The medical gentleman had arrived. He was taken up to Levison's room at once.

The whole party waited anxiously for news. It came at last.

The doctor's explanation was heard with amazement. Levison had been cruelly beaten—his back and arms showed weals and bruises caused by a rain of brutal blows. Someone unknown had beaten him savagely; but an examination of his clothes showed that he had not been robbed; the attack seemed to have been inspired by sheer unmeaning brutality. He had suffered as much from exposure as from the brutal beating; but he was in no danger. He would be ill—that was certain—but all he needed was careful nursing. That last item of information was a great relief to the St. Jim's party.

But who had done it—and why? That was a mystery—a mystery that puzzled and baffled all at Eastwood House.

CHAPTER 8.
Cardew's Punishment !

"**Y**OU'RE lookin' glum!"

Ralph Reckness Cardew strolled into Sidney Clive's room. He was tired of his own company; tired of speculating on the problem that troubled him. With an effort, Cardew had dismissed the matter from his mind: and he had strolled along to speak to Clive, feeling the need of company.

He expected to find Clive dressing for dinner at that hour. He found him sitting by a low fire in his room, with a dark and gloomy face.

"Haven't you heard?" muttered Clive.

"Anythin' happened?"

"Yes."

"Well, I haven't heard it," said Cardew. "I've been in my room, workin' out problems." His manner was light, but there was a shade of anxiety on his handsome face, as he looked at Clive. The thought was in his mind at once that some news had been heard of Mike Lomax's blunder—if after all Lomax had blundered. Cardew realised that it was necessary for him to be very careful.

Whether he repented of the wickedness into which his fierce resentment had hurried him, he hardly knew himself. But he knew that it was ruin to him if the truth ever came out. Even his nearest and dearest chums, Clive and Levison, must never suspect.

"Levison come in?" he drawled.

Clive nodded without speaking.

"Well, what's the jolly old happenin' that you're lookin' like

an owl about?" asked Cardew cheerily. "Has Gussy lost his latest top hat in a snow-drift?"

"Don't!" muttered Clive.

"Somethin' serious?

"Yes."

"Well, give it a name," said Cardew impatiently. "What's happened?"

"Levison——"

Cardew's face changed.

"Nothin's happened to old Ernest?"

"Yes."

"He told me he was going down to the village," said Cardew. "What's happened to him! Run over by a car——"

"No, no! He—he was found on the footpath——"

"The footpath!"

"Yes."

"In the park."

"Yes."

"Found?" repeated Cardew, in a voice so unlike his own, that it sounded strange and jarring to his ears: "Found? Did you say found? Was he hurt?"

"Yes."

"On the footpath in the park! Hurt?"

It seemed to Ralph Reckness Cardew that an icy hand was clutching at his heart. What had he done—what had he done?

He made a spring towards Clive, and caught him by the arm, so savagely that Clive gasped with pain. He shrank a little from the strange, terrible expression on Cardew's convulsed face.

"What had been done to him?" panted Cardew. "Quick —tell me—you fool, tell me!"

"He's been beaten——"

"Beaten!"

"Some ruffian seems to have set on him," groaned Clive. "He wasn't robbed—his watch and money are in his pockets. He was beaten with a cudgel—horribly—and left lying in the snow. He was insensible—when they found him—— I—I think he hasn't come to, yet."

Cardew stared at him. His grasp dropped from Clive's arm. His face was white, his eyes almost wild.

"Levison!" said Cardew, in a broken voice. "Levison! Old Ernie! My own pal—as good a pal as a fellow ever had! Oh, Heaven, I suppose this is what I deserve!"

"What do you mean?" muttered Clive. There was something in Cardew's look that almost scared him. "What——"

Cardew did not answer. He hurried out of the room, and went along to Levison's door. He tapped very softly, opened the door a few inches, and looked in.

He caught a glimpse of Ernest Levison in the bed, his unconscious face on the white pillow—of Frank, sunk deep in a chair, motionless, soundless. Doris, sitting by the head of the bed, glanced round swiftly, and put her finger to her lips.

Cardew made her a sign—an imperative sign; the girl rose silently, and crossed to the door.

"How is he?" breathed Cardew.

"He has not spoken yet."

"He is hurt?"

"Yes."

"But "—Cardew choked over the words—"Is there any danger?"

"The doctor thinks not."

Cardew felt his heart throb. A terrible fear had been upon him. He breathed more freely.

"I had to know!" he whispered, and he withdrew as silently as he had come. Doris returned to her chair by the bedside.

Cardew lingered in the broad corridor. He leaned on the oaken banister. He felt strangely tired and ill. There was a step below—Tom Merry was coming up.

Cardew's eyes gleamed at him.

The vengeance he had planned to fall upon Tom Merry had fallen upon his own chum—his best chum! It was a just punishment, so far as Cardew was concerned, for his wickedness. He felt that it was so, yet the sight of Tom Merry, well and fit, while his chum was stretched on a bed of sickness, roused deep bitterness in his breast. Wally of the Third was following Tom up the stairs, but Cardew hardly noticed the fag. He stepped towards Tom, as the Shell fellow reached the landing.

Tom's face softened as he saw the white misery in Cardew's handsome face. Evidently the disaster to Levison had hit the dandy of the Fourth hard.

"You've heard, of course?" said Tom.

"Yes—I've seen him. I—I suppose they don't know who did it," said Cardew.

"No. But the police will find him, I fancy, when Levison is well enough to give a description of him," said Tom. "The villain who did this won't escape unpunished, I am sure of that!"

Cardew winced.

Tom Merry paused a minute outside Levison's room, in the hope, perhaps, of hearing his voice. But all was silent, and Tom went on to his own room.

Cardew leaned on the banisters, sick and miserable. His wickedness had come home to him, and, like Cain of old, he felt that his punishment was more than he could bear. A wild impulse was upon him to descend to proclaim his guilt, to all the assembled house-party—to take as his just reward the horror and scorn and indignation in every face; then to go forth alone, despised, for ever shamed.

The voice of Wally of the Third came to him, low but distinct. He had hardly noticed the fag, but he realised that Wally was speaking to him—strange words for him to hear.

"You cur! You cur! You cur!"

Cardew turned a dull look on the fag. What was the boy assailing him for now—assailing a guest in his father's house? He hardly cared. He only stared dully at the red, almost flaming face of the indignant fag.

"You cur! You cur!" Wally's words came almost in a hiss between his teeth. "You've got to get out! Do you hear? You've got to get out of this house, you cur!"

Then Cardew understood.

Wally knew!

CHAPTER 9.
Get Out!

WALLY of the Third came closer to Cardew. He was trembling with passion, his hands were clenched. It seemed that it was only with difficulty that the fag restrained himself from dashing his clenched fists full into the face of the white, stricken junior standing before him.

"You cur!" Wally seemed unable to think of any other epithet. "Oh, you cur! You meant it for Tom Merry—and Levison got it! Your own pal! Oh, you cur!"

Cardew tried to pull himself together. How did Wally know? What did it all mean? He seemed dazed.

A minute or two before, the impulse had been on him to confess, to proclaim his guilt, to rush recklessly on his punishment. That impulse was gone now. At the thought of what would follow he shuddered in every fibre of his body. The look on Doris' face—when she knew—on Frank's! Death would be preferable to that! And Wally knew—he knew!

Not a word of denial came to Cardew's lips. He was not by nature given to lying. He was too reckless for that. And to save his life he could not have lied now. He looked at the indignant fag with haggard eyes.

"You're to go!" said Wally. "Do you understand? Do you want me to speak to my father—to Gussy? Will you go without a scene, or wait till you're kicked out, like the cur you are?"

Cardew made a gesture towards Levison's room.

"I can't go while he's like that!" he whispered.

"You're going, and at once! You sha'n't sleep another

night in this house!" said Wally between his teeth. "You cur!"

Cardew recovered himself a little.

"Come into my room," he said.

"No need! I've told you——"

"Come in, kid."

Cardew went to his room, and after a moment's hesitation Wally followed him. Cardew closed the door and faced the fag in the bright electric light.

"What do you know about this?" he asked. He seemed almost himself again now. His face was white, but calm; his voice cool and steady. Little outward indication was there of the misery and remorse that gnawed within.

"I saw you in the summer-house that day with that brute Lomax," muttered Wally. "I heard something. You told him to watch Tom Merry, the day he went to the abbey with Miss Fawcett, so that he would know him again. Lomax has done this."

"You've told Tom Merry?"

"No."

Cardew breathed more freely.

"I'd have warned him," said Wally. "I thought some rotten trick was going to be played—snowballing him, or something—some sort of a jape. I never thought of anything like this! I never knew there was a cowardly villain in this house!"

Cardew shrank a little.

"Only afterwards," continued Wally, "I found that Tom hadn't gone to the abbey ruins at all. Something happened to stop him."

"He did not go?"

"No; Levison went——"

"Levison!"

"Yes," said Wally savagely, "Levison went instead, for some reason. And your scoundrel, who was watching, must have taken him for Tom Merry, as he was with Miss Fawcett at the time and place you told him. When I found that that had happened I thought I'd hold my tongue. I didn't want to meddle, and I thought Tom was all right. I never dreamed it was anything but a jape of some sort. But when we found Levison I knew the kind of jape you'd planned with that brute. I knew then."

"So—so that was how!" Cardew spoke almost unconsciously. "And I—I never knew!"

"If you'd happened to know, you'd have warned your brute to be more careful, and Tom would have got this instead of Levison!" said Wally fiercely. "That's it, isn't it? Oh, you cur! That hound was watching the place for Tom, and if he'd known Tom by sight he'd have set on him. Tom was out at the same time as Levison. But he believed that Levison was Tom Merry! You couldn't even make a cowardly plot like this without bungling! I'm glad you bungled, too! I'm sorry for Levison—but better him than Tom Merry! You cur!"

"Are you going to tell them?"

"Yes, if you don't clear! You're not fit to stay in this house—or any decent house! If my father knew, he'd have the servants fling you out! If the Head knew, you'd never be allowed to go back to St. Jim's next term! You cur!"

"That's enough," said Cardew.

"You're going?"

"I'm going."

"The sooner the better," said Wally. "When Levison's able to speak he will give a description of the brute, and Lomax will be caught. He will give you away, most likely."

"He won't," said Cardew coolly. "It's worth his while to keep his mouth shut—even if they get him."

Wally clenched his hands.

"I've a good mind to go straight to the pater and tell him all that I know!" he said.

"There might be some difficulty in proving it," drawled Cardew. "A great deal of difficulty, I think."

Wally's face flamed at him.

"Let me pass! I'm going to my father!"

"No need for that," smiled Cardew—a ghastly smile. "I don't want a scandal—proved or unproved. I'm going. Will you give me time to pack my trunk, dear boy, after this exhibition of hospitality?"

Wally stepped to the door. His face was hard and set.

"If you're not gone in half an hour I shall go to my father and tell him the whole story!" he said.

And, with a look of scorn and loathing that brought a rush of crimson into Cardew's white face, the fag left the room.

Cardew stood for some minutes, silent, without movement. This was the end of it.

His dastardly plot had recoiled on his own head. His scheme of vengeance had laid his own chum on a bed of sickness. His wickedness, instead of being buried deep in the deepest secrecy, was known. He was ordered out of the house by a Third Form fag! And he had to go! He had to go—without a word to Levison, without a word to the faithful friend who had been struck down by his bravo's blunder!

This was the end and outcome of his long and bitter feud with Tom Merry—a feud begun in sheer idleness, perverse waywardness—which had led him from bad to worse, till it had landed him in crime! For this was crime!

This was the end—the end that he deserved. The brute whom he had employed had exceeded his instructions—as Cardew might have expected, from the nature of the man. And it was upon Levison that the man's savage brutality had been wreaked. This was what he deserved—and now he was going, creeping away like a thief in the night, leaving surmise, perhaps suspicion, behind him.

And there was no help!

A quarter of an hour later Ralph Reckness Cardew slipped quietly from the house. A note left on his dressing-table, addressed to D'Arcy, made his excuses—explained that he was called suddenly to his grandfather's home. That was Cardew's only farewell. He went without a word—and it was not till some hours later that Tom Merry & Co. knew that he had gone.

CHAPTER 10.
Forget and Forgive!

FOR three days the doctor's orders kept Levison of the Fourth to his bed; and for two or three days further he had to keep his room. Then he was able to rejoin the house-party, looking a little pale, but very like his old self. There was keen sympathy from everyone; but Levison was not a fellow to ask for sympathy or to care for it; he seemed to wish chiefly that the whole episode should be forgotten as speedily as possible.

But it was not so easy for such a matter to be dismissed. The brute who had attacked him had to be found and punished, and Levison had two interviews with the police on the subject. But he was able to give no description whatever of the man.

That was a disappointment to the police, and a surprise to Levison's comrades. The winter dusk, the suddenness of the dastardly attack, explained it, perhaps; yet it was strange that so keen and observant a fellow as Levison should have seen and noted nothing of his assailant. Whatever he knew or had seen, the fact remained that he gave no description of Mike Lomax; he simply stated that he had nothing whatever to say on that point. Neither did he advance any theory as to why the attack had been made.

Of all the St. Jim's party, only Wally knew why Levison was silent. From Levison's silence Wally realised that Levison knew or suspected. He was silent because to speak might have involved his own chum in disgrace and shame. And as Levison was silent Wally kept his own counsel—he did not even speak to Levison on the subject. He shrank from the terrible scandal that would have followed the exposure of the facts; and if Levison, the injured party, chose to hold his tongue, it was not for anyone else to speak. Cardew was gone, and it was best for the matter to die away into oblivion.

Levison was told that Cardew was gone, and made no comment. Only Wally of the Third knew that he guessed why the dandy of the Fourth had left.

Cardew certainly was not missed by the Christmas party at Eastwood House. Tom Merry & Co. wondered a little at his abrupt departure, but it came as a relief to them.

It was on the second day after Levison came down that he set out on a ramble by himself in the park, avoiding the company even of Doris and Frank. His ramble brought him to the little summer-house in the wood—lonely, banked round with drifting snow.

He glanced round him before he entered.

"You've come, old bean?"

Ralph Reckness Cardew stood there. His manner was light and airy, as of old; but there were lines in his handsome face, the imprint of troubled thought. Cardew's days had not been happy since the disaster to his chum.

"Yes—I had your letter," said Levison. He held out his hand frankly.

"Better let me tell you somethin' before you shake hands with me," smiled Cardew.

"You need tell me nothing," said Levison quietly.

Cardew started.

"You know?"

"Yes."

"Then D'Arcy minor has told, after all?"

"Wally?" repeated Levison. "He has told nothing. Does he know anything? How could he know?"

"He knew so much that he ordered me out of the house," said Cardew coolly. "That's why I went. I wasn't keen on leaving you without a word."

"Well, he has said nothing, if he knows," said Levison.

Cardew looked relieved.

"Then how do you know anything?" he asked.

"I've thought it out. I knew you were planning something, as I told you—something foolish, something wrong," said Levison. "I warned you, as you remember. When this happened—I knew. Not at the moment, of course—but thinking it over afterwards. I knew the man; I'd seen him at the abbey ruins, where I went instead of Tom Merry——"

"That's what did the mischief."

"There was no motive for the attack on me; the man was evidently put up to it. Nobody had a motive for that. But somebody had a motive for putting up an attack on Tom Merry. Cardew, I should never have dreamed that you were capable of it!"

"Neither should I—until I did it!" said Cardew. "But I never meant it to happen as it did. A thrashing—that was all I meant. And I never dreamed that the brute would make a mistake in his victim. But I'm not makin' excuses. It was the limit—the outside edge—I know that now. I knew it all the time, of course, but wouldn't see it till too late. They haven't got the man?"

"I gave no description of him."

"For my sake?"

"Yes."

Cardew was silent for a minute or two.

"I asked you to meet me here, to confess," he said. "That's not needed, as you know already. I'm prepared to face the music."

"There's no music to face," said Levison, with a faint smile.

"You mean you're takin' it quietly?"

"What else can I do? I don't want you disgraced—I don't want you punished. You know that. If it had happened to Tom Merry, and I'd guessed the truth, I should have been bound to speak out. It happened to me, and it's my own business—so I shall say nothing."

Another long silence. Cardew's face was quivering.

"I'd better go, then," he said. "I understand that it's all over—you've done with me. You can tell Clive, or he'll be puzzled when we go back to St. Jim's. Good-bye!"

He turned to the doorway.

"I shall tell Clive nothing," said Levison; "and it will make no difference when we get back to St. Jim's. You must have been mad to act as you did, Cardew. I've had a rotten time; but I'm glad I went through it instead of Tom Merry. It can be kept secret now. We've got to forget it."

"You mean that, Levison?"

"Of course I do."

Levison held out his hand again. This time Cardew took it.

. . . .

Ernest Levison said nothing of that meeting when he returned to Eastwood House. Cardew's name was hardly mentioned again among the St. Jim's party so long as the Christmas holidays lasted. As the vacation drew to its close and the new term neared Tom Merry thought of his rival, and wondered what would be the outcome of the feud when he met Cardew again at St. Jim's. Only Levison knew that there was a change in Ralph Reckness Cardew—and that his long contest with Tom Merry would take a new and surprising turn when the juniors met once more at the old school.

THE END.

Brief Introduction.

Jack Morton, the popular centre-forward of Boltwich, has succeeded in clearing himself of the charge of theft brought against him by his cousin, George Clifton. In addition, he has established his right to a share of his late grandfather's great fortune.

THE TRIERS!

(Conclusion.)

Jack's Homecoming!

IT was an hour later that Jack Morton entered the old cottage where he and his mother had spent so many happy years of their lives, and as he entered and saw the dear white head bent over her sewing in the old way, in the same old chair, he sprang forward with a glad cry.

"Mother!"

"My boy—my boy!"

They kissed one another, and in another minute the lad was telling the old lady everything of what had happened.

With many a startled and agonised gasp of surprise she listened to it. She could scarcely believe that she and Jack were coming into their own at last. But, like the good-hearted soul that she was, when at last Jack had got to the end of his telling, she begged him to have mercy on George Clifton.

Jack nodded.

"Yes, mother," he said, "that is why I did nothing at the time; though I think that it would have been easy enough for me to persuade the inspector to have arrested the fellow then and there. But it was difficult. Whatever George Clifton has done to me, I cannot forget that he is my own flesh and blood. And, quite apart from that, there is the further consideration that I would have had, probably, to have dragged old Graves into it—and I am very grateful to him!"

"Yes, indeed," agreed the old lady, "his daughter has been an angel to me, my boy, since all this trouble started. I hope that nothing happens to him!"

"Nothing shall happen to anyone if I can help it!" said Jack.

Then he started, for suddenly there had come to his ears again the now well-known chant:

"We want Jack Morton!"

He went to the window of the cottage, and, looking out, saw that the crowd had surrounded the little gate.

He went out.

"What is it, boys?" he asked.

"Have you forgotten there is a League match this afternoon, Jack?" they cried.

He started, and a broad grin came to his face.

"By Jove, I had!" he said. "But I'll come along now, and we will see what we can do with them. Just half a minute!"

He rushed back to his mother, explained the situation, promised her he would not be gone long, and then hurried back to the "boys."

The Last Game!

BY this time the town of Boltwich was getting somewhat used to the excitement and alarms in connection with Jack Morton, their youthful centre-forward; but this afternoon there was a record scene on the famous ground as Jack ran on to the field with the team.

The story had spread about Boltwich that he had been set free from the charge which George Clifton had brought against THE GEM LIBRARY.—No. 829.

him; but, even more, in the strange way that good news has of getting about a town, the news had spread, too, that there was queer work on foot, and that before very long folks would hear that Jack Morton had become a power in their midst, and was indeed going to become the head of Clifton's.

The cheers, then, were genuine and hearty, for the good people of Boltwich had endured the hardships put upon them by George Clifton for long enough, and they were delighted to think that a youngster who had proved himself such a good sport, always ready to play the game, and always ready to take the hard knocks of life with a smile, was going to take the place of a man who had invariably proved himself a bully and cheat.

The game commenced.

Boltwich were playing a very fast and clever team from the North of England, who never yet had suffered defeat on the Boltwich pitch, and who had come down again to teach the home lads a lesson or two.

But it was they who learned the lesson this afternoon.

From the kick-off—which the visitors took—Jack jumped right in, and, without a moment's hesitation, was down the field like a flash.

It was a bit of a fluke, of course, but it was that sort of fluke which, either in football, or in the bigger game of life, is often called genius, and it probably is, for the real genius is the man or the boy who knows how to take a chance while other people are thinking about it.

Anyhow, Jack got right down the field, and before the game had been in progress a full minute he had sent in a stinging shot, which had defeated the visiting goalie, and had notched the first point for the home side.

A remarkable scene followed. It was, of course, most regrettable; but the visitors, who knew about the trials and tribulations through which the youngster had passed, took it like good fellows.

The crowd broke on to the pitch then and there, and the game had to be held up for a few minutes while they raised Jack Morton shoulder high once again, and carried him round the ground.

"Good old Jack!" they yelled.

Then, as they passed the stands with him, Jack glanced round, and saw the place where his pals the Triers were all sitting, and, raising himself as best he could, he waved a cheery greeting to them.

"All the best, Jack!" cried the Triers, and he knew that in them he had friends for life.

Well, of one thing, at any rate, they could be sure, that now Jack Morton had come into his own, none of them need ever worry about the future.

At last the game was able to proceed, and there was no holding Jack or his team.

They were simply irresistible, and before the final whistle blew Jack had scored four times, and the visitors could certainly not go north again proudly declaring that they had never been defeated on the Boltwich ground.

* * *

Jack awakened next morning with that very pleasant feeling of wondering what had happened recently in his life to make him feel so very pleased with himself.

Then suddenly he remembered, and, looking up, realised that he must, after all the exhausting business of the last few days, have overslept himself, for there was his mother standing in the room at his side, handing him a cup of tea and a letter.

"A letter for you, dear boy," she said.

The lad took it in surprise, and then gave a gasp.

"It's from George Clifton!" he said. "You had better hear what he has got to say, mother!"

He opened the letter, and a moment later he was reading it to his mother.

"My dear Morton," Clifton had written.—"I shall be out of England by the time you read this, and I dare say that you will be glad to hear it. I have been thinking things over, and, on the whole, it seems to me that the best thing that I can do for everyone concerned, is to make a dash for it. I have a little money of my own, and I intend to go to a new country and start a new life.

"I don't say that I regret that I have done the things that I have, but I can say with perfect candour that I am very weary of all the worry and anxiety of not going straight, and so I am going to throw off all the old life, take a new name, and strike out for myself. At the same time as I write this, I am writing to my lawyers, making over all my share in our grandfather's business and estate to you, and you will not hear of me again.

"I have nothing more to say; but, perhaps, having done you many a bad turn, I may be allowed to wish you the best of good luck, and perhaps you, in return, will permit me to escape, and to live in peace. If you do, I can assure you that you will never hear of me again.

"Your cousin,

"GEORGE CLIFTON."

There were tears in the old lady's eyes as she looked down at Jack.

"Poor man!" she said.

Jack gave a grunt.

"I don't want his share," he said; "and if he does this, I shall keep his share for him. But at the same time I am jolly glad that he is out of the way; he was a bad egg, and there is no getting round that, mother!"

But George Clifton had gone, and a few days later Jack Morton had taken his place at the head of the big firm, and was safely in the saddle.

People expressed concern as to whether the lad would be able to cope with all the new responsibilities that had come his way; but those who had watched him play centre-forward so often were quite certain that he had in him all the makings of a great leader of men, even in their work, and there it is that a leader's qualities are most tried, and in a few weeks all Boltwich knew that the lad was more than equal to his job.

But he had retired from first-class football.

He started with Laurie Robson, his best pal, a club called the Triers, and before many seasons were out that club had become famous all over the land for fair play, good sportsmanship, and hard, honest playing.

THE END.

Are you reading "TOM OF THE AJAX"?

This splendid seasonable
yarn has been—

—written specially
for the GEM !

The Stolen Pie!

A Magnificent and Amusing
Story, introducing the old-
time favourites, Gan Waga,
the Eskimo, and Rupert
Thurston & Co.

By

SIDNEY DREW.

CHAPTER 1.
Some Uninvited Guests !

DARRANCOMBE HALL had come to Rupert Thurston through the death of his hard-riding, hard-drinking uncle, Dale Thurston, one of the last of the old-fashioned squires who loved a good horse and a good hound, and detested motor-cars and all new-fangled inventions like he hated poison. In his lifetime he had practically ignored the very existence of his nephew, but as he had died a bachelor and forgotten to make a will the hall and estate belonged to Rupert after the Government had helped itself to a substantial slice for death duties and other charges.

As Thurston had never visited Darrancombe since his boyhood, and had almost forgotten what the old gentleman was like, he was not prostrated with grief when the news of Dale Thurston's death reached him. He was in New York at the time, and, as the solicitor's letter had been following him about for weeks from place to place, the squire had been laid to rest in the family vault long before the new owner of Darrancombe Hall was aware that he had passed out of this life. Having been born with a silver spoon in his mouth, as the saying is, this unexpected addition to his fortune did not excite Rupert Thurston very much, and three months passed before he found time to drive down to Darrancombe, accompanied by his friend, Prince Ching Lung.

"From what I remember of it, Ching," he said, "it's a fine old place, and my uncle looked after it well. The lawyer told me it was in excellent repair. He never grudged money for the hall, his pack of hounds, and his wine-cellar. He hunted his pack for over forty years, and they'll expect me to keep it on. That would mean spending the winter down here, and I'm much too fond of a roving life to do that."

"With the Lord of the Deep in dry dock for a good many weeks you have time on your hands," said Ching Lung. "Hello, what's this?"

It looked like a police-trap. They were running into a quaint sleepy-looking village of thatched cottages when several men sprang out of the hedge and held a rope across the road. Thurston stopped his big car, and one of the men came forward and touched his cap.

"Begging your pardon, sir," he said, "but we be stoppin' all cars till we do find the right 'un. Be you Squire Thurston, if you please?"

"I'm Thurston of Darrancombe Hall, if that's what you want," said Rupert.

The man raised his hand and someone sounded a bugle. Cottage doors opened and cheering people rushed out of the cottages into the village street.

Others rushed out of the Darrancombe Arms, mostly red-coated gentlemen with faces of a similar hue, who mounted horses led by grooms, and then, with the huntsmen in front and the whipper-in behind, the Darrancombe hounds, thirty couples strong, came trotting across the village green.

Amid cheers for the squire, ropes were fastened to the car, and, surrounded by hounds and horsemen and his shouting tenants, the new squire and Ching Lung were dragged in triumph up the village street, past the inn and the old church, through the gateway of the hall, across the splendidly-timbered park, to the very door of the splendid house where the servants were assembled.

Then Rupert made some kind of a speech, which was cheered to the echo. Presently he found himself in the spacious entrance hall being introduced by his uncle's solicitor to the gentlemen in scarlet coats, riding-breeches, and glossy boots.

"I didn't expect this, Mr. Gigland," said Rupert, when he had time to take breath.

"I had to do it, sir," explained the solicitor. "They expected it, you know. Though I didn't know what time you'd arrive I made arrangements. A banquet to-night to the members of the hunt, and unlimited cold beef and refreshments to everybody outside. Refreshments also in moderation at the Darrancombe Arms to all comers, of course. The whole thing won't cost a great deal, and I wanted you to make a good impression."

"Oh, I don't mind what it costs," said Rupert. "Let them enjoy themselves, Mr. Gigland, and don't trouble about the expense."

There was a heavy raid on old Squire Thurston's wine-cellar that night, but at last Rupert's guests rode away in the moonlight, and Thurston and the prince, who had donned scarlet for the banquet like the rest of them, were left to smoke a last cigar in peace.

"You'll settle down and become a country squire yet, old chap," said Ching Lung. "This is a grand old place that has come to you."

"True enough, Ching, but there will have to be some alterations if I stay here," said Rupert. "Candles in massive silver candlesticks are pretty things to look at, Ching, but I prefer electric light. There isn't even a telephone in the place, and I believe with thirty-five bedrooms there are only two bath-rooms. We must alter all that. I can ride to hounds as well as most people, but I know nothing about hunting a pack, and that's what they seem to expect me to do. It's not in my line, and I don't intend to try it. I expect I shall end by letting the place if I can find a tenant."

While Rupert and the prince were chatting, a motor-car drove into the village in the clear moonlight. Darrancombe was fast asleep and as quiet as a graveyard. There were four gentlemen in the car,

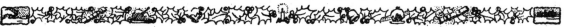

and they were all out of work. The car stopped before the inn.

"Bedad, get down and bang at the dure, Ben," said the driver, "and ax where we are."

"Not likely, souse me, and have a jug of water poured over me, my lad," said the person spoken to. "Hold easy a minute while I look at the sign-board."

It was rather a faded sign-board. There was a dim picture of some animal that might have been a fox or a poodle, but the lettering was more distinct.

"It's the Darrancombe Arms right enough, Barry," said the man who had gone to investigate. "There's some big gates slap ahead, souse me, so that ought to be the hall."

Five minutes later a heavy knocking at the massive front door of Darrancombe Hall startled Ching Lung and the new squire. All the servants had gone to bed. Thurston took up one of the massive silver candlesticks and Ching Lung unbarred the door and opened it.

"Sorry to trouble you so late, by honey, but could you oblige us with the loan of a spanner?" asked a familiar voice.

"And some suppers, Chingy," added another familiar voice. "We awful hungriness, old bean."

"Out o' work, souse me, and starving," said the man who had looked at the sign-board of the inn. "We ain't tasted a bite o' food for umpteen years."

"Oh, for the smill of a hambone or a boite from the wing of a bloater! Av ye don't take us in and grub us, we'll have to pawn the mother," said the gentleman with the Irish accent, dropping into poetry: "Bedad, and av ye dhroive us out, you'll foind your mother up the spout."

It was Ching Lung's motor-car, and large to go up a pawnbroker's spout, but as he did not wish to lose the car, and the house was Rupert Thurston's, he stood aside. The visitors, Mr. Thomas Prout, also on the books of that craft, and Mr. Gan Waga, were certainly out of regular employment while the yacht was in dry-dock, but they had been provided with comfortable quarters in Porthampton and their wages were being paid regularly.

"And how did you find us out, you blackguards?" asked the Squire of Darrancombe.

"It was this letter, sir," said Prout. "It said on it that if it couldn't be delivered to you aboard the yacht it was to be forwarded on to you at this place, by honey. And thinking it might be important——"

"You bagged my car out of the garage and treated yourselves to a joy-ride," said Ching Lung. "Things were getting a bit too slow for you ashore at Porthampton, I suppose. I've a good mind to throw you out again and make you walk back. What's that terribly urgent letter about, Rupert?"

"A bill from my bootmaker," said Rupert Thurston. "If you blackguards want anything to eat, go and find the larder, for I'm not going to waken the servants for your benefit. And you can sleep on the floor, which is the proper place for you. Why couldn't you stay away till you were asked?"

"Kick 'em out neck and crop, and be done with it," said Ching Lung. "Fire the whole bunch of them, and let's go to bed."

In spite of this chilly welcome, and Ching Lung's suggestion to pitch them out on their faces into the cold park, the three hungry mariners grinned, and clutching a candlestick, Gan Waga waddled out of the room, and, tilting his snub nose upwards, he sniffed the air.

"Bedad, bhoys, the Iskimo is on the scent," said Barry O'Rooney. "He'll smill the larder a moile off, and that's the only bit of use the fat rogue is in the wide worrld. Come quick and muzzle the rascal afore he ates the lot. Afther the spalpeen, or he'll ate the place bare, bones and all."

Clutching more silver candlesticks, the three hungry sea-dogs set sail in the wake of the Eskimo, whose unerring nose led him to the kitchen, and from the kitchen to the larder. In the kitchen the fire was still burning. Prout raked it together while the bo'sun lighted the lamps. It was a wonderful larder, and Rupert Thurston's guests at the banquet had not succeeded in emptying it. There was a whole salmon, a huge game pie that had not been cut, and a sirloin of beef as intact as when it came out of the oven. There were jellies and tarts, and trifles and blancmanges, and fruit salads, and cheese and celery, and nuts galore. There were also bottles of wine and bottles of ale and spirits still sealed and corked, which the butler had been too tired to restore to the cellar and put under lock and key.

"By honey, Mr. Rupert and the prince didn't exactly give us the glad eye, as they call it," said Prout, as he proceeded to carve the salmon, "but whether they meant it or didn't mean it, I'm glad I came! I suppose you couldn't manage a slice of this stuff, could you, Ben?"

"I could manage two better, souse me," replied the bo'sun. "So make it two, Tommy. One slice looks so lonely on a chap's plate!"

"And, bedad, Gan," remarked Barry O'Rooney, "you ate properly wid a knife and fork! None o' that disgusting finger business, and then wiping your hands on your hair. Give him some fish quick, Tom, for he's got his greedy little oies on that lovely game-poie, and he'll be snatching ut and bolting! Phwat a loife! Phwat a spread! For marcy's sake, Ben, don't let the monsther do ut! He's putting vanilla custard and vinegar on his salmon!"

"Yo' not knows what's goodness!" grinned Gan Waga, as he reached for the Worcester sauce. "M'yum! Custards and salmons, they just lovelifuls!"

After carving the salmon, Prout sharpened the knife and began to operate on the surloin of beef. Gan Waga could not keep his beady little eyes from the game-pie. It was large and oblong and beautifully brown and shiny. The Eskimo loved game-pie.

"Looks, Tommy—looks!" he said, in a hoarse whisper. "What that big blackness thing behinds yo', hunk?"

Prout, taken off his guard, turned his head, and Maddock and O'Rooney rose from their chairs to look. Gan Waga's arm went round that noble pie, and before they realised it the Eskimo and the pie were half-way up the staircase.

"The pie!" roared Barry O'Rooney. "The murthering thafe of an Iskimo has pinched ut! Have at the rogue!"

At the top of the staircase Gan Waga lost his bearings; but only for a moment. Clutching his prize, he waddled along a gloomy passage till he saw the bright, wintry moon shining through the front-light above the front door. The angry pursuers were not far away. Putting down the pie, Gan Waga turned the key and pulled back the bolts.

As Prout & Co., taken off their guard, turned their heads, Gan Waga's arms went round the noble pie, which he promptly collared.

"Souse me, we've got him!" growled Maddock. "He's gone out, and he can't run for toffee. We'll give him pinching pie, the fat waster!"

Over snow or ice or in the water the Eskimo could travel at great speed, but on land he was slow and clumsy. A capture seemed certain. But they had reckoned without the car, which still stood where they had left it.

"Ho, ho, hoo, hoo!" laughed the Eskimo. "The merry olds pie nots good fo' yo', dearies, 'cos it give yo' nightmares! Good-bye-e!"

Barry O'Rooney made a frantic plunge down the steps and a dive at the rear of the car. He missed by inches, and fell sprawling. Smoothly and swiftly the car ran over the grass, and came to a standstill in the open, where it was impossible to stalk it in the bright moonlight. Gan Waga raised the pie aloft and bowed to them.

"By honey," said Prout, grinding his teeth, "I hope it'll choke him! I didn't mean to eat any beef, but to save up for that!"

"So did I, souse me!" groaned the bo'sun. "I never see such a lovely pie in all my life! I only wish it was chock full of rat poison!"

Keeping a wary eye astern, so that he could make sail in case of pursuit, Gan Waga opened his knife, cut a wedge-shaped piece out of the pie, and munched joyfully. It was the very monarch of game-pies—a delicious mingling of pheasants, partridges, hare, and woodcock. Gan Waga patted himself and blinked upwards at the moon, heedless of scowling eyes and shaking fists and the horrid things Prout, Maddock, and O'Rooney were saying about him.

CHAPTER 2.
The Hunted Eskimo!

RUPERT THURSTON and Prince Ching Lung went to their bedrooms without troubling any further about the late-comers, for they knew that they were quite capable of looking after themselves. The beef and the other things were so good that the mariners did very well in spite of the regrettable absence of the game-pie. Though gone, it was not forgotten, and Barry recalled it as they sat in front of the kitchen fire, smoking their pipes.

"A dirthy thrick!" he said. "Didn't Oi warn ye he was watching that poie, and that he'd be afther snatching ut and bolting wid ut, the fat brigand?"

"And to catch us the silly way he did, souse me—that's what makes me so wild!" said the bo'sun. "Older than Adam that same trick is!"

"It's those rotten old tricks that come off," grunted Prout. "If he wolfs half that pie, by honey, he'll sleep for a week! If we could only get him napping, we could run him out about ten miles, chuck him off the car, and leave him to foot it back. There's nothing he hates worse than a long walk."

"Faith, that's a foine oidea, Tommy!" said Barry O'Rooney, rubbing his hands. "Let me get hould of him aslape, and, bedad, we'll give him all the walking he wants, the dishonest blatherskite! Ut sames murther to lave a noice foire loike this, but justice must be done, so Oi'll explore a few, bhoys."

Gan Waga had eaten all the game-pie he wanted to eat—for the time being. He could easily have driven the car a safe distance from the house, and slept in it quite comfortably; but he was not sleepy. Gan Waga felt thirsty, and he also felt lonely. He was not pining for the company of Prout, Maddock, and O'Rooney, although he was very friendly with the three mariners when it did not happen to be the other way about. Gan wanted Ching Lung, for with Ching Lung he knew he would be perfectly safe, ever if he had purloined the whole larder.

Under the white, silent moon the deserted park looked very ghostly. It was cold, too, but the Eskimo did not object to cold, but liked it. There was plenty of pie left, and Gan Waga did not intend to waste it. He got out of the car, carrying the remainder of the pie on a cushion, and waddled towards the house. Barry O'Rooney, who was watching from the door, gave a silent chuckle.

"Come along, young feller-me-lad!" he muttered. "Bedad, you don't know who's waiting for you! Oi'll tache you to pinch poies, you ugly haythen!"

Then Barry O'Rooney saw something else. A man stepped out the shadow of a tree and confronted the Eskimo. Cushion and pie slipped from the startled Eskimo's limp hands. The man had a big cudgel, and advanced brandishing it as if to strike. Self-protection being the first law of nature, Gan Waga made a clutch at the nearest available weapon, which happened to be the remains of the pie. He hurled it with both hands, and fled for the car. The man with the cudgel uttered a smothered kind of howl. From the doorway Barry O'Rooney saw him prance about on one leg, and then sit down. He got up, pranced about on the other leg, and then sat down again, this time on the cushion. Finally, he managed to erect himself on both legs, and then, shaking his cudgel, he set out across the grass after the terrified Eskimo, who was running his hardest.

"One of the gamekeepers," grinned Barry O'Rooney. "Bedad, Gan, ut's good for you, my bhoy, he did that slithering and skating, or he'd have had you! Och, he'll have you by the neck yet, av you don't put more pepper into ut! Long-legs wins, and the Iskimo is bate. Sprint, Gan, you fat tortoise, or ut's a woipe wid his shillelagh ye'll be getting! Murther and gridirons! Phwat's the mather wid the man? Are his boots soled wid oice?"

"Ooh! Wa-ooh!" shrieked Gan.

A prod in the back from the pursuer's cudgel elicited the shriek from the Eskimo. Another stride, and his hand would have been on Gan Waga's collar, and Barry was about to rush out to prevent the pie-stealer from being roughly treated, when the man seemed to skid as if he had trodden on something very slippery. For the third time in succession he sat down with a good deal of violence. He was a person of determination, for he was up again at once; but his slip had saved the Eskimo, for Gan Waga was in the car. The self-starter worked without a hitch, and once his hands were on the steering-wheel the Eskimo's courage and confidence came back to him.

"Good-bye-e!" he cried, though his voice was thin and breathless.

Still the man did not give up. Since his first smothered howl when the pie had hit him he had not uttered a sound. He continued to run after the car.

"Bedad, Oi'd bether fetch the others and stop this!" thought Barry. "There must be more keepers where Gan's going, or the chap knows he's running into a corner, or he wouldn't be following up. Sure, a hoiding wouldn't do that fat thafe of an Iskimo a bit of harrm, but the prince wouldn't loike it. Oi'll wager that av he does catch Gan he'll be in such a stew of a timper he'll use that ould blackthorn of his purty free!"

Barry hurried in, grinning all over his face, to impart the glad news. Darrancombe Hall was an ancient, rambling place, and in his haste Barry O'Rooney found the wrong staircase, and a very dark one. There were lots of stairs, but he put his foot in the wrong place. An anguished howl and a succession of bumps broke the placid stillness of the night. When Barry O'Rooney came to

A man, brandishing a stick as if to strike, stepped out of the shadows and confronted Gan Waga.

a full stop the gloom around him sparkled with stars which, like the particular stair he had tried to put his foot on, were not really there at all.

Barry got up, moaning, only to bang his head against a shelf, dislodging a couple of jars or bottles, that clattered down and broke. Evidently, by the smell, one was a bottle of pickles. Mingled with the aroma of vinegar was another scent quite familiar to him, but he did not stay to think what it was.

"Bedad, Oi'll have a lump on my head the soize of a punching-ball!" he groaned. "And Oi belave that rotten vinegar and sthuff has splashed all over me. Phwat a hole! No gas, no electric loight—only rotten ould paraffin lamps and candles. Ut's a marcy Oi didn't break a limb!"

This time Barry O'Rooney was wise enough to strike a match. The smell of pickles and the other smell, which was far stronger, accompanied him, for he had managed to smash a large bottle of anchovy sauce or essence of anchovy over his boots. He discovered the stairs to the kitchen, and went down. There were three chairs drawn up before the fire, but they were empty. Prout and Maddock had gone in search of something softer to spend the night on than kitchen chairs with wooden seats and backs. After that glorious supper they wanted easy chairs at least, with plenty of cushions, if they could not find couches or Chesterfields. And at the moment Barry was searching for them they were cuddling down to slumber in Rupert Thurston's drawing-room.

"Bad luck to thim for a brace of ugly desarters!" growled Barry. "Av Gan puts up a foight wid that keeper-chap there'll be a purty tale to tell. And av he wanted to tell the tale, he won't understhand the fellow's counthry accent, and ut's as sure as the nose on my face the man won't understhand Gan Waga's lingo. Drat the Iskimo! Pouf! Phwat's this awful smell Oi'm carrying about wid me? Phew! 'Ut's loike sthale fish. Phwat a loife, bad luck to ut!"

Barry did not intend to fall down any more flights of stairs, so he made no further search for Prout and Maddock. In spite of Gan Waga's evil deeds, he did not wish him to be ill-treated by an angry gamekeeper. The smell of fish reemed to grow more pronounced in the fresh air. There was no sign of the keeper, the car, or of Gan Waga. The Eskimo was a good driver, and, so long as he had room and petrol, and nothing went wrong with the works, he was not likely to be caught. Barry growled a few more growls, and set off in the direction that the car and its pursuer had taken.

And as Barry O'Rooney walked over the dewy grass of Darrancombe Park beneath the silvery moon, he left a sweet scent of essence of anchovy behind him.

Meanwhile, that low-down pie-snatcher Gan Waga crawled along and took a good look at the man whose unexpected appearance with the big stick had startled him so much, and to whom he had given the pie. He was a lean, bony man quite six feet tall, and he had a lot of black whiskers. When an Eskimo manages to grow whiskers at all it is always a very thin crop, and that perhaps is why Gan Waga disliked them. In addition to the black whiskers, the man also wore cord breeches, leather gaiters,

THE GEM LIBRARY.—No. 829.

thick-soled boots studded with hobnails, a grey coat with bulky pockets, a brown billycock hat, and the thick stick. He had a long, steady stride, and he kept it up.

"I run yo' offs yo' legses, my hairy old beans!" grinned the Eskimo, who was quite himself again. "Yo' have big, hard cornses on yo' par feet ifs yo' mean to follow me about all night!" He grinned, and then raised his voice. "How yo' wases, Charlie? Charlie can't catch me!"

Then Gan Waga looked ahead. He saw a lake and a long stretch of undulating park-land dotted with clumps of trees. It looked good going, though it was rather like a switchback; and, as he liked to see the gamekeeper run, he travelled slowly. The grim pursuer never varied his stride, but kept on at the same steady, swinging pace. The car bumped off the grass on to a gravelled road that seemed to make a circuit of the lake. Gan Waga kept to the road, and smiled back at the gamekeeper, who came crunching after him.

"Yo' be awfulness tired, old dears!" said the Eskimo sweetly. "Why yo' chasing me about, hunk? Yo' ought to be home in bedses, Charlie!"

"Wait till Oi do get 'old of you, me lad!" said the gamekeeper, speaking for the first time. "You'll be in bed for three solid months arter Oi done wi' you!"

"Come on the grass some morer, Charlie," said the kindly Eskimo, "and it not hurts yo' par feets so muchness!"

An ordinary man would have abandoned such a hopeless chase; but the gamekeeper was not an ordinary man. Gan Waga was going in the proper direction to suit him. Two of the under-keepers lived in a cottage at the head of the lake, and it was almost time for them fo come on duty and patrol the park. He had his whistle in his pocket, and he fancied that the fat, foreign-looking poacher in the motor-car would throw up his hands and surrender at the sight of a gun, and he cursed himself for having left his own gun behind.

Gan Waga put on speed and drew away, which gave him time to stop and light a cigar; but the gamekeeper did not halt. The Eskimo began to get tired of it, and thought he might as well go home. Doubtless Prout, Maddock, and O'Rooney would be asleep by this time. He was still thirsty after so much pie, but there was lots of water in the lake. Gan made another spurt, got down and drank out of his cupped hands, and waited in the car until the dogged gamekeeper came within earshot.

"I goings now, Charlie!" he said. "Yo' most champion runners, so yo' can chase yo'selfs all night! Shave yo' whiskers off next times, and then yo' not have so much weight to carry! I awful sadness to leave yo', Charlie, but I want some morer suppers! Chi-ike! Charlie can't catch me!"

The Eskimo waved a farewell. Another backward glance showed him the position of the house. The gamekeeper uttered a yell of rage, and hurled his cudgel after the Eskimo, who took the road round the lake. Further pursuit was utterly hopeless. Dashing into the shrubbery he found a hidden wire, and pulled it. As he rushed past the cottage at the head of the lake the Eskimo heard a terrific bang, so close to him that he fancied a tyre had burst. It was not a tyre,

however, but a spring gun the keeper had fired to warn his two comrades that evil-doers were about.

Fancying that he had been shot at, Gan Waga stooped low over the steering-wheel. The keeper was running to cut him off, but he had no possible chance of doing so. The car circled the lake at almost racing speed, and plunged into a dark tunnel of trees. When he emerged Gan Waga guessed rightly that the curving road would enter the main drive further on and bring him to the very steps of Darrancombe Hall.

And then, to his horror, the engine gasped and grunted and gave out. The tank was dry! There were some petrol-tins in the car, but they were dry also. In the shadows behind he saw—or imagined he saw—the dim figure of a running man. It was hardly possible that it could be his remorseless pursuer, unless he had found some amazing short cut; but the Eskimo was getting nervy.

He sprang out of the useless car and took to his legs. If he had been near the lake all would have been well, for he was like a seal in the water; but the lake was far away, and Gan Waga was sorrowfully aware that he was a poor runner. He was not much of a fighter, either, and he was also sorrowfully aware that the big, bony man with the whiskers would not be in a gentle mood. He gave another frantic glance over his shoulder, and there, without a doubt, was the remorseless pursuing shadow.

"Oh, mi! Oh dears, dears, dears!" groaned the Eskimo. "I wishes I never steal that rotten old pie! Ooh! Murders!"

Suddenly he saw a long, low building with an iron gate. It was impossible to reach the house before being overtaken, for it was too far away. If he could not run he might hide, and so evade the terrible man with the black whiskers who refused to be shaken off.

The iron gate ought to have been locked. The reason it was not locked was due to the fact that, for the first time in living memory, refreshments were being given away free at the Darrancombe Arms. In his hurry to get there before the last barrel ran dry the person in charge of the gate had neglected his duty. Gazing back, his little beady eyes round and scared, Gan Waga turned the handle and pushed.

Then Gan Waga uttered a weird howl of terror and anguish. Dim shapes rose out of the gloom and surrounded him. There was an uproar of horrifying sounds, and the darkness seemed filled with glaring eyes and gleaming teeth. The dark shapes leapt at him and hurled him from his feet by sheer weight, and galloped over him as he lay on his back gasping and moaning.

Gan Waga had opened the gate of one of the Darrancombe Kennels. There were fourteen couples of hounds in that particular kennel. They were pleased to see the Eskimo, and they had expressed their pleasure by jumping at him and knocking him down; but they were much more pleased to see the open gate. Out they streamed joyously, headed by old Shafter, the pick of the pack.

Two minutes later they had found the ruins of the pie and the cushion that was well smeared with it, and three minutes later they had torn the cushion to shreds.

Ching Lung started out of his slumbers. In his dreams he had been hunting, and the hounds were hot on the

Printed and published every Wednesday by the Proprietors, The Amalgamated Press (1922), Ltd., The Fleetway House, Farringdon Street, London, E.C.4. Advertisement offices: The Fleetway House, Farringdon Street, London, E.C.4. Registered for transmission by Canadian Magazine Post. Subscription rates: Inland and Abroad, 11s. per annum; 5s. 6d. for six months. Sole agents for South Africa: The Central News Agency, Ltd. Sole agents for Australia and New Zealand: Messrs. Gordon & Gotch, Ltd.; and for Canada, The Imperial News Co., Ltd. (Canada).—Saturday, December 29th, 1923.
DN

scent. He was dreaming still, he thought; but suddenly he sprang out of bed and rushed to the window. Sounds that fill a fox-hunter's heart with joy filled the midnight air—the music of a pack in full cry.

The prince flung up the window and leaned out, and at the same moment the window next his was opened, and Rupert Thurston's head and shoulders appeared.

"What in the name of wonder has happened?" cried Rupert Thurston.

"I don't know, old man, unless your park is haunted by a ghost-pack," answered Ching Lung. "Your hounds have got out, and, by the look of it, they've found a red-hot scent. Tumble into some clothes as fast as you can, and see what's the matter."

CHAPTER 3.
Treed !

IT was a very hot scent indeed—the result of the essence of anchovy on Barry O'Rooney's boots and the game-pie on the boots of the gamekeeper. Barry did not find the car, and he was beginning to think that Gan Waga had escaped from the park by another gate, when something happened. He heard a violent bang, and then the car came into view on the other side of the lake, plunged into an avenue of trees, and was lost to sight.

"Murther and onions!" thought Barry. "Surely the spalpeen daren't fire at Gan to hit! There he goes, anyway, the troublesome rogue, and bedad, av he's a grain of sinse left he'll scuttle into the house and loie low! A noice game this is, whin Oi ought to be aslape in my bed! Bad luck to the oily Iskimo!"

Barry had wandered a good way from the house. Feeling sure that Gan Waga was safe, he was about to return when he was suddenly seized from behind by the tall, bony man with the whiskers, neatly tripped, and deposited face downwards with his nose pressed hard into the dewy grass of Darrancombe Park. The bony man, who was very out of breath, took a seat on Barry's spine, and puffed and panted.

"G-g-g-ga!" remarked Barry O'Rooney furiously. "Ag-ag-g-g-ga!"

It was not a very brilliant speech, but it was all he could say at the moment, for the point of his chin was on a thistle, and his mouth was filled with grass. He made several furious and frantic heaves to try to dislodge his assailant, but the thin gamekeeper was fairly weighty. He had his whistle in his hand, but he was too short of breath to blow it, and when he attempted to do so the only sound was a thin and feeble squeak.

Barry dug his toes into the ground, worked the top of his head into the grass,

and tried to imitate a wild and unbroken broncho of the prairies by buck-jumping. It was a great and gallant effort. It ridded him of the gamekeeper, who was shot off so violently that he nearly swallowed the whistle. He aimed a blow at the supposed poacher as Barry O'Rooney was scrambling to his feet, and, before sitting down again, Barry retaliated. The gamekeeper found breath enough to say "Ouch!" And then, rubbing their heads, they sat and glared at each other.

"For a ha'porth of nuts, my noble lad," said Barry, "Oi'd set about you; and then, bedad, there'd soon be a funeral in your family! 'Oi'm a man of pace, but you thry to biff me again and nasty things will happen! There's only wan man aloive who has a chance to wallop me whin it comes to a foight, and that's Jack Dempsey—and Jack's too woise to thry ut on! You take me for a poacher, don't you, you unshaven ould rogue? Well, Oi'm not. Oi'm a guest at the hall, and Mr. Rupert Thurston's friend. Av you don't belave ut, bhoy, get up on your hind legs and Oi'll hammer some understanding into you!"

"W-wait till Oi gimme breath!" said the keeper, who was as game as any pheasant or partridge in the park, "and Oi'll kill 'ee stone cold, so Oi will!"

"Och, that's the way to talk, bhoy!" said Barry. "Be quick about ut, for, bedad, Oi'm losing me beauty-slape! Ut's long enough since Oi roighted wid a man wid whiskers, and ut'll be a change afther the clane-shaven wans. Av there's any little message you'd like to lave to your woife or mother, you'd betther tell me now, William, and Oi promise to deliver ut. As Oi towld you, Oi'm a man of pace, but Oi'm a proud O'Rooney of Ballybunion Castle, and the only O'Rooney who ever refused a challenge to foight was stone deaf, and didn't hear ut. Whin he did larn the truth and phwat he'd missed, ut preyed on the poor lad's moind so much that he doied of a broken heart. So up wid you, Willy, and shake hands, and then we'll settle ut loike gintlemen!"

The gamekeeper was quite willing. Barry looked at him sorrowfully in the moonlight.

"Sure, ut sames a pithy to spoil a good-looking fellow loike you, wid such a glorious set of whiskers," he said; "but if you will have ut, bhoy, put 'em up!"

"Howld aisy wan minute, darlint!" said Barry. "In the absence of a referee and seconds, how do we go? Phwat about the rules, William?"

"There be no rules, for Oi be goin' to polish 'ee off quick!" replied the gamekeeper. "And Oi'll tell 'ee for whoy. There be two sleepy louts in you cottage who wouldn't wakken oop and come to

help Oi when Oi touched off that gun, and when Oi be finished with 'ee, Oi be goin' to wakken they oop and rattle their thick heads together till Oi rattles 'em off. So just tak' that for a starter!"

Then the gamekeeper swung his fists and butted in at Barry O'Rooney with his head down, like a human battering-ram. A neat upward prod from Barry's right fist knocked his chin upwards again. Before he could recover, Barry O'Rooney gave him a pile-driver in the ribs that left the gamekeeper as limp and windless as a punctured tyre. Though a powerful man, and no doubt an awkward customer in a wrestling-match or in a rough-and-tumble, the gamekeeper was no boxer. As he swayed, with goggling eyes, Barry O'Rooney unclenched his fist, pressed the flat of his hand against the gamekeeper's face, and pushed. And down went the man with the whiskers!

"Phwat a foight!" said Barry sadly. "Willie, you've decaved me. You don't tell the truth, Willie. You—— Help! Phwat the—— Murther and onions! Phwat's this?"

There was only a rush of padded feet, for the hounds had finished the last portion of the run without a sound, on a scent of essence of anchovy that was hot enough to scorch the grass. They surged over Barry O'Rooney in a four-legged tide, and tumbled him on top of the gamekeeper. Barry O'Rooney staggered and shinned up a tree. The gamekeeper made a quick recovery and did the same, for to obtain the flavour of the game-pie the hounds were trying to chew his boots off.

And when Rupert Thurston and Ching Lung came along, armed with whips, there they found them.

Barry O'Rooney had not been bitten, but his trousers were in a hopeless state.

"And this is phwat Oi get for being koind!" he growled. "Bad luck to that haythen, poie-snatching Iskimo. There'll be red murther done this noight av Oi can lay hands on him. And thim trousers as good as new! There's only wan good Iskimo, and that's a dead wan! And bedad, he doies to-night!"

But you have to catch your Eskimo before you can kill him, and Barry O'Rooney's hideous threats did not disturb Gan Waga. Well over his fright, and fast asleep in the loft above the kennels, with the moonlight shining through a dusty little window on his plump and placid face, Gan Waga dreamed of game-pie spread with raspberry jam, and smiled blissfully in his sleep.

(*Another topping yarn of the amusing Gan Waga next week. Note the title: "GAN WAGA'S HUNTING!" By famous Sidney Drew.*)

My Readers' Own Corner

Tuck Hampers and Money Prizes Awarded for Interesting Paragraphs.

(If You Do Not Win a Prize This Week--You May Next!)

All Efforts in this Competition should be Addressed to : The GEM LIBRARY, "My Readers' Own Corner," Gough House, Gough Square, London, E.C.4.

THIS WINS OUR TUCK HAMPER!

"POOH !"

A nigger from North America had been for a short holiday in Canada, and on his return he told his mistress of his adventures. "And while I was dere, Miss Lucy, I went into de white man's church, and de white man, he took me all up de corridor an'——" "When you are speaking of a church, Sam, you should say 'aisle,' and not 'corridor.'" "He done took me all up de aisle, right up to de front, and he gone and set me on de front bench, Miss Lucy, in de middle of two white ladies. W'at you t'ink ob dat, Miss Lucy? Me, poor nigger man, in de middle ob de two white ladies on de front bench!" "That was all right, Sam, but you must not say 'bench.' You must say 'pew.'" "Pew, Miss Lucy, pew? Dat was w'at de two white ladies said!"—A Tuck Hamper, filled with delicious Tuck, has been awarded to I. D. Alnett, The Palace, Hampton Court.

LITTLE BY LITTLE !

"Very sad, very sad, sir!" said the doctor. "I greatly regret to tell you your wife's mind is completely gone." "Well, I'm not surprised, doctor," returned the husband. "She's been giving me a piece of it every day for the last fifteen years!"—Half-a-crown has been awarded to Edmund Lachapelle, 45a, St. Familes Street, Montreal, Canada.

NOT GUILTY !

A certain lady, upon engaging a new cook, was careful to impress upon her that no followers were allowed, and that the last cook was discharged through breaking that rule. Shortly afterwards, suspecting that everything was not all right in the culinary department, she paid a surprise visit to the kitchen, where, during a tour of inspection, she discovered a stalwart soldier standing bolt upright in a cupboard. "Bridget!" she cried. "What is this doing here?" "Faix, ma'am, he must have been left there by your last cook!" replied Bridget innocently.—Half-a-crown has been awarded to A. Goslett, Treaty Cottage, Albert Road, Woodstock, South Africa.

WHY NOT ?

A young man entered a cafe for dinner one day, and soon the band began to play all the liveliest tunes. After a while he got up from his table and walked up to the conductor of the band and said: "Do you play by request?" "Oh, yes, sir, we play anything by request," answered the conductor. "Well," remarked the young man, with a smile, "do you mind playing dominoes while I finish my dinner?" —Half-a-crown has been awarded to J. T. Hughes, 100, High Street, Connah's Quay, nr. Chester.

A NATURAL MISTAKE !

As no one else could be found, Skimpole was asked to play in a practice hockey match. He agreed, but as his time is chiefly taken up with the works of Professor Balmycrumpet, his knowledge of the game is decidedly limited, and he was repeatedly offending by raising his stick above his shoulder. "Sticks!" was repeatedly shouted at him, and thinking the players were alluding to his thin legs, he approached Kildare, who was refereeing the match. "I wish to protest against this vulgar abuse," he said. "I know my legs are not robust, but if those fellows don't stop calling them sticks, I shall certainly refuse to finish the match." "It's all right," said Kildare, smiling, "they're alluding to hockey sticks, not walking sticks!"—Half-a-crown has been awarded to P. Haslam, 152, Molyneux Road, Kensington, Liverpool.

TUCK HAMPER COUPON.

The GEM LIBRARY.

No attempt will be considered unless accompanied by one of these Coupons.

"TOM OF THE AJAX!" Rattling New Training-Ship Story in This Issue!

EVERY WEDNESDAY.

The GEM 2d

LIBRARY OF SCHOOL AND SPORTING STORIES

No. 830.
Vol. XXV.
January 5th, 1924.

DEFENDING HIS FOE!

Tom Merry hits out at Cutts, the bullying Fifth-Former, and saves his sworn enemy, Cardew, from a severe handling. (An exciting incident from the grand long complete school story of Tom Merry & Co. contained in this issue.)

Start the New Year well by getting the finest story-book obtainable — Specially compiled by Your Editor.

Ralph Reckness Cardew, junior captain of St. Jim's, is saved from serious trouble by another fellow's unselfish pluck; and that fellow is Tom Merry, the object of Cardew's relentless enmity!

TOM MERRY'S FOE!

A Rattling Story of St. Jim's, telling of further dramatic happenings in the great feud between Tom Merry and Ralph Reckness Cardew.

BY
MARTIN CLIFFORD.

CHAPTER 1.
Back to St. Jim's !

"HEAH we are again, deah boys !"

Arthur Augustus D'Arcy made that remark.

A swarm of St. Jim's fellows crowded the platforms at Wayland Junction. From all corners of the kingdom they were gathering for the new term.

There was a buzz of cheery voices, an incessant trampling of feet, a bumping of baggage, and shouting for porters. Fellows who knew one another exchanged greetings at the tops of their voices over countless intervening heads.

"Hallo, Tom Merry !"

"Cheerio, Gussy !"

"Haven't you washed during the vac, Trimble ? You don't look like it !"

"Keep off my feet, you ass !"

"Is that Gussy, the one and only——"

"Weally, deah boy——"

"Buck up, you fellows ! The local's going !"

There was a swarming across the bridge over the line to the platform where the local train for Rylcombe waited. Arthur Augustus D'Arcy waved a delicately gloved hand to his chums, Blake and Herries and Digby.

"Wally wound, you chaps ! We shall be left behind at this wate !"

Study No. 6 linked arms and shoved through the crowd. There were loud and wrathful protests on all sides as they shoved.

"Keep back !"

"Don't shove, you School House cads !" roared Fatty Wynn of the New House.

"Weally, Wynn, you are in the way," said Arthur Augustus. "In the circs, deah boy, we have no wesource but to shove."

"Yooop !" roared Fatty, as he sat down suddenly, and Study No. 6 trod gently over him.

"Whom are you shoving ?" demanded Figgins, also of the New House.

"You, old bean !" answered Blake genially; and, suiting the action to the word, he strewed George Figgins by the side of Fatty Wynn.

"Ha, ha, ha !"

"We're catching the first local," remarked Blake. "These New House bounders can wait for the second train."

"Yaas, wathah !"

"There's Kerr ! Give him a shove for luck !"

Kerr of the New House was not really in the way. But the chums of the School House were in great spirits, and they gave Kerr of the Fourth a shove for luck. Kerr sat down with a bump.

"Ow !"

"Take a little west, deah boy," said Arthur Augustus, as Study No. 6 pursued their destructive course.

Kerr scrambled up behind them.

The swarm of fellows had closed up, and a dozen pushing juniors intervened. Kerr could not reach the enemy, but he jerked an apple from his pocket, and took aim over a dozen heads. The silk hat of Arthur Augustus gleamed in the wintry sunlight, high over the tumult, like the plume of Navarre at the battle of Ivry. Only for a moment more did that gleaming topper gleam in the sunlight. Then Kerr's apple smote it, and it flew.

"Bai Jove !"

Arthur Augustus, suddenly hatless, halted.

"Come on !" roared Blake.

"My hat——"

"Come on !" shouted Herries.

"Yaas, but my hat——"

"Blow your hat !" howled Digby. "We shall lose the train !"

"Blow the twain !" retorted Arthur Augustus warmly. "I would wathah lose the twain than lose my hat !"

And Arthur Augustus plunged among innumerable legs in pursuit of his topper.

"Clear the way, there !"

"Gerrout !"

"Come on, Gussy !"

"Wats !"

The throng surged on to the local platform, carrying on Blake and Herries and Digby. Arthur Augustus was left in chase of his hat. It was a difficult chase. Redfern found the hat floating against his knees, and passed it on with a really good kick, considering how quick it was, and the hat sailed away across the platform. It almost bonneted Levison of the Fourth, who, however, headed it, and sent it sailing on. After it rushed Arthur Augustus, red and wrathful, with his celebrated eyeglass flying at the end of its cord.

He rushed into Clive and Cardew of the Fourth, and sent them spinning. Clive staggered against an automatic machine; Cardew staggered against Kangaroo of the Shell, and Kangaroo staggered in his turn.

Arthur Augustus had almost reached the elusive hat, when Levison minor of the Third passed it to Manners minor. Reggie Manners sent it sailing again, with a well-directed kick, over the head of its owner.

"You young wottahs !" roared Arthur Augustus.

"Ha, ha, ha !"

The swell of St. Jim's spun round after the hat.

It had dropped behind him, at the feet of three Shell fellows who were coming off the bridge over the line.

"Don't twead on my hat, Tom Mewwy !" yelled Arthur Augustus. "Keep your feet off my hat, Mannahs !"

The Terrible Three of the Shell halted.

"Dear me !" said Monty Lowther. "Here's Gussy playing a game of chasing his hat, like a kitten chasing its tail. All right, Gussy, we'll play !"

And Monty Lowther, who had evidently returned for the new term in his accustomed humorous state, proceeded to dribble the hat along the platform.

"You uttah wottah——"

"Pass!" roared Figgins.

"Here you are!"

"Ha, ha, ha!"

"Figgins, you bwute——"

"Take the pass, Fatty!" yelled Figgins.

"This way!" roared Fatty Wynn.

"You fwightful wottahs!" shouted Arthur Augustus. "You are wuinin' my hat!"

"Ha, ha, ha!"

"If you are askin' for a feahful thwashin'——"

"Pass! Pass!"

The hat sailed up and down the platform, looking less and less like a hat every moment. Fellows seemed to care little even whether they lost their train, so long as they obtained a free kick at the sailing topper. Even Blake took a kick at it—which could not be considered chummy, good chum as Blake was.

"Blake, you wottah!" gasped the breathless swell of St. Jim's.

"Ha, ha, ha!"

"Dig, you beast, if you kick my hat——"

Crash!

"Oh cwumbs! Stop it, somebody!"

Somebody stopped the hat. Kildare of the Sixth, captain of St. Jim's, came striding along the platform with Darrell, and he stopped the wrecked hat, quite unintentionally, with his nose. Kildare uttered a sharp exclamation as the unexpected missile smote him.

"Oh gad!"

"Ha, ha, ha! Goal!" yelled Monty Lowther.

The shattered hat fell at Kildare's feet. Arthur Augustus rushed up breathlessly, to be transfixed by the glare of the captain of the school.

"D'Arcy! Is that your hat?"

"Yaas, wathah!" gasped Arthur Augustus.

"Take a hundred lines!"

"Wha-a-at?"

"Play any more silly tricks, and I'll cane you."

"Bai Jove! Weally, Kildare——"

The great man of the Sixth walked on, unheeding. Arthur Augustus gathered up what was left of his hat. Blake yelled to him from an open carriage door.

"Come on, Gussy! We're moving."

Arthur Augustus raced for the carriage and jumped in. The train moved out of the station, crammed with St. Jim's fellows. They waved their hats and sent cat-calls at the fellows left crowding on the platform. But Arthur Augustus did not wave his hat, or his hand, or utter a word. He sat with his silk topper on his knees, gazing at it, and gazing, as if by force of gazing he could gaze it back into something like the shape of a hat. Until the train arrived at Rylcombe Arthur Augustus sat in mournful contemplation of that which had been a thing of beauty, but had not been destined to be a joy for ever.

CHAPTER 2.
Not a Double Event!

TOM MERRY looked thoughtful.

The new term was only a day old, and the Terrible Three were in their study, No. 10 in the Shell. Winter mists lay thick on the old quadrangle of St. Jim's, but inside Study No. 10 all was bright and cheery. Tom Merry stared at the glowing fire, and wrinkled his youthful brow in thought.

Manners and Lowther watched him, perhaps guessing what was in his mind, and waiting for him to speak.

"Give it a name!" said Monty Lowther suddenly.

Tom looked up.

"You're thinking about Cardew?" asked Manners.

"Well, yes."

Monty Lowther glanced at the study clock.

"You've been thinking for about ten minutes," he remarked. "Now let's have the result."

Tom laughed.

"It's a bit difficult," he said. "You know that Cardew of the Fourth bagged the junior captaincy last term, and I——"

"And you let him do it," said Monty.

"Well, it wasn't for me to make a fuss, if the fellows wanted a change," said Tom. "But never mind that."

"We do mind it, in this study," said Manners.

"We did, we do, and we shall!" added Lowther categorically. "But what about it now?"

"I thought I ought to give Cardew a chance to make good, and back him up," said Tom. "It turned out badly. He's made a fairly rotten junior captain, as I think all the school knows."

"Perfectly rotten!" agreed Lowther. "If you made up

your mind to it, Tom, you could hook him out of it, and down him, and it would be a case of as-you-were."

"Well, I don't know about that," said Tom thoughtfully. "I've been thinking of it during the holidays."

"I'm glad to hear it!"

"But I don't know. Certainly, I think the football would be safer in my hands than in Cardew's. But he was elected, and the election stands. But——" Tom wrinkled his brow again. "You know that Cardew made a feud of it; he wasn't content with being my rival, but had to constitute himself my enemy. We had trouble while we were staying at Gussy's place for Christmas."

"I know."

"Cardew left Eastwood House," went on Tom. "But—well, while he was there, and we were there, you know he played trick after trick on me, and that I lost my temper and smacked his face. It was understood that as soon as we got back to school I should give him a chance of returning that smack with interest—if he is able to add the interest," said Tom with a laugh.

"Which he couldn't do," said Manners.

"I've seen him once in the quad since we came back," continued Tom Merry. "He was walking with Levison and Clive, and he took no notice of me, or I of him. Some of the fellows are saying that he intends to cut me out of the football for the rest of the season, but I dare say that's only idle talk. But——"

Tom rubbed his nose thoughtfully.

"Go it!" said Monty.

"When he was bothering me so much at D'Arcy's place in the vac, I made up my mind to give him the licking of his life as soon as we were back at school. But he left, and I cooled down. I'd rather the thing dropped, if Cardew is willing. There's no need for us to punch one another that I can see."

"You never could let the sun go down on your giddy wrath, old scout," grinned Lowther.

"Well, I believe I've never felt vindictive," said Tom. "I hate to keep anything up against a fellow, if it can be helped. I'd rather let Cardew severely alone, all the more because I'm on friendly terms with his friends, Clive and Levison. That's what I was thinking out. There was an understanding about a meeting with the gloves on, but if Cardew says nothing about it, I suppose I need not."

And Tom looked inquiringly at his chums.

Both of them smiled.

It was like Tom Merry to forget old offences, even in the case of so persistent and irritating an enemy as Ralph Reckness Cardew had been to him.

"I'd rather you licked him," said Manners.

"Much rather," said Lowther.

"But if he doesn't begin——"

"Oh, he'll begin right enough," said Monty Lowther confidently. "Cardew hasn't done with you yet."

Tom looked a little worried.

"Blessed if I see why he should be so much up against me," he said. "I've never done him any harm, and he's done me a good deal. But suppose we let it go at that—leave Cardew alone, unless he goes on the war-path of his own accord?"

"I suppose you can let it go at that," assented Monty Lowther, rather reluctantly; and Manners nodded, after a pause. Both Tom's chums resented his loss of the junior captaincy more than Tom himself did.

"That's settled, then," said Tom cheerily. "It's rotten to begin the term with a row."

And Tom proceeded to sort out his books for prep, his chums following his example.

There was a tap at the study door, and it opened to admit Aubrey Racke of the Shell.

Racke of the Shell lounged into the study with an insolent air. The Terrible Three looked at him rather grimly. The blackguard of the Shell was not a welcome visitor in Study No. 10.

"Want anything?" asked Manners, with more directness than politeness.

"Nothin'."

"Take it and go, then," suggested Lowther.

"I've got a message for Tom Merry."

"Well, here's Tom Merry," said the owner of that name.

Racke sat on the edge of the table and swung his legs.

"I've come from Cardew," he explained.

"Oh!" said Tom, his brow darkening.

Monty Lowther grinned at Manners, who laughed. It did not seem, after all, that Tom's peaceable desires would be realised.

"Cardew's expected to hear from you before this," said Racke.

"Has he?"

"You had a row at D'Arcy's place over Christmas, I understand," drawled Racke. "You undertook to fight it out when you got back to St. Jim's. As Cardew hasn't heard from you, he's asked me to call in, as his second, and make the arrangements."

" ON THE ' BALL ' ST. JIM'S ! " Arthur Augustus D'Arcy's shining topper sailed up and down the platform, and fellows seemed to care little about their train so long as they obtained a free kick at it. *(See page 4.)*

"I should have thought he would have asked Levison or Clive," said Tom.

"Well, he asked me. Are you backing out?"

Tom Merry's eyes gleamed at the cad of the Shell.

"You can tell Cardew that I'll meet him when and where he likes," he answered quietly.

"Hear, hear!" said Manners and Lowther together.

"Mean that?" asked Racke.

Tom half-rose from his chair. Aubrey Racke s manner was as insulting as he could make it. But Tom sat down again.

"Yes, I mean it. Now get out, please!"

"Well, you see, you seemed so backward in comin' forward, you know," drawled Racke, "I really began to think it was an attack of cold feet in this study, or somethin' of the sort."

Monty Lowther rose to his feet with a gleam in his eyes.

"You really thought that, Racke?" he asked.

"Oh, yes!"

"Quite a mistake on your part," said Monty. "Quite, I assure you. Tom's ready to meet Cardew and give him the licking he was asking for all last term. Manners will second him, and I shall be at liberty to make a double event of it, with your assistance."

"What?"

"A double event will be quite interestin', and start the term in style," said Lowther. "Tom and Cardew, and you and little me, Racke. Who's your second?"

"I—I'm not fightin' anybody, you silly ass!" exclaimed Racke, with a considerable diminution of insolence in his manner.

"Your mistake. You keep on making mistakes," said Lowther genially. "You're fighting somebody. You're fighting me, you know."

"I'm not."

"You are, old man! Who's your second?" persisted Lowther.

"I'm Cardew's second, and so——"

"My dear man, Cardew can get another second, and a third and fourth, if he wants them. You're my mutton."

"Look here——"

"You wouldn't care to stand idly by while a fight is going on, with the warlike blood of the Rackes boiling in your veins," continued Monty Lowther. "Think of the Racke record in the war—always right at the front—at least, where the profiteering was going on. You'd be yearning for a scrap, Racke, and I'm going to oblige you. It's arranged?"

"It's not!" growled Racke, slipping from the table and moving towards the door. "I'll give Cardew your answer, Merry."

"Do!" said Tom, laughing.

"Don't forget your appointment with me, Racke," said Lowther.

"I've no appointment with you, you ass!" snapped Racke.

"Dear me," said Monty. "I begin to think that there must be cold feet in this study, after all; only dear old Racke must have brought them in with him."

"Ha, ha, ha!"

"Sure you don't want to fix up that appointment, Racke?"

"No, you dummy!"

"Then take your cold feet away, and yourself along with them," said Monty Lowther; "and you may as well take my boot, too!"

Racke made a jump into the passage as Monty Lowther advanced on him.

Crash!

A boot caught Racke as he escaped, and he staggered across the Shell passage.

THE GEM LIBRARY.—No. 830.

"Ow!"

Racke spun round in the passage and glared at Monty Lowther, smiling in the doorway, with a glare that ought to have withered the cheerful Monty on the spot.

"You rotter—ow!—you cad—wow! I—I—"

"Like to fix up that appointment, after all, and make a double event of it?" asked Lowther blandly.

Aubrey Racke slouched away down the passage without replying. Apparently it was to be, after all, only a single event!

CHAPTER 3.
Cardew's Way !

RALPH RECKNESS CARDEW yawned.

He seemed tired.

It was not prep that had tired him; he had not touched his prep. But since the opening of the new term Cardew had had several things to do, and a number of matters that required attention. The post of junior captain at St. Jim's was not all "beer and skittles," as Cardew found; and, although he cheerfully neglected all the duties that could be neglected, there were some that couldn't be treated in that easy manner. And so Cardew found his post a tiring one.

Levison and Clive were at work, setting Cardew an example that he did not follow. Cardew was stretched elegantly in the study armchair; a place he often occupied while his study-mates were at work. Possibly he found exertion enough in watching them.

"No prep this evening, Cardew?" asked Sidney Clive, rather sarcastically.

Cardew shook his head.

"Too exhaustin'," he explained.

"You may find Mr. Lathom still more exhausting in the morning."

"Old Lathom's an easy-goin' bird at the beginnin' of term," said Cardew easily. "Luckily, we're not in the Shell, under the eagle eye of Linton. I can manage Lathom."

Clive grunted, and dropped his eyes to his books again.

"There's a lot of work and responsibility on my hands, you see," went on Cardew plaintively. "I've had a lot to do. Interviews with Kildare, as head of the games—interviews with the Housemasters—no end of jawin'. Lots of things to fix up. I've made no end of arrangements for the term——"

"Good!" said Levison.

"I've forgotten most of them already."

"What?"

"Can't remember half of them," said Cardew coolly. "Dash it all, fellows here seem to want to make work of football. I always thought football was a game."

"You needn't have butted into Tom Merry's job if you didn't want to take the trouble he took," said Clive.

Cardew nodded.

"A hit—a very palpable hit!" he replied. "You're right, as you always are, with your solid common-sense, Clivey."

"Oh, rats!"

"But I did butt in, and here I am," said Cardew, "junior captain, with all sorts of worries and woes on my young shoulders. There's only one way of gettin' through my herculean task."

"What's that?"

"Leavin' it alone," said Cardew. "Jobs often do themselves if they're thoroughly left alone. Otherwise, they remain undone, and usually nobody's a penny the worse. There's a lot of unnecessary work done in this world. Leave things alone, and they right themselves somehow. What do you think of that for a programme?"

"All right for a lazy slacker," said Clive.

"Exactly; then it will suit me down to the ground. Hallo! Here's the one and only!"

Cardew smiled and nodded to Arthur Augustus D'Arcy as he appeared in the doorway of Study No. 9 in the Fourth.

But Arthur Augustus neither nodded nor smiled.

He fixed his eyes upon Cardew, and his eyeglass gleamed at the slacker of the Fourth.

"So glad to see you, old bean," said Cardew affably. "I missed you sorely, Gussy, when I was so suddenly called away from your hospitable home during the vac. I'd been goin' to ask you lots of important things, about silk hats and neckties and socks, and I never had the opportunity."

"Weally, Cardew——"

"Take a pew, old man. Let's have a friendly pow-wow," said Cardew. "It will interrupt these fellows' work, and it's always painful to me to see work goin' on."

"You are an uttah slackah, Cardew."

"Right on the nail," assented Cardew. "But take a pew. It makes me tired to see a fellow standin'."

"Wats! I have come heah to speak to you sewiously, Cardew."

"Here beginneth the first lesson," said Cardew. "Go it, Gussy. Anythin' to interrupt work."

"I heah that you have fixed up a fight with Tom Mewwy," said Arthur Augustus sternly.

Levison and Clive started and looked quickly at Cardew. That cheery youth smiled and nodded.

"You've heard right, old bean," he said.

"Is that how you are startin' the term, Cardew?"

"Just like that."

"I wegard it as wotten," said Arthur Augustus. "There were wows enough last term. Tom Mewwy has kept clear of you this term, as I know vewy well. I heah that you sent Wacke of the Shell to him as your second."

"Never thought of you," said Cardew regretfully. "I'd have asked you if I'd thought of it, Gussy."

"I should have uttahly wefused to act for you, Cardew."

"Then it wouldn't have been much use askin' you, would it?" asked Cardew agreeably. "What are you grousin' about, then?"

"I wepeat that I wegard it as wotten! I twust," said Arthur Augustus sternly—"I twust, Cardew, that you will withdraw this wotten challenge and pweserve the peace."

"What a trustin' fellow you are!" said Cardew admiringly. "I like a fellow with a trustful nature. So refreshin'!"

"Is that all you have to say, Cardew?"

"Oh, no! It's a fine evenin'!"

"What?"

"For the time of year, of course. We must expect a little mist," said Cardew gravely.

"You uttah ass!"

"But I hope the weather will get worse——"

"Worse?"

"Yes. That will stop the football!"

Arthur Augustus' eyeglass gleamed with scorn.

"It is weally not much use speakin' to you, Cardew," he said at last.

"Not much," agreed Cardew. "Yet you keep on doin' it. I suppose you find the impulse to wag your chin irresistible?"

Arthur Augustus breathed hard.

"I wecommend you, Cardew, to dwop this fight with Tom Mewwy and to give your whole attention to the duties you have taken on yourself," he said sternly.

"Jolly good advice!" assented Cardew.

"Then you will act on it?" asked Arthur Augustus, his noble brow clearing a little.

"Oh, no! I never act on good advice!" said Cardew cheerily. "Give me some bad advice and I'll see what I can do for you."

Arthur Augustus D'Arcy looked at Cardew—a long look—and then turned and walked out of the study. His temptation was strong to administer a "feahful thwashin'." Fortunately, he resisted the temptation.

"Dear old Gussy!" smiled Cardew, when the swell of St. Jim's had shaken the dust of Study No. 9 from his aristocratic feet. "Always a pleasure to see him and hear him chin. I believe his mission in life is to cheer fellows up and make a brighter St. Jim's."

"You're fighting Tom Merry?" asked Levison abruptly.

"Yes."

"You've asked that cad Racke to act as your second?"

"Yes." Cardew nodded. "You see, I knew you fellows would be against it, so it saved argument not to mention it to you till it was fixed up. Argument is a waste of energy."

"You're satisfied with what you are doing?"

"Quite!"

"Very well, then," said Levison quietly, and he said no more.

"You will come, of course?" said Cardew. "You disapprove, but you'll come. Only as 'lookers-on in Vienna,' as the johnny says in the play."

Levison shook his head without speaking.

"You, Clive?"

"No!"

"Then there will be only jolly old Racke to see me through," sighed Cardew. "As Racke seems to be my only friend, I think I'd better amble along to his study and give him a friendly word. Ta-ta!"

Ralph Reckness Cardew detached himself with an effort from the armchair and strolled out of Study No. 9. Clive called to him.

"Banker in Racke's study, I suppose?" he said.

Cardew smiled back from the doorway.

"You know Racke's little ways," he said. "When a fellow's in Rome he must do as Rome does—what?"

And Cardew walked away. Sidney Clive compressed his lips a little, and his eyes met Levison's for a moment. Ernest Levison shrugged his shoulders.

"I suppose it's no good talking to him!" said Clive.

"It never is!"

"This won't do!"

"I know it won't."

And prep went on in Study No. 9 rather moodily.

AN " UPHEAVAL " IN THE FIFTH FORM STUDY ! " You were askin' for fags, Cutts," said Cardew,"so we've come to oblige ! "   The juniors up-ended the table, and the crockery and the provisions shot off it in a crashing stream. *(See page 8.)*

CHAPTER 4.

Cardew Takes the Matter in Hand !

"CUTTS——"

    "The cad——"

    "The cheeky rotter——"

    "The rotten bully——"

Cutts of the Fifth was the topic. Gerald Cutts of the Fifth Form at St. Jim's often was the topic of indignant discussion among the juniors.

Cutts of the Fifth was not only a sportsman and a good deal of a blackguard—which did not concern the Lower School very much—but also he was a bully, which concerned them very much indeed.

In the junior Common-room a dozen fellows were discussing Cutts of the Fifth in tones of indignation and wrath.

Cardew strolled into the room while the discussion was going on. Cardew had been out of gates—possibly because he had business out of gates, and possibly because there had been games practice that afternoon.

Certainly it was not a junior captain's business to go out of gates when games practice was on. But Cardew had his own peculiar methods of dealing with the captaincy.

"Oh, here he is!" exclaimed Tompkins of the Fourth.

"Talkin' about me, dear boy?" asked Cardew cheerily.

"You've cut games practice this afternoon," said Blake.

"Yaas, wathah!" said Arthur Augustus D'Arcy.

"Pressure of important business," explained Cardew gravely. "I asked Talbot to take my place. Surely Talbot gave satisfaction?"

"Better than you could!" grunted Herries.

"Then all parties ought to be pleased," said Cardew. "But what's the matter with Tompkins?"

Clarence York Tompkins was the centre of the indignant group in the junior Common-room. Tompkins was red with wrath—which was very unusual with him, for Clarence York was a decidedly mild youth as a rule.

"It's that cad Cutts!" said Tompkins.

"Awful bounder, isn't he?" assented Cardew. "Quite a bad hat! And, what is worse, he has serious errors in taste. No harm in a chap bein' a blackguard—I'm a blackguard myself—but there are ways of doin' these things. But what has the unspeakable Cutts been doin' this time? You fellows look waxy."

"He has been twyin' to fag the Fourth," said Arthur Augustus. "A cheeky cad in the Fifth, you know, makin' out that he can fag fellows, like a Sixth Form prefect!"

"What a neck!" yawned Cardew.

"Made me fag for him!" howled Tompkins. "Fag for the Fifth, you know! Made me light the fire in his study, and laid into me with a fives-bat when I said the Fourth didn't fag for the Fifth!"

"It is imposs for this to be tolewated, you know," said Arthur Augustus. "Cutts would nevah have dared to fag the Fourth when Tom Mewwy was captain!"

"No fear!" said Digby.

"Tom Merry would have brought him up sharp enough!" said Blake. "But what's a chap to expect when the fellows have been crass asses enough to elect a lazy slacker captain of the House and the school?"

"Yaas, wathah!"

"Gently, old beans!" murmured Cardew. "Bein' kept out of gates by games practice—I mean by pressin' business of a personal nature—I wasn't on the scene when Cutts committed this crime. Therefore, how could I stop him? Even the great Thomas couldn't have done anythin' without bein' on the scene at the time."

"Well, you're on the scene now!" grunted Kangaroo of

the Shell. "What are you going to do? I hear that you've got a fight on with Tom Merry for Saturday afternoon."

"Quite so!"

"Well, most of the fellows will tell you that a junior captain has more important business than picking rows with the most peaceable chap in the House!" snapped the Australian junior. "And among other things, it's his business to keep our end up against the seniors when they get over the limit."

"Yaas, wathah!"

"What's the good of talking to Cardew?" said Blake scornfully. "What does he care about Cutts bullying and fagging the Fourth? He's too jolly busy dodging games practice, or playing banker in Racke's study."

Cardew's handsome face coloured a little. Whatever popularity he had had as junior captain seemed to be diminishing fast.

"Give a fellow a chance," he said. "If Cutts has committed this crime——"

"Oh, don't be an ass!"

"It is a crime to fag the Fourth," said Cardew gravely. "Why, I belong to the Fourth myself. He might have tried to fag me! That makes the matter really serious."

"Weally, Cardew——"

"If he has done this awful deed," said Cardew, "Cutts must be dealt with. I shall regard it as my bounden duty to strew the hungry churchyard with his bones."

"You uttah ass——"

"Or—as that would perhaps be a little too drastic even for Cutts of the Fifth—I think perhaps a raggin' would meet the case," said Cardew. "Cutts laid into you with a fives bat, Tompkins?"

"Yes, he did!" hissed Tompkins.

"How many?"

"Six—just as if he was a prefect!"

"Then I sentence Cutts of the Fifth to six," said Cardew calmly. "It only remains to carry out the sentence."

"Only!" jeered Dig.

"That's all!" said Blake, with deep sarcasm.

"That's all," assented Cardew He glanced at the Commonroom clock. "Cutts will be in his study now at tea. If Cutts is at home, it's a good opportunity to call on him. Anybody comin'?"

There was a buzz among the juniors.

"You mean it?" asked Blake.

"Naturally. I'm takin' this matter up as junior captain, and I'm goin' to try to prove myself worthy of my famous predecessor, the great and admired Thomas. I shall want some help. Cutts has asked for it, but he's not likely to take it from me without raisin' irrelevant objections. His objections will have to be overruled."

"Ha, ha, ha!"

"Weally, Cardew, if you mean business——"

"I—I say, it's jolly serious to rag the Fifth," said Tompkins. "The Housemaster might butt in."

"Or a prefect," said Crooke of the Shell. "You'd better go a bit slow, Cardew."

"Cutts has asked for it," said Cardew cheerily. "We can't refuse Cutts what he has asked for so earnestly. It wouldn't be kind."

He glanced over the juniors.

"I shall want you, Blake—and Herries, Digby, D'Arcy. Julian, Tompkins, Kerruish, and Kangaroo. I think that will be enough to overrule any irrelevant objections Cutts may raise to receivin' what he has so earnestly asked for. Are you ready?"

"Bai Jove!"

There was a momentary hesitation. A raid on the Fifth Form passage was not a simple undertaking, nor an easy one. Cutts of the Fifth was a powerful fellow, and it was probable that one or two others of the Fifth might be in his study. And certainly, at a call from Cutts, a crowd of the Fifth would turn out to drive an invading mob of juniors from the seniors' quarters. And the best fighting-men in the Lower School were not, of course, of much use against hefty seniors.

Cardew's eyes roamed over the group of juniors ironically.

"I asked you if you were ready," he remarked.

"Yaas, wathah!" said Arthur Augustus firmly.

"Yes!" said Blake. "We'll follow you if you'll lead—if you don't dodge round the first corner and scoot!"

Cardew shrugged his shoulders.

"Follow on, then!" he said.

With rather grim faces, the juniors he had named followed him from the room. They reached the corner of the Fifth Form passage in the School House. There Clarence York Tompkins paused.

"I—I say——" he stammered.

"Well?" smiled Cardew.

"I—I say, I hardly think it's worth while going for Cutts," said Tompkins. "I don't want a row."

"Dear man," said Cardew, "it's a little too late for that!

There's going to be a row—a royal row! But if you've got cold feet you can clear."

"I—I've got some lines to do."

"Go and do them," said Cardew politely. "You mustn't neglect lines—it would be disrespectful to our kind masters."

Tompkins disappeared.

"Any more of you fellows got lines to do?" asked Cardew satirically.

"No!" grunted Blake.

And the party marched on to Gerald Cutts' study in the Fifth Form passage.

CHAPTER 5.
Six for Cutts !

CUTTS of the Fifth was at tea in his study, with Gilmore, of the same Form. It was quite a nice tea, and there was a cheery fire blazing in the grate—the fire lighted by the hapless Tompkins under persuasion from the fives bat.

Cutts was in a good humour. Having licked Tompkins of the Fourth, and finally kicked him out of the study, Cutts was naturally in a good humour—such proceedings had a mollifying effect on his temper.

There was a tap at Cutts' study door, and he called out "Come in!" expecting to see Prye or St. Leger enter.

Instead of which, the door was opened by Ralph Reckness Cardew of the Fourth Form.

Cardew gave the Fifth-Formers a cool nod.

Cutts stared at him.

"What do you want?" he snapped. "Get out!"

"I hear that you've been lookin' for fags in the Fourth," said Cardew amiably. "We've come."

"Yaas, wathah!"

Cardew walked in, and D'Arcy followed, then Blake, and then the rest of the junior crowd. Cutts rose to his feet, puzzled. Gilmore stared at the juniors. The last of the invaders being in the study, the door was closed, and the key turned in the lock.

"Look here, what does this mean?" exclaimed Cutts. "If you kids are thinking of a rag——"

"Not a rag, old scout," said Cardew chidingly. "We've come to fag. We're goin' to fag for you, Cutts."

"I don't want a fag."

"Changed your mind?" asked Cardew. "A short time ago you were lookin' for fags in the Fourth Form. Now we've come to oblige you. Begin with the tea-table, you fellows, and make it nice and tidy."

"Yaas, wathah!" chuckled Arthur Augustus.

The fags, or raggers, whichever they were, began with the tea-table. It was a simple process, though it certainly did not make it nice and tidy. They up-ended the table, and the crockery and provisions shot off it in a crashing stream.

Crash! Crack! Smash!

"Ha, ha, ha!"

"You young villains!" roared Cutts.

He made a rush at the mob of juniors. They were ready for him. Five or six received him as he came on, and the next moment Gerald Cutts was rolling on his carpet, with the juniors clinging to him like cats.

"Back up, Gilmore!" yelled Cutts.

Gilmore backed up, but it was not of much use. Gilmore of the Fifth went to the floor, and Kangaroo sat on his chest, and Herries on his legs, while Kerruish took a businesslike grip on his ears, and banged his head on the floor.

Gilmore's wild yells filled the study.

"Keep that chap quiet!" yawned Cardew. "Sit on his head, or stuff somethin' into his mouth. Sorry, Gilmore, but you've got a rather unmusical voice, and my nerves are delicate."

"Groooooogh!" was Gilmore's reply, as a handful from a loaf was crammed into his mouth.

"You keep quiet, Gilmore, old top, and you won't get hurt," continued Cardew. "It's Cutts that we're here to deal with. You'd better take it quietly. Bang his head if he moves, Kerruish."

"What-ho!" grinned Kerruish.

Gilmore seemed of Cardew's opinion, that he had better keep quiet. At all events, he kept quiet. The odds were too heavy, and the door was locked against reinforcements. Gilmore decided to take it philosophically.

Cutts was struggling with savage determination.

But the raggers were equally determined, and there were too many of them for the bully of the Fifth.

Gerald Cutts was spread-eagled on the floor, with his nose grinding into the carpet.

A junior knelt on each arm and leg, and Gerald Cutts was pinned to the floor.

Cardew looked round the study.

"Where's the fives bat, Cutts?"

"You young hound——"

"I don't seem to see it. Where is it?"

"Help!" roared Cutts.

"Will you tell me where the fives bat is—the one you whacked Tompkins with?"

"No!" howled Cutts.

"Pull his ears till he does, Blake!"

"Ha, ha, ha!"

"Yow-ow-ow-wooop!" came in a fiendish yell from Cutts of the Fifth.

"Will you tell me now, dear boy?"

"In the cupboard!" gasped Cutts, almost speechless with rage.

"Thanks!"

Cardew sorted out the fives bat.

"Keep clear, you fellows!" he said.

"Yaas, wathah!"

Whack!

"Yow!"

There was a heavy knock at the door, and the voice of Lefevre, the captain of the Fifth, shouted through. Two or three more of the Fifth could be heard outside.

"What's this row?" shouted Lefevre.

"Not a row, dear man," answered Cardew coolly. "I've come here in my official capacity, as junior captain, to give Cutts six."

"Wha-a-at?"

"Gettin' deaf, old bean?"

"Open this door at once!" shouted Lefevre.

"But Cutts hasn't had his six yet."

Whack!

"Rescue, Fifth!" shrieked Cutts.

Whack!

"You cheeky young rascals, open this door!" roared the captain of the Fifth. "I'll teach you to come here ragging!"

"Thanks. We're not in need of any instruction on the subject, Lefevre. We know how."

Whack!

"They're really whackin' Cutts," came St. Leger's voice from the passage. "Poor old Cutts!"

Whack!

"Fancy Cutts gettin' six from the juniors!" chuckled another Fifth-Former. "Oh, my hat! Poor old Gerald!"

Gerald Cutts writhed with rage and pain. Cardew was laying on the strokes with great energy, and there was no doubt that Cutts was hurt. But he felt the bitter humiliation more keenly than the strokes of the fives bat.

"One more!" chuckled Blake. "Make it a good one, Cardew!"

"Yaas, wathah!"

Whack!

Undoubtedly the last whack was a good one. It elicited a fiendish yell from Cutts of the Fifth.

Outside, there was a sound of chuckling. Cutts of the Fifth was so lofty and supercilious a fellow, that his humiliation was not wholly unsatisfactory to his Form-fellows in the Fifth. The Fifth intended to avenge this affront to their dignity; meanwhile, they chuckled over Cutts' discomfiture.

"Is that enough, Cutts?" asked Cardew politely.

"Ow, ow! I'll—I'll—— Ow!"

"Are you sorry you fagged the Fourth?"

"Ow! I—I——"

"Are you sorry? If not, I regret to say that I shall have to begin again with the fives bat."

"I'm sorry!" gasped Cutts. And there was a fresh chuckle from the Fifth-Formers outside, as they heard that confession. They could hardly believe that the lofty Cutts had been brought so low. But he had!

"Good!" drawled Cardew. "Now, as we've done the business quite in the style of the late lamented Thomas, we may as well clear."

"You see what you'll get as soon as you open the door!" came the voice of the captain of the Fifth.

All eyes turned on Cardew. Cutts had been punished, and humiliated in a way he was not likely to forget for the remainder of the term. The dignity and independence of the Fourth Form at St. Jim's had been vindicated. But there was still retreat from the enemy's quarters to be contrived—and that was a problem for Cardew's strategy.

Cardew picked up the poker, and thrust it between the bars of the grate.

"Bai Jove!" murmured Arthur Augustus.

"Good!" grinned Blake.

As soon as the poker was heated red and glowing, Cardew twisted a handkerchief round the handle and drew it from the fire. Blake unlocked the door and threw it open.

"Now!" exclaimed Lefevre, making a stride into the study.

He halted suddenly.

"Put down that poker!" he roared.

Cardew made a pass at him with the glowing end of the poker, and Lefevre jumped back hurriedly into the passage. Cardew followed him out.

"You young rascal——"

"Put down that poker——"

"Keep back——"

"Follow the man from Cook's!" said Cardew, and he led the way down the Fifth-Form passage, red-hot poker in hand.

The Fifth-Formers backed into the study. They were prepared to mop up the passage from end to end with the cheeky juniors, but for the poker. But a red-hot poker put quite a different complexion on the matter.

Instead of handling the juniors, they hurled remarks from their study doorways as the enemy retreated—under guard of the red-hot poker.

"Bai Jove!" grinned Arthur Augustus D'Arcy, when the avengers were safe in the junior Common-room again. "Bai Jove, you know, Cardew is not such a wotten skippah aftah all, you know."

And all the fellows agreed that he wasn't.

"But Cutts will remember this, Cardew," remarked Blake. "You'd better keep your weather eye open for Cutts."

Ralph Reckness Cardew shrugged his shoulders carelessly. Evidently he was not alarmed.

CHAPTER 6.
Foes!

TOM MERRY paused before the notice-board, and glanced at a paper there, written in Cardew's elegant hand.

It was the list of players for the House match on Saturday afternoon; the first junior match of the new term.

Cardew's name, as captain, certainly should have been there; but Cardew's name was not there. Tom Merry's name, as that of the best junior footballer at St. Jim's, certainly should have been there also. But neither was Tom Merry's name there.

Tom wrinkled his brow a little.

After all the trouble that had occurred between him and the new junior captain, it seemed hard to believe that Cardew seriously planned to keep him out of junior football for the season. If that was really Cardew's object, there was strenuous resistance to be expected on Tom's part.

Cardew, through his second, had arranged the fight with Tom Merry to take place that afternoon in Rylcombe Wood. He had chosen that retired spot to avoid interruptions; and perhaps, too, Cardew did not want an audience. Bitterly determined as he was to beat his rival in fisticuffs as in other matters, Cardew probably knew very well that he had taken on an extremely difficult task, which it was doubtful if he could carry through.

If the fight ended in his defeat—as was likely enough—probably Cardew preferred not to have a ring of spectators staring at him at the time.

As Tom had agreed to meet him at any time and place specified, he had no objection to raise. But as the junior House match was taking place at the same time, it kept both of them out of the football.

A good many fellows were commenting on the football list. Talbot of the Shell was named as captain in Cardew's place. That was a wise choice on Cardew's part. Talbot was a good man for the post. But the comments of the juniors were derisive.

"Might as well make Talbot captain for good and all," remarked Blake. "Precious sort of a skipper to fix up a fight simultaneously with a House match!"

"Yaas, wathah!"

"I'm down to play for School House," remarked Manners. "That means I sha'n't be able to second you, Tom—if I play."

"You must play," said Tom at once.

"I'm down, too," said Lowther, frowning. "Look here, Tom, this looks to me as if Cardew's bent on keeping us both off the scene when you meet him and lick him."

"Pewwaps he doesn't want you fellows to see Tom Mewwy lick him," suggested Arthur Augustus D'Arcy.

There was a laugh.

"I would act as your second with pleasuah, Tom Mewwy," continued the swell of St. Jim's. "But Cardew has put me down to play—and Blake and Hewwies and Dig, too."

Herries grunted.

"He's put me down for goal," he said. "He did it before, and changed his mind. I rather think I sha'n't give him a chance to change his mind again. I'm not keen on playing under Cardew's lead."

"Well, he's put the whole study in," said Blake. "Better back up the House, Herries. Cardew can't very well let you down again, now your name's posted up in the list."

"Well, that's so," assented Herries.

"Tom Merry's left out!" giggled Trimble of the Fourth. "I agree with Cardew there! I never did think Merry much of a player."

"Weally, Twimble, you sillay ass——"

Tom Merry laughed. "Cheek" from Baggy Trimble was not likely to disturb his equanimity.

"It's silly rot," growled Kangaroo. "He's got my name

down, and I've a jolly good mind to tell him to cross it out and put yours in, Tom."

The captain of the Shell shook his head.

"Don't do that," he said. "Anyhow, I couldn't play this afternoon, as I've got to meet Cardew."

"Utter rot! No need for the scrap at all; and, anyhow, it could be put off. I'd speak to Cardew about it, if I were you."

Tom Merry nodded, deciding to act on the Australian junior's advice.

He looked for Cardew, and found that youth sunning himself by the steps of the School House in the quadrangle. Cardew gave him a nod, with a steely look in his eyes. Levison and Clive had been talking to Cardew, and both of them were frowning as they moved away. Both were down in the House eleven.

"Look here, Cardew," said Tom abruptly, "it's awkward our scrap coming off the same time as the House match. If you're going to keep on as junior captain you ought to be in the match."

"Thank you for tellin' me my duties," said Cardew. "When I want another tip from you I'll ask for it."

Tom set his lips.

"Most of the fellows think I ought to be in the team," he said.

"Most of the fellows seem to be rather asses."

"You don't care to postpone the scrap?"

"Not at all."

"If you hold me to my word, I shall turn up in Rylcombe Wood as arranged," said Tom. "But I think——"

"Never mind what you think, it's a fixture," said Cardew. "Will you excuse me for mentionin' that you bore me?"

"You've got my second down to play," said Tom.

"Can't you find another?"

"Yes; but——"

"What's the good of seconds?" yawned Cardew. "If you're left without one I'll tell Racke I don't want him, and make it square. I don't see why we can't settle our little differences by ourselves."

"I don't care one way or the other," said Tom curtly. "As a matter of fact, nearly every fellow I should care to ask is down to play football this afternoon."

"Well, Racke isn't down to play," grinned Cardew. "But I dare say he'd rather go off for a quiet smoke than turn up to second me in a scrap. I'll give him his head."

Tom looked at him fixedly.

"I think I know why you've arranged all this," he said. "You want the fight to take place without any witnesses."

"Why should I?" yawned Cardew.

"I don't know; unless it's to save your face when you get licked."

Cardew shrugged his shoulders.

"I'm not licked yet," he remarked.

"You will be," said Tom. "I fancy you know that you're not up to my weight. But have it your own way—with or without witnesses is all the same to me. The old oak in Rylcombe Wood at three."

"That's it."

"I shall be there," said Tom. "Are you taking gloves?"

Cardew's eyes glittered.

"No!" he said.

"Do you want me to take them?"

"No."

Tom knitted his brows.

"I don't like the idea."

"Dear me!" said Cardew lightly. "Racke said somethin' the other day about cold feet in your study. Was he right?"

Tom Merry did not answer that question. He turned his back on the dandy of the Fourth and walked away. Cardew, perfectly well aware of how narrow an escape he had had of being knocked spinning off the steps, smiled. Cutts of the Fifth came out of the School House as Tom walked away, and he looked at Cardew with a gleaming eye.

Cardew gave him a cool nod.

"Feelin' better for that battin', Cutts?" he asked genially.

Cutts made a motion towards him, clenching his hands. But he thought better of it and walked on. There were plenty of juniors within call, and Cutts was not looking for another ragging. He had already learned how little Cardew recked of his lofty position as a Fifth-Former.

Cardew laughed, dismissing Cutts of the Fifth from his careless mind. But, as a matter of fact, he would have done well not to dismiss Gerald Cutts so lightly from his thoughts.

CHAPTER 7.

The Worm Turns!

FIGGINS of the New House grinned.

Figgins seemed amused.

It had been the opinion of George Figgins at the time of the election that, for the sake of the school generally, the St. Jim's fellows should have rallied round and

elected a New House chap skipper. New House chaps saw the matter in the same light as Figgy, without a dissentient voice. School House fellows, on the other hand, saw it in quite a different light; and even fellows who did not like Cardew had voted for him, to escape the irretrievable disaster of getting a New House chap in as skipper. Views on this subject in the two Houses at St. Jim's were wide as the poles asunder.

The School House vote being numerically much stronger than that of the New House, Cardew had been elected, and Figgins & Co. gloomily prognosticated that St. Jim's would go to the dogs. And now, in Figgy's opinion, signs were strong that the school was already on its way dog-wards.

"First House match of the term, and the giddy captain absent!" said Figgins to his chums Kerr and Wynn. "That lazy slacker Cardew is junior captain of School and School House, and he's not turning up the first time his House goes into the field."

"Just like him!" remarked Fatty Wynn.

"I wonder how long the chaps will stand it," said Kerr. "Tom Merry was a good captain enough, School House chap as he is. But Cardew——" Kerr shrugged his shoulders expressively.

"I hear that he's put the Fifth in their place in his House," remarked Redfern.

Figgins sniffed.

"That's neither here nor there. Ought he to be here on the football ground, or ought he not?"

"He jolly well ought!" agreed Redfern.

"So glad to hear your opinion," said a gentle voice behind the New House juniors, and they turned to see Cardew.

The dandy of the Fourth was in Etons and an overcoat. Evidently he was not thinking of football that afternoon. He gave the rather grim-looking juniors a cool smile and nod.

"Not playing for your House—what?" said Figgins.

"Quite so—not!"

"Call that playing up as captain?"

"Dear man, my ambition is not to play up as captain. I find it a bore," explained Cardew.

"Why not chuck it up, then, and let a better man in?" demanded Figgins.

Ralph Reckness Cardew shook his head seriously.

"I've been thinkin' of chuckin' it up," he answered. "But I couldn't let a better man in—there isn't one at St. Jim's! Ta-ta!"

Cardew strolled on, smiling. Figgins resisted a strong inclination to go after him and punch him.

Cutts of the Fifth was strolling at a little distance. It was very unusual for the lofty Fifth-Former to turn up on little side; he could not be supposed to be interested in lower-school football. Kerr glanced at him, and saw that Cutts' eyes were on Cardew.

"He's stalking Cardew!" grinned the Scottish junior. "Look at him! I've heard that Cardew gave him six the other day for fagging the Fourth. I fancy Cardew would be safer on the footer-field this afternoon than off it!"

"Oh, that fellow can look after himself," said Figgins carelessly. "Hallo, here come the School House bounders!"

Smith major of the Fifth, in Norfolk jacket and whistle, little side with the School House footballers, but not to play. Cardew strolled round the field, nodding and smiling to fellows, apparently unconscious of the general condemnation of his line of conduct. Arthur Augustus D'Arcy gave him a glance of great severity.

"The cheek of that boundah weally passes all limits," he told Blake. "The least he could do is to keep out of sight if he is going to desert the side this afternoon."

"Sheer neck!" agreed Blake.

"He weally seems to be twyin' to make the whole school fed up with him," said D'Arcy. "He hasn't vewy far to go, at this wate."

"Cheeky cad!" grunted Herries.

Cardew called out cheerily to Levison and Clive as they lined up with the School House side.

"Play up, you chaps! Keep up the credit of the study."

His chums did not answer. They felt that Cardew was showing the worst of taste in sauntering on the field in that nonchalent manner in the circumstances. It really seemed that D'Arcy was right, and that Cardew was seeking to make the fellows "fed up" with his captaincy.

"If they keep up the credit of the study it's more than you will do, Cardew!" called back Blake.

"Right on the wicket, old bean!" assented Cardew.

"Oh, get out of sight, do!" growled Blake.

"Yaas, wathah!"

"Just goin', old top! So happy to oblige you," drawled Cardew; and, without waiting to see the ball kicked off, he strolled away towards the school gates.

And Gerald Cutts of the Fifth, who had been looking carelessly on, with his hands in his overcoat pockets, strolled in the same direction. Cardew was not giving a single thought

AT THE POINT OF THE POKER! Forced to back away from the glowing end of the red-hot poker Cutts & Co. are unable to wipe up the floor with Ralph Reckness Cardew and his followers. *(See page 9.)*

to Cutts of the Fifth, and it never occurred to him to glance back.

Had it occurred to him, and had he noticed the glitter in the eyes of Gerald Cutts, even Cardew might have taken the alarm. But he was thinking of other things, and he had forgotten the existence of the Fifth-Former to whom he had given six, and who, since that incident, had writhed under the mockery of his Form-fellows. It was an incident that Cutts was not likely to forget, even if the other seniors had allowed him to forget it, though Cardew dismissed it from his mind so carelessly.

Cardew turned out of the gates and sauntered down the lane, between hedges that glimmered with frost.

He turned into the footpath in Rylcombe Wood, and sauntered on at a leisurely pace, whistling. He was early for his appointment with Tom Merry, and had plenty of time on his hands.

The old oak in the glade was a well-known landmark, and it was by the old oak that the meeting was to take place. Cardew turned from the footpath and plunged into the wood. Once, as he thought he heard a footstep and a rustle, he glanced round; but he saw nothing in the frosty woods.

He reached the glade where the gnarled old oak stood, and found Aubrey Racke of the Shell there, smoking a cigarette.

Racke took the cigarette from his mouth, and nodded and grinned at the dandy of the Fourth.

The careless expression faded from Cardew's face; his features hardened and his eyes glinted.

"Early on the spot, you see," grinned Racke.

"I see."

"Merry won't be here till three."

"It's not far off three now, I think."

"Then I suppose I'd better get out of sight," chuckled Racke. "I suppose Tom Merry hasn't smelt a rat?"

Cardew shook his head.

"He wouldn't" agreed Racke. "I'm blest if I thought you'd pull it off, Cardew; but it was a good wheeze fixing it for the same time as the House match. That settled the

matter for most of the fellows; otherwise, a good many would have managed to get on the spot somehow."

"I know that."

"As the matter stands, Tom Merry will be here without even a second."

"Yes."

"And he doesn't suspect foul play?" said Racke, with contemptuous scorn.

Cardew winced.

What he contemplated could scarcely be called by any other name than the one Racke applied to it. But the words jarred on Cardew's nerves.

"He suspects nothin'," said Cardew, with a lightness he found it difficult to assume. "I don't like the fellow; but, to do him justice, he isn't your sort—or mine. He never suspects foul play, and if a fellow told him I was plannin' to get him alone here to take a rotten advantage of him he wouldn't believe a word of it."

"More fool he!" sneered Racke.

He extended his cigarette-case to Cardew. The dandy of the Fourth selected a smoke, but threw it away unlighted. Racke nodded.

"Wiser, when you're just goin' to fight," he agreed. "Smokin' won't help your wind. Not that it's likely to be a strenuous tussle—what? Ha, ha!"

Cardew did not reply. The black look was settling deeper on his handsome face. Racke watched him with a grin. He was quite ready to oblige the grandson of Lord Reckness in fair play or foul—especially if it was a move against Study No. 10. Racke had not forgotten Monty Lowther's boot, and other offences of the Terrible Three.

"It's all cut and dried?" he asked. "You're sure Tom Merry will come alone?"

"Quite sure."

"He's not to see me, and I'm to watch. If you get the better of him, I'm to remain simply a witness. That's the game."

"That was it!" said Cardew, in a low voice.

"If he begins to get the upper hand, somethin' is to hit him and give you a chance," grinned Racke. "Well, I must say he's askin' for it, in comin' here alone to meet a fellow he knows is his enemy. Catch me playin' the fool like that."

"Not likely," said Cardew, with a curl of the lip.

"I fancy not! I shall have to take jolly good care that Merry doesn't see me," said Racke. "A story like this wouldn't sound well in the Common-room, would it?"

"No!"

"But it's all right. You can't lick him——"

"Can't I?" said Cardew fiercely.

"No, you can't," said Racke coolly. "You know you can't, or you wouldn't be fixin' up this trick. You can't lick him, as I said; but you'll keep him too busy to be lookin' round him. I'll choose the right moment—you can trust me for that. I'll see that this stone catches him fair and square—and after that you ought to have a walk-over."

Cardew did not speak.

"He'll never know what hit him," went on Racke, with great enjoyment. "Afterwards, he may fancy it was some village kid chuckin' stones. Even if he suspected you of fixin' it up, he couldn't prove anythin'. And he won't even see me."

"You're safe," said Cardew contemptuously.

"If I weren't safe, I shouldn't take a hand in it," said Racke coolly. "I don't intend to be sent to Coventry by the whole school, and perhaps bunked by the Head! This infant!" He looked at his watch. "Merry's not due for ten minutes yet. Time for another smoke."

Racke of the Shell lighted a fresh cigarette. Cardew took a turn or two up and down the glade. His brow was growing blacker and blacker.

He had planned this, and his plan had been a success. Tom Merry—the last fellow in the world to suspect black treachery—had fallen blindly into the trap; it was not a difficult matter to hoodwink an open, frank nature like that. Cardew was to beat him by fair means if he could—he passionately hoped that he could. All his strength, all his courage, should be spent in the attempt. But if he could not beat his foe by fair means, defeat must be staved off. Fair play if possible—otherwise, foul!

Blacker and blacker grew Cardew's brow.

He had planned this—in cool blood, with a smile on his face, over a cigarette in Racke's study. He had carried through his scheme without repentance. But——

There was a "but."

Cardew was not the only fellow in the world who fancied himself to be worse than he was, and whose better nature rose within him, when the test came. As he paced there, thinking—thinking, the blackness grew in his frowning brow, and the dark blood surged in his cheeks. Was it really he, Ralph Reckness Cardew, who had planned this thing with the worst blackguard at St. Jim's—or was he dreaming? He turned suddenly on Racke.

"You rotter!"

Racke stared at him, as well he might. The cigarette dropped from his lips in his astonishment.

"Wha-a-at?" he stammered.

"You reptile! Get out!"

"What?" yelled Racke.

"Get out, while I keep my hands off you!" said Cardew, between his teeth. "I'm fed up with you! Get out!"

Racke stared at him, his eyes blazing with rage. He clenched his hands, and his voice was husky with rage as he spoke.

"You cur! You've changed your mind?"

"Yes. Get away from me!"

"You've changed your mind—after bringin' me here, and now you turn on me and call me names!" Aubrey Racke choked with rage. "Why, you cheeky cad, you—you——"

"I'm done with you! Get out!"

"Do you think Tom Merry won't keep the appointment?" hissed Racke. "Do you think you are gettin' out of the fight? Is that it? You're afraid to stand up to him in a fair fight, and you know it! You insolent rotter——"

Smack!

Aubrey Racke staggered back against the tree.

"Oh, you rotter!" he panted. "I—I——"

Cardew had broken with his valuable ally now, with a vengeance. Perhaps he was glad to make it impossible for himself to change his mind again. Certainly Aubrey Racke was not likely to help him now, in fair play or foul.

"Is that plain enough?" asked Cardew. "I'm done with you! You'd better go, Racke!"

"I—I'll go, but—but——"

There was a footstep, a rustle of branches. Racke broke off, and the two juniors turned, expecting to see Tom Merry. But it was not the captain of the Shell who appeared. It was Cutts of the Fifth—Cutts, with a mocking grin on his hard face, and a merciless glitter in his eyes.

THE GEM LIBRARY.—No. 830.

CHAPTER 8.
Cutts' Vengeance !

CUTTS of the Fifth stopped, and fixed his eyes on the two juniors. There was a light cane under his arm, and he let it slip down into his hand. Cardew eyed him coolly. It was easy to guess that Gerald Cutts' intentions were hostile; but Cardew was insensible to fear. Racke looked from one to the other, and the rage in his face gave place to a grin of triumph. He knew all about the ragging of Cutts, and he knew that the vengeful Fifth-Former had followed Cardew to this lonely spot to "take it out" of him.

What Racke would have done but for his sudden break with Cardew, was uncertain. It was not likely that he would have backed up the Fourth-Former in a struggle with so redoubtable an adversary as Cutts of the Fifth Form. As matters stood, he openly rejoiced in seeing Cardew cornered by his enemy.

Cutts raised his hand, and pointed in the direction of the distant footstep.

"You can hook it, Racke."

"Just goin'," said Racke coolly.

And with a leer at Cardew he went, and his footsteps died away in the wood. Ralph Reckness Cardew did not move. He knew that Cutts' grasp would be upon him the moment he attempted to follow Racke. He knew that there was serious trouble for him now, and he faced it with his usual icy coolness.

Gerald Cutts stood silent, without moving, till Racke's footsteps had died away in the underwoods. His eyes were on Cardew like a cat's.

"You're takin' it coolly!" he remarked.

"Takin' what?" drawled Cardew.

"You know what I've run you down for."

"Because you're so fond of fashionable society?" suggested Cardew. "Because pushin' outsiders always like to thrust themselves on a gentleman, asked or unasked."

Cutts set his teeth.

"You batted me the other day," he said.

"Oh, yes!" said Cardew, as if making an effort to remember. "I believe it was you I batted, Cutts. I know it was some bullyin' cad!"

"The Fifth haven't let me forget it yet."

"Bit of a come-down, wasn't it?" agreed Cardew. "You carry your head so jolly high, Cutts—though there's little or nothin' in it—that there's bound to be a sort of general rejoicin' when you're taken down a peg or two. And it's a bit of an event for a Fifth-Former to be given six by the Fourth."

"I think you'll be sorry for that six, by the time I've given you sixty!" said Cutts, with deadly calmness. "You're for it, Cardew! I can't imagine what made you come here, to this lonely place, alone, exactly as I should have wanted you to. But it's very convenient."

A dark and bitter look came over Cardew's handsome face. It was his own intended treachery that had brought him alone to that lonely place. There was self-mockery in the bitterness of his look. His treachery, so tardily repented, had placed him at the mercy of an enemy who knew no mercy. He might have said, with Laertes of old, "I am justly slain with mine own treachery!"

Cutts made a stride towards him. Cardew put up his hands. He knew that he was no match for the Fifth-Former; there was only one junior at St. Jim's who could have hoped to stand up to Cutts of the Fifth in a fight, and that was Tom Merry of the Shell. But there was no escape, and Cardew intended to fight as long as his strength lasted. At least, he would not submit tamely.

Cutts burst into a harsh, mocking laugh, as the Fourth-Former put himself in an attitude of defence.

"You'll make it worse for yourself," he remarked.

He came on grimly.

Cardew was fighting the next moment. So fierce and savage was his resistance, that for a few moments the powerful Fifth-Former was held. And luck favoured Cardew at the outset, and he landed a heavy blow fairly in Cutts' right eye that made him stagger back dizzily.

An oath dropped from Gerald Cutts' lips, and he rushed furiously on the junior.

It was impossible for a Lower boy, of Cardew's light build, to resist that savage rush. He went down like a ninepin. Cutts lost his footing and sprawled over him. A second more, and he had a sinewy knee planted on Cardew.

"Now, you young cad——"

"You coward!" breathed Cardew.

He twisted round, and struck up at the Fifth-Former. Cutts' bending face caught the blow, and his nose streamed red. He returned it with a savage blow that dazed the junior.

Cardew still resisted; but Cutts dragged him over, dragged his hands together, and knotted a short, thick cord about his wrists. It was evident that the bully of the Fifth had come

CUTTS' REVENGE! Enraged to a pitch of ungovernable fury Cutts stood over Cardew, swishing his cane in the air. Lash! Lash! Lash! The blows came down with all the force of Cutts' powerful arm. *(See this page.)*

prepared. Cardew, with his hands tied, was wrenched to his feet.

"Now!" breathed Cutts.

He dragged the junior to a tree-stump, and forcibly bent him over it. The ends of the cord were securely tied to jutting knots in the stump.

Cutts stepped back.

Cardew was quite helpless now, and "bending over" in the approved fashion for punishment. The dandy of the Fifth paused to dab his nose with his handkerchief, and to feel his eye with his finger—an eye that was already growing purple. Cutts' face was white with rage. He had intended to thrash Cardew without mercy; but he had not expected any serious resistance—far less any serious damage to himself. But he knew now that he was going to have a black eye, and that knowledge enraged him to a pitch of ungovernable fury.

He looked about in the frosty grass for the cane he had dropped, and picked it up. Then he stood over Cardew, swishing the cane in the air.

Lash!

The blow came down with all the force of Cutts' powerful arm. In spite of Cardew's courage, a cry of pain burst from his lips.

"That touches you, does it?" snarled Cutts.

He raised his arm again.

"You rotten bully!" breathed Cardew.

Cutts laughed.

"You gave me six!" he said "I've givin' you sixty—and a few over for this eye! Look out!"

The cane slashed down again. This time Cardew uttered no cry; he set his teeth like iron, and by sheer force of will kept back every sound of pain. Again the cane lashed.

Lash! Lash!

Cardew's face was white, and set hard. A Head's flogging was nothing to the punishment he was receiving now. But still he bore it in iron silence.

Lash!

"What's this—what——" It was a breathless voice, as Tom Merry of the Shell ran through the bushes. "Cutts—you brute—you bully! Stop!"

CHAPTER 9.
Just Like Tom!

TOM MERRY was a few minutes late for his appointment. He had stopped to see the kick-off in the House match; and then a vigorous attack by Figgins & Co. on the School House goal had held him chained to the spot, to see how it turned out, and then a smart rally of the School House held him still enchained. But he remembered at last his appointment with Cardew, and tore himself away from the football-field, leaving New House and School House going great guns, cheered by crowds of juniors of both Houses.

Tom Merry looked at the clock tower, and hurried away towards Rylcombe. It was already close on three o'clock, and his meeting with Cardew was to take place at three, in the heart of Rylcombe Wood. The Shell fellow broke into a run.

He was sprinting along the footpath when he almost ran into Racke of the Shell. Racke called to him.

"Hold on, Merry!"

Tom paused in his sprint.

"Can't stop, Racke; I'm late already."

"It's all right; Cardew doesn't expect you," said Racke. The cad of the Shell was keenly anxious that Tom should not arrive on the scene until Cutts had had time to finish with Cardew. Racke's was not a forgiving nature, and Cardew's change of mind—and of manners—dwelt bitterly in his revengeful mind.

"Not expecting me!" said Tom, stopping. "How's that?"

"It's all off, you see," explained Racke. "Cardew got me there——"

(Continued on page 16.)

The St Jim's News

EDITORIAL!

By Tom Merry.

WE were talking about adventure the other day in our study, and it occurred to me that it would be a jolly good idea to have the subject in the "St. Jim's News."

Adventure is one of the most wonderful words in the English language, in my opinion. It brings up all sorts of ideas to one's mind, and probably no two people imagine the same thing when they hear it. One would picture exciting events in South America; another would think of stirring scenes such as we hear about in connection with Antarctic Expeditions; while I don't suppose there's one of us who hasn't imagined himself the hero in some thrilling adventure.

Seeing that it was a topic likely to interest everybody, I spoke to the other fellows about it, and they were all very keen. They turned in yarn after yarn, and it took me some time to make my final selection. I was sorry to have to turn Kerr's yarn down, but I am afraid it was rather too wild and woolly for the "St. Jim's News." Anyway, it won't stop him from contributing to another issue.

The Towser yarn is first-rate, but there's more Herries about it than Towser, I can assure you; though Herries declares he can understand that dog as well as he would if it could talk, and sometimes I think he can. It doesn't do to take too much notice of Gussy's remarks on Towser.

The great George Alfred Grundy has excelled himself! It was unfortunate for him that we heard the real truth about his thrilling adventure, but we weren't at all surprised. It was just like old Grundy! When he found that the cat was out of the bag he nearly went mad, and threatened to smash us and our study to smithereens if we put his story in print. So we are looking out for earthquakes now!

To hear him on the subject of adventure you would think that it was something very different from my dictionary version of it. I looked it up, and it says that an adventure is "an event the issue of which is determined by chance"! When I told George Alfred that, he said: "Rats!" I must say that I think it's a bit tame, too.

The yarn of Digby's I should very much liked to have turned down, but, as it deals with myself, it would have been unsportsmanlike of me to confine it to the wastepaper basket. How Digby got to know of the affair beats me. I suppose Trimble's tattling tongue had got busy.

Tom Merry

THE GEM LIBRARY.—No. 830.

HEROISM!

By
George Alfred Grundy.

OF course, I don't see why I should waste my time turning out stuff for Merry, but seeing that he thought this week's "News" would not be complete without a contribution from me, I thought I might as well oblige.

All the same, I consider that it's absurd to ask a fellow like me to write about adventure in the skinny space of a column. If I'd been asked to write a book on the subject, there'd have been some sense in it.

You see, I'm a fellow who goes in for adventure as naturally as a donkey goes for carrots; and it's a funny thing, but I'm always the hero in my adventures. (Naturally.—Ed.)

Of course, it's no good going in for adventure if you haven't got plenty of pluck.

The latest affair was the other night in the village. I'd had a special late pass to go and see some friends, and it was very dark when I started back to the school. I was going down the High Street when I heard a bloodcurdling yell in one of the little side streets.

For a moment my heart stood still with horror. I felt certain that someone was being murdered—a yell like that could have meant nothing else.

Did I hesitate? Not for an instant! There was no telling what danger I might be running into, but I dashed in the direction from which the scream had come, and when I got near enough I saw that a gang of hooligans had got someone down on the ground!

I rushed at one of them and bowled him over with a blow from my mighty fist, and in a flash I swung round and caught another of them on the side of the jaw.

Perhaps they thought there was an earthquake breaking out; but whatever they thought, the effect of my attack was marvellous.

The two I had bowled over scrambled to their feet, and then they all ran for their lives! Really, I was surprised myself at the easy victory.

I assisted their victim to his feet, and was relieved to find that he wasn't much hurt; only badly shaken up. He was trembling with fear, though, and I could see that he had had a nasty shock, for he could not control his voice enough to speak.

I didn't worry him, because I knew he would soon pull himself together, and when he did he thanked me, with tears in his eyes, for saving his life. He said he was certain that if I hadn't arrived at the moment I did he would have been killed.

It's splendid to be a hero.

(We happened to hear afterwards that the "gang of hooligans" was a couple of Fourth Form youngsters from Rylcombe Grammar School ragging another kid!—Ed.)

A FEW GROWLS!

BY TOWSER.

I'VE been asked to say what I know about adventure. If I'd been asked to say what I don't know about it, I could have answered easily enough. I should just have growled: "Nothing!"

My life is all adventure. Directly I step out of my kennel I meet with an adventure of some kind, and when I go to the village with my master—well, there's nearly always trouble in some way or another, which is a very strange thing, because I'm as peaceful as a lamb.

I'll just tell you about a funny little affair the other day. I went into the village with my master, and we were walking along the street as quietly as a couple of old ladies. Suddenly a girl came round a corner a little way in front of us, and she had a dog with her—one of those fluffy things with little legs and a silly kind of bark—Poms, I believe they're called.

Well, of course, I never take any notice of things like that, and I pretended not to see it, but just after the girl had turned the corner a fellow came round, rather in a hurry. He happened to overtake the girl and the dog just as they were going to pass my master and me.

He was going to hurry along between us when he suddenly saw me, and darted aside; why he should do so I don't know, because I was perfectly clean, having had a bath only the day before.

Anyhow, he bumped into the girl and nearly knocked her over. Now, although I don't like Poms, I must say the one who was with that girl had got plenty of pluck, and was pretty sharp, too. He darted forward, and in a jiffy he had got a piece out of the leg of that fellow's trousers.

Evidently nobody noticed the actual deed but me, but you can imagine my surprise when the fellow started hopping about on one leg and accusing me of biting him! Well, you could have knocked me down with a fishbone! I might say that he wouldn't have got off so lightly if I'd gone for him!

At first I didn't take much notice, but when I heard him threatening to go to the police station, and demanding my master's name and address, I thought I'd better look into the matter. I smiled (people never seem to like it when I smile!) and strolled up to the man's leg to examine the damage more closely.

Before you could have said "Jack Robinson" that leg, and the rest of the fellow with it, was on the way to the end of the street at top speed, and in less than a minute it disappeared round the corner!

My master didn't say anything as we walked on: he just bent down and patted my head.

FIGGINS' FIDDLE!

By Robert Arthur Digby.

'**W**HAT on earth's that?"

Tom Merry laid his pen gently upon the study table, sat bolt upright, and listened.

A slight sound had broken the stillness of the night. It was only slight, but it was curious, weird, and uncanny.

The time was well after eleven o'clock. The remainder of the school was wrapt in slumber.

Tom Merry had obtained permission from his Form master, Mr. Linton, to stay up beyond his usual bed time to finish the editorial of the "St. Jim's News." He had almost finished when the curious sound came to his ears.

For a moment Tom Merry was startled. But he pulled himself together.

"Blessed mouse, I suppose," he muttered.

He sat motionless, straining his ears for a repetition of the sounds.

It came again. A strange wailing squeak, ending in a long-drawn-out moan. Very faint, but obviously quite near at hand.

"It's not a mouse!" he muttered. "And it doesn't sound human. What the dickens can it be?"

Tom Merry peered round the study, bewildered.

"Wonder if it's from the passage?" he muttered. "Probably one of the chaps having a game."

The sounds came again. This time quite distinctly from without the study in the passage beyond.

Rising softly from his chair, Tom Merry switched off the light, tip-toed to the study door, cautiously turned the knob and peered without into the dark, black corridor.

But he heard nothing. The strange sounds had ceased. Everything was now quiet and still.

"Perhaps my imagination," he said sleepily. "I'll get to bed, and finish the editorial first thing in the morning I've done enough for to-night."

Closing the study door after him, Tom Merry groped his way along the passage towards the staircase leading to the Shell dormitory.

He stopped suddenly, however, as the wailing sounded again. This time ending in an uncanny shriek.

Merry was convinced, now, that it was something more than imagination. And although his nerves were fairly steady, he felt a slight tremor run down his spine.

What could it be? What should it be? Should he go back and investigate? Or—— No, he'd awaken Manners and Lowther first.

Swiftly mounting the staircase, he tiptoed towards the Shell dormitory.

Manners and Lowther were asleep. But a gentle shake of their shoulders soon awakened them to the fact that something was wrong.

"Come quickly, chaps!" whispered Tom Merry tensely. "There's something jolly mysterious downstairs. The queerest noises imaginable."

Slipping trousers and coats over their pyjamas, Manners and Lowther, with thumping hearts, followed Tom Merry along the corridor, and passed noiselessly down the stairs. Everywhere was silent and still.

Half-way along the Shell passage Tom Merry halted. A faint, far-away sound reached his ears, ending in a ghostly, uncanny moan.

"Hush!" he breathed. "Listen, chaps! Can you hear anything?"

"I can!" murmured Lowther. "What the dickens is it? It's jolly rummy!"

Manners shivered a little.

"What are we going to do?" he muttered.

"Going on, chaps, or——"

"Yes, certainly we are. If it's anyone having a joke at my expense, I'm going to collar him; and the joker's going to get it in the neck."

And with Lowther bringing up the rear, the trio crept forward along the passage.

A dozen yards from their study they halted. The wailing came again, distinctly, within a few yards of the crouching juniors. But they could see nothing.

"Come along, chaps!" whispered Merry tensely. "We'll fathom this blessed mystery."

Creeping along the passage wall, they reached their study. Tom Merry opened the door, and the three juniors passed within.

The fire, still flickering, cast weird, ghostly shadows upon the walls.

"Switch the light on, Tom," whispered Manners, "then we'll get a candle and search the passage. The sounds came from there, I'm certain."

Fortunately, there was a piece of candle on the mantelpiece. Monty Lowther applied a light from the fire, and holding it aloft, led the way into the passage.

The Terrible Three stood and peered around, utterly bewildered. They could see nothing. No sign of anyone, or anything.

Midnight boomed its mournful notes from the old clock-tower. As the last note died

away there came a faint, but fearful, moan —very near, almost at their feet.

The juniors stood tense, scarcely daring to breathe, yet trying to penetrate the darkness beyond the candle's glimmer.

Suddenly Monty Lowther gave a gasp, and bounded forward.

"What's this, chaps?" he cried quickly.

He had picked something up from the floor. It was a small oblong wooden box with a round hole in the top. Two or three strings were fastened at either end of the box, running across the hole.

Tom Merry gazed at the thing in disgust.

"Oh, my blessed hat!" he cried "Figgins' home-made string fiddle! Have we ever been had?"

There was a gasp of relief.

"B-but, I say, chaps! What's caused the giddy rumpus?" asked Manners. "The thing couldn't make those noises on its own. Someone must have——"

"I've got it!" said Lowther quickly.

"Crumbs!" said Tom Merry. "It's not pins. It's Figgins' tame porcupine!"

"There's something inside here. Half a tick, I'll just feel and—— Yar-o-o-o-oh! Yaro-o-oh!"

Monty Lowther dropped the instrument as though it had suddenly become red-hot. His yells of anguish rang through the night.

"What the thump——" began Merry.

"There's a thousand blessed pins inside there!" howled Lowther, nursing his fingers. "If Figgy's done this, I'll spiflicate the ass!"

Tom Merry bent down and picked the box up gingerly.

"Come inside the study, chaps!" he said. "We'll have a look at it. Figgy wouldn't do a trick like that. He'd bar putting— Crumbs, they're not pins, either. It's something alive! It's Figgy's tame porcupine."

"Oh, my hat!" shrieked Manners. "We've been spoofed! That accounts for the queer noises we heard. Every time the blessed thing moved, its stiff quills caught the strings. The joker must have known that you were sitting up, Tom."

"Yes, he did," said Tom Merry. "He's done us fairly this time. But we'll collar the bounder in the morning, chaps!"

"Yes, rather!"

And they did.

"ADVENCHAHS!"

By Arthur Augustus D'Arcy.

ADVENCHAH! Bai Jove, yes! I considah that's a toppin' subject to talk about. When Mewwy spoke to me about it, he said: "Could I w'ite anything on advenchah?"

Bai Jove! That was widiculous, of course! If he'd said "would" instead of "could" he would have shown his common sense, because there isn't a fellow in St. Jim's who knows more about advenchah than I do. Why, bai Jove, I've had enough advenchahs of my own to fill a woppin' big book.

There was that affair of my twousahs when that howwid bwute Towsah wan between

my legs in the High Stweet and made me sit down in a puddle. Then there was the case of my best toppah, bai Jove, when I found that Blake's white mice had made a nest in it! (Not exactly an adventure, Gussy, except for the mice!—Ed.)

I knew old Tommy would put his spoke in before long; he always does, y'know. He came in and looked ovah my shouldah just now. Weally, it's too bad intewwuptin' a fellow when he's w'iting' about advenchah; puts him wight off his stwoke.

Let's see, where had I got to? Bai Jove, yes—the white mice in my toppah! Wotten affair that was. Evewyone used to say when I went near them after that: "Oh cwumbs, what a howwid smell of mice!"

Bai Jove! I'm wandewin' away fwom my subject—as the parson would say. Advenchah, isn't it? Weally, y'know, I'd almost forgotten all about it!

Of course, it all depends on a fellow's ideahs of advenchah. It's not so easy to w'ite about advenchah as it sounds. (He made out that it was the simplest thing possible when I asked him!—Ed.) What one

fellow might think was an excitin' advenchah I might think nothin' of. (Quite likely.— Ed.)

The twouble is that I've had so many advenchahs that I don't know which one to w'ite about. I've had at least twenty with that beast Towsah, but I expect you've heard about most of those. That animal's been more twouble to me than anything at St. Jim's, y'know; it isn't wight that a fellow should be allowed to keep a bwute like that to wowwy evewybody else. What would the Head say if I was to ask permission to keep a lion?

Bai Jove, I can hear old Tommy comin' along the cowwidor again. I must buck up!

"Time's up, Gussy?"

"I've hardly started yet, deah boy!"

"Sorry; it's time to go to press! Come on with that wot!"

"Weally, y'know, I haven't started on my advenchah yet. I——"

(But Tom Merry had picked up the copy and bolted.)

"TOM MERRY'S FOE!"

(Continued from page 13.)

"You!"

"Yes; I was to chuck a stone at you from behind a tree, if you began to get the better of him," said Racke coolly. "Catch on? That's why Cardew fixed it up for the same time as the House match, and managed to have no seconds, and the fight out of gates."

"Impossible!"

"Honest Injun!" said Racke.

"And you——" exclaimed Tom, his eyes blazing at the blackguard of the Shell.

"I was only pullin' his leg, you see," said Racke, backing away a pace. "I let him run on, till a few minutes ago, and then I told him I'd have nothin' to do with it. See?"

Tom eyed him.

"It looks as if there's some truth in what you say, Racke," he answered quietly. "Cardew's rather queer arrangements look like it. If he thought of playing such a dirty trick, I hope he changed his mind."

"He didn't; it was I——"

Tom interrupted him scornfully.

"You'd have played it out—that's your sort, Racke," he said. "It's not Cardew's sort, I believe. Anyhow, I know he isn't dodging a fight; he's got plenty of pluck. I'm going on."

"I tell you——"

"Oh, rats!"

Tom Merry started on again, and Racke caught him by the arm and pulled him to a halt.

"Look here, Tom Merry, I tell you——"

"Let me alone!"

Tom Merry angrily shook off the grasp of the Shell fellow, and ran on. Racke stood in the footpath, and looked after him with a sneering grin.

"After all, he can't handle Cutts," he murmured. "And I suppose he wouldn't chip in to help Cardew, anyhow! I know I wouldn't in his place! Cardew's for it!"

And with that satisfactory reflection, Aubrey Racke walked on towards the school.

Tom Merry, giving no further thought to the cad of the Shell, ran lightly along the grassy footpath, and turned off through the wood towards the glade of the old oak. Cardew's first—and only—cry of pain reached his ears as he hurried on through the thickets. He started as he heard it.

"What the thump——" he ejaculated. He quickened his pace, and ran breathlessly into the glade. Then he saw.

Tom Merry burst on the scene, breathless with haste, his eyes blazing with indignation. He had come there to fight Ralph Reckness Cardew—he had almost come there to be a victim to Cardew's treachery. But he did not think of that now. The junior, his hands tied to the tree-stump, was writhing under the savage lashes of the cane, and Tom caught a glimpse of his white, set face and the bitter pain in it. That was more than enough for Tom.

"Cutts, you bully!" he panted.

Cutts spun round in astonishment. Tom Merry's arrival there was a complete surprise to him.

He glared angrily at the Shell fellow.

"Clear off!" he exclaimed sharply. "You've no business here, Tom Merry!"

Without answering, Tom Merry sprang at him and wrenched the cane from his hand. So sudden was his action that the cane was whirling away among the tree-tops before Cutts realised what was happening.

"You rotten bully!" shouted Tom.

"You—you——" stuttered Cutts.

Cardew looked round. He could not escape from his position, bound as he was; he could render no aid to Tom Merry if the captain of the Shell took up his cause against so formidable an adversary as the big Fifth-Former. Not to save his life would Cardew have called to his enemy for aid. But there was a gleam of hope in his pale face now. Tom Merry's look and words showed that there was little doubt of the line he would take.

Cutts raised a hand that trembled with rage.

"Get out of this, Merry, or I'll give you the same as I'm givin' Cardew!"

"Let him loose at once!" rapped Tom Merry.

"Wha-a-at?"

"Stand aside while I do it, then, you rotter!"

Tom Merry came fearlessly on. Cutts sprang in his way, his fists clenched.

THE GEM LIBRARY.—No. 830.

"You—you dare to stand up to me, Tom Merry——"

"Yes, you cur!"

Tom Merry sprang back, but only to throw off his coat and cap and then his jacket. Cutts glared at him in angry amazement, scarcely believing that the Shell fellow seriously intended to stand up to him in defence of Cardew. But he soon had proof of it.

"Now, you cad——" exclaimed Tom.

"I'll smash you!" roared Cutts.

He came on with a rush. Cardew had been swept under by such a rush; but Tom Merry was made of more sinewy stuff. He met the rush with left and right, and it was Cutts who staggered back, and, stumbling over Cardew, fell to the ground.

"Well hit!" shouted Cardew involuntarily.

Cutts of the Fifth sprawled, breathless, amazed to find himself on the ground, amazed, and boiling with rage.

"Look out!" panted Cardew.

Tom Merry was looking out. Cutts scrambled to his feet and came at the Shell fellow like a tiger.

What followed was wild and whirling. Cardew, staring on, strained frantically at the cord on his wrist, passionately eager to get loose and go to the help of his defender. But he could not get loose—he was too securely tied for that—and he could only look on at the hardest fight Tom Merry had ever put up since he had come to St. Jim's.

For in weight, in muscle, in strength, in reach, Cutts of the Fifth was far and away ahead of the junior. And he had skill in boxing, too—which he needed now. At the first glance it would have been said that Tom Merry had no chance of success—that in a minute or less he would be as helplessly at the bully's mercy as Cardew now was.

But it did not prove so. Tom was as light as an eel on his feet, and a great deal quicker in movement than the big Fifth-Former. And he was strong and sturdy, though nowhere near the size and weight of Gerald Cutts. And he was the best boxer in the Lower School at St. Jim's, and that counted for a great deal.

Again and again a quick leap, a side-step, a backward spring, saved him from Cutts' heavy attack; and when he had a chance he never lost it. Cutts' right eye, already half-closed by Cardew, was quickly closed entirely, and there was a blue bruise forming under the other. His nose streamed crimson.

Tom Merry showed signs of severe punishment, too. But he did not heed his punishment.

It was Cutts who first drew back from the struggle. Deep down, the bully's heart was craven.

He backed away, panting; and as he backed Tom Merry came on with a lightning rush. Cutts' defence was nowhere; and Tom's right crashed into his face, followed up by his left under the chin. Cutts staggered back and fell heavily.

Tom Merry stood over him, panting. The Shell fellow seemed hardly aware that blood was streaming from his nose, oozing from his mouth, and that a dozen bruises showed on his face. He was ready for Cutts when the Fifth-Former came up to the scratch.

Gerald Cutts staggered up.

But he did not come on. Possibly if he had pushed the fight to the last extremity Cutts might have triumphed. But a fight to a finish with an adversary who was game to the last gasp was not in Gerald Cutts' line. He did not come on.

"Beaten, by gad!" yelled Cardew, as the Fifth-Former backed away.

Cutts' face flamed with rage. That taunt brought him on again, and he rushed savagely at Tom Merry.

Tom Merry went down, but he was up again like a cat, fighting desperately—hammer and tongs, hammer and tongs—till Cutts panted:

"Stop!"

The Fifth-Former dragged himself loose, and, without a look at Tom, plunged into the bushes. He disappeared, and Tom Merry stood panting, almost reeling with his exertions, and wondering whether he had, in actual fact, beaten Cutts of the Fifth in a stand-up fight. But there was no doubt of it—he had!

Cutts was gone, and Tom Merry leaned against the old oak to get back his breath. He passed his hand dazedly before his eyes and blinked at Cardew.

There was a strange expression on Cardew's face as Tom stepped towards him and cut the cord with his penknife. Cardew rose from the stump, his eyes strangely on Tom Merry.

"You're hurt!" he said at last.

"Yes, a bit," gasped Tom.

"I never saw such a scrap! And I—I was goin' to scrap with you!" Cardew laughed. "You wouldn't have left much of me, I suppose."

"Cutts hasn't left much of me, I think," said Tom Merry ruefully. "We shall have to put off our little affair, after all, Cardew. I couldn't stand up to a bunny rabbit now."

"Put it off!" said Cardew slowly. "Oh, yes, we'll put

(*Continued on page 20.*)

This splendid yarn of the
quaint Gan Waga-

—has been specially written for
the GEM, so don't miss it !

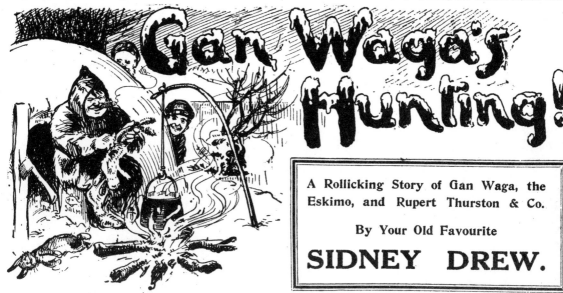

Gan Waga's Hunting!

A Rollicking Story of Gan Waga, the
Eskimo, and Rupert Thurston & Co.

By Your Old Favourite

SIDNEY DREW.

CHAPTER 1.
The House Wreckers!

SNOW may not be pleasant stuff for
people who are inclined to have
red noses or suffer from chilblains,
but away from towns where the
traffic churns it into black slush, it can
often transform ugliness into beauty.
Darrancombe Village did not need snow
to render it beautiful, for at all seasons it
was one of the prettiest villages in
England, and England can boast of pos-
sessing the prettiest villages in the whole
wide world.

But with snow on its thatched roofs, on
trees and hedgerows, and on the village
green, and icicles hanging from the
eaves, Darrancombe resembled a charm-
ing Christmas card designed by a first-
class artist. And when Squire Thurston's
hounds came through, the scarlet coats of
the huntsmen and whip gave it a charm-
ing touch of colour. The hounds, of
course, were merely out for exercise, for
beneath the snow the ground was frozen
as hard as rock, and until a thaw came
there could be no hunting. The Darrancombe foxes were having a holiday and
running up bills against the squire for
ducks, fowls, and geese that disappeared
mysteriously, leaving only a few feathers
behind to tell the tale.

The railway-station was two miles
away, and after tramping two miles
through the snow, it was only natural
that Mr. Thomas Prout should enter the
quaint village inn to obtain something to
keep out the cold. There he discovered
a couple of friends of his—Mr. Benjamin
Maddock, and Mr. Barry O'Rooney,
playing a game of dominoes in the cheerful warmth of a roaring fire of logs.

"By honey, you're a couple of nice
pals, you are !" said Prout. "Why
couldn't you come and meet me or send
a car? I telegraphed, didn't I ?"

"Swate bhoy of moine," said Barry
O'Rooney, pushing the dominoes aside,
"so you did. Exactly four minutes ago
your telegram came. Oi'd been round to
the post-office to inquire, and when ut did
arroive the kid brought ut in to us. You
see, darlint, that blizzard on Thursday
noight flattened out a lot of the telegraph woires. Ben and me reckoned
that av the thrain didn't get lost, you'd
be here sooner than the message."

"Have a drink and don't grouse,

Tom," said Maddock. "What's the best
news from Porthampton, souse me ?"

"Not much," answered Prout. "It's
a sight colder there than it is here. The
painters have had to pack up, for it froze
their brushes stiff. They're putting a
new engine in the yacht. It's a big job,
and she don't look like getting out of
dock afore the spring. I fetched your
packets along, and little you deserve
them, either. You ought to have been
paid off instead of drawing full wages
while you're lounging ashore doing
nothing but eat and drink."

They were undoubtedly having an easy
time of it while the yacht Lord of the
Deep was being reconditioned and re-
fitted. Maddock and O'Rooney grinned
as Prout threw down a couple of plump
envelopes containing their month's pay.
Not only were they receiving full wages,
but they were living on the fat of the
land free of charge at Darrancombe Hall
as Squire Thurston's guests.

"There are toimes, bhoys, whin the
thought that Oi was ever fool enough to
come to say has brought bitther tears to
my broight blue oies," said Barry
O'Rooney, as he pulled a packet of
Treasury notes out of his envelope.
"There are toimes—and this is wan of
them—whin the same thought makes my
heartt bubble wid joy. Oi'm niver
happier at say than whin Oi'm ashure
and the spondulicks are rolling in. How
many of these have you pinched, Tom ?"

"Mine seem all right, souse me," said
Maddock, "so he must be turning honest
in his old age. This is a very nice life,
this is, and while it lasts I'll not try to do
any man out of a job. You'll pay what
we owe, won't you, Tommy, and save us
the trouble of unbuttoning our coats
again to get at the money."

"I'll see you both shot first !" growled
Prout. "I say, how's that Eskimo going
on? Has he gone mad lately ?"

"Bedad, since the frost and snow came
the spalpeen has been as loively as a
linnet," answered Barry O'Rooney.
"There's three or four inches of oice on
the lake. Good luck to the oice and the
snow for clearing that oily Iskimo out of
the house. He's built himself a snow
igloo and put on an ould suit of mangy
sealskin. All the baste wants now to
make him really happy, is a few walruses
and a bunch of Polar bears."

"We've got a good hour to kill afore
lunch," said Maddock the bo'sun, con-
sulting a large silver watch. "Let's go
round and have a look at the reptile and
push his igloo flat. There's nothing so
bad for a chap as idleness. If we dance
on his igloo, he'll have to build another,
souse me, and it will be a kind action, for
it will keep the blubberbiter out of mischief. There's nothing I hate worse than
an idle man, barring whelks."

Passing the main entrance, they
walked through the crisp snow to a door
in the wall of the park. In the centre of
the snow-clad lake was a small island on
which a few leafless willows grew, and
here Gan Waga the Eskimo had built his
igloo, a dome-shaped snow hut with a
tunnel for a front door, and a slab of ice
for a window. Outside this mansion thin
smoke was rising from a wood fire over
which an iron pot was suspended. The
owner of this palace was squatting outside it in his front garden, skinning a
rabbit.

"Bedad, ut remoinds me of the toime
Oi discovered the North Pole," said
Barry O'Rooney. "Ahoy, blubberbiter !
How d'ye foind things at all, at all ?"

Gan Waga's sealskin costume looked
rather patchy where the fur had worn off
it. He smiled at his visitors and reached
for a hatchet with a bright, keen edge.
As hatchets are rarely used for skinning
rabbits, the action seemed to suggest that
the Eskimo had a suspicious mind.

"Oh, I all merry and brightness !" he
said cheerfully. "So yo' back, hunk,
Tommy, old dear, and justs as ugliful as
ever."

"I don't think," said Prout. "And a
very nice house ours is, by honey, a
lovely house, bath-room, drawing-room,
and billiards-room all complete. I don't
see no garage, so p'r'aps you've given up
your Rolls-Royce, Gan. I should like a
house like that myself, only I don't think
I could run to the rent. Warm in winter
and cool in summer, ain't they? Hot
water all over, day and night, and
electric lifts to every floor. And what a
jolly kitchen !"

"Bedad, next to the swate home of my
childhood's days, Ballybunion Castle,
ut's the foinest place Oi ever clapped oies
on," said Barry O'Rooney. "None of
your silly towers and ugly chimney-pots,

bhoys, but all as smooth and lovely and round as a dumpling, and so clane. And Oi loike the front dure. No silly stheps to wash, and no silly brass knockers and dure-knobs to polish. Och, ut's a gem of a house, and Oi suppose you'll grow some roses round the dure, Gan, whin summer comes again. But phwat is home, however beautiful, widout a woife? There ought to be a Mrs. Blubberbiter. Oi can imagine her shoving out her head to welcome you, Gan, her face all smoiles and shining wid blubber, whin you come back at noight wid a walrus undher wan arrm, and a barrel of whale-oil undher the other. In my moind's oie Oi can see her sylph-loike forrm as graceful as a sack of flour wid a rope tied round ut, chivvying you round the garden wid a harpoon, because you forgot the bear's grease for her bonny black hair. Phwat a lovely vision of domestic bliss! Wance more whin Oi shut my oies Oi can see——"

Carried away by these beautiful imaginings, Barry O'Rooney closed his eyes once too often. Maddock gave him a violent push. In happy England it is not only considered a breach of good manners to enter a gentleman's house without being invited to do so, but it is also a breach of the law. Barry staggered and reeled up against the igloo. Had it been built in the land of Gan Waga's birth, it might have withstood the shock; but it was too frail. As Barry O'Rooney, unable to save himself, went sprawling across it, the roof caved in, and Barry O'Rooney, except for his boots, was lost in the ruins.

The rabbit hurled after him by the owner of the wrecked mansion smote Maddock on the back of the head as he fled with Prout across the frozen lake. When they gained the bank they stopped to look back and grin. O'Rooney, very red in the face, had just heaved himself out of the wreckage. He vanished again as Gan Waga jumped at him.

Boots and clenched fists emerging from the tossing snow, and yells and grunts told of fierce strife.

"Souse me, I hope Gan will give it him good and hard, Tom," said the bo'sun. "It's a low-down trick to wreck a man's home."

"Nearly worse than murder," Prout agreed. "Only a heartless rogue could do a thing like that. And after praising the house like he did, too!"

"Let's go away," said Maddock. "I can't bear such sights. And besides, by honey, don't forget that the blubberbiter can hop along over snow faster than we can. When he's finished with Barry he may take it into his thick head to make sail after us with that nasty little chopper. Ugh! Fair disgusting!"

The bo'sun had been the cause of it all, but instead of going back to rescue Barry O'Rooney, he turned away callously and abandoned him. Barry, having spat the snow out of his mouth, bawled for mercy, and informed the angry Eskimo, who was on top of him, in a tired voice, that he had his fingers crossed. Then they both crawled out of the ruins of the igloo, for Gan Waga granted the truce Barry had appealed for, it being quite understood that when a gentleman asks for mercy and declares he has his fingers crossed, it is unfair to hit him. All the same, the Eskimo grasped his hatchet.

"Gan, bhoy," said Barry O'Rooney, scooping out the cold snow that lay between his collar and his neck, "ut's a moighty shame your noice house has got busted, but, honour broight, my swate youth, Oi didn't do ut. Phwat Oi mane to say is that Oi didn't do ut intentionally. Wasn't Oi imagining all koinds of lovely things for you and roses round the dure wid both oies shut toight? Arrah,

THE GEM LIBRARY.—No. 830.

then, whoy this thusness? Ut was that rogue Maddock who shoved me, bad luck to him, and may his shadow never grow whiskers. And for that man's voile act Oi'm banged on the nose, biffed in the ear, pounded in the ribs, choked wid snow, thrampled on in forrty-noine different places. Gan, ould sport, ut's in my moind to give you a real fourpenny wan and knock your thick head clane over the wall of the parrk, only you did ut out of ignorance, and, besides, you have that ugly chopper. Instead, Oi howld out the hand of friendship. Let us be brothers, and give ut the bo'sun harrd in the neck for this foul deed. Phwat sayest thou, my homeless blubberbiter? Spake on!"

Gan Waga rose and picked up the rabbit. Grasping that skinless rodent by its hind legs he swung it close to Barry O'Rooney's ear and spoke.

"Hops it quickfuls, yo' uglifuls old rascals," said Gan Waga.

Having no appetite for uncooked rabbit just then, Barry O'Rooney departed. When out of the immediate danger-zone, he lingered.

"Oi'll tell you phwat Oi'd do wid them ruins, Gan," he said. "Oi'd build a snow man wid a face on him about as handsome as your own and just as loike you as possible. Then Oi'd get a bucket of boiling wather and pour ut over the face. Afther that, Oi mane av Oi was you, Oi'd take that little hatchet, cut a hole in the oice, and shove mesilf through ut, and everybody would be happy. And, bedad, Oi'm joyful that Oi did bust your rotten old house."

Left alone in the bleak and desolate snow, the Eskimo sat down and crooned a sad little song to himself in his native tongue as he cut up the rabbit. A bleak wind began to blow as he put more sticks under the fire, and grey clouds drifted across the wintry sky. When the pot was simmering, Gan Waga lighted a cigar and lay down with a heap of snow for a pillow. Suddenly the parkland was blotted out in a smother of falling flakes.

Half an hour later, the Eskimo was lost to view. He had found another house without having had the trouble to build it. The snow had covered him, and only a small hole from which an occasional puff of cigar-smoke ascended betrayed the fact that there was something alive beneath it. Then the cigar went out, and so did the fire, extinguished by the drifting snowflakes, and Gan Waga fell asleep, only to start up with a howl wearing the iron pot as a helmet and drenched with luke-warm rabbit stew. And then Gan Waga heard roars of laughter.

CHAPTER 2.
A Raid That Failed!

THE people who did the laughing were Rupert Thurston, Squire of Darrancombe, and his almost inseparable friend Prince Ching Lung, for Gan Waga was not laughing at all. The squire and the prince stood with the snow up to the knees of their rubber boots. They had come out to see how the Eskimo was getting on in what to him was delightful weather. They had not missed the igloo, for they were not aware that Gan Waga had built one. They did see his cooking-pot and something else that as owner of a pack of fox hounds interested Mr. Rupert Thurston a good deal.

A couple of fine foxes had been attracted by the appetising scent of Gan Waga's rabbit stew. Thurston pulled Ching Lung behind a tree. After a preliminary sniff or two one of the foxes

gave a well-judged spring and managed to balance himself cleverly on the swaying pot. Then he put in his head and the gulping noises he made as the stew slipped down his throat roused the envy of the second fox. There was not room for two of them. For a second or so they snarled and struggled and yapped, the pot swinging, and then toppling from its hook, the pot turned over and fell, Gan Waga started up out of the snow, and two scared foxes, one going north and the other south, streaked away across the snow-clad lake for their lives.

"Ha, ha, ha, ha, ha!" laughed the prince and the squire of Darrancombe. "Oh, ha, ha, ha, ha, ha!"

Gan Waga ridded himself of his iron hat, scraped some of the warm stew out of his eyes, grasped his hatchet and prepared to murder somebody or other.

"Kamerad!" yelled Ching Lung and Rupert Thurston, holding up their hands. "We surrender."

"We didn't do it, Gan," added the prince. "It was a couple of foxes after your fodder. And do put your tin hat on again, my fat and beautiful one, for it suits you splendidly. You only want a silk band round it and a feather stuck in it and you'd look a jolly handsome chap."

Gan Waga did not think that Ching Lung and Thurston would play such a shabby trick on him, but he was not quite convinced of their innocence until he saw the tracks of the foxes in the snow. A rub with a handful of snow removed the stew from his face and hair and a roll in it cleansed his sealskin suit after a fashion.

"It seems to me, Chingy, old dear, I jolly badness downs on my luck," he sighed. "That my igloo, those lumps. That wickedful rascal, Barry O'Loonatic, he smash that flatness fo' me. And my niceness rabbit-stew, he goned west, too, Chingy. Yo' and yo' rotten old sneak-thief foxes, Ruperts. What yo' gotted all those silly hounds fo' if yo' can't catch the foxes? How I go on, hunk, if I nots able to make a stews without having it pinched?"

"Only an insane idiot with a nice warm house to go to and lots of good food would want to boil rabbits out in the snow," said Rupert Thurston. "Only that or a savage."

"Well, yo' catch yo' savages foxes," said the Eskimo. "All the idjitness seem morer to keeps all those hounds eating their heads off. Fifty or sixty hounds and idjits on horses in red coats and sometimes they never catches one fox in a day. That's what I calls idjitness, Chingy. I catch twenty foxes in a day easiness."

"My poor fat friend, my forlorn Eskimo pal from the ice-bound land of Blubberipook, you don't understand the noble sport of fox-hunting and never will," said Ching Lung. "A fox is a sacred sort of animal. He must not be trapped, shot, or poisoned. He must die only one way, to be bowled over by the pack. Men who trap, shoot, or poison foxes are in this country boiled in oil. A queer sort of game killing foxes with hounds, Gan, and an expensive one. I'll wager it costs Rupert a pile of money every fox his pack roll over. A jolly lot more than eighteen-pence a time, eh, Rupert?"

"I not care what it cost, Chingy," said Gan Waga. "Tells yo' old foxes not to touch my stews no more, Ruperts, or I make them sorriness for it."

The Eskimo declined to go back with them. After the sharp snowfall, the temperature had fallen, and it was bitterly cold. They left Gan building another igloo.

"Queer merchant, but I suppose he's happy," said Thurston.

"As happy as a hungry thrush with a big fat worm, old scout," answered Ching Lung, "but like the worm he'll turn. If Barry O'Rooney and his two accomplices start smashing down his homesteads, he'll get ratty. He'll also get ratty if the foxes make free with any more of his Irish stew. You ought to have warned him."

"I think there are only a couple of foxes in the park, and I don't want foxes in the park," said the squire. "If he can rid me of them so much the better. If what Prout says about the yacht is correct we shall be stuck down here for a couple of months. It's not likely that we shall actually bore each other to death, but I'm tired of shooting, and you're much too hot for me at billiards. So let's hope this beastly Arctic weather will break and give us a chance to go hunting."

It did not take Gan Waga very long to construct another igloo. Later he chipped away the ice in various places round the little island to protect himself from intruders and covered these man-traps with snow, for Gan did not feel inclined to build igloos to give other people the pleasure of pulling them down. Then he visited the snares he had set for rabbits. There was no wild thing, furred or feathered, that the Eskimo could not trap. There were eight rabbits in his snares. He skinned a couple of them and put them in the pot and hung the others in a willow tree out of the reach of foxes. Then, having relighted the fire and cut a dead branch for fuel, the Eskimo put on a pair of snow-shoes he had made that morning and went to Darrancombe Hall.

Thurston's servants could not make the Eskimo out at all. They could quite understand the positions of Prout, O'Rooney and Maddock, but the squire and the prince seemed to look upon the snub-nosed gentleman with black, tallowy hair as an equal. Gan Waga certainly looked upon himself an anybody's equal. He clumped over the Turkey carpet in his snow-shoes and stopped as he saw O'Rooney and Prout smoking their pipes in front of a blazing fire.

"Some folks, bedad," said Barry, "go through loife, Tom, and never do wan koind action, not even to plase a friend. Oi axed that Iskimo to do wan koind little thing for me, and he hasn't done it, a throiling little favour that wouldn't have taken foive minutes. Oi only axed him to cut a hole in the oice on the lake where the wather was noice and dape and he wouldn't do it. Would you belave ut, only a toiny koind action loike that?"

"He's got a nasty mind, by honey," said Prout. "I can't bear these foreign chaps, with oily noses, flat noses, mouths like open cellar flaps and eyes like two currants stuck in a lump of dough. What's the use of talking to such riff-raff about kind actions. The only thing they understand is a biff on the ear from an honest British fist. That's the only way to larn 'em, my lad. An Eskimo, a dog, and a walnut tree, the more you biff 'em the better they be."

"Yo' comes near my igloo any morer and I do some biffingnesses, old dears," said Gan Waga. "I going to watch outs. You dare comes and I shows you, my mouldy old bananas. Yo' t'ink it a merrifuls jokes, breaking ups my happy homes, hunk? Yo' dares come nears and yo' gets swatted hards, that's all."

"Phwat d'ye mane dare? Whoy, you overgrown barrel of whale oil, av you give me any sauce, Oi'll be along to-noight and roll on your ould snow shack. Grab him and shove his head in the coal-box, Tommy, and shut the lid. He's daring

us, d'ye notice—daring us! He's gone clane up the loop."

"Oh, gets offs it," said Gan Waga. "This is what I comed fo', so takes yo' great ugly hoofs off it."

In his indignation, Barry O'Rooney had risen and was standing on the edge of a fine bearskin rug. Gan Waga gave the rug a tremendous jerk and Barry seated himself unexpectedly in Prout's lap. This abrupt action shot some of the hot ashes from Prout's pipe down O'Rooney's collar and he got up quickly and danced about clawing madly at his spine. By the time he had cooled down, Gan Waga and the bearskin rug were gliding away over the snow to the igloo.

"What a blunderer you are, Barry, by honey," grumbled Prout. "making me waste half a pipe of 'baccy, and 'baccy the price it is."

Barry felt the blisters on his neck very tenderly, clenched his fist, and glared at Prout. The arrival of the butler made him gulp down his wrath.

"Excuse me, gentlemen," said the butler, "but there has been an accident —a burst water-pipe. Unfortunately, it has flooded both your bed-rooms. There's a large, airy room on the ground floor. The housekeeper wishes me to ask if you would mind occupying it if she had two beds put up till she can make other arrangements?"

"Never a bit!" said Prout. "We're old sailors, by honey, and we could sleep on planks with spikes in them. Ask the lady to stick up a bed for Maddock, for we're used to being together. What rotten things do happen on land, Barry! All the time I've been at sea I can't remember a bust water-pipe, though I've had a busted water-spout drop on me. What with pipes busting, kitchen boilers exploding, and chimneypots blowing off, I wouldn't live ashore for a pension. It ain't safe!"

"Nor me!" said Barry O'Rooney. "Oi don't loike policemen, especially noight policemen. The very fact that they have 'em shows that the place must swarm wid rogues and rascals. We want no police aboard, Tom; so the merry ould say for me all the toime, bhoy!"

Presently Maddock joined them, and they were invited to inspect their new

quarters. It was a long, low-ceilinged room in the front of the house, and three nice beds had been placed in it with crimson eiderdowns and feather pillows.

"There's a bath-room through that door," said the butler; "but only cold water, I'm sorry to say. And I can only give you candles. The late squire was very old-fashioned, and I must say Darrancombe Hall is a bit out-of-date. I'm pleased to learn that the new squire is making big alterations in the spring—electric light, lifts, telephones, and central heating. On your next visit, gentlemen, I have no doubt we shall be able to make you much more comfortable."

"If I never get anything worse than this you won't catch me grumbling a lot, souse me!" said Maddock. "Hi, Tom! You're nearest! Pick up the fender quick, my lad, and sling it at that! Never mind breaking a few panes of glass as long as you hit it hard!"

There was a face at the window—the plump, grinning face of Gan Waga, the Eskimo—but, like most beautiful things, it quickly faded away and vanished.

After dinner Thurston asked the prince to excuse him, and went to his desk to write some letters.

"I'm off to have a pow-wow with Gan," said Ching Lung. "I shall be back in less than an hour. Where are the three wasters?"

"Playing billiards, I think, Ching. I heard the balls clicking as I came past the billiards-room."

"Then they're out of mischief, and not trying to rag the Eskimo," said Ching Lung. "I'll just wade along and find out what he's up to."

The sky was bright, with frosty stars shining down on a white and silent world. Ching Lung was wise enough to whistle when he reached the edge of the lake; and Gan Waga, who knew that whistle, dived out of his igloo, with a shout of warning.

"Don't yo' moves, Chingy, till I fetches yo'!" he cried. "Else yo' get a wet shirt, old dear! I dugged a lot of holes, so be very carefulness!"

Gan Waga guided Ching Lung safely to the igloo; and, crawling through, the prince squatted down on the bearskin

" Yarooooh ! " cried Gan Waga, as the contents of the stewpot trickled all over him, and the two foxes went streaking across the snow-clad lake for their lives !

rug to smoke a cigarette. The Eskimo's lighting and heating apparatus consisted of one candle, but the snow-hut was bright and fairly warm.

"Rupert says you may snare those foxes if you want to, Gan," said Ching Lung. "He thinks there are only two in the park—and he doesn't like them in the park."

"Old Rupert not know muchness, Chingy, ifs he thinks there only twos," said Gan Waga. "I bet there's twenty-twos and morer. I catches them quick-fuls when I starts. I jolly soons——"

The Eskimo raised a warning hand and leaned forward to listen. Ching Lung had sharp ears, but he heard nothing. The grin of joy that suddenly widened Gan Waga's mouth told him that something was going to happen very cheerful from the Eskimo's point of view.

"They coming, Chingy!" chuckled Gan Waga, rubbing his hands together. "Dears, dears! They comings to push my igloo overs, Chingy, all three of them!"

"Careful, old warrior!" said Ching Lung. "Make sure, Gan. It may be one of the gamekeepers, and if you drown a gamekeeper the coroner will be rude to you."

For all Gan Waga knew about coroners, a coroner might have been something to eat. He listened again.

"Three of thems, Chingy! I hears the snow crunch, crunch, crunch!" he whispered. "Ha, ha, ha! I only hopes they do try to push my poor old igloo flat!"

Gan Waga wormed his way through the tunnel, and Ching Lung followed. If Prout, Maddock, or O'Rooney got hurt or wet, the prince was of opinion that they fully deserved it.

Even if it is an easy thing to push down a man's house, no honest-minded person would ever dream of doing so. And to steal out in the still and gloom of the night for such a fell purpose was monstrous. The three mariners seemed to want to make a kind of hobby of it.

Three dark figures, outlined clearly against the white background of snow, were slowly approaching the lake. Of course, Gan Waga had dared them to come, and threatened to swat them hard if they did come; but that was a poor excuse to descend three strong on that solitary and simple-minded Eskimo.

"Whisht! Go aisy, bhoys!" said Barry O'Rooney. "Oi spoy feetprints in snow. Somewan has come along in front of us and left his thracks. Phwat says Sexton Blake?"

"The prince, souse me!" said Maddock. "You don't need to call in Sexton Blake to know that. That's a foot, Barry —not a great beetle-smasher, like yours!"

"Bedad, then, the prince is unlucky!" grinned Barry O'Rooney. "Av he's foolish enough to kape bad company, he'll have to go through ut! We'll do ut in sthyle; not wan of your chape smashes, but a rale collapse! Get round the igloo, and when Oi say the worrd fall on ut loike wan man. Then up, bhoys, and scuttle for home, swate home. And by the toime they've done bellowing and got the snow out of their oies they'll never know we've been there."

"They'll see our tracks, silly!" said Prout.

"And phwat matther av they do see our thracks? How were we to know the prince was insoide? Oi ax you that. Aren't we gentlemen? Would we ever dhrame of being so unmannerly as to peep through a strange window to see who was insoide? A swate little house, isn't ut? Wan of the happy homes of England! How beautiful they sthand, wid roses round the dure! Oi'll wager Gan has gulped down enough rabbit-stew for six—the fat glutton—and gone to slape to dhrame about more grub! Grub, grub, grub, and still more grub— whale-oil and blubber and butther and tallow candles and bacon-fat and suet— that's all he lives for!"

"Shut up!" said Maddock. "Give it a rest, for the sake of Mike, Barry! Can't you keep that chin of yours from wagging for ten seconds at a stretch? Souse me! If he is asleep, he sleeps light, and his great ugly ears are as sharp as needles! If he hears us he won't stop inside to have the shack shoved down on him; he'll pop out of his hole quick as a weasel. Besides, you chump, he ain't likely to be asleep, with the prince there. The proper way is to rush it and get it over quick."

"That's the ticket, by honey!" agreed Prout. "Of course he isn't asleep! Rush in, push in, and rush out! Go!"

The house-wreckers made a dash for the ice, though it was not a very tremendous dash owing to the depth of the snow.

"Murther! Ow! Help! Oi'm gone!" shrieked the frenzied voice of Barry O' Rooney.

"Souse me! What—— Ow! Help!" shrieked the no less frenzied voice of Benjamin Maddock, the bo'sun.

The ice had given way beneath their feet, and feet foremost they sank into the icy flood, squirting up fountains of water. For the moment Prout had escaped. He tried to grab at the nearest head, which happened to be the bo'sun's, and stopped a snowball, thrown by an unseen hand, with his left ear. To level things up, a second snowball smote him in the right ear. Not liking it at all, and heedless of the frantic yells of his drowning comrades, Prout passed the igloo and Gan Waga's fire across the little island. It seemed safer to go that way, but unfortunately it was not so, for the Eskimo had fortified his igloo very effectively. There was a third splash and a third howl.

"Got him, Chingy!" shouted Gan Waga, dancing in his delight. "He inside too, Chingy—rights in the merry old soup. Dears, dears! Oh, ha, ha, ha, haah!"

The water was not very deep, but it was very cold, and as soon as the unhappy housebreakers discovered that they were more likely to freeze to death than drown, they stopped caterwauling and got out. As they slunk away Gan Waga hugged Ching Lung and wept a little on the bosom of the prince's fur overcoat.

(Continued on next page.)

TOM MERRY'S FOE!
(Continued from page 16.)

it off! You came here to fight me, Tom Merry. What did you interfere with Cutts for?"

Tom stared at him.

"Wouldn't you have interfered?" he demanded.

Cardew shrugged his shoulders.

"I hope so; but probably not."

"Rot!" said Tom, dabbing his streaming nose with his handkerchief. "Oh, my hat! I feel pretty done! Ow!"

"I should have been pretty done if you hadn't come up!" said Cardew quietly. "Cutts was givin' me jip, and he meant to give me more! But I think you've got worse than I should have got. You chipped in on my account—like a fool!"

"Thanks!" said Tom, still dabbing.

"Like a fool!" repeated Cardew deliberately. "But—but I'd give most of the things I possess, Tom, to be a fool like you! Can you guess that I had Racke here to play foul if you got the better of me? I'm glad to say I changed my mind and kicked him out—some rag of decency left that I'd overlooked, I suppose. When we were at Eastwood House at Christmas, Tom, you smacked my face, and I've thought of nothing since but revenge. You can smack it again if you like."

"I don't like—and I'm sorry——"

"That's all right! I asked for it, same as I've asked for what you've given Cutts. This fight of ours isn't postponed; it's off. No need for you to demonstrate that you can lick me; you've licked Cutts, who is good for three of me. Still, we'll have it out one of these days if you're keen on it."

"I'm not keen on it."

"There's a pool in the wood where you can bathe your face," said Cardew. "Let me help you; you're fairly done! And—and if you feel inclined to kick me, go ahead! I don't mind!"

"Fathead!" said Tom, laughing.

He leaned on Cardew's arm as they went through the wood. No one seeing them then would have guessed that the two juniors were rivals and foes.

Tom Merry, indeed, did not know whether Cardew was still his enemy in the following days. Cardew seemed to avoid him. He was still junior captain, and Tom Merry's name did not appear in the football list. On all sides it was felt that Cardew's tenure of the junior captaincy was precarious, and that a struggle was coming between Cardew and Tom Merry—a struggle the result of which was doubtful, but which was certain to be determined and obstinate. Possibly even Ralph Reckness Cardew himself did not fully know whether, after what had happened in the wood, he was still Tom Merry's Foe.

THE END.

(Another extra-long school story of Tom Merry & Co. next week, chums: "JUST LIKE CARDEW!" By Martin Clifford. Don't miss this splendid treat!)

"Do yo'—do—do yo' think they—they come backs any morer, Chingy?" he sobbed.

"I cannot tell, dear heart, but I think not," said the prince, as he watched the half-drowned mariners footing it over the snow. "Why do you ask? Do you wish them back?"

"Yes, Chingy, I do," said the Eskimo, "only so that I could push them in again. Oh, ho, ho, ho, hooh! Oh, dears, dears! I tink I shall starts to laugh in a minute, Chingy. We swatted and biffed them lovelifuls, hunk? Ha, ha, ha, ha, haah! I teaches them to push over my igloos! I larn them, and I'll larns them morer soonfuls, old ducks!"

CHAPTER 3.
A Good Catch!

PROUT, Maddock, and Barry O'Rooney were too tough and seasoned for their soaking to do them much harm. They were miserable, and they were also angry. They slunk into the house, and were glad that they had not to go upstairs, for it is not easy to climb a staircase when wearing trousers frozen at the knees almost as stiff as boards. Their fingers were so numbed that they could scarcely get their clothes off, but they towelled each other briskly till the circulation came back again.

"It's not worth dressing again to-night!" growled Prout as he wiped out his damp pipe. "It's lucky I've got a watertight 'baccy-pouch, so I'm getting into bed to have a smoke. If your 'baccy's wet, Ben, sing out, and I'll sling mine across to you. By honey, we didn't half fall into it, did we? Drat that blubber-chewing Eskimo!"

"Bedad, he must have bored holes all round that rotten oiland!" said Barry O'Rooney. "Br-r-r! Oi'm about as cowld as a frog in a snow-blizzard, and Oi can't kape my knees from hitting aich other. Bad luck to Gan Waga! Br-r-r! Me-my teeth are beginning to rattle! Ochone! They must have fetched these sheets straight off the oice afore they put them on the bed! Tommy, be a sporrt. Shove your head out of the dure and yell to the butler chap to bring a hot-water bottle!"

"And some hot rum, souse me, Tommy!" added the bo'sun. "Tell him to put plenty of rum in it, with some lemon and two lumps of sugar, and make it boiling hot!"

"If you want hot-water bottles and hot rum, my lads, get 'em for yourselves," said Prout. "I'm feeling cosy at last, and, by honey, I'm not shifting out of it till morning!"

"Ochone! Oi'm sure my fate have dhropped off, for Oi can't faal thim!" moaned Barry O'Rooney. "Phwat a loife. Fool that Oi was ever to lave swate Ballybunion and come to say. Who stharted that stunt about going out and bashing in the igloo? Show me the man and let me currse him! Where's my fate? Oi must have left them in my boots, for Oi'm sure they're not in bed with me. That treacherous monsther! Oi hope Oi haven't lost my fate, for Oi'm longing to kick him!"

"There's no getting away from the fact, it was the Eskimo's game," said Prout. "He got us fine that go, by honey, but our turn next. I can wait, so good-night, boys!"

Prout knocked the ashes out of his pipe, and extinguished the candle by squeezing the wick between his finger and thumb.

"You were in bed last, Ben," said O'Rooney. "Did you lock the dure?"

"I ain't sure, but I think I did," answered the bo'sun. "If you think I

The ice gave way beneath the housebreakers' feet and they sank into the icy flood. "Ha, ha, ha!" laughed Gan Waga, as he pelted them with snowballs from the bank.

didn't, show a leg and lock it yourself. I'm fed-up to the teeth, souse me, and I'm going to sleep!"

There was one person in Darrancombe who did not sleep that night, and that person was Gan Waga the Eskimo, for Gan Waga the Eskimo was hunting. To be more accurate, Gan Waga had gone trapping, which is not exactly the same thing. The keen weather had made the wild creatures fiercely hungry, and therefore bolder and less cautious. The Eskimo understood their ways, and he could have taught Rupert Thurston's head gamekeeper in a few hours more than he had learned in years. And if Gan had cared to turn poacher he would have sent the head gamekeeper raving mad, for in a week he would have stripped the park bare of fur and feather.

And Gan Waga's trapping was very successful, considering that he was trying to capture one of the wariest of all four-footed beasts. In the grey of the dawn he shouldered two bulky sacks and plodded away, keeping a wary look about him, though there was not much danger of encountering any of the keepers in such weather and at such an hour. Curiously enough, the moment Gan Waga mounted the steps of Darrancombe Hall the front door was opened by Prince Ching Lung.

"S-sh! Don't make a row!" said the prince, who was wearing a dressing-gown and slippers. "Did you do any good?"

"Nines of them, Chingy," grinned the Eskimo. "I knew betterer than Rupert. I gotted nines, but I not gotted them alls, Chingy."

"Where?"

"In a strong sacks, Chingy. They not started to fight yet, but they will if I nots let them out sooness. I let them outses, Chingy, and then I go backs to my igloo and have some rabbit stew fo' breakfasts and play shut-eye, fo' I a bit tiredness."

"Well, I promised to open the door for you at six, and here I am!" said Ching Lung. "I didn't expect you to trap nine live foxes, though I know you're a real dandy at the game. Rupert will be jolly pleased, for he has too many foxes.

They won't do in that sack, for, if they don't bite their way out, they'll start scrapping with each other, or get smothered. Where can you put them where they'll be safe till we can take them outside and turn them down?"

Gan Waga smiled in the pale light of the candle Ching Lung was holding, and pointed across the hall.

"They be all rights in the sacks, Chingy," he said. "I shoves them in theres. Yo' only gotted to tell the huntsman to fetch them."

Gan Waga went out to fetch the sack, but before bringing it in he cut a short slit in it, knowing well what would happen and very quickly, for no sack with the tiniest slit in it will hold a fox for long. Then Gan Waga crossed the hall and turned the handle of the door. He could have howled with delirious joy when the door which Maddock had not locked swung open. Gan Waga tiptoed in and placed the writhing, evil-smelling sack at the foot of Barry O'Rooney's cot.

"So that's done, Chingy!" he said. "I gladness I catch those foxes for old Ruperts! Dears, I tiredness! I smoke one of yo' cigarettes, and then I goes."

Ching Lung had no idea that the room was tenanted, but he knew it before Gan Waga had finished his cigarette, for three howling, bare-footed men in night attire bolted out of it, their eyes goggling and their hair standing on end.

By the light of his candle Ching Lung saw foxes scurrying over the cots, foxes trying to climb the window curtains, and foxes trying to scurry up the chimney! Foxes, foxes everywhere, and not a hound to hunt them.

On his way back to his igloo Gan Waga fell down in the snow seventeen times through laughing so much.

THE END.

(Look out for another of the ripping yarns by famous Sidney Drew. Meanwhile, make a point of reading: "'HAT-TRICK' GUY!" a rattling football story, written specially for next week's GEM.)

Tom Gale, the plucky young hero of
the Ajax, goes through—

—much trouble in this powerful
and thrilling instalment!

TOM of the AJAX
by ROLAND SPENCER

A Thrilling, True-to-Life Training-Ship Story.

The Scissor Trap!

A S the steamer's bows sawed up
and down in the great hole it had
torn in the plates of the Ajax,
pandemonium reigned on that
low-positioned deck of the ship.

Boys ran shouting in terror here and
there, tripping over the hems of their
long nightshirts. Dicky West had been
flung against the lockers; while Tom,
gasping with horror, stared round and
shouted for order. His voice was
drowned in the melee.

Desperate, the lad realised that something must be done to maintain order.
He leaped up and charged, shouting, for
the crowd of boys fighting and pushing
and yelling at the ladderway leading to
the decks above. It was a bottle-neck
there, resulting in such a crush as Tom
had never before witnessed on the ship.

Above the shouts of terror came cries
of pain, as younger boys were crushed
and pressed against the railings on either
side of the ladderway. Tom meant to
get there and force some sort of order.
It was his duty as a chief petty officer.

The young leader of the Hoods, however, tripped over his nightshirt, and fell
flat on the deck, the heavy fall winding
him. But he at once scrambled to his
feet, and found that he had fallen on his
own working-clothes, thrown on to the
deck at the first impact of the collision.

Like a flash, Tom drew on his trousers
over his nightshirt. He had noticed that
the long garments were impeding the
movements of the others, and making
panic worse than ever. Then he rushed
at the surging mass near the ladderway.
Above the cries, shouts from the steamer
and the upper deck of the Ajax could
now be heard. But the orlop deck was
the greatest danger point in the ship.

The young chief of the Hoods sprang
over the heads of the boys at the outskirts of the throng, bearing them down
under him. Stoniky Burr had been one
of the panic-stricken fighters, pushing
and crushing down the smaller boys. It
THE GEM LIBRARY.—No. 830.

was he who first went down under Tom's
attack.

"Order!" bawled Tom, and his voice
at once quietened the din immediately
around him. Tom seized his opportunity. "Parade in front of your
hammocks!" he yelled. "Chiefs of
divisions, march off! Quickest way!
Don't be a lot of idiotic fools—fighting
like a school full of girls because someone
yelled 'Mouse!'"

This raised a laugh, and the din subsided as if by magic.

"Chief P.O.'s, get busy!" roared Tom,
in a pretended rage. "Let's hear from
you! Back, you Grenvilles! Hi, there!
If you Blakes want to disgrace the ship,
you can. The other divisions won't!"

Tom gave the lead himself by yelling
to all the Hoods to get back to their
hammocks. He led the way for his own
division, and the rest, though some of
the smaller boys were white with terror,
placed themselves under the orders of
their leaders.

WHAT HAS GONE BEFORE!

*TOM GALE, a sturdily-built youth and chief
petty officer of the starboard watch aboard the
famous old training-ship Ajax, which is moored
near the southern bank of the River Thames a
quarter of a mile down the river from Fleethithe,
falls foul of
STONIKY BURR, C.P.O. of the port watch, a
bully of the first water.
DICKY WEST is a cheerful ginger-headed youth
and a staunch chum of Gale's
Trouble arises when Tom Gale is detailed,
together with Stoniky Burr, as a hare in a cross-
country hare-and-hounds that is to take place.
Burr—unlike Tom, whose whole heart and soul is
in the chase—soon gets fed-up, and suggests holding back. But not so with Tom. He is anxious
to elude the hounds, who are hot in chase. Burr's
anger is at once aroused, and when Tom is running
across a plank bridge Burr manages a spill, and
Tom falls headlong into the creek below. Hot
words and a fight follow, and Burr is thrashed
and left. It is then that a mysterious, sinister
man in green spectacles approaches Burr. He
gives his name as KALCHE, and he enlists the aid
of Burr in a plot against Tom Gale, without,
however, giving any reason for this.
Later, when on the water, Burr tries to force Tom off, but he
himself is precipitated into the water and is
rescued by Tom, although the latter realises that
Burr's attempt was deliberate.
Tom is puzzling the whole thing out in his hammock at night, when he is startled by a rending
crash, and he feels the Ajax quiver from stem to
stern. The next moment he utters a startled cry
as a jagged hole appears in the ship's side, torn
like paper by the stem of a huge red-rusty steamer
which crashes into the Ajax.*

(Now read on.)

Thus, as Mr. Landfar, the chief officer-
instructor, and Mr. Dennithorne of the
"physical jerks" class came leaping
down the ladderway, they were agreeably surprised to see that there was not
a break-neck panic in progress on the
orlop deck.

The Grenville division nearest to the
staircase, began to scramble up hurriedly
for the upper deck. They were followed
by the Blakes, but Tom noticed that
Stoniky Burr, in the rear of the Blakes,
looked back and then dodged behind the
ladderway.

Tom was about to see the Hoods off
in the wake of the Blakes, when a series
of yells sounded out from above. The
clang of the steamer's engine-room telegraph followed, the churn of her screw,
and then the great rusty bows began to
draw out from the hole in the side of
the Ajax. Tom shouted a warning to
the boys of his division to stand clear,
and a voice boomed out through a megaphone from the quarter-deck of the Ajax.

"Full speed ahead, you on the
steamer, there!" bawled the officer.
"Keep her jammed in! We're
damaged!"

At that instant the lights on the orlop
deck went out, and again shouts of terror
sounded out from the boys, the roar of
the chief officer-instructor, and Mr.
Dennithorne bawling for order echoing
above the din. Tom felt the air from
the hole in the ship, now that the bows
of the steamer had drawn out, blow cold
on his face again. He shouted to the
Hoods to stand fast, but a startled
exclamation terminated his order.

Out of the darkness a pair of hands
had gripped his throat. They seemed to
be choking the life out of him. He
struggled, but he was forced back—back
towards the hole in the training-ship's
side.

It was all so unexpected that it seemed
to overwhelm the plucky youngster, but
he clawed at his assailant's arms and
grabbed at his face. He could feel the
heavy breathing close to his cheek. Then
the flash of a lantern from the steamer's
bows shone through the hole and lit up
the face of the person attacking him.

Stoniky Burr!

Swiftly dodging down, Tom let drive at Burr's body. What was the fellow's game? Why was he attacking just now—at this desperate moment for them all? Had he suddenly gone mad?

Young Gale fought like a tiger. Burr and he swayed about in the now even thicker darkness, the noise of their fighting drowned by the shrieks of the boys and the vibrating roar of distress from the steamer's siren. Through it all, Tom heard the shouts from the deck of the steamer:

"All clear ahead to ram home sir! Ay, ay; a hair-line! Full speed ahead, there!"

The steamer's engine-room telegraph rang out, followed by the powerful stamp and quiver of her engines. Tom felt, rather than saw that the great rusty craft was forging ahead again to jam her bows back into the hole in the Ajax, to hold them there with her beating screw to minimise the inrush of water through the hole.

Burr was clinging to Tom like a tiger to its prey. Tom lashed out weakly, for Burr's grip had left him breathing with difficulty. Then the bully of the Ajax crashed his head into Tom's teeth, and the young leader of the Hoods went back with a strangled cry.

Tom was suddenly conscious that he was in the open air, but he had nothing solid below him. His brain worked like lightning. He was through the hole in the training-ship's side.

The steamer's bows were crashing in again. He would be crushed to death when rusted steel should meet the jagged torn edges of the plates of the Ajax. Young Gale's feet were scraping on the edge of the torn wooden orlop deck of the training-ship. His hand had caught a curled and jagged strip of steel hanging from its mother plate. The lad pulled himself up, meaning to scramble into the hole again, for he was actually outside, and could see things dimly, but instead of leaping in he sprang back with a swift cry of fear.

The great rusty bows of the steamer were just boring forward into the hole. Tom saved himself by a hair's breadth, and that only by diving backwards into the water between the steamer and the Ajax. The lumpy, curdling, troubled water met the back of his head like the blow from the hand of a giant.

Luckily, Tom did not lose consciousness. His head rose above the surface, and he saw through the wraiths of fog the rusty steamer towering above him on one side and the tall black and white side of the Ajax on the other. The steamer's heel had been caught by the tide and was being pressed down river, while her stamping engines and thrusting screw kept her great bows jammed tightly into the hole in the Ajax.

A swift exclamation escaped Tom at the realisation of his new danger. The steamer was closing in towards the Ajax! He would be caught like a badger in a hole! He would be crushed like an egg-shell under a steam-hammer.

His heart seemed to miss a beat, as he struck out desperately down the tide, arm over arm, lashing the water to foam as he swam. Could he race the tide and so defeat the scissor trap into which he had fallen? Would he clear before rusty iron crashed against painted steel?

<hr />

A Fight for Life!

THE swirling waters helped Tom. As the great bulk of the two vessels moved closer and closer, the water was squeezed out of place, assisting the natural current of the ebb.

Tom Gale got clear under the steamer's high quarter, just when both fabrics quivered and groaned, as eight thousand tons brought up solid against the four thousand of the training-ship.

The plucky young Hood felt a wave of relief surge in his breast as he swept clear of the two ships, but he had only escaped one danger to be swirled in a riot of lashing and curdling water into another. He struck out gamely for the great, slimy, weedy mooring chains at the stern of the Ajax, but he could make no headway against the current, and was whisked clear without being able to get within fifteen yards of the chains.

"Well, I'm alive and kicking," said Tom to himself. "But I've no sense of direction. Goodness knows where I am swimming to. Must keep on, though, to prevent cramp."

His teeth were chattering with the cold and the reaction, but he put his head down to it and swum on with an easy side-stroke—a stroke with which he had once swum over two miles in a swimming test. The water was choppy, but, being swept along with the current as he was, and closed in by a narrow circle of fog, the direction of the water's run could not be determined by him. He did not know whether he was swimming with, across, or against the current.

Sounds, muffled and mysterious through the fog, conveyed nothing to him. And soon even they could not be heard, for the water became very broken and lumpy.

"A tide-rip," muttered Tom. "Must be the one off——"

He broke off suddenly. He had distinctly heard the thump of a screw. He began to tread water, cocking his head to listen intently. Yes, it was an approaching steam-driven vessel. He listened for the sound of its siren.

It came soon, seeming to rip through the fog, so near it was. Tom turned quickly and looked in the direction of the sound. He trod water briskly, all his nerves strung up to highest tension. If the boat should run him down, that would be an end of him for sure.

"Must be a tug just put out from the shore," muttered the young swimmer, peering into the whiteness ahead of the narrow rim of tossing water. "Gosh, I can hear the wash now! Jingo, it must be quite close!"

Bracing himself for the task in mind that of throwing himself sideways if the stem of the tug should be pointing direct for him—Tom waited with his heart in his mouth.

The wash could be heard like a roaring torrent in his ears now. Then, quick as a thought, a dark form leapt swiftly

out of the mists with its red and green eyes and the white glimmer of the mast-head light above.

Straight at Tom it came, and the plucky youngster literally threw himself sideways. The wash of the boat had him in its grip. It surged the lad under, almost choking the life out of him, and Tom struggled frantically to keep himself down, fearful as he was of the beating screw of the little vessel.

His ears buzzed and his head felt fit to burst. He remained below water as long as he could, then struck out savagely for the surface for a breath of life-giving air.

His head shot up from the depths, and as he filled his lungs with a hiss, he saw the stern light of the tug just glimmering away in the thickness of the foggy night.

Full of thankfulness at his escape, though his half-formed idea of bawling for help had been frustrated, Tom swam steadily on on his breast. He followed the direction of the tug with his eyes, then set off at right-angles, trying to sense his direction by the feel of the wind on his face.

How much longer Tom swam he could not judge. He only knew that he was getting to the last of his strength. His arms were becoming leaden and the ginger he had previously put into the kick with his legs was now beyond him. He could only go steadily and hope for the best.

Blue with cold, aching in every limb, sluggish of movement and laboured of breathing, the only thing in Tom that remained buoyant was hope. And that seemed to brace him up to keep on keeping on. It was all he could do.

Like a giant of blackness the coaster sprang forward from the mists, pointing dead for the buoy. Tom Gale shouted in a frenzy of alarm, and dragged himself to his feet, clinging desperately to the reeling cage-work of his refuge.

"While there's life there's hope," he chattered through his teeth. "Better this than being squashed by the steamer or churned to death by a tug's screw."

Tom now realised that he was doing little more than supporting himself, while the tide swirled him rapidly seawards. The brave lad struck out as strongly as he could, but it was a very weak best, and the boy could not but realise that he was about done.

He floated on his back for a luxurious two minutes, but had to get down to his stroke again to try to keep the blood circulating through his veins. He trudged for a few yards, just like a dog swims, then a swift cry, half of alarm and half of delight, escaped him!

He had seen somthing! A dim, ghostly light glimmering in the thickness ahead. But it disappeared suddenly.

Then he heard something! The clank of a ring-bolt and the rattle of chain on iron, followed by an ominous swirling and sugging of water.

The sounds were ones Tom could easily interpret. It was a buoy, swirling and swinging in the tide. It must be a gas-buoy, for he had seen the light. He hardly had time to think about it, when the black, conical shape leapt at him from the fog, and the rushing tide crashed the lad heavily against the swirling monster.

Weak hands clutched at the hanging chains and slipped off the weeds clinging to the buoy. The tide gripped the boy's legs and swept them round the side of the rounded buoy, but gamely he hung on, his fingers seemingly having no grip left in them.

He held, though! And he was able to raise his right hand and get hold of one of the uprights of the cage-work of the buoy. Then he began to claw upwards, to try to haul himself to comparative safety, clear of that gripping and tearing water.

How he managed it, Tom never knew; but at last he was lying round the upper part of the buoy, clinging to the conical cage-work with the light flashing its double flash out into the fog every five seconds.

The down-river wind seemed to be cutting through him like a knife, but Tom knew that the buoy was his only salvation, so he fought to retain his senses. It was a terrific effort of will, but Tom won! He clung there shivering and longing for the fog to lift and for rescue to come to him. He could keep covering and uncovering the light, if the fog cleared, so that someone would come out to investigate, find him, and take him ashore.

The boy went through the plan in detail, again and again, during those terrible hours on the heaving and clanking buoy. It would work without a hitch. Only let the fog lift.

Suddenly, Tom's deadened senses were on the alert. He heard the rattle of sheetblocks as a big sailing craft manoeuvred somewhere a little up-river. He knew the sound well—had heard it often through the steel side of the Ajax while lying wakeful in his hammock. A sailing craft gybing!

Young Gale dragged himself to a sitting position. He shouted, but the weakness of his own voice frightened him. He realised the present futility of shouting, so just waited, strung up to high tension by the suspense. Would the approaching craft come near enough to hear a cry, sent out at just the right second?

A steady surging in the water was the next sound that came to the boy's ears. The rumbling of agitated canvas had ceased; the sails were once more 'asleep'—filled out on the other gybe by the fresh wind. Tom could hear the drone of a voice—"Four fathom; three-an'-a-half"—as a man made soundings with the lead; could even now hear the creaking of the jaws of the gaffs and booms. Then, like a giant of blackness, above which was a pinnacle of leaning canvas dissolving to nothingness overhead in the fog, the coaster sprang forward from the mists, pointing dead for the buoy!

The lad shouted in a frenzy of alarm, and dragged himself to his feet, clinging desperately to the reeling cage-work of his refuge. A shout rang out from the foredeck of the coaster.

"Hellum har-rd up! Battery Ledge Buoy!"

There was a shouted order from aft, followed by the grinding of the wheel-chains as the rudder was forced promptly over, then the clumping of two pairs of seaboots on the wooden decks, the roar of disturbed canvas, jerking of sheets and rattling of masthoops, followed by a sickening crash as the vessel's booms smashed over on to the other gybe! Tom felt the wash from the seemingly over-powering mass of the boat surging about his knees, the buoy lurched heavily, nearly throwing the exhausted youngster off. But in a flash, being a sailor, he knew that danger of collision was past. The helmsman of the ketch—for coasting ketch it was—had gybed all standing to alter course and escape collision.

The coaster was smashing by! Tom had not been seen! The lad shouted as loudly as he could, but the men on the coaster had other work to do than stand and gape at the buoy. The youngster felt the chance of rescue again slipping from his grasp, for the ketch was now well clear—her jibboom already disappearing in the fog down the tide.

Tom's senses seemed to reel. This was almost beyond human endurance. But a heavy bump on the buoy brought him back to quick thought, and, no sooner seeing than understanding, the lad braced himself for a spring. The boat which was being towed by the coaster had swerved as the ketch suddenly altered direction, and had hit the buoy before being jerked clear by its mother craft.

Even as he tightened his muscles Tom felt that this was further torture—another chance of escape being snatched from him. The boat was now a couple of yards from the buoy, the painter snaking in the water, loose, to the counter of the ketch. In another second it would tauten, and the boat would be jerked round and away before Tom's feet could clatter on to its bottom-boards. Then he would fall into the water and lose boat, buoy, and all other slender chances of life! For Tom was about at the last of his strength.

Another hour would see him senseless, with nerveless fingers slipping from the buoy, to let his exhausted body slide down into the yellow depths of the river-mouth.

Even as he doubted his ability to spring to the boat he was in mid-air, hurtling towards his last chance of rescue. He saw the boat's painter tautening, and saw the boat itself jerk round while he was still in mid-air. Then, joy of joys, his bare feet thumped into the stern-sheets, and he crumpled up, completely at the end of his strength.

The lad did not immediately lose consciousness. He heard a shout—it seemed from afar, a disjointed, mumbling sort of string of words:

"Split me . . . in the boat. . . . Ay, ay, jumped over from the buoy. . . . Lyin' senseless now . . ."

"Haul in, then, ye fool . . . Get 'im aboard . . ."

A jerky sort of motion that seemed very pleasant followed. Then——

"Blink me eyes, if it ain't a trainin'-ship boy . . . From the Ajax, o' course . . ."

The voices trailed off into nothingness; but before the exhausted youngster had entirely lost his senses one burning realisation was throbbing in his brain.

He was saved!

The Fight in the Lane!

TWENTY minutes later, with his clothes steaming before the stove in the cabin of the coaster, and clad in a pair of tarry trousers and a shirt—the property of the mate, and consequently about six sizes too big for him—Tom learned that he was aboard the 250 tons coasting ketch Breadwinner, bound round the Ness for Great Yarmouth.

The skipper—a big, bearded man with a tanned, hard-bitten face—sat sucking at a clay pipe in the little cabin as he surveyed the youngster. Tom was still looking very exhausted, but he was built of tough stuff, and where many other boys would have been utterly played out, he was already feeling almost chirpy again.

"So y'mean t'say, lad, that yer've spent most o' the night on that there buoy?" said the skipper of the Breadwinner, in amazement. "Shiver me, if that don't beat all! But I reckon it's mighty lucky we blew along when we did. You couldn't ha' stuck it much longer, I'll warrant!"

Tom nodded.

"That's a fact! I was just about done!"

Briefly he told the wondering old coasting skipper how he had come to be on the buoy at all. The other whistled.

"Sounds more like a bloomin' cinema show, don't it?" he said at last. "You're mighty lucky not to be feedin' the fishes in Sea Reach by now!" He puffed thoughfully at his pipe. Up above Tom could hear the grate of the wheel-chains, the creaking of the mizzen-boom, and the occasional patter of reef-points on the sail, like a flurry of rain on a window-pane, every time the running ketch yawed so that the wind was partly spilled from her sails.

"We're bound for Great Yarmouth, as I say," went on the skipper. "Can't put you ashore afore we get there, y'know. But wi' this wind we'll be there in twenty-four hours, especially if this blamed fog lifts soon."

Out of the murk the fog-bell of the Chapman lighthouse, off Canvey Island, came to their ears. The skipper glanced at the clock on the fore bulkhead. Six o'clock.

"This fog should be liftin' mighty soon," he said.

He was right. With the coming of day the fog winnowed to little more than trailing mist-wraiths. The sun soon dried these up, and, climbing up on deck, Tom found the broad waters of the Thames estuary bathed in the glorious light. Off Leigh the bawley-boats were running seawards. Tom drew a deep breath. A true sailor at heart, the sight

There was a trampling of feet, and Tom felt the grip on his shoulder relax as the boys of the starboard watch came dashing upon the scene.

quickened his pulses, causing his eyes to shine.

All that day the Breadwinner ran before the wind. The sight and feel of the sea did more to pull Tom round after his terrible ordeal than all the tonics and rubbing of the skipper. By nightfall he was almost his old self again.

He turned in at last, in an unoccupied bunk in the cabin. He fell asleep to the sound of washing waves, creaking spars, and the occasional slap of a halliard against one of the masts. Throughout the night the Breadwinner ran on, lifting forward powerfully as the waves rolled under her quarters. When dawn broke the roar of the anchor-chain woke Tom. They were at Yarmouth.

"I wonder what they're thinking on the old Ajax?" the youngster mused, as he sat in the ketch's boat later that morning, as it was rowed shorewards. "And I wonder what damage the old ship suffered? I'll see by the papers."

The skipper of the Breadwinner shook hands warmly with the youngster as they said good-bye at the police-station to which he had accompanied Tom. The police, who seemed to imagine at first that it was a case of a runaway, telegraphed to the Ajax. Tom had learned with great relief that the ship was safe.

An hour later a reply to the wire came through, and Tom was put in charge of the guard of a train bound Londonwards. The train steamed slowly out of the station, gathered speed, and soon the beautiful Suffolk countryside was flying by rapidly.

It was, however, a tedious journey for Tom to Fleethithe; but at last, when

evening was closing in, the training-ship youngster alighted at his destination.

"Rum! Doesn't seem to be anyone to meet the prodigal son," he told himself, as he glanced round the familiar station. "I didn't expect a red carpet and a band, but I should have thought someone—even if it was only old Dicky—would have been sent along."

Outside the station he looked round again. Once more his hopes were dashed. So, with a shrug of the shoulders, Tom set off briskly to walk the two miles that separated him from the training-ship.

The sun was setting as he left the houses of Fleethithe, and when he turned down the long, tree-bordered lane known as Black Dell Lane, that led to the jetty opposite the Ajax, the lonely road ahead was gloomy with the swift-gathering darkness.

"This is a cheerful home-coming, I don't think!" said Tom to himself. "Still, I suppose I must reckon myself mighty lucky to be doing this home-coming stunt at all."

His feet crunched softly in the road, the only sound that broke the somewhat eerie silence of that gloomy spot. Black Dell Lane, dark and shadowy at the best of times, was not a cheery thoroughfare on a dark night. Tom, anxious for the warmth and light aboard the Ajax, quickened his steps.

"I wonder why on earth no one was at the station?" he repeated, puzzled. "I——"

He broke off abruptly. The next instant he had leaped backwards, a swift, startled cry breaking from him, for out

of the darkness to his right a shadowy form had come leaping. Tom had a swift glimpse of a long, sallow face, and then he was struggling desperately, senses whirling, with his unknown adversary.

A dozen conflicting thoughts raced through his brain. What could it mean?

Even as he asked himself the question his fist crashed home with staggering effect on the jaw of the man who had attacked him so suddenly, so mysteriously. Tom, taken off his guard though he had been, was fighting now with all the fierce determination of his dogged pluck. The man came at him again. Tom saw the bearded face contorted with fury in the dim light. Again the youngster sent the other reeling back with a straight left that would have felled a professional pugilist. And this time the strange figure of the darkness lay where he fell, apparently knocked clean out!

Tom was breathing hard, trying to collect his wits. Then he heard swift footsteps behind him, and was just in time to swing round and meet the attack of another dark figure that came leaping at him through the gloom.

The next instant Tom was fighting in desperate silence against two more assailants—men whose purpose in attacking him he had no further time to wonder over.

The youngster had retreated till his back was against the hedge, only his exceptional skill as a boxer enabling him to gain that strategic position. One swift glance up and down the dark lane had showed him that it was deserted, and he knew that in that lonely spot the chances were a hundred-to-one against anyone turning up to help him against the terrible odds.

Already the man lying in the road was staggering to his feet, cursing, to come forward menacingly towards the combatants. Three to one! In his heart Tom knew the game was up.

But he fought on, with teeth clenched. His blood was up, and he scarcely felt a stinging blow on the side of the head as a clenched fist crashed on his temple. He felt his own fist smash into the open, gaping mouth of the man—felt the skin of his knuckles break on the other's teeth. And then another blow struck Tom between the eyes. He crashed back into the hedge, blinded and dizzy, the next moment strong hands had grasped him, pinning him down, and a harsh voice grated in his ear:

"Lie still, you cub! Lie still, or——"

But that last blow had finished the youngster. He had not even the power to struggle as he was hauled roughly to his feet. Dimly he heard muttered voices, felt himself half-led, half-carried down the lane. A black shape loomed up before him. A motor-car was waiting there, and already one of the men had set the engine purring.

The door was opened swiftly. Strong arms thrust him forward.

It was the sight of that waiting car that roused Tom from the dizzy stupor into which that smashing blow had sent him. He had no time to wonder as to the reason. All he realised was that these mysterious assailants meant to abduct him. In a flash the dazed stupor fell from him.

With a sudden fierce twist he flung himself free. There was a shout of rage from the bearded figure who had started the car. He came in leaping pursuit, and in the light of the car's headlamps, which he had switched on, the man's eyes gleamed strange and green. Green spectacles. Tom sprang aside, struck out at a second assailant, and then his heart gave a bound of joy.

Down the lane, from the direction of the river, he heard the crunch of feet, the rattle of wheels. But above those sounds came to his ears the words of a song that he had heard only in one place —aboard the Ajax:

"There's good chaps in the port watch—
    As good as on the sea!
But my number's two-'itty-fi',
    So starboard's the watch for me!"

A fatigue party of the starboard watch from the training-ship—it could mean nothing else! And two-fifty-five—Dicky West's number!

Tom turned to race towards the oncoming youngsters. But a foot was thrust out before he could get clear away, and he went sprawling. The next instant he was lying in the road, pinned down by the man on top. A hand came groping for his mouth, but not before he had yelled with all the power of his lungs:

"Help! Quick—Ajax! Ajax!"

Then the hand closed over his mouth, choking back the words. But as it did so he heard an answering shout come out of the darkness—a shout of amazement. Then he heard the racing of footsteps down the lane. Boys of the starboard watch were racing to the rescue!

Perplexity!

"FORRARD the starboard watch!"

It was the voice of Dicky West that Tom heard echoing down the lane as the training-ship youngsters came racing through the darkness to where the young leader of the Hoods lay pinned beneath the man with green spectacles.

He heard the muttered oath that broke from his captor, felt the grip on his shoulder relax in sudden startled doubt. Then the boys of the starboard watch were in among them, fists flashing!

The man with the green spectacles— Kalche—sprang to his feet and struck out at the surging crowd of youngsters round him. Tom dragged himself to his feet, saw the whirling shapes of the combatants as they fought in the light from the car's lamps. Then Dicky West was at his side.

"By gum, Tom!"

Tom laughed shakily.

"Guessed right first time, Dicky!" he said. "They attacked me. I don't know what it means—who they are——"

A reeling form staggered back towards them—one of Kalche's men, driven back by the fist of one of the youngsters of the Ajax. He regained his balance immediately and turned to race off into the darkness. But Tom sprang forward, and his leg shot out. The man crashed heavily, and then Tom and Dick were the centre of a struggling group, as half a dozen youngsters fought to drag down the third man.

"Into the car, fools! Into the car!"

It was the voice of the man in green spectacles, almost incoherent with fury and chagrin. His two companions heard it, and sprang for the waiting motor.

"Don't let 'em get away! Catch hold of the rotters!"

Dicky West was yelling gleefully. Dick always enjoyed a scrap. But although there were a dozen youngsters against the three men, those three were desperate. Boys fell back like ninepins before the heavy blows, and the next instant Kalche was at the driver's seat.

The car's engine was still running, and as Kalche opened the throttle he jerked in the clutch. The motor-car leapt

forward like a live thing, and the next moment, with a powerful roar from its exhaust, it had flashed past where Tom and Dicky West were standing. They leapt back just in time, and stood panting in the dark road as they watched the ruby rear-light disappearing down the lane.

"They've got away, blow 'em!" gasped Dicky. "Of all the rotten luck!"

Tom did not answer. His brow was wrinkled. What could it all mean? Who could these men be? And what possible object could there have been for their mysterious attack?

The other youngsters clustered round Tom, asking a dozen questions at once. Tom told his brief story.

"Hanged if I know much more than you chaps do!" he concluded. "It's an absolute mystery! And now they've got away, it doesn't look as if we shall ever find a solution to it!"

Dicky West grunted.

"I should say it is a thundering mystery! It's rum enough to beat the band, this is! What do chaps like that, with a car and all, want with you, Tom?" He broke off with a puzzled frown, to add: "But what are you doing here? We were just off to the station to get some stuff that's turning up there by the seven-thirty train. We were told you'd be blowing along in that train, too. We were to meet you."

Tom felt his jaw tenderly where it had come into hearty contact with a man's fist.

"Some mistake over the train, then— that's all," he said. "I turned up by the train before that. Seems to have been unlucky I did, too! What are you chaps fetching from the station?"

"Oh, some junk or other for patching up the hole that steamship kindly made for us in the orlop deck," answered Dicky. "Three hundredweight of special-sized bolts, or something. There's only a temporary patch there now. Lucky the old Ajax wasn't sunk, too, I can tell you! But the ship that rammed us had the sense to keep her nose in till the engineers on the Ajax were ready with a standard patch. That's a wooden one, you know. But what about you?" he added quickly. And there was something in Dicky's voice that told Tom more than mere words could do. "We all thought you were done for, till we heard from the police at Yarmouth."

"No, I'm far from done for," said Tom shortly. He did not intend to mention Burr's part in the affair till he and Dicky were alone together. "Well, I suppose I'd better blow along with you to the station. And I'll just drop in at the police-station to let 'em know what's happened in the lane. We failed to catch the swabs, but the police may have a bit more luck. They'd got their number-plate covered, I noticed; but we can give a description of the car, at any rate."

The youngsters returned down the lane to where the two handcarts had been left. On the way to the railway-station Tom told his story to the police, and the inspector set off immediately to the Ajax for an interview with Commander Boyce.

Tom had a rousing reception on the orlop deck when he had reported himself and had finished with his interviews with various officers. There was only one youngster who was not pleased to see him, and that boy was Burr.

The bully of the Ajax had learnt of Tom's arrival before he saw him, so that Tom had missed the queer look that had leapt into Burr's eyes at the news that

(Continued on opposite page.)

Printed and published every Wednesday by the Proprietors, The Amalgamated Press (1922), Ltd., The Fleetway House, Farringdon Street, London, E.C.4. Advertisement offices: The Fleetway House, Farringdon Street, London, E.C.4. Registered for transmission by Canadian Magazine Post. Subscription rates: Inland and Abroad, 11s. per annum; 5s. 6d. for six months. Sole agents for South Africa: The Central News Agency, Ltd. Sole agents for Australia and New Zealand: Messrs. Gordon & Gotch, Ltd.; and for Canada, The Imperial News Co., Ltd. (Canada).—Saturday, January 5th, 1924.

Tom Gale was back aboard the ship. But Tom's own eyes were grim as he found an opportunity of taking Burr aside that evening in a deserted corner of the mess-deck.

"What was the idea, Stoniky," asked Tom bluntly, "shoving me through the hole that night?"

Burr had dropped his eyes. He was scowling, but there was also a look of fear on his face.

"What d'you mean?" he stammered. "I—I dunno what you mean."

Tom chuckled grimly.

"You don't—eh? Well, let me tell you, my bonnie lad, that I jolly well know who it was who shoved me through the hole when the ship was rammed! It was you! And I mean to know the reason why! See?"

"Don't talk like a fool, Gale!" snarled Burr. "I didn't know. It was as dark as pitch, and I got the wind-up and made a bolt for the ladder-way. I know I banged into someone—knocked someone flying. But you must be mad to accuse me of—of——"

He broke off, stammering

Tom shrugged his shoulders.

"Oh, cut out that yarn, Stoniky! Think I don't know jolly well? You tried to do for me on the yardarm that same day, only it didn't come off! For some reason of your own you're out to make things hot for me, Stoniky! Goodness knows why. But I can look after myself. But let me tell you this. I can fight my own battles; but if I see you trying the same game as you're playing with me on anyone on this ship who's not able to stand up to you I sha'n't take it in my own hands to interfere."

"What, you'd go and peach, you sneak?" sneered Burr.

Tom did not answer, but swung on his heel and strode off towards the ladder-way leading down into the orlop deck.

Burr stood looking after the young leader of the Hoods with darkened eyes.

And then on the lower deck, as he made his way towards the Hood division's section, Tom Gale came to a sudden standstill. His lips opened in a low exclamation; a swift thought had flashed into his mind

"By gum!" he muttered, his face startled. "I wonder? No, hang it, it's not possible!"

But as he turned in that night the thought returned to him, in spite of his words. Could it be that there was some strange connection between Burr's sudden hatred and equally sudden wealth, and with that other attempt on Tom by the man of the green spectacles in Black Dell Lane?

He shook himself impatiently.

"Rot!"

But there was a thoughtful frown on Tom's face as he turned over to go to sleep.

Sleep did not come at once. Before Tom's eyes there was a hideous gleam from countless green eyes. The young C.P.O. turned over, with a grunt, and half buried his head under his blanket in an effort to get rid of the mocking eyes. But still he saw them.

He made up his mind that he had not seen the last of the man with the green spectacles, and that it behoved him to keep his own eyes wide open for further trouble.

He was to be glad that he made that resolution!

(There will be another thrilling instalment of this grand new serial next Wednesday. In the meantime, all my readers who like stories of the sea should start reading " Topsail Tony ! " by the famous David Goodwin, in our companion paper, the " Boys' Friend," now on sale.)

My Readers' Own Corner.

Send Your Latest Ribtickler to Me !

TUCK HAMPERS AND MONEY PRIZES AWARDED FOR WIT !
(If You Are Not a Prizewinner This Week You May Be Next.)

All Attempts in this Competition should be Addressed to : The GEM, " My Readers' Own Corner." Gough House, Gough Square, London, E.C.4.

THIS WINS OUR TUCK HAMPER.

BOTH WRONG !

Two dear old ladies were listening to the band, and arguing whether the piece being played was the Barcarolle from the "Tales of Hoffman" or the "Soldiers' Chorus from "Faust." At last one said that she would go round to the side of the band-stand and see if it was written up. When she returned she said, "Matilda, we were both wrong. It is not the Barcarolle from the ' Tales of Hoffman,' neither is it the Soldiers' Chorus from ' Faust.' It is the Refrain from ' Spitting '!"—A Tuck Hamper has been awarded to Sidney Lemel, 9, Ebbsfleet Road, Cricklewood, London, N.W.2.

IT WORKED !

"Good morning, madam," said the canvasser. "Here is a polish for cleaning silver—best on the market." "Don't want any !" snapped Mrs. Jones. "Sorry to have troubled you, madam, but I thought the lady next door was mistaken !" "What did she say ?" "She said I need not waste my time calling here, as you had no silver to clean." "The impudent thing ! Give me half a dozen boxes !"—Half-a-crown has been awarded to William Mitchell, 5, North Shore Street, Campbeltown, N.B.

NO SALE !

A man was looking at some new trunks displayed outside a shop. The dealer, with an eye to business, politely asked him if he'd like to buy one. To his astonishment, the man said: "What's the use of a trunk to me ?" Whereupon the dealer replied: "Why, to put your clothes in, of course !" The Man (indignantly): "What! And go naked? Not me !"—Half-a-crown has been awarded to H. Preston, 31, Archway Road, Highgate, London, N.19.

A SLIGHT MISTAKE!

A gentleman went into a barber's shop in London for a hair-cut one very foggy day. When he was seated the barber tucked the cloth round his neck and remarked : "Very thick, sir !" "Yes," said the gentleman, "but I'd like it cut short." "Oh," exclaimed the barber, "it's not the 'air of the 'ead I mean, but the hair of the hatmosphere !"—Half-a-crown has been awarded to Miss Margaret Leslie, 41, Loons Road, Dundee.

IT JUST DEPENDED !

Mrs. Terrace was engaging a new cook. After interviewing a large number of equally large ladies, she at last picked on one Irish woman who seemed to be as nearly perfect as any cook can be nowadays. "I thing we can arrange the matter of wages," remarked Mrs. Terrace. "What is your name ?" "Mrs. O'Shannessey, ma'am," was the answer, accompanied by a beaming smile. "Do you expect to be called Mrs. O'Shannessey ?" asked Mrs. Terrace. "Oh, no, ma'am," responded the applicant, "not if you have an alarm clock !"—Half-a-crown has been awarded to Malcolm G. Chattin, 1, Selborne Street, Walsall, Staffs.

HIS SUPERIOR KNOWLEDGE.

Two Highlanders, in London for the first time, were greatly amazed at the heavy street traffic. While they were standing awestruck on the pavement, a water-cart passed, spraying the dusty streets. "Hey, mon !" yelled Donald, running after the cart. "Ye're losin' a' yer water !" "Come back, ye old fule," called his companion after him. "Dae ye no' ken that's tae keep the bairns frae sittin' on the back o' the cart ?"—Half-a-crown has been awarded to Donald Macfarlane, 48, Second Avenue, Clydebank, Scotland.

CORN-ERED !

An old gentleman walked up the steps of the Corn Exchange. "Is this the Corn Exchange ?" he asked. "Yes, sir," replied the commissionaire. "Then can you do anything with this corn on my foot ?" asked the old man. "I want to get rid of it !"—Half-a-crown has been awarded to Ian Wright, 11, Inchaffray Street, Perth, N.B.

THAT'S ALL !

"Now, children," said the school teacher, "can any of you tell me of a greater power than the King ?" "Yes, ma'am !" cried a little boy eagerly. "Very well, you may tell the class," said the teacher. "An ace of trumps !" came the lad's unexpected reply.—Half-a-crown has been awarded to Jas. McCollam, Coast Guard Cottages, Magheramorne, Co. Antrim, Ireland.

TUCK HAMPER COUPON.

THE GEM LIBRARY.

No attempt will be considered unless accompanied by one of these Coupons.

Your Editor Chats With His Readers.

Address all letters: The Editor, The "Gem" Library, The Fleetway House, Farringdon Street, London, E.C.4. Write me, you can be sure of an answer in return.

My Dear Chums,—This week two special duties must come first. As a start, I want to wish you one and all the happiest possible New Year, with plenty of prosperity and good days in which to enjoy it. In the second place I must refer to the wonderful kick-off programme of the "Gem."

ON TOP!

Of course, the old and well-recognised position of the "Gem" is the outstanding fact. The success of the stories of St. Jim's is unqualified. No drum, big or otherwise, is required to emphasise the fame and appeal of the series.

WITH A BANG!

Next week's yarn is tremendous. It brings a much vexed question to a head. Mr. Martin Clifford marshals his facts like a first-class military commander. I want to impress upon you that the tale of Tom Merry and Cardew next Wednesday is one to put the old paper several pegs higher.

"JUST LIKE CARDEW!"
By Martin Clifford

This dramatic wind-up to a wonderful series showing the bitter feud between Tom Merry and Cardew is simply astounding. Truth may be stranger than fiction, but fiction which owes its popularity to a deep knowledge of human nature on the part of the writer is, often enough, the strangest of either. Next week's story is out and out convincing. You know something of the odd, fantastic temperament of Cardew. He likes to win, but once he has won he is disgusted with the result of victory. I'll be bound you have run up against just such a walking contradiction in your tramp through the world.

MARTIN CLIFFORD'S STAR TURN!

There need be no hesitation in so styling this splendid yarn. We see Cardew the possessor of the spoils of conquest, as it were. And he feels fed up with himself, with St. Jim's, and with the world in general. It is natural enough, of course. Cardew's eccentricities are not really so uncommon, only in his case these conflicting idiosyncrasies are more pronounced. Only one more word concerning this glorious story, which will be in your hands next week, and I have done. There is poetic justice in it. We get an election. There is, of course, enormous excitement over this contest. And what happens? Who said stalemate? Well, just wait and see!

A SLIGHT DIFFICULTY!

Over and over again I feel nonplussed. Suggestions come in asking me to bring into the limelight again certain characters who have scored in former tales. All this is generous and complimentary to authors, but it puts the editor in a dilemma. You know the "Gem" is prepared considerably in advance of publication. That being so, it is next door to impossible to run in some special story to please a reader. A series of yarns has to come to an end. You would hardly believe, too, the eagerness for novelty among large numbers of my supporters. I am just saying this to show that it is not easy to carry on for ever and a day with, say, Anthony Sharpe, or some other favourite. It has to be turn and turn about. The same remark applies to some of the St. Jim's characters. Not that I like to cause any disappointment.

"'HAT-TRICK' GUY!"

You will be interested in the doings of this formidable goal-scoring centre-forward, who makes his bow on Wednesday next. "Hat Trick" Guy has the happy knack of scoring three or more goals in every match in which he plays, and the developments, as may be expected, are sensational and thoroughly novel. It is really a top-hole story of a most vivid and original sort. Look out for it. The author has all the mysteries of footer in the palm of his good right hand.

"TOM OF THE AJAX!"

Our serial is going ahead like a house afire. Tom Gale is up against an inveterate enemy in the person of the wearer of the green spectacles, but though driven to the wall, Tom finds there is still plenty to fight for, while he is not without friends. In next week's instalment the bully, Stoniky Burr, plays a considerable part, and is responsible for heaps more trouble.

THE "HOLIDAY ANNUAL!"

There are still a few copies left over of the prize book of the season. If you have not secured one, now's the time.

Your Editor.

GREAT SCHOOL, FOOTBALL, AND TRAINING-SHIP STORIES INSIDE !

EVERY WEDNESDAY.

The GEM 2ᴰ

No. 831.
Vol. XXV.
January 12th,
1924.

LIBRARY
OF
SCHOOL AND SPORTING STORIES

FORCING A FIGHT!

"You're a liar, Tom Merry!" said Cardew deliberately.　"Don't I speak plainly enough?"　(A tense scene from "JUST LIKE CARDEW,"—this week's great school story.)

Your Editor Chats With His Readers.

Address all letters: The Editor, The "Gem" Library, The Fleetway House, Farringdon Street, London, E.C.4. Write me, you can be sure of an answer in return.

OUR COMPANION PAPERS.

"THE BOYS' FRIEND" Every
                              Monday
"THE MAGNET"   Every Monday
"THE POPULAR"   Every Tuesday
"JUNGLE JINKS"   Every Thursday
"THE HOLIDAY ANNUAL"
                  Published Yearly.

My Dear Chums,—Next week's issue of the GEM is likely to be memorable. There is nothing new about that, since in a sense every number of the famous paper can lay claim to this distinction. But next Wednesday I have another of the extra long St. Jim's yarns which you all like. This tale is a real mystery one, and it brings that first favourite, Eric Kildare, well into the glare of the limelight.

"ERIC KILDARE'S SECRET!"
By Martin Clifford.

This grand extra long story of St. Jim's is our big star turn for next week. It shows Kildare faced with a dilemma of the trickiest sort—just the sort of thing which would have puzzled the cleverest detective. Immediately after bidding farewell to his cousin, who has come to St. Jim's to take leave of the skipper, Kildare comes into contact with a down-at-heels party of the most unattractive kind.

A SPORTSMAN'S ACTION!

Just what the unprepossessing personage confides to Kildare you will learn when the next issue of the GEM is in your hands. It is a tale which starts you wondering, and then keeps you on the tenterhooks of anxiety right away to the end. Kildare is not so much nonplussed as pained. He is a fellow who always sees where duty lies. There never was any shilly-shally nonsense about the school captain. He plays up to a very strange responsibility, which comes suddenly upon him—right out of the blue, as it were—and the resulting complications and tragic difficulties will be followed with breathless interest. A magnificent yarn, this, worthy of a series which has won world-wide fame.

OLD-TIME LURE!

A friendly letter reaches me from Toronto which in its main purport has, to my mind, a very curious bearing on next week's tale of St. Jim's. My Canadian correspondent speaks very frankly about the unfailing charm of the stories of St. Jim's, but, for all that, he is what I should term a harker back. He keeps on looking over his shoulder at the past. Some of the former tales struck him so keenly, and have left so vivid a remembrance that he is disposed to be hypercritical of what is happening now. He pleads for more and more of the real atmosphere of St. Jim's. I am sure he will see these few lines. Let me advise him to read the coming yarn very carefully. It is just precisely what he asks for, or I am much mistaken.

"THE WRONG FILM!"
By Sidney Drew.

This is a real scream, written in Sidney Drew's most amusing vein. You will roar with laughter at the manner in which Ching Lung and Gan Waga merrily turn the tables on Prout, Maddock, and O'Rooney. See it next week, and grow fat, for laughter has that effect.

THE TUCK HAMPER.

Somebody told me the other day that there were no new jokes. I hesitate to believe it, though one may have to range the world to discover the scintillating novelty in the shape of a quip. But sometimes the old joke with a new beard and side-whiskers is welcome. They get a cordial reception from me. Send them in—the brightest you can find. I read them all. Often enough some quaint wheeze, venerable enough, starts one on a new tack—I mean, some jokelet of the sort which caused Methuselah to tumble out of his rocking-chair, overcome with mirth. Anyway, the Tuck Hamper rolls merrily on its way. It is a distinguished feature of the GEM.

"TOM OF THE AJAX!"
By Roland Spencer.

Get your chums to read this fine serial. Be assured that next week's instalment is a bit thrillier than ever. Tom Gale is still pursued by an enemy whom he cannot throw off. This foe in the green spectacles can be followed in his turn with interest, for round his sinister personality hangs a mystery of the most amazing kind. The yarn grips all along because of the knowledge of the presence of what may be termed the hidden hand. Something rather uncanny is at work behind, and the unseen danger becomes more oppressive and realistic as the tale proceeds.

A GROWL!

Just a word must be dropped in here regarding a growl that reaches me from Australia. A staunch supporter of the Companion Papers says that there is not enough of my Chat. "Give us a whole page, as you used to do of old," says the writer. I am much obliged to him for the hint. But, as to a whole page, that wants finding. Who wishes to turn the printer's hair white before its time? Week in, week out, I am faced with the same genial old difficulty—namely, how to pack in all the good features which are prepared for the GEM. Then there may be readers who say, "Who wants Chat?" I am not saying there are. All experience goes to show that a little corner of Chat is welcome. Anyway, I shall not lose sight of the suggestion.

"FOOTBALLERS' NAMES" COMPETITION.

NOTE.—All those of our readers who took part in this great picture-puzzle competition will be glad to know that the time for sending entries was extended by three days after the closing date previously announced. Towards the last, so huge was the demand for the GEM that many readers were late in obtaining their copy, and to give all our friends an equal chance of entering the competition we accepted efforts up to the first post on Friday, December 21st. We are now grappling with the adjudication, and are making every effort to give you the result at an early date. Watch out for it!

TO ALL WHOM IT MAY CONCERN!

This concerns a vast number, as a matter of fact. It is a hint to all my numberless readers to drop me a line whenever they feel inclined to give me a leg up with a smart suggestion, or when they think my advice might be useful. I am always pleased to hear.

Your Editor.

Now that he has wrested the junior captaincy from his rival, Cardew becomes slacker than ever! The juniors consider that he has overstepped the mark, and take matters into their own hands again.

JUST LIKE CARDEW!

A Most Remarkable New Extra-Long Complete Story of the World-Renowned Tom Merry & Co. at St. Jim's. By Famous

MARTIN CLIFFORD.

CHAPTER 1.
Fed-Up with Cardew.

"LEAVE the talkin' to me, deah boys."

"Br-r-r-r-r!"

"I do not wegard that as an intelligible wemark, Blake. You fellows had bettah leave the talkin' to me——"

"You've done enough talking for a dozen already," remarked Herries. "Take a rest."

"Weally, Hewwies——"

Bang!

Jack Blake knocked at the door of Study No. 10 in the Shell, in the School House at St. Jim's.

It was a forcible knock, and it sent Tom Merry's door whirling open.

"Hallo!" ejaculated Tom.

Tom Merry was kneeling before the study fire, making toast. Manners and Lowther were busy with the tea-table. Tom was giving his whole attention to the toast; but there was an air of expectation about his study-mates, and they had looked at one another, and at the door several times, before Blake of the Fourth hurled it open.

Tom Merry looked into the passage in surprise. It was crowded with juniors.

Blake and Herries, Digby and D'Arcy, were in the van. Behind them came Talbot of the Shell, and Kangaroo, and Dick Julian, and Wildrake, and a dozen more fellows.

Manners and Lowther did not seem surprised. In fact, they seemed to have been expecting this numerous visit.

"Oh, here you are!" said Monty Lowther.

"Yaas, wathah, heah we are," said Arthur Augustus D'Arcy. "I was just mentionin' that the fellows had bettah leave the talkin' to me. I am goin' to put it vewy plain to Tom Mewwy."

"Ring off, Gussy!"

"Weally, Blake——"

"We've come——" began Digby.

"It's a deputation," explained Blake. "A deputation to interview you, Tom Merry, in the name of the House."

"Yaas, wathah!"

"Oh!" said Tom. "You haven't come to tea? I was just thinking that the toast wouldn't go round."

"Weally, Tom Mewwy——"

Tom Merry rose from the fireplace with a ruddy countenance. He looked rather regretfully at the tea-table. Having lately come in from a tramp in the snow, Tom was ready for tea—more than ready. But a House deputation was a House deputation, and Tom Merry politely gave the deputation his best attention.

"You see——" said Herries.

"Yaas, wathah, you perceive, deah boy——"

"This is how it is——" began Julian.

"We——" commenced Kerruish.

Tom Merry raised his hand.

"One at a time!" he suggested. "It's easier to follow a solo than a chorus. What's the game?"

"Bai Jove!"

The deputation crowded into the study. Manners and Lowther took their places along with the deputation; evidently they were "in it," whatever the game was. There was not room for the whole deputation in Study No. 10, so fellows who could not squeeze in formed an overflow meeting in the passage outside.

"Pway leave the talkin' to me, you fellows," repeated Arthur Augustus D'Arcy. "As a fellow of tact and judgment I——"

"Dry up, Gussy!"

"I wefuse, in the circs, to dwy up, Blake. I am goin' to point out to Tom Mewwy——"

"Order!"

"The fact is——" said Blake.

"Leave it to me," said Manners. "You see, Tom——"

"It's like this," explained Monty Lowther. "The long and the short of it is, Tom, that the House is fed-up with Cardew, and wants you back as junior captain."

"Hear, hear!" said the whole deputation.

"That's it!" said Blake.

"Just that!"

"Yaas, wathah!"

"Oh!" said Tom Merry, frowning a little.

"In the circs, deah boy——"

"As matters stand——"

"With the school going to the dogs——"

"The football mucked up——"

"Order!" bawled Blake. "For goodness' sake let a fellow speak!"

"Weally, Blake——"

"Better choose a spokesman," said Tom Merry, laughing. "At this rate you won't be finished by bed-time. And there's prep, not to mention tea."

Blake glared round at the deputation. Blake had constituted himself spokesman. Unfortunately, D'Arcy had done the same, and so had Julian and Kerruish. And all the other fellows appeared to think that the matter could not be properly elucidated without parenthetical remarks from themselves.

"Let a chap speak!" said Blake.

"Yes. I'm the chap!" remarked Lowther. "Now——"

"Weally, Lowthah——"

"I'm the chairman of this deputation!" roared Blake. "Shut up, the lot of you. Now, here's the case in a nutshell, Tom Merry. Last term you were junior House captain, and junior captain of the school. Cardew managed to boost you out of the job."

"Yaas, wathah! I considah——"

"Cardew was elected junior captain," said Tom Merry mildly. "I'm sorry if the fellows ~~e not satisfied with their choice. But there it is. Cardew of the Fourth is junior captain."

"We're fed-up with Cardew."

"Yaas, wathah!"

"What sort of a captain is he?" demanded Blake. "He goes wandering out of gates when there's a House match on. He forgets the dates of School matches. He shirks games practice. He's just a slacker."

"A fwightful slackah!"

"He was elected," continued Blake. "It was a pity, but there it was. Lots of us only voted for him to keep out the New House candidate. But I'm blessed if I don't almost think a New House man would have made a better captain. Figgins, for instance——"

"Yaas, wathah!"

"Of course, the junior captain ought really to be selected from the Fourth Form, and from Study No. 6," said Blake. "In our study we're agreed on that."

"But other studies seem to differ," grinned Kangaroo.

"But for the good of the school, and to save St. Jim's from going to the dogs," continued Blake, rather grandly, "we're putting aside all personal claims, and we're going to back you up, Tom Merry."

"Yaas, like anythin', old scout."

"That's what this deputation has come for," said Blake. "We want you to put up again for the captaincy, Tom Merry, and we promise you our hearty support."

"Hear, hear!"

"We want you to appeal to Kildare of the Sixth, as head of the games, to order a new election," went on Blake. "That's easy enough. And, if you put up as a candidate, you'll sweep the board."

"And then things will be as they used to be," said Julian. "We've had enough of Cardew."

"More than enough."

"Too much—tons too much!" said Kerruish. "I dare say he's all right in his way, but he's no good as captain."

"Rotten!" said Wilkins of the Shell. "Why, he leaves you out of the matches, Tom Merry!"

"I don't believe he ever wanted to be captain, seriously," said Monty Lowther. "It was one of his stunts. Anyhow, he doesn't want to do a captain's duties."

"He wanted to show what he could do if he liked," remarked Manners. "I really fancy that Cardew is as much fed-up with the captaincy as we are with him."

"Anyhow, we're fed-up with him, right up to the chin," said Blake. "We want you back, Tommy."

"Hear, hear!"

"Now, are you putting up?"

The deputation looked at Tom Merry, and waited for his answer. There was a silence.

Tom Merry's face was very thoughtful.

"I twust, Tom Mewwy," said Arthur Augustus, breaking the silence, "that you are not goin' to wefuse to wally wound at the wequest of your loyal followahs?"

"Play up, Tom!" said Talbot of the Shell, in his quiet way. "You know that we've got a rotten skipper,' and we want you back. If you'd put up a fight for it, Cardew would never have got in."

"Well, he was elected," said Tom slowly.

"There was a feahful lot of twickewy in the election, deah boy."

"I dare say there was; but fellows were not bound to vote for him if they didn't choose. They wanted a change, and they got a change," said Tom. "I know jolly well, of course, that Cardew isn't any good as skipper, especially in football. I think the House and the school want a new captain. But I——"

"Cut out the buts," said Herries.

"But," repeated Tom firmly, "I don't feel disposed to go in against him. If the House and the school wanted me—well, they had me, and they changed me for Cardew. I don't think I ought to try to turn him out——"

"As he did you!" grunted Herries.

"I'm not taking Cardew as an example to follow," said Tom, rather dryly.

"Yaas, but——"

"You say yourself that we want a new captain!" growled Blake.

"I agree to that. I suggest Talbot——"

"Rot!" said Manners and Lowther together, and Talbot of the Shell smiled.

"Well, that's not a bad suggestion," admitted Blake. "If you won't stand, Tom, we'll back up Talbot against Cardew."

"Hear, hear!" said the deputation.

"And I'll back him up!" said Tom heartily. "Let it go at that!"

"Very well. Talbot's the man!"

"Bravo, Talbot!"

"Hold on!" broke in Talbot of the Shell quietly. "I'm not the man! I'm not standing! Tom Merry's the man we want; and, in any case, I shall not put up as a candidate."

"Now, look here——" said Tom persuasively.

"Bosh!" said Talbot. "You're the man, Tom, and sooner or later you'll have to come round. Make it sooner."

"Make it now!" urged Julian.

"Yaas, wathah!"

Tom Merry shook his head.

"If there's a new election, I'll agree to put up as a candidate," he said. "That's all I can say. I can't take any steps to turn Cardew out. It would be a bit too much like the way he treated me. Which, as I've said, is an example I don't care to follow. You'd better tell Cardew you're fed-up with him, and leave it at that."

"That would only make him hang on!" growled Blake. "You know what an obstinate mule he is."

"Yaas, wathah!"

"Look here, Tom Merry! We jolly well want you, and if you don't take the lead, you'll take a ragging!" roared Herries.

"Ha, ha, ha!"

"Bump him!"

"'Yes,' or 'No'?" demanded Blake.

"No!" said Tom.

"Bump him!"

"Here, hands off, you silly asses!" roared Tom Merry, as the deputation made a rush at him. "Hold on, you chumps! Oh, my hat!"

"Ha, ha, ha!"

Bump!

Tom Merry smote his own study carpet forcibly with his person. It was a heavy smite, and he roared.

"There!" gasped Blake. "That's a warning. Now you'd better think it over, Tommy, or there's more in store!"

"Yaas, wathah!"

"Ha, ha, ha!"

The deputation crowded out of the study, leaving Tom Merry sitting on the carpet, gasping for breath. Manners and Lowther remained in Study No. 10, grinning.

"You silly asses!" gasped Tom. "Why didn't you back me up? Ow!"

"Serves you jolly well right!" said Manners.

"Jolly good mind to bump you again!" said Monty Lowther.

"Ow!"

Tom Merry picked himself up, and set his collar and tie straight. There was no doubt that the deputation of the Lower School had been in earnest; they wanted Tom Merry, and they had shown it forcibly. But Tom's determination was unchanged. Ralph Reckness Cardew, duly elected junior captain of St. Jim's, had no attack on his position to fear from the rival he had supplanted.

CHAPTER 2.
A Ragging in Study No. 9 !

"NOW for Cardew !"

"Yaas, wathah !"

The junior deputation, having finished with Tom Merry—for the present—proceeded along to the Fourth Form passage. They stopped at No. 9, the study that belonged to Cardew, Levison, and Clive. Blake thumped at the door and hurled it open.

Levison & Co. were at tea. Levison and Clive looked rather surprised when the crowd appeared in their doorway. Cardew smiled—perhaps guessing why they had come. Cardew could not have failed to be aware that his system was not popular with the School House fellows—or the New House, for that matter. Indeed, on a good many occasions the new junior captain seemed to have deliberately set out to make his followers fed-up with him.

The actual fact was that Cardew, having attained the goal of his idle ambition, had tired of it, as he tired of most things. He had set out to give Tom Merry a "fall," and in that he had succeeded completely. He had started the contest idly, in his whimsical humour, and it pleased him to show what he could do if he liked. But the duties and responsibilities of the post he had gained did not please him in the very least, and he coolly let them slide.

Bitterness had crept into the contest, on Cardew's side, at least; but for that, it was probable that Cardew would have thrown the thing up before now. He had been Tom Merry's rival, and he had become Tom Merry's enemy—or the rival his enmity had been black and bitter. But that, too, had changed, partly owing to circumstances, and partly to Cardew's own volatile and changeable nature.

That his followers were fed-up with his ways was no secret to him; and, if he had not known it, the looks of the deputation would have enlightened him. But he greeted Blake and his army with a polite nod and smile.

"Trickle in, old beans," he said. "So glad to see you! You ought to have told me you'd asked these fellows to tea,

THE DEPUTATION ! Tom Merry rose from the fireplace as the swarm of juniors entered the study. " You haven't come to tea ? " he asked. " The fact is," said Blake, " we are fed-up with Cardew as captain. We want you to put up again, Tom Merry, and we promise you our hearty support ! " (See page 4.)

Levison. I'd have given a more extensive order at the tuck-shop."

"But I didn't !" said Levison.

"Then you, Clive——"

"I didn't, either," said Sidney Clive, laughing.

"Dear me !" said Cardew. "Then they must have come unasked. I take this as a great compliment, my young friends—one more proof of the irresistible attractions of my society."

"We haven't come to tea !" bawled Herries.

"Wathah not !"

"Never mind. Stay to tea now you're here," said Cardew gracefully. "Sit down—there's some chairs—and a box or two—and the floor is clean and commodious."

"Weally, Cardew——"

"We've come on business!" exclaimed Blake, planting himself in front of the dandy of the Fourth, with a grim brow.

"What a horrid word," said Cardew. "I never could give my attention to business matters. Call another time, if you don't mind."

"We do mind !" hooted Herries.

"It's about the football, and the captaincy !" said Blake.

"Dear me !"

"The Abbotsford match comes off on Saturday."

"Does it ?"

"Have you forgotten the Abbotsford match ?" howled Dig.

"Abbotsford !" said Cardew, in a reflective sort of way. "Bless my soul ! Now I come to think of it, there is a cricket match with Abbotsford."

"Cricket !" shrieked Blake.

"Yes—no—football, of course," said Cardew, with a cheery smile. "Right you are—football !"

The deputation glared at Cardew.

"Have you thought about the team yet ?" asked Blake, breathing hard.

"Is there any hurry ?"

"Have you thought about the matter at all ?"

"Oh, yes ! I was thinkin' only yesterday what a bore it is."

"Bai Jove !"

"It is, isn't it ?" asked Cardew. "But the fact is, I've been havin' a little argument in committee. I'm goin' to think the matter out very seriously, of course."

"When ?"

"Dear man, you mustn't fire questions at your skipper in this way. I may find a few minutes some time."

"I suppose that's meant to be funny ?" asked Blake, after a pause.

"Not at all. I fully intend to find a few minutes, to think about the Abbotsford match," said Cardew blandly.

"Do you think that's good enough for us ?"

"I think it will have to be."

"You weren't at games practice this afternoon," continued Blake.

"Games practice is a bore, like most other things."

"Do you intend to play in the Abbotsford match, or are you standing out, as you've done before ?"

"Who knows ?" said Cardew.

"Don't you know ?" roared Blake.

"I least of all," said Cardew cheerily. "It depends largely on how the spirit moves me at the time."

"Bai Jove !" ejaculated Arthur Augustus. "I wegard that as sheeah cheek, Cardew."

"Go hon !"

Blake looked round at the deputation. They were all footballing fellows, who played for the House, or were eager to do so. Cardew's nonchalant way had an exasperating effect on all of them.

"That's the sort of captain we've got," said Blake. "We could get a new election if Tom Merry took it up, and put it to Kildare. He won't. We seem to be landed with this rotten slacker. Well, if he's going to stick on to the job, he's going to do the job, or take the consequences."

"Yaas, wathah !"

"Collar him."

Cardew made a bound out of the armchair. His nonchalance vanished all of a sudden as the deputation reached for him.

A dozen hands grasped him.

"Put his head in the coal-box first," said Blake.

"Ha, ha, ha !"

Cardew struggled desperately. What effect he had expected his ' cheek ' to produce upon the juniors cannot be said; but, apparently, he had not expected this. This was what happened, however.

"Bear a hand," Cardew yelled to his chums, as he was dragged struggling to the coal-box.

Levison shrugged his shoulders, and Clive laughed. They had exhausted their eloquence on Cardew, without producing any perceptible effect on the slacker of the Fourth. Now the fellows were taking more drastic measures, and Levison and Clive had no sympathy to waste on the slacker.

"You've asked for that," said Sidney Clive. "I hope it will do you good, Cardew."

"You rotter !"

"If you don't want the job, chuck it up," suggested Clive. "Nobody asks you to keep it on."

"Yaas, wathah—wesign, and we'll let you off the waggin', Cardew," said Arthur Augustus.

"Go and eat coke !"

"Bai Jove ! Wag him, deah boys !"

Cardew, struggling furiously, had his well-brushed head jammed into the coal-box. Blake stirred up the coals with a poker, while the dandy of the Fourth's head was held there.

When Cardew's head was withdrawn, there was a yell of laughter in the study. He was as black as a sweep, and gurgling with rage.

"Hand us that ink, Levison," said Blake.

Levison shook his head. He would take no hand in the ragging of his chum, though he was not prepared to intervene in his behalf.

But Kerruish handed over the ink, and Blake proceeded to pour it on the thick coal-dust on Cardew's head.

Ink ran down in streams, streaking Cardew's face, and running into his collar.

"Any jam in the cupboard?" asked Blake.

"Yaas, wathah."

Arthur Augustus handed out a pot of jam. Blake ladled it out over Cardew's coaly and inky head.

Cardew had ceased to struggle now; he was held too firmly for resistance. Under coal dust and ink and jam, his face was white with rage.

"There, I think that will do," said Blake, surveying him. "He looks a ripping object, I must say."

"You rotters !" panted Cardew.

"This is a tip," explained Blake. "Just a warning of what you've got to expect, if you go on as you've started. The football list is to be out by Friday afternoon. See ?"

"Hang you."

"If it isn't, look out for more squalls. And you've got to play in the match."

"I'll suit myself about that," gasped Cardew.

"You won't, if you stick on as skipper. You'll play up, and if you shirk it, you'll get a real ragging—this is a joke to it. Understand ?"

"Get out of my study."

"I think we're finished here," said Blake. "Come on, you fellows."

"Ha, ha, ha !"

The deputation crowded out of the study, laughing. Cardew stood in the middle of the room, almost unrecognisable under coal dust, ink, and jam. He gave his chums a glare, and then glared into the glass. Then he rushed from the study in search of a bath-room.

That evening there was much chuckling in the junior common-room over the ragging of Ralph Reckness Cardew. The fellows expressed the hope that it would do him good. But fellows who knew him well did not think that that hope was likely to be realised.

CHAPTER 3.

A Chance for Grundy !

GRUNDY of the Shell bestowed a lofty frown upon Cardew, the following day, as he came on him in the Form-room passage. Cardew greeted him with a pleasant nod—Grundy's frown was the grim response. George Alfred Grundy, apparently, was not feeling kindly towards the dandy of the Fourth.

"Lookin' for you, old bean ?" said Cardew.

"Look for somebody else, then," growled Grundy. "You're a slacking rotter, Cardew, and I'm done with you."

"Not really ? Unsay those cruel words !" urged Cardew, and Wilkins and Gunn, who were with Grundy, chuckled. Grundy reduced them to gravity with a ferocious glare.

"I'm done with you," he repeated, waving a large hand at Cardew. "You ought to be sacked from your job. You got me to back you up in the election, making out that you'd give me a chance in the matches—a chance I've never had from that ass Merry. You promised me——"

"I don't remember makin' any promise," said Cardew meekly. "But——"

"Practically," said Grundy. "You said you'd give every good man a chance as soon as you had the football in your hands."

"But that doesn't apply to you, old bean."

"I don't want any cheek !" roared Grundy. "For two pins I'd dust up the passage with you, junior captain or not. You're no good. The election ought to be cancelled. Lot of silly rigmarole about elections at this school, in my opinion. I think——"

"But I want you——"

"No good wanting me," interrupted Grundy, "I refuse to have anything to do with you."

"But I was going to ask you——"

"The answer's ' No ' before I know what you want," said George Alfred Grundy, "and I don't want to know."

"I want you——"

"Bosh !"

"To play——"

"Eh ?"

"In the Abbotsford match."

"What ?"

"Centre-half," said Cardew. "Are you on ?"

Grundy & Co. gazed at Cardew in sheer astonishment. Grundy was astonished at having his claims recognised at last, after so many rebuffs and disappointments. Wilkins and Gunn were still more astonished. Grundy being the very worst footballer at St. Jim's, and indeed in the whole wide world, it was amazing to hear that he was selected to play in a school fixture.

"Is this a joke ?" gasped Wilkins.

"Not at all," said Cardew blandly. "I'm making up my team for Abbotsford. Grundy's my man if he'll play."

"But he can't play !" ejaculated Gunn.

"What's that ?" roared Grundy.

"I—I mean——"

"I'm your man, Cardew," said Grundy cordially. "Let bygones be bygones. If you're able to see my form now I can excuse you for being a silly idiot before. I'm your man."

TAKEN PRISONER! Hardly had Ralph Reckness Cardew left his study than he was stopped by a sudden rush. Before he knew what was happening he was whirled off his feet, and rushed away. *(See page 9.)*

"Then you're down to play," said Cardew.

"Good."

Ralph Reckness Cardew strolled on smiling. Wilkins and Gunn wore an expression that could only be described as flabbergasted. George Alfred Grundy smiled genially.

"Not a bad skipper, Cardew," he remarked. "A bit of a slacker, but after all he's got an eye to a fellow's form. Tom Merry would never have played me for school or House either."

"I should jolly well think he wouldn't," gasped Wilkins.

"What?"

"I—I mean——"

"Cardew's the man for my money," said Grundy. "I can see now that I did right in backing him up in the election. Fellows are talking of a new election now."

"The sooner the better, I should think," murmured Gunn.

"I shall back Cardew up, of course—a really good skipper," said Grundy. "Of course, properly speaking, I ought to be junior captain of the school. But I must say we've got a good man in Cardew."

George Alfred Grundy strolled away in a state of great satisfaction. Naturally, he was not slow to impart the glad news to others.

It was the first time Grundy had been asked to play for school; and he was greatly elated. The fact that any side Grundy played for was doomed to defeat did not worry Grundy; he was unaware of the fact.

The news was received in the Common-room with a roar of laughter. Fellows did not seem to take it seriously.

That was natural enough. Grundy's style in football was uncommon—it was a style that could not be sufficiently uncommon. Charging his own forwards off the ball from behind, tripping up the halves in his own team, barging into the backs at critical moments, were among Grundy's minor sins as a footballer. He had been known to send the ball right into his own goal—he had been known to punch the referee

for a difference of opinion. The bare idea of Grundy in a school or house team made the St. Jim's fellows shriek.

"But it's true!" roared Grundy, indignant at this reception of the glorious news.

"Ha, ha, ha!"

"Bai Jove, you know, Gwunday will be the death of me," gasped Arthur Augustus D'Arcy. "My weal opinion is, Gwunday, that you are too funnay to live."

"Cardew's told me——" howled Grundy.

"What a joker that fellow Cardew is!" chuckled Blake. "It's too bad to pull Grundy's silly leg like this."

"Yaas, wathah! But Gwunday ought not to be ass enough to take it sewiously."

"It's quite serious!" yelled Grundy.

"Ha, ha, ha!"

"Oh, you're a set of puddenheads!" snorted Grundy. "You'll see my name up in the list."

"Ha, ha, ha!"

There were no believers. Indeed, Grundy's great news was soon bandied about the house, as a screaming joke, under the title of "Cardew's Latest." Fellows roared over it in the studies. The cream of the joke was that Grundy took it seriously and really supposed that he was going to play for St. Jim's against Abbotsford.

But George Alfred's vindication was coming.

After tea Ralph Reckness Cardew was seen to post up a paper on the Common-room wall and walk airily away. There was a rush to read the paper, which contained the list of the team for the Abbotsford match on the morrow.

A crowd of fellows read the paper, and there was a gasp of stupefaction. For prominent among the names written there, in Cardew's elegant hand, was the astonishing name:

G. A. GRUNDY.

"Grundy!" shouted Kangaroo of the Shell. "Rot!"

"Trimble, too!" roared Blake.

"Twimble, bai Jove!"

"And Racke——"

"And Crooke——"

"And Mellish——"

"And Clampe, and Chowle! Great pip!"

The juniors could scarcely believe their eyes. Tom Merry, indeed, rubbed his eyes as he read. Grundy of the Shell—Baggy Trimble, the fat slacker of the Fourth—Racke and Crooke, the black sheep, who hated football—and the rest of the list almost on a par with them! Yet there it was—the official list of players selected for the match at Abbotsford. Ralph Reckness Cardew's own name was here—the only footballer's name in the list. Even his chums, Clive and Levison, were left out.

"This must be some sort of a silly joke!" said Tom Merry.

"Yaas, wathah!"

Grundy of the Shell came into the Common-room. He glanced round with a grin on his rugged face.

"I hear the list's up," he said. "My name's there, I fancy, what?"

"Oh, yes—and a lot more to match!" said Blake sarcastically.

Grundy pushed through the crowd and looked at the list. The sight of his own name gave him satisfaction. But he started at the others.

"Trimble—Racke—Crooke—great Scott! Cardew can't really be thinking of playing that lot!" he ejaculated.

"Might as well play them as you," grunted Herries.

"It can't be serious," said Monty Lowther. "It's one of Cardew's idiotic jokes. Let's go and see him about it."

A dozen fellows rushed away to Study No. 9 in the Fourth to interview the junior captain and ask him what the thump he meant. Cardew was not there—and Levison and Clive knew nothing of the matter. In fact, they declined to believe in the existence of that remarkable football list until they had gone down to the Common-room and seen it with their own eyes.

Cardew, for reasons of his own, kept out of sight. There was deep discussion on the subject; and it was Blake who hit upon what was soon generally considered as the explanation.

"This is Cardew's answer to the ragging we gave him," he said. "He's going to chuck the Abbotsford match away just to show us that he can do as he likes."

"But are we going to let him?" demanded Manners.

"No fear!"

Cardew was not seen till nearly bed-time. Then he was surrounded by an angry and inquiring crowd. He assumed an expression of surprise.

"Not satisfied with the list?" he asked, elevating his eyebrows. "My dear man, I've given the matter a lot of thought, as I told Blake I would. The team's all right."

"All wrong, you mean!" hooted Herries.

"So glad to have your opinion," said Cardew politely. "I stick to my own, all the same."

"You're really thinking of taking that crew over to Abbotsford?" exclaimed Tom Merry.

Cardew gave him a curious glance.

"Why not?" he asked.

"About a thousand reasons why not, I should think!" exclaimed the captain of the Shell. "It will be throwing the match away, and making us all look asses."

"You really think so?" asked Cardew.

"Certainly I do."

"What a pity your opinion isn't of any consequence, then!" smiled Cardew.

"Wha-a-at?"

"You ought to have remained junior captain," said Cardew, with a smile. "Then you'd have had the job on your hands. At present it's on mine. My idea is to try new blood, you know—give new fellows a chance."

"Such as Grundy!" hooted Blake.

"Such as Grundy," assented Cardew.

"You silly ass!"

"Dear man, and you voted for me in the election!" sighed Cardew.

"Only to keep out the New House man."

"I jolly well wish we had the New House man!" howled Kangaroo. "Figgins wouldn't play the fool like this."

"It's a bit too late to think of that, isn't it?" smiled Cardew.

"Look here——"

"You howling ass!"

"You cheeky chump!"

Cardew smiled, and walked away with his hands in his pockets. Bed-time came, and Kildare and Darrell, of the Sixth, came to shepherd off the Shell and the Fourth to their dormitories. But it was long before the juniors slept that night. Discussion raged long and fiercely on the subject of the Abbotsford match, especially in the Fourth Form dormitory. In that dormitory Cardew was subjected to a running

fire of objurgations, to which he did not pay the slightest heed. While the Fourth Form told him what they thought of him, Ralph Reckness Cardew slumbered peacefully.

CHAPTER 4.

Drastic Measures!

THERE was considerable excitement in the Lower School of St. Jim's the following morning.

Even yet the fellows could scarcely believe that Cardew was serious in intending to take that hopeless crowd over to Abbotsford for the match in the afternoon.

The members of Cardew's eleven found themselves extremely unpopular; but they did not seem to mind.

Grundy was satisfied with his own selection, and, though he was not satisfied with the rest, he felt that his own wonderful play would probably pull the game out of the fire. Racke and Crooke openly grinned at the exasperation of the juniors. They were looked down on as slackers and black sheep, and it was quite certain that they would not exert themselves in the match. The school record was nothing to them. Certainly, they liked to be able to say that they had played for the school; but their play certainly was not likely to reflect any credit on their school. Baggy Trimble was quite gleeful at the prospect, especially at the exasperation of all the fellows he liked.

Levison and Clive were dismayed. But their remarks to Cardew on the subject were received only with airy persiflage, and they soon gave it up. It was clear that Cardew meant to go on his own wilful way. He was junior football captain, and he had the final voice in the selection of the team. He declared that he was trying "new blood"; quite a good idea in its way, but evidently only a pretext in this case.

But it was difficult to see what was to be done. Blake of the Fourth, and some other fellows, took the resolve of appealing to Kildare, as senior captain of the school and head of the games. Kildare heard them out with a thoughtful brow, and shook his head.

"You had a good skipper in Tom Merry," he said. "As a majority voted for Cardew, it appears that you wanted a change. Now you're asking me to interfere and over-rule the captain you elected yourselves. I can't do it."

"As head of the games you've got authority," said Blake.

"Quite so, and I shall exercise it if it's needed. But I don't feel called upon to interfere with Cardew."

"But——"

"That's all!" said Kildare.

And Blake & Co. went, furious.

"After all, we did elect Cardew," remarked Dig. "It was to keep the New House man out; but there it is. It's a bit thick to ask Kildare to drop down on the man we elected ourselves."

"Yaas, wathah! All the same——"

"Cardew's not going to turn St. Jim's junior football into a farce," said Blake, between his teeth. "If he won't chuck it, and if Kildare won't make him chuck it, somebody else will make him. We'll jaw this over, and find a way."

And Blake and a few choice spirits retired to Study No. 6, to jaw the matter over, after dinner, and find a solution. Meanwhile, Tom Merry was giving the matter some deep thought.

The outcome of Tom's cogitations was a visit to Cardew's study. He found that cheerful youth sprawling in the arm-chair, smoking a cigarette. Cardew nodded to him genially.

"Trot in, old bean! Glad to see you!" he said airily.

Tom Merry came in.

"It will soon be time to start for Abbotsford," he said.

"Yes; I've asked Trimble to let me know when the brake appears in the offing. Trimble's my inside-left, you know."

"Are you serious about that, Cardew?"

"Quite."

"You think you've got a winning team?"

"Well, football is full of chances," said Cardew gravely. "I think that I've mentioned that I'm trying new blood."

Tom Merry made an effort to keep his temper. He knew that it was of no use quarrelling with the airy dandy of the Fourth.

"I'm not asking to play myself," he said quietly. "You seem bent on keeping me out of the football this season; but let that go. But surely, Cardew, you don't want to muck up the school football?"

"Why not?"

There really was no reply to be made to that question, and Tom Merry did not attempt to answer it.

"I suppose it's no use my asking you to think better of it?" he said, after a pause.

"Well, no; though I'd like to oblige you," smiled Cardew. "You did me a good turn a week or two ago, you know."

"I know you're my enemy, though I never gave you any cause," said Tom. "We've had plenty of trouble, I know. But what have the other fellows done for you to serve them like this?"

RALPH RECKNESS CARDEW

who has held the reins as junior captain for the past few weeks.

"Haven't you heard of the raggin' in this study?"

"So that's your motive?"

"That and other things," Cardew laughed. "You wouldn't understand if I explained. But you're mistaken on one point. I'm not your enemy, Tom Merry."

"I'm glad to hear that, at least," said Tom dryly.

"I mean it." Cardew's face became earnest. "I'm not a fellow to forget an injury or a service. Cutts of the Fifth had me at his mercy in the wood the other day, and I was booked for a terrific hiding. You chipped in, and handled him."

Tom Merry passed his hand over his nose rather ruefully. That feature still bore signs of his terrific combat with Cutts of the Fifth—a combat which had been the talk of the St. Jim's juniors for days.

"I've treated you rottenly all along the line," went on Cardew calmly. "Naturally, when you saw me in Cutts' grip, I expected you to let him go ahead, and take it out of me. Instead of which, you stood up to a fellow twice your size and weight, and got me clear. I told you at the time you were a fool to do it, and that I'd like to be such another fool, instead of my esteemed self! I meant that. I suppose you thought I'd forgotten all about the matter by this time?"

"Well——" Tom hesitated.

"I hadn't," said Cardew. "I remember it. I dare say I shall make it up to you in the long run. Who knows?"

"If you feel under any obligation to me," said Tom, "you can wipe it out by playing square in the football. I don't ask you to play me or my friends. But don't take a rotten side into the field from sheer silly caprice."

Cardew smiled.

"That's all right," he said. "The fellows elected me, didn't they? Oughtn't they to have a lesson, after turning down a jolly good skipper and electing a jolly bad one?"

Cardew's tone was final.

"Then there's nothing more for me to say," said Tom, and he turned his back on Cardew and quitted the study with a gloomy brow.

Cardew smiled, and finished smoking his cigarette. Having finished it and thrown the stump into the ashes in the grate, he rose and stretched himself and strolled from the study.

He did not stroll very far.

Three paces from the doorway of Study No. 9 he was stopped by a sudden rush. Before he knew what was happening he was whirled off his feet and rushed away.

CHAPTER 5.
Left in the Lurch.

"WHERE'S Cardew?"

A dozen fellows asked that question, but nobody seemed able to reply. The brake was waiting to take the footballers over to Abbotsford, and Cardew's remarkable team were ready to start. But Ralph Reckness Cardew did not seem ready to start with them.

Baggy Trimble had gone to his study to tell him that the brake was ready. But he had not found Cardew there.

"The silly ass!" exclaimed Grundy. "Keeping us waiting! We shall be late for the match at this rate!"

"Oh, never mind," yawned Racke. "What does it matter?"

Grundy snorted.

"Bai Jove, where's Cardew, you fellows?" exclaimed Arthur Augustus D'Arcy, coming up to the waiting group.

"Goodness knows!" growled Grundy.

"What are you goin' to do if he doesn't turn up?" asked Arthur Augustus D'Arcy, with a smile on his face.

"Oh, I can captain the team, if it comes to that!" remarked Grundy. "I'll put another man in."

"Bai Jove!"

"Levison, seen Cardew?" shouted Chowle.

"No!" answered Levison curtly.

"He's got to be found!" growled Crooke. "The silly ass! Is this another of his silly tricks?"

A good many fellows were looking for Cardew. But the dandy of the Fourth was not to be found. It really looked as if Cardew, after arranging for that remarkable team to represent St. Jim's on the football field at Abbotsford, had deliberately absented himself. Some of the fellows remarked that it was not surprising. Nobody could really want to show up at football with players like Grundy and Trimble and Crooke. Quite an army of fellows gathered round the brake, discussing Cardew's strange absence.

Where was Cardew?

The question was asked on all sides without an answer being forthcoming.

It might have been noted that Study No. 6 Blake and Herries and Digby and D'Arcy—smiled at one another and exchanged glances of intelligence. But most of the fellows were thinking of Cardew, not of Study No. 6.

Tom Merry was brought on the scene by the news that Cardew had disappeared, while the team was waiting to start. It was a puzzle to Tom. It was hard to believe that Cardew had deliberately gone out and left his team in the lurch; but if that was not the case, where was he? A score of fellows pointed out to Tom that Cardew, being off the scene, it was up to him to take the Abbotsford match in hand. Tom Merry shook his head very decidedly.

"Rot!" was his answer. "I'm not even a member of the eleven! It's up to Talbot."

"Talbot!" repeated Grundy.

"Talbot's vice-captain," said Tom Merry. "If the captain chooses to vanish just before the match, it's up to the vice-captain, isn't it?"

"Well, I suppose so," said Grundy slowly. "But Talbot isn't playing in this eleven at all, as it happens."

"He will be!" said Blake.

"Yaas, wathah!"

"Well, I've no objection to Talbot as captain," said George Alfred Grundy generously. "Let him come along!"

Study No. 6 grinned at one another. Half a dozen fellows rushed in search of Talbot of the Shell.

Tom Merry walked away. He had the interests of St. Jim's junior football at heart, but he was not disposed to butt in where he had no official concern.

It was agreed on all hands that, as Cardew evidently was not going to appear, it was "up" to Talbot. Even the remarkable eleven did not dissent from that.

Their dissent would have made no difference, had they

TOM MERRY from whom the captaincy has been won and whose reinstatement is imminent.

dissented. Cardew, in his official capacity, had to be regarded. Nobody was likely to regard Racke or Crooke or Trimble or Grundy.

Tom Merry and Manners and Lowther walked together to Big Side, to look on at a senior match. Kildare's eleven were playing the New House that afternoon. But the Terrible Three had been only a few minutes on Big Side when Wally of the Third came panting up to them.

"Pull up your socks, Tom Merry!" bawled D'Arcy minor. "You're wanted!"

"How's that?" asked Tom, looking round.

"Talbot wants you!" grinned the fag. "He's making some changes in the team. Lowther's wanted, too!"

"Oh!" ejaculated Tom.

Monty Lowther chuckled.

"Looks as if Cardew's wonderful eleven is doing a fade-through," he remarked. "I suppose there isn't a man in it that Talbot would be willing to take over to Abbotsford."

The Terrible Three hurried away. In the quad Racke and Crooke passed them, scowling. Evidently the two black sheep had been dropped out of the team.

"Look here, Tom Merry!" It was Baggy Trimble's voice. "I jolly well object to your bagging my place in the eleven!"

"Your place!" exclaimed Tom.

"Talbot's turned me down!" said Trimble, with a deeply injured look. "Turned me down after I was specially selected to play!"

"Ha, ha, ha!" roared the Terrible Three.

"Look here, you know, I think——"

But the Shell fellows did not wait to hear what Baggy Trimble thought. They hurried on to the brake. Loud yells greeted them as they arrived. Clampe and Chowle, who were New House fellows, were arguing with Figgins & Co., also of the New House. It appeared that Talbot had called on Figgins and Wynn and Kerr for their services, and Clampe and Chowle raised objections to leaving the team. Figgins & Co. were overruling their objections by the simple process of knocking their heads against the side of the brake. The wild yells of Clampe and Chowle rang far and wide, amid howls of laughter.

Clampe and Chowle were soon convinced that they were no longer members of the St. Jim's junior eleven. They escaped from the grasp of Figgins & Co., and fled for their lives.

"I shall want you, Tom," said Talbot of the Shell, with a smile. "I'd rather you captained the team——"

"Bosh!" said Tom. "I'll play under you as skipper, if you like."

"Right-ho, then!"

"How many of Cardew's men have you got left?" asked Manners.

"None!" answered Talbot briefly.

"Ha, ha, ha!"

"Look here——" Grundy of the Shell was roaring, with a voice like unto that of the Bull of Bashan. "Look here——"

"Dry up, Grundy!"

"I'm a member of this team, ain't I?" bellowed Grundy. "Am I a member of this football eleven or not?"

"Not!"

"Cardew specially told me——"

"Blow Cardew!"

"My name's up in the list——"

"That list's cancelled."

"It isn't cancelled!" roared Grundy. "I don't consent to its being cancelled. I object strongly!"

"Well, you can go on objecting, while we get off to Abbotsford," said Blake. "Buck up, you fellows, or we'll be late."

"Yaas, wathah!"

Talbot's hastily recruited team was complete. They crowded into the brake—Talbot, Tom Merry, Lowther, Blake, D'Arcy, Figgins, Kerr, Wynn, Redfern, Kangaroo, and Levison. As many other fellows as the brake would hold crowded in to accompany them to Abbotsford. George Alfred Grundy, crimson with wrath and indignation, voiced his objections at the top of his voice, and made a rush to get a place in the brake. Grundy did not get into the brake—he found himself sitting on the hard, cold ground in a breathless state. The brake rolled off without him.

"Oh, my hat!" gasped Grundy, as Wilkins and Gunn helped him to his feet. "Oh crumbs! The cheek of it!"

"Come away, old fellow," said Wilkins, trying not to grin.

"Come away!" repeated Grundy wrathfully. "I'm going to play at Abbotsford, you dummy."

He rushed after the brake.

"Oh crumbs!" said Gunn, staring after him.

Grundy flew down the road after the brake. There was a roar of laughter from the footballers in the vehicle.

"Here comes Grundy!"

"Bai Jove! Gwunday's aftah us."

"Ha, ha, ha!"

"Stop!" roared Grundy.

The brake slowed on the rise in the lane, and Grundy overtook it, and grabbed hold. He was seized by half a dozen hands above, and held. His cap was jammed down his back, and Redfern squeezed an orange into his collar. Then he was dropped into the road, on the top of the rise, and the brake rolled on.

Grundy sat, breathless, in the road.

"Ow! Oh! Gug-gug-gug!" were his remarks, as he sat and blinked after the disappearing brake.

"Ha, ha, ha! Good-bye, Grundy!"

"Grooooogh!"

The brake was out of sight when Grundy felt equal to staggering on. Pursuit was hopeless; moreover, Grundy did not want any more oranges squeezed down his neck. In great wrath and indignation, George Alfred gave it up, and he tramped back to St. Jim's a sadder if not a wiser Grundy.

CHAPTER 6.
In Durance Vile !

RALPH RECKNESS CARDEW sat silent.

He was seated on an empty trunk, in the top box-room in the School House. A box-rope fastened him to the trunk; it was wound and knotted about him with great security. And there was an ample reason for his silence—a large duster that was fastened over his mouth.

Fortunately, Cardew had the healthy habit of breathing through his nose. Otherwise, he might have been in danger of suffocation, for the duster was fastened very effectively.

His eyes were gleaming with rage as he sat.

There was another fellow in the box-room—George Herries of the Fourth. George Herries was standing at the little window, looking over a wide view of frosty roofs and frosty branches.

He took no notice of Cardew—save when he moved a little. Then Herries' eyes would dwell upon him for a watchful moment.

Cardew quivered with rage as he sat.

It had not even occurred to his mind, wary as he usually was, that drastic measures like this would be taken.

But they had been taken—and they had been completely successful. Study No. 6 had collared the junior football captain, and rushed him away, struggling, up the box-room stairs. In the little room they had secured him with the box-rope and the duster, and left him with the door locked on him. Not till the brake had started for Abbotsford did George Herries arrive to keep him company.

Herries, at the little high window, had a view of the distant senior football-ground, and he was interested in Upper School football. He would have preferred to accompany the team to Abbotsford, but Study No. 6 had agreed that somebody should be left in charge of Cardew; and as Herries was not playing, he remained.

Cardew, sitting on the box, stared at him with furious eyes. He had heard three strike from the clock-tower, and he knew that St. Jim's junior footballers must have arrived at Abbotsford, and that the game would have started.

He knew why he had been kidnapped in this extraordinary manner. Study No. 6 had told him that much.

Cardew had carried matters with a high hand, and he realised now that other fellows could be high-handed, too—and still more so!

"Good man!" ejaculated Herries suddenly. Kildare of the Sixth had just scored against the New House.

Herries turned from the window. He grinned at the furious face of Ralph Reckness Cardew.

"Feel a bit cramped?" he asked.

Cardew did not answer—for good reasons. George Herries consulted his watch.

"It's half-past," he remarked. "I'm afraid you'll have to sit there till four, Cardew."

Cardew glared at him.

"You see, you're not to be depended on," explained Herries. "It would be just like you to scoot across to Abbotsford and butt in somehow. Blake thinks the match had better be over before you are let loose. What do you think?"

No reply came from the angry mouth under the duster.

"Talbot's taken over a winning team, if that's any comfort to you, old scout," added Herries. "I rather fancy we shall beat Abbotsford. Don't be sulky—you asked for this, you know."

IN DURANCE VILE! Quivering with rage, Ralph Reckness Cardew sat tied to an empty trunk in the box-room, a large duster fastened over his mouth, while Herries, standing by the window, kept a watchful eye on him.
(See page 10.)

Herries turned to the window again and resumed watching the game on Big Side.

Cardew sat motionless, consumed with rage. He had already tried his strength on the box-rope, and found that there was nothing doing. He had to wait, with what patience he could muster, until George Herries chose to release him.

It was fortunate for Herries that he was able to watch the senior House match from the window. Otherwise, he certainly would have found his vigil a tiresome one. Cardew found it tiresome enough. The minutes crawled by on leaden wings to the bound junior sitting dumb on the trunk.

It was not till the senior House match was finished that George Herries turned to the prisoner.

"You can cut now," he said.

And he started unfastening the box-rope. The duster was jerked off, and Cardew had the use of his voice.

"You rotter!" he gasped.

"Go it!" said Herries.

"I'll smash you when I get loose."

"You're welcome to all the smashing you can do. I sha'n't be sorry to give you a hiding," answered Herries cheerfully.

The rope was loose at last, and Cardew staggered from the trunk. He chafed his wrists, breathing hard. Herries opened the box-room door.

"Getting on with the smashing before we go down?" he asked.

Cardew's answer was a savage rush.

"Ready, old man!" chuckled Herries.

They were fighting fiercely in a moment more. Cardew's fury, so long pent up, found a vent in a fierce attack, and Herries was driven round the box-room. But Herries was a sturdy fellow, and he knew something about boxing. The dandy of the Fourth found himself stopped, and Herries

stood up to him, giving blow for blow, and certainly handing out as much punishment as he received.

For fully five minutes the combat raged, and then the two juniors, breathless, separated and glared at one another.

Both of them had streaming noses and other damages.

"Minute's rest?" suggested Herries, and he took out his handkerchief to dab his nose.

Cardew gave him a look, and walked out of the box-room. It was not much use fighting Herries; though the attack had solaced him a little when he was released. He went down the box-room stairs, and as he came into the Fourth Form passage there was a shout from Baggy Trimble.

"Here's Cardew!"

"He's turned up!" shouted Julian. "I say, where have you been all this time, Cardew?"

Cardew did not answer. He strode away to his own study, entered it, and slammed the door. But the news had spread that Ralph Reckness Cardew had reappeared after his mysterious absence; and a few minutes later the door was thumped open, and George Alfred Grundy strode into Study No. 9.

"So you've turned up?" bawled Grundy.

Cardew gave him a scowl.

"Where have you been?"

"Find out!" snapped Cardew.

"You left us in the lurch."

"Oh, get out!"

"Do you call that playing the game?" roared Grundy. "Do you know that I was dropped out of the team by that ass Talbot?"

"Don't worry, you silly ass."

"Worry?" roared Grundy. "I'll worry you! This is one

of your jokes, I suppose—pulling my leg, by Jove! I'll worry you."

He rushed at Cardew. That exasperated youth met him half-way, and Study No. 9 was the scene of a terrific combat. Grundy was a hefty fellow, and Cardew, good boxer as he was, was scarcely a match for the burly Shell fellow. The uproar in the study brought a crowd of fellows along the passage, and they stared into Study No. 9 and chortled.

"Cardew's getting it!" yelled Baggy Trimble. "Serve him jolly well right for letting us all down! Go it, Grundy."

"Ha, ha, ha!"

"Give him jip, Grundy!" howled Mellish.

Grundy had Cardew's head in chancery by this time. He was wrathful and indignant, as was natural, with his belief that Cardew, in his whimsical humour, had made a fool of him, and let him down at the last moment by way of a joke. Grundy wanted Cardew to understand exactly how he regarded a joke of that kind, and he certainly made his meaning clear.

"Here, don't slaughter him, Grundy!" exclaimed Wilkins at last. "Leave some of him, old chap."

"Ha, ha, ha!"

"I'll smash him!" roared Grundy.

Wilkins and Gunn ran into the study and dragged the excited Grundy away. Cardew staggered to the wall, and leaned on it breathlessly. Grundy gave him a glare.

"Perhaps he's had enough," he panted.

"Looks as if he has," grinned Wilkins. "Come on."

And the great Grundy suffered himself to be led away. Cardew kicked the door shut after him.

Then he sank into an armchair, gasping for breath. It was not Cardew's lucky day.

CHAPTER 7.
A Slight Mistake !

TOM MERRY & CO. returned in cheerful spirits from Abbotsford in the winter dusk.

Talbot had led his team to victory; Abbotsford School had been beaten by two goals to one; a result very different from that which would have been achieved but for the kidnapping scheme carried out in so masterly a manner by Study No. 6.

Herries met the returning footballers with a rather swollen nose, but a grin on his face

"All serene?" he asked.

"Wight as wain," answered Arthur Augustus D'Arcy. "We've beaten them, deah boy. How's Cardew?"

"What's happened to your nose?" asked Blake.

"Cardew!" explained Herries. "But his nose is the same, only more so. He seemed annoyed."

"Ha, ha, ha!"

"I hear that he's had a fight with Grundy since then. Grundy seemed to think that Cardew has let him down."

"Ha, ha, ha!"

Study No. 6 went in to tea in great spirits. They felt that they had saved the situation, and that they deserved well of their country. Of the kidnapping scheme they had said no word to the other fellows—outside Study No. 6 nobody but Cardew knew why he had failed to turn up for Abbotsford.

"There'll be a wow about it, of course," remarked Arthur Augustus D'Arcy, as the four sat down to tea. "But we don't mind a wow! I considah that we acted with gweat tact and judgment."

Blake looked thoughtful.

"If Cardew makes a fuss, we can stand it," he said. "But I think very likely he won't. The whole school will cackle at him if it comes out—and he don't like looking ridiculous. But I don't care a rap how he takes it, for one."

"Wathah not."

Tom Merry looked into Study No. 6 on his way to his study.

"You fellows heard anything of Cardew yet?" he asked.

"I believe he's in his study," grinned Herries.

"He had gone out this afternoon, I suppose?"

"No, I think he was in the School House all the time."

"It's jolly queer."

"Yes, isn't it?" said Blake blandly.

"Yaas, wathah."

And a smile went round Study No. 6. Tom Merry looked a little puzzled. But Lowther was calling him from the passage, and the captain of the Shell went on without asking further questions.

The Terrible Three were sitting down to tea when the door of Study No. 10 opened, and Ralph Reckness Cardew looked in. He stepped into the study, and fixed his eyes on Tom Merry with a bitter expression.

"So you're back," he said.

"Yes, here we are again," answered Tom cheerily.

"We've beaten Abbotsford," added Monty Lowther

THE GEM LIBRARY.—No. 831.

politely. "I'm sure that news will please you, Cardew—you're so keen on football."

"And so concerned about the school record in games," remarked Manners satirically.

Cardew's eyes gleamed.

"And you think you can play a trick like this without being called to account, Tom Merry?" he asked.

Tom stared at him.

"Trick! A trick like what?"

"You are not making out, I suppose, that you don't know why I missed Abbotsford to-day," sneered Cardew.

"I haven't the faintest idea why you missed Abbotsford, and I don't care a rap," retorted Tom Merry. "I suppose you were slacking about as usual."

"Liar!"

"Wha-a-a-t?"

"Don't I speak plain enough?" sneered Cardew.

Tom Merry jumped up from the tea table.

"Quite plain enough to make me throw you out of the study," he exclaimed, and he rushed at the dandy of the Fourth.

Cardew faced him with his hands up, his look black and bitter. But he was no match for the captain of the Shell. He went through the study doorway whirling, and landed in the passage with a crash.

Tom stood in the doorway with flashing eyes.

"Now come back and repeat what you said," he panted.

"I'll repeat it fast enough—I'll shout it from the house-tops, if you like," exclaimed Cardew, staggering to his feet, crimson and breathless. "I'll have you turned out of the junior club for the trick you've played on me to-day."

"Bai Jove!"

The "row" in the Shell passage had brought most of the fellows out of their studies, among them Blake & Co.

"Bai Jove! You are labahin' undah a misappwehension, Cardew," Arthur Augustus tried to explain.

"I think the fellow's wandering in his mind," said Tom Merry contemptuously. "What trick does he think I've played him?"

"The dear man's put it down to you," grinned Blake. "Put it down to Study No. 6, Cardew. It was a little stunt of our own."

"Yaas, wathah!"

"Little us, and nobody else, and we're ready to answer for it," said Digby, "and we're ready to play the same game over again, every time you try to muck up the footer."

"You bet!" said Herries.

"But what——" exclaimed Tom Merry, mystified.

Blake waved his hand towards Cardew.

"He can tell you, if he likes. We don't mind. If he cares to take it before the head of the games, we're ready to walk to Kildare's study with him."

"Yaas, wathah! Weady and willin'!"

Cardew panted for breath. He had taken it for granted, without thinking of a doubt, that Tom Merry, his old rival, had been at the bottom of the kidnapping. But he realised his mistake now.

"You—you—— Then you didn't know what had happened?" he stammered, quite taken aback.

"I don't know that anything happened!" snapped Tom. "What the thump are you driving at? What's all this mystery about?"

"You—you didn't know I was kept away?"

"How the thump should I know?"

"I—I thought——"

"Were you kept away?" demanded Tom, something of a light breaking on his mind.

"Yes," panted Cardew.

"Yaas, wathah!" chuckled Arthur Augustus.

"And—and I thought——" stammered Cardew.

"You thought!" snapped Tom scornfully. "You thought! And you come to my study and call me a liar, because you thought! I think you ought to be jolly well ashamed of yourself!"

Cardew drew a deep breath.

"Perhaps you're right," he admitted. "In fact, I know you are. I—I—I'm sorry!"

And with that rather unexpected apology, Ralph Reckness Cardew turned and walked away, leaving the passage in a buzz behind him.

CHAPTER 8.
The Election !

"ELECTION on Wednesday!"

"Bai Jove!"

"Good news!"

It was good news to a good many fellows, and surprising news, too. But there it was, on the notice-board, signed by Kildare of the Sixth. On Wednesday at three o'clock, in the lecture-room, a new election was to take place for the selection of the junior captain of St. Jim's.

"Wippin' news!" said Arthur Augustus D'Arcy, and his view was shared by all Study No. 6.

"Ripping news !" said Monty Lowther, in Study No. 10, and Manners and Tom Merry heartily agreed.

"Ripping news !" said Figgins, in the New House. "We're going to have another chance for this House, you fellows." And Kerr and Fatty Wynn agreed that it was ripping.

There had been a good deal of excitement and speculation in the Lower School, after the incident of the Abbotsford match. The right story of what had happened that day was not generally known. Cardew having decided to keep his own counsel, Study No. 6 had done the same, in spite of many inquiries and much surmise.

But that most of the footballing fellows were thoroughly fed-up with Cardew was no secret, and it was known that trouble must come, and Tom Merry was urged on all sides to take up the gage of battle and give his rival a fall. But Tom steadily declined to take the lead against the junior captain; and then, unexpectedly, it became known that Cardew himself had requested the head of the games to appoint a new election. Some airily explained to Kildare that they didn't seem satisfied with the present state of affairs; and, as a matter of fact, Kildare himself was very far from satisfied, and was glad to take the opening that Cardew's request gave him.

So now it was settled, and the notice was on the board, and the Lower School was in a ferment on the subject.

Why Cardew was taking the chance was a mystery, even to his own chums, Clive and Levison. But he was taking it, and of his own accord. At the last election the School House had rallied round him, to keep out the New House candidate; but crowds of fellows were heard to say now that they would prefer the New House man to Cardew. Which was a proof of how thoroughly fed-up they were with their present captain, for, generally, the whole School House would have agreed that there could not be a skipper chosen from the New House, without St. Jim's going rapidly to the dogs in consequence.

Cardew still had a party—not a party to be greatly proud of, however. Racke & Co., the slackers of the school, backed him up, chiefly from dislike of Tom Merry and his partisans. Some other fellows thought he might be given another chance. And a few, perhaps, had in view generous spreads in Study No. 9 and invitations to Reckness Towers. A good many fellows who had supported him on the last occasion, regarding it as "sporting" of him to put the matter to the test again, resolved not to vote at all. They did not care to help re-elect him, but did not feel disposed to take a hand in turning him out.

It was probable, therefore, that the poll would be a more limited one than was usual in such cases; a circumstance that inspired hope in Figgins & Co.

When the School House voted en bloc in school elections the New House was too powerfully outnumbered to have much chance for its candidate. But when the School House vote was split, there was a chance for the New House. And the fact that many voters were to abstain from voting at all, increased that chance—for there were not likely to be many abstentions in the New House ranks.

Figgins & Co. beat up voters on all sides, and rallied the juniors of their own House. In the School House a crowd of fellows did electioneering business for Tom Merry. Electioneering was not in Tom's own line; he simply declined to have anything to do with it. He was there to be voted for if the fellows wanted him to be captain of the Lower School. And he left it at that. He declined to ask anybody for a vote. Indeed, he told Baggy Trimble that, if Baggy had the cheek to vote for him, he would kick Baggy.

But though Tom Merry went on his way and made no sign, his friends pushed his cause in both houses, and with great energy. Arthur Augustus went so far as to suggest that anybody who did not vote for Tom should be given a feahful thwashin'.

Cardew did not display the energy he had displayed earlier. There were no royal spreads in Study No. 9, no vague promises; in fact, there was no trickery. Apparently Cardew wanted to be elected fairly and squarely this time, if elected at all.

All the Lower School looked forward to Wednesday, and there was much counting and re-counting of possible votes. Three candidates were nominated—Tom Merry, Cardew, and George Figgins. All calculations showed that the voting was likely to be close.

In resigning his place as junior captain of the school,

Cardew had resigned also that of junior House captain. That was an affair that concerned the School House alone, and Kildare had appointed Tuesday evening for the House to choose a new captain. It was a small affair compared with Wednesday's election, but fellows attended it eagerly, regarding it as a straw which would show which way the wind was blowing. And there were loud cheers from Tom's partisans when he was declared junior House captain, with a majority of a dozen votes in his favour.

"It's going our way," Monty Lowther remarked, in Study No. 10 afterwards. "You'll be elected junior captain of the school to-morrow, Tom."

Tom Merry nodded.

"It looks like it," he said. "But there's many a slip, you know. Still, let's hope for the best."

"Anyhow, you're junior House captain now, and it's the first step," said Manners. "That was how Cardew started when he began his campaign. He got in as House captain, and started giving you trouble. You can give him a Roland for his Oliver now, Tom."

"H'm!" said Tom.

"We'll jolly well make you!" declared Lowther warmly. "This study is up against Cardew all along the line. If he keeps the School captaincy, you're going to give him trouble as House captain, do you hear?"

Tom Merry shook his head.

"We've got to think of the school," he said. "Things would go to pot with House captain and School captain jibbing at one another. If Cardew remains junior captain of St. Jim's, I shall try to make the best of it—not the worst."

"Fathead!"

Tom Merry laughed.

"I suppose you're right, Tom," said Monty Lowther, after a long pause. "But you're really a bit too good for this jolly old world, you know. If you play the game, Cardew won't."

"No reason why I shouldn't, if he doesn't."

"Oh, bow-wow!"

"But we're going to win," said Manners. "The trouble is, so many fellows saying they're not going to vote. They backed up Cardew last time, and don't like to turn him down now. But I believe most of them hope you'll get in, Tom."

"Hoping isn't enough," growled Lowther. "They ought to vote."

"Well, so long as they don't vote for Cardew, it's something," said Manners. "I think we're going to pull it off."

Over in the New House there was something like equal confidence in Figgins' study.

"I fancy we're really going to pull it off this time," George Figgins declared to Kerr and Fatty Wynn. "It will be rather a catch for St. Jim's, having a New House junior skipper."

"No end of a catch," agreed Kerr.

"We'll celebrate it, if you get in, Figgy," said Fatty Wynn. "We'll stand the biggest spread that ever was stood at St. Jim's."

"Trust you to think of that!" chuckled Figgy.

In Study No. 9 in the Fourth it was difficult to tell whether Ralph Reckness Cardew was feeling confident or not. Whatever he thought on the subject he kept to himself, and even Levison could not guess his thoughts. Clive and Levison had not voted in the House captain election on Tuesday evening, and they did not intend to vote in the School captain election on the morrow. Cardew was their chum, but they wanted Tom Merry for their captain. Cardew's best friends could not say that he had been a success or a credit to the school in his new role. It was Cardew who gave them the news how Tuesday's election had gone, when he strolled into Study No. 9 afterwards.

"You've got a new House captain," he announced.

"Tom Merry?"

"Yes."

"Good!" said Clive frankly.

"Very good!" said Cardew with a laugh. "Some of the fellows are sayin' that it's an omen for to-morrow, and that Thomas will romp home, back into his old job."

"I think it's very likely," said Levison.

"So do I," agreed Cardew. "It will be a close thing, anyhow." He gave a deep yawn. "Frightful bore, these school elections, what?"

"No reason why you should go in for them, if you find them a bore," said Ernest Levison dryly.

"Is there ever any reason for anythin' I do?" yawned Cardew. "Hallo, here's jolly old Trimble! Roll away, Baggy!"

"I want to speak to you in private, Cardew," said Baggy Trimble mysteriously.

"Shout it out!"

"But it's private."

"Your mistake; it isn't. Say it and bunk, or, better still, bunk without sayin' it."

"Look here, you've been kicked out of the House captaincy," said Trimble warmly. "I offered to vote for you—"

"For half-a-crown," assented Cardew. "You did, old fat bean. I'm glad I kept the half-a-crown in my pocket."

"Of course, I was going to vote out of friendship," said Trimble. "You might have lent me half-a-crown. That would have nothing to do with it, of course. But about to-morrow?"

"Ring off, and roll."

"It's more important to-morrow," said Trimble, blinking at him. "If Tom Merry gets in as junior captain of

school, where do you come in, Cardew? Now, I've got a lot of influence. You know how popular I am in both houses. Exerting my influence, I can turn the scale in favour of any candidate."

"Oh, my hat!"

"If I throw my weight into the scale, something's bound to happen," said Trimble impressively.

"If you throw your weight anywhere, something would happen, I fancy," agreed Cardew. "Somethin' like an earthquake."

"Ha, ha, ha!"

"You silly ass!" roared the fat junior. "Look here, I'm going to back you up to-morrow. I'm down on Merry, and we don't want Figgins, a New House cad, for captain. I'm your man, Cardew!"

"Thanks!"

"Pure friendship, you understand," said Trimble.

"I understand," grinned Cardew.

"Good! That's settled," said Trimble. "I—I suppose you could lend a fellow five bob?"

"Easily."

"Thanks, old man." Baggy Trimble held out a large, fat, and far from cleanly hand.

Cardew stared at it.

"Soap!" he said.

"Eh?"

"And hot water——"

"What?"

"And a scrubbin' brush, and a little Sanitas."

"You—you—you——" gasped Trimble. "You funny idiot! Are you going to lend me five bob, or are you not going to lend me five bob?"

"I'm lendin' you nothin' but a boot, old bean, and here it is!"

"Yaroooh!"

Baggy Trimble departed hurriedly from the study. He put a fat and furious face into the doorway a minute later, and roared:

"Yah! I'm going to vote for Figgins! Yah!"

Then he disappeared, narrowly escaping a-cushion that hurtled from Study No. 9.

"There's a vote gone," sighed Cardew, sinking into the armchair. "By the way, as the votin' to-morrow is sure to be close, do you fellows know whether the rules allow a candidate to vote?"

"It's allowed," said Levison, "but it's not the thing. I'm quite sure that neither Tom Merry nor Figgins will vote for himself."

"But it's permitted?"

"Oh, yes!"

"Then I think I shall vote."

"It's rotten bad form to do anything of the kind, Cardew," said Sidney Clive rather gruffly.

"Think so?"

"Don't you think so yourself?"

"That depends," yawned Cardew. "In my case, I don't think so. Anyhow, I fancy I shall vote. Now don't give me a sermon, old bean—give me the Latin dick, and let's have a dig at this rotten prep."

And prep proceeded in Study No. 9 in a rather grim silence.

CHAPTER 9.
Just Like Cardew!

"WALLY wound!" said Arthur Augustus impressively. It was Wednesday afternoon.

After dinner that day the electioneering was fast and furious. The three rival candidates preserved an attitude of lofty confidence, or, at least, indifference. But their followers canvassed for votes on all sides, and there was keen enthusiasm, and many disputes and arguments, and some punching of noses.

But even as three o'clock, the hour of the election, drew near, nobody could make a good guess at the result. All that was certain was that the voting would be close.

It was a fine afternoon, and a half-holiday, and a good many fellows were tempted out of gates, which made the result more uncertain than ever. Nobody was bound to turn up for the election if he did not choose to do so, and fellows who were not keen on it gave it a miss. The immediate followers of the three candidates were keen enough, but there were a good many indifferent, especially among fellows who had backed up Cardew last time and did not care to back him up again, and yet hesitated to turn against the fellow they had once elected.

The lecture-hall was not at all crowded by three o'clock, and it became clear that the number of abstentions would be very considerable.

"Wally wound," repeated Arthur Augustus, as Study No. 6 made their way to the lecture-room. "I say, Gwunday, are you wallyin' wound?"

Grundy of the Shell gave a snort.

"I'm standing out," he snapped. "Catch me voting for

A TERRIFIC COMBAT! The uproar in the study brought a crowd of fellows along the passage, and they stared into Study No. 9 and chortled. "Cardew's getting it!" yelled Baggy Trimble. "Serve him jolly well right for letting us all down. Go it, Grundy!" (*See page 12.*)

Tom Merry. He's told me plainly that he'll never put me in the school eleven, or the House eleven either."

"But it would be wathah wotten if he agweed to play a dud, wouldn't it, old chap?" asked Arthur Augustus innocently.

"You silly ass!"

"Weally, Gwundy——"

"And I'm rot voting for Cardew," said Grundy. "He's let me down once, and he'd do it again. And, of course, I wouldn't vote for Figgins, a New House bounder. So I'm standing out, and so are Wilkins and Gunn. I'd jolly well whop them if they voted when I stood out."

"Bai Jove!"

Grundy stalked away in lofty dignity. No candidate who refused to recognise his football claims was worthy of his support, in his opinion, and the great Grundy was determined to ignore the election. However, in spite of being ignored by the great Grundy, the election proceeded.

Kildare and Darrell of the Sixth came into the lecture-room on the stroke of three to conduct the proceedings. The captain of St. Jim's glanced over the gathering, rather surprised to note that there were so many absentees. However, that was no concern of his, and he directed the door to be closed and locked when the last stroke of three had died away.

Arthur Augustus D'Arcy jammed his celebrated eyeglass into his eye and glanced round anxiously. Tom Merry, George Figgins, and Ralph Reckness Cardew were all present, and they were duly proposed and seconded, and the two prefects proceeded to the count.

"How many fellows do you make pwesent, Blake?" whispered Arthur Augustus, who had already counted the assembly thrice with three different results.

"A hundred," said Blake, "and nearly half of them New House chaps."

"Ninety-three," said Dig.

"You mean eighty-nine," said Herries.

"Bai jove—I make it a hundwed and twenty——"

"Silence!"

"Ordah, there, you fellows—don't keep on talkin' while the count's goin' on. I feel suah, Blake, that there are ovah a hundwed——"

"Silence!"

"Weally, you know——"

"Shut up, D'Arcy!"

"Bai Jove!"

Kildare and Darrell completed their counting and compared notes. They were observed to shrug their shoulders, and the juniors gazed at them anxiously, keen to hear the result.

"Weally, you fellows, I feel quite on tentah-hooks, you know——"

"Silence!"

Kildare announced the result—a result that made the St. Jim's juniors stare.

"One hundred and twenty votes have been recorded. The voting is equally divided: Tom Merry, forty; Cardew, forty; Figgins, forty."

"Bai Jove!"

"Oh, my hat!"

There was a buzz of surprised voices. Everyone had expected the voting to be very close; but nobody had looked for this outcome. The three candidates had tied.

"Well, that beats it!" murmured Figgins to his chums.

"Rotten!" muttered Monty Lowther in Tom Merry's ear, and Tom nodded and smiled.

Cardew gave the captain of the Shell a curious glance. He stepped towards Kildare.

"I ask for a re-count," he said.

"The counting is quite correct."

"Very likely; but I believe a candidate is entitled to claim a re-count," drawled Cardew; "I claim it!"

"Very well!" said Kildare quietly. "The votes will be counted over again, you fellows."

"I twust some silly ass will change his mind and vote for Tom Mewwy," murmured Arthur Augustus.

"Yes, rather."

"Hands up for Tom Merry!" called out Kildare.

Forty right hands went up. And then, slowly, but surely, a forty-first hand was raised.

There was a gasp throughout the meeting. For the. last hand that went up was that of Ralph Reckness Cardew!

Every eye turned on Cardew.

He did not seem to observe it. He stood with his hand raised over his head, his face expressionless.

"Bai Jove! Do you see that, you fellows?" gasped Arthur Augustus.

Tom Merry stared at his rival blankly.

Kildare fixed his eyes on Cardew grimly.

"What does this mean?" he snapped.

"Candidates are allowed to vote, I understand," yawned Cardew.

"You're voting for Tom Merry?" exclaimed Kildare.

"Why not? He's a better man for the job than I am."

"Wha-a-t?"

"You're bound to count in my vote, dear man! Get on with it!"

"Well, my hat!" ejaculated Tom Merry.

In the midst of an excited buzz and some laughter the counting was completed. The result was known in advance now, but the juniors listened while the captain of the school announced it.

"Tom Merry, forty-one votes. Cardew and Figgins, forty each. Tom Merry is duly elected junior captain of St. Jim's."

"Hurrah!"

"Good old Tom Merry!"

"Well, it's all right, so long as it's not Cardew," remarked Figgins philosophically.

"Hurrah!"

Tom Merry's supporters closed round him and bore him out of the lecture-room shoulder-high in triumph amid laughter and cheers. Figgins & Co. cheerily joined in the cheering. Ralph Reckness Cardew sauntered away with his hands in his pockets, nonchalant as ever, having once more demonstrated that the only thing that was to be expected of him was the unexpected!

Tom Merry was back in his old place—junior captain of St. Jim's, and there were few fellows who were not, after all, satisfied with that result of the prolonged contest. The contest was over now—Cardew of the Fourth was no longer his rival, and evidently no longer his enemy. Cardew's amazing action had surprised all the school—Tom Merry as much as the rest; but on reflection the fellows agreed that it was just like Cardew!

THE END.

(There will be another magnificent story of Tom Merry & Co. in next week's GEM. Note the title, chums : " ERIC KILDARE'S SECRET ! " By Martin Clifford.)

My Readers' Own Corner

TUCK HAMPERS AND MONEY PRIZES AWARDED FOR WIT!

THIS WINS OUR TUCK HAMPER.

FULLY EXPLAINED !

A negro met an acquaintance, also coloured, and was surprised to see that his friend was wearing a new suit, new hat, and new shoes. "Hey, boy," he said, "how come you dressed up this way? Is you got a job?" "I'se got somethin' better'n any job," replied the other. "I'se got a profession." "What is it?" "I'se a orator." "What's a orator?" "Don't you know?" replied the resplendent one, in surprise. "Well, I'll tell you what a orator is. If you was to walk up to a ordinary man, and arsk him how much was two and two, he'd say 'four,' but if you was to ask a orator, he'd say: 'When in de course of human events it becomes necessary to take the numeral of de second denomination and add it to de figger two, I says unto you, and I says it without fear of successful contradiction, dat de result will invai'ably be four.' Dat's a orator."—A Tuck Hamper filled with delicious tuck has been awarded to Edward B. McManus, 47, Oxford Road, Waterloo, near Liverpool, Lancs.

NOT SO SIMPLE.

A schoolmaster one day asked a dunce of the class some simple questions in arithmetic. He was surprised to find that he got the correct answers, and when he had finished questioning, he turned smilingly on the boy and said: "Correct! Sit down!" The youngster did. "Now," resumed the master, addressing the same boy, "let's see if you have enough sense to ask me some questions." The boy thought for a minute, and then asked: "Please, sir, what would four yards of calico cost if cotton was twopence a reel?" "I think you take me for a fool!" angrily retorted the master. "Correct!" meekly returned the boy. "Sit down!"—Half-a-crown has been awarded to C. W. Chapman, 80, Haylings Road, Leiston, Suffolk.

HIS VERDICT !

Smith, who had been entertained by a South African magnate, in his gorgeous house, at a very poor and insufficient dinner, was asked by his host: "What do you think of my dining-room?" "Well," said Smith, surveying the auriferous deposits on the ceiling, "I should have preferred less gilding and more carvings!"—Half-a-crown has been awarded to M. Curtis, 12, Upper Conduit Street, Leicester.

MUSICIANS ALL!

"Father," said the bad boy of the family, "is an adept at blowing his own

trumpet, while mother is equally expert at harping on one string; mother-in-law has to play second fiddle, and Aunt Kate leads a humdrum existence; grandpa gives every night a solo on his nasal organ, without the stops; uncle spends his time wetting his whistle; John is fond of his pipe, and Emily is for ringing the changes on her lovers—and I'm a bit of a lyre myself."—Half-a-crown has been awarded to Cecil A. Hiscock, 440, Garratt Lane, Earlsfield, S.W. 18.

ONE TO JOHN BULL!

"Gee, that's a cute little church!" said the American, as he viewed St. Paul's. "Yes," was the reply, "that's St. Paul's!" "Very cute; but a mere cruet beside some of ours." Then they travelled to Trafalgar Square. "Gosh, what's that?" said the American, pointing to Nelson's Column. "That? Oh, that's the pepper-box to fit your cruet!" was the calm reply.—Half-a-crown has been awarded to Ernest C. Higgs, Globe Works, Clapton Park, E. 5.

A GOOD RETORT !

A woebegone tramp called at a house to ask for aid. The door was opened by a woman of angular proportions, severe in demeanour and uncertain age and temper. Having heard the object of his visit, she observed in raspy tones. "I shall not give you anything. If you had been wise you would not have come here. Do you know who I am?" The tramp replied he had not the pleasure of knowing her. "Well, I am a policeman's wife, and if he was here he would take you, and very quickly, too!" The tramp looked at her for a moment, and then said: "I believe you, ma'am. If he took you, he'd take anybody!"—Half-a-crown has been awarded to E. Furlong, 11, Bradstone Avenue, Phibsboro, Dublin, Ireland.

You will always remember "Hat-Trick" Guy—

—after you have read this topping tale.

"HAT-TRICK" GUY!

A Sensational Soccer Story

BY

ERNEST JAMES.

CHAPTER 1.

Found—A Centre-Forward !

JOHN MANNINGS, manager of Norwood Celtic Football Club, paused on his way to his office beneath the grand-stand to watch the practice taking place upon the playing-pitch.

Jeffrey Willis, Celtic's inside-left, had secured the ball which the goalkeeper had just punted down the field, and now, as John Mannings watched from behind the goal-mouth, the youngster sent in a first-time shot, guaranteed unstoppable. With a sudden herculean spring, Billy Brown endeavoured to keep his charge intact, but it was to no avail, for the spinning leather whizzed like a thing of life past his outstretched fingers, and the next moment was twirling at the back of the net.

"Good shot, Willis!" cried John Mannings, smiling pleasantly. "That's the kind to give 'em on Saturday, lad!"

Jeff Willis returned the encouraging smile, and then he was after the ball again with Charlie Bates, the outside-left, hot upon his track.

Norwood Celtic were in their first season of League football. Previously, they had figured only in amateur circles; but, with Haversham United dropping out of the League at the end of the previous campaign, the Celtic, having greater ambitions than playing friendly games for the rest of their existence, had sought, with other clubs, election to the vacant position. And the Celtic had gained their ambition, for at the League committee meeting they had been elected with thirty-two votes.

To say that such a grand old sportsman as John Mannings was delighted at the success of his club, is to put the matter mildly. He was positively jubilant, and he straightway set himself the task of strengthening the team in readiness for the opening match. Up and down the country did the manager go, but, to his consternation, he only managed to secure the services of one player of any note.

Almost at his wits' end, John Mannings sat himself down to think upon returning from a fruitless journey to Bolton. What about the boys who had been playing for the Celtic during the preceding season?

He had quite forgotten their existence in the moment of his jubilation when Celtic had gained election to the League, and had thought only of footballers with big names. That had hardly been playing fair with the fellows who had been so keen on the Celtic winning their matches when they had been mere amateurs. Success to a certain degree had now descended upon Norwood Celtic, so why not ask the old team if they would be willing to play for the club now that it had turned professional? Yes, that was the thing to do without a doubt

Accordingly, the manager had called them together, and to a man the boys had agreed to continue being members of the club. Several, of course, found it impossible to turn professionals, but they signed amateur forms nevertheless, and decided to turn out whenever they were free, if the club wanted them.

Time drew on, and with but a few days to go to the opening match of the season the Celtic experienced a bad piece of luck. Billy Thomas, their centre-forward, met with an accident whilst out on his motor-bike, and when picked up was found to have broken his leg. And so bad was the injury that the doctor had told John Mannings that it was doubtful whether Thomas would again be able to play football.

The question of who was to fill Thomas' place in the side was a hard one, and within three days of the game with Leaminster Rovers it had not been settled. Thomas, it had definitely been stated, would not be able to play again for at least a year. Of the three reserves Celtic boasted, one was a goalkeeper, and the other two half-backs. In their respective positions all three were good and capable players. But as centre-forward not good enough. Each had had a trial, but had proved not worth persevering with.

However, such was the unhappy state of affairs that it seemed that one of the three would have to be included in the side to meet the Rovers. Who that one would be had yet to be settled, and the committee had decided to leave the selection of the team until the morning of the match. Not that they held out hopes that John Mannings would, in the meantime, be successful in securing a centre-forward elsewhere. As a matter of fact, that possibility did not even enter their minds.

As Billy Brown flung himself full length across the goalmouth and turned a shot from Charlie Bates neatly round the post, John Mannings came out of a deep reverie, and, with a helpless shrug

of his shoulders, proceeded on his way. John had been thinking of the centre-forward berth again. Who was to fill it? That question was continually recurring in his brain.

Reaching the aperture beneath the grand-stand, the manager almost collided with Sam Jackson, the trainer, who was just coming out to the ground.

"Good-morning, Mr. Mannings!" said Sam respectfully. "There was a phone call for you about a couple of minutes ago. Your son, I——"

"My son!" exclaimed John Mannings. "Ah, yes, of course!"

For the moment the manager had quite forgotten that his son, Guy, was due home that day.

Guy was the elder of John Mannings' two boys, and his school career at Claremont was now finished. He had, however, several reasons for not wishing to leave Claremont, the chief being that Philip, his younger brother, remained behind. Between Guy and Phil there had existed at school a strong brotherly love, and it was therefore only natural that they did not wish to part. But part they had to, nevertheless.

"Did he say where he was ringing up from, Sam?" asked the manager, breaking a short silence.

An eager look had come into John Mannings' steel-grey eyes as he asked the question. And the manager's change of visage was brought about by a great inspiration which had suddenly come to him.

"Yes, Mr. Mannings," replied Sam Jackson. "He said——"

"Yes, yes! Where, man—where?" interrupted the manager excitedly.

"From home and——"

But John Mannings was gone. Without waiting to hear what else the trainer had to say, he had darted through the door beneath the grand-stand. And as, after tapping his forehead significantly, Sam Jackson strolled across the pitch to where the players were still at practice, the manager was already in his office, with the telephone receiver jammed to his ear.

Impatiently John Mannings waited for the operator to put him through to his home. The proposition, brought about by the sudden happy thought which had struck him, that he wished to put to his son, Guy, could not be delayed a minute. Therefore, it can easily be understood that, after several seconds had elapsed and he had not got through to his number, he began to stamp his foot quite angrily upon the floor.

A voice came suddenly over the wire. John Mannings recognised it immediately as belonging to George Wright, his manservant.

"Mr. Mannings speaking," he said into the transmitter. "Is Master Guy there? No! Then where the dickens is——"

"Hallo, dad!"

John Mannings let go of the telephone receiver as if it had suddenly become red-hot, and, springing to his feet, he dashed across the room. Standing just inside the door, which had opened noiselessly, was his son Guy, an expansive smile upon his handsome, clean-cut features.

In his excitement at seeing the youngster again, John Mannings almost knocked him over as he rushed up to him.

"Steady, dad!" said Guy, laughing, catching hold of his father's arm to save him from falling. "Anybody would think you hadn't seen me for years. Why, I was only home on holiday a couple of months ago."

Gasping for breath, and, consequently, unable to speak coherently for a while, the manager of Norwood Celtic Football Club led his son over to his desk, and, to Guy's surprise, forced him into the saddlebag armchair.

"What's the game, dad?" asked Guy, thinking that his father had suddenly taken leave of his senses.

By this time John Mannings had sufficiently recovered his breath to speak clearly.

"The game, my boy," he replied, opening a drawer and taking out a printed form, "is this. You sign here!"

He placed the form in front of Guy, and jabbed a finger on a blank space which had obviously been left for a signature.

Wondering, Guy Mannings glanced down at the sheet of paper before him, and as he read the words thereon his bright blue eyes opened wide in amazement. Quickly he looked up into his father's smiling face.

"Dad, what—what—what are you getting at?" he stuttered.

"I'm getting at nothing, my lad," returned his father. "What I am trying to get, however, is your signature to that form."

"But—but——"

"Now don't start arguing, Guy!" said John Mannings severely. "Time's precious. Probably it would be best for me to explain to you what I am after."

"Perhaps so," murmured Guy faintly.

"It's like this, son," continued the manager of Norwood Celtic, "we play a League match, as no doubt you are aware, on Saturday. The team will consist of all last season's players, with the exception of an outside-left named Charlie Bates. Bates, by the way, was secured from Burbridge Albion. But—and here is the trouble—we haven't a centre-forward——"

"And you want me to fill the breach?" interrupted Guy eagerly, now that he was beginning to understand what his father was driving at.

"Precisely," said his father, with a smile. "Billy Thomas would have led the side on Saturday, but for the fact that he broke a leg a few weeks ago and left us stranded. Not one of our reserves is a centre-forward, although we should have been compelled to have included one against Leaminster Rovers, if we did not find a man to take Thomas's place in the meantime. Now, you see how things stand, and I hope you will sign as an

amateur and play for the club. It will mean hustling to get your papers through in time for you to play on Saturday, so get a move on, Master 'Hat Trick' Guy!"

Guy smiled at mention of his nickname. At Claremont he had been football captain and centre-forward of the first eleven. And he had earned himself the nickname "Hat Trick" Guy, and this on account of the happy knack he had of scoring three or more goals in a match. Without a doubt, it had been Guy's prolific goal-scoring that had won for Claremont the Public Schools' Championship three years in succession.

Guy picked up a pen from his father's desk and dipped it in the inkwell.

"I'm on if you think me good enough, dad," he said cheerily.

"Good enough!" retorted John Mannings. "I should think you are! It's certain that I would not have wasted my time in explaining to you all the club's trouble if I thought otherwise. I don't believe in favouritism, son or no son. You can play footer with the best of 'em, and I expect you to have a lot to do in realising my ambition. That ambition, my lad, is to see the Celtic finish well up in this its first season in the League. And there's something else. We have got to win next Saturday's match, so see that you are in fine trim, and have your shooting boots with you. Now sign, Guy, please!"

With a flourish Guy applied his signature to the form. He handed it to his father, who folded it and carefully stowed it in an inside pocket.

"And now, Guy," said the manager of Norwood Celtic, clasping the youngster's hand, "you ask Sam Jackson, the trainer, to rig you out with some togs, and get in some practice with the boys at once. You'll find them out on the pitch. Meanwhile, I'm off to get your papers through so that you will be able to show Leaminster what you are made of on Saturday."

Thus it came about that Norwood Celtic discovered a centre-forward at the eleventh hour. And with the signing on of "Hat Trick" Guy it seemed that the club's troubles were at an end.

CHAPTER 2.
Blackmail !

"THE beastly cad!"

Guy Mannings' face flushed angrily, and, clenching his teeth, he crushed the letter which he had been reading tightly in his hand.

It was the eve of the big match, and Guy, when he had come down to breakfast, had heard from his father that his papers had come through from the League. Besides the news that he was now eligible to play for Norwood Celtic, John Mannings told his son that already the newspapers were remarking upon the great capture the club had made in obtaining his services.

Guy had read a copy of "Town Sport" himself, and had been amused by the glowing account given therein of his prowess when at Claremont. Reference was also made to his nickname and how he had earned it.

After a hearty meal, Guy, as happy as the proverbial sandboy, had proceeded to the library in his home, and, taking up a book, had settled himself in a comfortable armchair to read. But he had not been there for more than five minutes when his peace of mind was disturbed. George Wright, his father's manservant, entered with a letter addressed to him. Wondering, the youngster opened the

envelope and glanced hurriedly at the message contained therein, and immediately his high spirits vanished, leaving him perfectly wretched. The note, of a distressing nature to Guy, came from Kebble, a village near Claremont, the youngster's old school, and ran:

"Dear Sir,—I should like to see you on business at twelve o'clock to-day. Meet me outside of the post-office in East Norwood. Of course, I have no need to mention the steps I shall take if you do not come along.

"Yours faithfully,
"MIKE HUNT."

Guy groaned as he realised all that the letter meant, and for the moment he felt that if he had his brother Phil within distance he would kick him hard for having been such a silly young ass when he had first come to Claremont.

Guy well remembered how Phil had got into the scrape which had involved him as well. He remembered, too, the man Mike Hunt, a bookmaker of disrepute, who did business with Percy Cavendish & Co., the "smart set" at the school. Unfortunately, Phil had been taken up by Cavendish and his cronies directly he had set foot within the precincts of Claremont, and before Guy could step in the damage was done.

Cavendish had put Phil wise to a way of making money easily, and that way was to wager on horse-racing. The youngster received the tip to put "all he had" on Rocky Tops in the Dishem Stakes, and when he protested against gambling he was told he wasn't a sport.

Now, Phil rather prided himself on being a sportsman, and had then informed Cavendish & Co. that he only had a shilling to his name. Immediately the difficulty was got over. The young rascals had said that their bookmaker only ran credit accounts, and so it came about that Phil had written out a wager putting five pounds on Rocky Tops.

The sequel had followed quickly. Rocky Tops lost its race, and when Mike Hunt, who was the bookmaker, applied for his money, Phil hadn't got it to pay up. Several weeks passed, and Hunt threatened to expose Phil to his headmaster if he didn't pay in a few days. Scared, and at his wits' ends, the youngster had approached Cavendish & Co. and asked them to lend him the money. But the "smart set," laughing gleefully at Phil's awkward predicament, had refused. Phil then told his wretched story to his brother; and Guy, after giving him a lecture, went all haste to Mike Hunt's house in the village. By promising to pay within three months, Guy, by giving the bookmaker an I O U for the amount owing to him by his brother, managed to extract from the man the slip on which Phil had made his wager on Rocky Tops.

It was a splendid piece of self-sacrifice that Guy had made, for he had taken the burden off his brother's shoulders and had placed it upon his own instead.

Yes, Guy remembered it all. And the three months' grace which he had succeeded in obtaining from Hunt was up to-day.

Where was he to get the money from to pay the man?

Guy had only ten shillings in his possession. He knew that it was useless to approach his father and inform him that he was in the debt of a bookmaker. Being somewhat of a martinet, and having such a great affection for his sons, Guy knew that the old sportsman would be broken-hearted if he learned that he had incurred a racing debt. Neither could Guy explain to his father that the•

debt was in reality his brother's. No, he decided to keep the whole affair a secret, if he could, for he realised that if he did tell his father, as likely as not he would disown him for having disgraced the family name.

What could he do? Guy sat and thought the matter out, but he could not get any nearer to solving the problem.

Suddenly he started. The clock on the mantelpiece was striking the hour of eleven. He had been sitting in the library ever since ten minutes past nine, and at twelve o'clock he was due to meet Mike Hunt.

Wretchedly Guy got to his feet, and, passing out of the room, made his way downstairs to the hall. Reaching for his cap, he opened the front door, and, banging it after him, he quickly gained the

"But you can't!" cried Guy, clenching his fists. "He doesn't owe you a penny. It is I who am in your debt, and you know it, you rascal!"

Mike Hunt grinned.

"That may be," he said. "But you can't deny the fact that you have taken the debt off your brother's shoulders."

Guy was silent. True he could not deny that fact. If he were asked whether the debt were his or really his younger brother's, he could only admit that it was Phil's.

"So you have nothing to say to that, eh?" grinned Hunt. "Still, what I want to know is whether you have my money?"

Guy shook his head.

"Then," said the bookmaker in bullying tones, "I shall report your brother

Without a word, Guy followed the man until at length he passed into the park and sat down on a seat. There was no one in sight, and Mike Hunt was satisfied. He rolled himself a cigarette and lighted it, and then turned to Guy, who had seated himself next to him.

"Now, Mister Mannings," he said, in an oily tone, "I have heard that you are playing for Norwood Celtic on Saturday."

Guy started. The proposition had something to do with the Norwood Celtic—Leaminster Rovers match. He had half suspected as much.

"Well," continued Mike Hunt, in the same oily strain, "you have got to play the worst game of your life. You've got to do your best to let the side down. None of the 'hat-trick' business—

Endeavouring to avoid collision with the Rovers' left-back, Guy tripped over a piece of turf and pitched headlong to the ground. As he fell his fist met the ball and sent it goalwards. "Hands!" roared the crowd.

road. With dragging footsteps the youngster made off in the direction of the post-office. In ordinary circumstances he could have done the distance well inside forty minutes, but when at last he did reach his destination it wanted but a few minutes to twelve.

Mike Hunt was awaiting him already, and the bookmaker grinned evilly when he saw Guy approaching with downcast face.

"So you've come, young feller-me-lad," he said, as Guy came level with him.

Guy gave a start, for as yet he had not seen the man.

"Yes," he said quietly, looking up into the man's coarse features.

"Well, you know what I'm after," said Mike Hunt, with a sneer. "Suppose you thought you could get away with it when you left the school. Not so, my young buck. I am here to collect the dibs, otherwise I'm going to see the headmaster of Claremont and inform him that your brother is the one really in my debt——"

to Dr. Dennis unless you agree to a proposition I am going to put to you."

Guy looked sharply at Mike Hunt. That the man was an unscrupulous rascal and always ready to do anything to gain his own ends, he knew. At Claremont, Guy had heard of several underhand schemes which Hunt had participated in and which, had they come to the notice of the police, would have landed him in gaol. And the youngster was quite sure that the proposition which the bookmaker was now going to put to him, was of a shady nature.

Guy was on the alert. But he decided to hear what it was all about, for he knew that Hunt's threat to expose his brother was no idle one.

"And what is the proposition, Mr. Hunt?" asked Guy quietly.

Mike Hunt looked about him. The post-office was situated in a side street in the town, but for all that, quite a good number of people passed to and fro.

"We'll walk along the road a bit," said the bookmaker meaningly. "Better to discuss business in a nice quiet spot."

savvy? If the Celtic win, I go straight to Dr. Dennis. If they lose, I'll give you back your I O U and cry quits. Is it a deal?"

For a moment Guy felt as though he would rush straight at the rascal and hit out right and left. The rascally proposal made the youngster see red, and his fist clenched tightly. But it was only for the fraction of a second that the bookmaker was in any danger from the boy. Suddenly the colour ebbed from Guy Mannings' face, leaving him pale to the lips. He shrugged his shoulders helplessly. His position was all the more awkward by reason of the fact that his father expected him to play the game of his life against Leaminster Rovers. Yet, how could he do his best for the side when his brother was in danger of being disgraced if the Celtic should win? He must save Phil whatever the cost.

Probably he could get out of playing in the match on Saturday. But that, he realised, was impossible, for his father would want to know what was wrong,

THE GEM LIBRARY.—No. 831.

and to plead that he was ill was an absurd excuse to make.

"Is it a deal?" repeated Mike Hunt, as he impatiently watched the working of Guy's face.

Guy's mind was made up in an instant then. He had again determined to make a sacrifice for his brother's sake.

"I'll do as you wish," muttered the youngster, between dry lips.

Mike Hunt grinned with evil satisfaction.

"Thought you would, my lad," he said lightly.

"And about the I O U?" asked Guy eagerly.

"I'll send it to you directly the Celtic have lost," replied the bookmaker.

And without another word he rose to his feet and strode away in the best of spirits. By offering long odds against Norwood Celtic winning their match with Leaminster Rovers, the rascally bookmaker had hopes of receiving quite a number of wagers backing the home club—wagers which would be losing ones now that he had bribed "Hat-Trick" Guy to play it low. Guy watched Mike Hunt out of sight. Sick at heart, the youngster surveyed his unenviable position. To save his brother, he would be letting his father down. But then he would be saving his father's son. Guy smiled faintly as he thought of that. But his mind was made up. On Saturday against Leaminster Rovers he would play the worst game of his career—muff passes, put in weak shots at goal, and do everything he could which would have a lot to do with the letting down of his side. And all this for his brother's sake.

CHAPTER 3.
The Match!

"AND now for a really ripping game of footer—I don't think!"

Guy Mannings flung his football rig into his gladstone bag, and, with a grunt, crossed over to his bed-room window.

Gazing out across the fields, he could just see the well-appointed football ground of the Norwood Celtic Club, and the crowds of Soccer enthusiasts flocking in at the different turnstiles to witness the match with Leaminster Rovers.

It wanted but half an hour to kick-off, and Guy was apparently in no great hurry to get up to the ground for the game. As a matter of fact, he didn't really wish to go at all.

After his father had departed earlier in the morning, the youngster had retired to his bed-room and had been there ever since, thinking of the hopeless position in which he was placed. But although he would have liked to have been able to do his best to help the Celtic win the game against Leaminster and thus realise his father's ambition, Guy felt that at all costs he must save his brother Phil from disgrace. His decision was made up. He had agreed with Mike Hunt to play the worst game of his career against the Rovers, and he was going to do so for his brother's sake.

At last Guy turned from the window, and, picking up his bag, he went downstairs to the hall. Reaching for his cap, he quickly left the house and made his way towards the football ground.

Down one street, then along another he strode, but without noticing the passers-by. Once a friend hailed him, but he proceeded on his way without heeding the cheery greeting.

"Hallo, Guy!"

The youngster had reached the players' entrance to the football ground, THE GEM LIBRARY.—No. 831.

and was about to pass through the gate when a hand was laid upon his shoulder. With a start he swung round and faced the beautiful girl who had accosted him.

"Er—good-morning, Miss Summers!"

Guy flushed to the roots of his hair, and raised his cap awkwardly. The girl looked surprised, but gave him a pleasant smile nevertheless.

Miss Summers, daughter of the chairman of the Norwood Celtic Football Club, took a big interest in the great winter game, and, whenever she found it possible, she attended the matches played on Manor Field. And, of course, it was natural that she always looked forward to seeing Norwood Celtic emerge from their games victorious.

"So you are playing for the club, Guy?" said the young lady, with a touch of satisfaction in her voice.

"Yes," answered Guy quietly.

"Then we shall win this afternoon, for sure," continued Miss Summers lightly. "And I shall expect you to have a lot to do with the victory, Guy. Don't forget that nickname of yours. Live up to it, won't you?"

"If I—I—I can," said Guy, with a wry smile.

Sylvia Summers looked eagerly at her friend. She had known Guy for years, and he had always appeared to her to be a light-hearted boy, with not a care in the world. But now, it seemed to Sylvia, that there was something radically wrong with the youngster—that he had a heavy burden upon his shoulders.

"Is there anything the matter with you, Guy?" she asked, with concern.

Guy Mannings flushed again.

"Oh, no!" he said hastily. "Nothing at all. I'm feeling a bit nervy. Most young chaps suffer from nerves when they are going to play in their first big football match, you know."

Miss Summers smiled. Guy's reply satisfied her, for she had heard that nearly every footballer is a victim to "stage-fright" in his initial game with a big club.

"Well, you'll soon get over the nerve trouble, Guy, once you get going," said Miss Summers. "And than, don't forget that I shall expect to see you scoring goals every other minute. Cheerio!"

And, without giving Guy time to answer, she proceeded on her way.

With a deep sigh, Guy Mannings passed into the ground en route for the dressing-rooms beneath the grand-stand. To deliberately play a bad game and let his side down was all the more revolting to him now that Miss Summers expected him to help Norwood Celtic to victory against Leaminster Rovers. Still, he mused, as he changed into his football rig some minutes later, he must save Phil from the hands of Mike Hunt if he could, and the only way he could do that was by letting the Celtic down. That he——

"Ready, boys?" asked Reg Parsons, the captain of Norwood Celtic, picking up a practice ball and glancing round the dressing-room.

There was a chorus of assent from the players, and as they followed Reg Parsons through the door leading out on to the playing pitch, Guy Mannings came out of his reverie and quickly brought up the rear.

"Here they are!"

"Come along, my bonnie boys!"

"Where's 'Hat-Trick' Guy?"

Norwood Celtic's ground was packed to its fullest capacity, and as the crowd caught sight of the home team's colours emerging from the aperture beneath the grand-stand, a terrific roar split the heavens. Then, to add to the hideous din, came a salvo from bells and rattles.

Drowned by the cataclysm of noise, the band out in the centre of the playing pitch ceased abruptly, and the musicians beat a hasty retreat.

With long, springy strides, Billy Brown made tracks for one of the goals, and no sooner did he place himself between the sticks than Charlie Bates sent in a long ground shot which beat him all ends up.

"That's the idea, boy!"

"Where did that one go to, Billy?"

The crowd voiced its appreciation of Bates' magnificent shot in no uncertain fashion. As yet the football "Fans" were not sure who was who of the two new members of the Celtic team, but whether the ball had been put into the goal by Bates, the new outside-left, or by "Hat-Trick" Guy did not matter overmuch to them, anyway. What they did care, however, was that it had been put there by one of the new recruits, and it was obvious that he could shoot with effect.

Meanwhile, Billy Brown had picked the ball out of the net, and there was a comical expression upon his handsome clean-cut features as he sent it out to where Guy Mannings, spick and span in his trim black-and-white striped jersey and white knickers, was standing eager for a chance to have a pot at goal.

As the leather came to him Guy trapped it neatly, and pushing it forward a yard or so he let fly.

Boomph!

The ball whizzed through the air with the speed of an express train, and it made straight for the left-hand top corner of the net. Billy Brown, with a "do or die" expression upon his face, made a strenuous leap sideways, but his outstretched fingers touched nothing more solid than air.

"Goal!"

"'Ware the sharpshooters!"

The terrific yell announced to the bewildered Billy Brown that he had been beaten for the second time that afternoon, and the youngster felt like kicking himself for his sorry display. But although he had had his charge penetrated so easily on each occasion, Billy Brown quickly realised that no matter who the goalie, those two shots would have taken a bit of stopping.

"Here come the Rovers!"

"Hurrah!"

In spite of the fact that the Rovers' supporters were outnumbered by at least three to one, the roar which greeted the visitors was no half-hearted one. The vocal explosion and the terrific din of bells and rattles must have been heard for miles around, but no sooner did the referee and linesmen put in an appearance than the sound ceased with startling abruptness, and every pair of eyes was turned upon the centre of the playing pitch to witness the toss for choice of ends.

In answer to the referee's summons upon his whistle, the rival skippers trotted to the middle of the pitch. The trio gripped palms, and then up went the coin. John Smith, the visiting captain, guessed correctly, and he set Reg Parsons and his men to face what little wind was blowing across the ground. This necessitated a change of ends, but Mr. Jennings, the referee, did not waste any further time once the players were in position.

Pheep!

Guy Mannings touched the ball to Jeff Wilson on his left, and Jeff, in his turn, transferred the leather to Charlie Bates on the wing.

"Now then, the Celtic, let's have one for a start!"

"Set 'em alight, my bonnie boys!"

A frenzied yell went up on all sides as Charlie Bates, with the leather literally glued to his toe, dodged first one and then another of his opponents on his dash to the corner flag. But the fleet little winger did not like the look of the Rovers' giant of a right-back who suddenly took an interest in things, and came thundering across the turf to intercept him. With a quick glance to his right, Bates saw that Guy Mannings was well positioned to receive the ball, and, as the opposing back bore down upon him, he sent in his centre as straight as a die to where the young centre-forward was standing.

As Guy trapped the leather and set off for goal, the Rovers' centre-half-back dashed after him with a determined expression upon his rugged features. But Guy could move when he liked, and he had little difficulty in shaking off his pursuer. He was in the penalty area now, and it looked as though it was any odds on him scoring a goal when, in endeavouring to avoid collision with the Rovers' left-back who suddenly made his appearance, he tripped over a piece of turf and pitched headlong to the ground. As he fell the youngster's arm shot out straight before him and his fist came in contact with the ball, sending it hurtling goalwards.

"Hands!" roared the crowd, and the referee's whistle shrilled.

"Hard luck, 'Hat-Trick'!"

The visitors' goalkeeper grinned as the ball trickled into the net from Guy Mannings' fist. Bill Turner had not troubled to keep the leather out once the whistle had gone for hands, for he did not mind allowing the ball to pass him when it didn't mean a goal for the opposing side.

A trifle dazed, Guy staggered to his feet, and as he retreated down the field for the free kick against him he determined that next time there would be a different tale to tell.

With a hefty kick, Peter Fleming sent the ball hurtling into the home side's territory, where the Rovers' inside-right fastened on to it like lightning and made a dash for goal. But Arthur Cummings was not destined to cover much ground on this occasion. He suddenly found himself confronted by Celtic's left-half who, with almost comparative ease, took the ball from his toe and sent it across to "Tiny" Phelps, the home side's outside-right.

To the accompaniment of a terrific yell from the Celtic's supporters, "Tiny" Phelps, with the leather under perfect control, made off down the touch-line with a speed worthy of a sprint champion. Reaching the corner flag, he steadied himself for a centre. Then, describing an arc, the ball came whizzing into the Rovers' goalmouth, where half a dozen players made a concerted leap to get their heads to it.

"In with it, 'Hat-trick'!"

"Now then, my bonnie boys!"

"Goal!"

Jumping higher than the rest, "Hat-trick" Guy managed to bring his tousled head into contact with the ball and to turn it into the net well out of the reach of Bill Turner's outstretched fingers.

As he trotted back to the centre of the pitch Guy smiled with satisfaction as he heard his name shouted on all sides. But the youngster did not forget to realise that he owed "Tiny" Phelps a great deal for that, his initial goal for Norwood Celtic.

From the moment of the resumption of the game Leaminster Rovers attacked hotly, to get on level terms; but they might as well have been up against a brick wall as to endeavour to get through the rock-like defence put up by

The ball came whizzing into the Rovers' goalmouth where half a dozen players made a concerted leap to get their heads to it. Jumping higher than the rest, "Hat-Trick" Guy met the ball with his tousled head and directed it into the net, well out of the goalie's reach.

Billy Brown and the Celtic's two brilliant backs. Anyhow, the interval arrived with Norwood Celtic still holding on to their one-goal lead.

But after the few minutes' intermission, so determined was the Rovers' attack that the Celtic defence wavered, and Arthur Cummings, seizing a grand opportunity, equalised with a rasping ground-shot which beat Billy Brown all the way.

Heartened by their goal and the encouraging shouts from their supporters, the Rovers were quickly into the picture again. Straight from the kick-off Arthur Cummings secured possession, and with a delightful solo run he got the ball to within a dozen yards of the Celtic's goal-mouth. Without hesitation the inside-right sent in a scorcher, and Billy Brown did well to tip the flying leather over the bar.

From the corner-kick the game took a sudden change in favour of the home side. As the leather soared into the goalmouth Billy Brown made a determined spring. His fists caught the ball a resounding thwack, and away it went up the field to where Guy Mannings was standing on the alert. Unmarked, and with only the Rovers' two backs between him and the goal, Guy was off like a flash, and so fast was he that he was through them before they realised what was happening.

Boomph!

As straight as a die Guy sent the ball for the left-hand side of the net, and although Bill Turner flung himself full length across his charge, he was beaten hopelessly. As a matter of fact, he was a second too late, and before he had made his herculean effort the leather was already in the net.

"Played, my lad!"

"We want the hat-trick now! What about it!"

And the hat-trick the enthusiastic "fans" had, for shortly afterwards Bill Turner found himself suddenly called upon to intercept a centre from Charlie Bates. The ball came flashing in towards the goal-mouth, and, at the same time as Turner leaped, Guy Mannings did the same.

Crash!

The two collided, and the next moment they found themselves on all fours at the back of the net, with the ball twirling dizzily beside them.

"Well played, Mannings!"

"Good old 'Hat-trick'!"

The thunderous cheer which rent the air as the referee pointed to the middle of the pitch was the loudest ever heard upon the Celtic's ground. Pandemonium seemed suddenly to have been let loose, and the barbaric sound did not cease right up to the final whistle, when the home side retired victorious by three goals to one. The hero of the hour was, of course, Guy Mannings, who had lived up to his nickname. But once in the dressing-room the youngster felt a sudden icy chill creep over him.

Instead of letting his side down, he had from the first whistle entered into the game heart and soul, and had been responsible for his side's victory. He had quite forgotten Mike Hunt's proposition and his brother's awkward predicament in his excitement, and now he knew that Phil was in grave danger of being expelled from Claremont.

Sick at heart, Guy finished changing, and then went along to his father's office,

(*Continued on page* 28.)

Although driven to the wall by the bullying Stoniky Burr—

—Tom Gale stands up for himself as stoutly as ever.

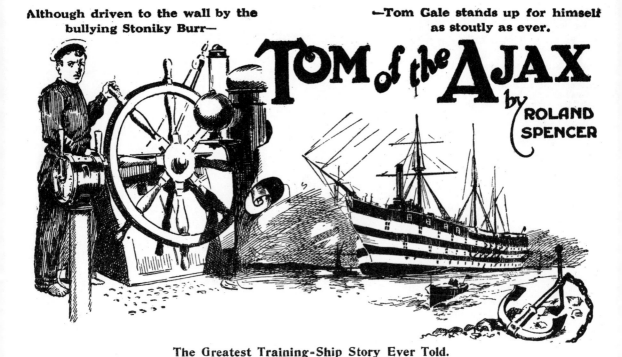

TOM of the AJAX
by ROLAND SPENCER

The Greatest Training-Ship Story Ever Told.

Gale's Ajax.

THE usual first early morning sounds on the decks of the Ajax the hurrying feet of the bugler on duty—broke the stillness of the dark morning, and terminated with the blaring call to all that it was time to get up.

The boys tumbled out of their hammocks promptly, for the Ajax was a strict ship, and often an officer followed up the bugle-call pretty closely.

Dicky West was out of his hammock like a sackful of coals tumbling into a cellar. The red-headed young Hood jerked at Tom's hammock.

"Show a leg, Tom! Up you get, if you don't want to be tipped out!"

Tom rolled sideways, capsizing his hammock, and was soon dressing with the rest.

"How goes it this merry morn, Tom?" asked Dicky. "Not like you to stick asleep with the bugle bellowing in your ears. Been dreaming of those chaps who attacked you in Black Dell Lane yesterday, or what?"

"P'r'aps so," admitted Tom. "I wish I knew a bit more about that rum business. But I feel as fit as a fiddle, anyway, for my two days' holiday. Wish I was still on the Breadwinner!"

"Well, buck up, old chap, or you'll be last dressed. Nice thing for a chief P.O., that!"

As the training-ship boys dressed they threw off their sleepiness. The chatter became louder, until the orlop deck sounded like a monkey-house. Boys began to lark about as they waited for chums to get ready to go up to the upper deck to the wash-house.

Before long, over two hundred bright and shining faces were waiting impatiently at the mess-tables on the lower deck for the Hot Dick and toke—porridge and bread in training-ship slang—to be served out.

Breakfast over, Tom Gale, Dicky West, and a few other mowers of the Hoods, ran off to prepare for their

attendance in the class-room of the navigation class. Mr. Cosine was the officer-instructor of navigation, and the navigation class was the only school work which Tom and his class-mates attended. Having passed successfully through the standards, and having chosen the Mercantile Marine as a career, they were being versed in the use of ships' instruments, logarithms, the heavenly bodies, and the hundred-and-one other things necessary in the training of a merchant ship's mate.

Though Tom was keen on the work, the officer-instructors were well aware that there was a bit of reckless devilry in the youngster. No one was more aware of this than Mr. Cosine. Though Tom never stooped to anything underhand in the way of japes, he seldom lost an opportunity of raising a laugh in class.

"Remember all that stuff about Mercator's charts?" asked Dicky, as the two chums walked along the corridor towards the class-room. "Old Cosine will be hot

WHAT HAS GONE BEFORE!

TOM GALE, a sturdily-built youth and chief petty officer of the starboard watch aboard the famous old training-ship Ajax, which is moored near the southern bank of the River Thames, a quarter of a mile down the river from Fleethithe, falls foul of

STONIKY BURR, C.P.O. of the port watch, a bully of the first water.

DICKY WEST is a cheerful ginger-headed youth and a staunch chum of Gale's.

Trouble arises when Tom Gale is detailed, together with Stoniky Burr, as a hare in a cross-country hare-and-hounds that is to take place. Hot words and a fight follow, and Burr is thrashed and left. It is then that a mysterious, sinister man in green spectacles approaches Burr. He gives his name as KALCHE, and he enlists the aid of Burr in a plot against Tom Gale, without, however, giving any reason for this.

Later, when on the yardarm, sixty feet above the water, Burr tries to force Tom off, but he himself is precipitated into the water and is rescued by Tom, although the latter realises that Burr's attempt was deliberate.

Tom is puzzling the whole thing out in his hammock at night, when he is startled by a rending crash, and he feels the Ajax quiver from stem to stern. The next moment he utters a startled cry as a jagged hole appears in the ship's side, torn like paper by the stem of a huge red-rusty steamer which crashes into the Ajax. In the ensuing melee a pair of hands grip at Tom's throat, and he recognises the face of Burr. Before Tom can recover he is sent hurtling off the ship into the water. He escapes, however, and is returning to the ship when he is waylaid by Kalche. His cries for help are answered, and a crowd of the Ajax boys rush to the rescue.

Tom then resolves to keep his eyes wide open for any further trouble from Kalche.

(Now read on.)

on it to-day. He's going to fire questions at us, and we've got to answer 'em, you'll remember."

"Gee-whiz—yes!" exclaimed Tom. "I'd forgotten that. What with falling out of that hole in the orlop deck when we were rammed, and having a nice, comfy night on a gas-buoy—well, I've not been able to think of things like charts!"

The chums clattered into the class-room, where a chattering babel of voices heralded the fact that work was due to begin. Tom and Dicky took their seats, and entered with gusto into the paper-pellet battle that spread to their corner on their arrival. Stoniky Burr, who was also a member of the class, was on "snags" duty at the door—that is, he was keeping cave.

Mr. Cosine was late, and Tom, always ready for a lark, left his seat, and walked over to the blackboard that was let into the bulkhead opposite the boys' desks.

"Chaps," he began, bowing to the class, "the lightning artist will now portray the noble figurehead of our ship—Ajax, the warrior."

With that, young Gale, who was clever with the pencil, chalked a very clever likeness of Ajax, with javelin upraised. The youngster, encouraged by the yells of delight from his class-mates, dashed a huge pipe between the thick lips of the figure, substituted a rakish-looking, though rather battered "topper" for the helmet, and finally added a few straight lines radiating from the noble Grecian nose of the hero. Altogether, it looked as though Ajax had not yet recovered from the effects of a night ashore. The nose Tom had given him was obviously a fiery red, apparently the effects of rather more drink than was good for the ancient Greek.

Under this work of art Tom scrawled:

"AJAX ON THE SPREE!"

The boys rolled in their seats, yelling with delight. But suddenly the class-room was plunged into silence by Stoniky Burr at the doorway. The bully of the Ajax hissed out "Snags!" and scuttled to his seat, where he bowed his head over his exercise-book like the rest.

Tom seized the duster, but, to his horror and surprise, Mr. Cosine stepped into the room before he could apply the cloth to the board. Burr must have waited till the master was close to the doorway before giving his warning.

Tom was caught red-handed!

The Challenge!

MR. COSINE gazed at the blackboard as though he had seen a ghost. Then he turned a frigid stare on Tom.

"Gale!" rasped the tall, severe-looking navigation master, his keen, steely eyes flashing from the youngster to the board. "Gale, I needn't ask if this work of genius is yours. You may think it extremely funny, but to my mind it is a joke that is in the worst of taste. That noble figurehead of the bows of this ship, scarred with the shot of Trafalgar as it is, is something of which you should be proud. You evidently regard it simply as a butt for low jokes. You will write out for me five hundred times, 'Ajax defended the ships.' Bring the lines to me to-morrow. Now erase every trace of your—er—art, and get back to your place!"

Tom rubbed away lustily at the blackboard, and returned to his seat by Dicky West. There was a low chuckle from Burr. He and his chum Hemming were grinning hard.

The questions regarding charts on Mercator's projections were then fired at the class. The boys did well, and Mr. Cosine became almost genial. He expanded like a flower in spring as he talked of hemispheres, true and magnetic charts, the meaning of the numbers dotted over the faces of the charts. He touched on the "station painter," and a description of this simple instrument for finding the ship's position from three visible points of land in coastwise navigation. When at last he came to an end he was almost purring.

Once free of the class-room, Tom laid a heavy hand on Stoniky Burr's shoulder as the big, loose-limbed fellow tried to slip away to the orlop deck ahead of the rest.

Tom swung the bully round to face him.

"What's the game, Stoniky?" cried Tom. "What was the idea—eh?—waiting till Mr. Cosine was close before saying 'snags'? It was to land me in for it, of course. You're no better than a peach, you rotter!"

"I didn't see him!" snarled Burr. "I—I was watching your drawing."

"Now you're coal-bunking!" snapped Tom. "A chap on snags duty can't see and hear if an officer enters the corridor a long way down. If you'd not been a cad, you'd have warned me in time to rub out that drawing. As it is, you've landed me for lines, and I've a thumping good mind to have you out for it. But you're hardly worth it, Stoniky."

"Have me out if you like!" snarled Burr. "I'm not afraid of you, Gale! It's a bodge-up saying I knew Cosine was coming. You're saying it to turn the other chaps against me. You're always doing that!"

"Oh, rot!" cut in Dicky West. "Think the chaps don't know well enough that you knew old Cosine was near? Still, it's the sort of thing we expect from you. Even the chaps in your own division know the rotter you are!"

"They don't say so, anyway!" cried Burr, clenching his fists, and glancing with angry eyes at the group of Blakes that stood near by. They were all smaller boys, and they dropped their eyes. Burr glared triumphantly at Dick and Tom.

"No, they don't say so!" agreed Tom, with a dry laugh. "More shame to them for thinking what they won't say out loud!"

Tom swung on his heel, and he and Dicky strode off, leaving the Blakes round their bullying leader. But boys of other divisions still carried on with the good work of slating Burr.

After dinner, the mowers, who had finished with the ordinary school work of the ship, and were attending either the navigation or the advanced Navy class, had training of a practical kind to carry out. Sometimes this was rope-work, gun-practice with the guns on the main-deck, or sail-making.

But this afternoon, the fire-buckets of the ship having become worn and dingy, they were set to work at repainting them. The officer-instructor of practical seamanship, who mixed the paint, explained the proportions of white lead, pigment, driers, and linseed oil as he worked. Then the youngsters got busy with the brushes.

"Jingo, hanged if this don't remind me of old Ajax's nose—the one you drew on the board this morning!" chuckled Dicky

"Snags!" cried Stoniky Burr. The warning cry came too late, however, for before Tom Gale could apply the cloth to the board, Mr. Cosine stepped into the room. Tom was caught red-handed!

West, as he applied his bright red paint carefully.

A laugh went round, though Stoniky Burr, a member of the group in which Tom and Dicky were working, simply scowled. But suddenly a queer gleam came into his eyes, and he glanced furtively round to see if the instructor were out of earshot. An idea had flashed into Burr's brain.

"You're pretty smart at japing," he sneered suddenly, turning to Tom. "I'll dare you to slip over the forecastle one night and paint the old figurehead's nose red—not just do it on the board! Suppose you'd funk a thing like that?"

"Well, you'd better go on supposing," replied Tom. "Think I'm going to carry out a jape just because you dare me to do it, Burr?"

"What a caper it would be!" chuckled another fellow of the group. "Why doesn't Stoniky do it himself?"

Burr glanced across at Hemming. His crony looked up.

"Gale never minds a jape he can't get landed too heavily over," grinned Hemming nastily. "But he funks anything really worth while!"

"Hemming's right!" put in Burr unpleasantly. "Gale carries through his reputation for daring japes by swank. He'd funk doing a thing like painting the nose of the figurehead. 'Sides, he's too much of a wet to be able to carry through the joke properly!"

Tom said nothing. It didn't seem worth while. But a tall boy near the outskirts of the group chipped in:

"I believe Gale really is funking it! Going to do it, Tom?"

Tom flushed.

"Why on earth should I?" he exclaimed, looking up from his pail. "I don't funk it, of course, but I'm hanged if I'm going to do a thing just because I'm dared to do it, anyway, not by a navy-neck like Burr!"

The bully of the Ajax scowled. But he brightened up as another fellow chimed in:

"I really believe Tom does funk it! Own up, Tom! You're windy, aren't you?"

"I'll punch your scumyum knob, shipmate, if you say that again! Shut up, and stop skulking!" cried Tom.

But he coloured as glances were thrown in his direction. Those glances, and the half-suppressed chuckles, told him well enough what his shipmates were really thinking.

In the Storm!

JUST after dark that night the figure of a boy stole forward, under the shadow of the life-net beneath the yards of the foremast, past the cat-heads of the ship, from which hung the anchors used for demonstration purposes, and right up into the eyes of the Ajax.

A coil of stout rope hung on a belaying-pin here in the foremost point of the vessel. Tom Gale—for it was he—unhooked the coil, and softly carried it further aft, along the starboard side. He belayed the rope to the fife-rail on the rigging at that part, and threw the coil into the blackness below, where the water gurgled round the training-ship.

"There," he breathed, "that'll fall alongside the port near my hammock. I'll show 'em if I'm afraid to paint old Ajax's nose red! I can shin up this rope and do the trick to-night. It'll mean being up here first thing in the morning to shove the rope back in the eyes, where it belongs, but I can easily do that."

He turned to make his way softly back. Then he paused as his eyes surveyed the sky doubtfully.

"Whew! It looks as if it's going to be a dirty night, though. Still, I'll chance that, What a lark it'll be! Crumbs, the ship'll be in an uproar!"

Chuckling at the thought of the sensation the jape would cause, Tom descended to the ladder-way from the deck. As he left the upper air a sighing gust of wind whisked round the companion and followed him down the ladder-way.

"Gee, it's going to blow some to-night!" he muttered. "There'll be some 'jowlers' slapping against the sides at the orlop deck level, so if I do make a noise, it won't be heard."

With that, Tom joined Dicky, who was waiting for his chum on the main deck. They had a job on hand. Tom was skipper of the football team that was to play for the Starboard Watch against the Port, and the eleven still had some vacant places to fill.

But it was soon time to turn in. Tom undressed with the rest, but he did not let himself fall asleep. He had not even mentioned his daring jape to Dicky, who was soon snoring in his hammock as though nothing short of a thunderbolt and a couple of earthquakes would wake him.

Tom waited till all was quiet on the orlop deck, save for snores and the sounds of the buffeting gusts of wind from outside, and the slam-slam of the lumpy seas, or "jowlers," as they dashed against the steel sides of the ship.

The Ajax was, in outer shape, exactly like the wooden warship of old whose name she bore. Indeed, the training-ship had been started on that old vessel, which had sailed in Nelson's fleet in its day. But as the old ship became too foul for a training-ship, a new vessel was built of steel and fitted for training-ship requirements. The original figurehead of the old Ajax had been built into the stem-head of the new ship, This mighty carved figure of teak, fifteen feet from top to bottom, now hung out over the waters of the historic Thames, as if thinking of bygone days, when the water creamed and hissed under it as the stout old heart of oak was sailed into the battles that made Britain mightier than ever.

But Tom did not think of all this as he squirmed out of the port near his hammock late that night, feeling the wind wet with spray on his face, the squalls filling his lungs till he gasped with the pressure.

The daring lad gripped the rope that swayed about near the small square

imitation gun-port, then dragged himself out into the windy blackness of the night.

Up, up the shaking rope went the youngster, hand over hand, occasionally forced to stop as a fresh squall crushed him against the deathly-cold, painted steel plates of the ship. Distant thunder was rumbling continuously, and the waves lashed mournfully against the bluff bows of the ship, far below him.

A streak of lightning flashed out suddenly, lighting up the wild scene of the river in the storm. The white-topped, bulky waves were savage and snarling, running with the tide as they were. After the flash of brilliant lightning the night seemed blacker than ever, and the lash of the waves and the moan of the wind more eerie than before. Still Tom swarmed upwards, laughing recklessly, his nightshirt and trousers wet through with the flung spray.

"Once let me get alongside old Ajax and I'll soon have the job done!" he chuckled. "I'll make the old buffer pay for those lines!"

At last he gripped the rounded, smooth rail of the bulwark of the forecastle deck. There he rested, peering cautiously over to make sure that the officer of the watch was nowhere near. The ship's search-light was sweeping up and down the shore-line. The beams could not light up the figurehead, at any rate on the riverward side, so once in position with his paint-brush he could work unseen by anyone on the deck of the ship.

Softly and slowly Tom slipped forward, taking cover in the flashes of lightning, more frequent now. He found the paint-brush and small pot of red paint where he had concealed it. Taking the handle of the pot in his teeth, Tom slithered over the side of the ship near the butts, or stops for the butt of the bowsprit.

He gripped a bobstay, and worked his way hand over hand along the stout steel rope till he was in a position from which he could begin operations with the paint-brush.

Another streak of blinding lightning from directly overhead lit up the strange scene, and by its light Tom was able to shift his perilous position slightly—to get his right foot in the mouth of the towering figurehead, resting his weight on the thick lower lip. In that flash he saw the great helmeted head, nearly five feet from helmet-tip to chin, the big blind eyes staring out across the river, the great, straight-bridged nose, almost a foot in length, all ready, simply begging to be painted red.

In an instant darkness closed in on him again, and the thunder crashed out. Tom chuckled again as he got his paint-brush ready, forced his toe further into the mouth of the figure-head, and gripped harder on the bob-stay with his left knee. It was a perilous position, for foothold was insecure, and Tom had to have his hands free for painting.

The squalls were buffeting him savagely, and jerking at his body as if anxious to wrest him from his precarious position and dash him down into the depths below, where he would most assuredly be forced under the Ajax's bluff bows by the racing ebb tide.

The thought made Tom shiver slightly, but he gripped the harder with the crook of his knee and waited for the next streak of lightning. It came, and by its light Tom meant to make a dab at the nose of the figurehead, thus finding the right place from which he could work by the feel of the shape of the nose.

The streak came, but Tom suddenly stiffened. Something seemed to crack in his brain, and the paint-brush was

Tom Gale stared down in horror at the white upturned face of the officer of the watch. Then, at a sudden sound from behind, he turned swiftly round, to see three figures that fought and swayed in the broken moonlight.

arrested in its journey towards the wooden nose of the figure. In the blackness that followed Tom felt himself in another generation. He could hear the wash of the water under the bows, imagined the creaking of straining spars, the rumbling of bellying canvas, and the twang of taut bowlines.

He fancied he could feel the lift of a great ship under wind pressure. He imagined this noble carved figure—great lumps of teak spliced together as it was—at the head of the line-of-battle ships, right in the van of the fleet.

Mr. Cosine had told them the story—the enclosing of the ships of the enemy, Nelson's immortal signal, the opening of fire, with the roar of cannon and the hiss of ball and grape-shot. The Ajax was one of the ships to the fore to lead the attack! Then the further signal, "Engage the enemy more closely!"

The Ajax, with the tremendous pressure of wind in her mighty expanse of canvas, was steered towards the tall ships of the enemy. The blind eyes of the big carven image were turned unflinchingly towards the peril—right into the teeth of the hissing grape and chain shot and the shattering cannon-ball.

Fearlessly, steered by fearless men, the great oaken fabric crashed into close fighting, led by this same carven image, all scarred and torn already by the enemy guns. So the ship was locked in the deadly conflict.

Tom felt sick. Had he, Tom Gale, really thought of painting the nose of this glorious mass of spliced teak a bright red, just to raise howls of laughter from unthinking minds, and a general rumpus on the ship—just for a joke? The lad began to climb back along the

bobstay, feeling a trifle cowed and very much ashamed of himself.

"What a cad I've been!" he gritted through his teeth. "I could kick myself to think I meant to do it. The chaps can think me all the cowards in the world, but I'll not touch that old figurehead except to honour it! Anyway, I've learnt something to-night the other chaps 'll never experience—old Ajax and I are pals!"

The lad gained the forecastle deck, hid the paint-pot, scouted down the bulwarks to where the rope leading down to the orlop deck ports still swung, and snaked down into the blackness and slipped overside. He slid down the rope and was soon beside his hammock. He listened intently. There was no sound save the heavy breathing of his shipmates, and the now gentler slapping of the waves against the ship's side.

The lightning had stopped. The short blow was dying down. It almost seemed that the gods were calming down now that the attempted outrage had not been committed. And Tom Gale turned into his hammock in his wet nightshirt.

What had made Tom so suddenly alter his mind about the jape? What had been the cause of light streaming in on his careless mind? It was what he saw in that last glaring streak of lightning—a jagged and zig-zag scar across the huge wooden face of the figurehead, the place where a round of chain-shot had hit it 'way back in Nelson's day, at the great naval action of Trafalgar!

Tom went to sleep a sadder but a wiser boy. He woke in the morning feeling little refreshed by his broken night's sleep. He was first above, intending to haul in the rope that he had used to shin up the night before, and

then to go to the wash-house to plunge his head under the cold water and try to cool his throbbing brow.

The decks seemed deserted. At the fore rigging Tom climbed up on the rail to see the figurehead again before securing the rope—to bid the wooden statue a mute good morning, and to thank his stars that he had at the last moment drawn back from carrying out his rather low-down jape.

He raised himself to his full height on the rail—only to reel back with a swift cry of sheer amazement.

The nose of the figurehead was gleaming in the weak morning sunlight a bright, glaring red!

❦❧❦❧❦❧ Downfall ! ❦❧❦❧❦❧

"CRUMBS!"

Tom felt like rubbing his eyes. He leaned over the bulwarks again, looking along the black curve of the ship's side towards the great wooden figurehead that reared itself majestically beneath the raked bowsprit. His lips were wide with mute amazement.

There it was, gleaming and brilliant—a nose as fiery-red as any pillar-box. Tom could scarcely believe his senses. Had he dreamed that he had refrained at the last moment? Had he actually carried his scheme through, after all?

"Am I going balmy—or what is it?" muttered Tom slowly. "Hang it, I know I didn't do it! But——"

He climbed down from the bulwark and went for'ard to get a closer view.

But there was no doubt about it; the nose of Ajax was the colour of a ripe tomato.

Tom whistled softly.

"Great elephants! I didn't do it, but someone jolly well has! Who on earth ——"

"What's the matter, Gale?"

Tom swung round. An officer had come along the deck behind him. It was Mr. Cosine.

"I—I was just looking," stammered Tom, "at—at——"

Mr. Cosine's steely-grey eyes fixed the youngster with a penetrating gaze. It was evident that his suspicions were aroused, and Tom longed for the deck to open and drop him to the safety of the main deck. He knew that there was going to be a row, and by bad luck it seemed that he would be playing a star part in it.

Mr. Cosine walked to the bulwark and leaned over, looking for'ard. Tom watched his face with trepidation. He saw Mr. Cosine's eyes search for a moment along the length of the ship; and then suddenly the master's lower jaw seemed to drop from its socket. His eyes bulged. His face seemed to turn a queer watery green. Altogether, Mr. Cosine rendered a very passable imitation of a stranded codfish.

Tom stepped back. But the next moment the master's eyes were on him. They no longer bulged—they seemed to bore holes through Tom, sharp as gimlets.

For a minute the master struggled to express his feelings. Then he rasped out:

"So you were not content with your performance on the blackboard yesterday, Gale! Your artistic abilities required a wider scope!"

Tom shuffled awkwardly. He was innocent, but he knew that he would have difficulty in persuading the angry navigation master of that fact. There was no doubt about it, he was well in the soup!

"No, sir, I didn't do that!" he managed at last.

The gimlet-eyes surveyed Tom doubtfully. Mr. Cosine, though hard and severe, was not a bad sort at heart, and he did not believe that Tom would lie to him. But then his eyes suddenly contracted. His glance had fallen to Tom's hands, and something there had leapt out to his sharp eyes instantly. His lips tightened.

"Gale, let me look at that hand!"

Tom glanced down at his right hand, and a startled look leapt into the youngster's eyes. Slowly he raised it. There in the nails was a lingering trace of scarlet which had not been washed out—mute evidence against him.

"Paint—red paint! What have you to say?" Mr. Cosine's eyes were hard. "Gale, you have been lying to me!"

Tom shook his head, but his eyes dropped.

"I—I didn't paint the figurehead, sir!" he repeated doggedly. "This paint —we were painting the fire-buckets yesterday——"

He broke off, stammering. He knew that he had not got paint on his hands then; it must have been last night.

"Did you get that paint on your hands when painting the fire-buckets?"

Tom did not reply. His chin was set doggedly. Mr. Cosine was frowning heavily; he could only believe now, though half against his will, that Tom had been lying to him.

"You have nothing to say, Gale? Really, I think you had better have
THE GEM LIBRARY.—No. 831.

owned up in the first place." He turned to the bulwarks again, and his eyes fell on the rope below. "That rope—did you put that rope there?"

"Yes, sir," answered Tom quietly. He might as well admit what he could not deny. "But all the same I didn't paint the figurehead—on my honour!"

There was contempt in the master's face as he turned again to Tom. Then he swung on his heel.

"I will leave this matter to Mr. Landfar, who, no doubt, will carry it to the commander," he said quietly.

Tom watched the tall, spare figure disappear down the ladder-way into the main deck. His cheeks were flaming. He had given his word of honour, and had still been disbelieved. The commander would be told that he had done this low-down act—— Anything might happen now.

Then hope revived in him. Someone had done it; and, unless the fellow was an utter outsider, he could not stand by and allow an innocent party to suffer. The chap would own up—for certain he would own up!

But there was a shadow still in the youngster's eyes as he turned away. Then he came to a sudden standstill. A burly figure had appeared from the door of the wash-house, an unpleasant grin on his face. Tom realised in a moment that Burr, the bully of the Ajax, had been listening to all that had passed between himself and Mr. Cosine.

"So you're going to get it in the neck for your little jape!" chuckled Burr. "Serve you jolly well right!"

Tom's eyes flashed.

"Suppose you're bucked, anyway!" he said hotly. "As a matter of fact, I didn't do it, I tell you. It was a rotten trick to do, and I chucked the whole idea, although I got out to do it, I admit. Someone else——"

He broke off. He had noticed a queer look in Burr's eyes. Tom's teeth came together with a click. It had come over him in a flash. Was this the fellow who had painted the figurehead?

"Someone else did it," Tom repeated slowly, his eyes fixed on Burr's. "Suppose you couldn't name him for me?"

"What do you mean?" cried Burr angrily. "Me? What should I know about it? You did it yourself, and you know it; and now you're trying to shift the blame on me!" He looked round quickly. "Suppose you hope there's an officer about to hear you! Well, there isn't, and you'll have to pay for your own jape! It's no good trying to shift the blame to me, you funk!"

"Funk—eh?" Tom's voice was quite cool, but there was a look in his eyes that Burr did not quite like. He stepped back in alarm. "That's a word I don't like, Stoniky Burr, and I'm hanged if I don't make you eat it!"

They were alone there, out of sight behind the wash-house, and Tom was in no mood to stand much from Stoniky Burr. Though Burr was bigger than Tom, he secretly feared the young chief petty officer of the Hood division ever since his licking by the Fleet during the last paper-chase. But there was no avoiding a scrap now, and Burr put up his hands.

It was a brief scrap, but what there was of it was pretty hot. It was interrupted by the bugle for breakfast, but by that time Burr had a black eye and a nose that was nearly as scarlet as that of the figurehead of the training-ship. Tom, too, had honourable wounds to show, but he had given far more than he had received.

"I think that'll do for the present, Stoniky!" he observed calmly, turning away for a quick wash before answering the bugle's summons. "Just a little reminder that your manners need improving!"

Tom did not enjoy his breakfast. If, as he firmly believed, Burr was the one who had painted the nose of Ajax, he could not hope for a confession from that quarter.

Things looked black for the Hood youngster. By this time the whole training-ship was buzzing with the news, and a murmur of continual chuckling buzzed throughout the mess-deck. Tom was the object of most eyes. It was evident that the youngsters of the training-ship, like Mr. Cosine, believed him to be the midnight painter.

"I tell you I know nothing about it, Dicky!" Tom confided to his chum. "I climbed out, and then changed my mind. It wasn't that I funked the consequences, as you know well enough, but it suddenly struck me what a rotten thing it was to do to that fine old figurehead. Why, that Ajax has fought with Nelson! I wouldn't touch it for anything—not now!"

Dicky nodded.

"I believe you, of course, old man. But I'm afraid you'll have a job to persuade the commander."

"You're right, Dicky," said Tom gloomily. "Hallo! What do you want?"

His last words were addressed to an excited youngster of the Raleigh division who had come running up.

"The commander wants you in his quarters!" puffed the other breathlessly. "You're in for it hot, Gale!" he added by way of encouragement.

Without a word Tom strode off. Dicky West watched the retreating figure with a worried look in his usually laughing eyes.

The quarter of an hour that followed seemed interminable to Dicky West. He wandered aimlessly round the orlop deck, waiting. Then at last a quick exclamation escaped him as he saw Tom's figure appear at the foot of the ladder-way.

Dicky raced towards him. His heart fell at the sight of his chum's face—Tom's face strangely white and lined. Tom's eyes were almost tragic.

"What's happened?" muttered Dicky in a low voice.

Tom glanced down at his arm, where his chief petty officer's badge had been but twenty minutes ago. There was a gasp from Dicky when he saw that that badge was no longer there.

"You—you——" he stammered.

Tom nodded, the ghost of a tragic smile twisting one corner of his lips.

"Disrated," he said simply.

————

A Fight in the Dark !

IT was a bad blow for the Hood division when they heard the news. Tom had been a popular officer, and only a few of the meaner spirits among them took advantage of the youngster's downfall. But the Blakes, led by Stoniky Burr, did not let Tom forget his troubles that day

Dicky West had been sent for, and returned with the news that he had been promoted to the rank of chief P.O. of the division in Tom's place, whilst a

Printed and published every Wednesday by the Proprietors, The Amalgamated Press (1922), Ltd., The Fleetway House, Farringdon Street, London, E.C.4. Advertisement offices: The Fleetway House, Farringdon Street, London, E.C.4. Registered for transmission by Canadian Magazine Post. Subscription rates: Inland and Abroad, 11s. per annum, 5s. 6d. for six months. Sole agents for South Africa: The Central News Agency, Ltd. Sole agents for Australia and New Zealand: Messrs. Gordon & Gotch, Ltd.; and for Canada, The Imperial News Co., Ltd. (Canada).—Saturday, January 12th, 1924.

youngster named Brown—a rather quiet, thoughtful fellow, who seemed to be in a perpetual day-dream, and in consequence had been nick-named Jemima—was made petty officer in Dicky's stead.

"The question is, since you say you didn't do it, who did do it?" said Dicky to Tom, as they turned in that night. "Some low-down swab, anyway, not owning up."

"I believe Burr's the chap," said Tom. "Though I must say I hadn't thought before that he would have had the pluck. He probably thought he would be able to land me with it somehow; if necessary, I dare say he would have sneaked about what I'd said last night about doing it. For some reason, Stoniky's got a down on me. Shouldn't wonder if he even hopes to make things too hot to hold me on board the ship—to get me to make a bolt for it."

"Well, if it is Burr, we'll land him with it sooner or later," muttered Dicky West fiercely. "Tom, I hate being chief P.O. like this, when you've no right to have been disrated. But it can't be helped, and I'll do all I can, of course, to find out who the chap is who actually did do the painting of old Ajax's nose. We'll find him sooner or later—Burr, or whoever it is."

Tom dropped at last into a troubled sleep. Everything seemed to have gone wrong during the last few days—it was as though some malignant fate was dogging his footsteps. His dreams were haunted by the face of Burr.

And then suddenly Tom found himself awake and alert. What was it that had broken in upon his restless sleep? Some sound—he seemed to be conscious of soft footsteps, stealing with cat-like stealth past the hammocks of the sleeping boys.

Without making a sound himself he turned his head. Bright moonlight was streaming in through the windows fitted into the imitation gun-ports. And suddenly a dark figure moved across one of those bright shafts of light on the port side of the deck. Tom drew his breath sharply. It was the figure of his dreams—the figure of Stoniky Burr.

He could not mistake that clumsy, heavily-built frame. Already it had been swallowed up again in the black shadows, but a moment later the silent figure had passed, a black shape, through another stream of moonlight. Where was Burr going? Tom raised himself softly on to one elbow, peering through the darkness, his ears straining for every faint whisper of sound.

"What the dickens——" he muttered to himself.

It might be, of course, that Burr was simply off to play some practical joke on someone. It was a favourite trick of his to let a sleeper's hammock down, in spite of the strict orders against this dangerous so-called joke. But something in Stoniky's manner told Tom that Burr was on more serious business to-night.

He heard the ghostly footfalls that still came to his ears from the darkness turn towards the ladderway leading up into the lower deck. Tom frowned, puzzled. But the next instant he was slipping softly from his hammock, a sudden idea burning in his mind.

What if Burr had remembered some clue that might lead to the discovery of his guilt—if it was he who was guilty—in connection with the painted figurehead? Even now, perhaps, he was on his way to the upper deck to destroy some clue, to keep the blame fixed on Tom for good.

It was the work of an instant for Tom to slip to the foot of the ladderway and up into the lower deck in silent pursuit. He followed Burr up the second ladderway into the main deck—it was obvious

that the bully of the Ajax was on his way to the upper deck.

Tom was breathing quickly, excitedly. He had lost sight of Burr now in the all-enveloping darkness, but without waiting, the Hood youngster slipped up on to the upper deck. The cold night air fanned his face as he stood looking round in the bright moonlight.

All was very still. He could hear every gurgling ripple that chuckled beneath the training-ship, could make out the distant engine-throb of a tug whose starboard light could be seen drifting down-river in the darkness. Then suddenly his attention was riveted. It seemed to Tom that he had seen a shadow move in the gloom at the break of the poop.

Keeping in the shadow of the high port bulwark, the youngster started to make his way swiftly aft. He had already glanced round to make sure that there was no sign of the officer of the watch. His bare feet made no sound on the smooth deck-boards, and then suddenly a startled cry broke from him as he felt his feet caught under him.

He sprawled headlong, to crash heavily on to a dark form that was lying in the shadow, ominous and still. For an instant Tom's heart seemed to miss a beat.

Dim in the gloom, as he struggled up, he made out the white face, with its closed eyes, of the officer of the watch. The officer was lying in a huddled heap, terribly still. Something seemed to grip Tom's nerves with icy fingers as he stared down in horror at that white, upturned face. He had forgotten Burr. And then an abrupt sound behind him made him swing round swiftly.

His lips opened in dumb, startled amazement. For three figures had suddenly leapt to life in the black shadows at the break of the poop—three figures that fought and swayed in the broken moonlight.

Tom saw a fist flash through the air, heard the sickening jolt as it crashed home. One of the three staggered and almost fell as the blow struck. Then the fight was over as soon as it had begun, and two of those dark figures turned in panic to race away.

But the other man was after them with swift, silent strides. It was like a shadow-show of phantoms. The two turned at bay against the starboard bulwark, the third man standing there in the moonlight, cornering them. Tom saw the black outline of his head—a fine head, with its strong jaw and straight nose—heard the sudden laugh of sheer dare-devil delight that broke from that dark figure, a laugh that somehow thrilled Tom through and through.

What could it all mean? It was like the weird imaginings of a dream. And then Tom saw something that sent him racing over the deck towards the shadowy three, to the help of the man who, single-handed, had cornered two. For what he had seen decided in a flash for Tom which side he meant to take.

In the moonlight, gleaming like cat's eyes from the dimly white face of the man crouching back against the bulwark, had come flashing out to him two glistening circles of green.

It was the man with green spectacles!

(There will be another grand long instalment of this powerful serial next week, chums. You will be held spellbound by the fearless "Avalanche" Hume, Gates new acquaintance, who is on the track of the man with the green spectacles. A word about next week's GEM—now make a point of ordering it well in advance, otherwise you may be disappointed.)

"HAT-TRICK GUY!"

(Continued from page 21.)

intending to inform him of his debt to Mike Hunt.

"Just the chap I want to see," said John Mannings, grasping his son's hand. "You were splendid, my boy, and here's a present for you, to show my appreciation of what you've done for the club to-day! Don't spend it recklessly, though!"

John Mannings handed Guy a slip of paper which the boy recognised instantly to be a cheque. And it was for five pounds—the exact sum owing to the rascally bookmaker, Mike Hunt!

Muttering his thanks, Guy almost ran from the room and out of the club-house. But he did not wend his footsteps towards his home. Instead, he set off for the railway station, and there he had little difficulty in getting the booking clerk, who he knew fairly well, to change the cheque. Then, with the five one-pound notes securely stowed away in his breast-pocket and a railway ticket for Kebble, he raced up on to the platform. Five minutes later he was off to find the rascally bookmaker.

. . . .

Mike Hunt received the surprise of his life when he opened his door to find Guy Mannings standing on the doorstep.

Guy quickly explained his presence, and, showing the man the five pounds, he demanded the incriminating I O U.

At first Mike Hunt refused to make the exchange; but when Guy threatened to inform the police of his underhand schemes the rascal parted without another murmur.

Happy with the success of his visit to Hunt, Guy went along to Claremont and saw his brother. And the two brothers sat down to a right royal feast to celebrate not only their escape from the hands of the blackmailer, but also to commemorate the Celtic-Rovers match, in which Guy had lived up to his nickname, "Hat-trick" Guy!

THE END.

(Look out for another topping yarn of the amusing Gan Waga and Rupert Thurston & Co. in next week's GEM entitled "THE WRONG FILM!" By Sidney Drew. Don't miss it.)